Will   Irma   Taranee   Cornelia   Hay Lin

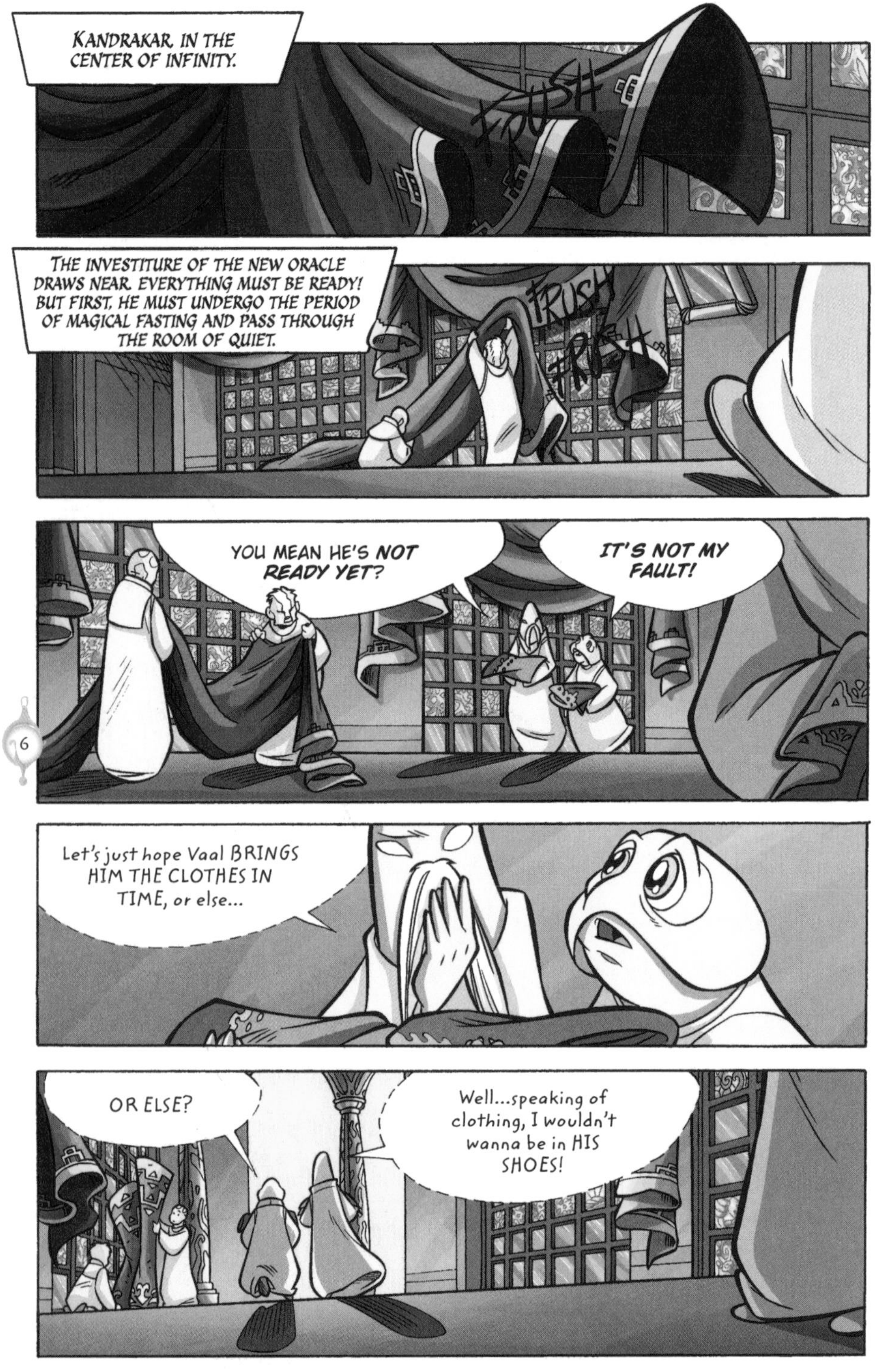
KANDRAKAR, IN THE CENTER OF INFINITY.
FRUSH
THE INVESTITURE OF THE NEW ORACLE DRAWS NEAR. EVERYTHING MUST BE READY! BUT FIRST, HE MUST UNDERGO THE PERIOD OF MAGICAL FASTING AND PASS THROUGH THE ROOM OF QUIET.
FRUSH
FRUSH
YOU MEAN HE'S NOT READY YET?
IT'S NOT MY FAULT!
Let's just hope Vaal BRINGS HIM THE CLOTHES IN TIME, or else...
OR ELSE?
Well...speaking of clothing, I wouldn't wanna be in HIS SHOES!

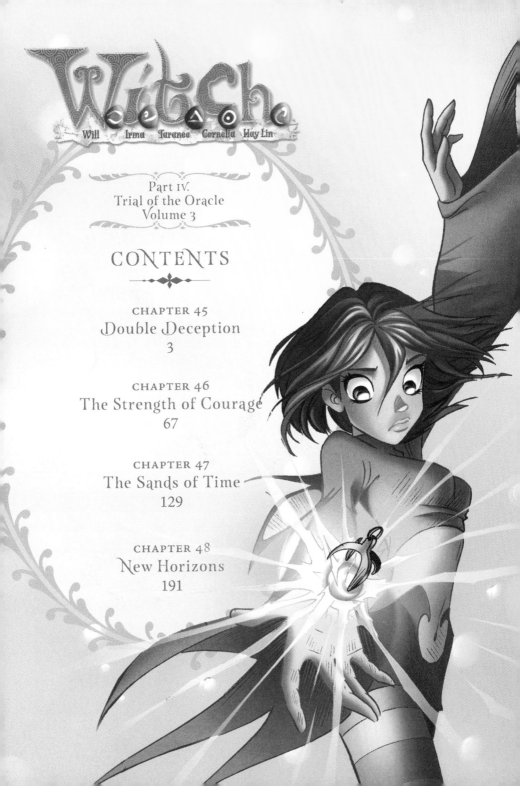

W.i.t.c.h.

Will Irma Taranee Cornelia Hay Lin

Part IV.
Trial of the Oracle
Volume 3

CONTENTS

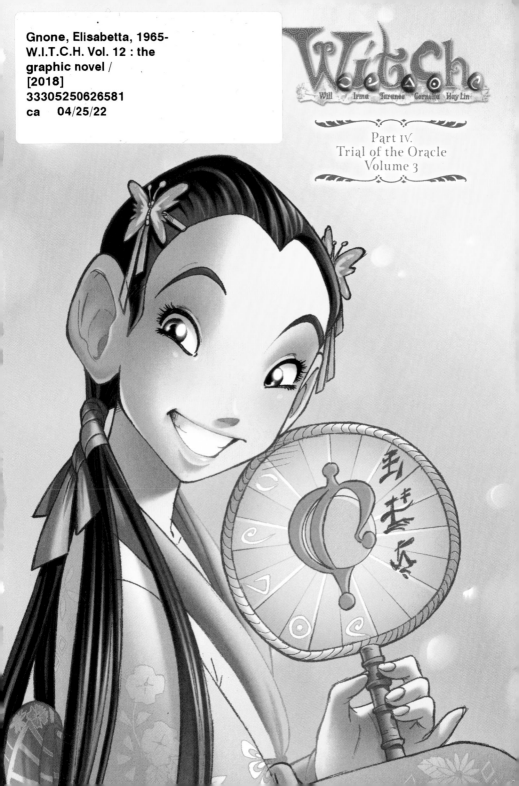

W.i.t.c.h.

Will Irma Taranee Cornelia Hay Lin

Part IV.
Trial of the Oracle
Volume 3

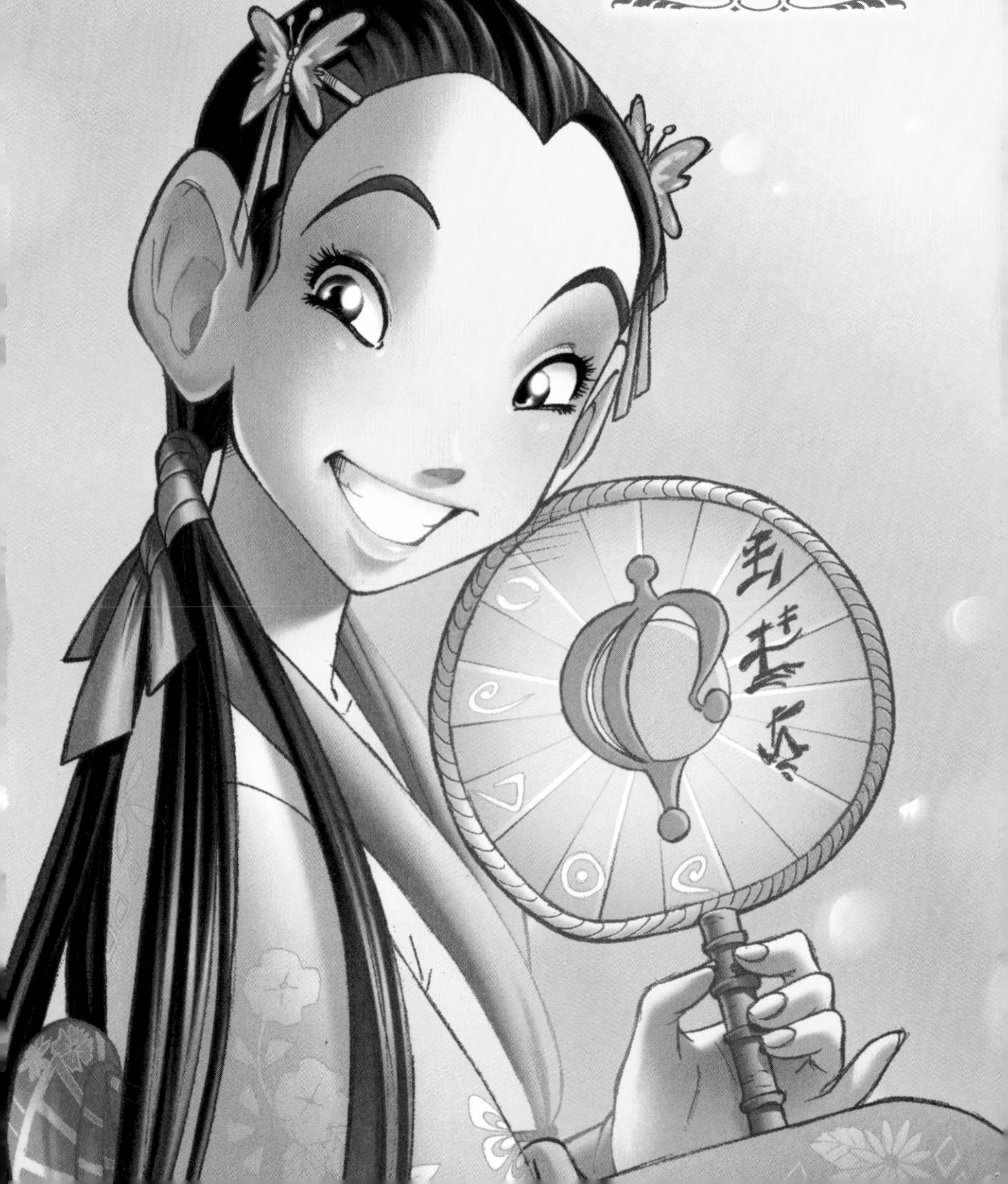

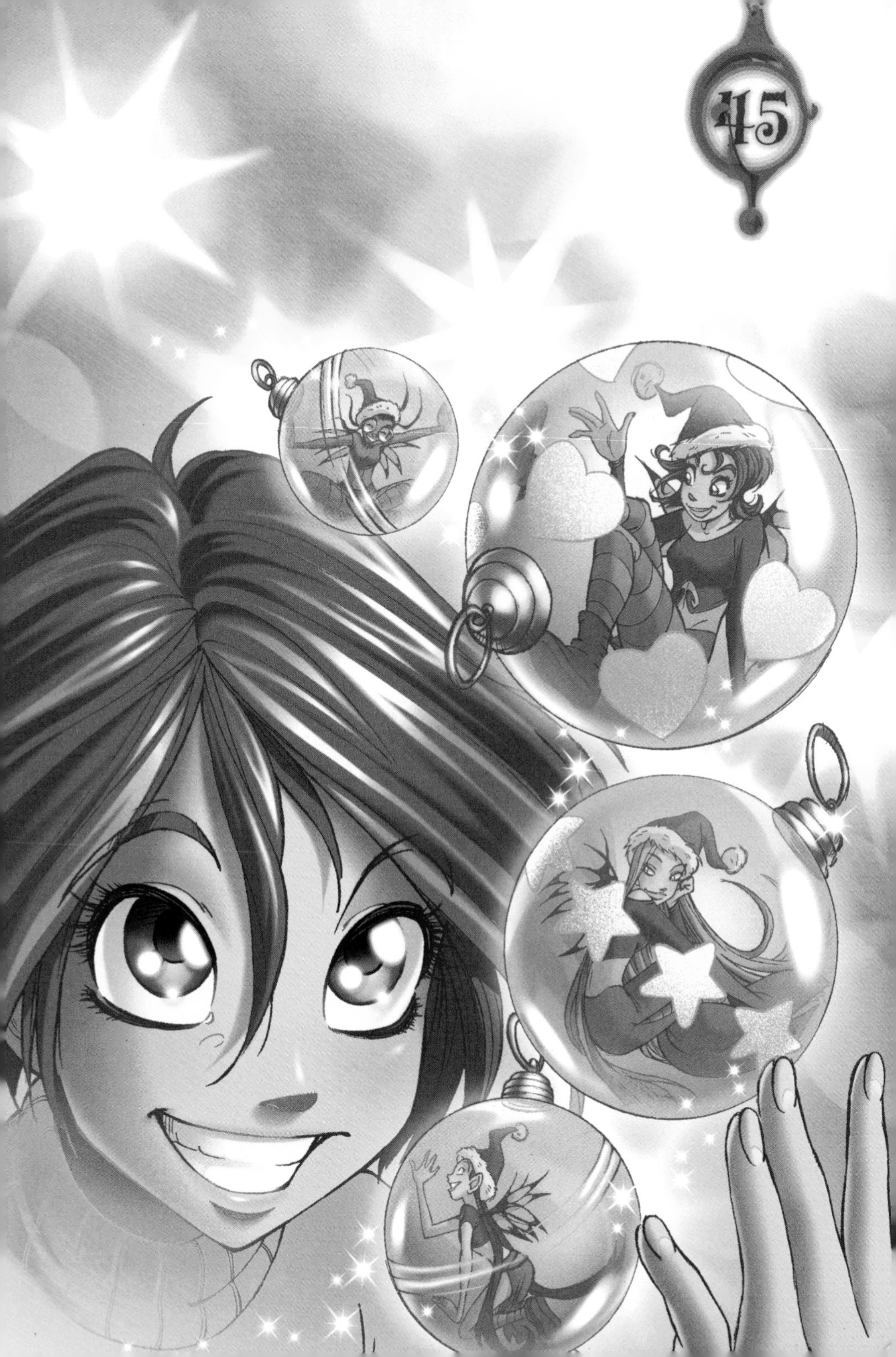
45

Double Deception

"A usurper has taken the place of the Oracle."

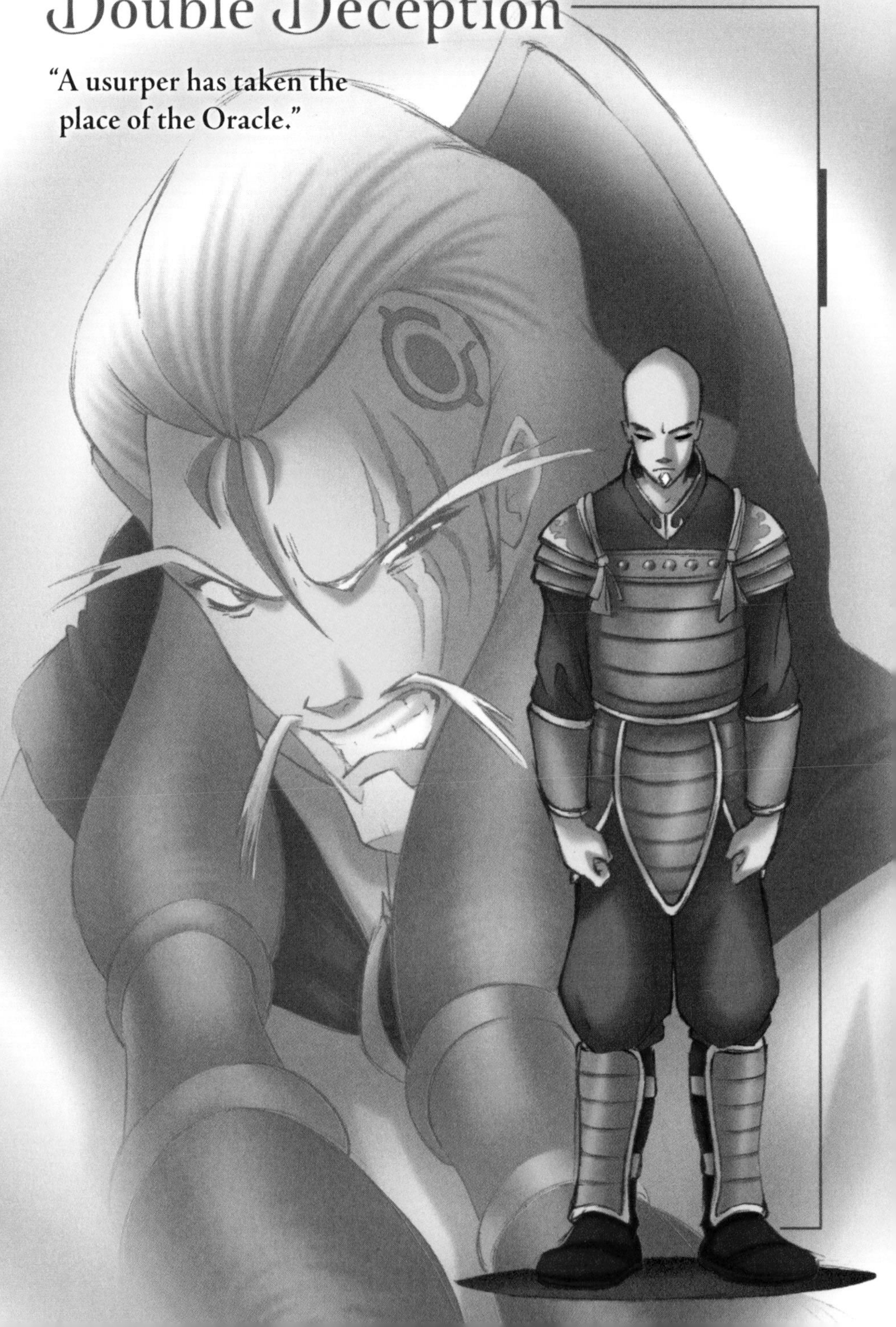

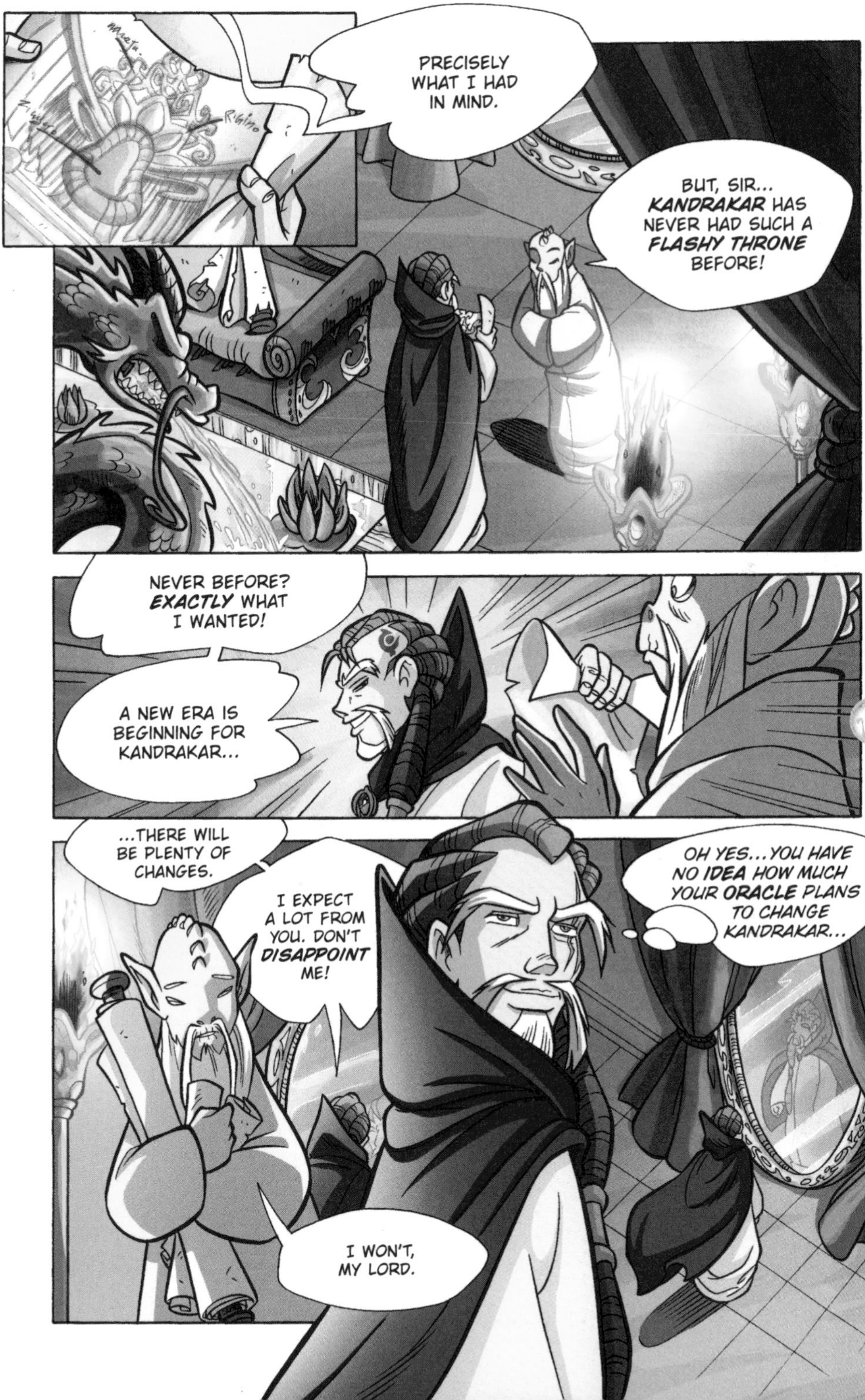
PRECISELY WHAT I HAD IN MIND.
BUT, SIR... **KANDRAKAR** HAS NEVER HAD SUCH A **FLASHY THRONE** BEFORE!
NEVER BEFORE? ***EXACTLY*** WHAT I WANTED!
A NEW ERA IS BEGINNING FOR KANDRAKAR...
...THERE WILL BE PLENTY OF CHANGES.
I EXPECT A LOT FROM YOU. DON'T ***DISAPPOINT*** ME!
*OH YES...YOU HAVE NO **IDEA** HOW MUCH YOUR **ORACLE** PLANS TO CHANGE KANDRAKAR...*
I WON'T, MY LORD.

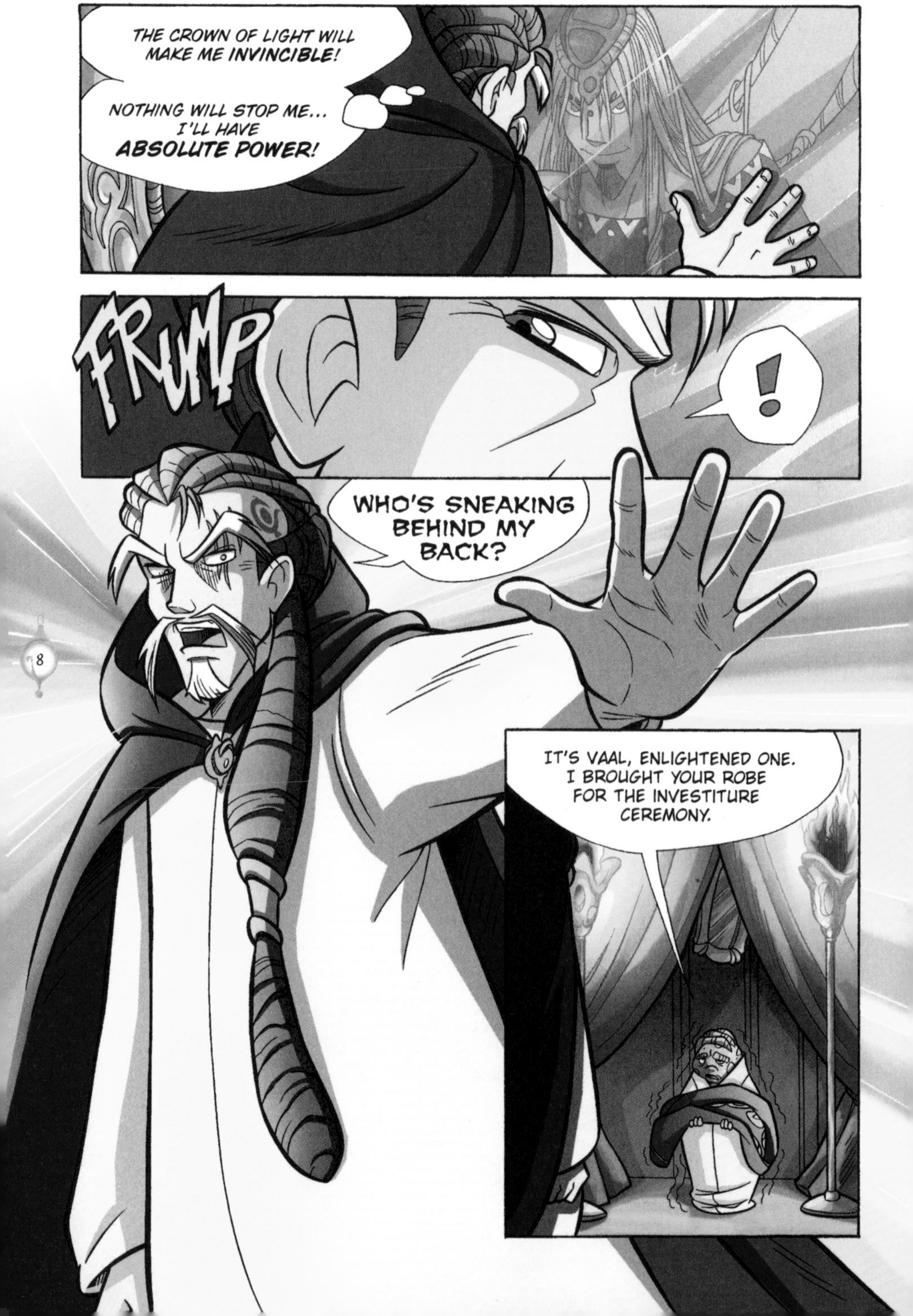
THE CROWN OF LIGHT WILL MAKE ME INVINCIBLE!
NOTHING WILL STOP ME... I'LL HAVE ABSOLUTE POWER!
FRUMP
!
WHO'S SNEAKING BEHIND MY BACK?
IT'S VAAL, ENLIGHTENED ONE. I BROUGHT YOUR ROBE FOR THE INVESTITURE CEREMONY.

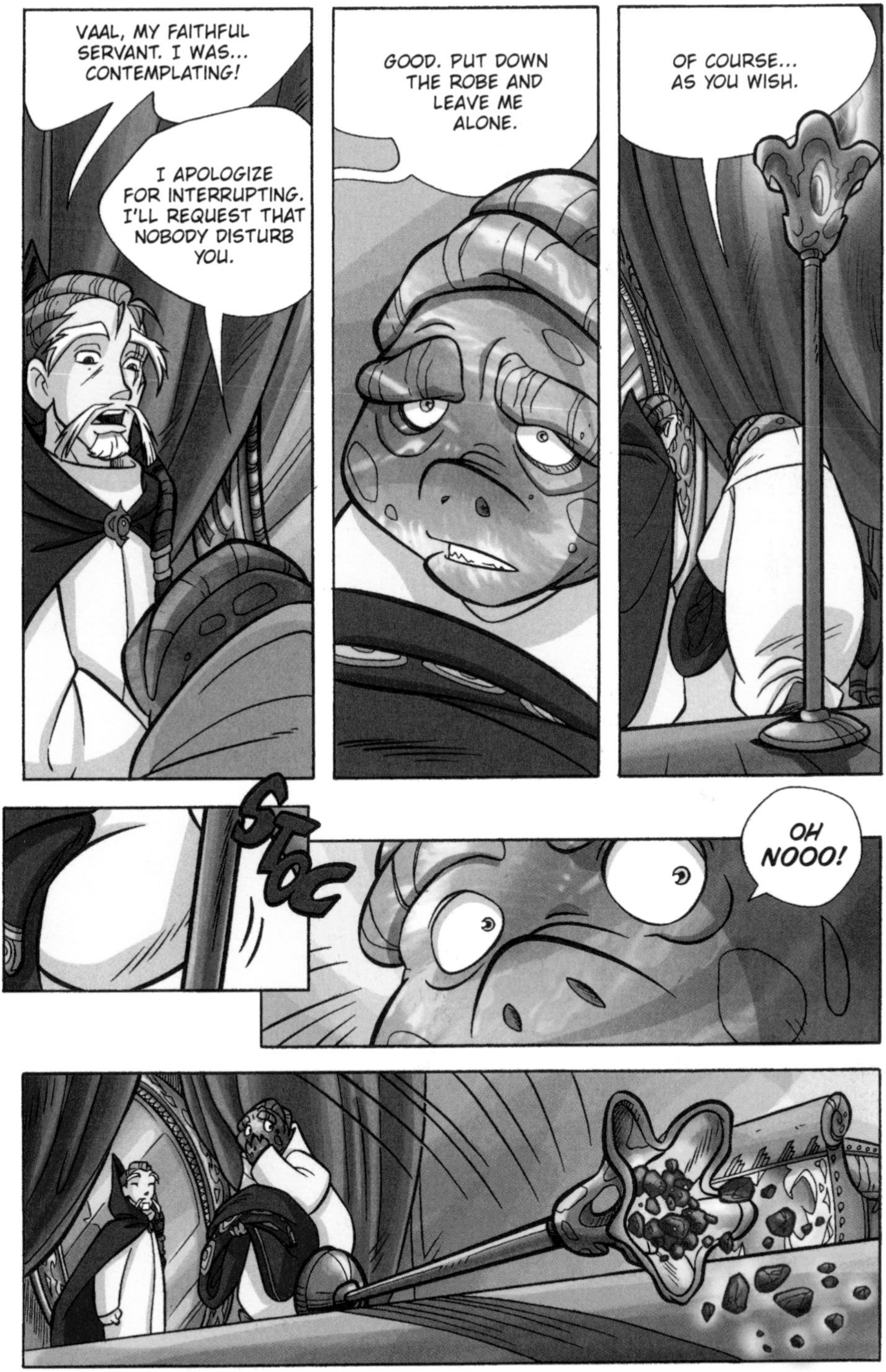
VAAL, MY FAITHFUL SERVANT. I WAS... CONTEMPLATING!
I APOLOGIZE FOR INTERRUPTING. I'LL REQUEST THAT NOBODY DISTURB YOU.
GOOD. PUT DOWN THE ROBE AND LEAVE ME ALONE.
OF COURSE... AS YOU WISH.
STOC
OH NOOO!

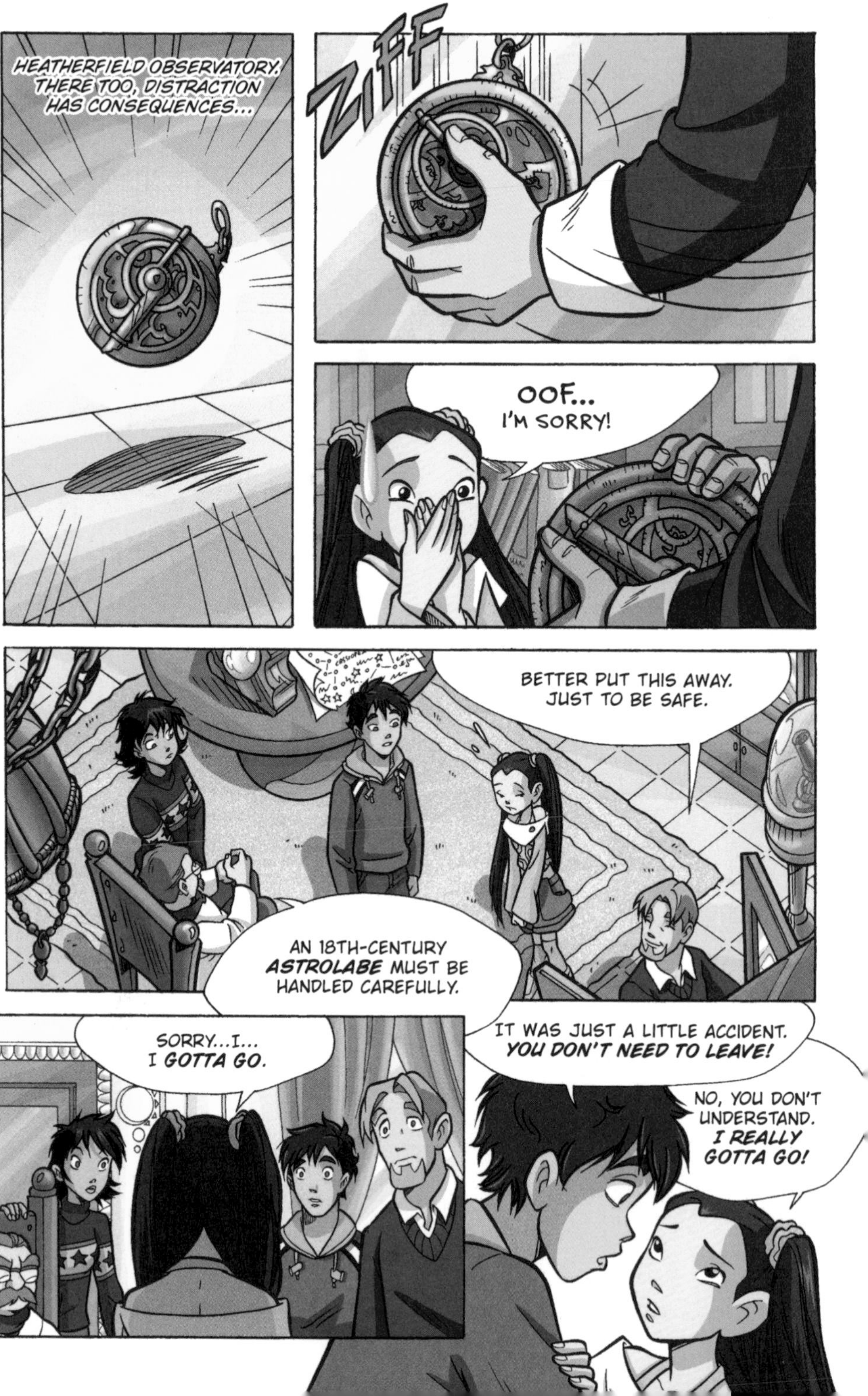
HEATHERFIELD OBSERVATORY. THERE TOO, DISTRACTION HAS CONSEQUENCES...
ZIFF
OOF... I'M SORRY!
BETTER PUT THIS AWAY. JUST TO BE SAFE.
AN 18TH-CENTURY ASTROLABE MUST BE HANDLED CAREFULLY.
SORRY...I... I GOTTA GO.
IT WAS JUST A LITTLE ACCIDENT. YOU DON'T NEED TO LEAVE!
NO, YOU DON'T UNDERSTAND. I REALLY GOTTA GO!

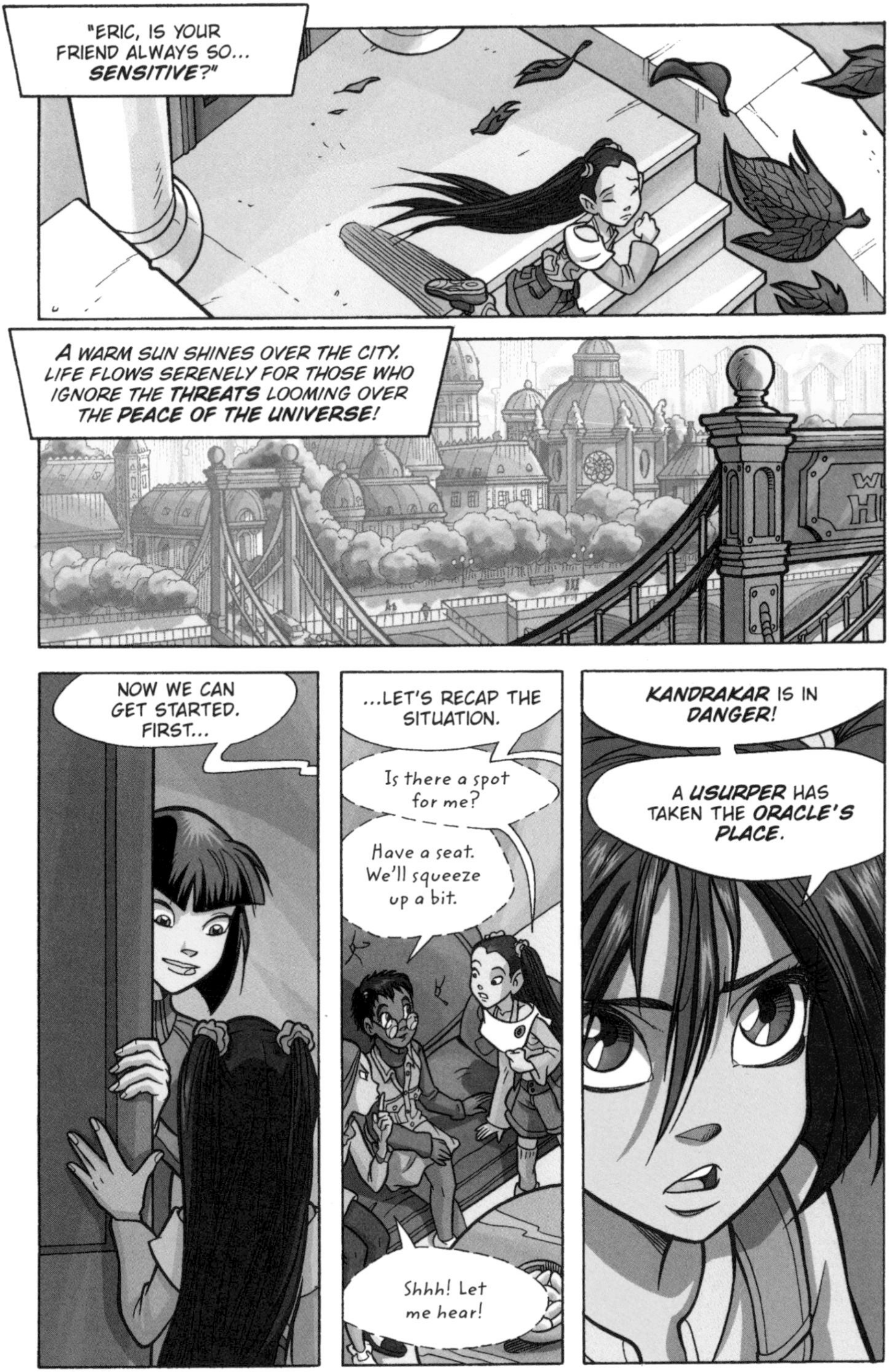
"ERIC, IS YOUR FRIEND ALWAYS SO... SENSITIVE?"
A WARM SUN SHINES OVER THE CITY. LIFE FLOWS SERENELY FOR THOSE WHO IGNORE THE THREATS LOOMING OVER THE PEACE OF THE UNIVERSE!
NOW WE CAN GET STARTED. FIRST...
...LET'S RECAP THE SITUATION.
Is there a spot for me?
Have a seat. We'll squeeze up a bit.
Shhh! Let me hear!
KANDRAKAR IS IN DANGER!
A USURPER HAS TAKEN THE ORACLE'S PLACE.

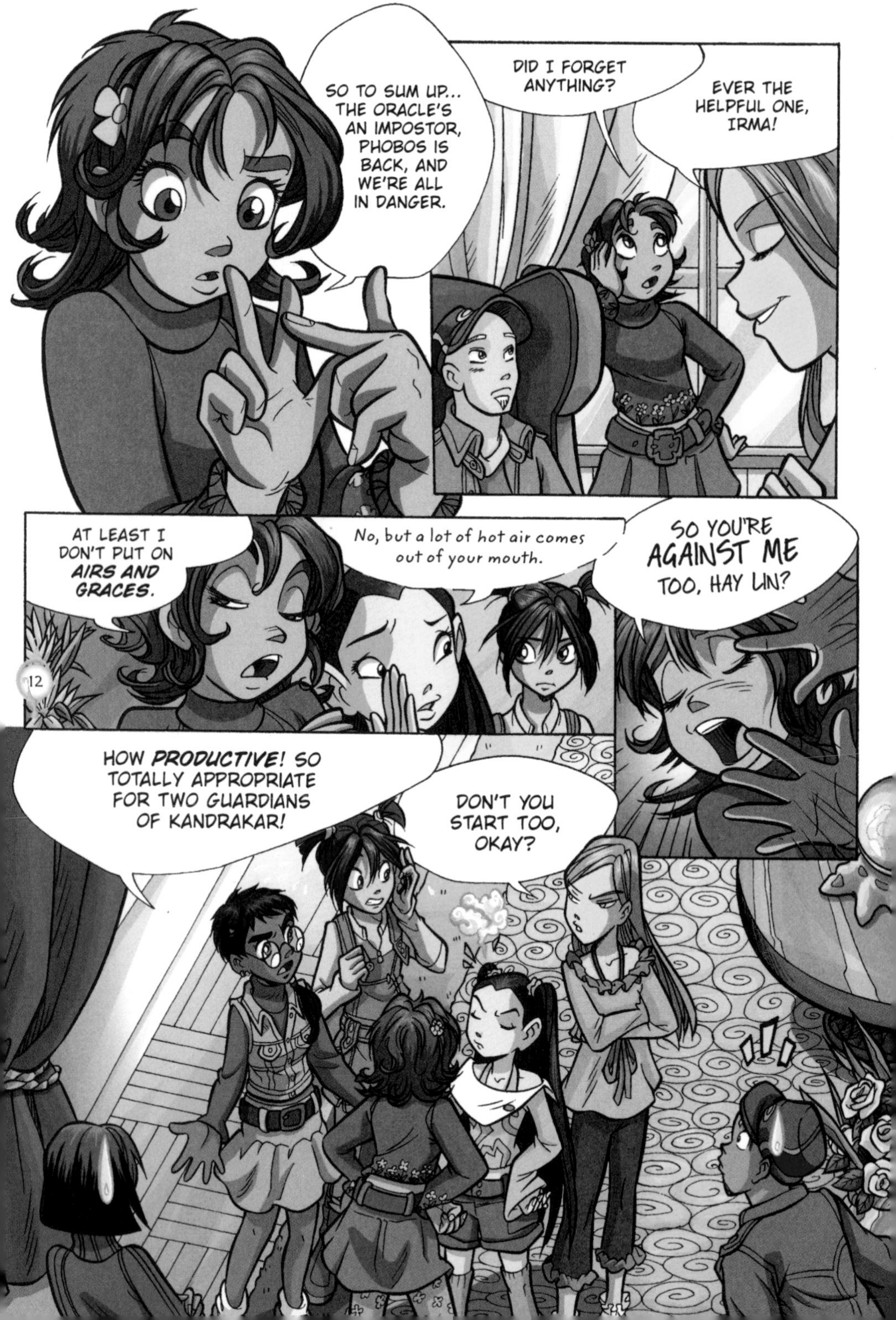

SO TO SUM UP... THE ORACLE'S AN IMPOSTOR, PHOBOS IS BACK, AND WE'RE ALL IN DANGER.
DID I FORGET ANYTHING?
EVER THE HELPFUL ONE, IRMA!
AT LEAST I DON'T PUT ON AIRS AND GRACES.
No, but a lot of hot air comes out of your mouth.
SO YOU'RE AGAINST ME TOO, HAY LIN?
HOW PRODUCTIVE! SO TOTALLY APPROPRIATE FOR TWO GUARDIANS OF KANDRAKAR!
DON'T YOU START TOO, OKAY?

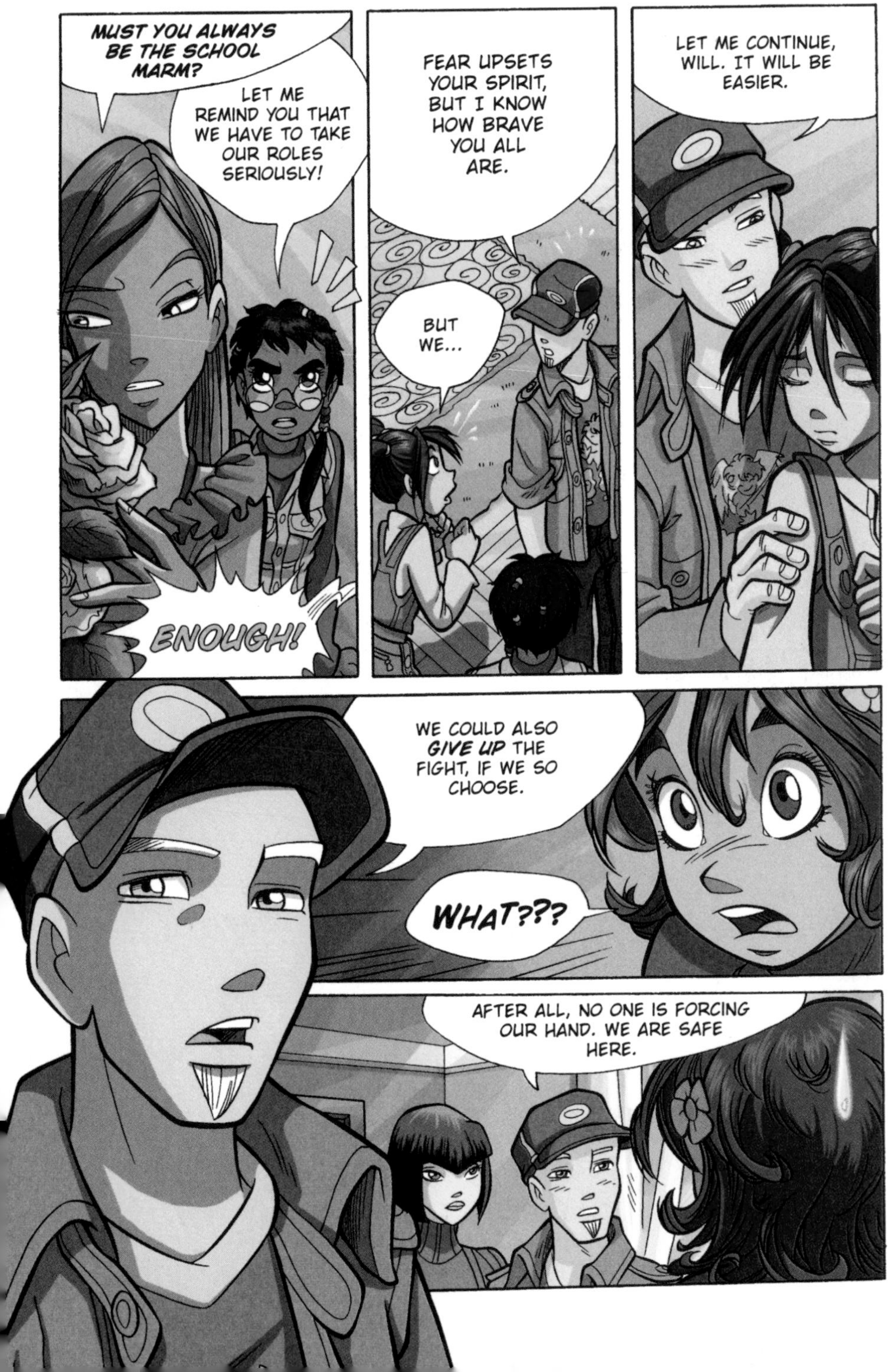
MUST YOU ALWAYS BE THE SCHOOL MARM?
LET ME REMIND YOU THAT WE HAVE TO TAKE OUR ROLES SERIOUSLY!
ENOUGH!
FEAR UPSETS YOUR SPIRIT, BUT I KNOW HOW BRAVE YOU ALL ARE.
BUT WE...
LET ME CONTINUE, WILL. IT WILL BE EASIER.
WE COULD ALSO GIVE UP THE FIGHT, IF WE SO CHOOSE.
WHAT???
AFTER ALL, NO ONE IS FORCING OUR HAND. WE ARE SAFE HERE.

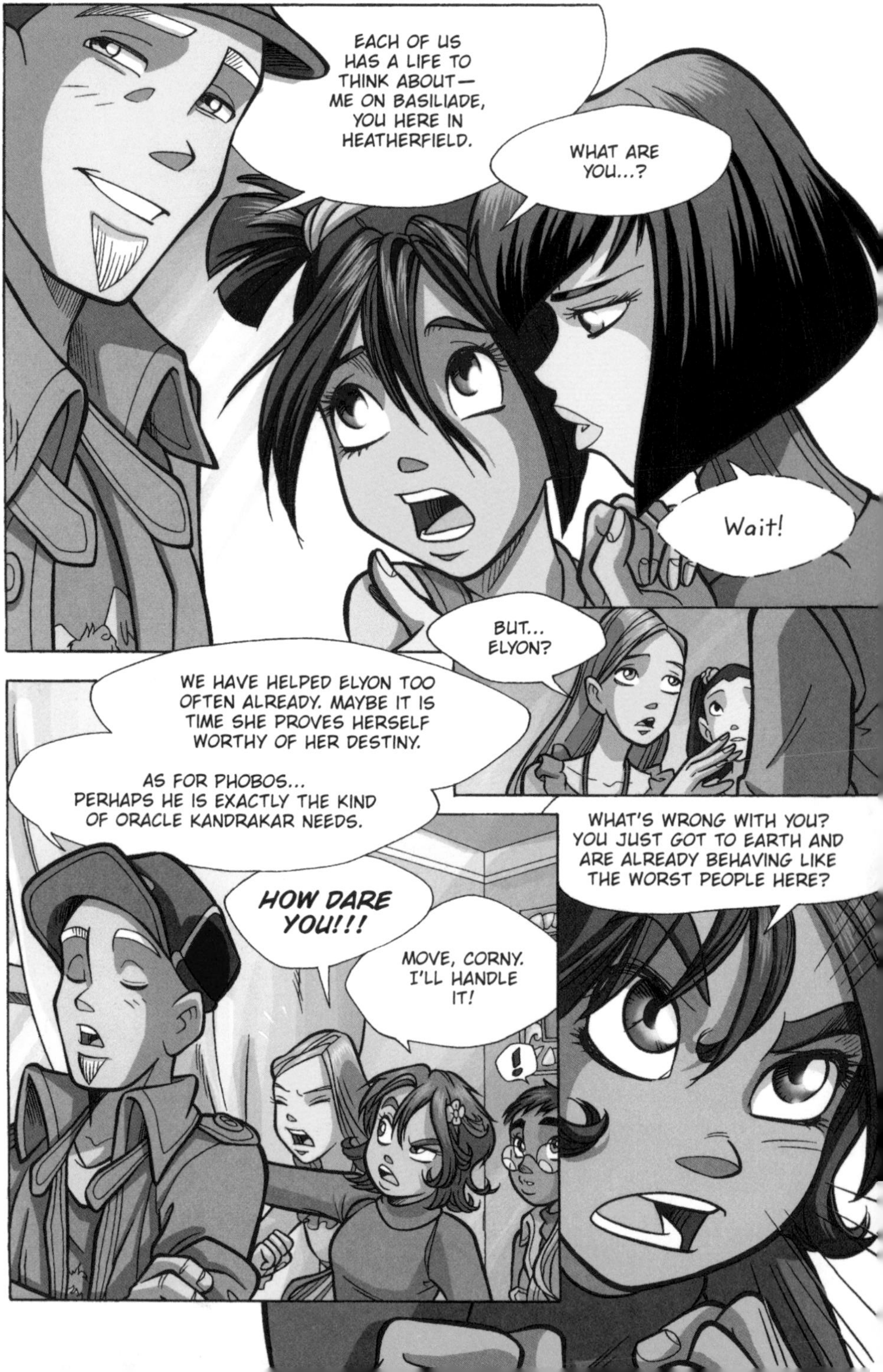
EACH OF US HAS A LIFE TO THINK ABOUT— ME ON BASILIADE, YOU HERE IN HEATHERFIELD.
WHAT ARE YOU...?
Wait!
BUT... ELYON?
WE HAVE HELPED ELYON TOO OFTEN ALREADY. MAYBE IT IS TIME SHE PROVES HERSELF WORTHY OF HER DESTINY.
AS FOR PHOBOS... PERHAPS HE IS EXACTLY THE KIND OF ORACLE KANDRAKAR NEEDS.
HOW DARE YOU!!!
MOVE, CORNY. I'LL HANDLE IT!
!
WHAT'S WRONG WITH YOU? YOU JUST GOT TO EARTH AND ARE ALREADY BEHAVING LIKE THE WORST PEOPLE HERE?

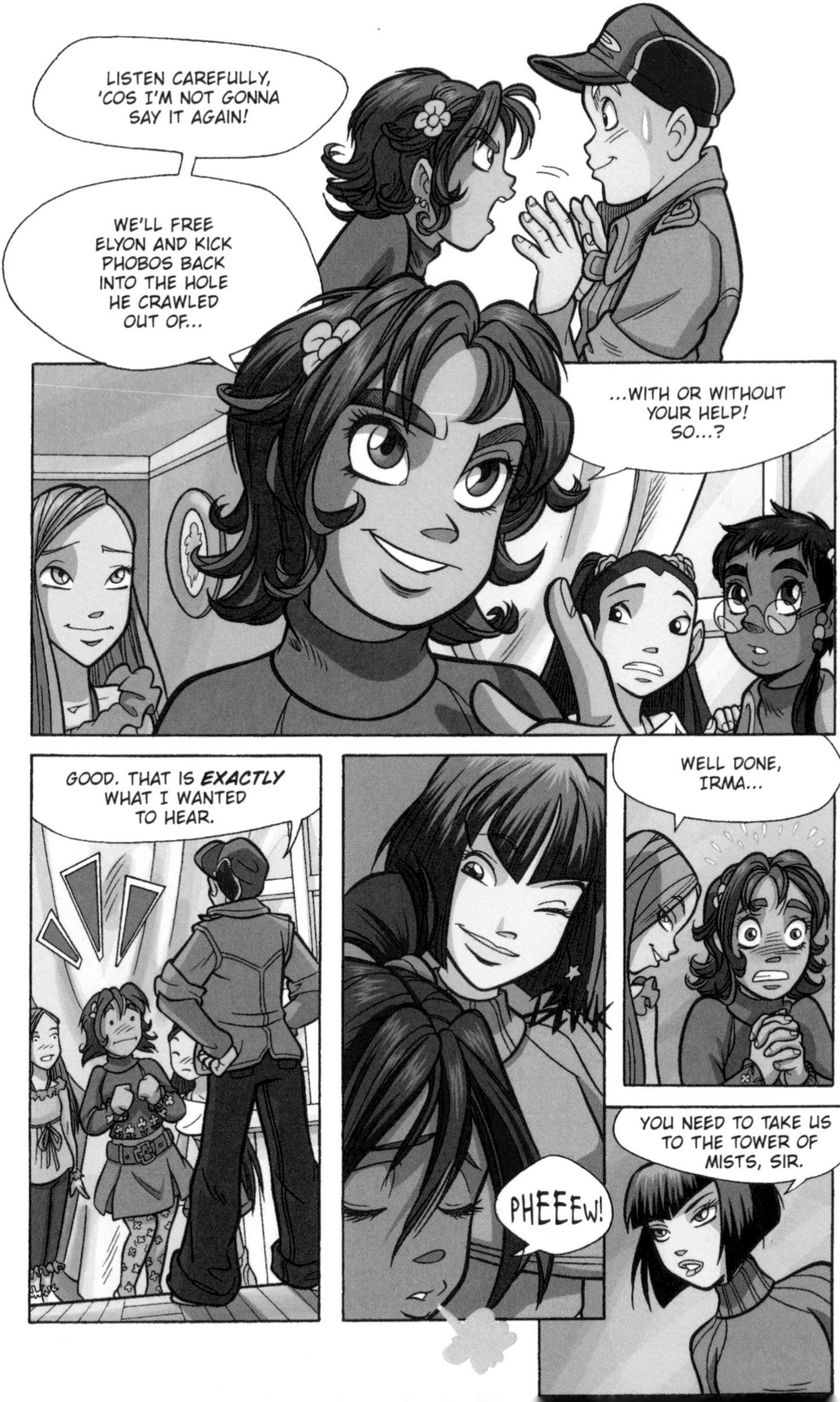
LISTEN CAREFULLY, 'COS I'M NOT GONNA SAY IT AGAIN!
WE'LL FREE ELYON AND KICK PHOBOS BACK INTO THE HOLE HE CRAWLED OUT OF...
...WITH OR WITHOUT YOUR HELP! SO...?
GOOD. THAT IS ***EXACTLY*** WHAT I WANTED TO HEAR.
PHEEEW!
WELL DONE, IRMA...
YOU NEED TO TAKE US TO THE TOWER OF MISTS, SIR.

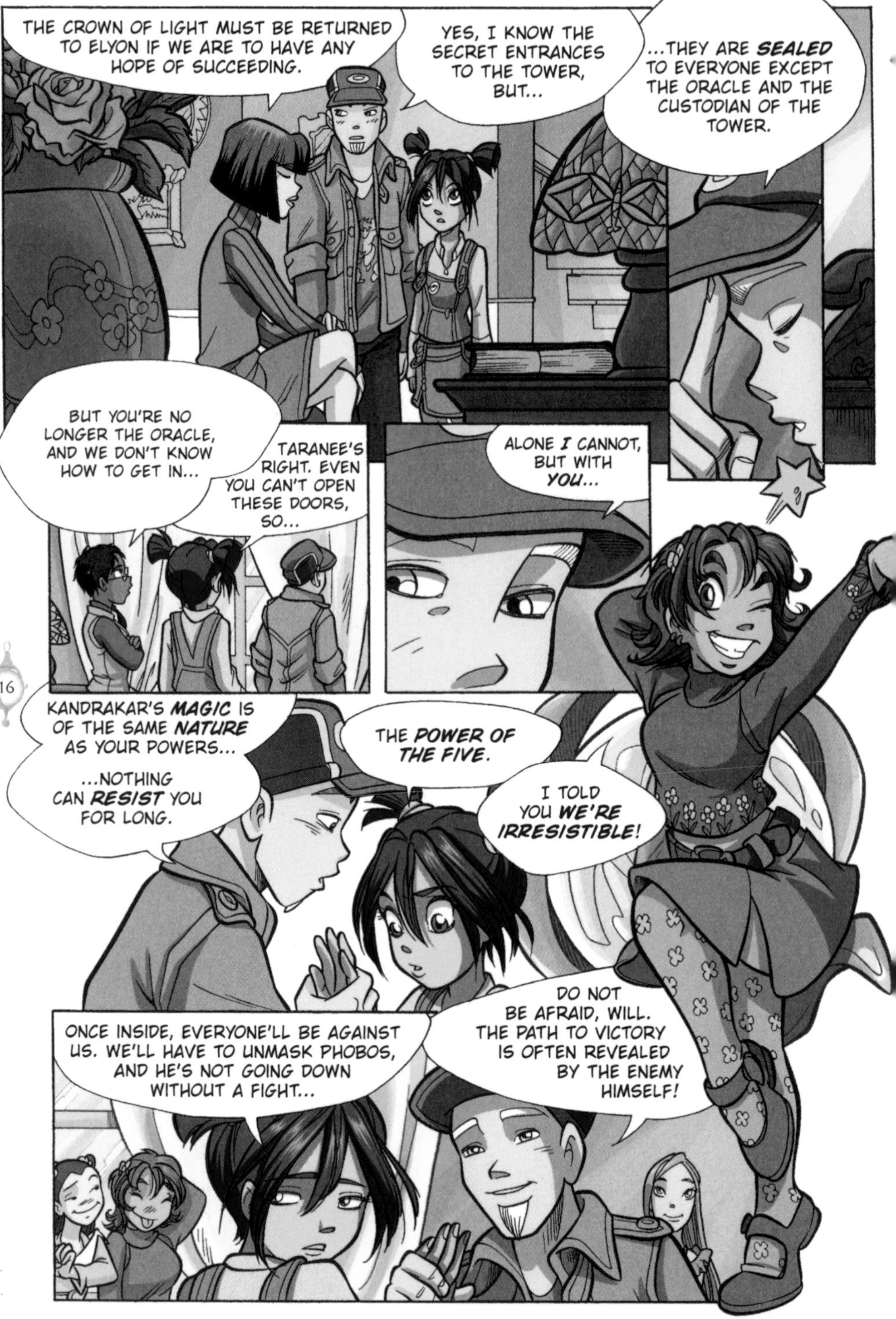

THE CROWN OF LIGHT MUST BE RETURNED TO ELYON IF WE ARE TO HAVE ANY HOPE OF SUCCEEDING.
YES, I KNOW THE SECRET ENTRANCES TO THE TOWER, BUT...
...THEY ARE **SEALED** TO EVERYONE EXCEPT THE ORACLE AND THE CUSTODIAN OF THE TOWER.
BUT YOU'RE NO LONGER THE ORACLE, AND WE DON'T KNOW HOW TO GET IN...
TARANEE'S RIGHT. EVEN YOU CAN'T OPEN THESE DOORS, SO...
ALONE ***I*** CANNOT, BUT WITH ***YOU***...
KANDRAKAR'S ***MAGIC*** IS OF THE SAME ***NATURE*** AS YOUR POWERS...
...NOTHING CAN ***RESIST*** YOU FOR LONG.
THE ***POWER OF THE FIVE***.
I TOLD YOU ***WE'RE IRRESISTIBLE***!
ONCE INSIDE, EVERYONE'LL BE AGAINST US. WE'LL HAVE TO UNMASK PHOBOS, AND HE'S NOT GOING DOWN WITHOUT A FIGHT...
DO NOT BE AFRAID, WILL. THE PATH TO VICTORY IS OFTEN REVEALED BY THE ENEMY HIMSELF!

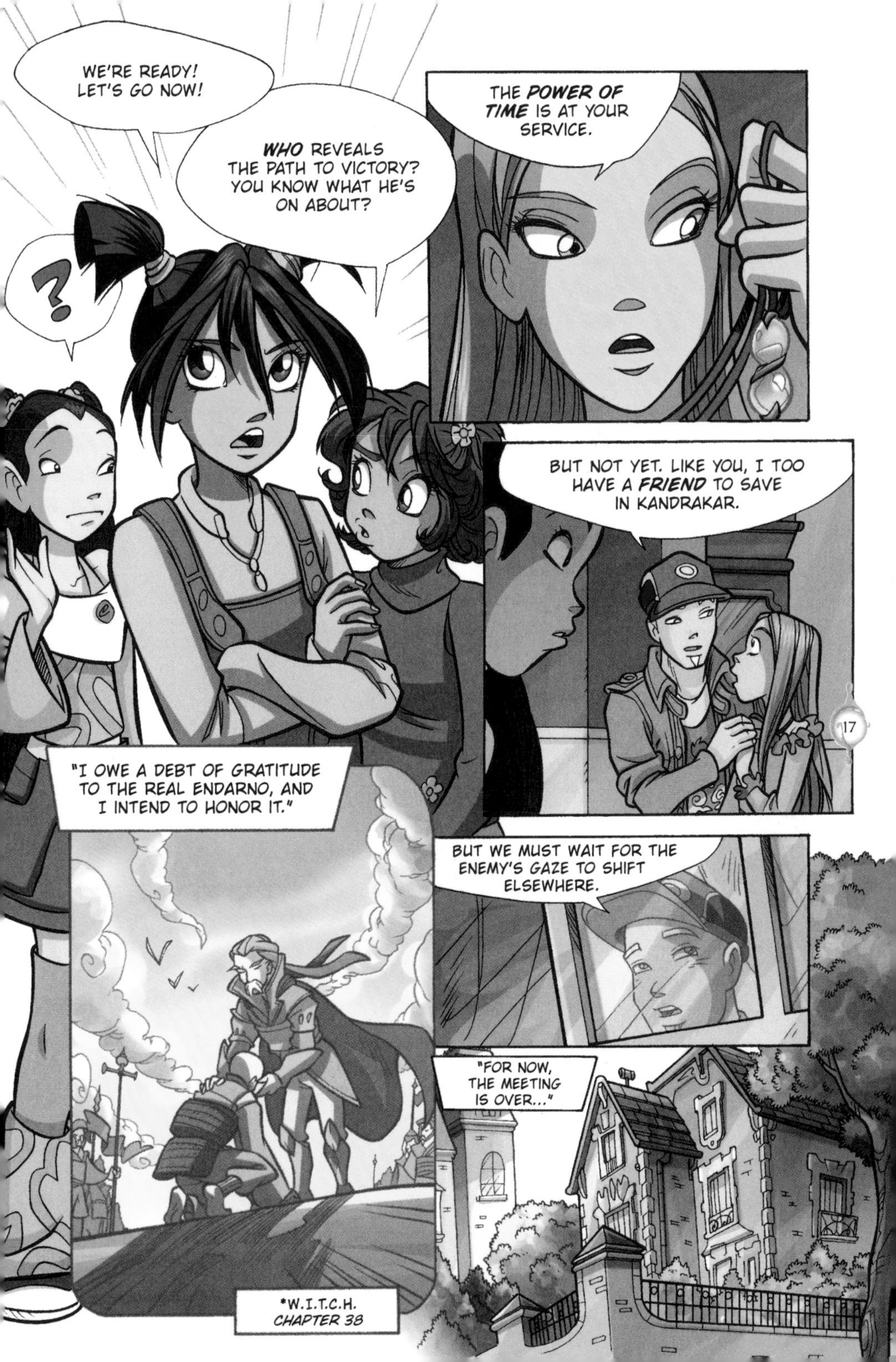
WE'RE READY! LET'S GO NOW!
WHO REVEALS THE PATH TO VICTORY? YOU KNOW WHAT HE'S ON ABOUT?
?
THE POWER OF TIME IS AT YOUR SERVICE.
BUT NOT YET. LIKE YOU, I TOO HAVE A FRIEND TO SAVE IN KANDRAKAR.
"I OWE A DEBT OF GRATITUDE TO THE REAL ENDARNO, AND I INTEND TO HONOR IT."
*W.I.T.C.H. CHAPTER 38
BUT WE MUST WAIT FOR THE ENEMY'S GAZE TO SHIFT ELSEWHERE.
"FOR NOW, THE MEETING IS OVER..."

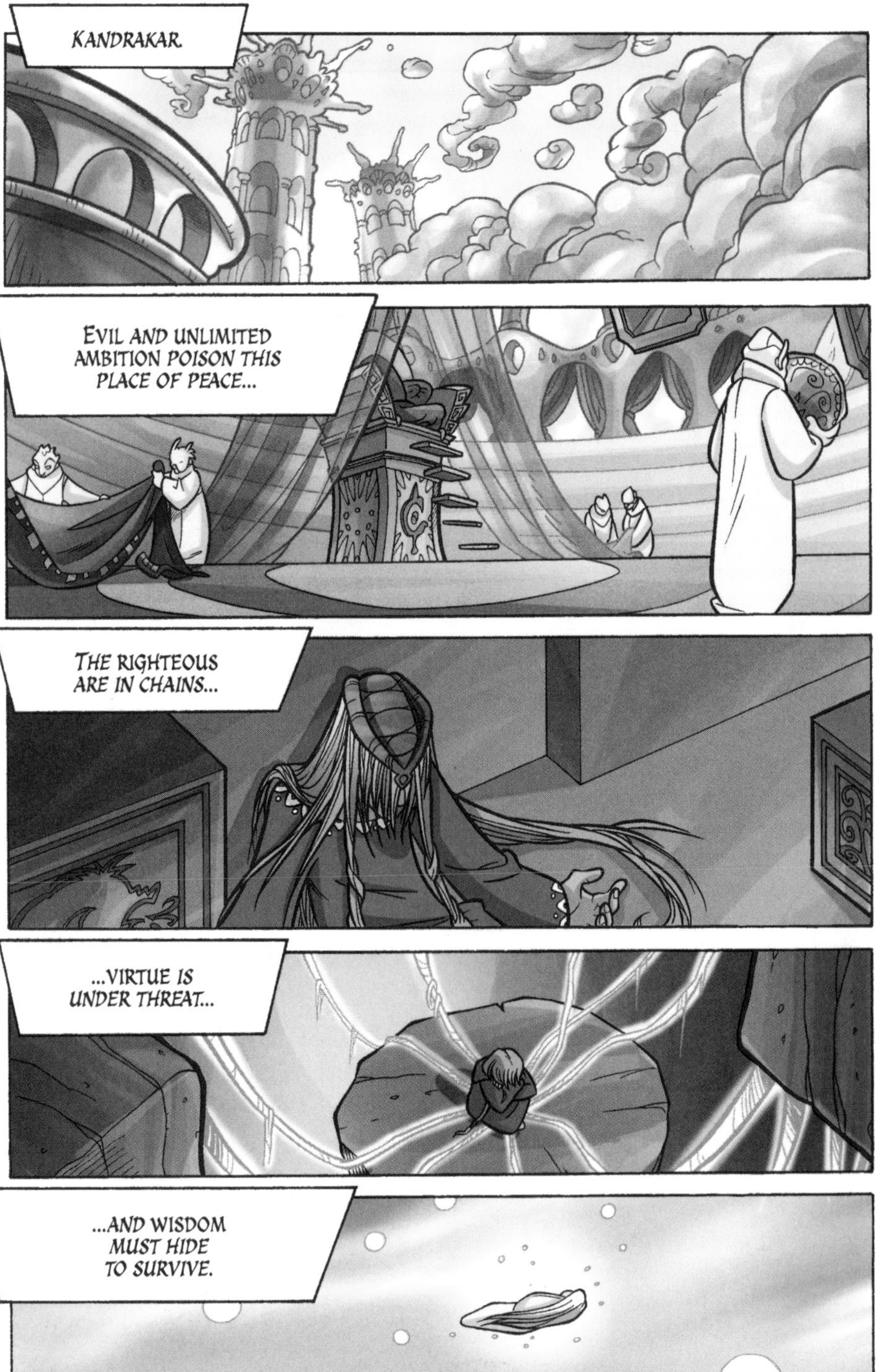
KANDRAKAR.
EVIL AND UNLIMITED AMBITION POISON THIS PLACE OF PEACE...
THE RIGHTEOUS ARE IN CHAINS...
...VIRTUE IS UNDER THREAT...
...AND WISDOM MUST HIDE TO SURVIVE.

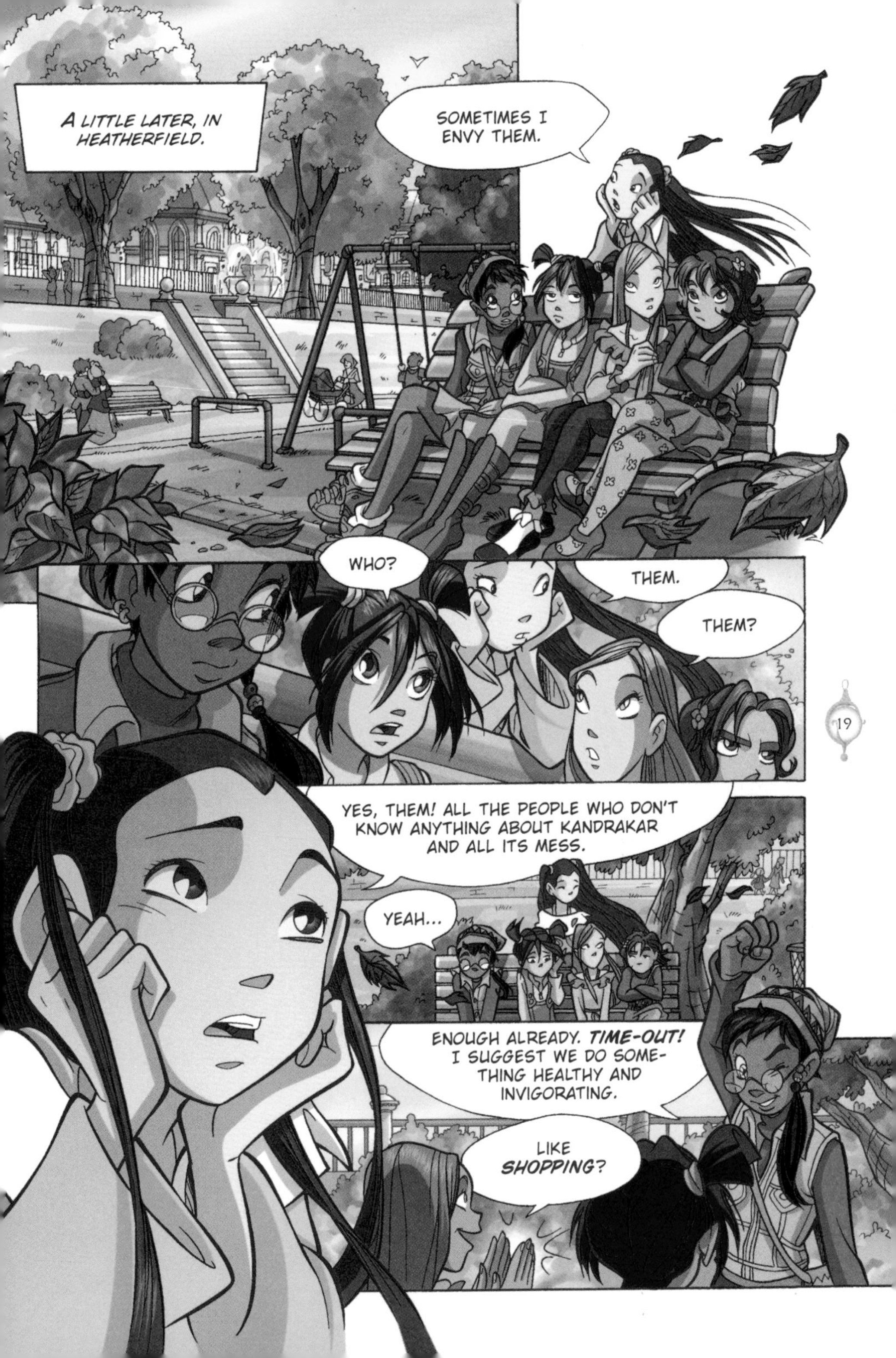
A LITTLE LATER, IN HEATHERFIELD.
SOMETIMES I ENVY THEM.
WHO?
THEM.
THEM?
YES, THEM! ALL THE PEOPLE WHO DON'T KNOW ANYTHING ABOUT KANDRAKAR AND ALL ITS MESS.
YEAH...
ENOUGH ALREADY. **TIME-OUT!** I SUGGEST WE DO SOMETHING HEALTHY AND INVIGORATING.
LIKE **SHOPPING**?

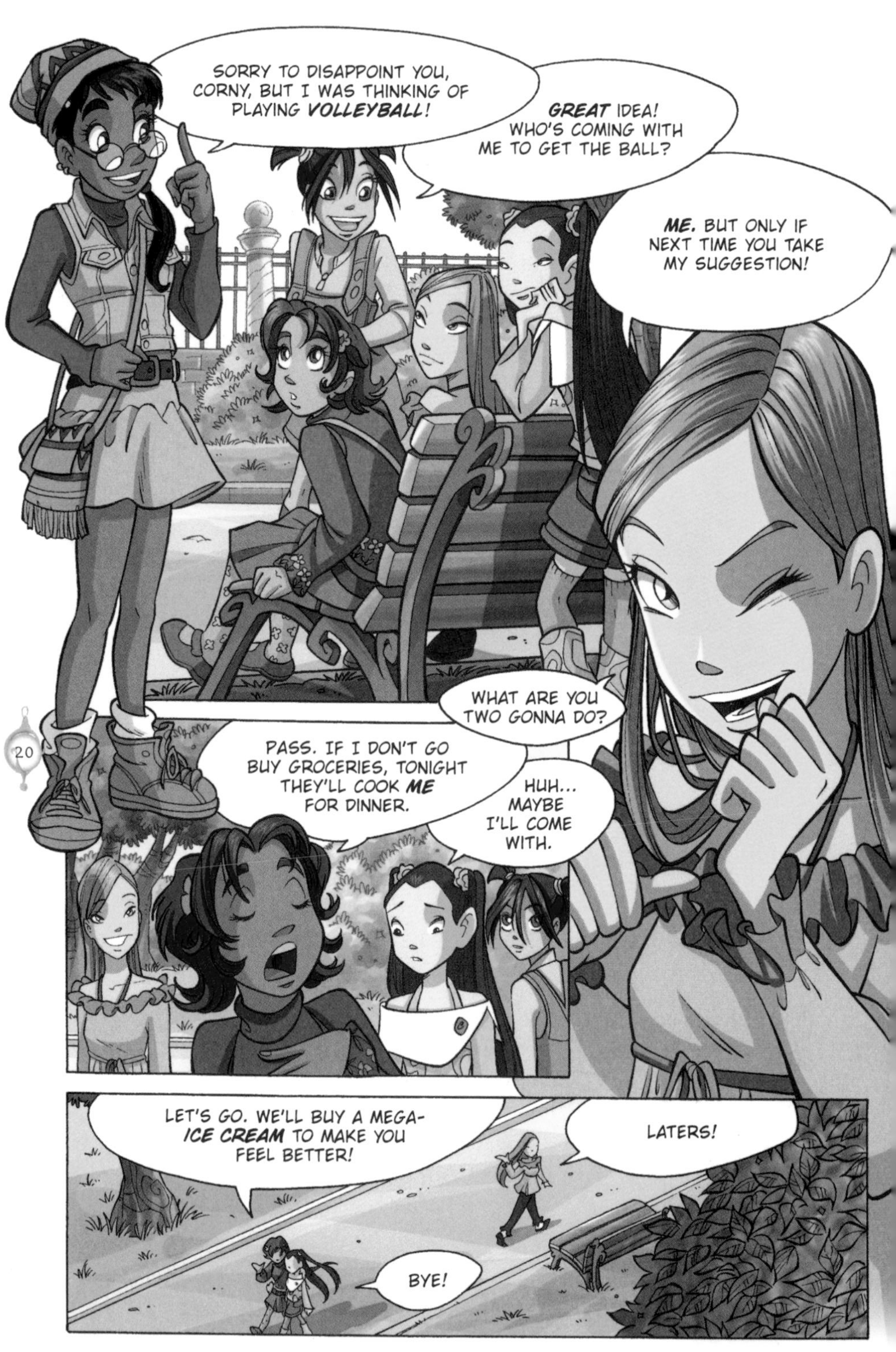
SORRY TO DISAPPOINT YOU, CORNY, BUT I WAS THINKING OF PLAYING **VOLLEYBALL**!
GREAT IDEA! WHO'S COMING WITH ME TO GET THE BALL?
ME. BUT ONLY IF NEXT TIME YOU TAKE MY SUGGESTION!
WHAT ARE YOU TWO GONNA DO?
PASS. IF I DON'T GO BUY GROCERIES, TONIGHT THEY'LL COOK **ME** FOR DINNER.
HUH... MAYBE I'LL COME WITH.
LET'S GO. WE'LL BUY A MEGA-**ICE CREAM** TO MAKE YOU FEEL BETTER!
LATERS!
BYE!

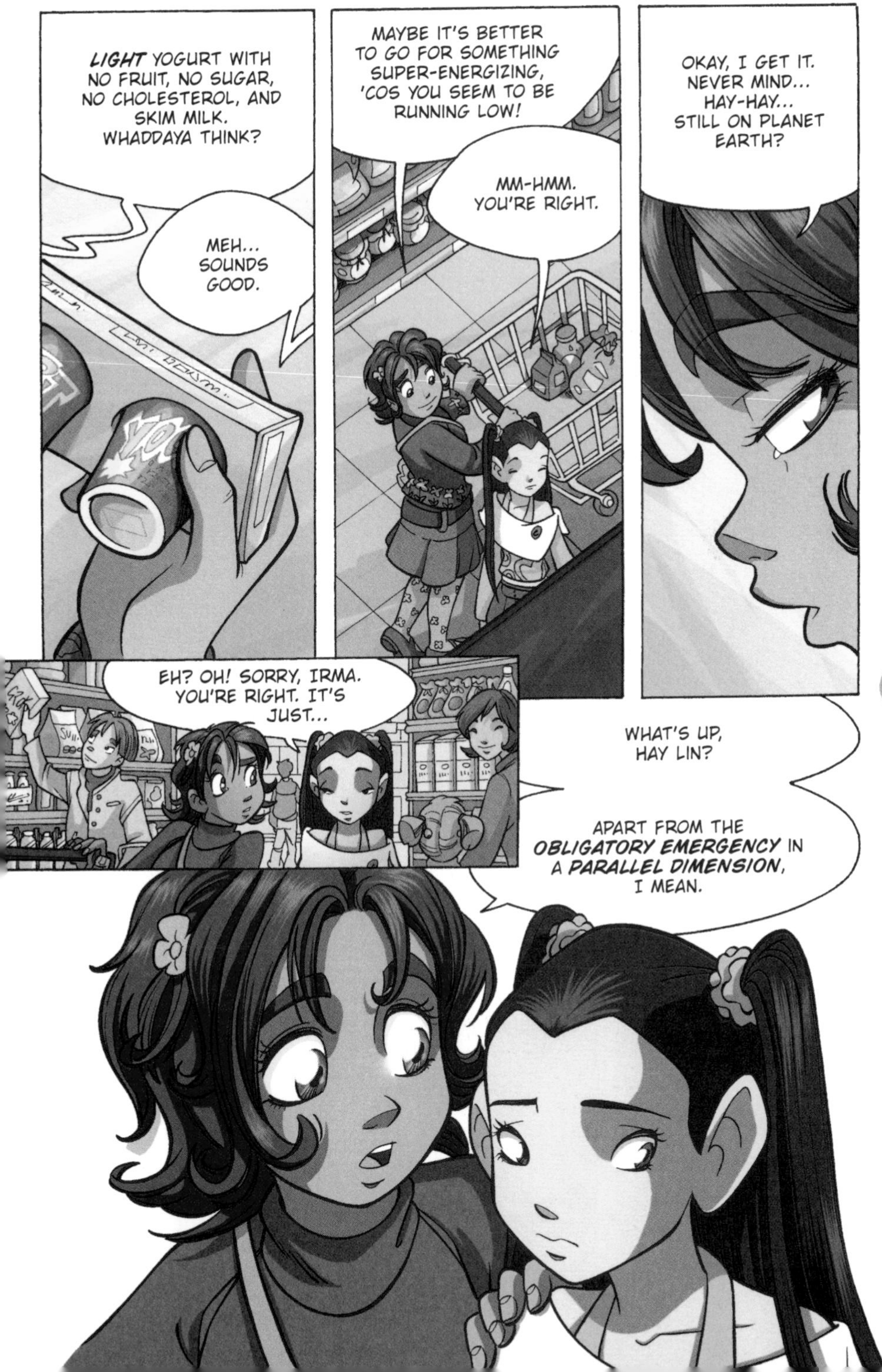
LIGHT YOGURT WITH NO FRUIT, NO SUGAR, NO CHOLESTEROL, AND SKIM MILK. WHADDAYA THINK?
MEH... SOUNDS GOOD.
MAYBE IT'S BETTER TO GO FOR SOMETHING SUPER-ENERGIZING, 'COS YOU SEEM TO BE RUNNING LOW!
MM-HMM. YOU'RE RIGHT.
OKAY, I GET IT. NEVER MIND... HAY-HAY... STILL ON PLANET EARTH?
EH? OH! SORRY, IRMA. YOU'RE RIGHT. IT'S JUST...
WHAT'S UP, HAY LIN?
APART FROM THE OBLIGATORY EMERGENCY IN A PARALLEL DIMENSION, I MEAN.

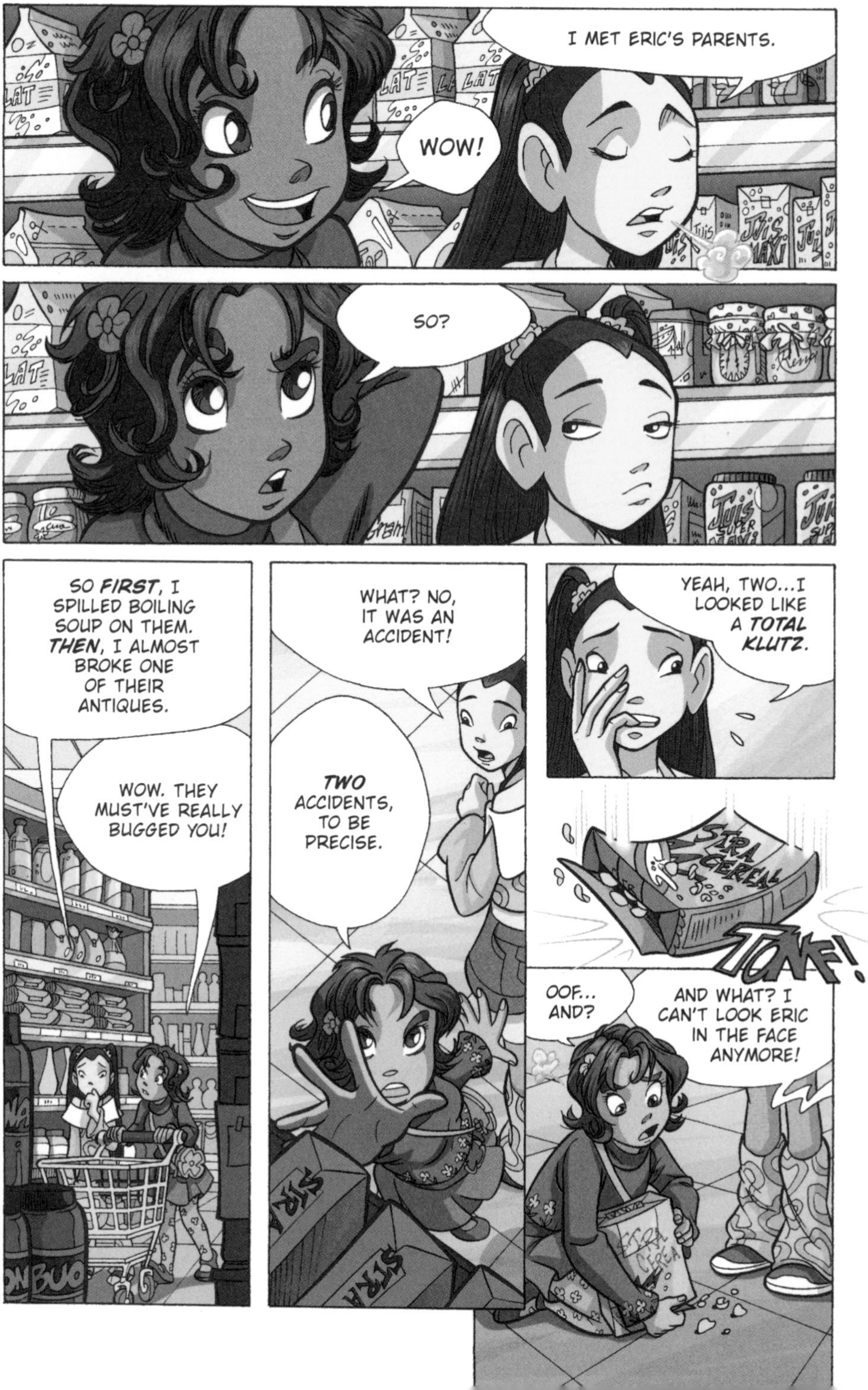
I MET ERIC'S PARENTS.
WOW!
SO?
SO *FIRST*, I SPILLED BOILING SOUP ON THEM. *THEN*, I ALMOST BROKE ONE OF THEIR ANTIQUES.
WOW. THEY MUST'VE REALLY BUGGED YOU!
WHAT? NO, IT WAS AN ACCIDENT!
TWO ACCIDENTS, TO BE PRECISE.
YEAH, TWO...I LOOKED LIKE A *TOTAL KLUTZ*.
STRA CEREAL
TONF!
OOF... AND?
AND WHAT? I CAN'T LOOK ERIC IN THE FACE ANYMORE!

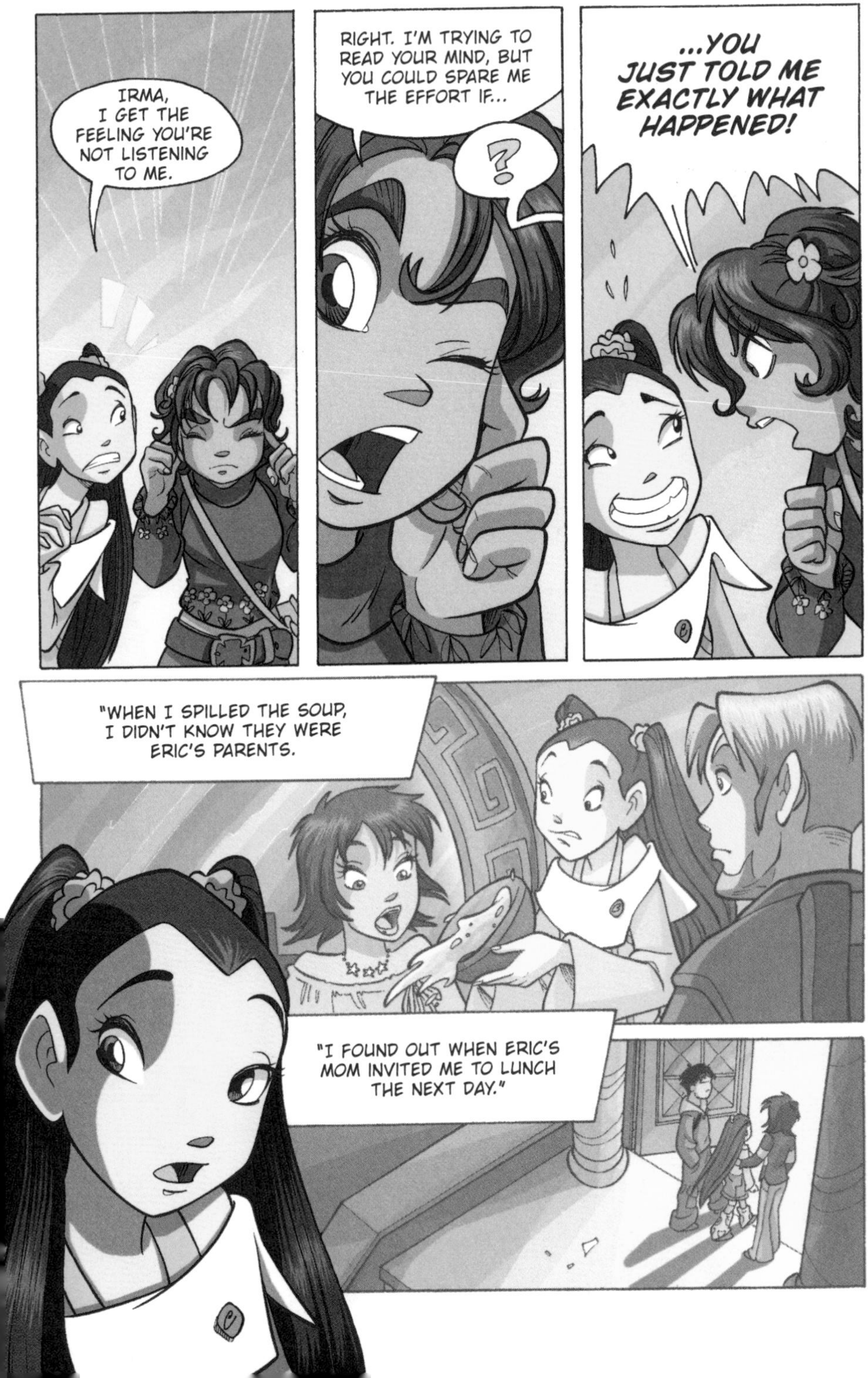
IRMA, I GET THE FEELING YOU'RE NOT LISTENING TO ME.
RIGHT. I'M TRYING TO READ YOUR MIND, BUT YOU COULD SPARE ME THE EFFORT IF...
?
...YOU JUST TOLD ME EXACTLY WHAT HAPPENED!
"WHEN I SPILLED THE SOUP, I DIDN'T KNOW THEY WERE ERIC'S PARENTS.
"I FOUND OUT WHEN ERIC'S MOM INVITED ME TO LUNCH THE NEXT DAY."

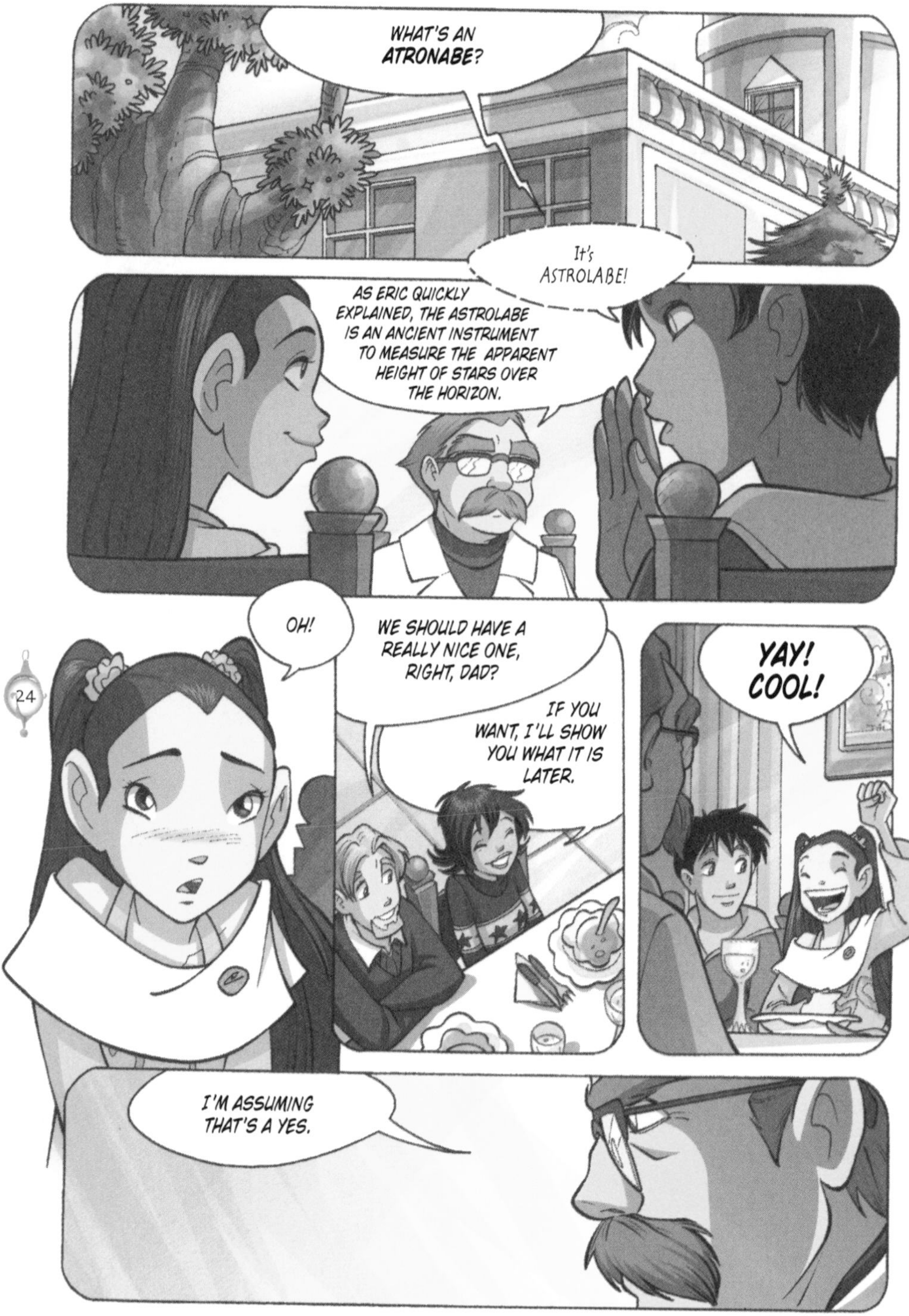
WHAT'S AN ATRONABE?
It's ASTROLABE!
AS ERIC QUICKLY EXPLAINED, THE ASTROLABE IS AN ANCIENT INSTRUMENT TO MEASURE THE APPARENT HEIGHT OF STARS OVER THE HORIZON.
OH!
WE SHOULD HAVE A REALLY NICE ONE, RIGHT, DAD?
IF YOU WANT, I'LL SHOW YOU WHAT IT IS LATER.
YAY! COOL!
I'M ASSUMING THAT'S A YES.

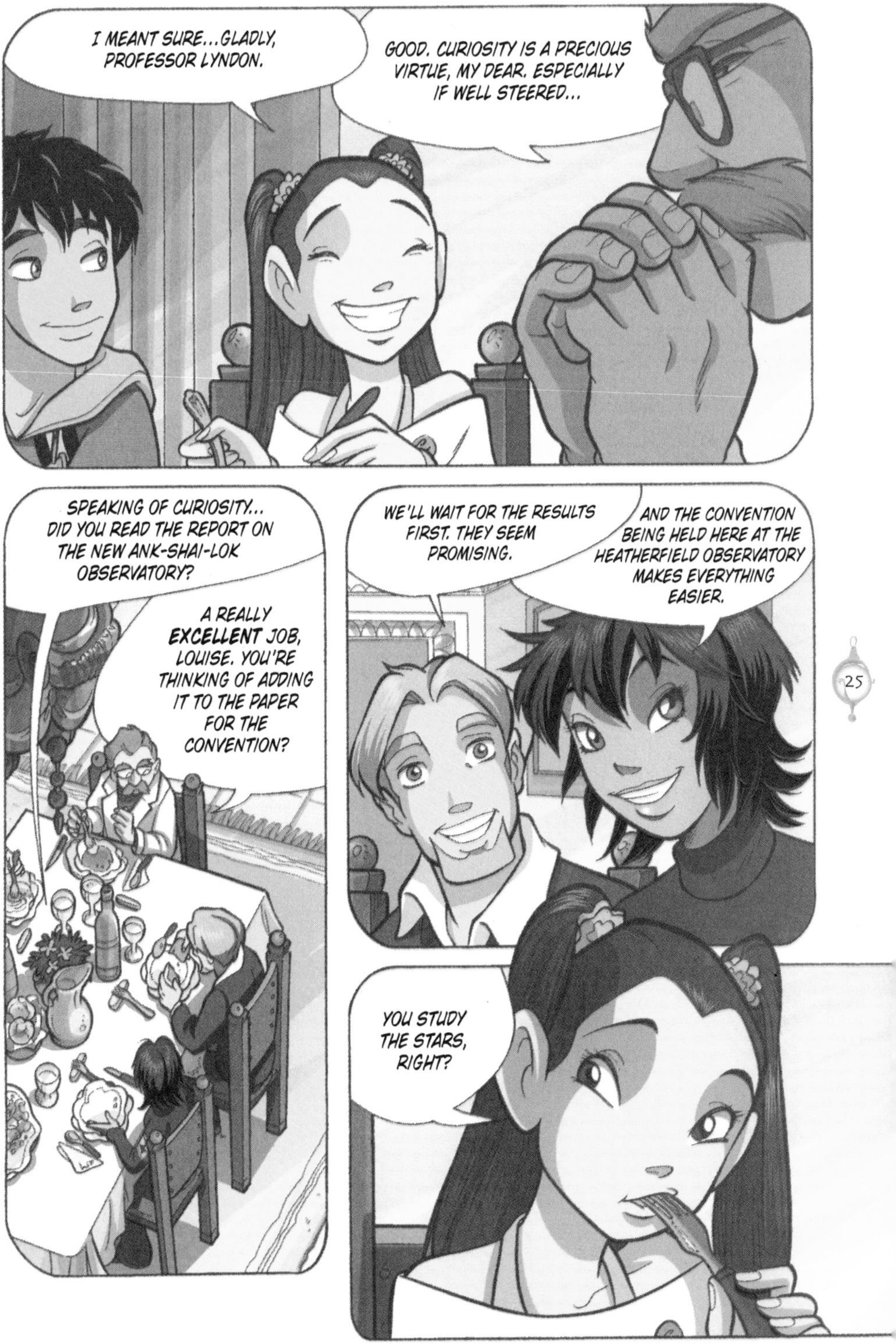
I MEANT SURE...GLADLY, PROFESSOR LYNDON.
GOOD. CURIOSITY IS A PRECIOUS VIRTUE, MY DEAR. ESPECIALLY IF WELL STEERED...
SPEAKING OF CURIOSITY... DID YOU READ THE REPORT ON THE NEW ANK-SHAI-LOK OBSERVATORY?
A REALLY **EXCELLENT** JOB, LOUISE. YOU'RE THINKING OF ADDING IT TO THE PAPER FOR THE CONVENTION?
WE'LL WAIT FOR THE RESULTS FIRST. THEY SEEM PROMISING.
AND THE CONVENTION BEING HELD HERE AT THE HEATHERFIELD OBSERVATORY MAKES EVERYTHING EASIER.
YOU STUDY THE STARS, RIGHT?

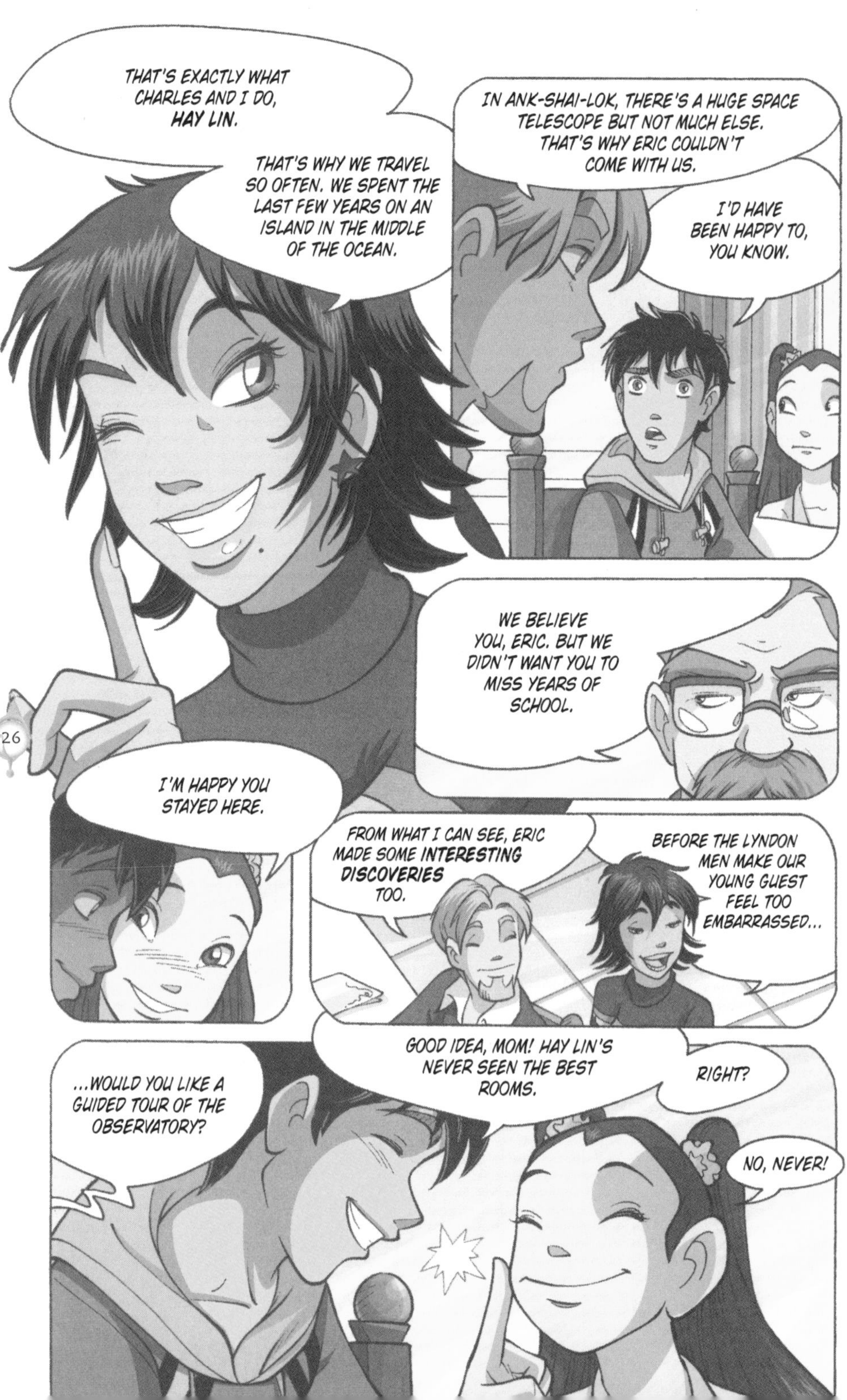
THAT'S EXACTLY WHAT CHARLES AND I DO, **HAY LIN.**
THAT'S WHY WE TRAVEL SO OFTEN. WE SPENT THE LAST FEW YEARS ON AN ISLAND IN THE MIDDLE OF THE OCEAN.
IN ANK-SHAI-LOK, THERE'S A HUGE SPACE TELESCOPE BUT NOT MUCH ELSE. THAT'S WHY ERIC COULDN'T COME WITH US.
I'D HAVE BEEN HAPPY TO, YOU KNOW.
WE BELIEVE YOU, ERIC. BUT WE DIDN'T WANT YOU TO MISS YEARS OF SCHOOL.
I'M HAPPY YOU STAYED HERE.
FROM WHAT I CAN SEE, ERIC MADE SOME **INTERESTING DISCOVERIES** TOO.
BEFORE THE LYNDON MEN MAKE OUR YOUNG GUEST FEEL TOO EMBARRASSED...
...WOULD YOU LIKE A GUIDED TOUR OF THE OBSERVATORY?
GOOD IDEA, MOM! HAY LIN'S NEVER SEEN THE BEST ROOMS.
RIGHT?
NO, NEVER!

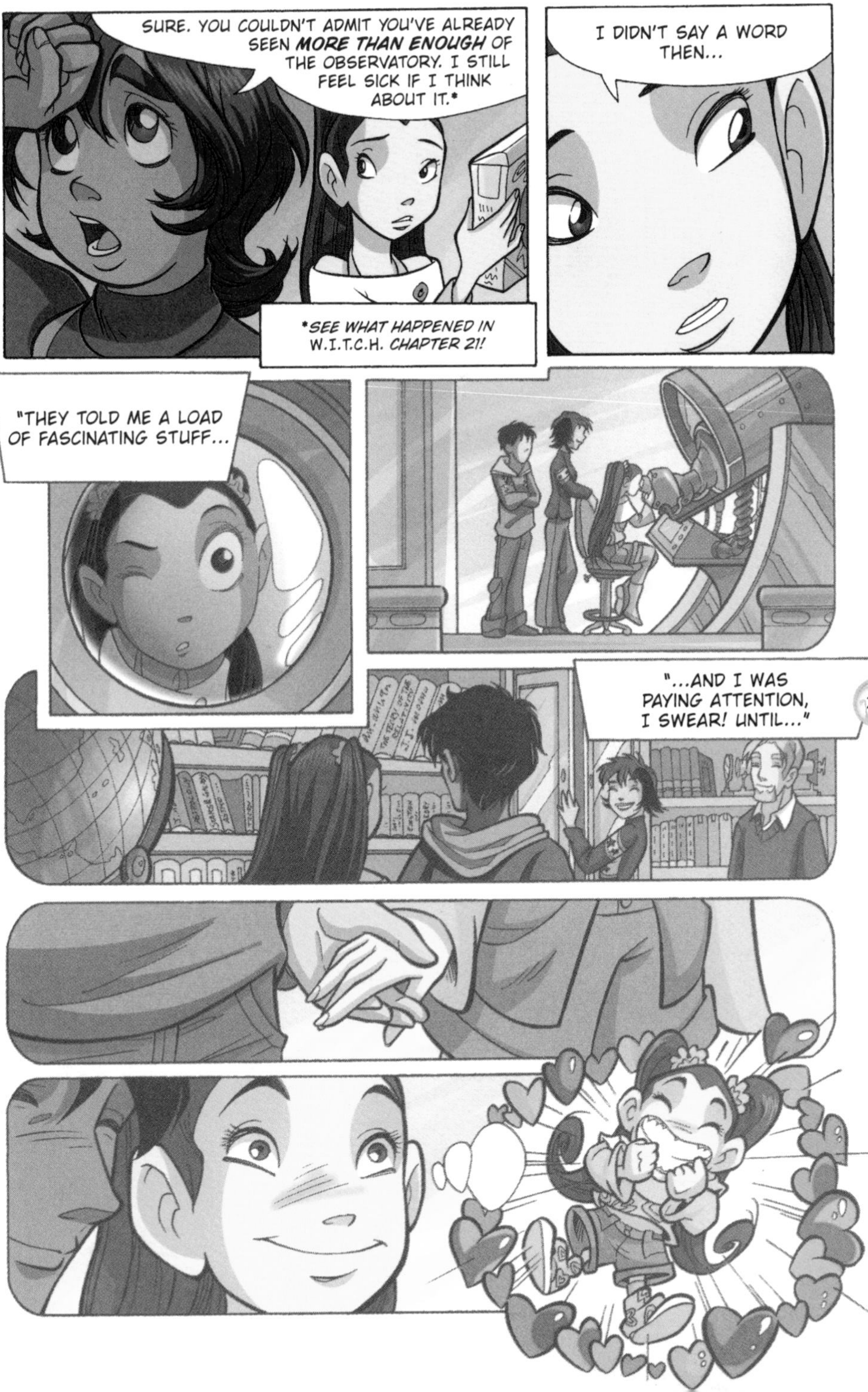
SURE. YOU COULDN'T ADMIT YOU'VE ALREADY SEEN **MORE THAN ENOUGH** OF THE OBSERVATORY. I STILL FEEL SICK IF I THINK ABOUT IT.*
*SEE WHAT HAPPENED IN W.I.T.C.H. CHAPTER 21!
I DIDN'T SAY A WORD THEN...
"THEY TOLD ME A LOAD OF FASCINATING STUFF...
"...AND I WAS PAYING ATTENTION, I SWEAR! UNTIL..."

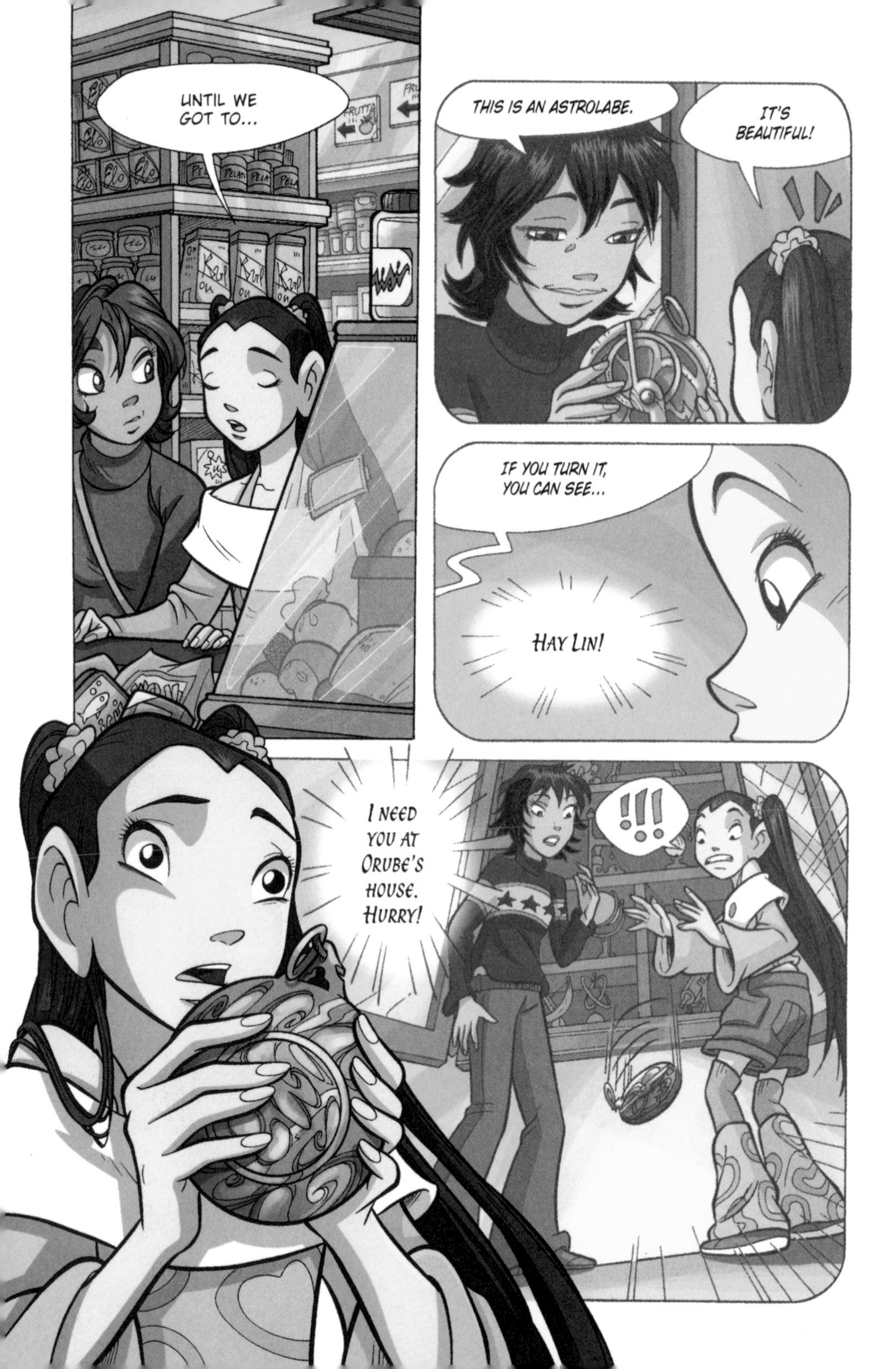
UNTIL WE GOT TO...
THIS IS AN ASTROLABE.
IT'S BEAUTIFUL!
IF YOU TURN IT, YOU CAN SEE...
HAY LIN!
I NEED YOU AT ORUBE'S HOUSE. HURRY!
!!!

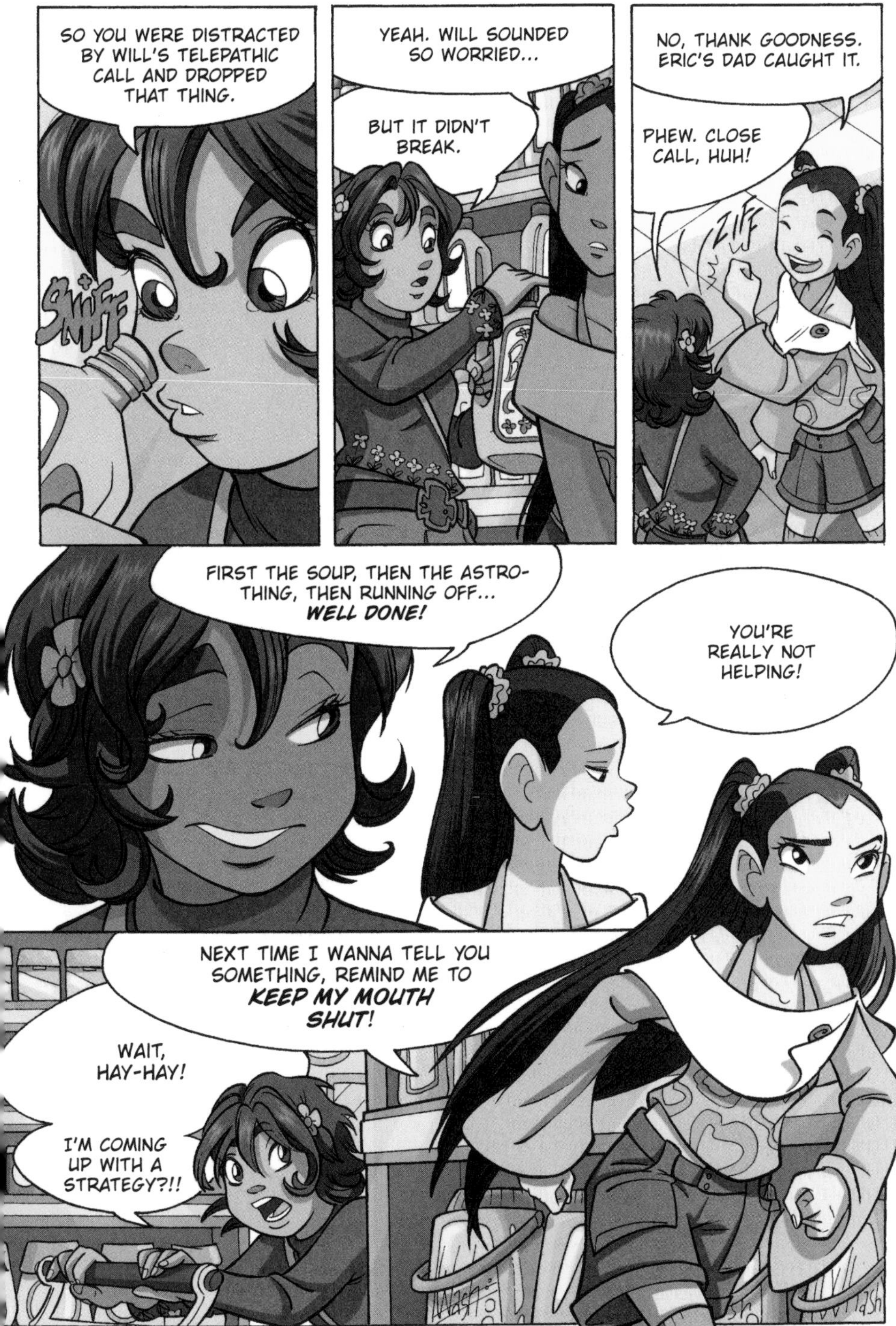
SO YOU WERE DISTRACTED BY WILL'S TELEPATHIC CALL AND DROPPED THAT THING.
SNIFF
YEAH. WILL SOUNDED SO WORRIED...
BUT IT DIDN'T BREAK.
NO, THANK GOODNESS. ERIC'S DAD CAUGHT IT.
PHEW. CLOSE CALL, HUH!
ZIFF
FIRST THE SOUP, THEN THE ASTRO-THING, THEN RUNNING OFF... **WELL DONE!**
YOU'RE REALLY NOT HELPING!
NEXT TIME I WANNA TELL YOU SOMETHING, REMIND ME TO **KEEP MY MOUTH SHUT**!
WAIT, HAY-HAY!
I'M COMING UP WITH A STRATEGY?!!

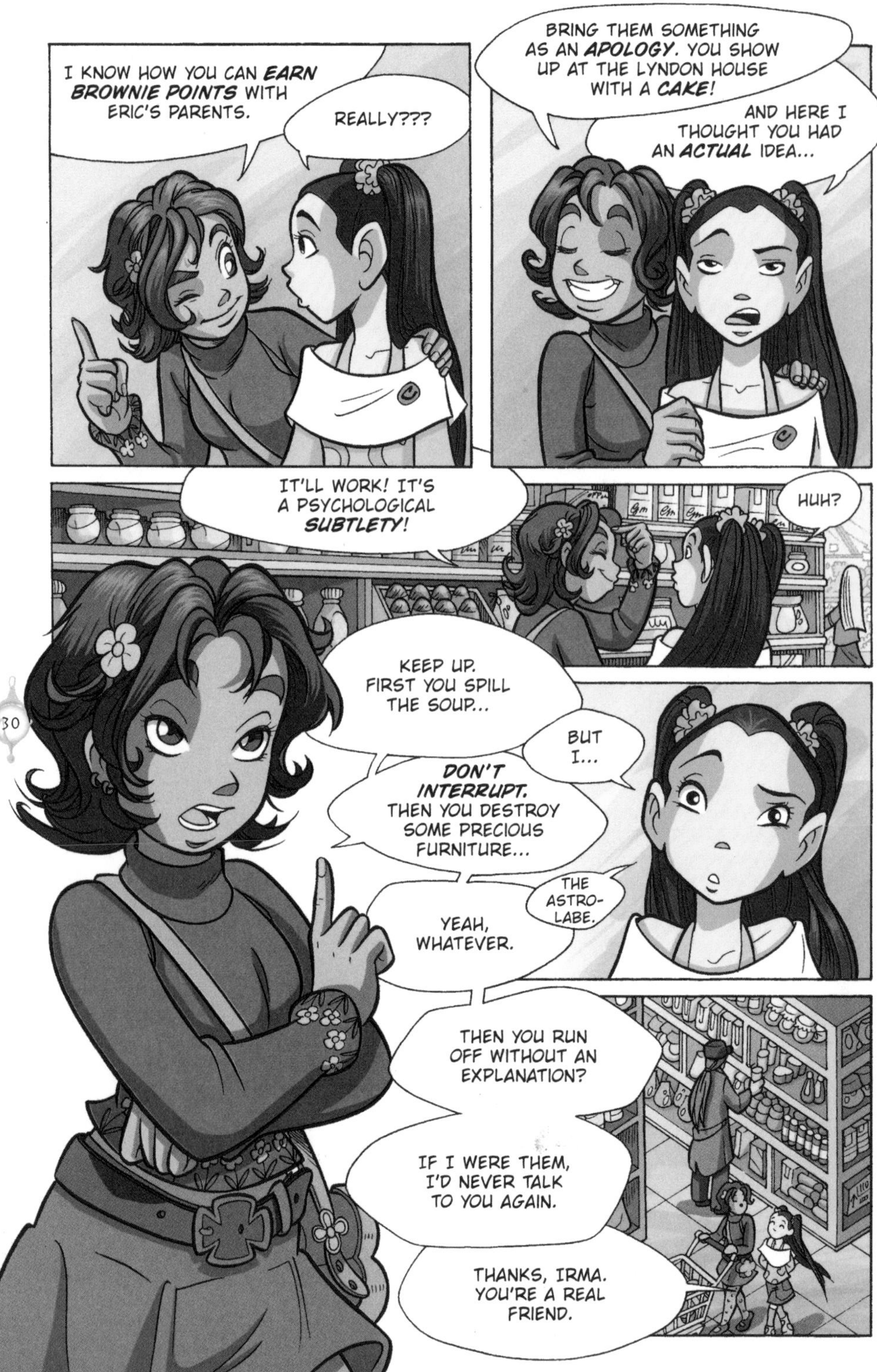

I KNOW HOW YOU CAN ***EARN BROWNIE POINTS*** WITH ERIC'S PARENTS.
REALLY???
BRING THEM SOMETHING AS AN ***APOLOGY***. YOU SHOW UP AT THE LYNDON HOUSE WITH A ***CAKE***!
AND HERE I THOUGHT YOU HAD AN ***ACTUAL*** IDEA...
IT'LL WORK! IT'S A PSYCHOLOGICAL ***SUBTLETY***!
HUH?
KEEP UP. FIRST YOU SPILL THE SOUP...
BUT I...
DON'T INTERRUPT. THEN YOU DESTROY SOME PRECIOUS FURNITURE...
THE ASTRO-LABE.
YEAH, WHATEVER.
THEN YOU RUN OFF WITHOUT AN EXPLANATION?
IF I WERE THEM, I'D NEVER TALK TO YOU AGAIN.
THANKS, IRMA. YOU'RE A REAL FRIEND.

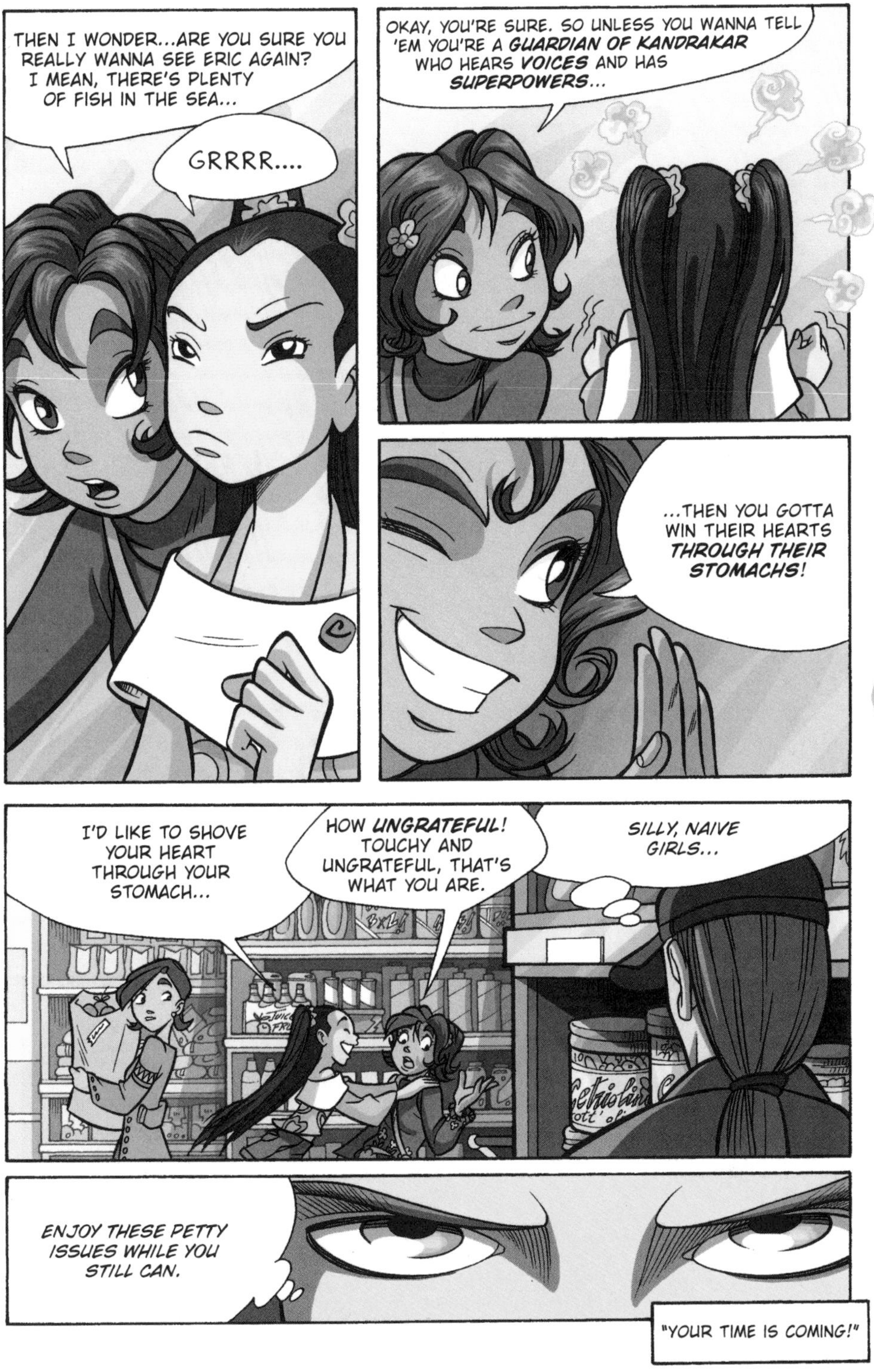
THEN I WONDER...ARE YOU SURE YOU REALLY WANNA SEE ERIC AGAIN? I MEAN, THERE'S PLENTY OF FISH IN THE SEA...
GRRRR....
OKAY, YOU'RE SURE. SO UNLESS YOU WANNA TELL 'EM YOU'RE A GUARDIAN OF KANDRAKAR WHO HEARS VOICES AND HAS SUPERPOWERS...
...THEN YOU GOTTA WIN THEIR HEARTS THROUGH THEIR STOMACHS!
I'D LIKE TO SHOVE YOUR HEART THROUGH YOUR STOMACH...
HOW UNGRATEFUL! TOUCHY AND UNGRATEFUL, THAT'S WHAT YOU ARE.
SILLY, NAIVE GIRLS...
ENJOY THESE PETTY ISSUES WHILE YOU STILL CAN.
"YOUR TIME IS COMING!"

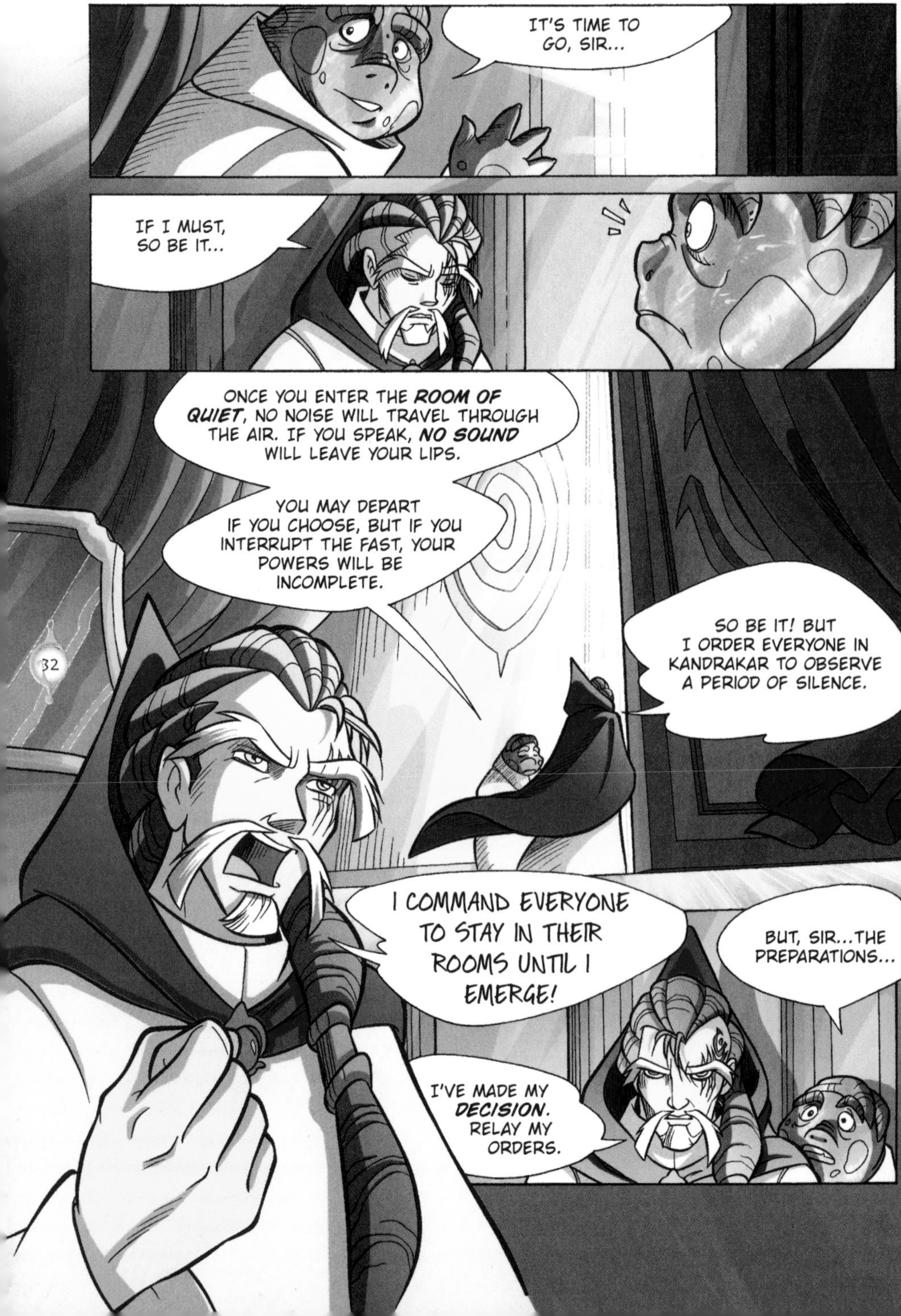
IT'S TIME TO GO, SIR...
IF I MUST, SO BE IT...
ONCE YOU ENTER THE **ROOM OF QUIET**, NO NOISE WILL TRAVEL THROUGH THE AIR. IF YOU SPEAK, **NO SOUND** WILL LEAVE YOUR LIPS.
YOU MAY DEPART IF YOU CHOOSE, BUT IF YOU INTERRUPT THE FAST, YOUR POWERS WILL BE INCOMPLETE.
SO BE IT! BUT I ORDER EVERYONE IN KANDRAKAR TO OBSERVE A PERIOD OF SILENCE.
I COMMAND EVERYONE TO STAY IN THEIR ROOMS UNTIL I EMERGE!
BUT, SIR...THE PREPARATIONS...
I'VE MADE MY **DECISION**. RELAY MY ORDERS.

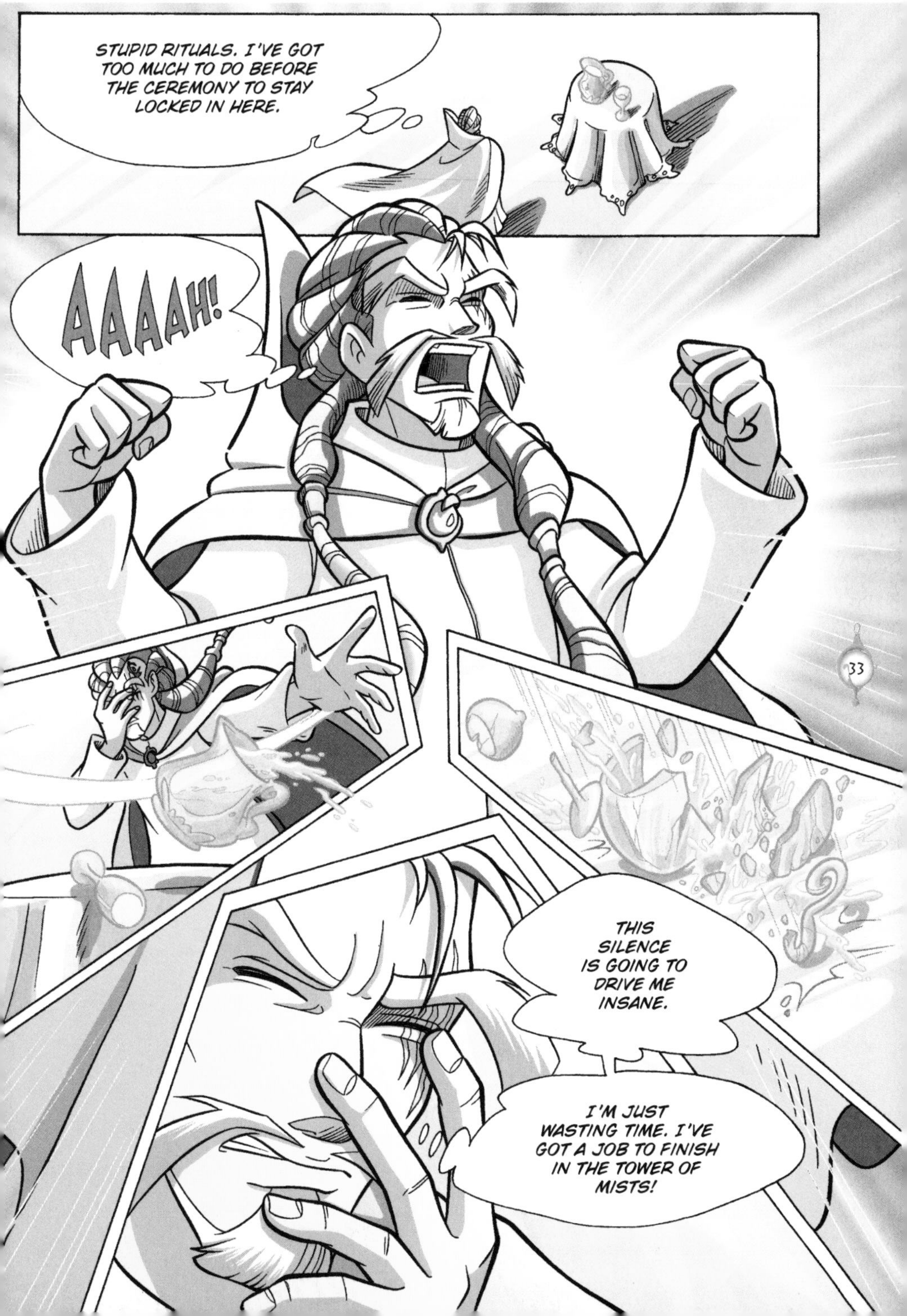
STUPID RITUALS. I'VE GOT TOO MUCH TO DO BEFORE THE CEREMONY TO STAY LOCKED IN HERE.
AAAAH!
THIS SILENCE IS GOING TO DRIVE ME INSANE.
I'M JUST WASTING TIME. I'VE GOT A JOB TO FINISH IN THE TOWER OF MISTS!

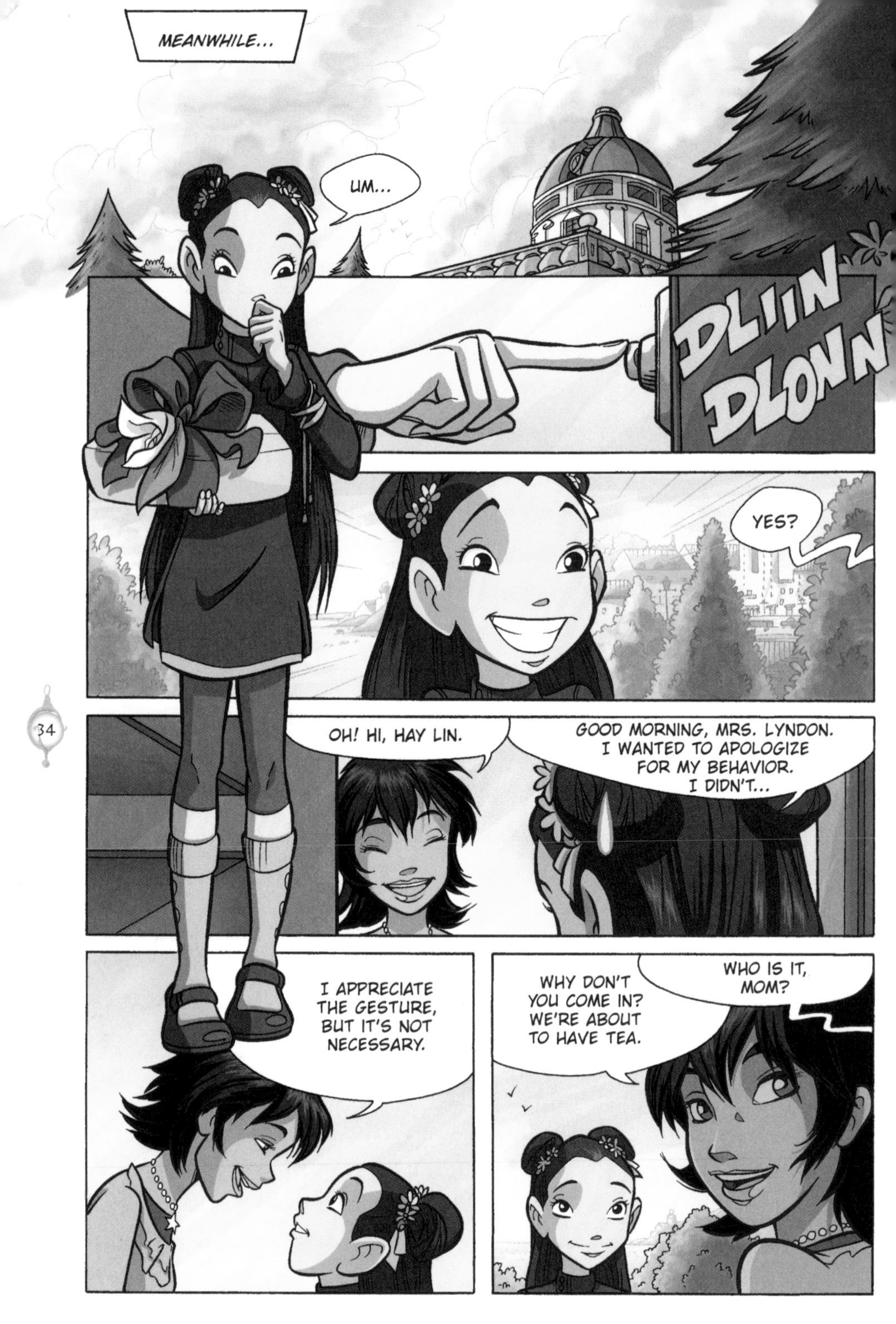
MEANWHILE...
UM...
DLIIN DLONN
YES?
OH! HI, HAY LIN.
GOOD MORNING, MRS. LYNDON. I WANTED TO APOLOGIZE FOR MY BEHAVIOR. I DIDN'T...
I APPRECIATE THE GESTURE, BUT IT'S NOT NECESSARY.
WHY DON'T YOU COME IN? WE'RE ABOUT TO HAVE TEA.
WHO IS IT, MOM?

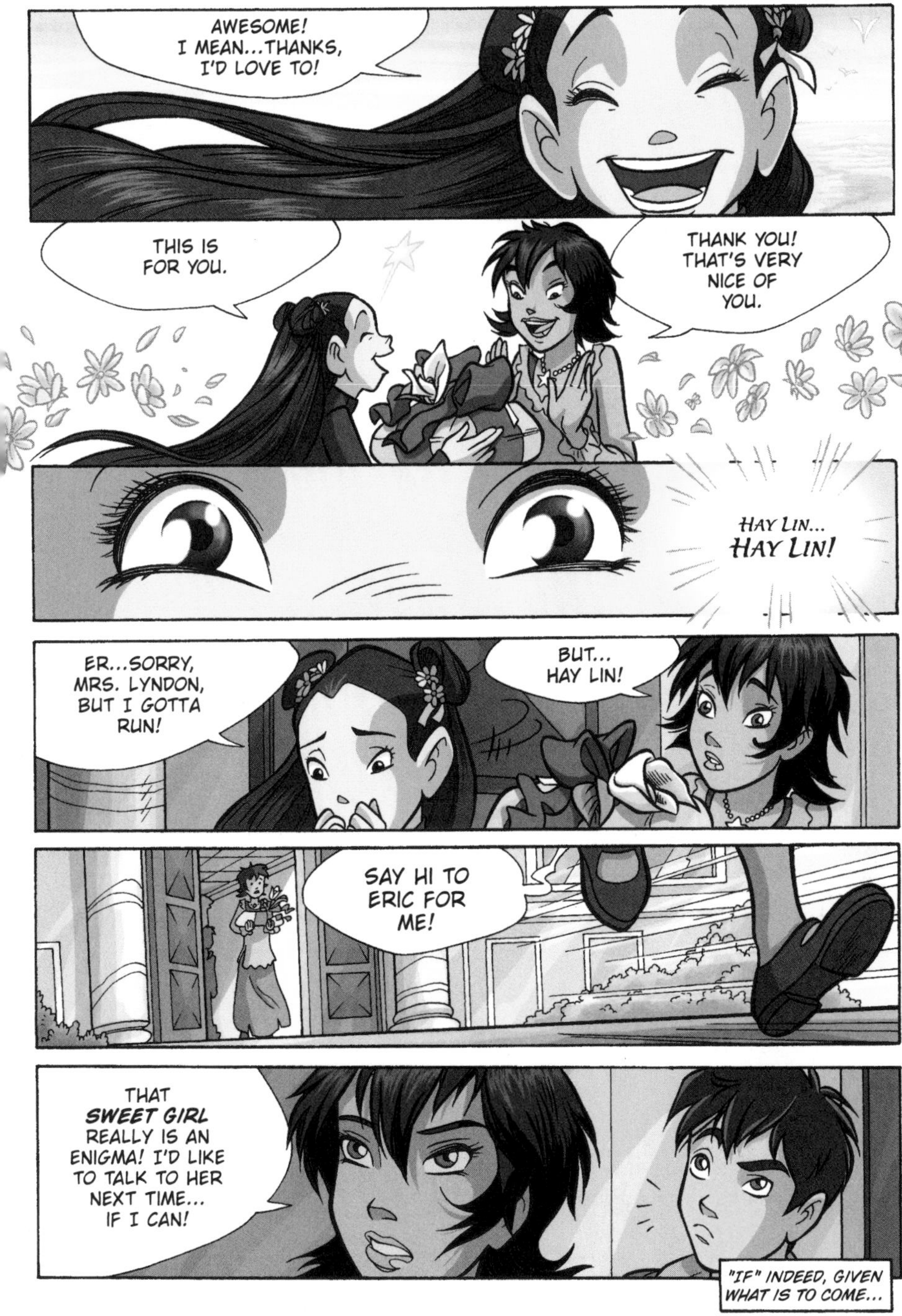
AWESOME! I MEAN...THANKS, I'D LOVE TO!
THIS IS FOR YOU.
THANK YOU! THAT'S VERY NICE OF YOU.
HAY LIN... HAY LIN!
ER...SORRY, MRS. LYNDON, BUT I GOTTA RUN!
BUT... HAY LIN!
SAY HI TO ERIC FOR ME!
THAT **SWEET GIRL** REALLY IS AN ENIGMA! I'D LIKE TO TALK TO HER NEXT TIME... IF I CAN!
"IF" INDEED, GIVEN WHAT IS TO COME...

Will   Irma   Taranee   Cornelia   Hay Lin

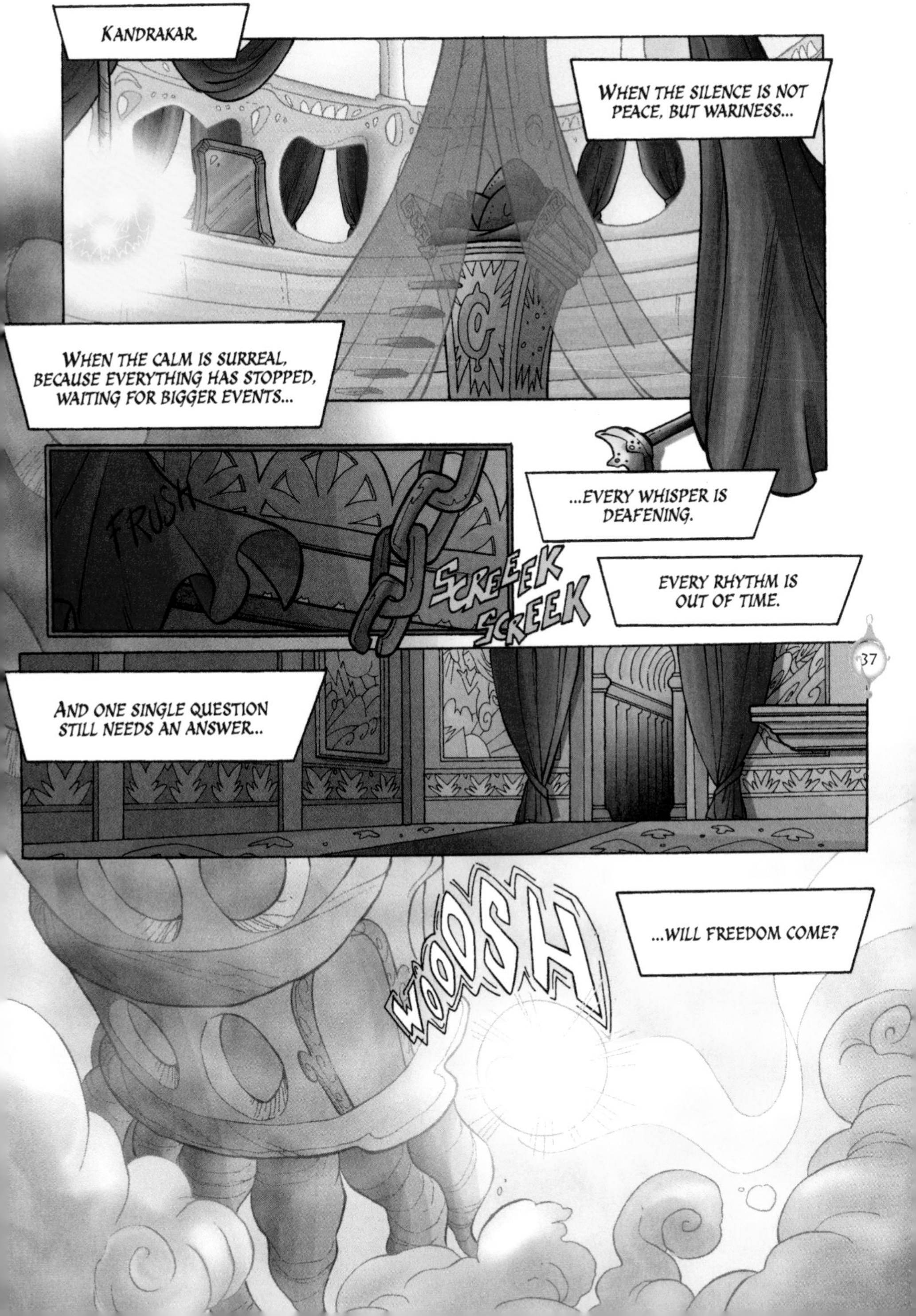

KANDRAKAR.
WHEN THE SILENCE IS NOT PEACE, BUT WARINESS...
WHEN THE CALM IS SURREAL, BECAUSE EVERYTHING HAS STOPPED, WAITING FOR BIGGER EVENTS...
FRUSH
SCREEEK SCREEK
...EVERY WHISPER IS DEAFENING.
EVERY RHYTHM IS OUT OF TIME.
AND ONE SINGLE QUESTION STILL NEEDS AN ANSWER...
WOOOSH
...WILL FREEDOM COME?

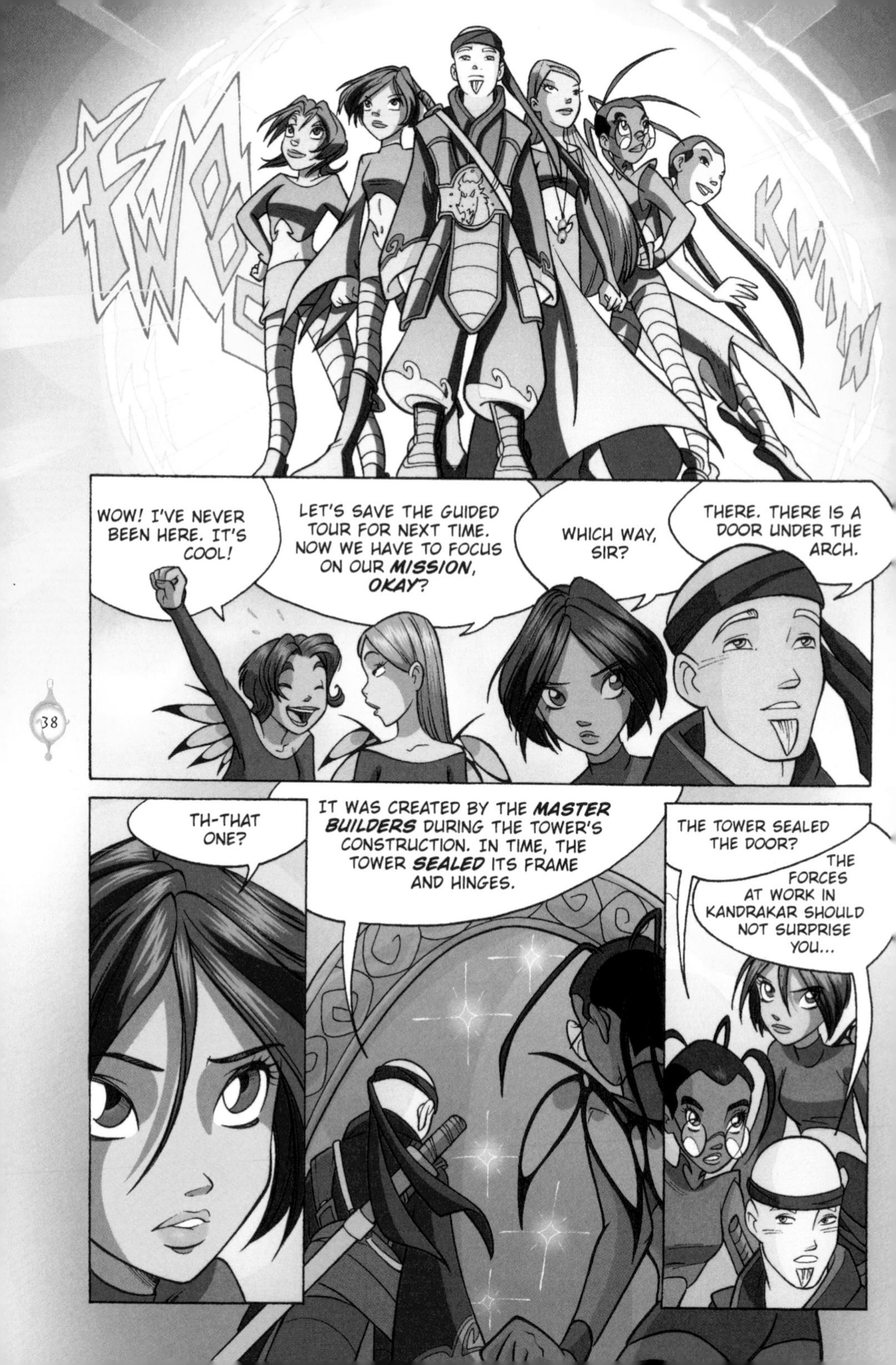
WOW! I'VE NEVER BEEN HERE. IT'S COOL!
LET'S SAVE THE GUIDED TOUR FOR NEXT TIME. NOW WE HAVE TO FOCUS ON OUR MISSION, OKAY?
WHICH WAY, SIR?
THERE. THERE IS A DOOR UNDER THE ARCH.
TH-THAT ONE?
IT WAS CREATED BY THE MASTER BUILDERS DURING THE TOWER'S CONSTRUCTION. IN TIME, THE TOWER SEALED ITS FRAME AND HINGES.
THE TOWER SEALED THE DOOR?
THE FORCES AT WORK IN KANDRAKAR SHOULD NOT SURPRISE YOU...

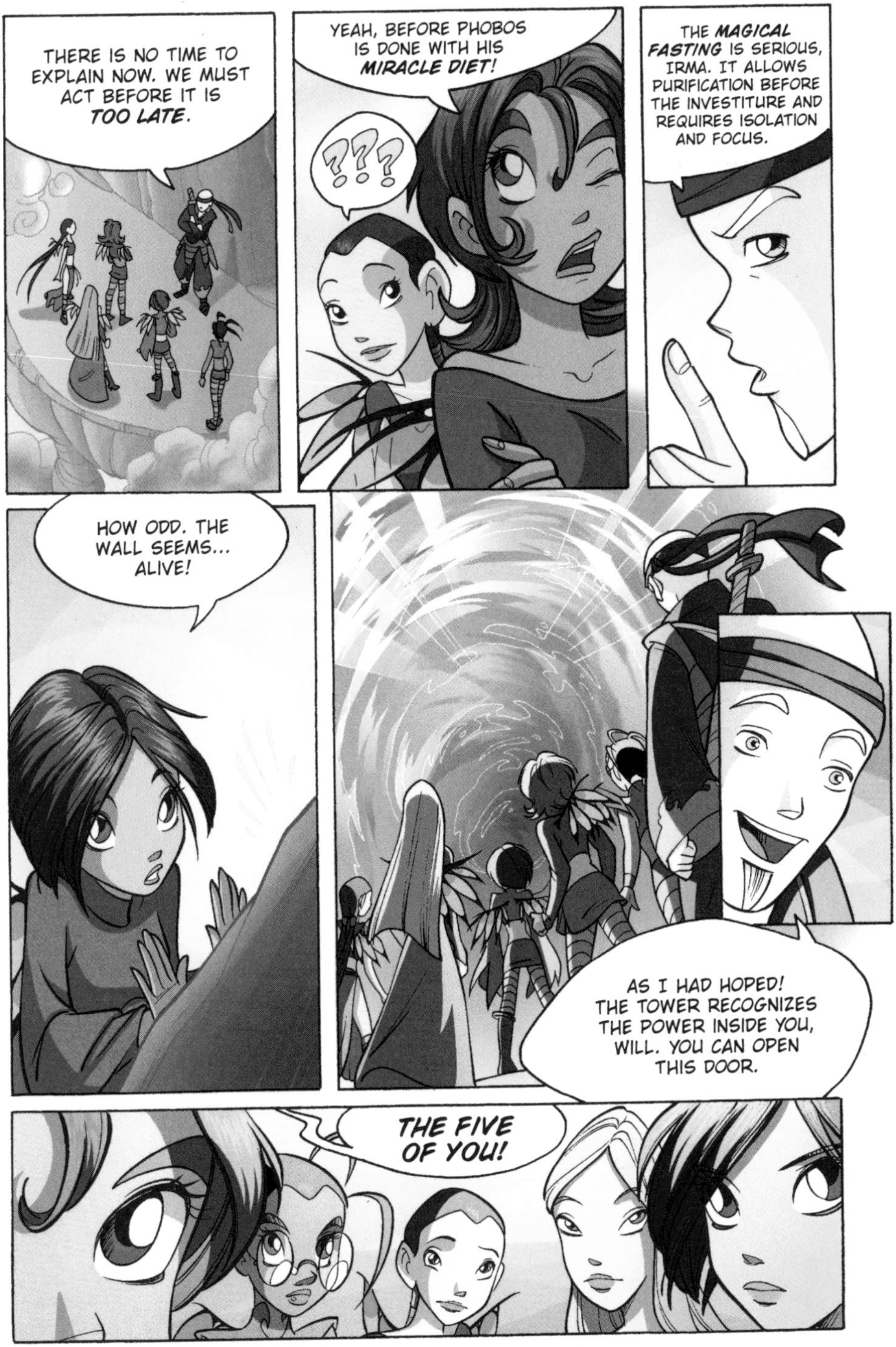
THERE IS NO TIME TO EXPLAIN NOW. WE MUST ACT BEFORE IT IS *TOO LATE*.
YEAH, BEFORE PHOBOS IS DONE WITH HIS *MIRACLE DIET*!
???
THE *MAGICAL FASTING* IS SERIOUS, IRMA. IT ALLOWS PURIFICATION BEFORE THE INVESTITURE AND REQUIRES ISOLATION AND FOCUS.
HOW ODD. THE WALL SEEMS... ALIVE!
AS I HAD HOPED! THE TOWER RECOGNIZES THE POWER INSIDE YOU, WILL. YOU CAN OPEN THIS DOOR.
THE FIVE OF YOU!

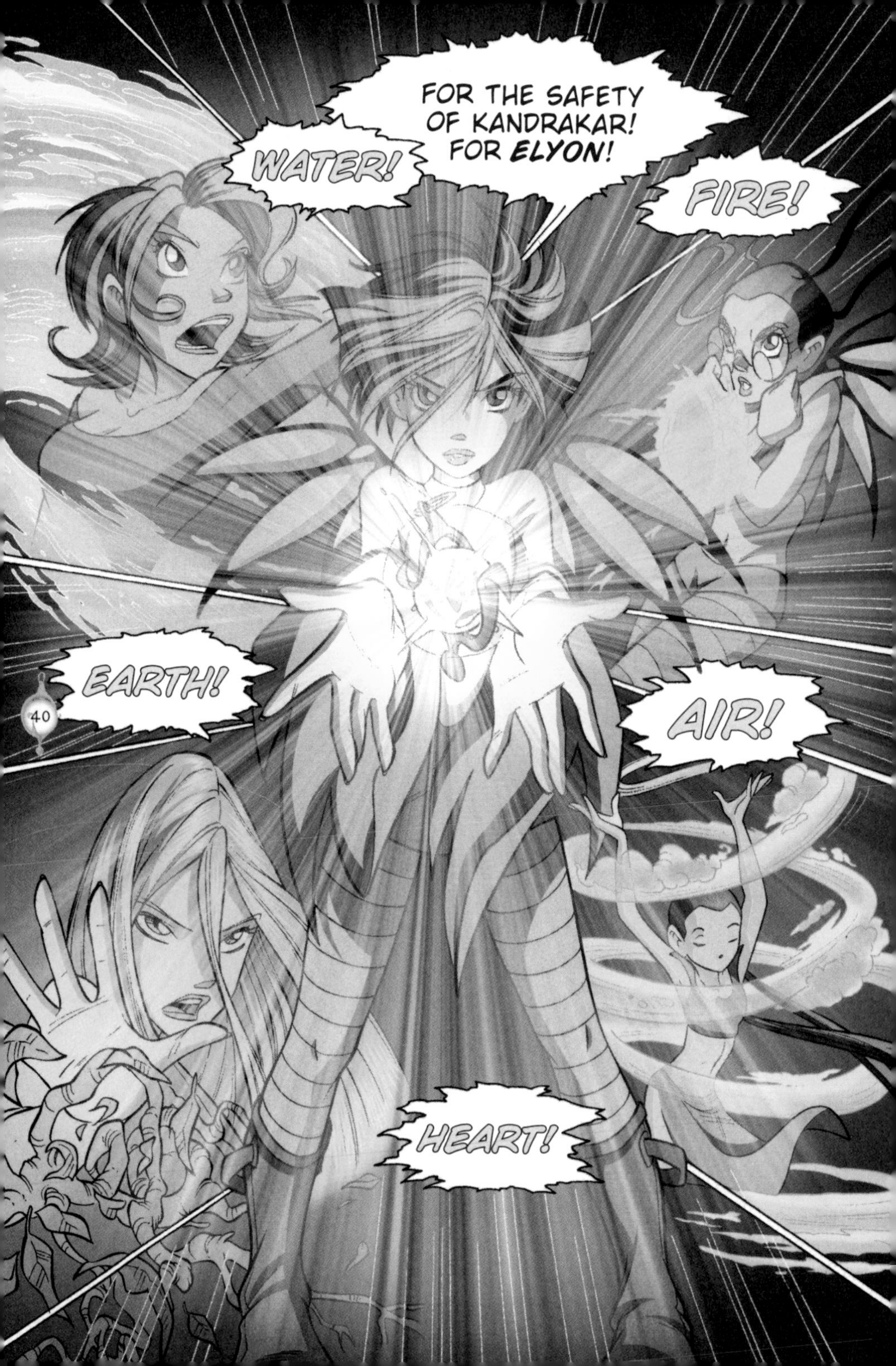
FOR THE SAFETY OF KANDRAKAR! FOR ELYON!
WATER!
FIRE!
EARTH!
AIR!
HEART!

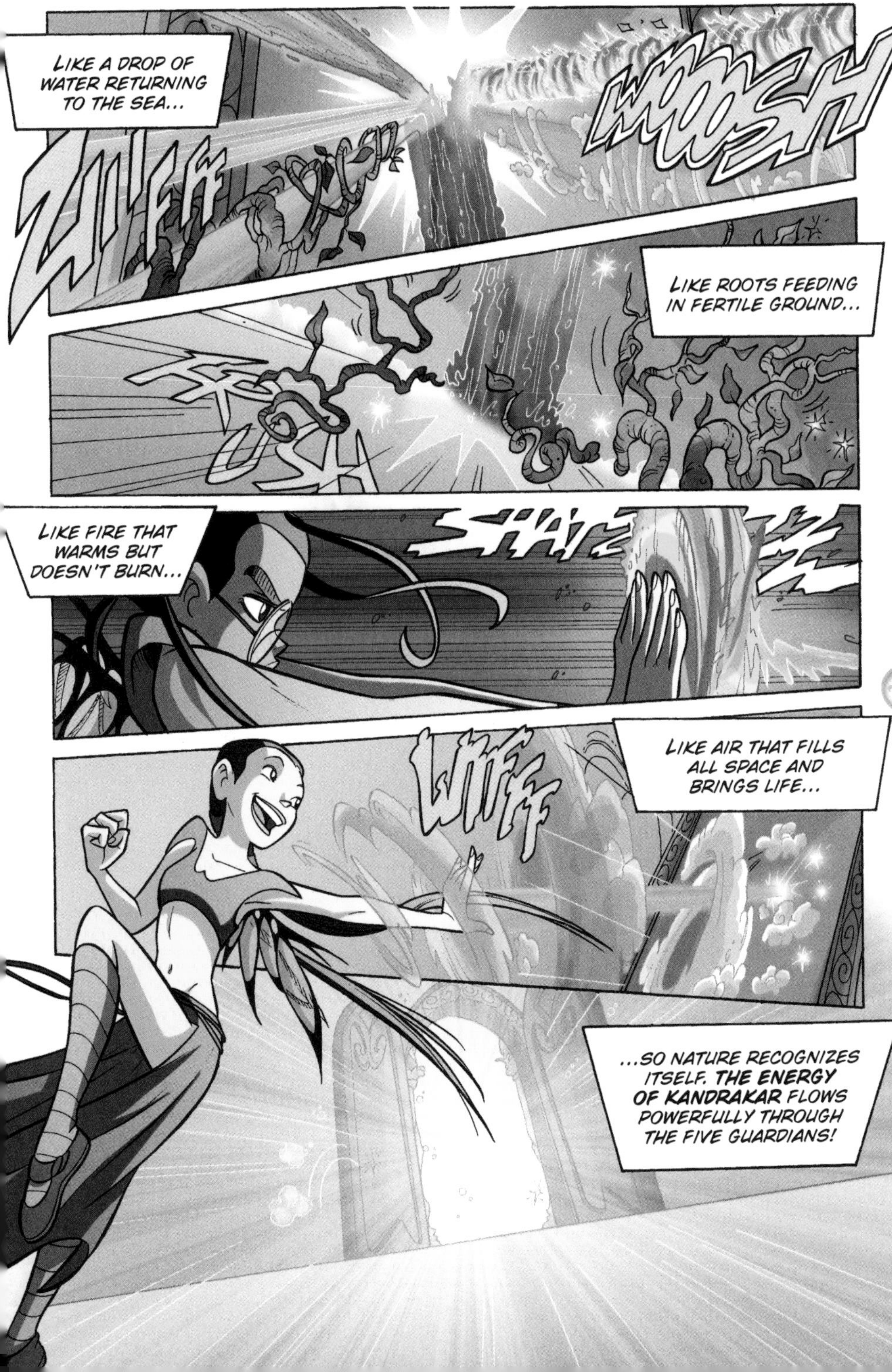
LIKE A DROP OF WATER RETURNING TO THE SEA...
WOOOSH
LIKE ROOTS FEEDING IN FERTILE GROUND...
LIKE FIRE THAT WARMS BUT DOESN'T BURN...
LIKE AIR THAT FILLS ALL SPACE AND BRINGS LIFE...
...SO NATURE RECOGNIZES ITSELF. **THE ENERGY OF KANDRAKAR** FLOWS POWERFULLY THROUGH THE FIVE GUARDIANS!

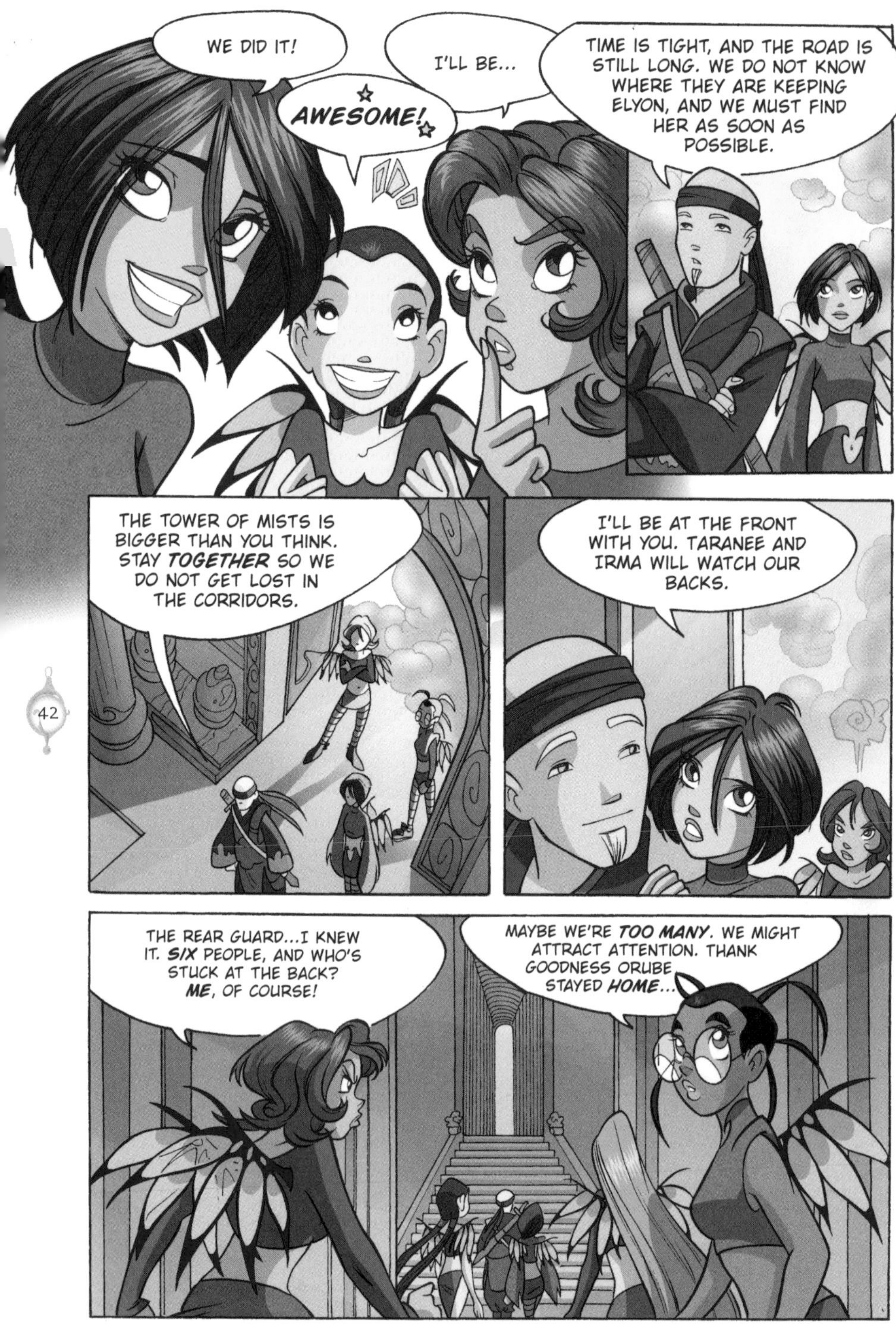

WE DID IT!
AWESOME!
I'LL BE...
TIME IS TIGHT, AND THE ROAD IS STILL LONG. WE DO NOT KNOW WHERE THEY ARE KEEPING ELYON, AND WE MUST FIND HER AS SOON AS POSSIBLE.
THE TOWER OF MISTS IS BIGGER THAN YOU THINK. STAY TOGETHER SO WE DO NOT GET LOST IN THE CORRIDORS.
I'LL BE AT THE FRONT WITH YOU. TARANEE AND IRMA WILL WATCH OUR BACKS.
THE REAR GUARD...I KNEW IT. SIX PEOPLE, AND WHO'S STUCK AT THE BACK? ME, OF COURSE!
MAYBE WE'RE TOO MANY. WE MIGHT ATTRACT ATTENTION. THANK GOODNESS ORUBE STAYED HOME...

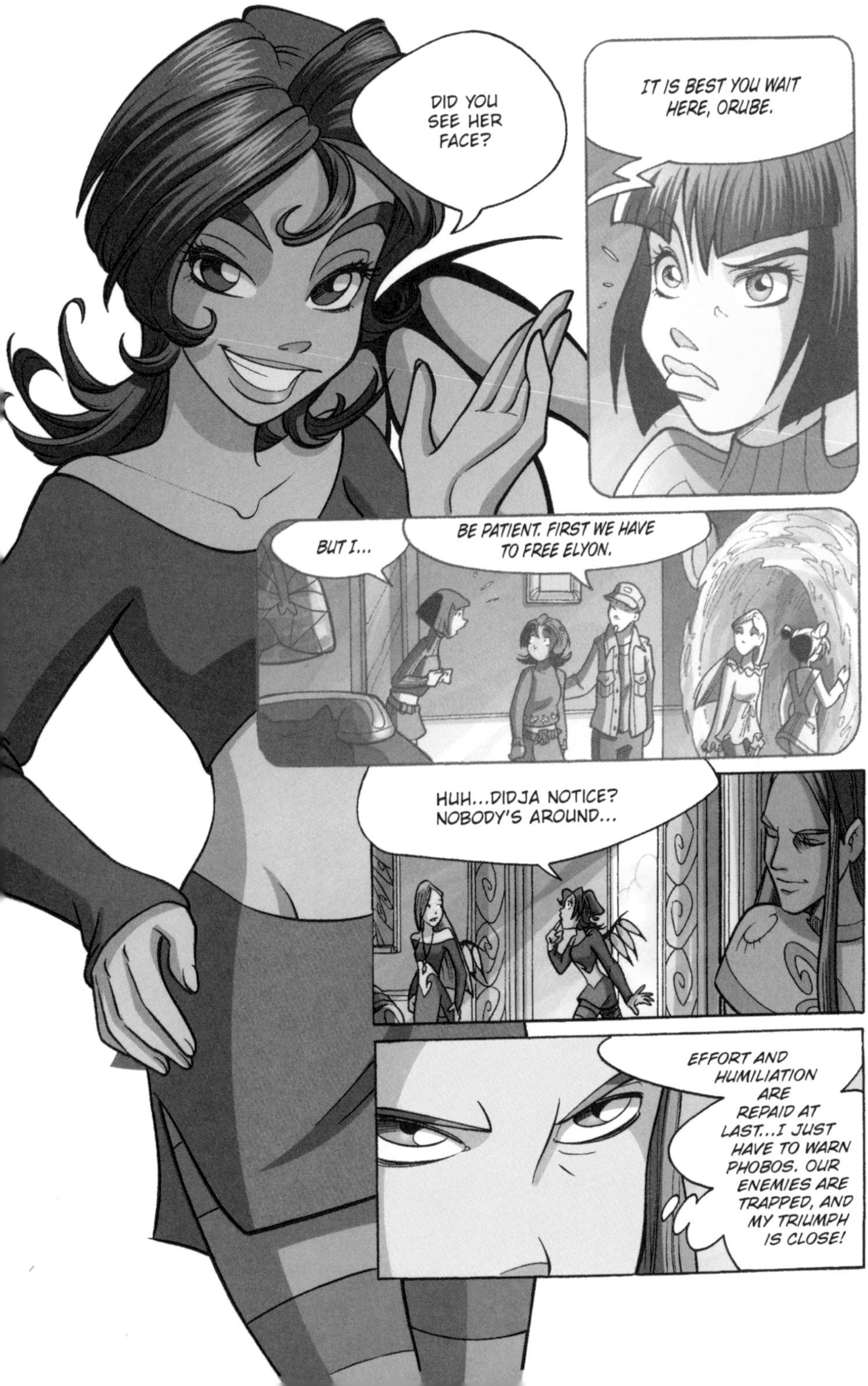
DID YOU SEE HER FACE?
IT IS BEST YOU WAIT HERE, ORUBE.
BUT I...
BE PATIENT. FIRST WE HAVE TO FREE ELYON.
HUH...DIDJA NOTICE? NOBODY'S AROUND...
EFFORT AND HUMILIATION ARE REPAID AT LAST...I JUST HAVE TO WARN PHOBOS. OUR ENEMIES ARE TRAPPED, AND MY TRIUMPH IS CLOSE!

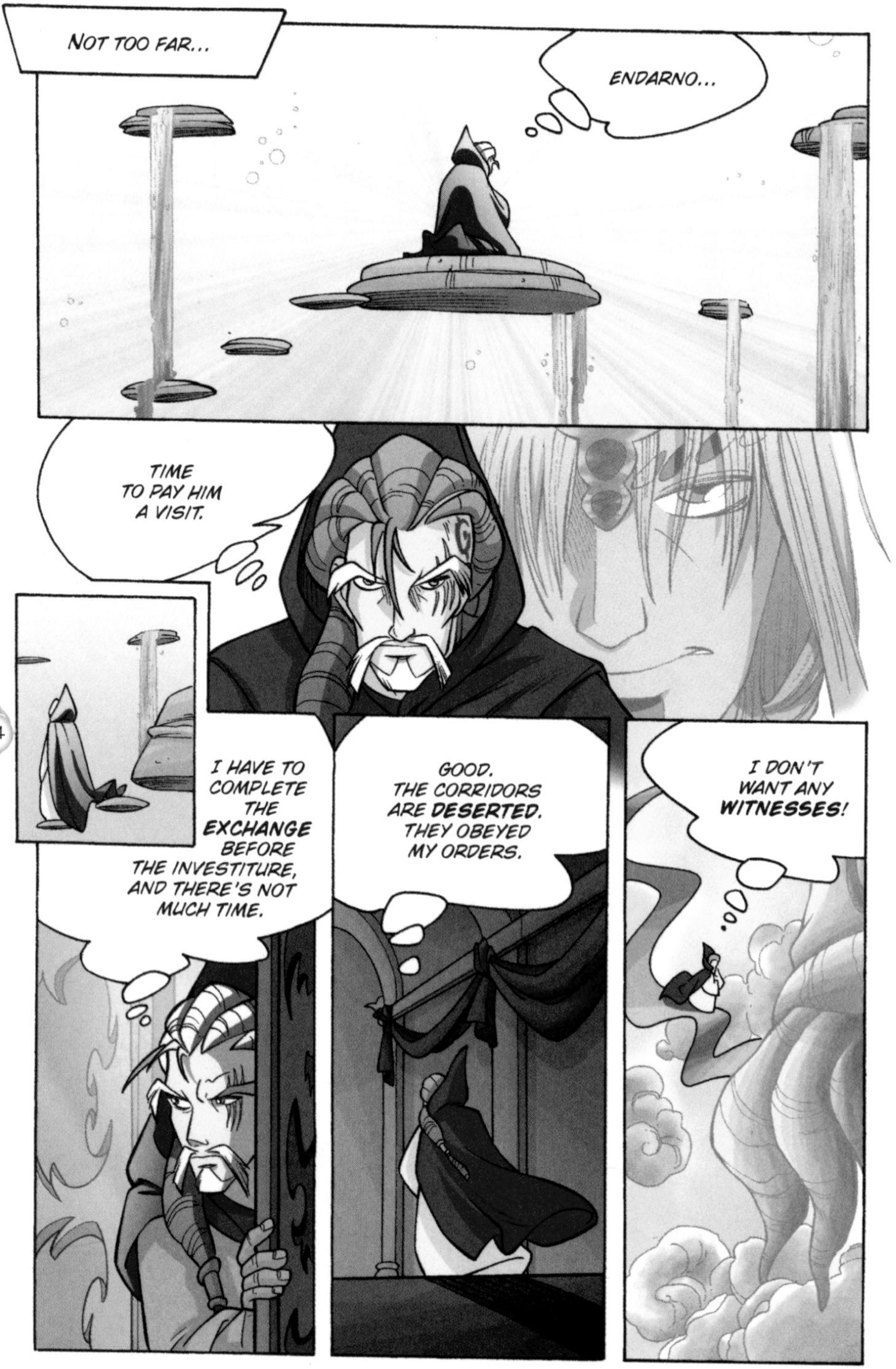
NOT TOO FAR...
ENDARNO...
TIME TO PAY HIM A VISIT.
I HAVE TO COMPLETE THE **EXCHANGE** BEFORE THE INVESTITURE, AND THERE'S NOT MUCH TIME.
GOOD. THE CORRIDORS ARE **DESERTED**. THEY OBEYED MY ORDERS.
I DON'T WANT ANY **WITNESSES**!

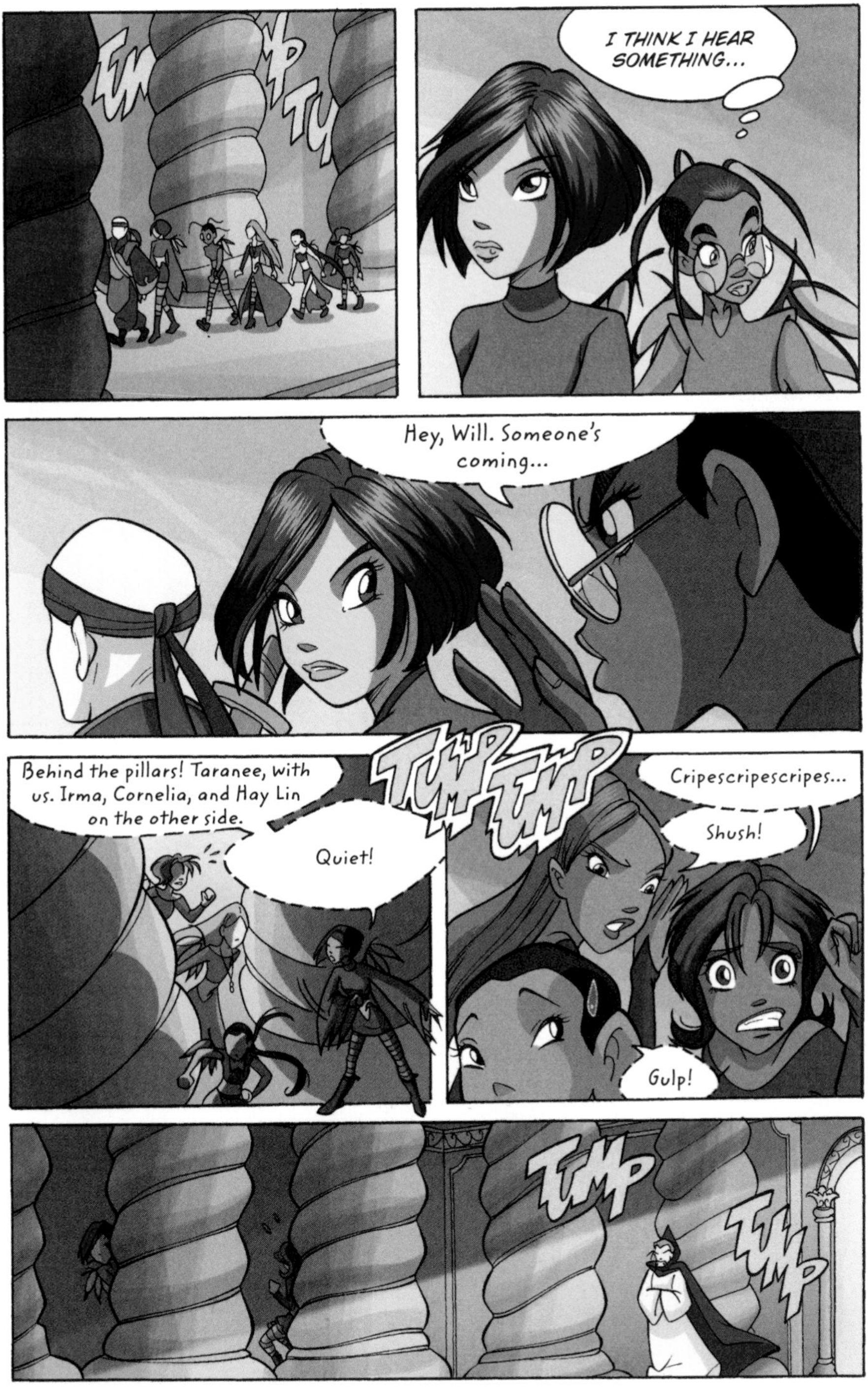
TUMP
TUMP
TU
I THINK I HEAR SOMETHING...
Hey, Will. Someone's coming...
Behind the pillars! Taranee, with us. Irma, Cornelia, and Hay Lin on the other side.
Quiet!
TUMP TUMP
Cripescripescripes...
Shush!
Gulp!
TUMP
TUMP

Phew! He's gone. He didn't see us! HE DIDN'T SEE US!

AH!

?

Cripescripes-cripes!

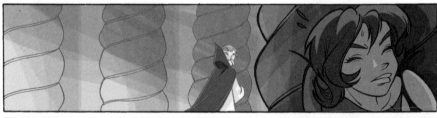

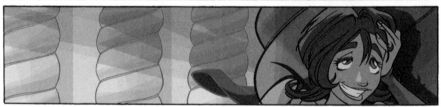

He's gone. We can get out.

WHAT'S PHOBOS DOING HERE?

HE MUST HAVE TAKEN A BREAK FROM FASTING. LUCKILY, HE DOES NOT YET HAVE FULL POWERS AND DID NOT SPOT US...

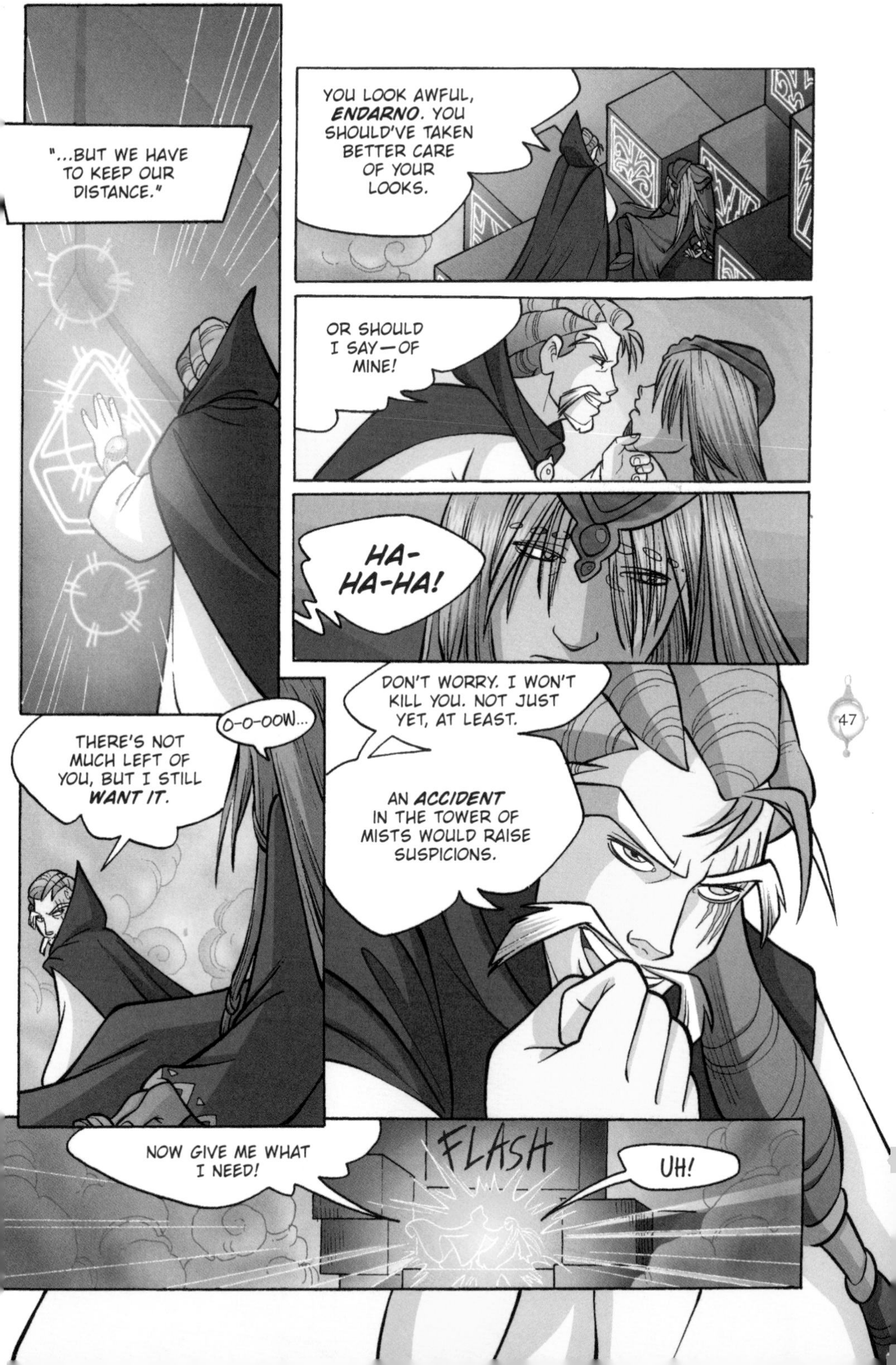
"...BUT WE HAVE TO KEEP OUR DISTANCE."
YOU LOOK AWFUL, ***ENDARNO***. YOU SHOULD'VE TAKEN BETTER CARE OF YOUR LOOKS.
OR SHOULD I SAY—OF MINE!
HA-HA-HA!
THERE'S NOT MUCH LEFT OF YOU, BUT I STILL ***WANT IT***.
O-O-OOW...
DON'T WORRY. I WON'T KILL YOU. NOT JUST YET, AT LEAST.
AN ***ACCIDENT*** IN THE TOWER OF MISTS WOULD RAISE SUSPICIONS.
NOW GIVE ME WHAT I NEED!
FLASH
UH!

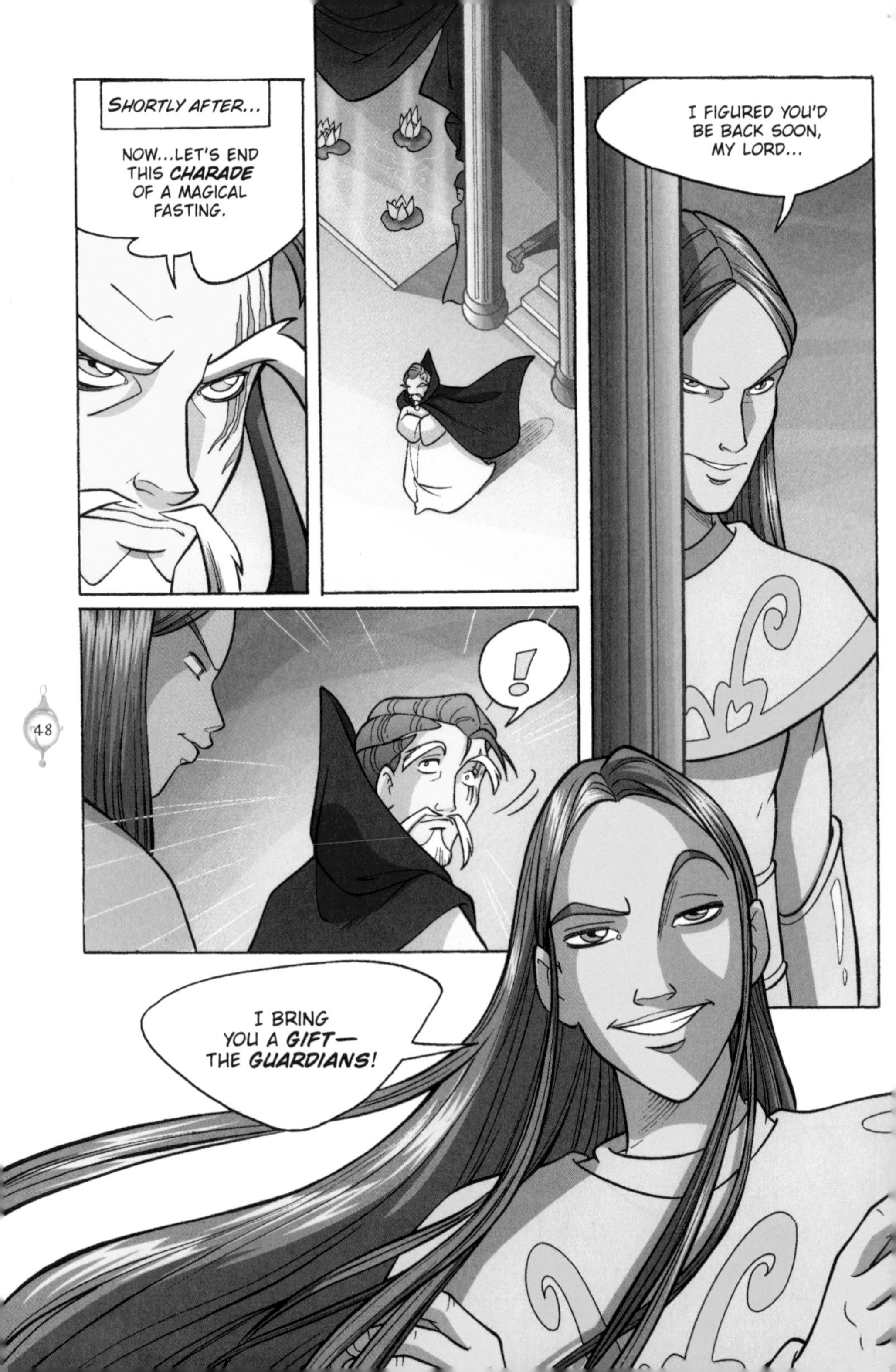
SHORTLY AFTER...
NOW...LET'S END THIS CHARADE OF A MAGICAL FASTING.
I FIGURED YOU'D BE BACK SOON, MY LORD...
!
I BRING YOU A GIFT— THE GUARDIANS!

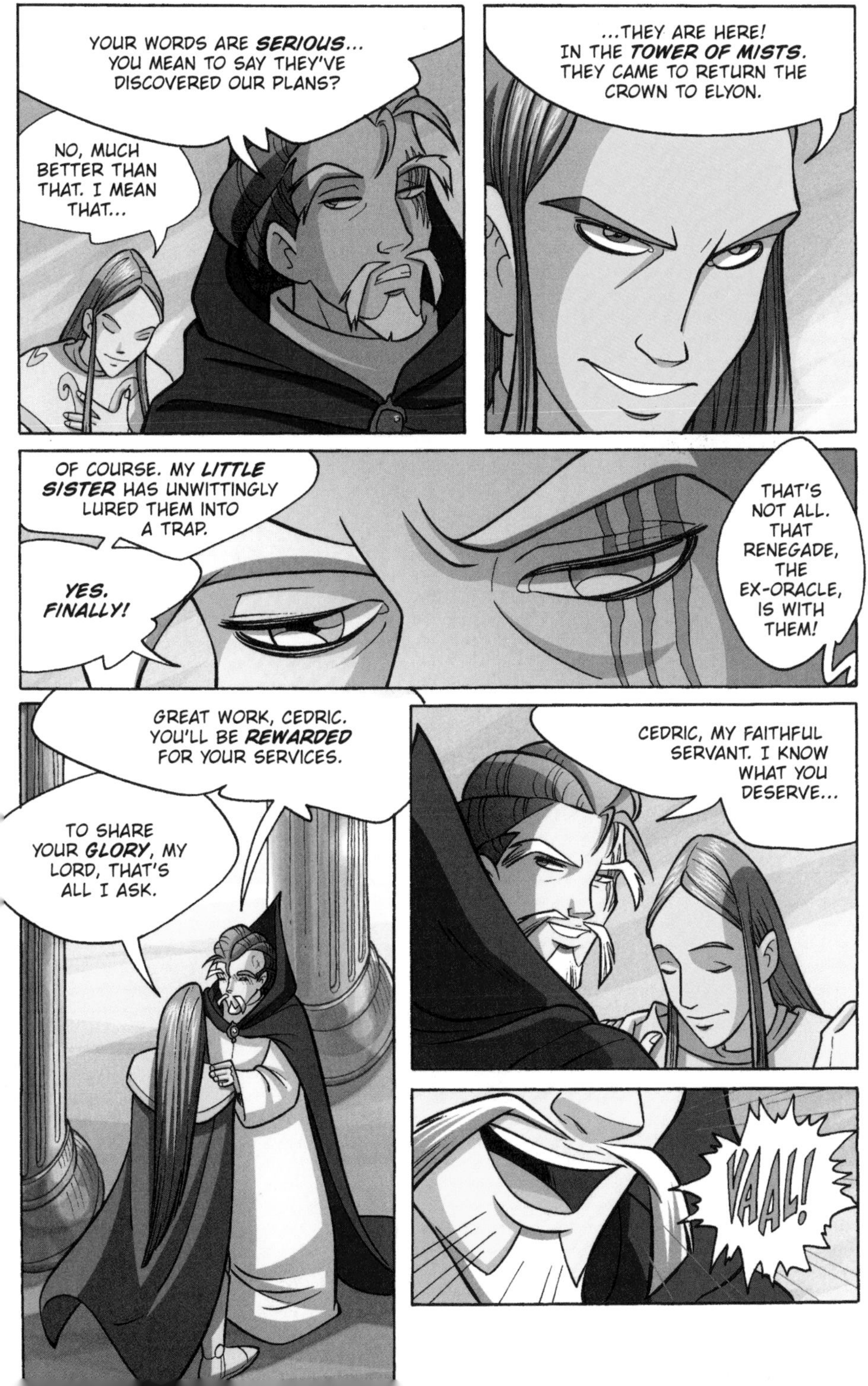

YOUR WORDS ARE SERIOUS... YOU MEAN TO SAY THEY'VE DISCOVERED OUR PLANS?
NO, MUCH BETTER THAN THAT. I MEAN THAT...
...THEY ARE HERE! IN THE TOWER OF MISTS. THEY CAME TO RETURN THE CROWN TO ELYON.
OF COURSE. MY LITTLE SISTER HAS UNWITTINGLY LURED THEM INTO A TRAP.
YES. FINALLY!
THAT'S NOT ALL. THAT RENEGADE, THE EX-ORACLE, IS WITH THEM!
GREAT WORK, CEDRIC. YOU'LL BE REWARDED FOR YOUR SERVICES.
TO SHARE YOUR GLORY, MY LORD, THAT'S ALL I ASK.
CEDRIC, MY FAITHFUL SERVANT. I KNOW WHAT YOU DESERVE...
VAAL!

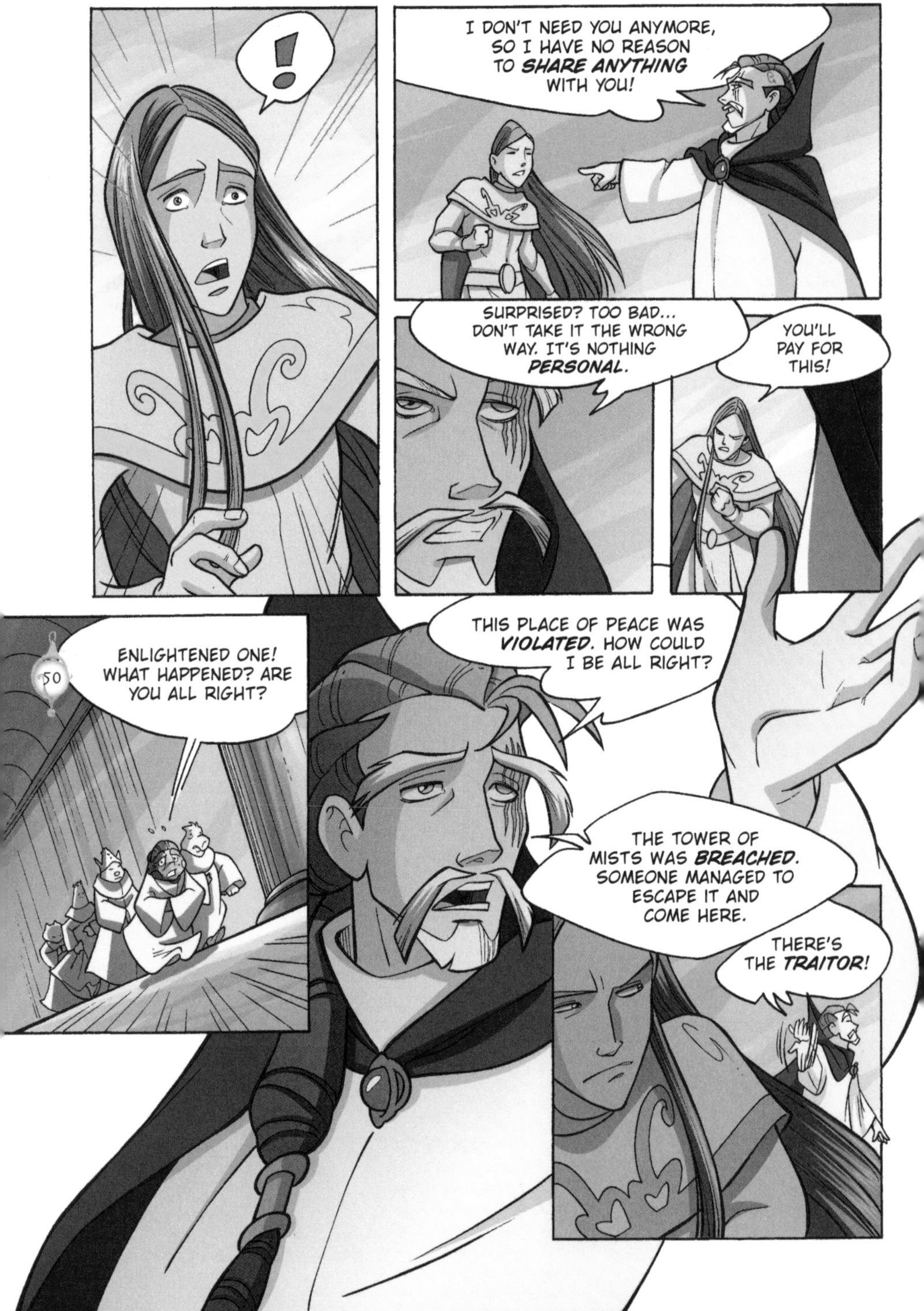
!
I DON'T NEED YOU ANYMORE, SO I HAVE NO REASON TO SHARE ANYTHING WITH YOU!
SURPRISED? TOO BAD... DON'T TAKE IT THE WRONG WAY. IT'S NOTHING PERSONAL.
YOU'LL PAY FOR THIS!
ENLIGHTENED ONE! WHAT HAPPENED? ARE YOU ALL RIGHT?
THIS PLACE OF PEACE WAS VIOLATED. HOW COULD I BE ALL RIGHT?
THE TOWER OF MISTS WAS BREACHED. SOMEONE MANAGED TO ESCAPE IT AND COME HERE.
THERE'S THE TRAITOR!

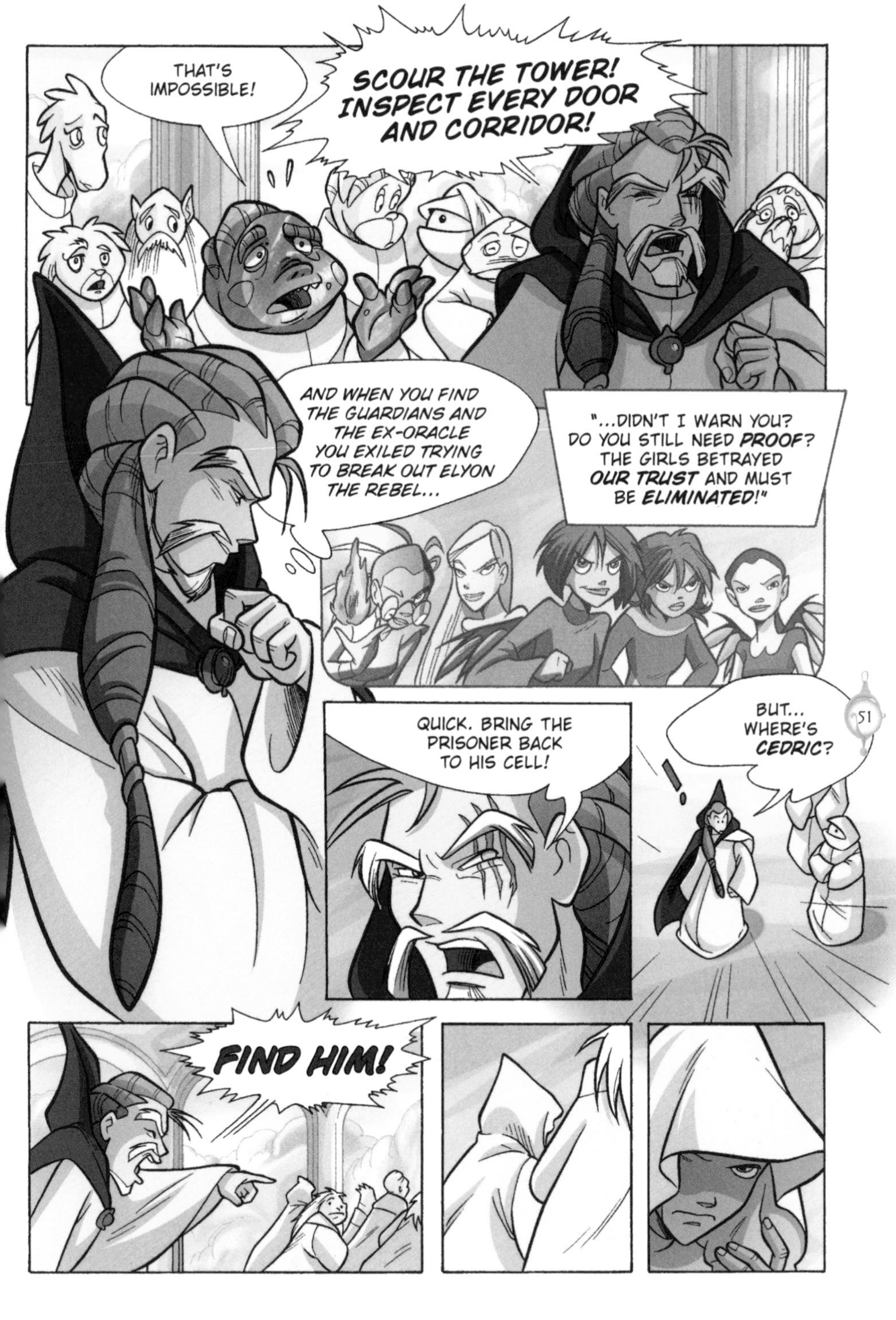
THAT'S IMPOSSIBLE!
SCOUR THE TOWER! INSPECT EVERY DOOR AND CORRIDOR!
AND WHEN YOU FIND THE GUARDIANS AND THE EX-ORACLE YOU EXILED TRYING TO BREAK OUT ELYON THE REBEL...
"...DIDN'T I WARN YOU? DO YOU STILL NEED PROOF? THE GIRLS BETRAYED OUR TRUST AND MUST BE ELIMINATED!"
QUICK. BRING THE PRISONER BACK TO HIS CELL!
BUT... WHERE'S CEDRIC?
!
FIND HIM!

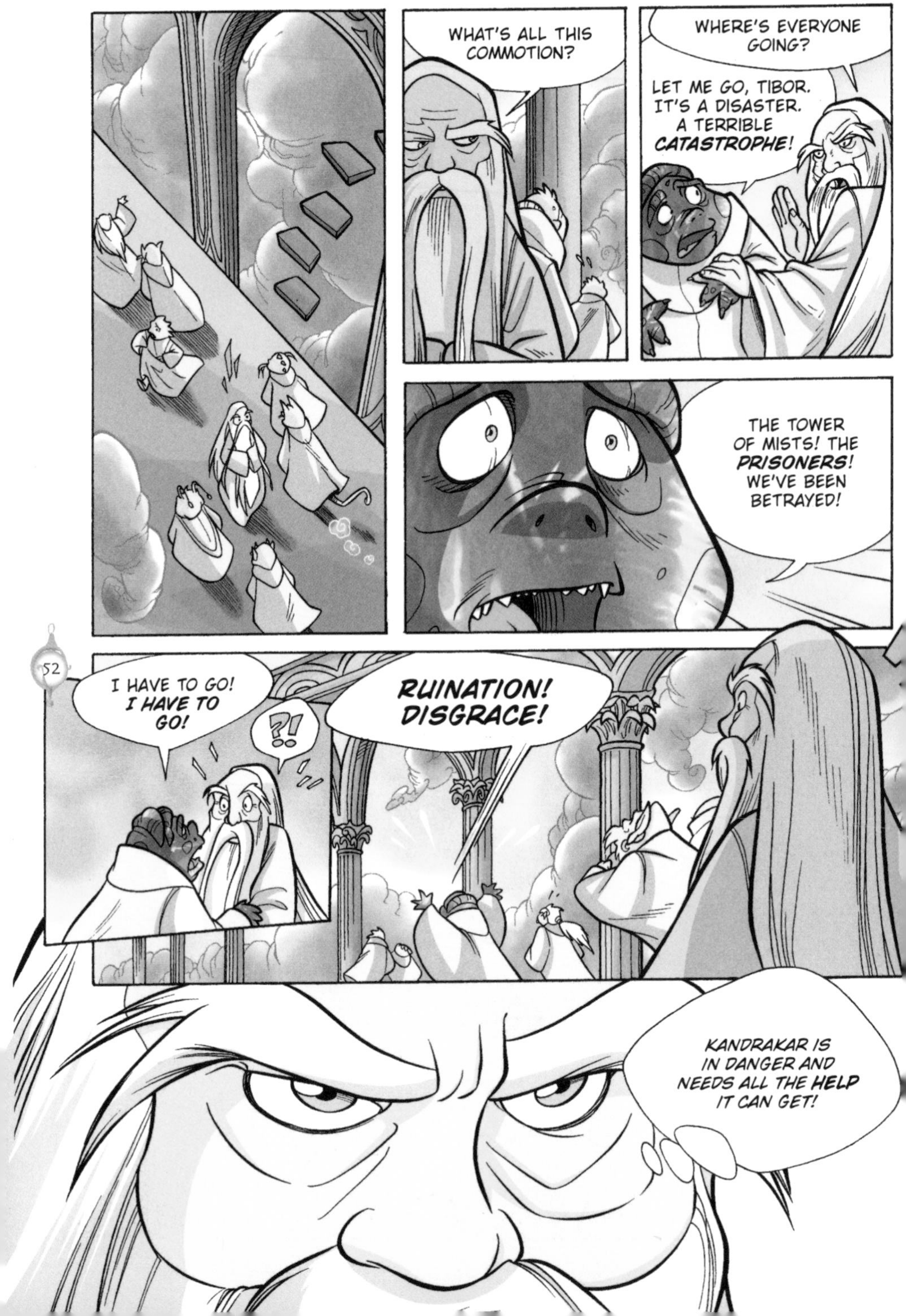

WHAT'S ALL THIS COMMOTION?
WHERE'S EVERYONE GOING?
LET ME GO, TIBOR. IT'S A DISASTER. A TERRIBLE CATASTROPHE!
THE TOWER OF MISTS! THE PRISONERS! WE'VE BEEN BETRAYED!
I HAVE TO GO! I HAVE TO GO!
?!
RUINATION! DISGRACE!
KANDRAKAR IS IN DANGER AND NEEDS ALL THE HELP IT CAN GET!

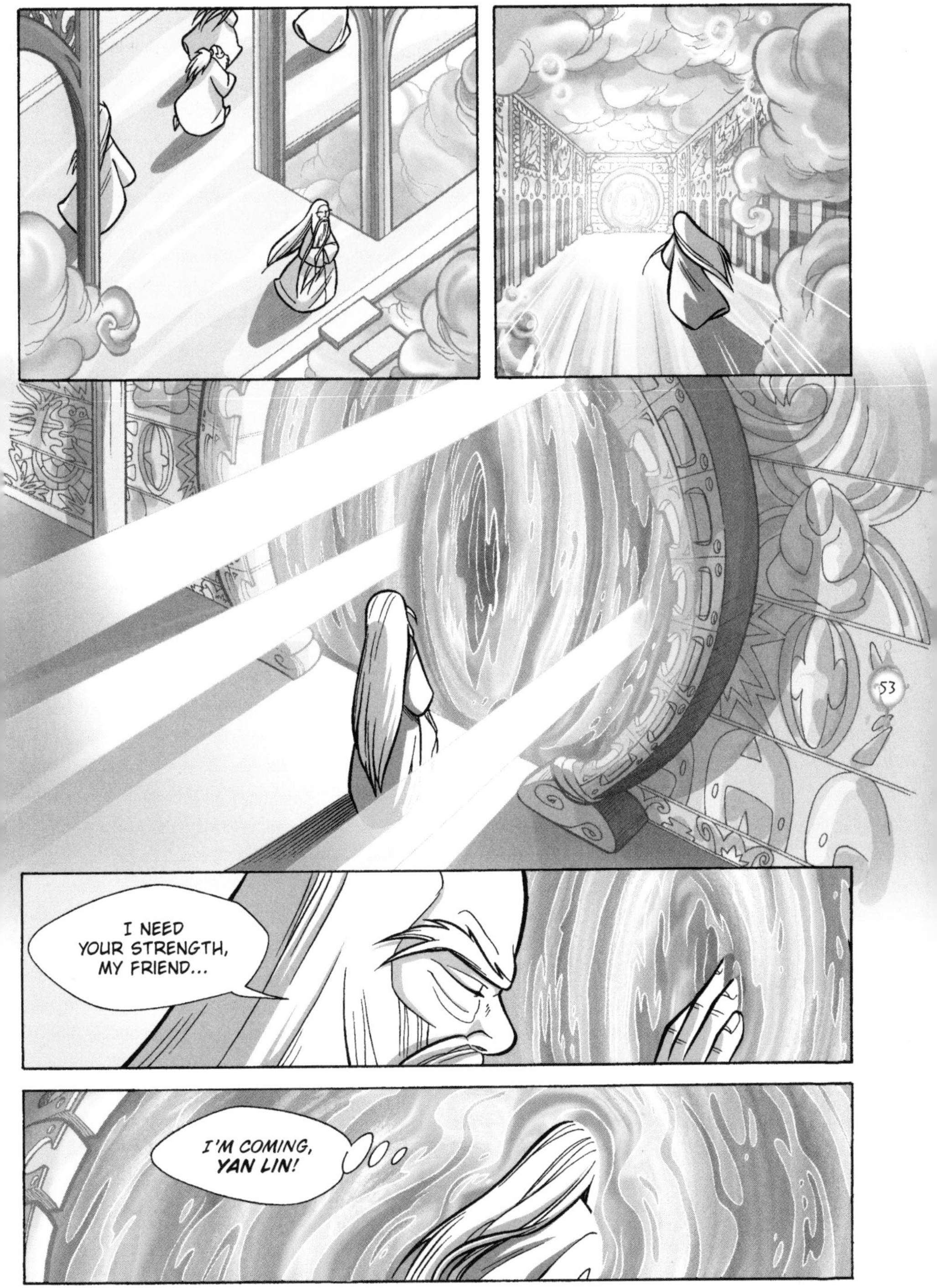
I NEED YOUR STRENGTH, MY FRIEND...
I'M COMING, **YAN LIN!**

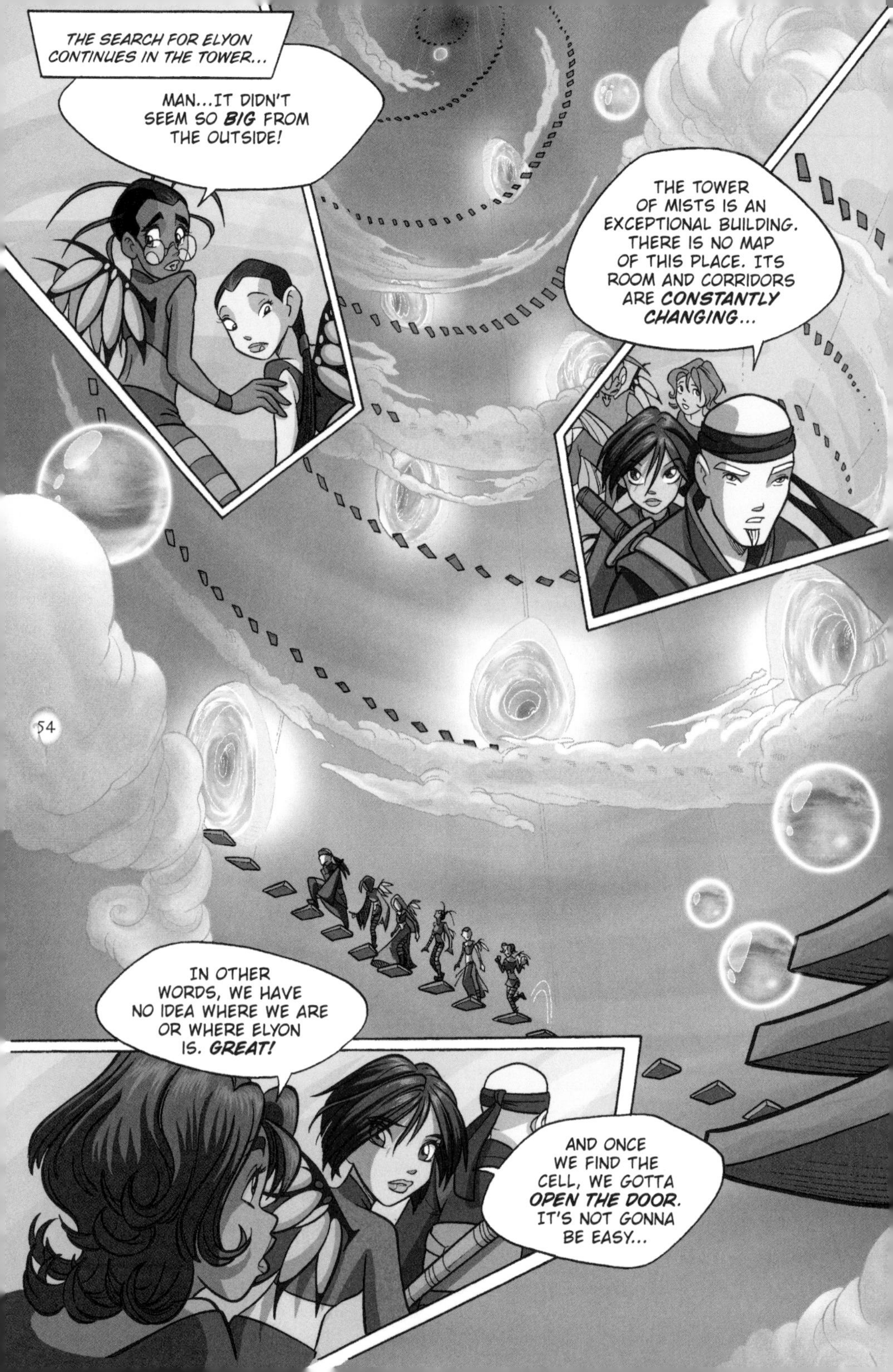
THE SEARCH FOR ELYON CONTINUES IN THE TOWER...
MAN...IT DIDN'T SEEM SO BIG FROM THE OUTSIDE!
THE TOWER OF MISTS IS AN EXCEPTIONAL BUILDING. THERE IS NO MAP OF THIS PLACE. ITS ROOM AND CORRIDORS ARE CONSTANTLY CHANGING...
IN OTHER WORDS, WE HAVE NO IDEA WHERE WE ARE OR WHERE ELYON IS. GREAT!
AND ONCE WE FIND THE CELL, WE GOTTA OPEN THE DOOR. IT'S NOT GONNA BE EASY...

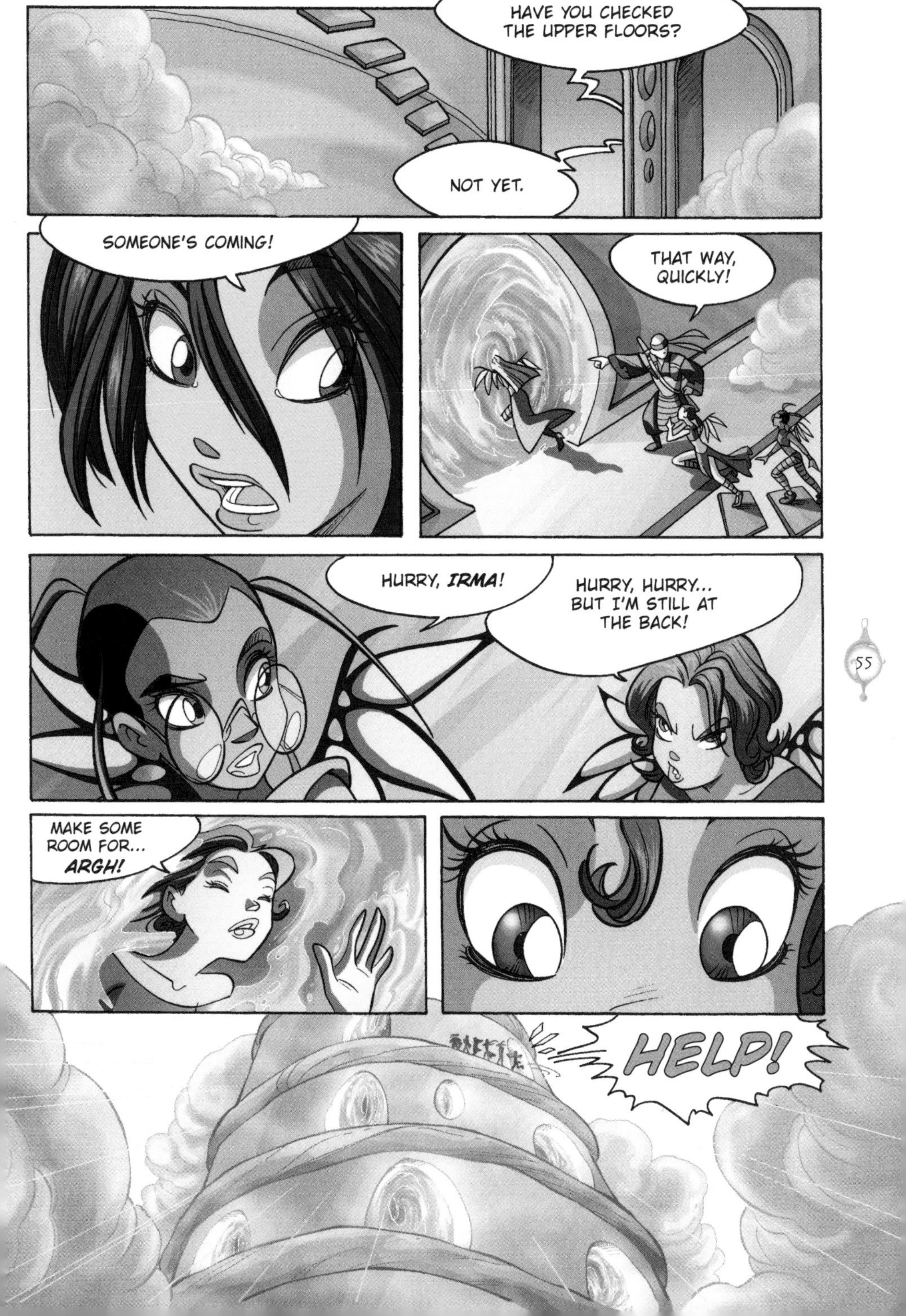
HAVE YOU CHECKED THE UPPER FLOORS?
NOT YET.
SOMEONE'S COMING!
THAT WAY, QUICKLY!
HURRY, **IRMA**!
HURRY, HURRY... BUT I'M STILL AT THE BACK!
MAKE SOME ROOM FOR... **ARGH!**
HELP!

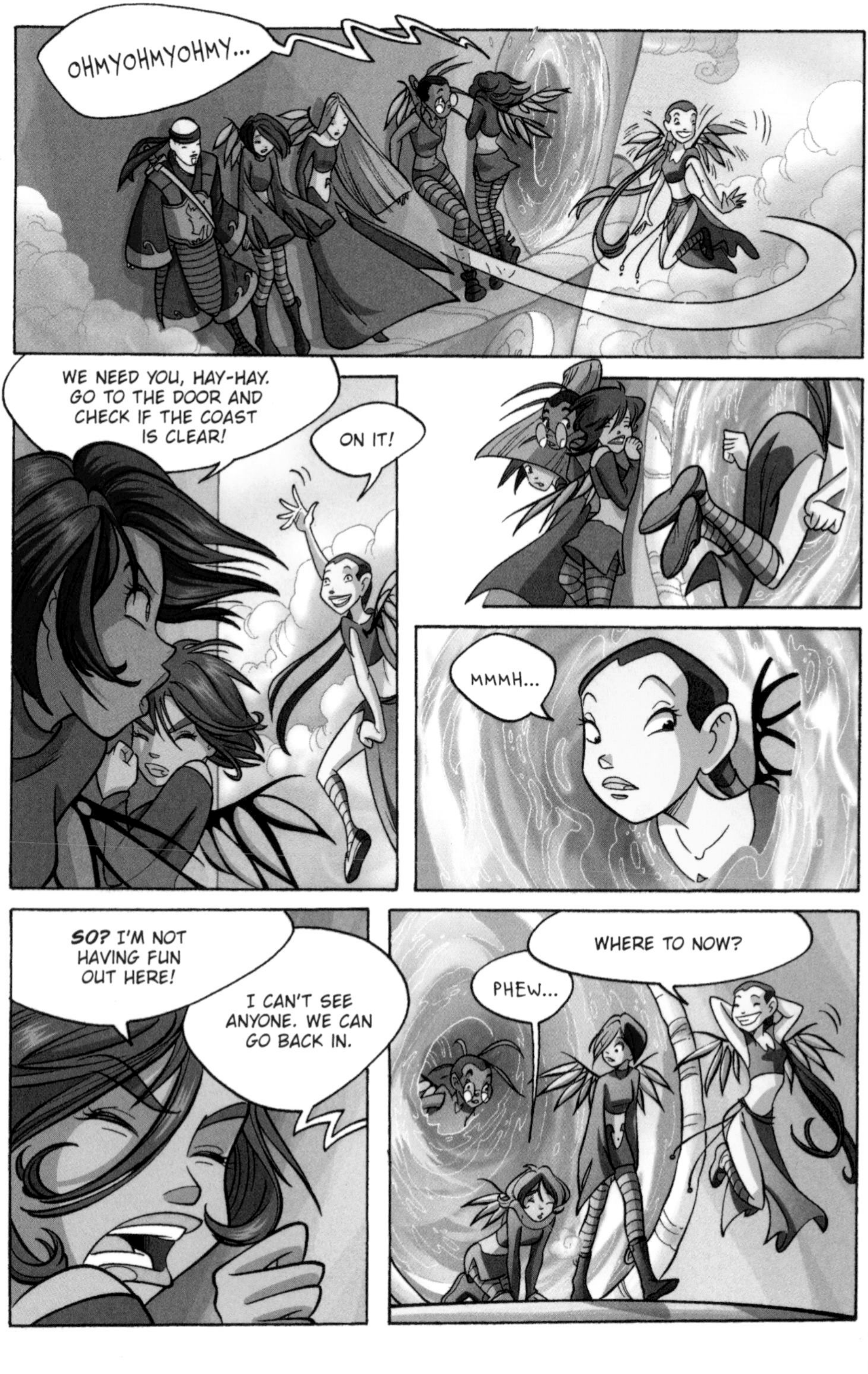
OHMYOHMYOHMY...
WE NEED YOU, HAY-HAY. GO TO THE DOOR AND CHECK IF THE COAST IS CLEAR!
ON IT!
MMMH...
SO? I'M NOT HAVING FUN OUT HERE!
I CAN'T SEE ANYONE. WE CAN GO BACK IN.
WHERE TO NOW?
PHEW...

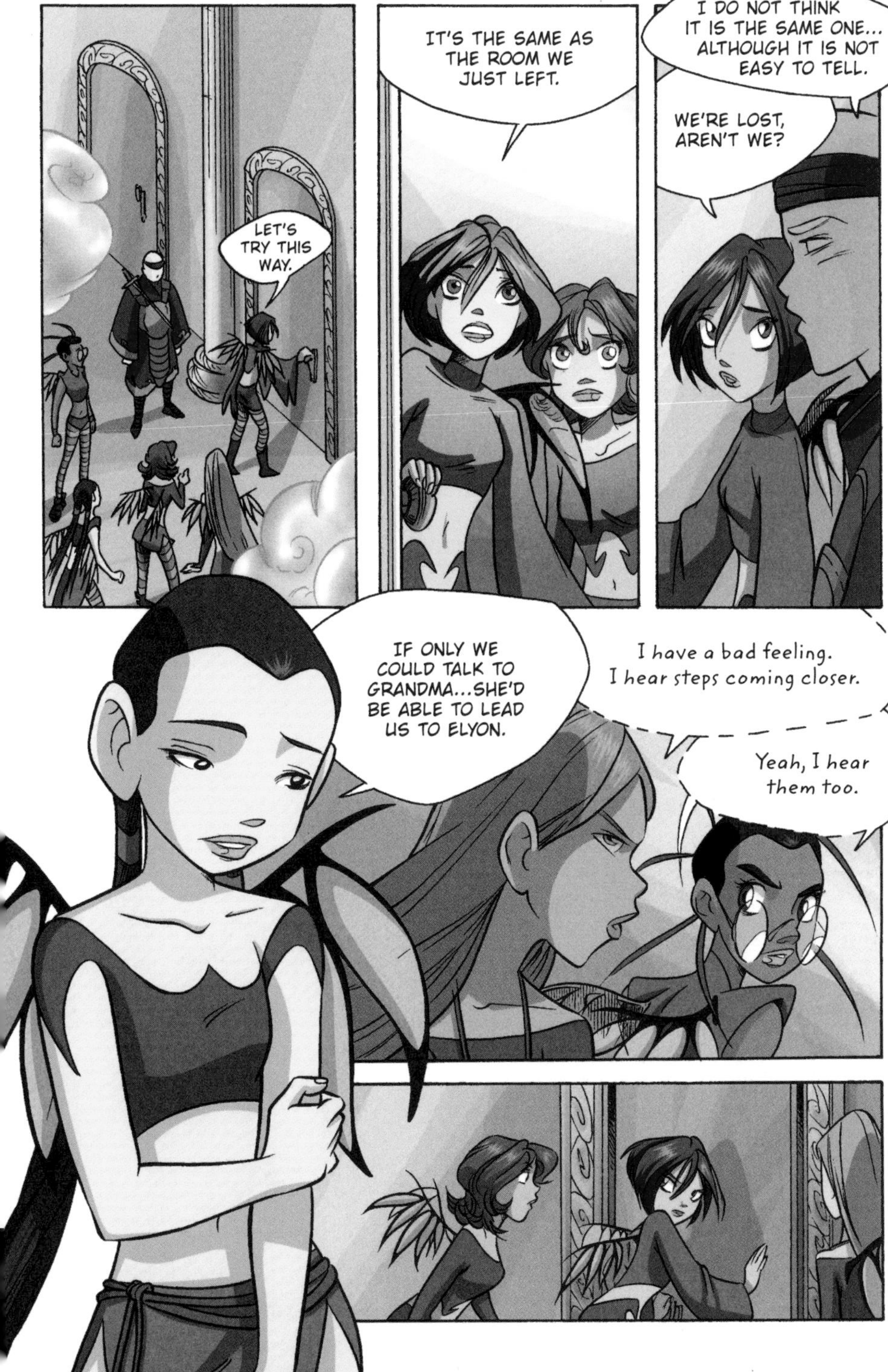
LET'S TRY THIS WAY.
IT'S THE SAME AS THE ROOM WE JUST LEFT.
I DO NOT THINK IT IS THE SAME ONE... ALTHOUGH IT IS NOT EASY TO TELL.
WE'RE LOST, AREN'T WE?
IF ONLY WE COULD TALK TO GRANDMA...SHE'D BE ABLE TO LEAD US TO ELYON.
I have a bad feeling. I hear steps coming closer.
Yeah, I hear them too.

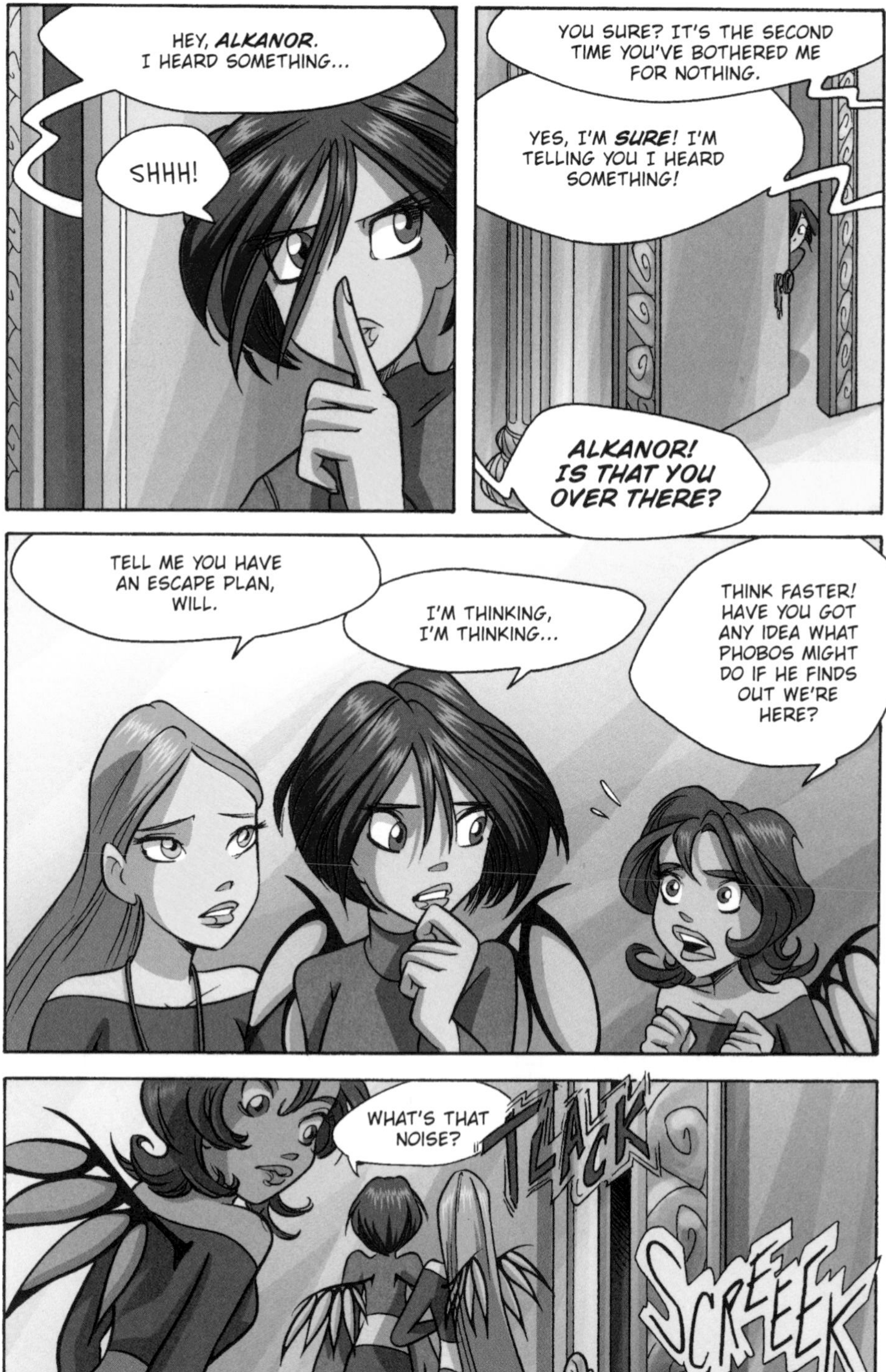
HEY, ***ALKANOR***. I HEARD SOMETHING...
SHHH!
YOU SURE? IT'S THE SECOND TIME YOU'VE BOTHERED ME FOR NOTHING.
YES, I'M ***SURE***! I'M TELLING YOU I HEARD SOMETHING!
ALKANOR! IS THAT YOU OVER THERE?
TELL ME YOU HAVE AN ESCAPE PLAN, WILL.
I'M THINKING, I'M THINKING...
THINK FASTER! HAVE YOU GOT ANY IDEA WHAT PHOBOS MIGHT DO IF HE FINDS OUT WE'RE HERE?
WHAT'S THAT NOISE?
TLACK
SCREEEK

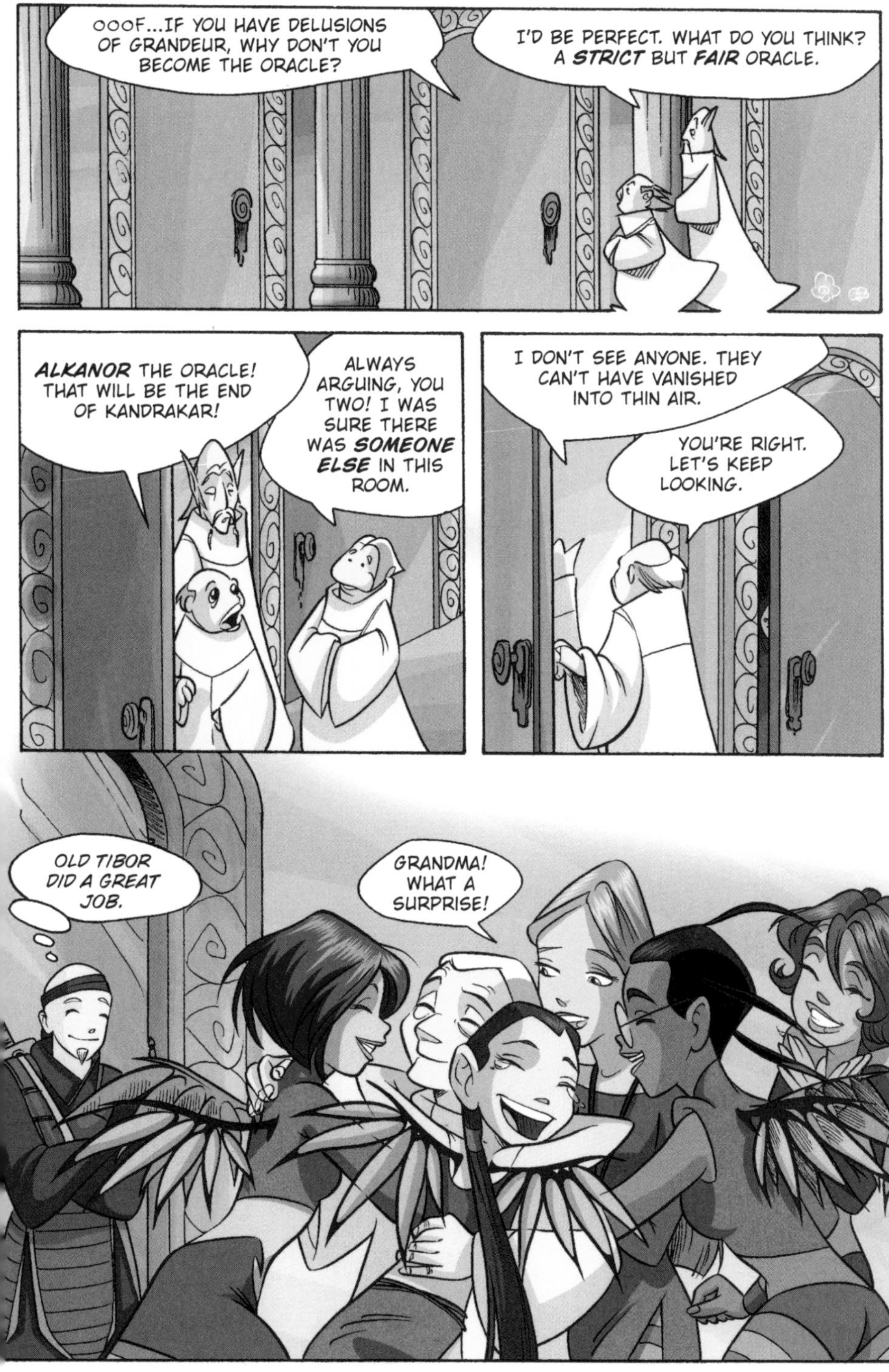
OOOF...IF YOU HAVE DELUSIONS OF GRANDEUR, WHY DON'T YOU BECOME THE ORACLE?
I'D BE PERFECT. WHAT DO YOU THINK? A **STRICT** BUT **FAIR** ORACLE.
ALKANOR THE ORACLE! THAT WILL BE THE END OF KANDRAKAR!
ALWAYS ARGUING, YOU TWO! I WAS SURE THERE WAS **SOMEONE ELSE** IN THIS ROOM.
I DON'T SEE ANYONE. THEY CAN'T HAVE VANISHED INTO THIN AIR.
YOU'RE RIGHT. LET'S KEEP LOOKING.
OLD TIBOR DID A GREAT JOB.
GRANDMA! WHAT A SURPRISE!

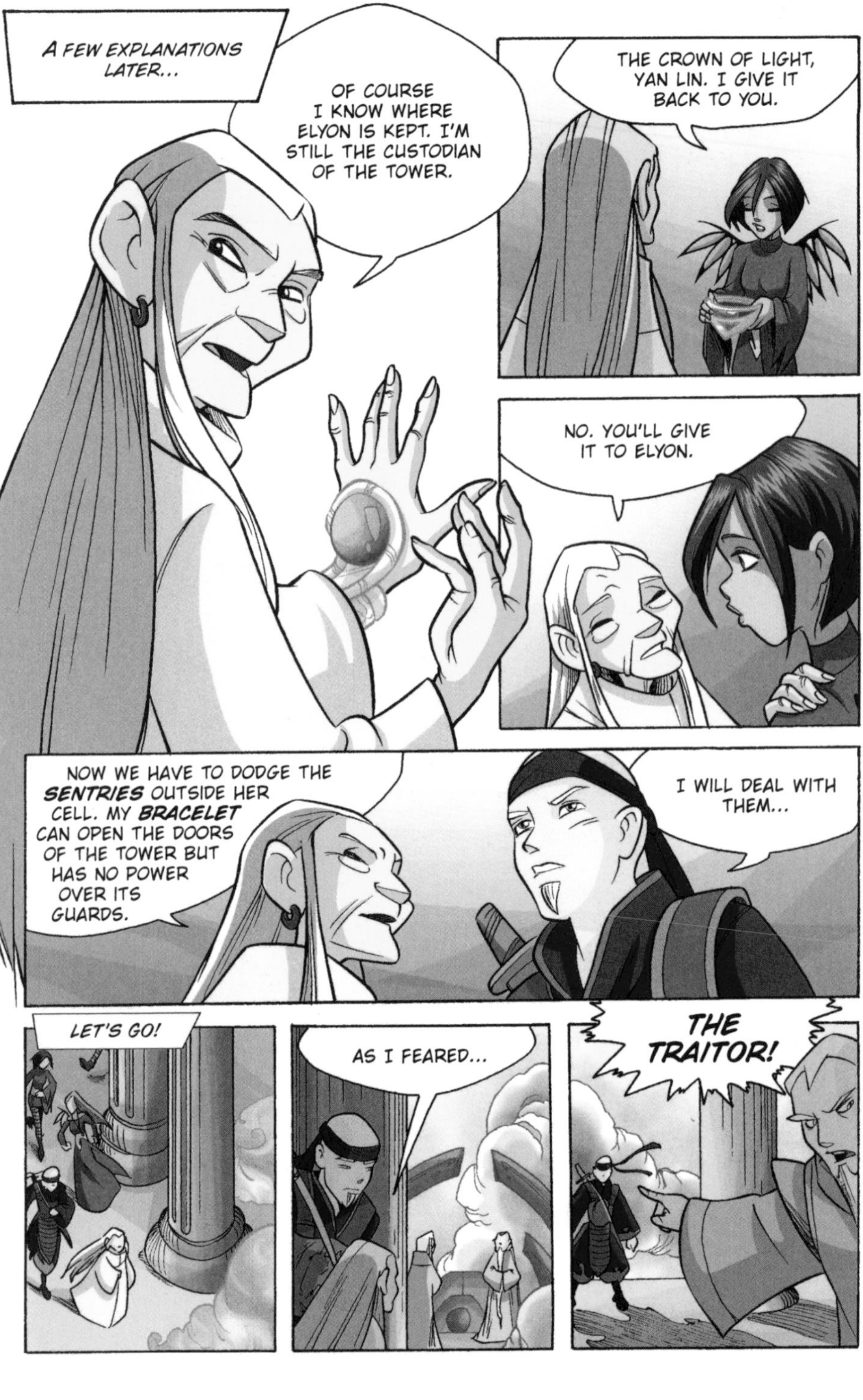
A FEW EXPLANATIONS LATER...
OF COURSE I KNOW WHERE ELYON IS KEPT. I'M STILL THE CUSTODIAN OF THE TOWER.
THE CROWN OF LIGHT, YAN LIN. I GIVE IT BACK TO YOU.
NO. YOU'LL GIVE IT TO ELYON.
NOW WE HAVE TO DODGE THE **SENTRIES** OUTSIDE HER CELL. MY **BRACELET** CAN OPEN THE DOORS OF THE TOWER BUT HAS NO POWER OVER ITS GUARDS.
I WILL DEAL WITH THEM...
LET'S GO!
AS I FEARED...
THE TRAITOR!

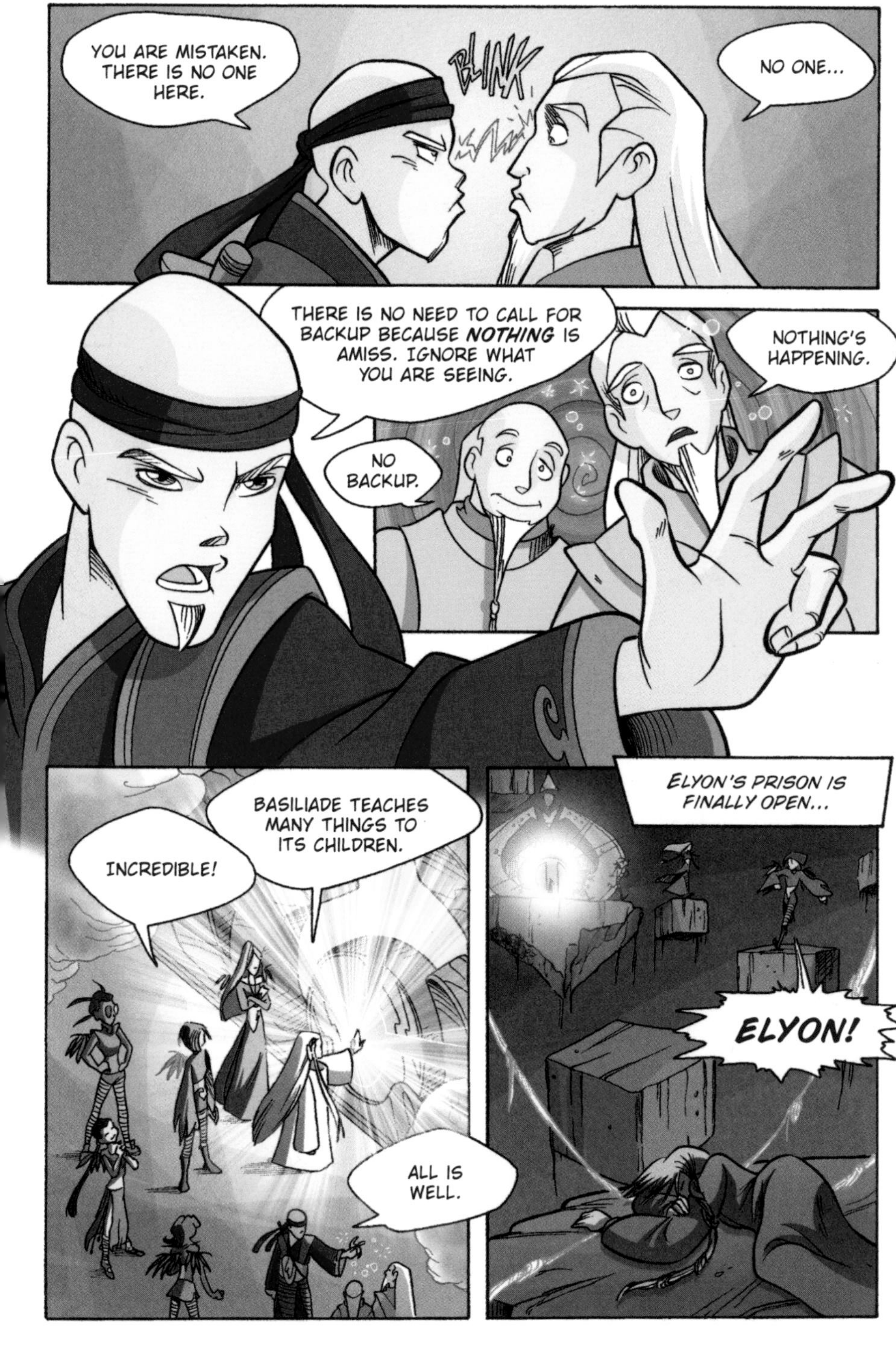
YOU ARE MISTAKEN. THERE IS NO ONE HERE.
BLINK
NO ONE...
THERE IS NO NEED TO CALL FOR BACKUP BECAUSE *NOTHING* IS AMISS. IGNORE WHAT YOU ARE SEEING.
NOTHING'S HAPPENING.
NO BACKUP.
INCREDIBLE!
BASILIADE TEACHES MANY THINGS TO ITS CHILDREN.
ALL IS WELL.
ELYON'S PRISON IS FINALLY OPEN...
ELYON!

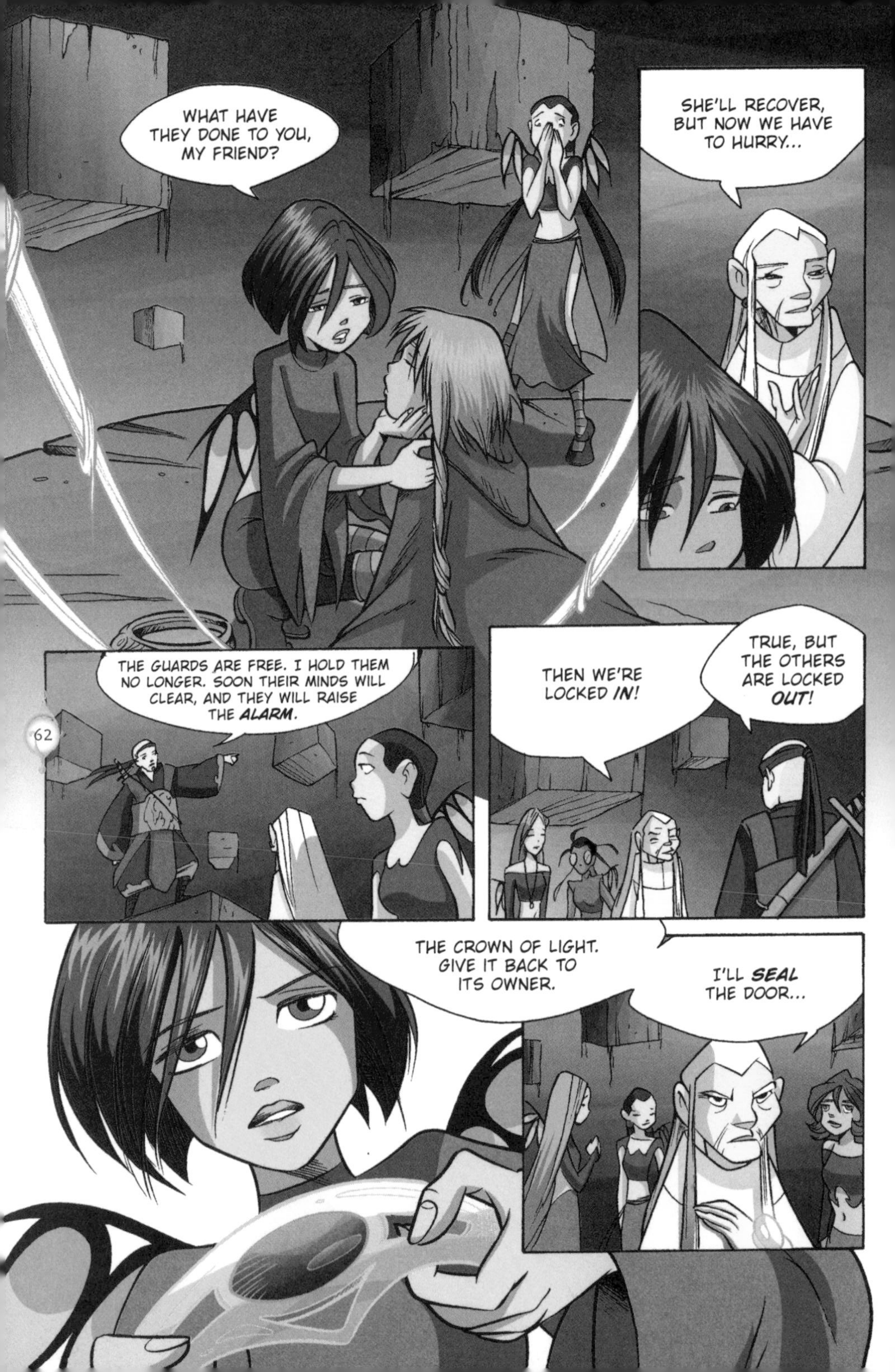
WHAT HAVE THEY DONE TO YOU, MY FRIEND?
SHE'LL RECOVER, BUT NOW WE HAVE TO HURRY...
THE GUARDS ARE FREE. I HOLD THEM NO LONGER. SOON THEIR MINDS WILL CLEAR, AND THEY WILL RAISE THE *ALARM*.
THEN WE'RE LOCKED *IN*!
TRUE, BUT THE OTHERS ARE LOCKED *OUT*!
THE CROWN OF LIGHT. GIVE IT BACK TO ITS OWNER.
I'LL *SEAL* THE DOOR...

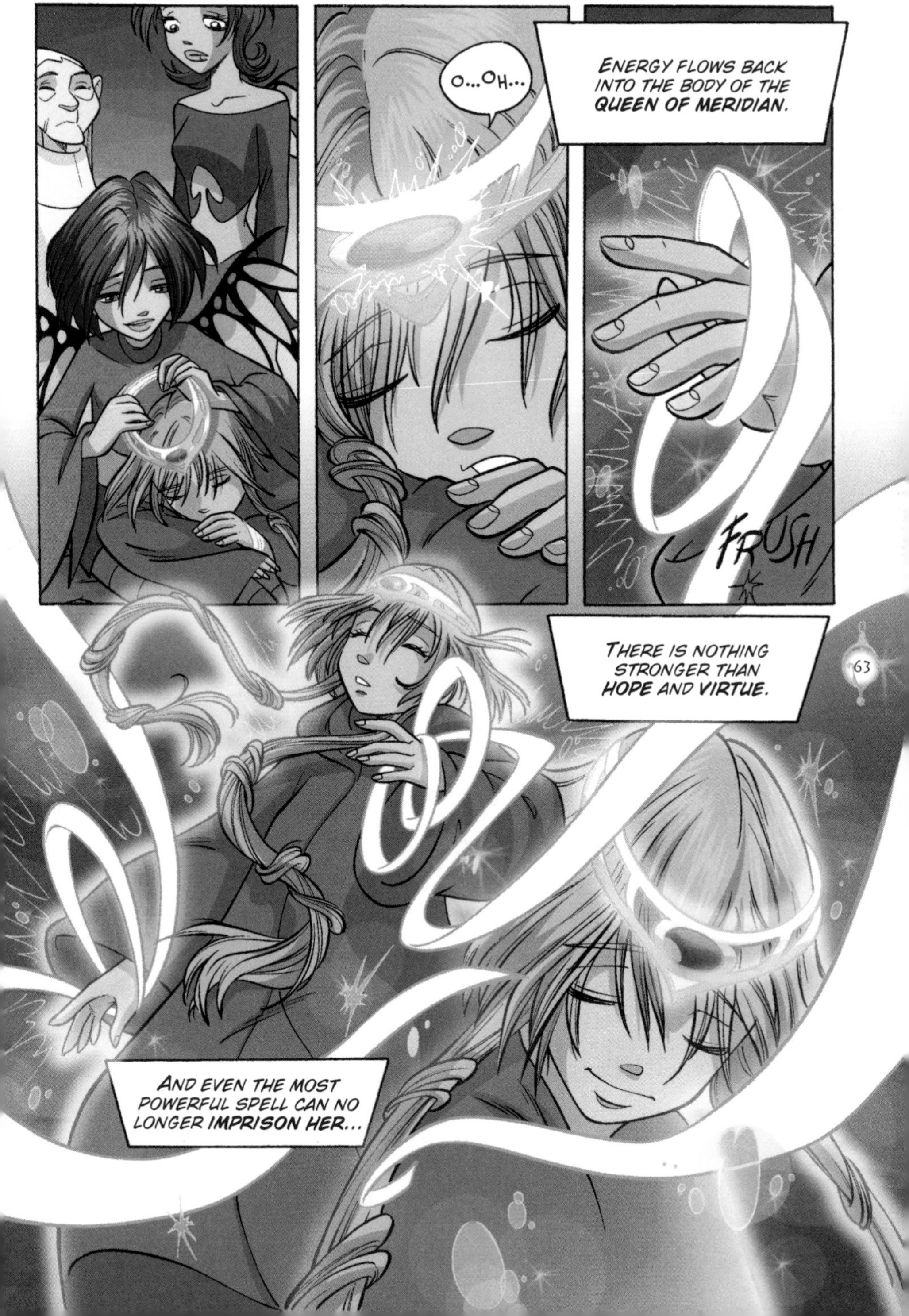
O...OH...
ENERGY FLOWS BACK INTO THE BODY OF THE QUEEN OF MERIDIAN.
FRUSH
THERE IS NOTHING STRONGER THAN HOPE AND VIRTUE.
AND EVEN THE MOST POWERFUL SPELL CAN NO LONGER IMPRISON HER...

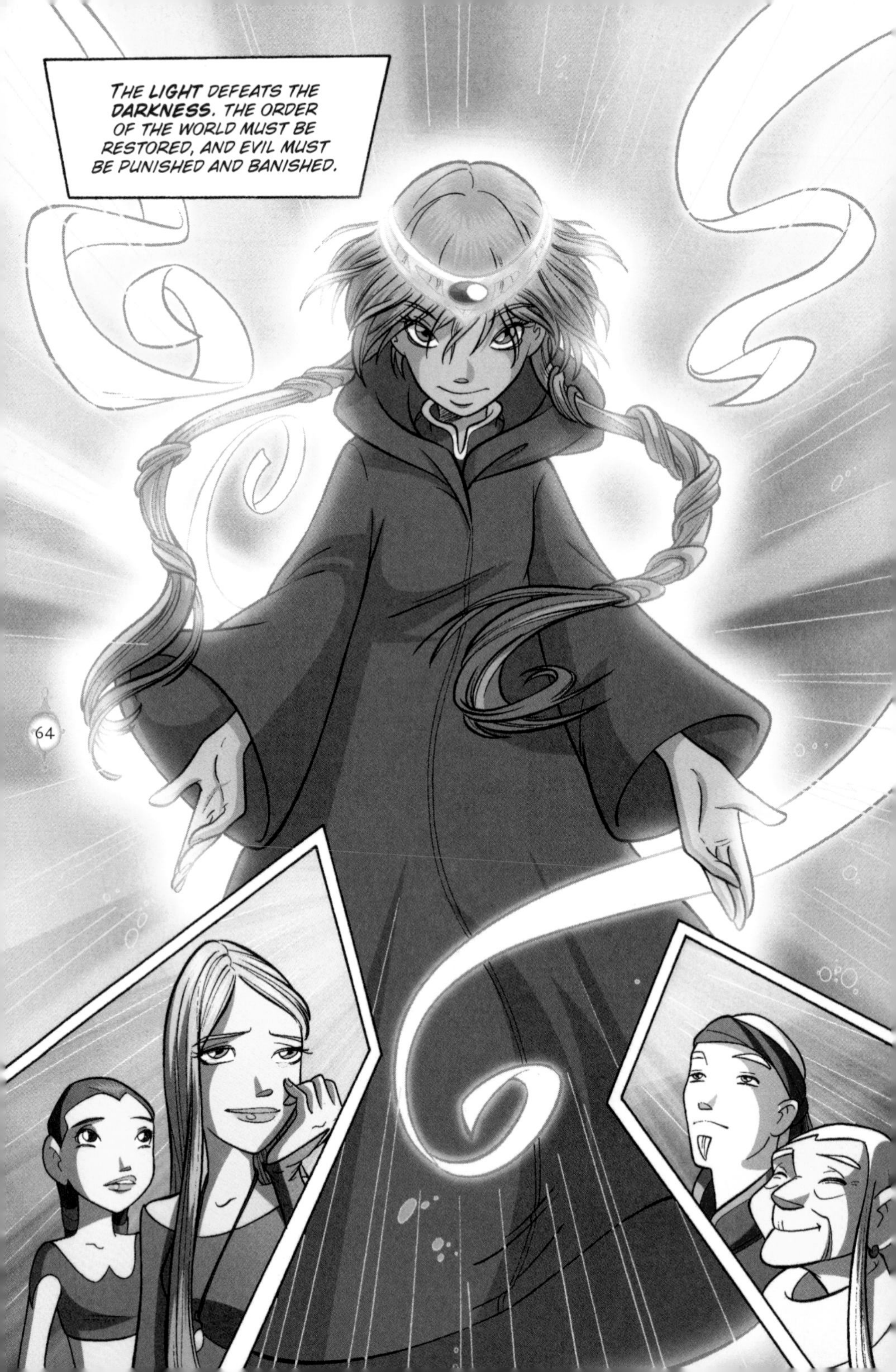
THE **LIGHT** DEFEATS THE **DARKNESS**. THE ORDER OF THE WORLD MUST BE RESTORED, AND EVIL MUST BE PUNISHED AND BANISHED.

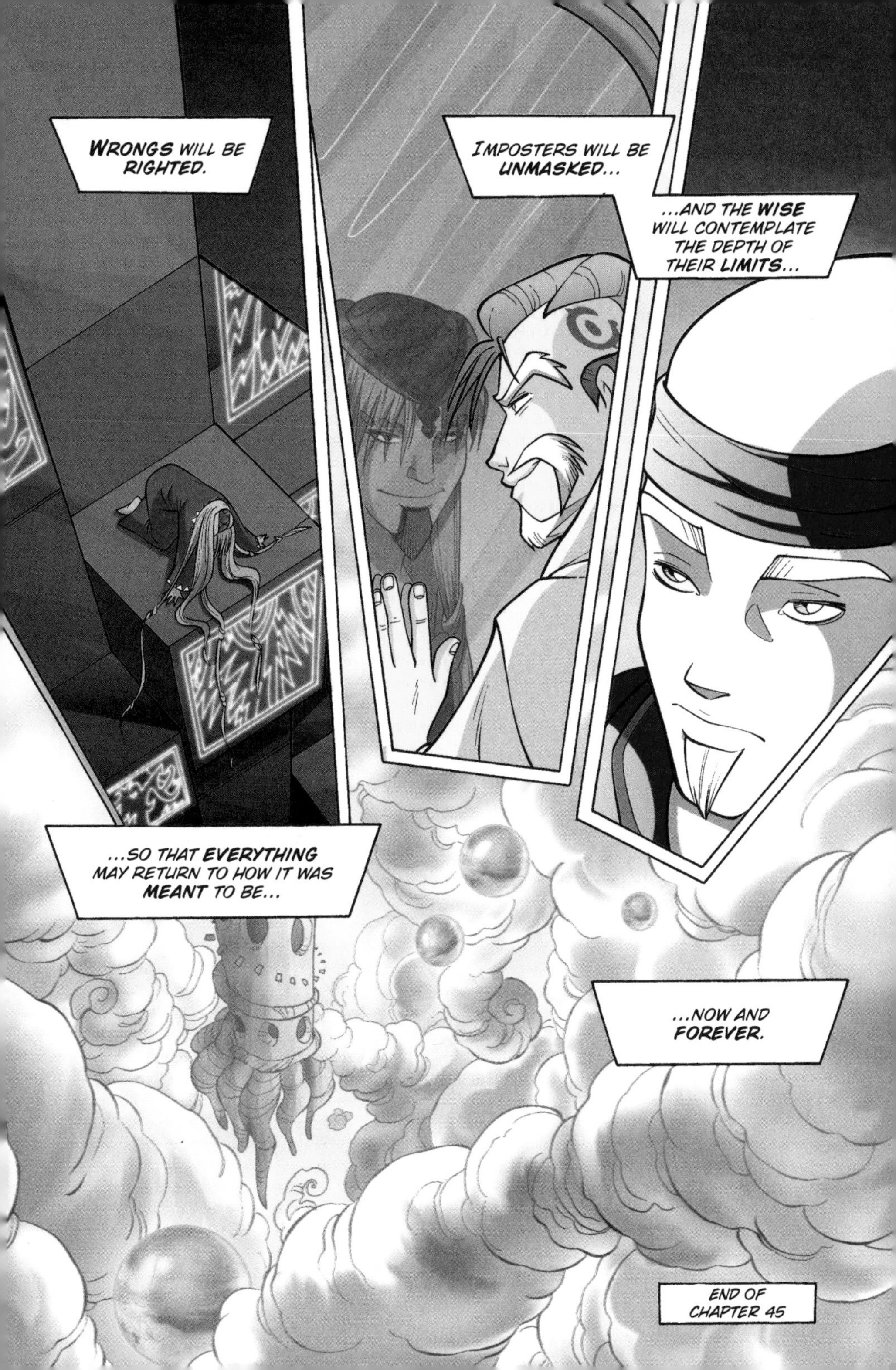
WRONGS WILL BE RIGHTED.
IMPOSTERS WILL BE UNMASKED...
...AND THE WISE WILL CONTEMPLATE THE DEPTH OF THEIR LIMITS...
...SO THAT EVERYTHING MAY RETURN TO HOW IT WAS MEANT TO BE...
...NOW AND FOREVER.
END OF CHAPTER 45

W.i.t.c.h.

Will Irma Taranee Cornelia Hay Lin

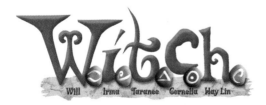

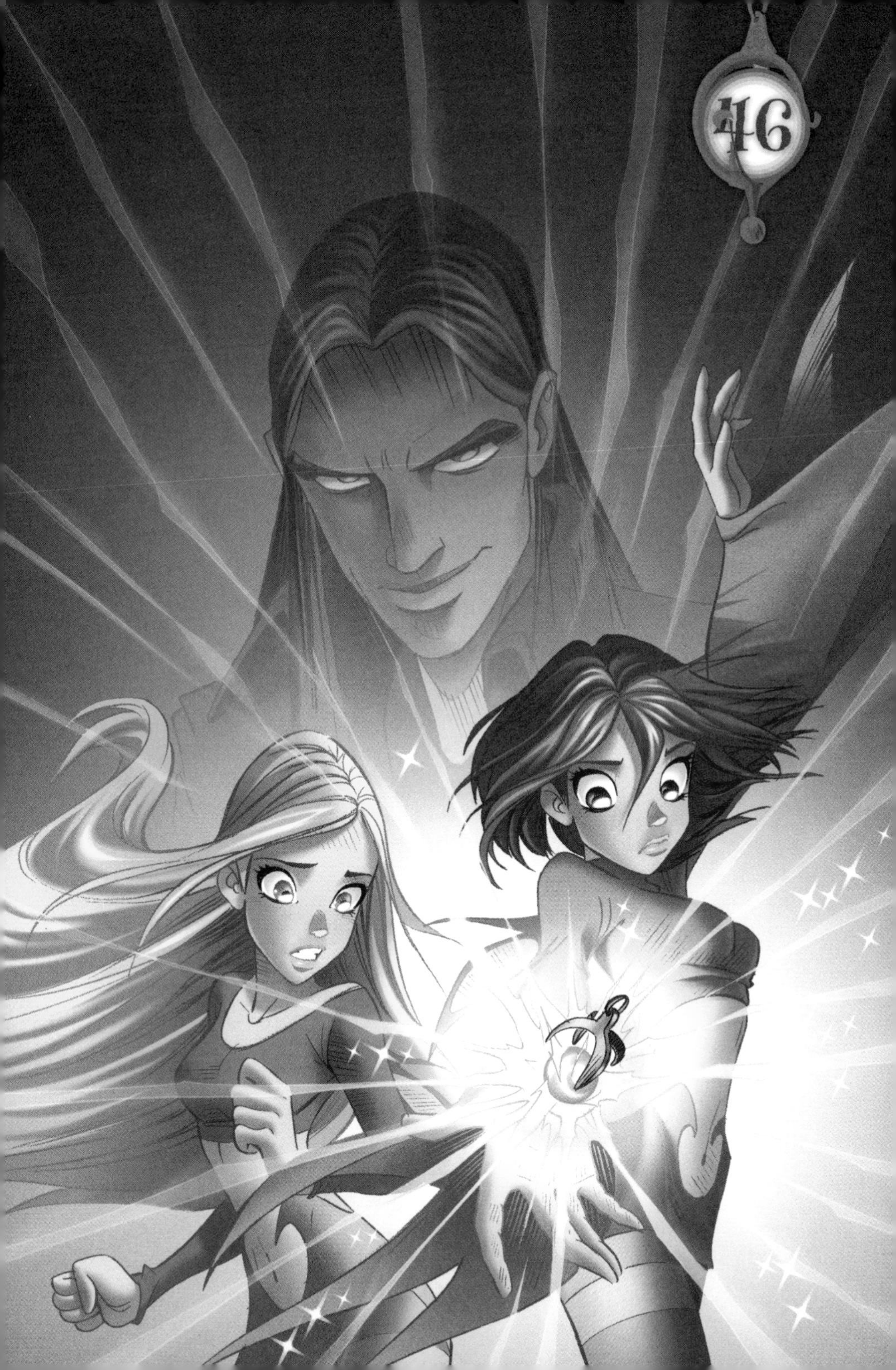
46

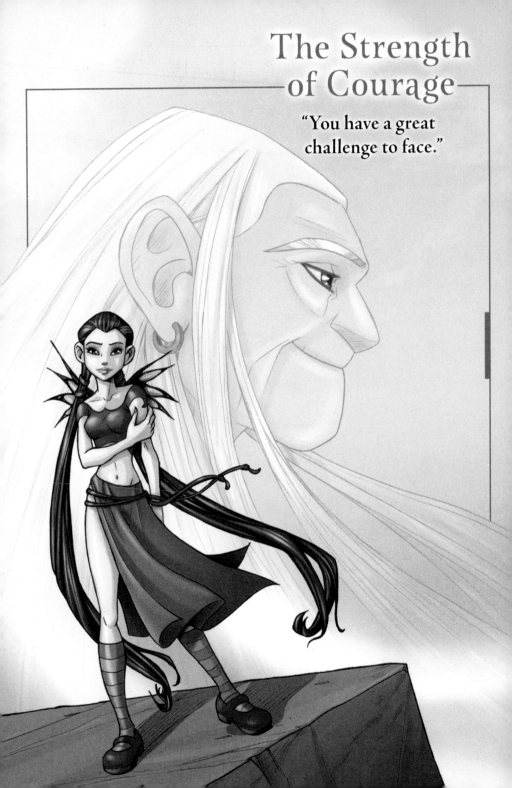

The Strength of Courage

"You have a great challenge to face."

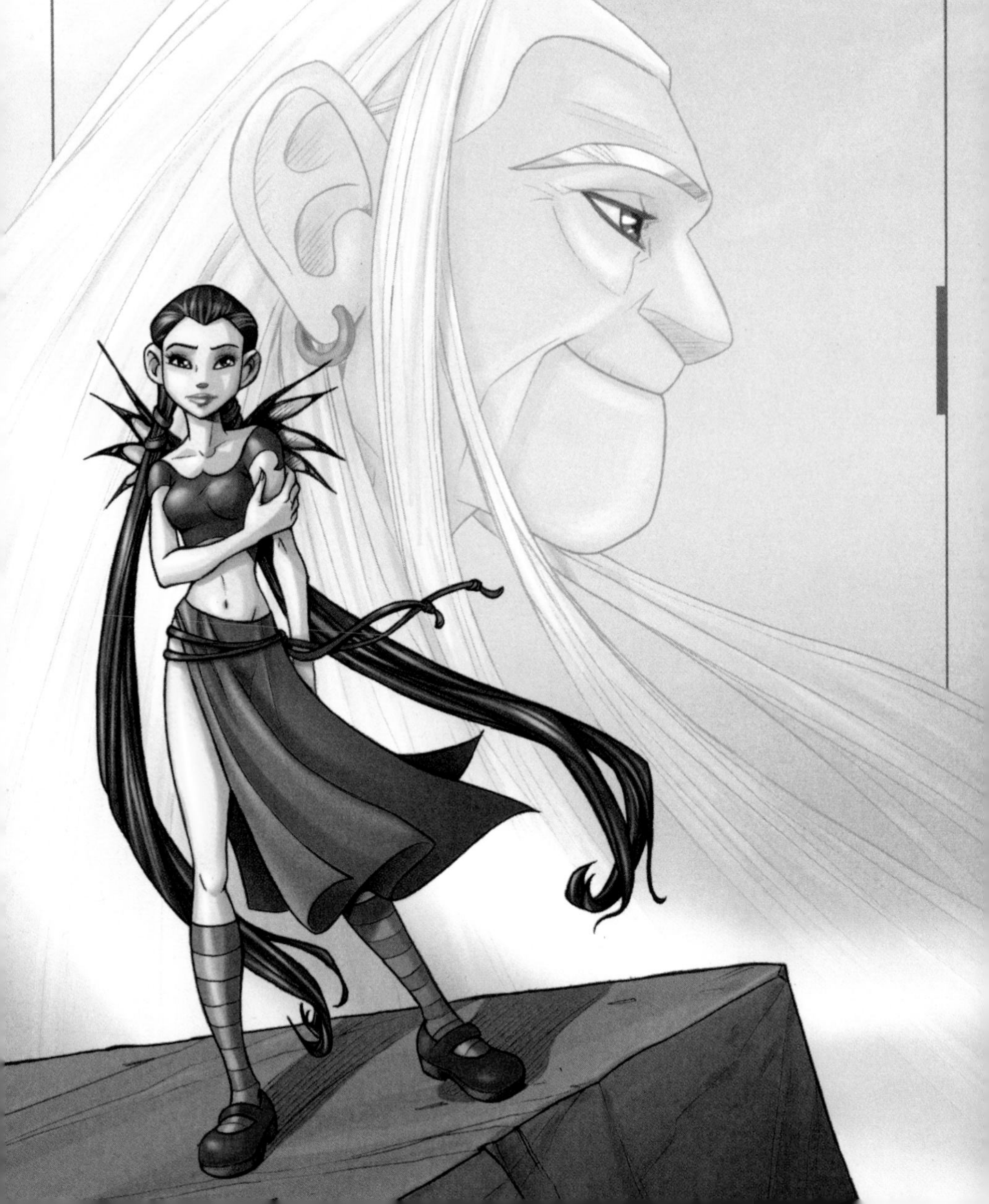

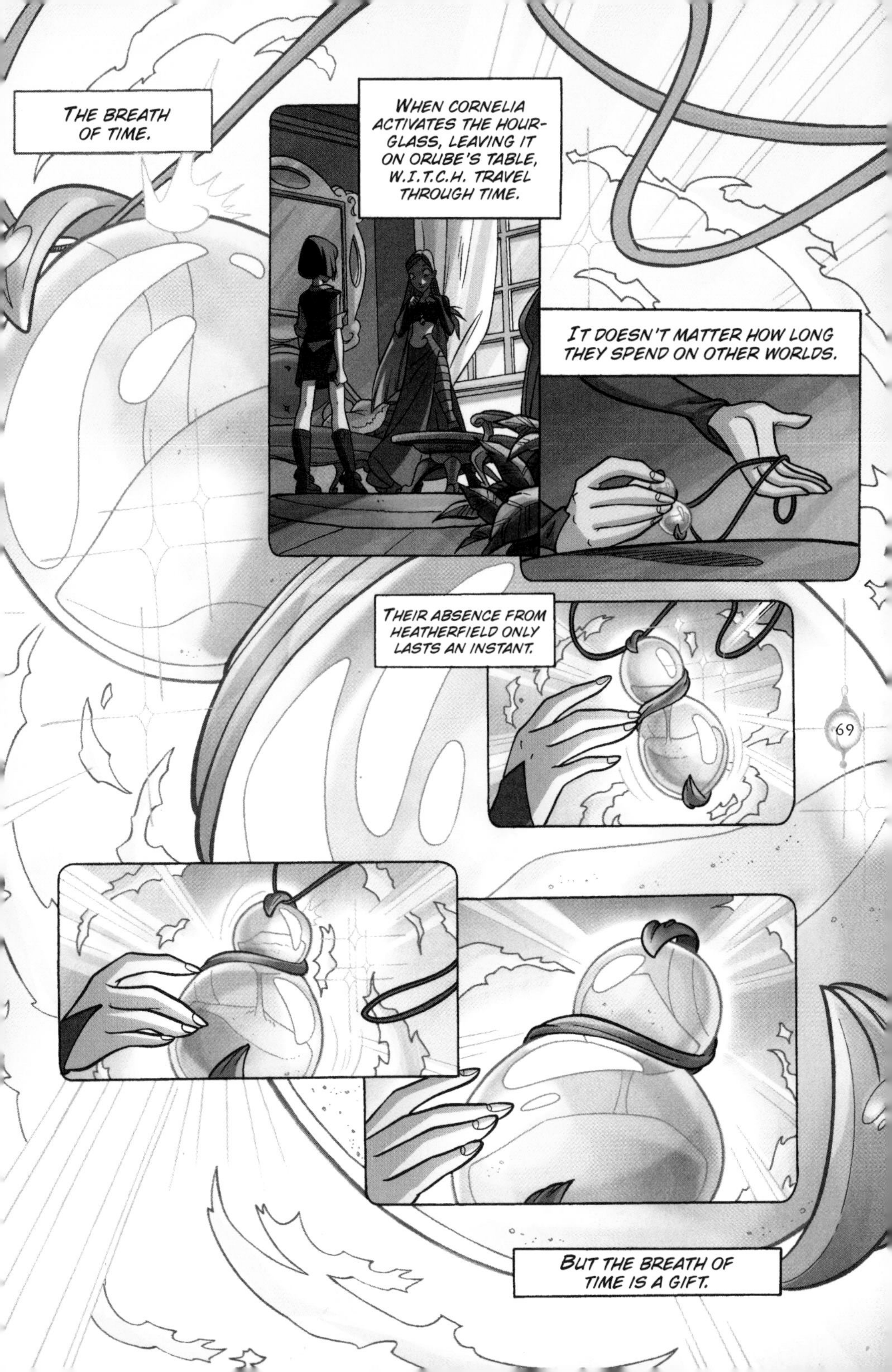
THE BREATH OF TIME.
WHEN CORNELIA ACTIVATES THE HOUR-GLASS, LEAVING IT ON ORUBE'S TABLE, W.I.T.C.H. TRAVEL THROUGH TIME.
IT DOESN'T MATTER HOW LONG THEY SPEND ON OTHER WORLDS.
THEIR ABSENCE FROM HEATHERFIELD ONLY LASTS AN INSTANT.
BUT THE BREATH OF TIME IS A GIFT.

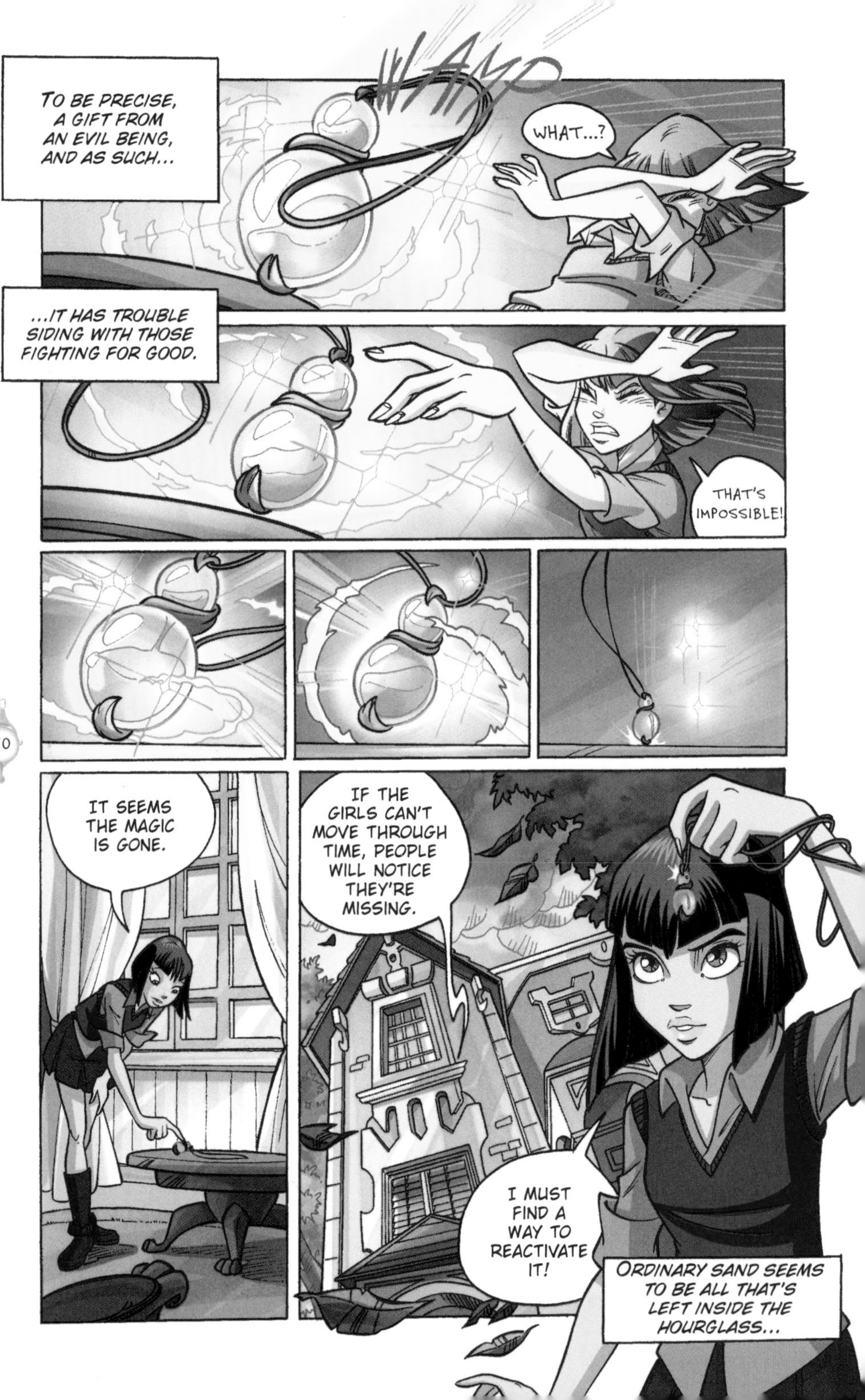
TO BE PRECISE, A GIFT FROM AN EVIL BEING, AND AS SUCH...
WAMP
WHAT...?
...IT HAS TROUBLE SIDING WITH THOSE FIGHTING FOR GOOD.
THAT'S IMPOSSIBLE!
IT SEEMS THE MAGIC IS GONE.
IF THE GIRLS CAN'T MOVE THROUGH TIME, PEOPLE WILL NOTICE THEY'RE MISSING.
I MUST FIND A WAY TO REACTIVATE IT!
ORDINARY SAND SEEMS TO BE ALL THAT'S LEFT INSIDE THE HOURGLASS...

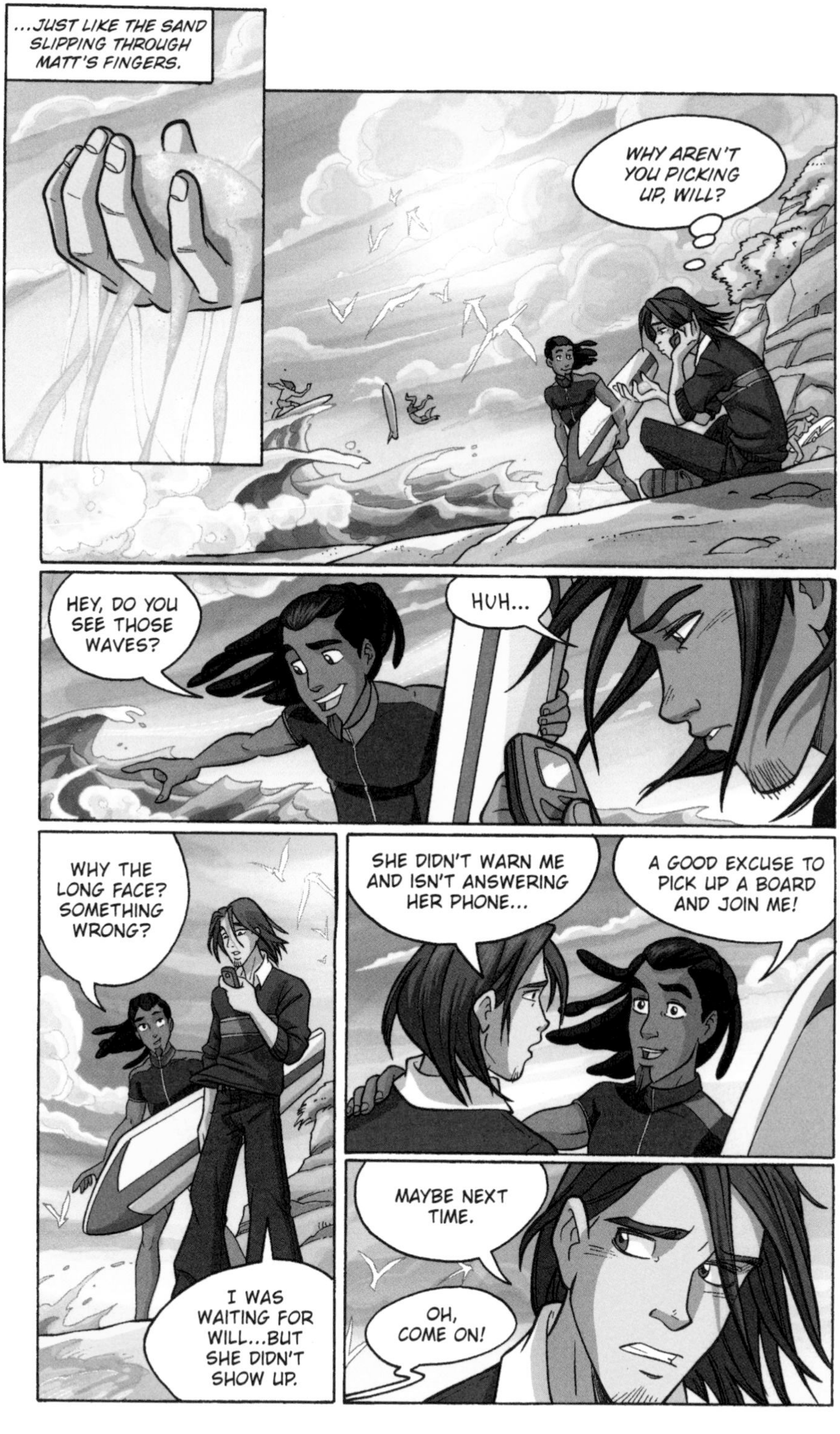

...JUST LIKE THE SAND SLIPPING THROUGH MATT'S FINGERS.
WHY AREN'T YOU PICKING UP, WILL?
HEY, DO YOU SEE THOSE WAVES?
HUH...
WHY THE LONG FACE? SOMETHING WRONG?
I WAS WAITING FOR WILL...BUT SHE DIDN'T SHOW UP.
SHE DIDN'T WARN ME AND ISN'T ANSWERING HER PHONE...
A GOOD EXCUSE TO PICK UP A BOARD AND JOIN ME!
MAYBE NEXT TIME.
OH, COME ON!

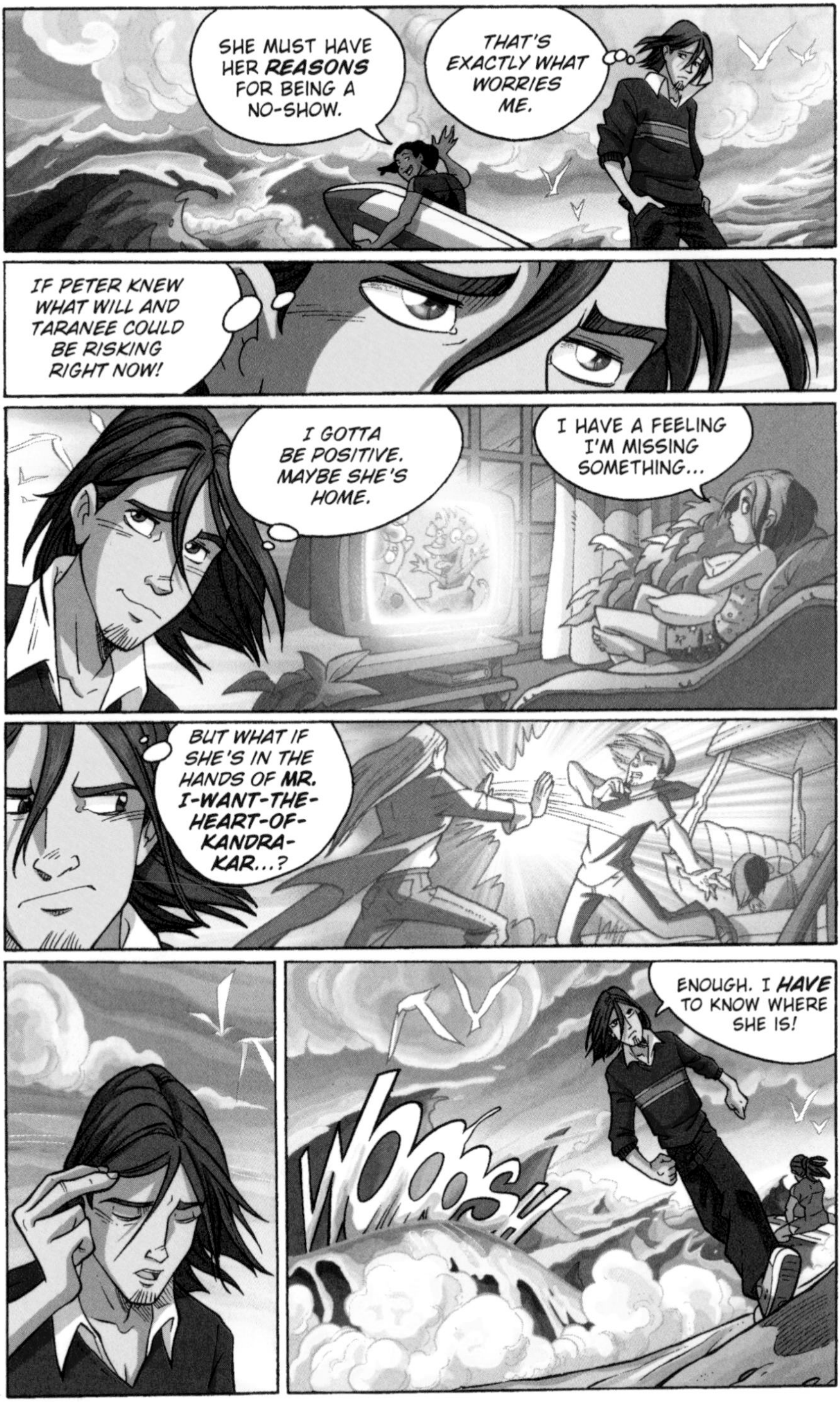

SHE MUST HAVE HER REASONS FOR BEING A NO-SHOW.
THAT'S EXACTLY WHAT WORRIES ME.
IF PETER KNEW WHAT WILL AND TARANEE COULD BE RISKING RIGHT NOW!
I GOTTA BE POSITIVE. MAYBE SHE'S HOME.
I HAVE A FEELING I'M MISSING SOMETHING...
BUT WHAT IF SHE'S IN THE HANDS OF MR. I-WANT-THE-HEART-OF-KANDRAKAR...?
ENOUGH. I HAVE TO KNOW WHERE SHE IS!
WOOSH!

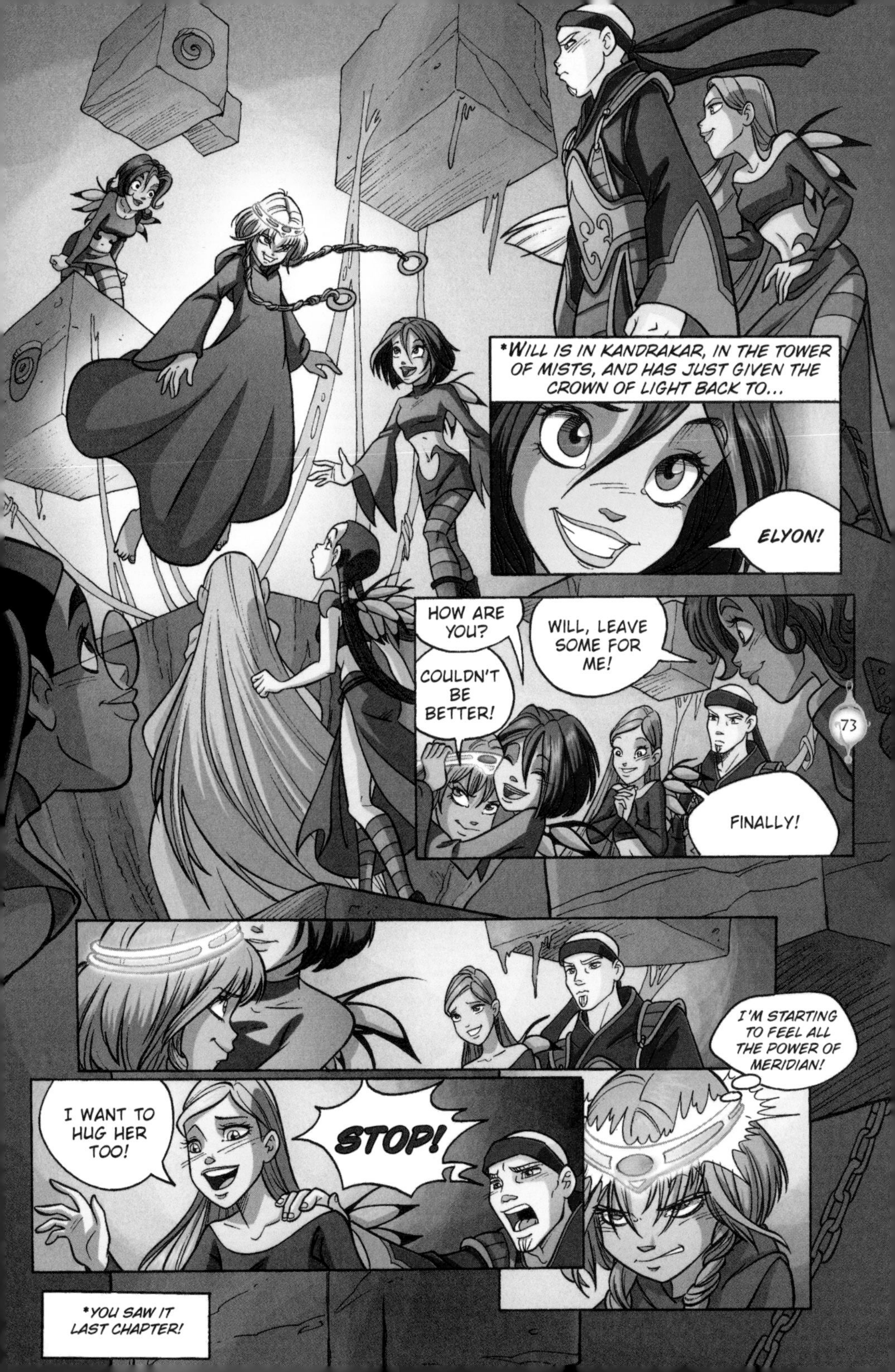

*WILL IS IN KANDRAKAR, IN THE TOWER OF MISTS, AND HAS JUST GIVEN THE CROWN OF LIGHT BACK TO...
ELYON!
HOW ARE YOU?
COULDN'T BE BETTER!
WILL, LEAVE SOME FOR ME!
FINALLY!
I'M STARTING TO FEEL ALL THE POWER OF MERIDIAN!
I WANT TO HUG HER TOO!
STOP!
*YOU SAW IT LAST CHAPTER!

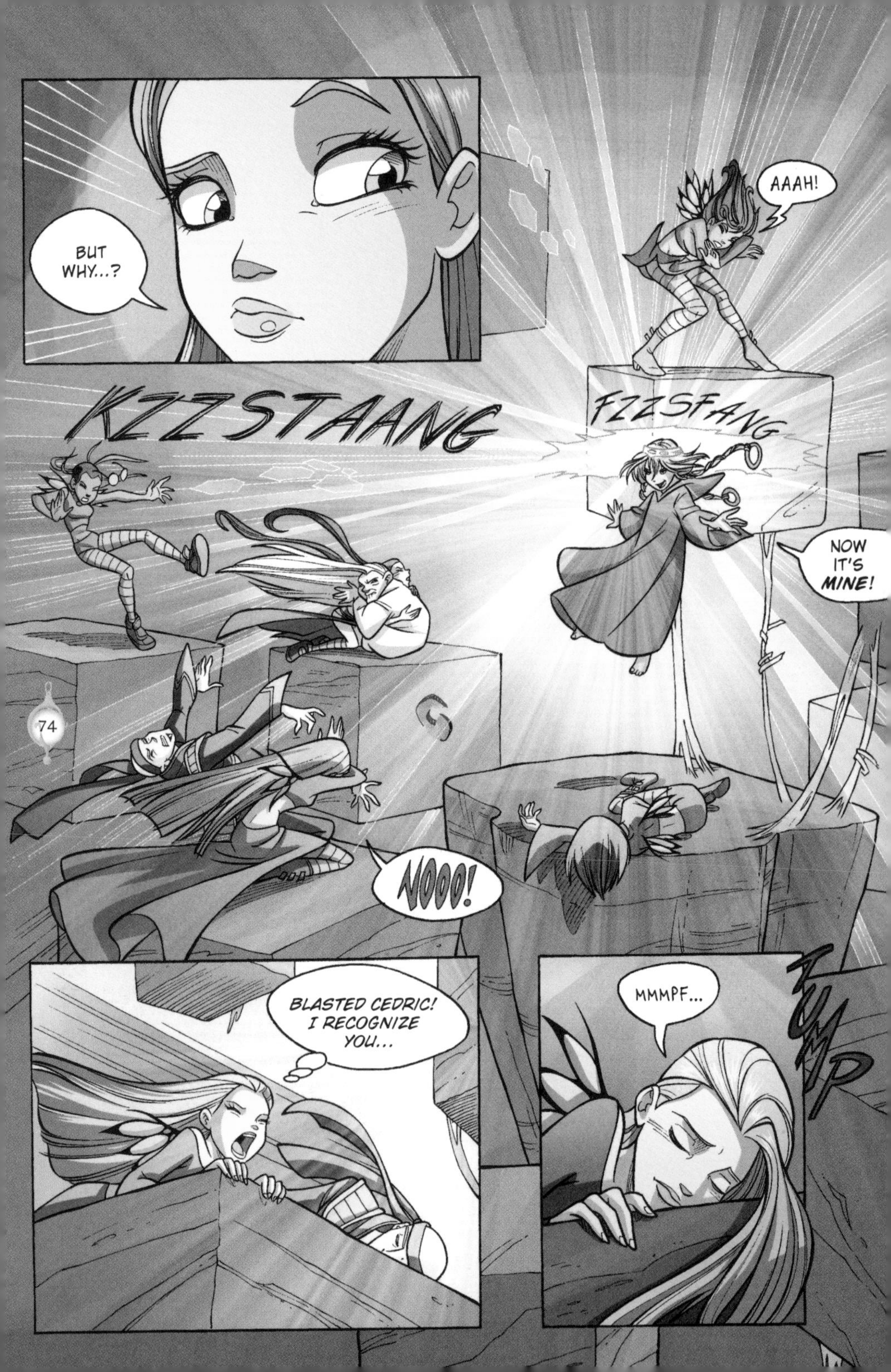

BUT WHY...?
AAAH!
KZZSTAANG
FZZSFANG
NOW IT'S *MINE!*
NOOO!
BLASTED CEDRIC! I RECOGNIZE YOU...
MMMPF...
THUMP

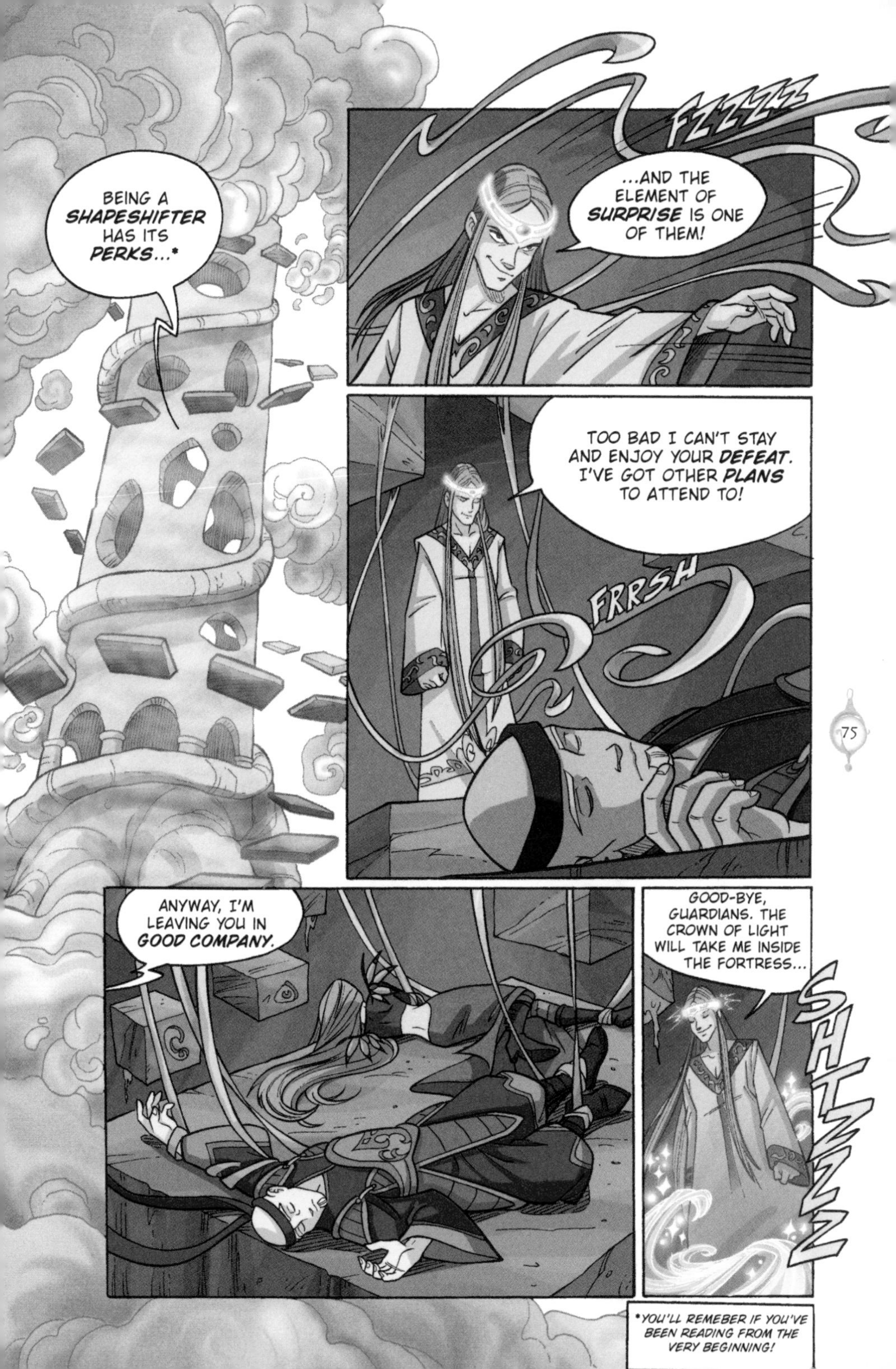
BEING A *SHAPESHIFTER* HAS ITS *PERKS*...*
FZZZZZ
...AND THE ELEMENT OF *SURPRISE* IS ONE OF THEM!
TOO BAD I CAN'T STAY AND ENJOY YOUR *DEFEAT*. I'VE GOT OTHER *PLANS* TO ATTEND TO!
FRRSH
ANYWAY, I'M LEAVING YOU IN *GOOD COMPANY*.
GOOD-BYE, GUARDIANS. THE CROWN OF LIGHT WILL TAKE ME INSIDE THE FORTRESS...
SHIMMMM
*YOU'LL REMEBER IF YOU'VE BEEN READING FROM THE VERY BEGINNING!

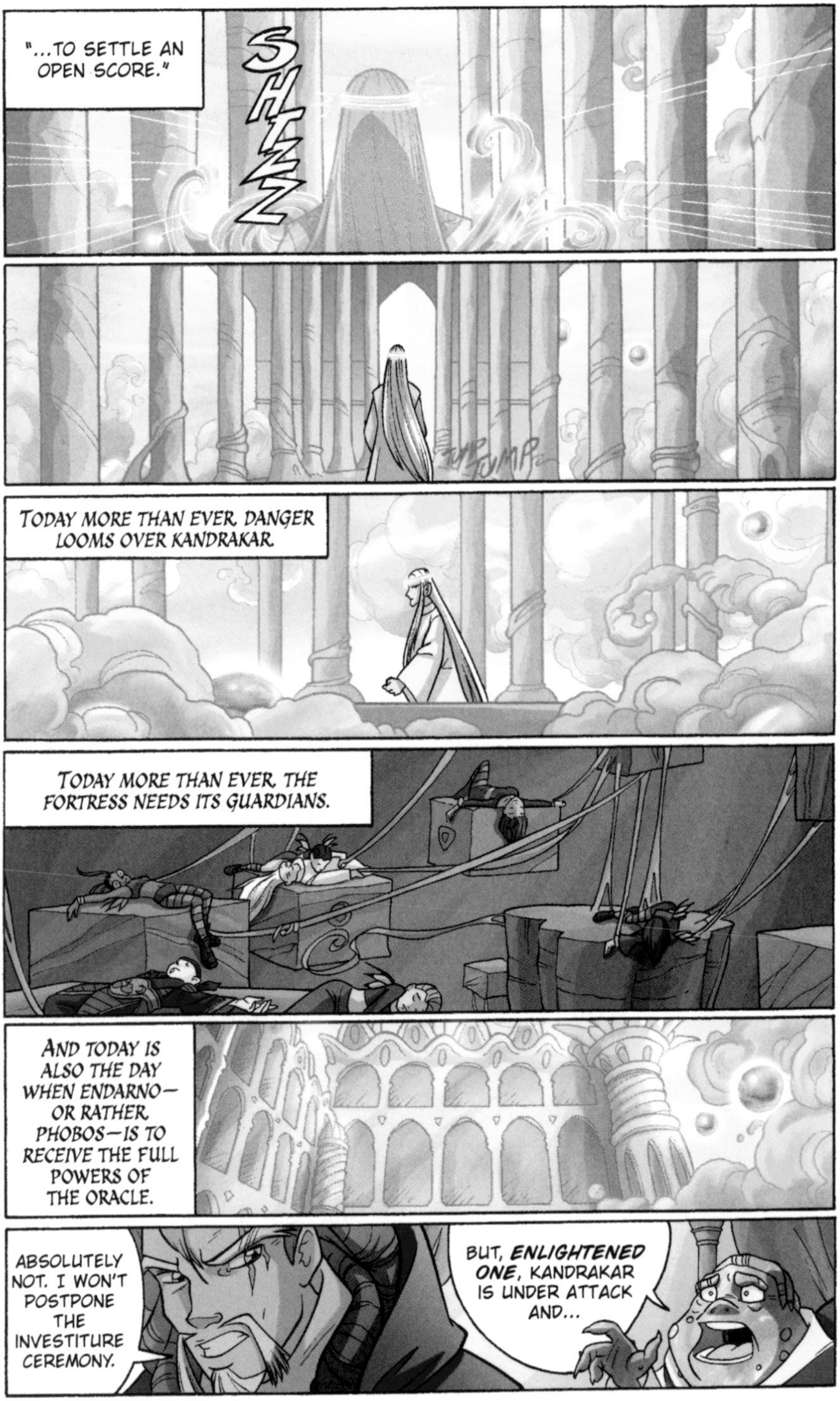
"...TO SETTLE AN OPEN SCORE."
SHIZZ
TUMP TUMP
TODAY MORE THAN EVER, DANGER LOOMS OVER KANDRAKAR.
TODAY MORE THAN EVER, THE FORTRESS NEEDS ITS GUARDIANS.
AND TODAY IS ALSO THE DAY WHEN ENDARNO—OR RATHER PHOBOS—IS TO RECEIVE THE FULL POWERS OF THE ORACLE.
ABSOLUTELY NOT. I WON'T POSTPONE THE INVESTITURE CEREMONY.
BUT, *ENLIGHTENED ONE*, KANDRAKAR IS UNDER ATTACK AND...

THAT WON'T BE NECESSARY.

STOP! HOW DARE YOU BARGE IN HERE WITHOUT...

I'M SURE THE *FUTURE ORACLE* WILL GRANT ME AN AUDIENCE. I BRING GOOD NEWS.

HOLD YOUR TONGUE. THE COUNCIL CAN'T BOW BEFORE A TRAITOR AND HIS ACCOMPLICES.

THE SITUATION IS UNDER CONTROL, AND THE *ESCAPED PRISONER* IS SECURED.

GOOD.

I'M GLAD TO SEE YOU BACK ON THE SIDE OF JUSTICE, HONORABLE *YAN LIN.*

VAAL, PROCEED WITH THE CEREMONY.

YES, MY LORD.

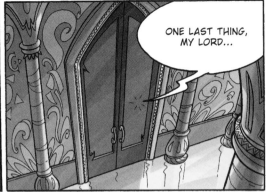

I HAVE A BAD FEELING.

ONE LAST THING, MY LORD...

SPARE ME YOUR *SHAPE-SHIFTING* TRICKS, CEDRIC. I KNEW IT WAS YOU.

HA-HA-HA!

NOT ONLY DID YOU BETRAY ME...YOU UNDER-ESTIMATED ME!

THE CROWN OF LIGHT!

INDEED. I TOOK IT FROM ELYON AND DEFEATED THE GUARDIANS, HIMERISH, AND YAN LIN.

WHAT DO YOU WANT, THEN?

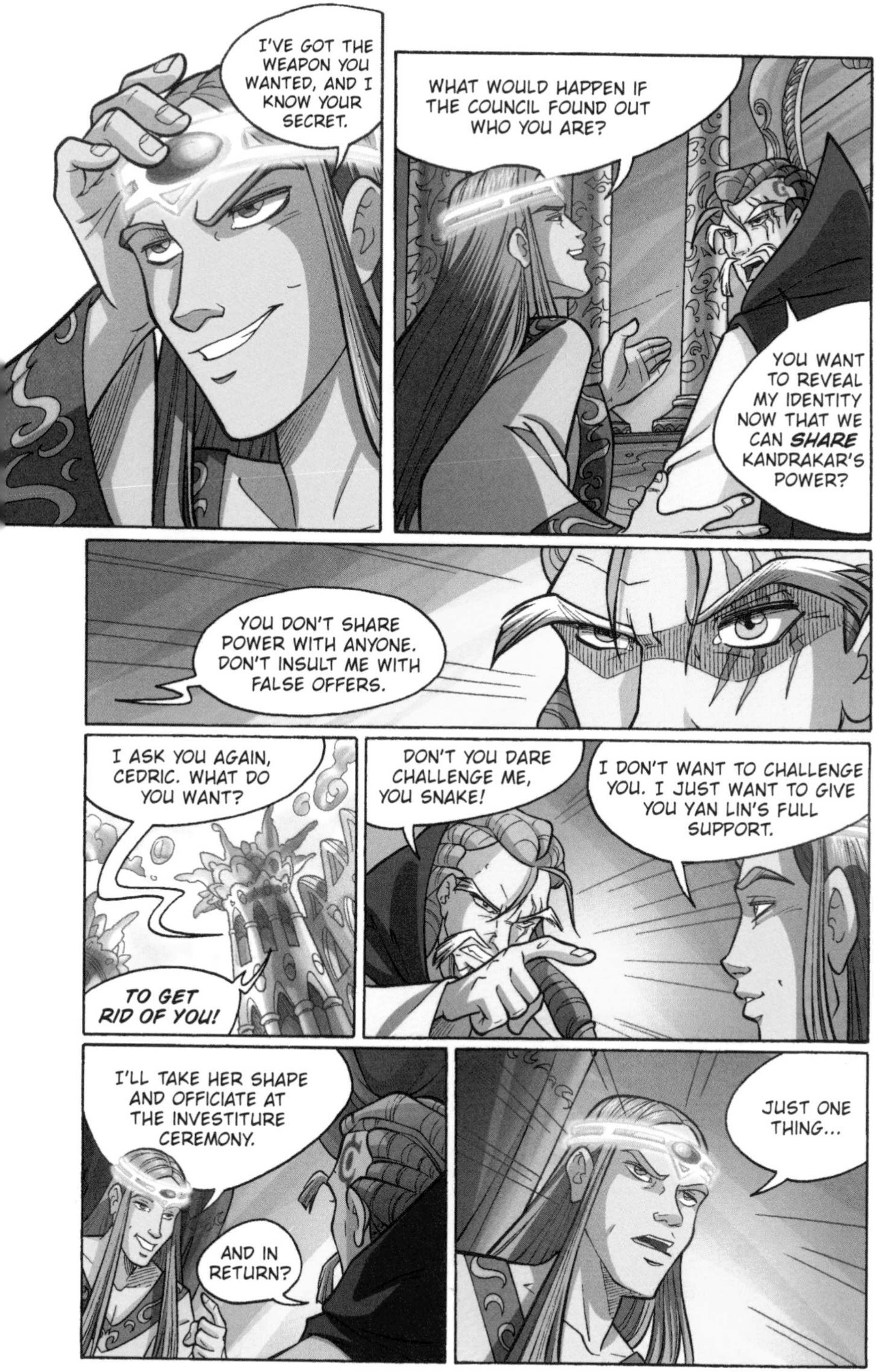
I'VE GOT THE WEAPON YOU WANTED, AND I KNOW YOUR SECRET.
WHAT WOULD HAPPEN IF THE COUNCIL FOUND OUT WHO YOU ARE?
YOU WANT TO REVEAL MY IDENTITY NOW THAT WE CAN **SHARE** KANDRAKAR'S POWER?
YOU DON'T SHARE POWER WITH ANYONE. DON'T INSULT ME WITH FALSE OFFERS.
I ASK YOU AGAIN, CEDRIC. WHAT DO YOU WANT?
TO GET RID OF YOU!
DON'T YOU DARE CHALLENGE ME, YOU SNAKE!
I DON'T WANT TO CHALLENGE YOU. I JUST WANT TO GIVE YOU YAN LIN'S FULL SUPPORT.
I'LL TAKE HER SHAPE AND OFFICIATE AT THE INVESTITURE CEREMONY.
AND IN RETURN?
JUST ONE THING...

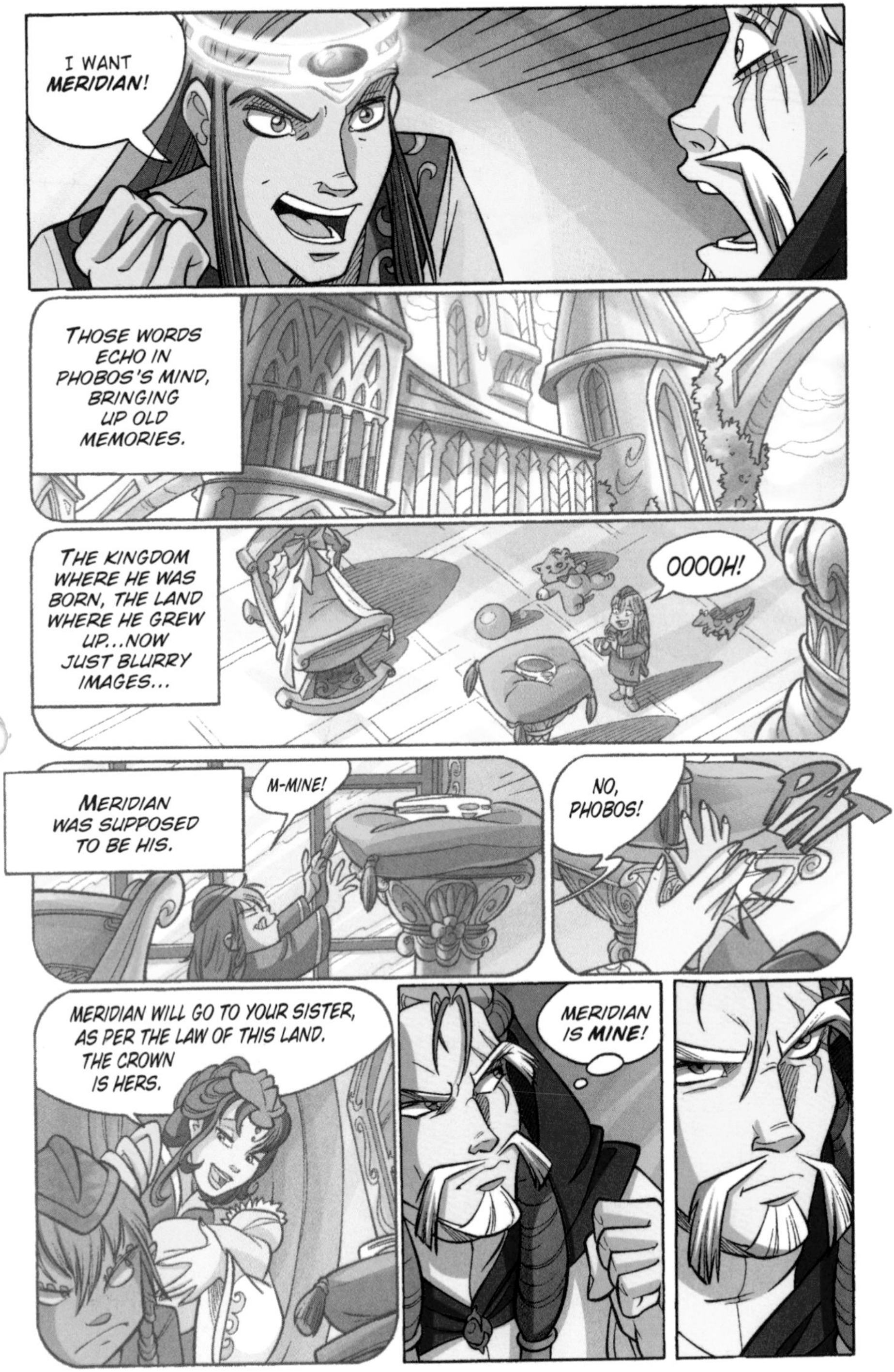
I WANT MERIDIAN!
THOSE WORDS ECHO IN PHOBOS'S MIND, BRINGING UP OLD MEMORIES.
THE KINGDOM WHERE HE WAS BORN, THE LAND WHERE HE GREW UP...NOW JUST BLURRY IMAGES...
OOOOH!
MERIDIAN WAS SUPPOSED TO BE HIS.
M-MINE!
NO, PHOBOS!
PAT
MERIDIAN WILL GO TO YOUR SISTER, AS PER THE LAW OF THIS LAND. THE CROWN IS HERS.
MERIDIAN IS MINE!

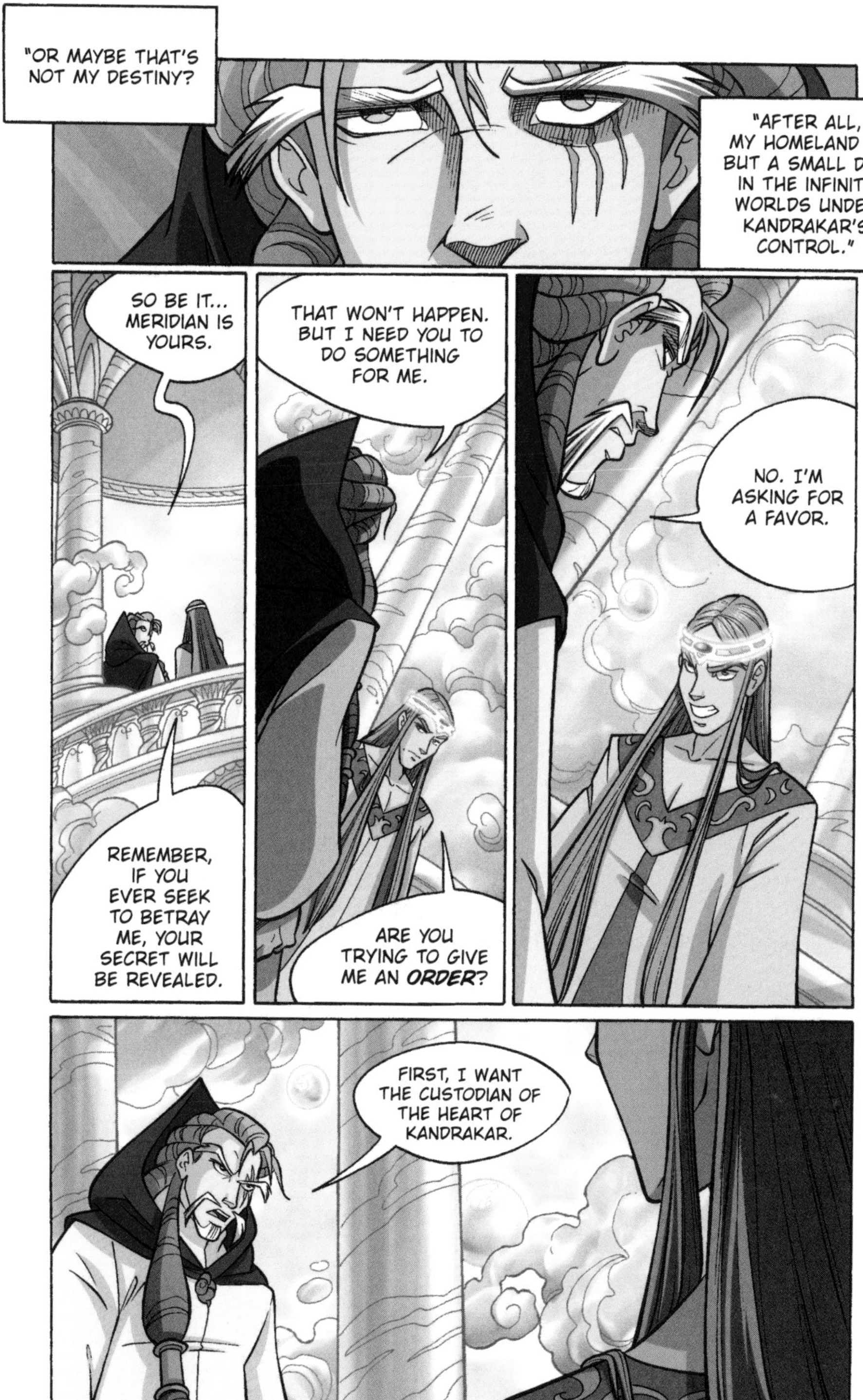
"OR MAYBE THAT'S NOT MY DESTINY?
"AFTER ALL, MY HOMELAND IS BUT A SMALL DOT IN THE INFINITE WORLDS UNDER KANDRAKAR'S CONTROL."
SO BE IT... MERIDIAN IS YOURS.
REMEMBER, IF YOU EVER SEEK TO BETRAY ME, YOUR SECRET WILL BE REVEALED.
THAT WON'T HAPPEN. BUT I NEED YOU TO DO SOMETHING FOR ME.
ARE YOU TRYING TO GIVE ME AN ***ORDER***?
NO. I'M ASKING FOR A FAVOR.
FIRST, I WANT THE CUSTODIAN OF THE HEART OF KANDRAKAR.

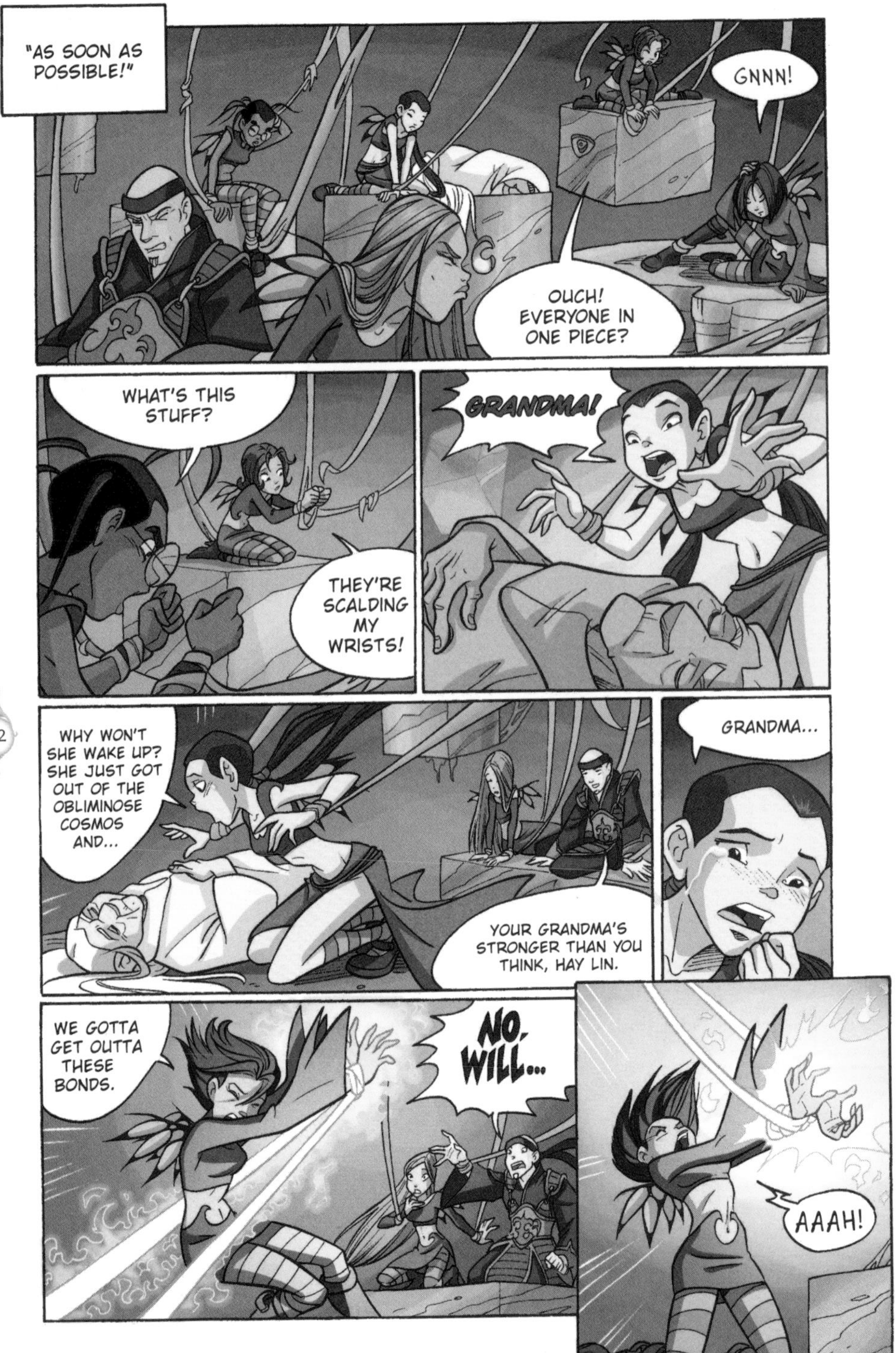
"AS SOON AS POSSIBLE!"
GNNN!
OUCH! EVERYONE IN ONE PIECE?
WHAT'S THIS STUFF?
THEY'RE SCALDING MY WRISTS!
GRANDMA!
WHY WON'T SHE WAKE UP? SHE JUST GOT OUT OF THE OBLIMINOSE COSMOS AND...
YOUR GRANDMA'S STRONGER THAN YOU THINK, HAY LIN.
GRANDMA...
WE GOTTA GET OUTTA THESE BONDS.
NO. WILL...
AAAH!

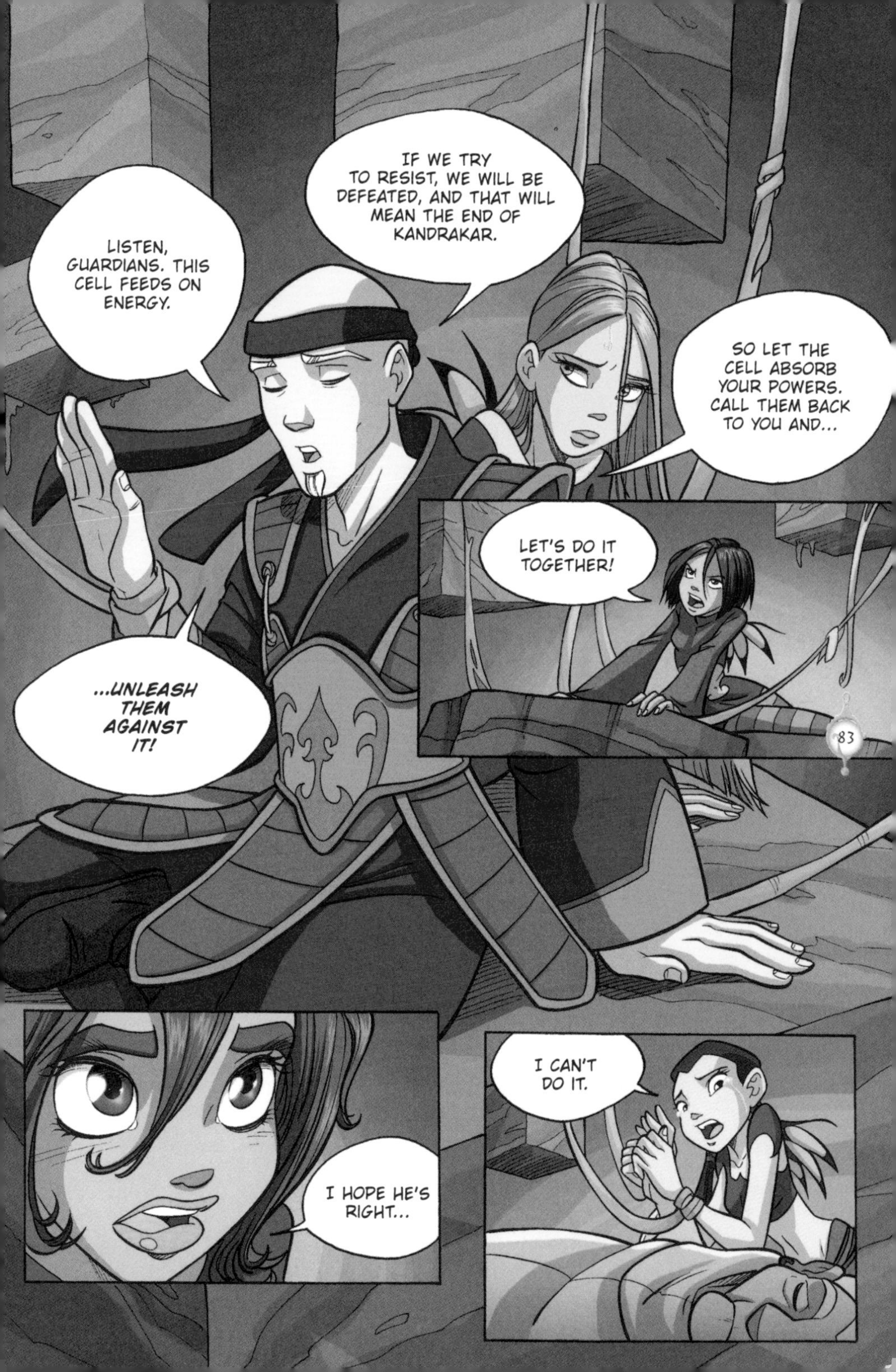
LISTEN, GUARDIANS. THIS CELL FEEDS ON ENERGY.
IF WE TRY TO RESIST, WE WILL BE DEFEATED, AND THAT WILL MEAN THE END OF KANDRAKAR.
SO LET THE CELL ABSORB YOUR POWERS. CALL THEM BACK TO YOU AND...
...UNLEASH THEM AGAINST IT!
LET'S DO IT TOGETHER!
I HOPE HE'S RIGHT...
I CAN'T DO IT.

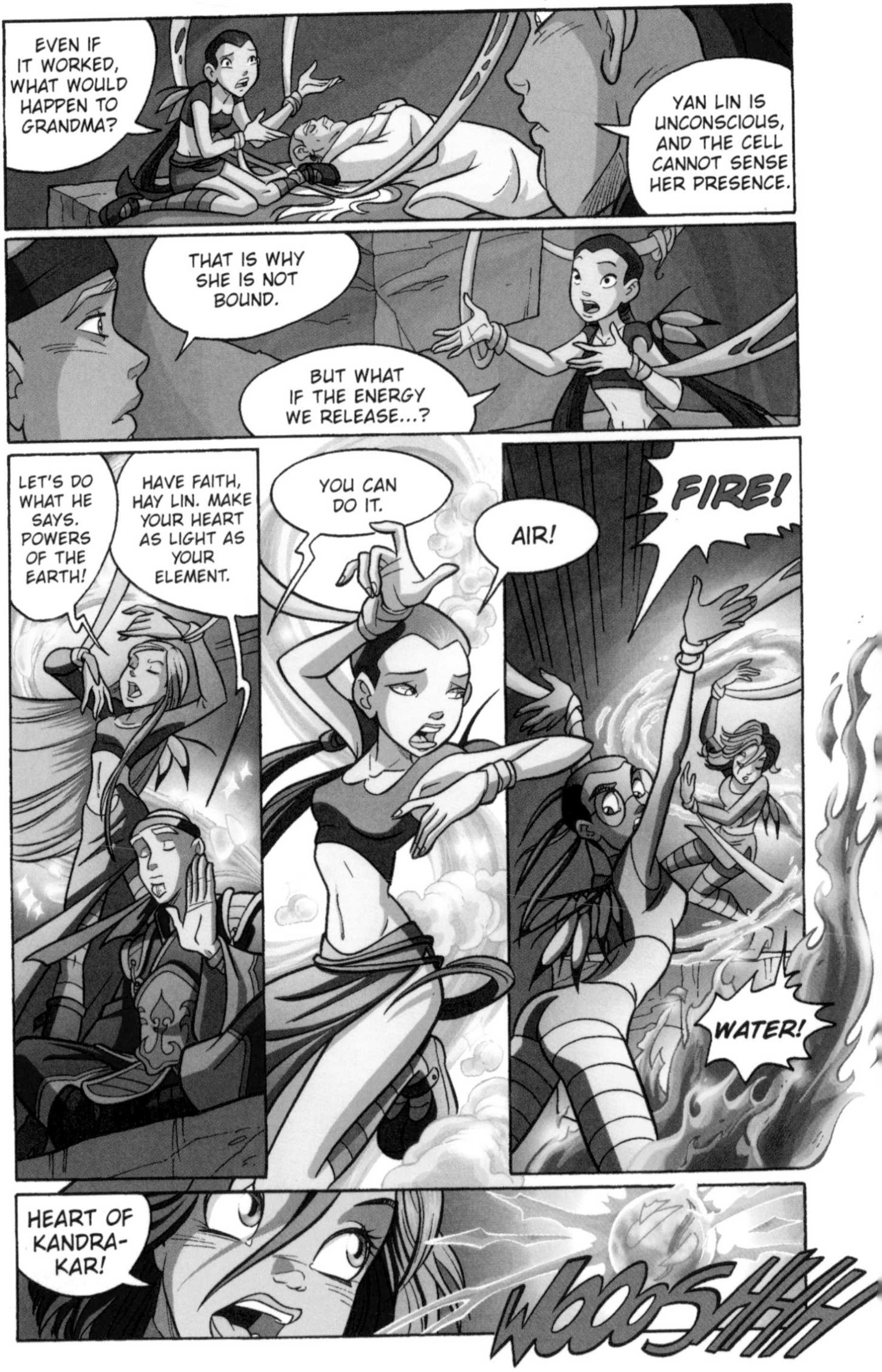
EVEN IF IT WORKED, WHAT WOULD HAPPEN TO GRANDMA?
YAN LIN IS UNCONSCIOUS, AND THE CELL CANNOT SENSE HER PRESENCE.
THAT IS WHY SHE IS NOT BOUND.
BUT WHAT IF THE ENERGY WE RELEASE...?
LET'S DO WHAT HE SAYS. POWERS OF THE EARTH!
HAVE FAITH, HAY LIN. MAKE YOUR HEART AS LIGHT AS YOUR ELEMENT.
YOU CAN DO IT.
AIR!
FIRE!
WATER!
HEART OF KANDRA-KAR!
WOOOSHHH

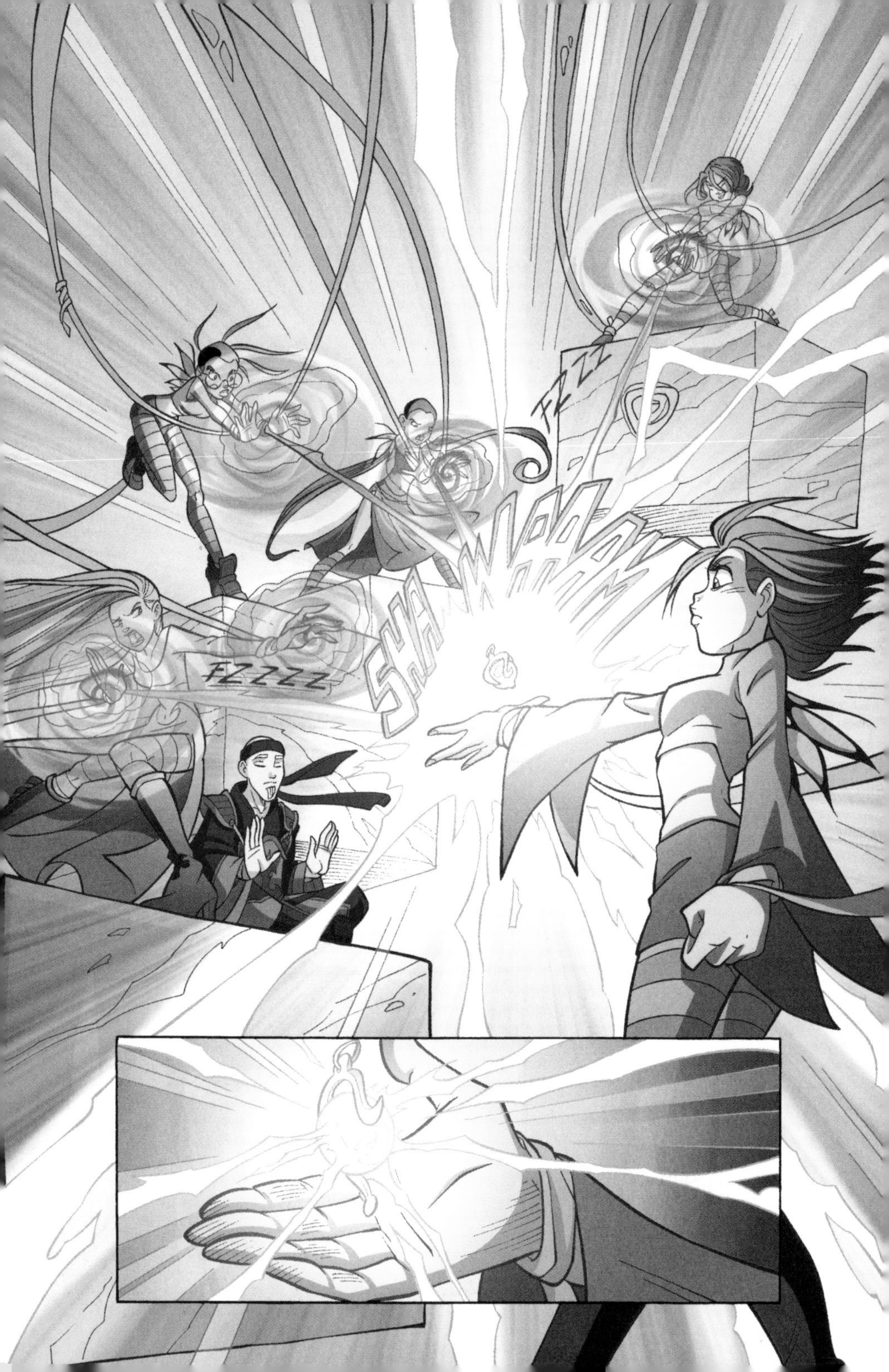
FZZZ
SHAWAAAM
FZZZZZ

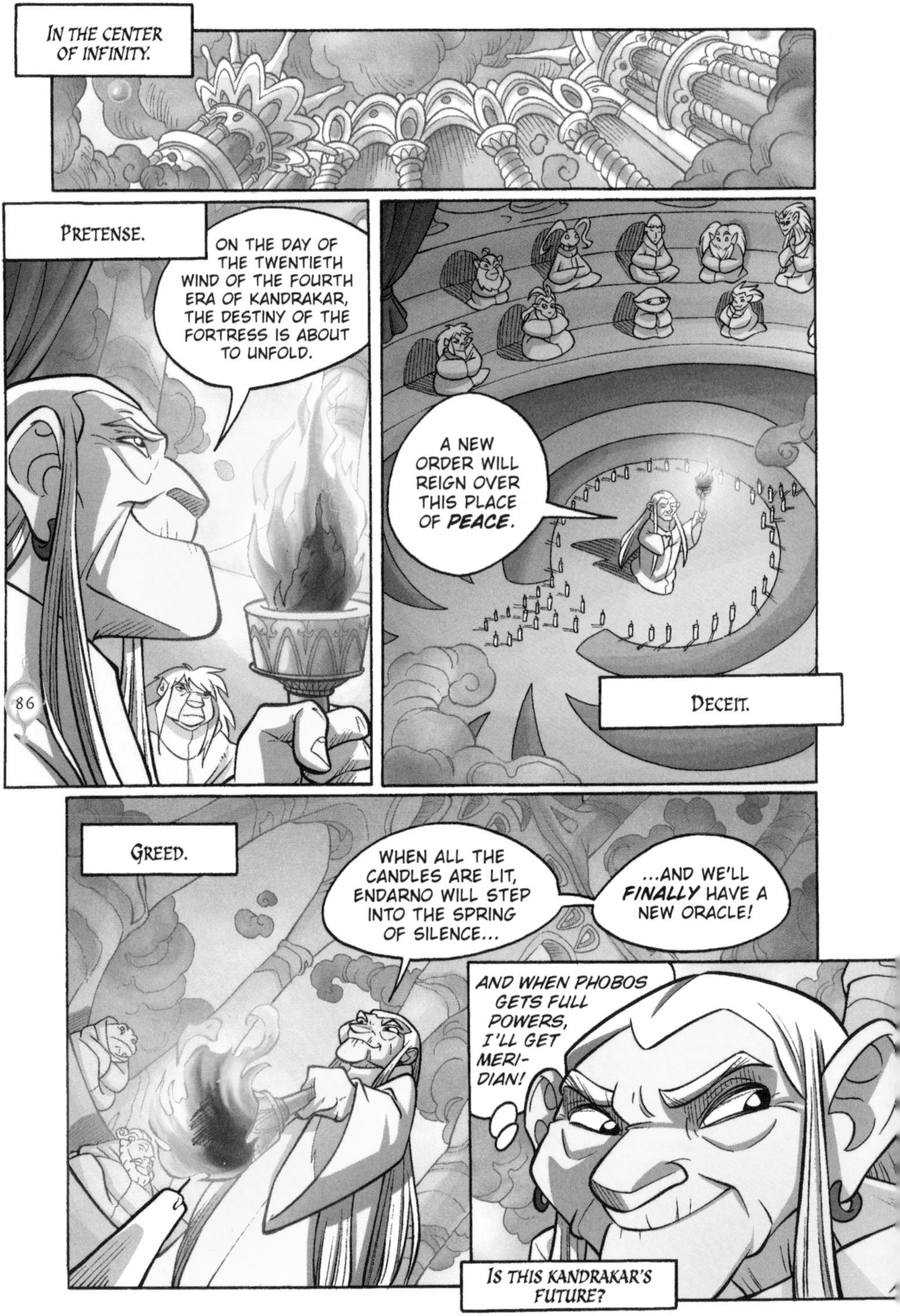
IN THE CENTER OF INFINITY.
PRETENSE.
ON THE DAY OF THE TWENTIETH WIND OF THE FOURTH ERA OF KANDRAKAR, THE DESTINY OF THE FORTRESS IS ABOUT TO UNFOLD.
A NEW ORDER WILL REIGN OVER THIS PLACE OF ***PEACE***.
DECEIT.
GREED.
WHEN ALL THE CANDLES ARE LIT, ENDARNO WILL STEP INTO THE SPRING OF SILENCE...
...AND WE'LL ***FINALLY*** HAVE A NEW ORACLE!
AND WHEN PHOBOS GETS FULL POWERS, I'LL GET MERI-DIAN!
IS THIS KANDRAKAR'S FUTURE?

IN THAT INSTANT, YAN LIN—THE REAL YAN LIN—OPENS HER EYES IN THE TOWER OF MISTS.

GRANDMA, ARE YOU OKAY?

UM... I'VE BEEN BETTER.

IT'S SO GOOD TO HEAR YOUR VOICE AGAIN!

WE DID IT! WE'RE *INVINCIBLE!*

IS EVERYONE ALL RIGHT?

MORE THAN WE DARED HOPE.

THE *BRACELET* OF THE TOWER'S CUSTODIAN OPENS EVERY CELL. IT'LL HELP YOU FIND WHO YOU'RE LOOKING FOR. GIVE IT TO HIMERISH.

WHY? YOU'RE NOT COMING WITH US?

YOU HAVE A *HUGE CHALLENGE TO FACE,* AND I NEED TO GET BACK ON MY FEET.

I'D ONLY BE A BURDEN.

THEN I'M STAYING WITH YOU.

I THOUGHT I WAS TOO OLD TO NEED A *NANNY!*

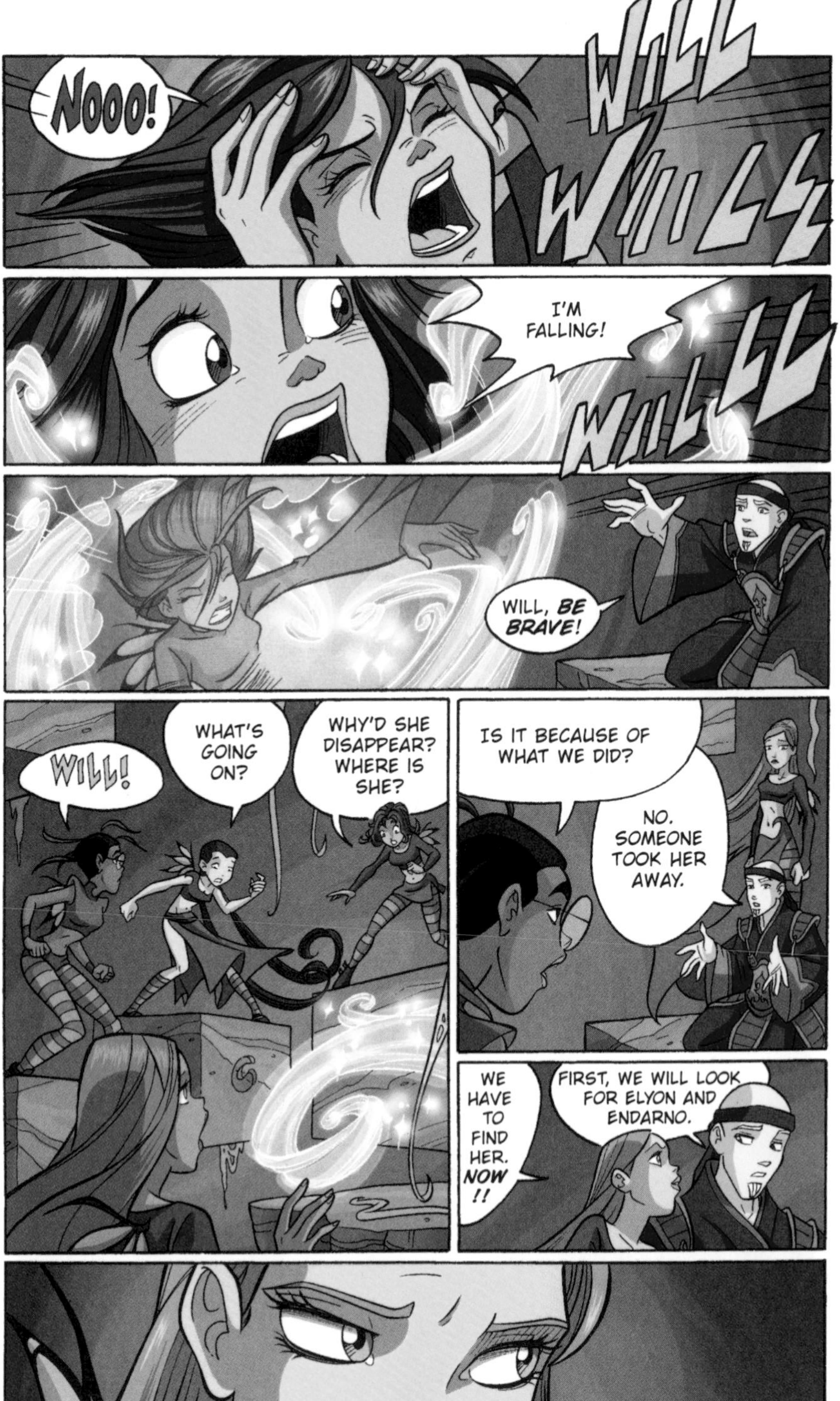
NOOO!
WILL
WILLL
I'M FALLING!
WILLL
WILL, BE BRAVE!
WILL!
WHAT'S GOING ON?
WHY'D SHE DISAPPEAR? WHERE IS SHE?
IS IT BECAUSE OF WHAT WE DID?
NO. SOMEONE TOOK HER AWAY.
WE HAVE TO FIND HER. NOW!!
FIRST, WE WILL LOOK FOR ELYON AND ENDARNO.

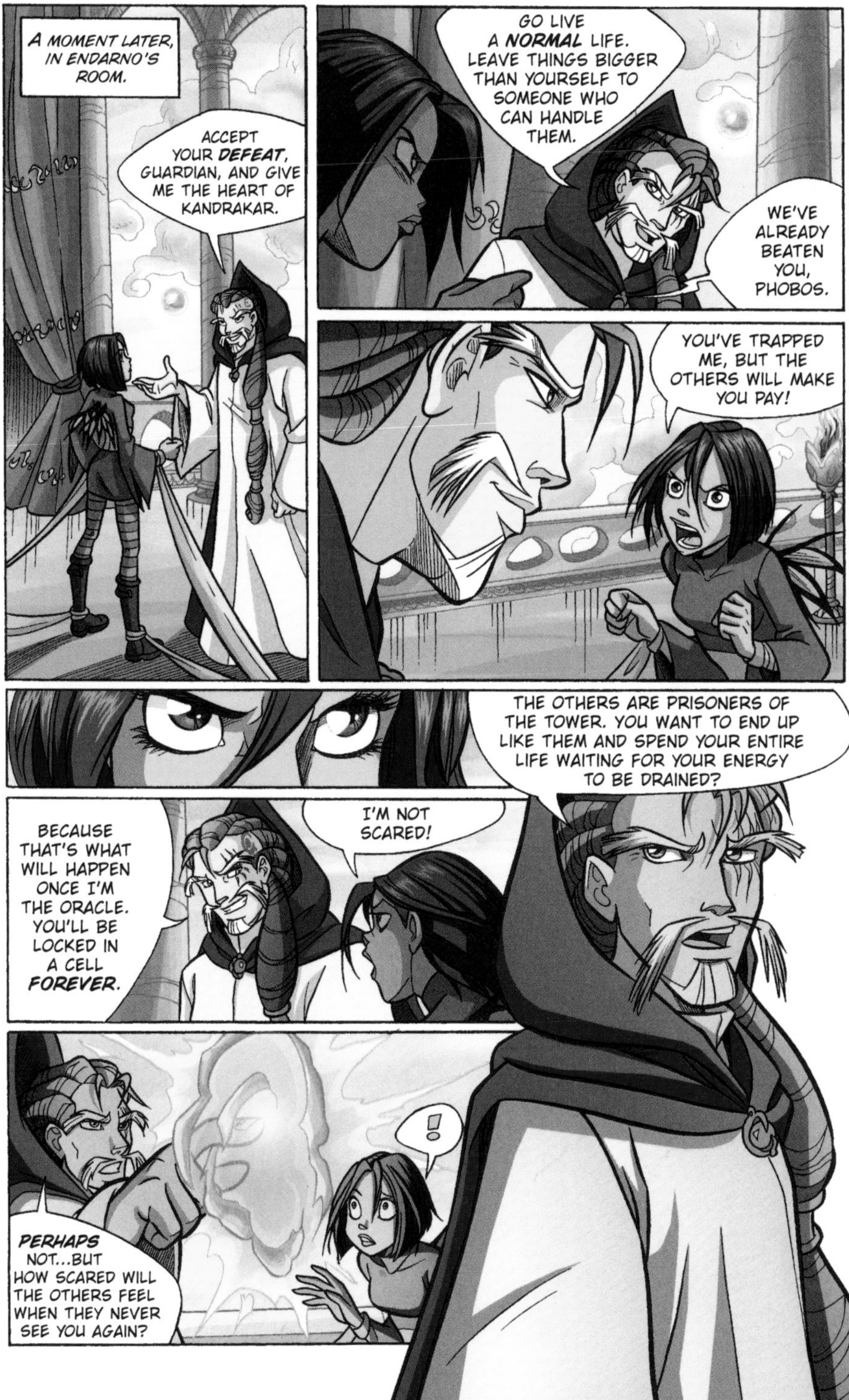
A MOMENT LATER, IN ENDARNO'S ROOM.
ACCEPT YOUR **DEFEAT**, GUARDIAN, AND GIVE ME THE HEART OF KANDRAKAR.
GO LIVE A **NORMAL** LIFE. LEAVE THINGS BIGGER THAN YOURSELF TO SOMEONE WHO CAN HANDLE THEM.
WE'VE ALREADY BEATEN YOU, PHOBOS.
YOU'VE TRAPPED ME, BUT THE OTHERS WILL MAKE YOU PAY!
THE OTHERS ARE PRISONERS OF THE TOWER. YOU WANT TO END UP LIKE THEM AND SPEND YOUR ENTIRE LIFE WAITING FOR YOUR ENERGY TO BE DRAINED?
BECAUSE THAT'S WHAT WILL HAPPEN ONCE I'M THE ORACLE. YOU'LL BE LOCKED IN A CELL **FOREVER**.
I'M NOT SCARED!
!
PERHAPS NOT...BUT HOW SCARED WILL THE OTHERS FEEL WHEN THEY NEVER SEE YOU AGAIN?

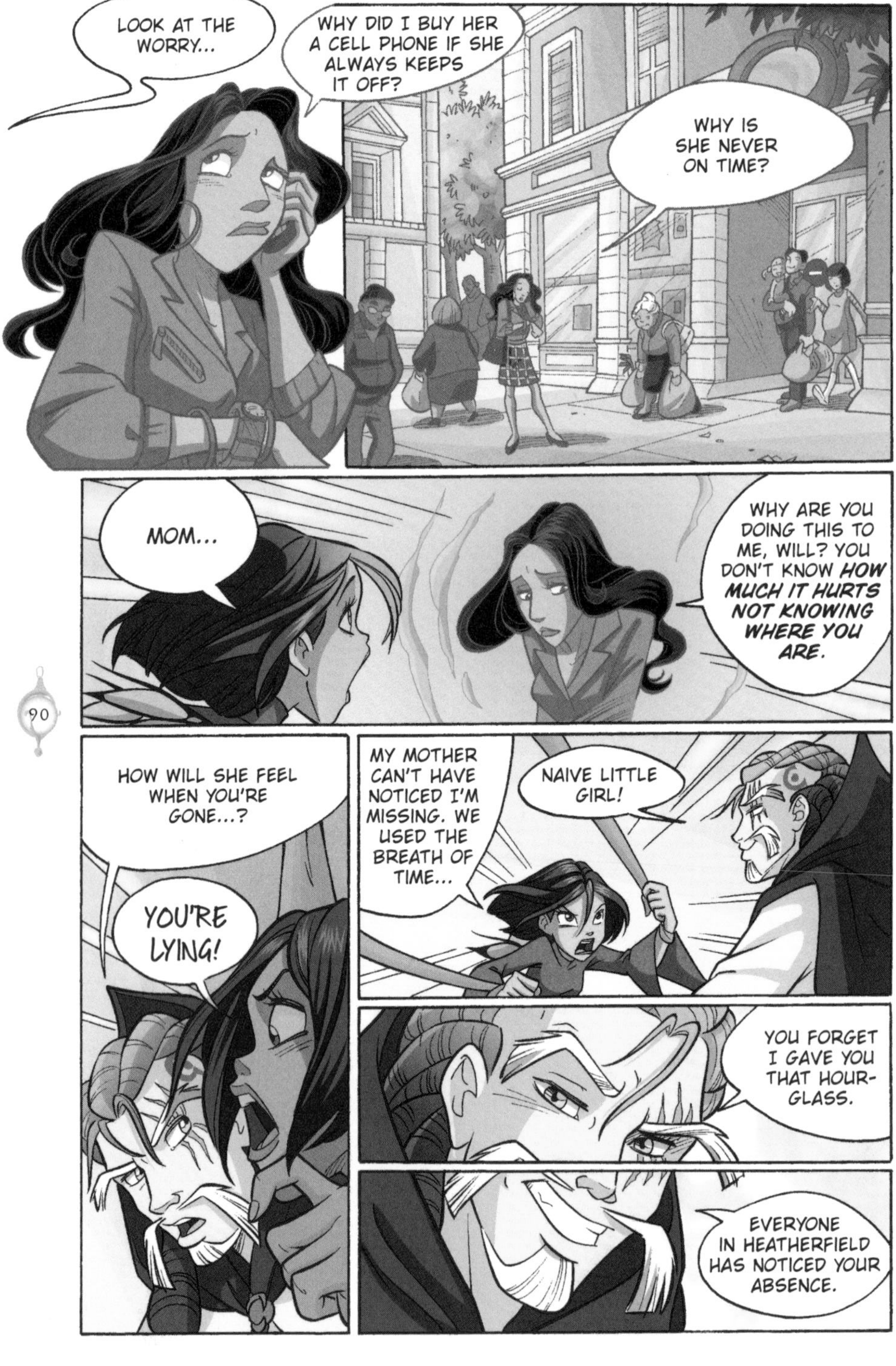
LOOK AT THE WORRY...
WHY DID I BUY HER A CELL PHONE IF SHE ALWAYS KEEPS IT OFF?
WHY IS SHE NEVER ON TIME?
MOM...
WHY ARE YOU DOING THIS TO ME, WILL? YOU DON'T KNOW HOW MUCH IT HURTS NOT KNOWING WHERE YOU ARE.
HOW WILL SHE FEEL WHEN YOU'RE GONE...?
YOU'RE LYING!
MY MOTHER CAN'T HAVE NOTICED I'M MISSING. WE USED THE BREATH OF TIME...
NAIVE LITTLE GIRL!
YOU FORGET I GAVE YOU THAT HOUR-GLASS.
EVERYONE IN HEATHERFIELD HAS NOTICED YOUR ABSENCE.

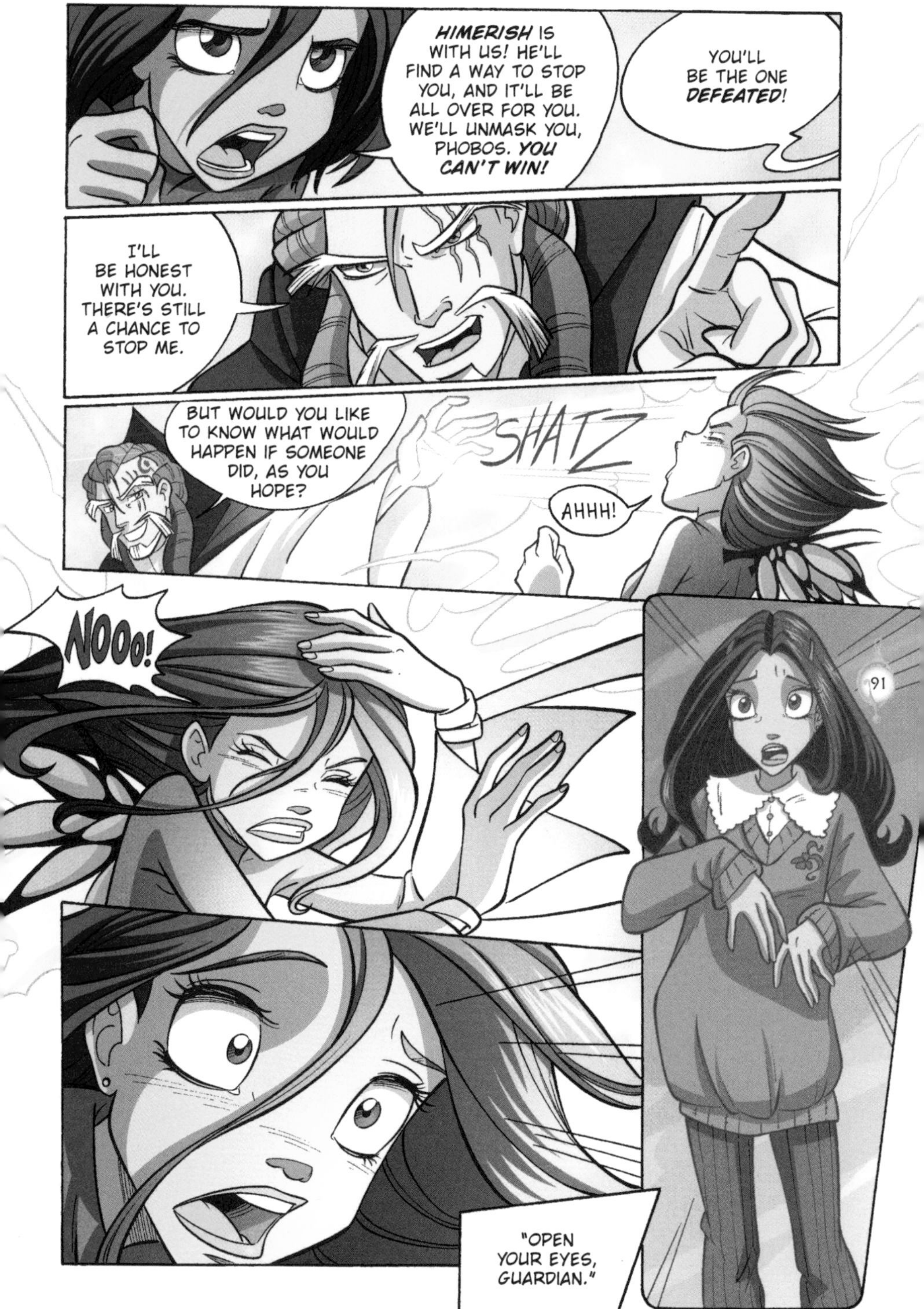

HIMERISH IS WITH US! HE'LL FIND A WAY TO STOP YOU, AND IT'LL BE ALL OVER FOR YOU. WE'LL UNMASK YOU, PHOBOS. **YOU CAN'T WIN!**
YOU'LL BE THE ONE **DEFEATED!**
I'LL BE HONEST WITH YOU. THERE'S STILL A CHANCE TO STOP ME.
BUT WOULD YOU LIKE TO KNOW WHAT WOULD HAPPEN IF SOMEONE DID, AS YOU HOPE?
SHATZ
AHHH!
NOOo!
"OPEN YOUR EYES, GUARDIAN."

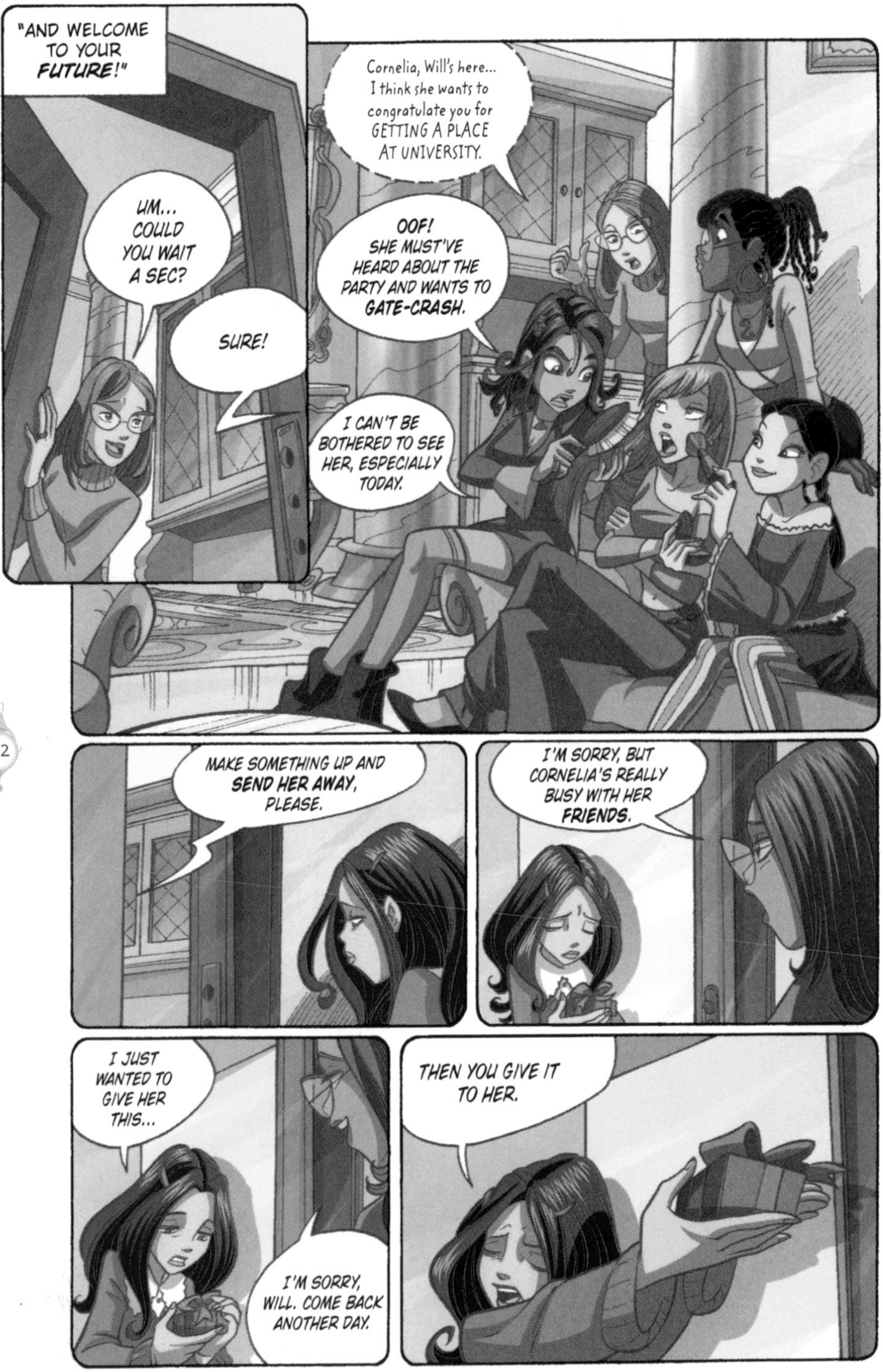
"AND WELCOME TO YOUR FUTURE!"
UM... COULD YOU WAIT A SEC?
SURE!
Cornelia, Will's here... I think she wants to congratulate you for GETTING A PLACE AT UNIVERSITY.
OOF! SHE MUST'VE HEARD ABOUT THE PARTY AND WANTS TO GATE-CRASH.
I CAN'T BE BOTHERED TO SEE HER, ESPECIALLY TODAY.
MAKE SOMETHING UP AND SEND HER AWAY, PLEASE.
I'M SORRY, BUT CORNELIA'S REALLY BUSY WITH HER FRIENDS.
I JUST WANTED TO GIVE HER THIS...
I'M SORRY, WILL. COME BACK ANOTHER DAY.
THEN YOU GIVE IT TO HER.

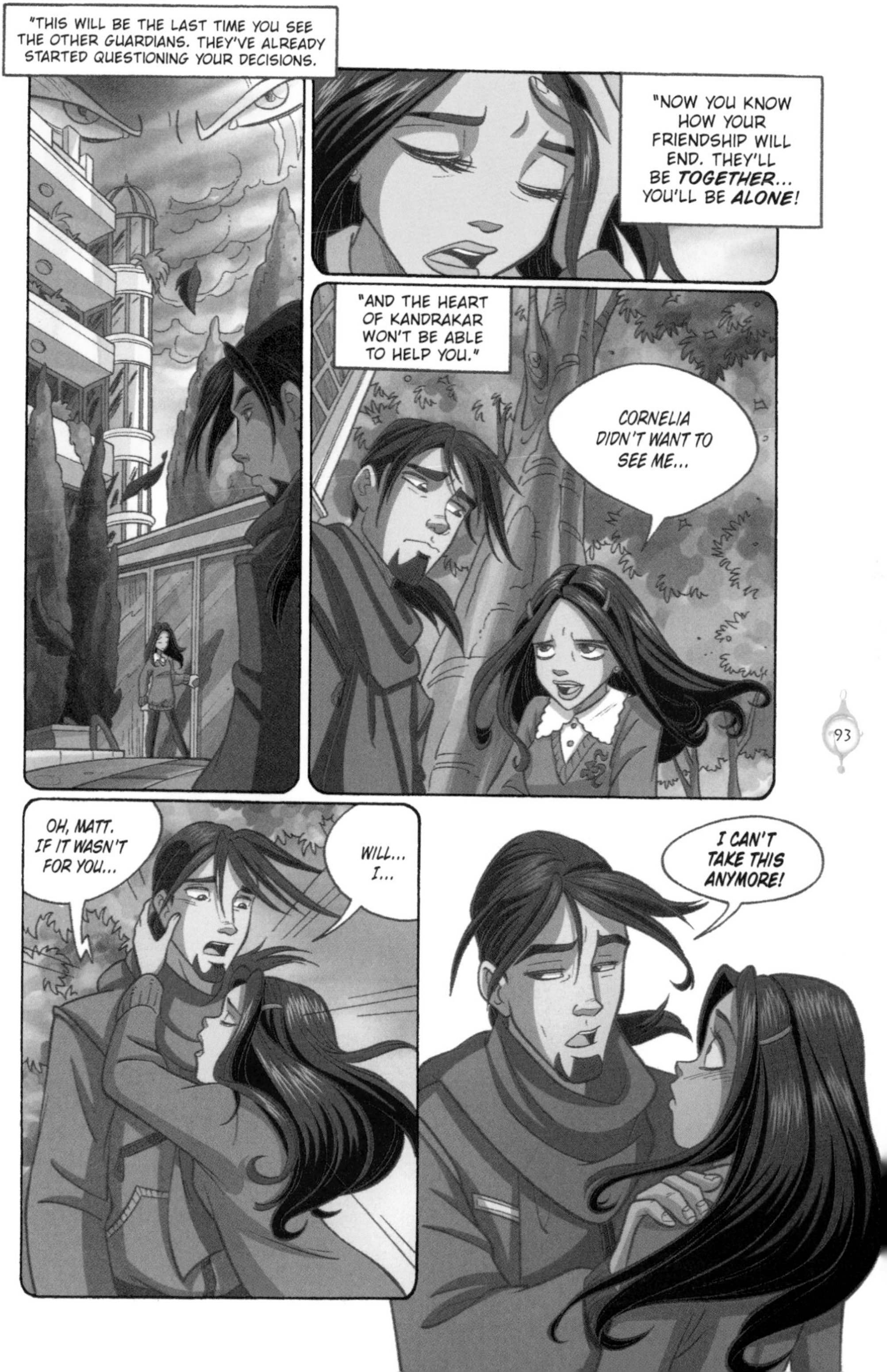
"THIS WILL BE THE LAST TIME YOU SEE THE OTHER GUARDIANS. THEY'VE ALREADY STARTED QUESTIONING YOUR DECISIONS.
"NOW YOU KNOW HOW YOUR FRIENDSHIP WILL END. THEY'LL BE TOGETHER... YOU'LL BE ALONE!
"AND THE HEART OF KANDRAKAR WON'T BE ABLE TO HELP YOU."
CORNELIA DIDN'T WANT TO SEE ME...
OH, MATT. IF IT WASN'T FOR YOU...
WILL... I...
I CAN'T TAKE THIS ANYMORE!

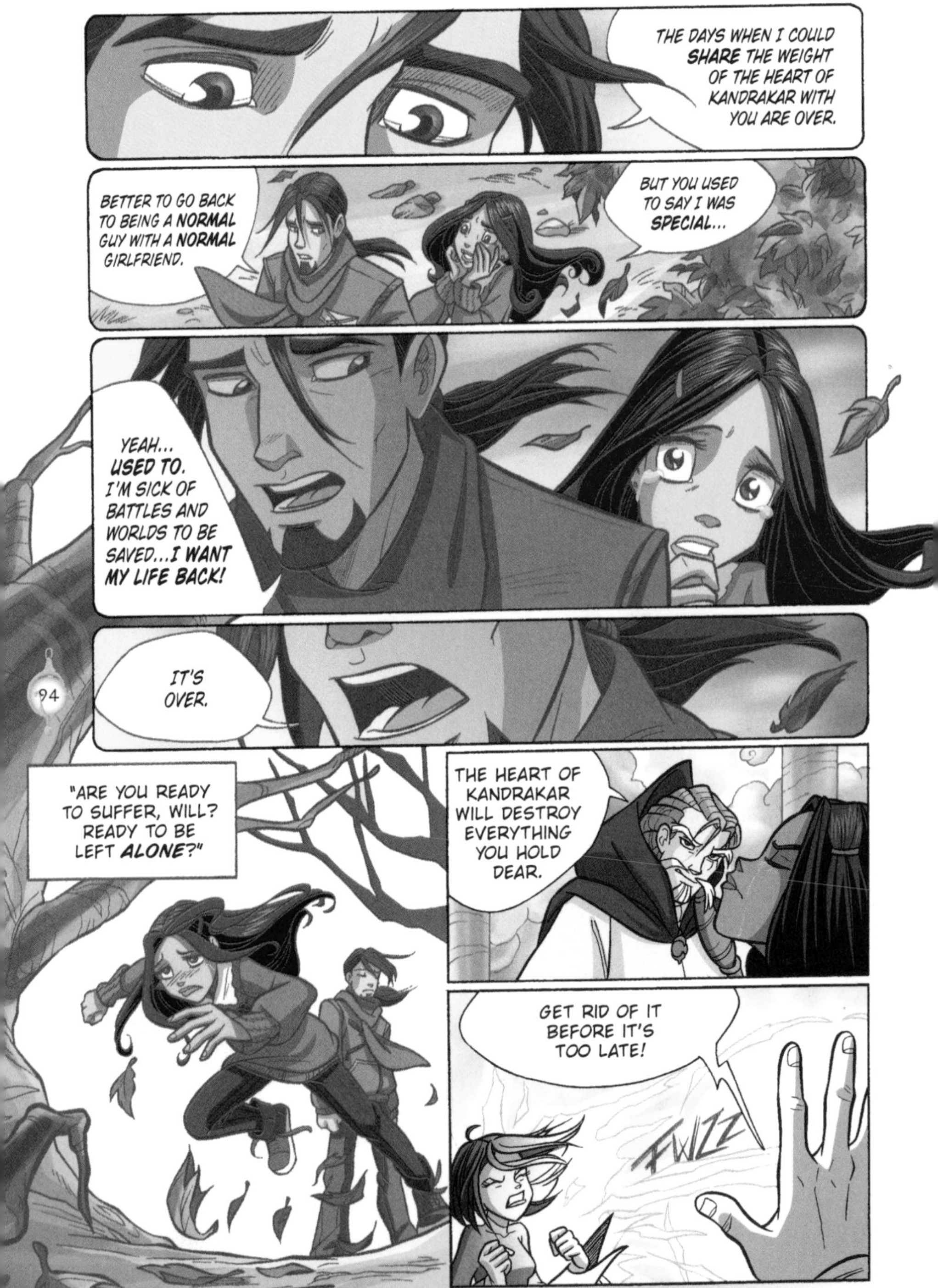

THE DAYS WHEN I COULD SHARE THE WEIGHT OF THE HEART OF KANDRAKAR WITH YOU ARE OVER.
BETTER TO GO BACK TO BEING A NORMAL GUY WITH A NORMAL GIRLFRIEND.
BUT YOU USED TO SAY I WAS SPECIAL...
YEAH... USED TO. I'M SICK OF BATTLES AND WORLDS TO BE SAVED... I WANT MY LIFE BACK!
IT'S OVER.
"ARE YOU READY TO SUFFER, WILL? READY TO BE LEFT ALONE?"
THE HEART OF KANDRAKAR WILL DESTROY EVERYTHING YOU HOLD DEAR.
GET RID OF IT BEFORE IT'S TOO LATE!
FWIZZ

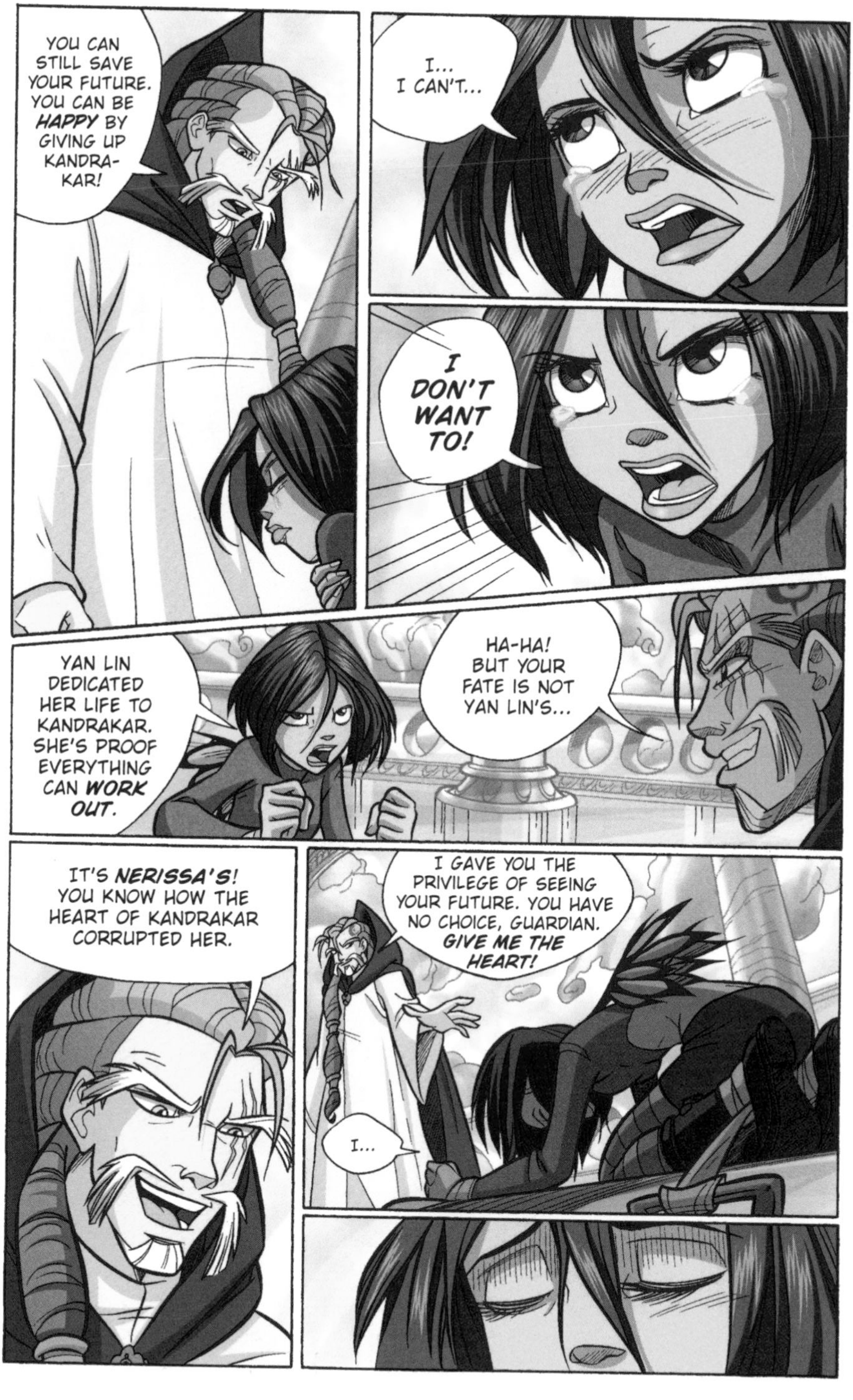

YOU CAN STILL SAVE YOUR FUTURE. YOU CAN BE HAPPY BY GIVING UP KANDRA-KAR!
I... I CAN'T...
I DON'T WANT TO!
YAN LIN DEDICATED HER LIFE TO KANDRAKAR. SHE'S PROOF EVERYTHING CAN WORK OUT.
HA-HA! BUT YOUR FATE IS NOT YAN LIN'S...
IT'S NERISSA'S! YOU KNOW HOW THE HEART OF KANDRAKAR CORRUPTED HER.
I GAVE YOU THE PRIVILEGE OF SEEING YOUR FUTURE. YOU HAVE NO CHOICE, GUARDIAN. GIVE ME THE HEART!
I...

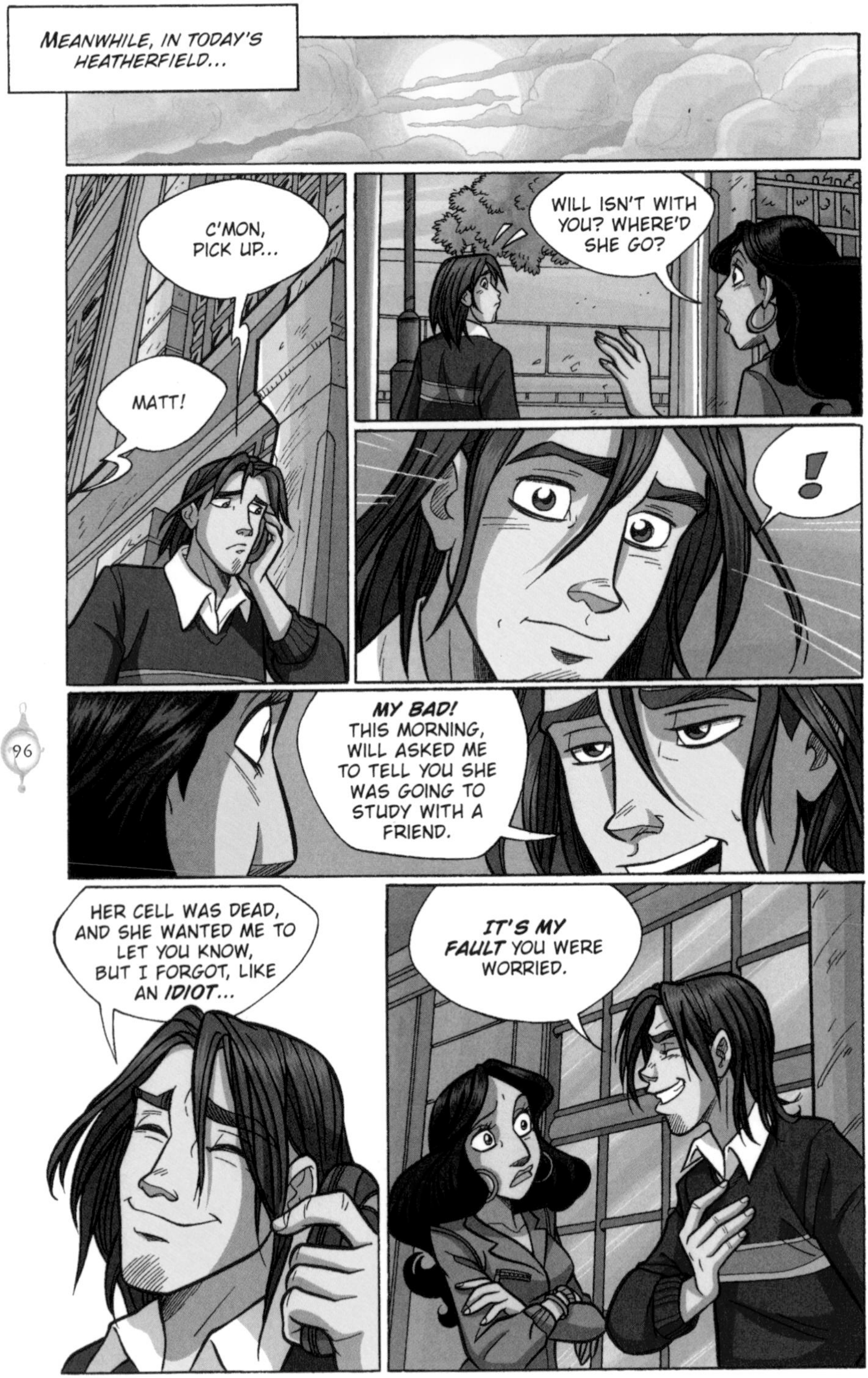
MEANWHILE, IN TODAY'S HEATHERFIELD...
C'MON, PICK UP...
MATT!
WILL ISN'T WITH YOU? WHERE'D SHE GO?
!
MY BAD! THIS MORNING, WILL ASKED ME TO TELL YOU SHE WAS GOING TO STUDY WITH A FRIEND.
HER CELL WAS DEAD, AND SHE WANTED ME TO LET YOU KNOW, BUT I FORGOT, LIKE AN IDIOT...
IT'S MY FAULT YOU WERE WORRIED.

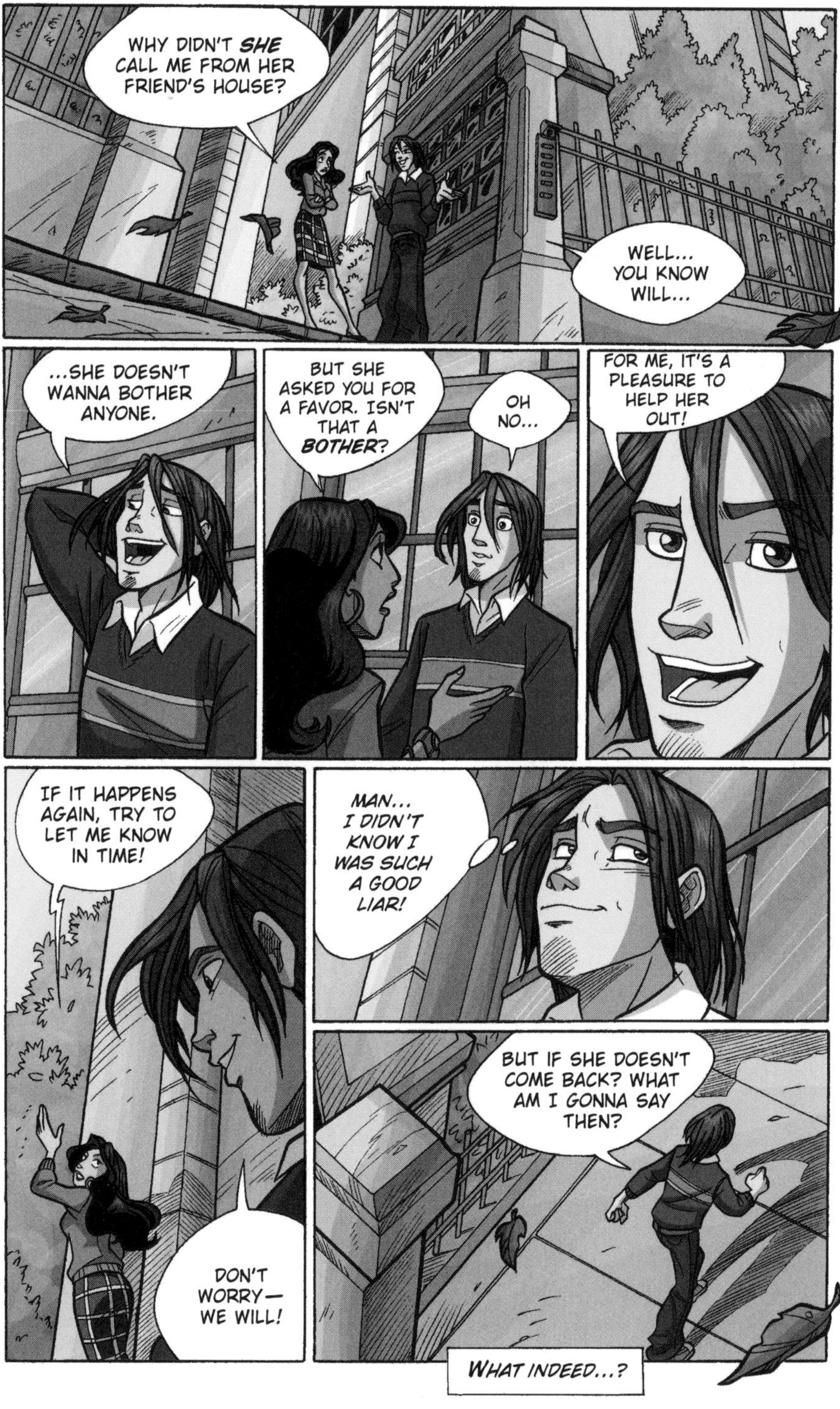
WHY DIDN'T **SHE** CALL ME FROM HER FRIEND'S HOUSE?
WELL... YOU KNOW WILL...
...SHE DOESN'T WANNA BOTHER ANYONE.
BUT SHE ASKED YOU FOR A FAVOR. ISN'T THAT A **BOTHER**?
OH NO...
FOR ME, IT'S A PLEASURE TO HELP HER OUT!
IF IT HAPPENS AGAIN, TRY TO LET ME KNOW IN TIME!
DON'T WORRY— WE WILL!
MAN... I DIDN'T KNOW I WAS SUCH A GOOD LIAR!
BUT IF SHE DOESN'T COME BACK? WHAT AM I GONNA SAY THEN?
WHAT INDEED...?

W.i.t.c.h.

Will   Irma   Taranee   Cornelia   Hay Lin

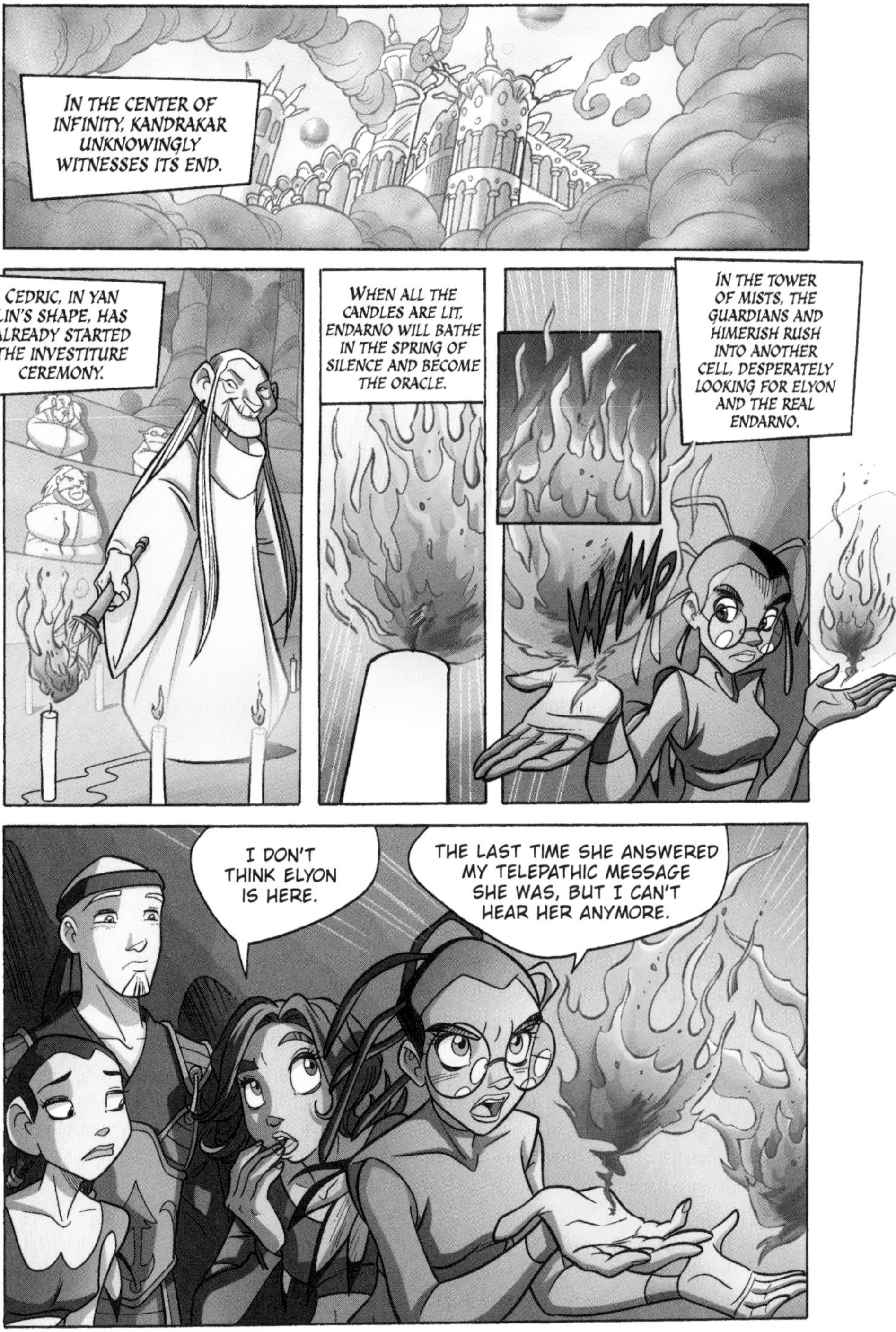
IN THE CENTER OF INFINITY, KANDRAKAR UNKNOWINGLY WITNESSES ITS END.
CEDRIC, IN YAN LIN'S SHAPE, HAS ALREADY STARTED THE INVESTITURE CEREMONY.
WHEN ALL THE CANDLES ARE LIT, ENDARNO WILL BATHE IN THE SPRING OF SILENCE AND BECOME THE ORACLE.
IN THE TOWER OF MISTS, THE GUARDIANS AND HIMERISH RUSH INTO ANOTHER CELL, DESPERATELY LOOKING FOR ELYON AND THE REAL ENDARNO.
WAMP
I DON'T THINK ELYON IS HERE.
THE LAST TIME SHE ANSWERED MY TELEPATHIC MESSAGE SHE WAS, BUT I CAN'T HEAR HER ANYMORE.

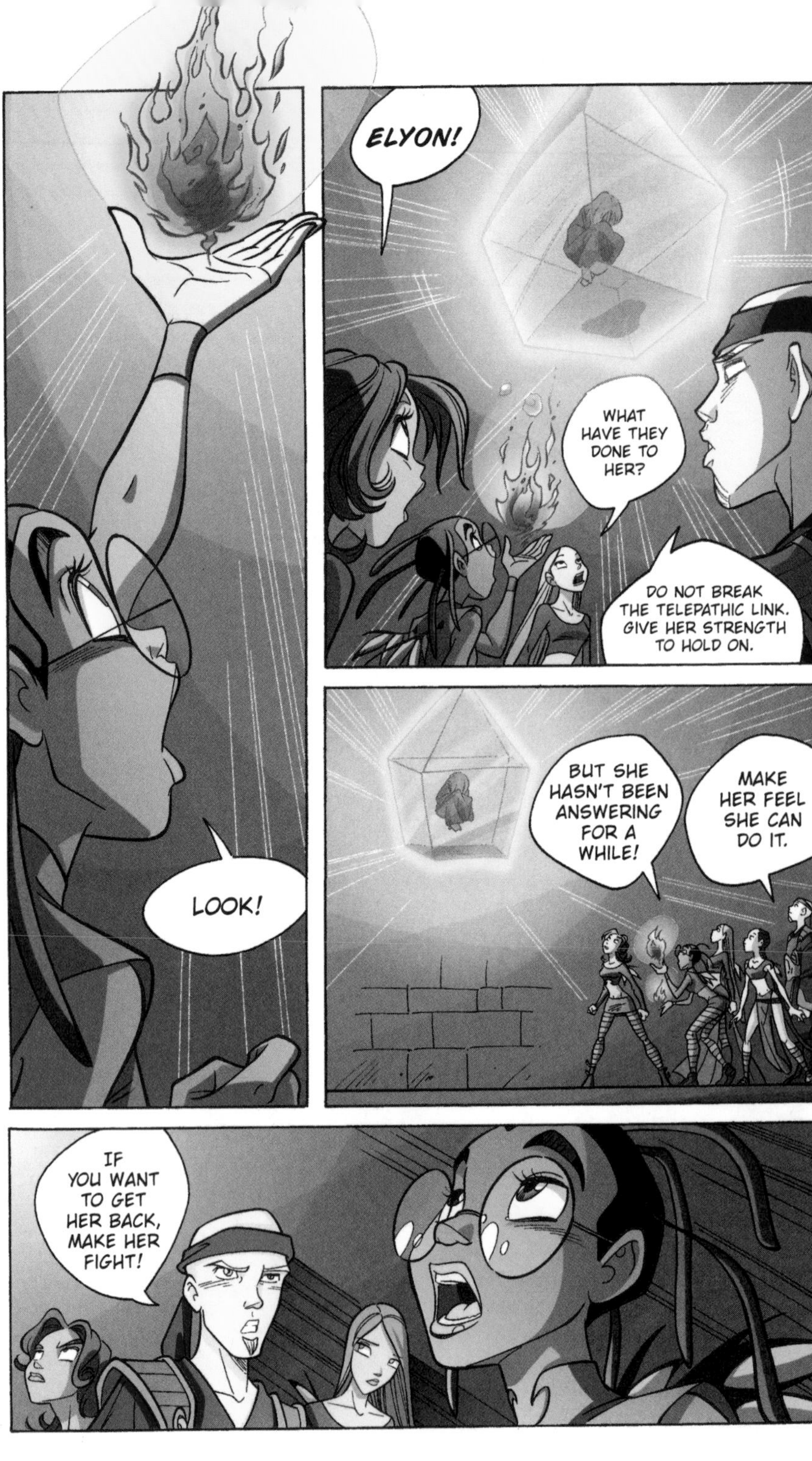
LOOK!
ELYON!
WHAT HAVE THEY DONE TO HER?
DO NOT BREAK THE TELEPATHIC LINK. GIVE HER STRENGTH TO HOLD ON.
BUT SHE HASN'T BEEN ANSWERING FOR A WHILE!
MAKE HER FEEL SHE CAN DO IT.
IF YOU WANT TO GET HER BACK, MAKE HER FIGHT!

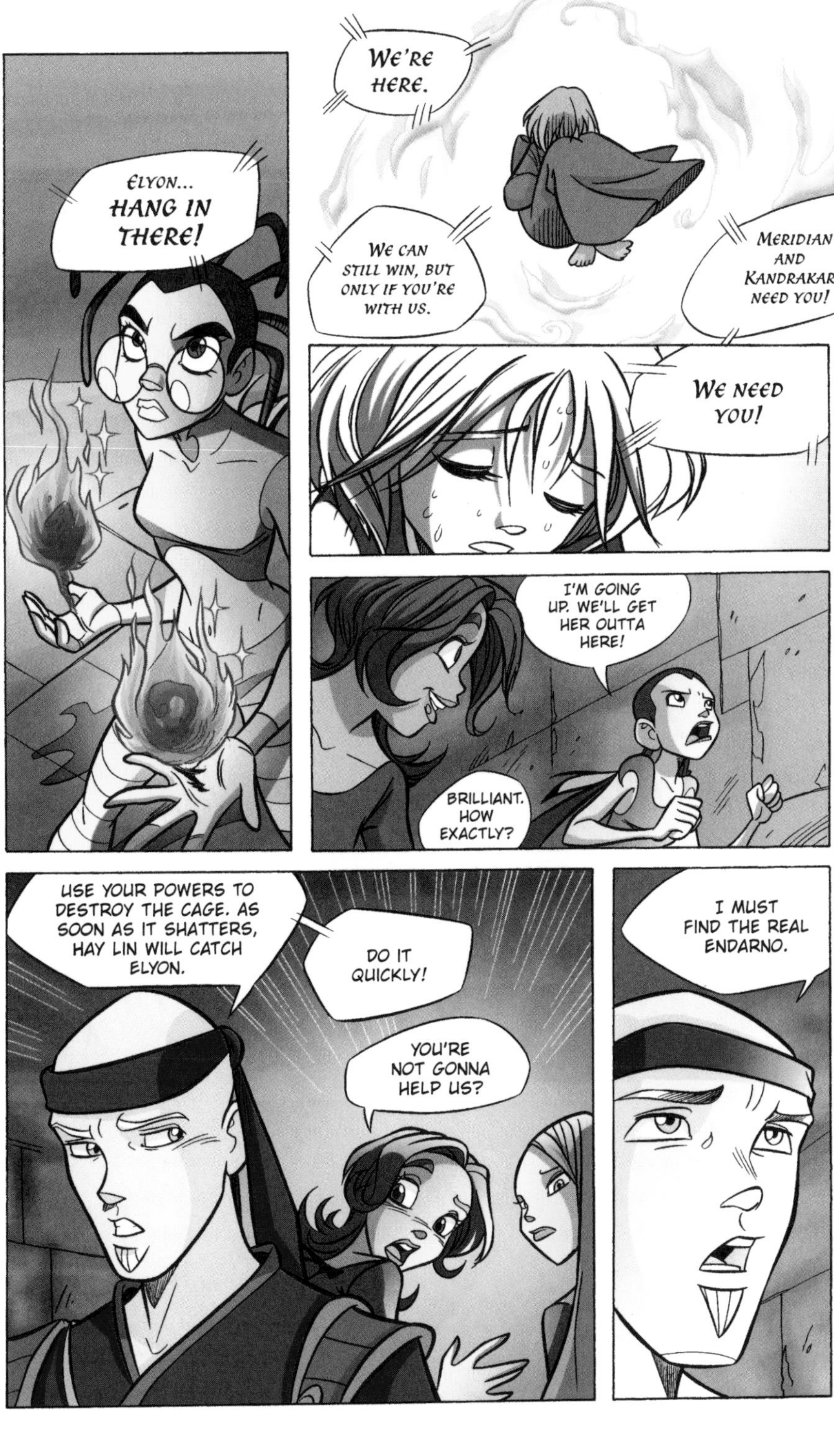
Elyon... HANG IN THERE!
We're here.
We can still win, but only if you're with us.
Meridian and Kandrakar need you!
We need you!
I'M GOING UP. WE'LL GET HER OUTTA HERE!
BRILLIANT. HOW EXACTLY?
USE YOUR POWERS TO DESTROY THE CAGE. AS SOON AS IT SHATTERS, HAY LIN WILL CATCH ELYON.
DO IT QUICKLY!
YOU'RE NOT GONNA HELP US?
I MUST FIND THE REAL ENDARNO.

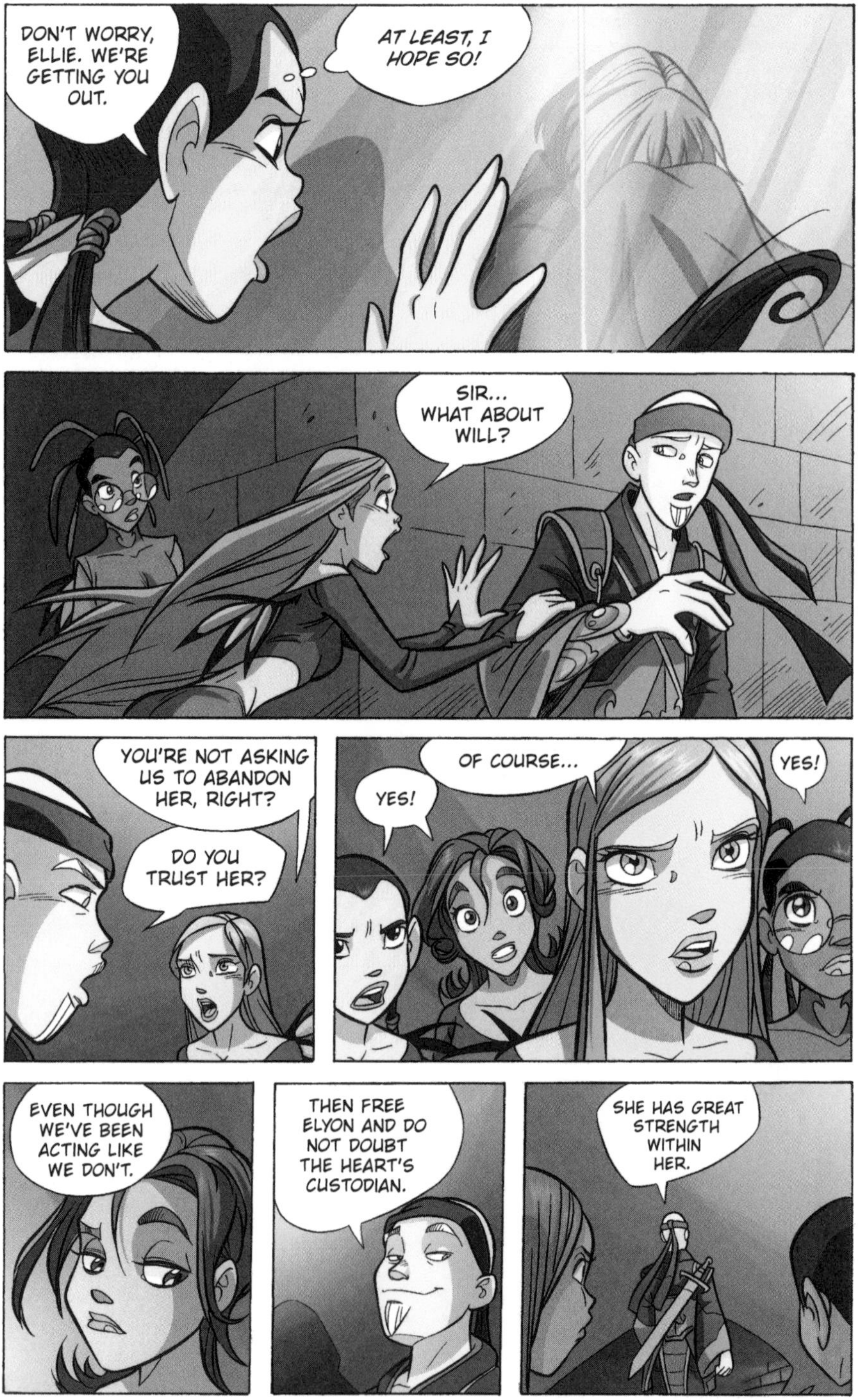
DON'T WORRY, ELLIE. WE'RE GETTING YOU OUT.
AT LEAST, I HOPE SO!
SIR... WHAT ABOUT WILL?
YOU'RE NOT ASKING US TO ABANDON HER, RIGHT?
DO YOU TRUST HER?
OF COURSE...
YES!
YES!
EVEN THOUGH WE'VE BEEN ACTING LIKE WE DON'T.
THEN FREE ELYON AND DO NOT DOUBT THE HEART'S CUSTODIAN.
SHE HAS GREAT STRENGTH WITHIN HER.

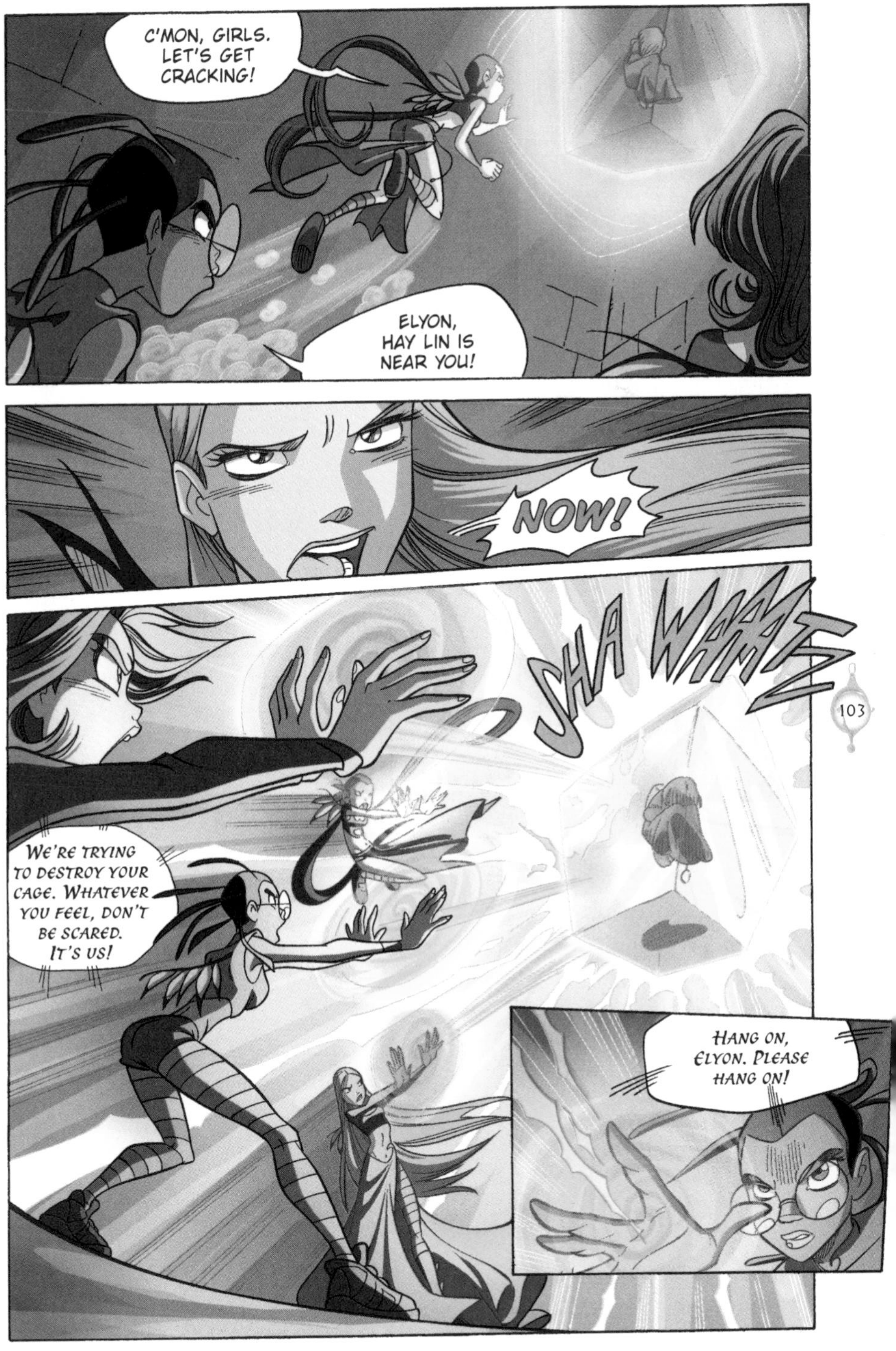
C'MON, GIRLS. LET'S GET CRACKING!
ELYON, HAY LIN IS NEAR YOU!
NOW!
SHA WAAAZ
WE'RE TRYING TO DESTROY YOUR CAGE. WHATEVER YOU FEEL, DON'T BE SCARED. IT'S US!
HANG ON, ELYON. PLEASE HANG ON!

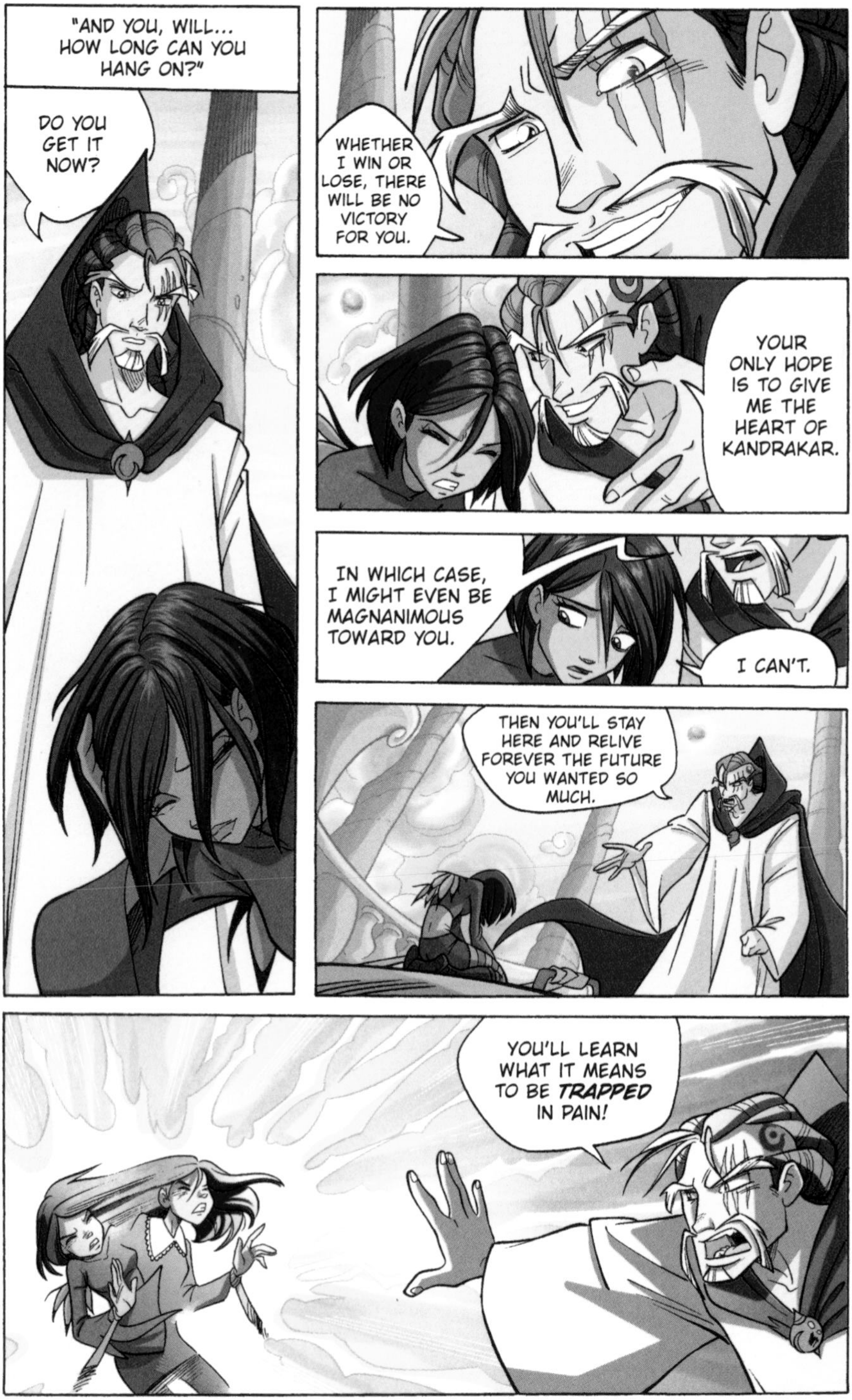
"AND YOU, WILL... HOW LONG CAN YOU HANG ON?"
DO YOU GET IT NOW?
WHETHER I WIN OR LOSE, THERE WILL BE NO VICTORY FOR YOU.
YOUR ONLY HOPE IS TO GIVE ME THE HEART OF KANDRAKAR.
IN WHICH CASE, I MIGHT EVEN BE MAGNANIMOUS TOWARD YOU.
I CAN'T.
THEN YOU'LL STAY HERE AND RELIVE FOREVER THE FUTURE YOU WANTED SO MUCH.
YOU'LL LEARN WHAT IT MEANS TO BE *TRAPPED* IN PAIN!

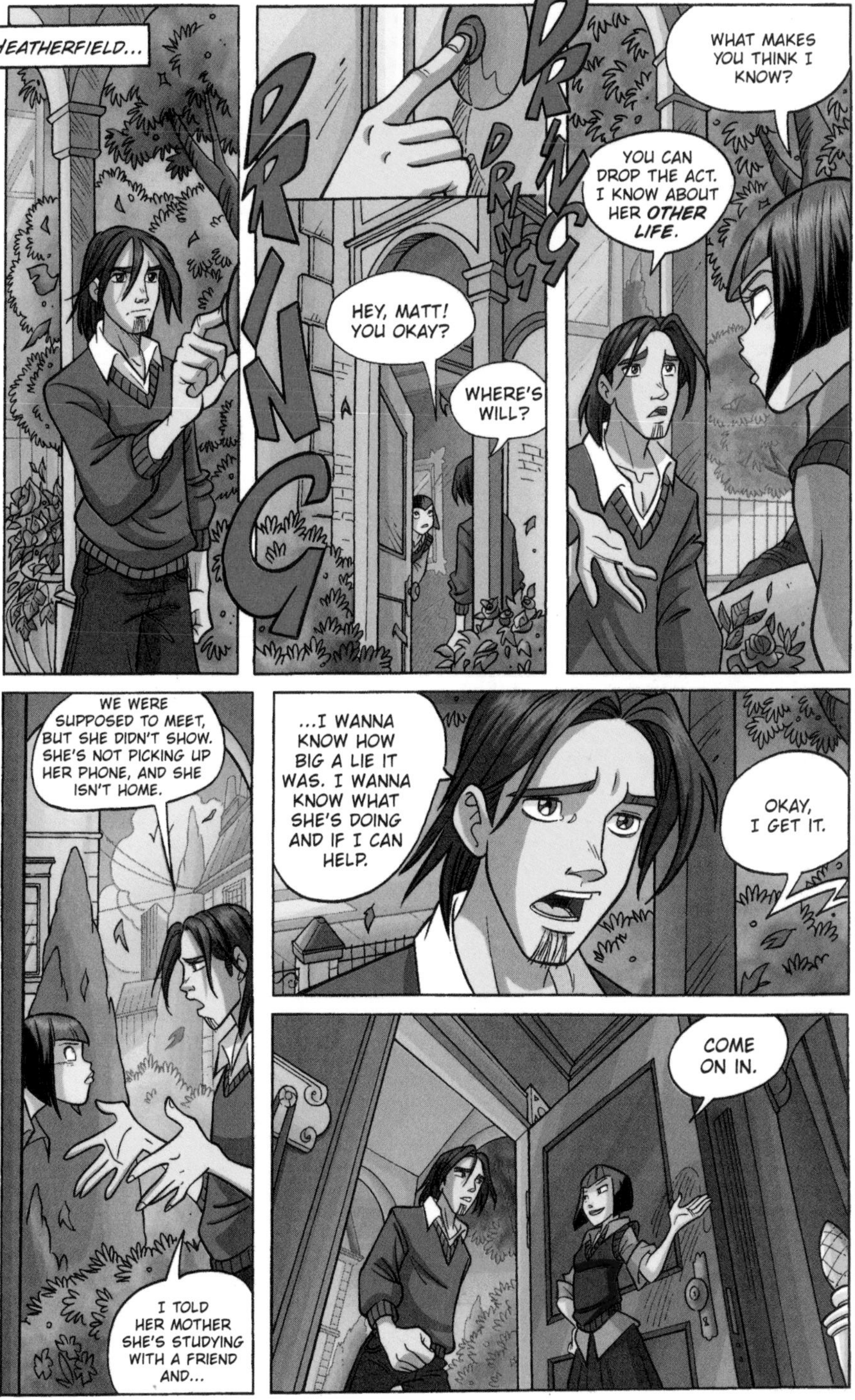
HEATHERFIELD...
DRING
DRING
DRING
DRING
HEY, MATT! YOU OKAY?
WHERE'S WILL?
WHAT MAKES YOU THINK I KNOW?
YOU CAN DROP THE ACT. I KNOW ABOUT HER **OTHER LIFE**.
WE WERE SUPPOSED TO MEET, BUT SHE DIDN'T SHOW. SHE'S NOT PICKING UP HER PHONE, AND SHE ISN'T HOME.
I TOLD HER MOTHER SHE'S STUDYING WITH A FRIEND AND...
...I WANNA KNOW HOW BIG A LIE IT WAS. I WANNA KNOW WHAT SHE'S DOING AND IF I CAN HELP.
OKAY, I GET IT.
COME ON IN.

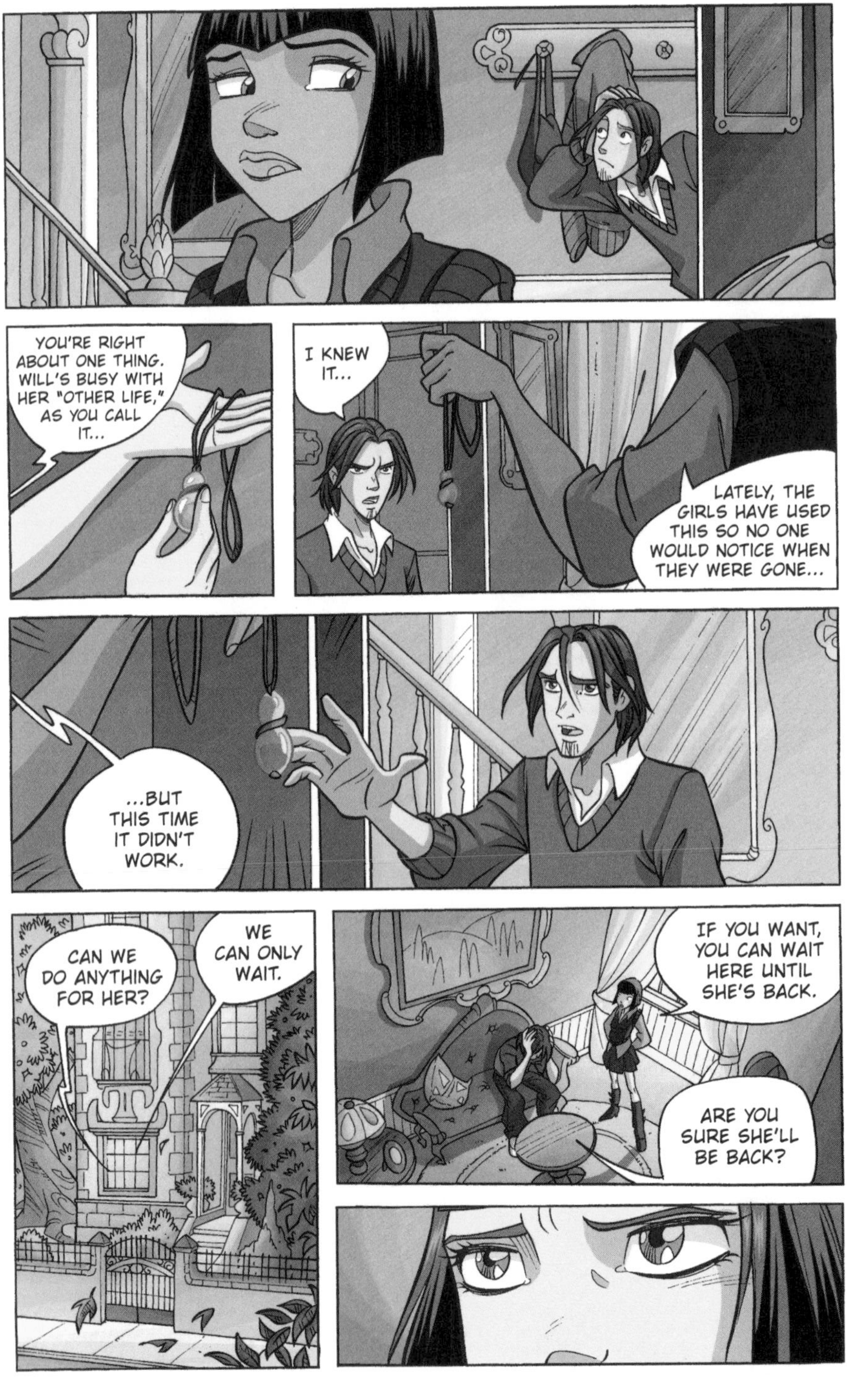
YOU'RE RIGHT ABOUT ONE THING. WILL'S BUSY WITH HER "OTHER LIFE," AS YOU CALL IT...
I KNEW IT...
LATELY, THE GIRLS HAVE USED THIS SO NO ONE WOULD NOTICE WHEN THEY WERE GONE...
...BUT THIS TIME IT DIDN'T WORK.
CAN WE DO ANYTHING FOR HER?
WE CAN ONLY WAIT.
IF YOU WANT, YOU CAN WAIT HERE UNTIL SHE'S BACK.
ARE YOU SURE SHE'LL BE BACK?

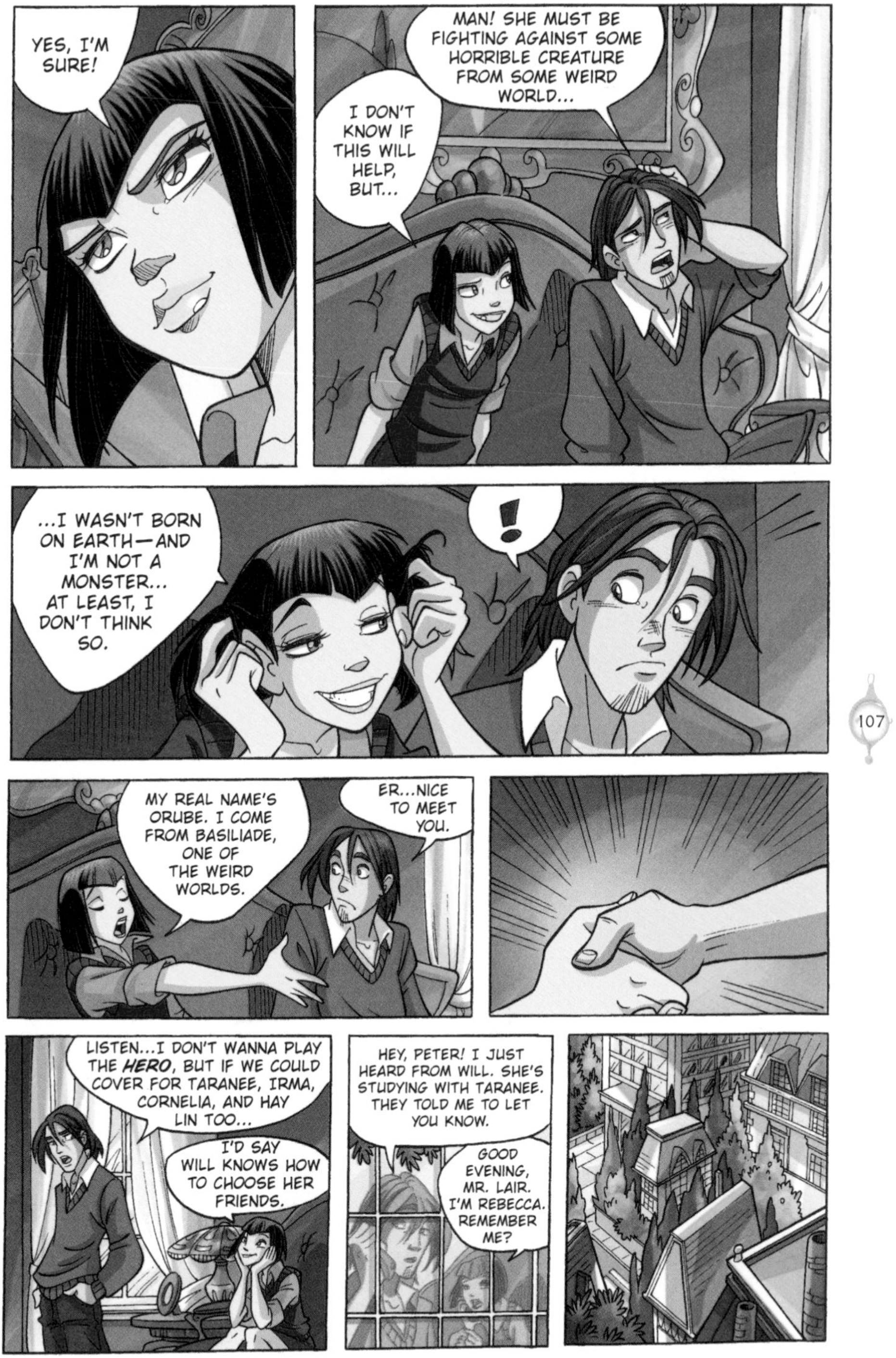
YES, I'M SURE!
MAN! SHE MUST BE FIGHTING AGAINST SOME HORRIBLE CREATURE FROM SOME WEIRD WORLD...
I DON'T KNOW IF THIS WILL HELP, BUT...
...I WASN'T BORN ON EARTH—AND I'M NOT A MONSTER... AT LEAST, I DON'T THINK SO.
!
MY REAL NAME'S ORUBE. I COME FROM BASILIADE, ONE OF THE WEIRD WORLDS.
ER...NICE TO MEET YOU.
LISTEN...I DON'T WANNA PLAY THE ***HERO***, BUT IF WE COULD COVER FOR TARANEE, IRMA, CORNELIA, AND HAY LIN TOO...
I'D SAY WILL KNOWS HOW TO CHOOSE HER FRIENDS.
HEY, PETER! I JUST HEARD FROM WILL. SHE'S STUDYING WITH TARANEE. THEY TOLD ME TO LET YOU KNOW.
GOOD EVENING, MR. LAIR. I'M REBECCA. REMEMBER ME?

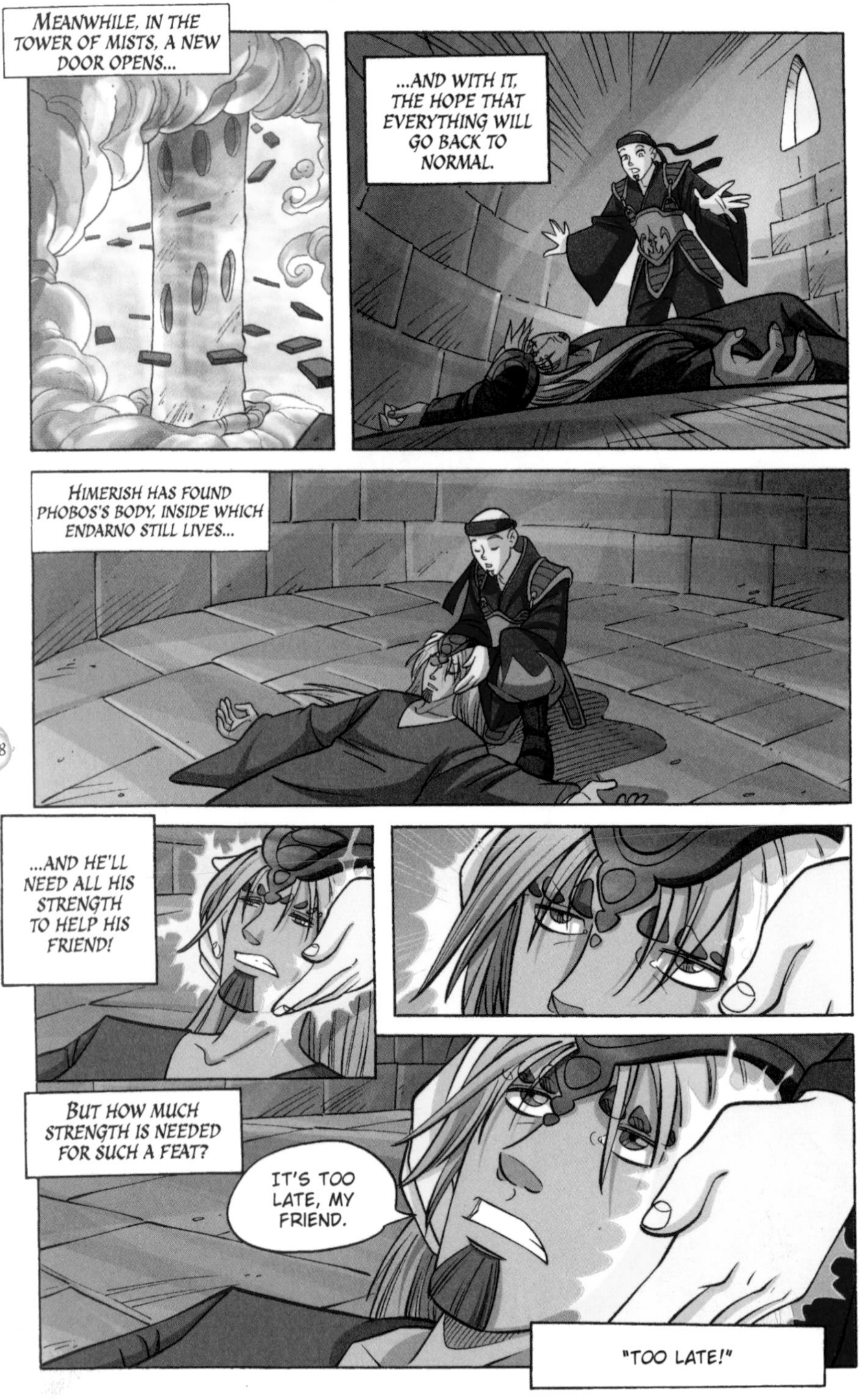
MEANWHILE, IN THE TOWER OF MISTS, A NEW DOOR OPENS...
...AND WITH IT, THE HOPE THAT EVERYTHING WILL GO BACK TO NORMAL.
HIMERISH HAS FOUND PHOBOS'S BODY, INSIDE WHICH ENDARNO STILL LIVES...
...AND HE'LL NEED ALL HIS STRENGTH TO HELP HIS FRIEND!
BUT HOW MUCH STRENGTH IS NEEDED FOR SUCH A FEAT?
IT'S TOO LATE, MY FRIEND.
"TOO LATE!"

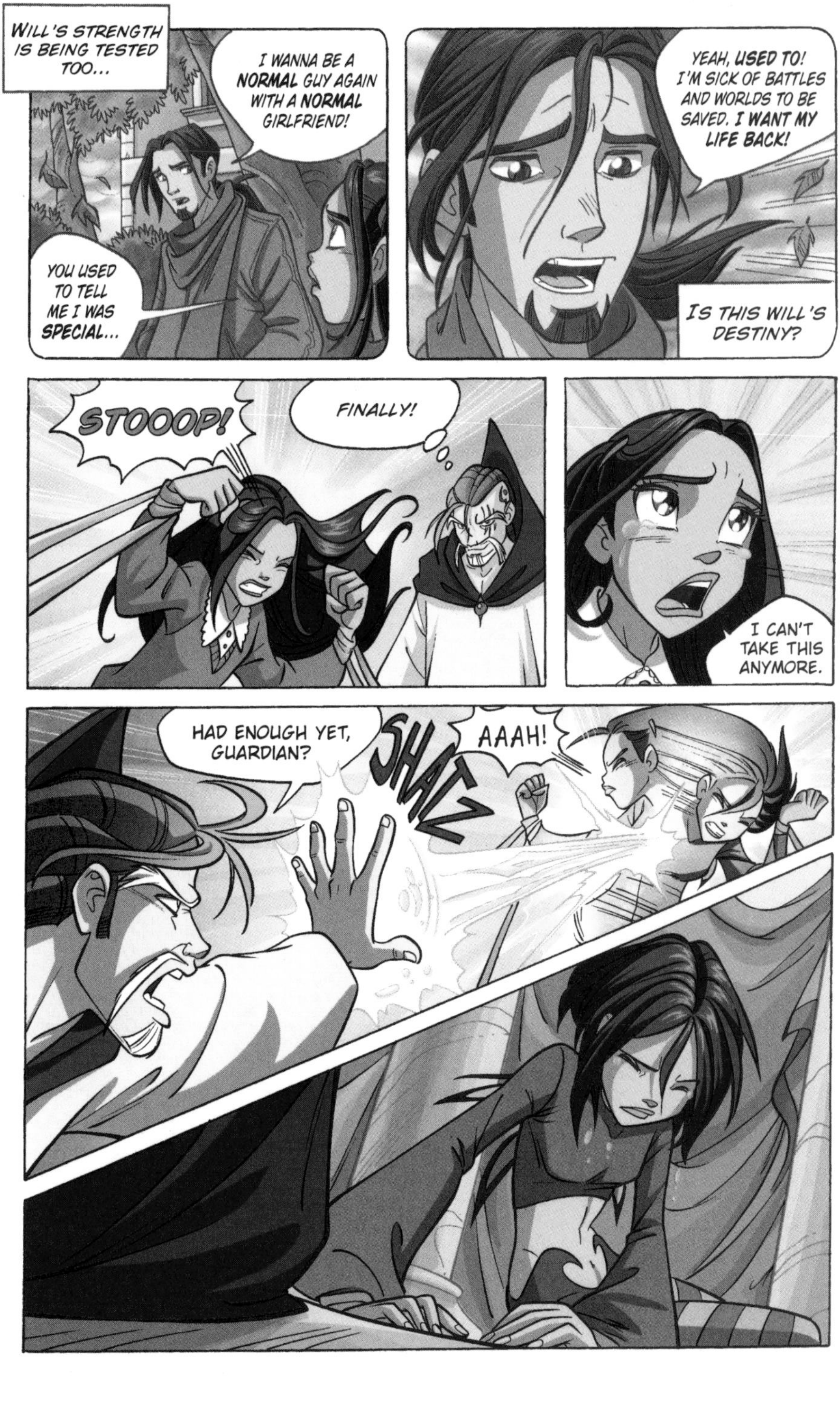

WILL'S STRENGTH IS BEING TESTED TOO...
I WANNA BE A NORMAL GUY AGAIN WITH A NORMAL GIRLFRIEND!
YOU USED TO TELL ME I WAS SPECIAL...
YEAH, USED TO! I'M SICK OF BATTLES AND WORLDS TO BE SAVED. I WANT MY LIFE BACK!
IS THIS WILL'S DESTINY?
STOOOP!
FINALLY!
I CAN'T TAKE THIS ANYMORE.
HAD ENOUGH YET, GUARDIAN?
SHATZ
AAAH!

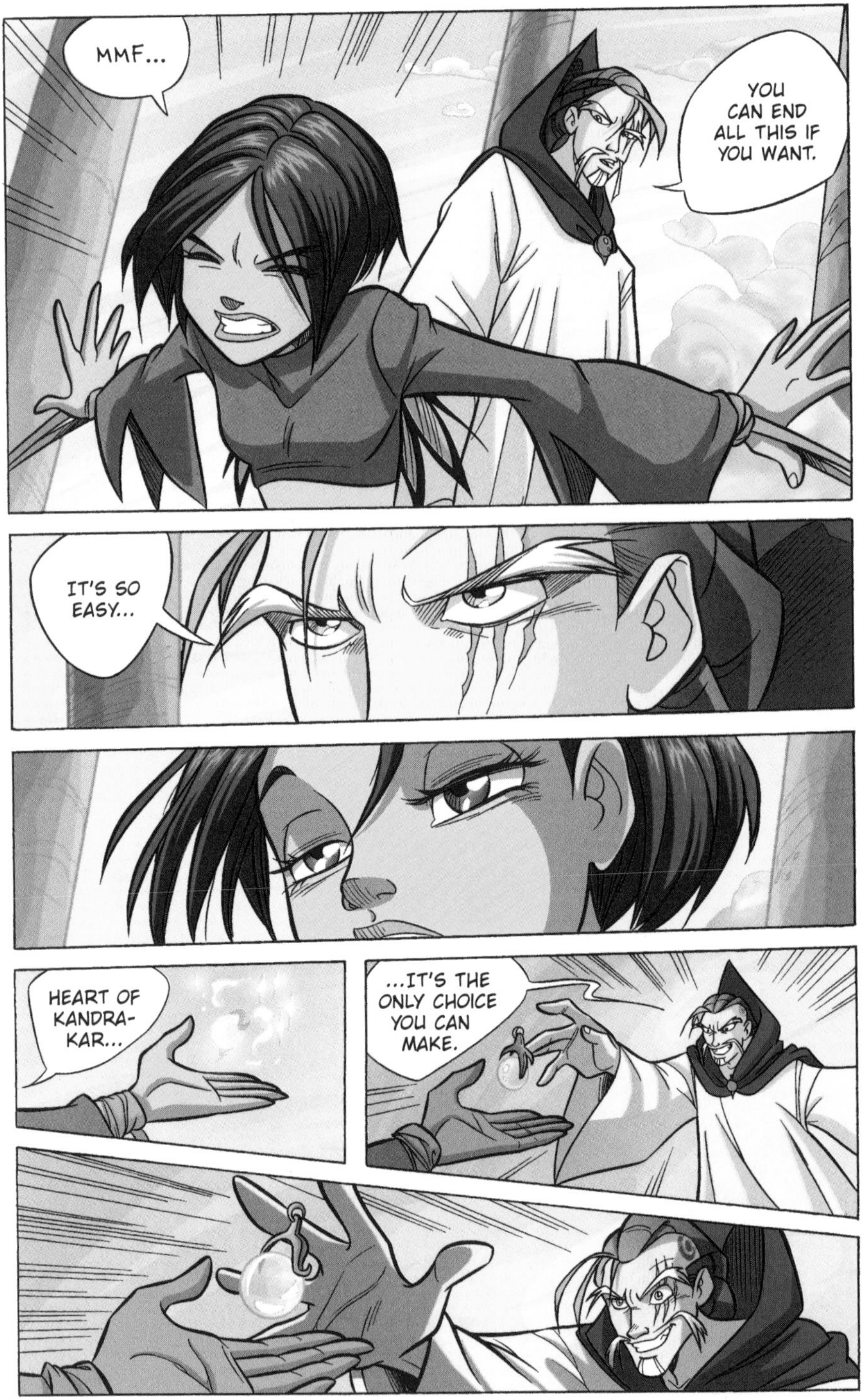
MMF...
YOU CAN END ALL THIS IF YOU WANT.
IT'S SO EASY...
HEART OF KANDRA-KAR...
...IT'S THE ONLY CHOICE YOU CAN MAKE.

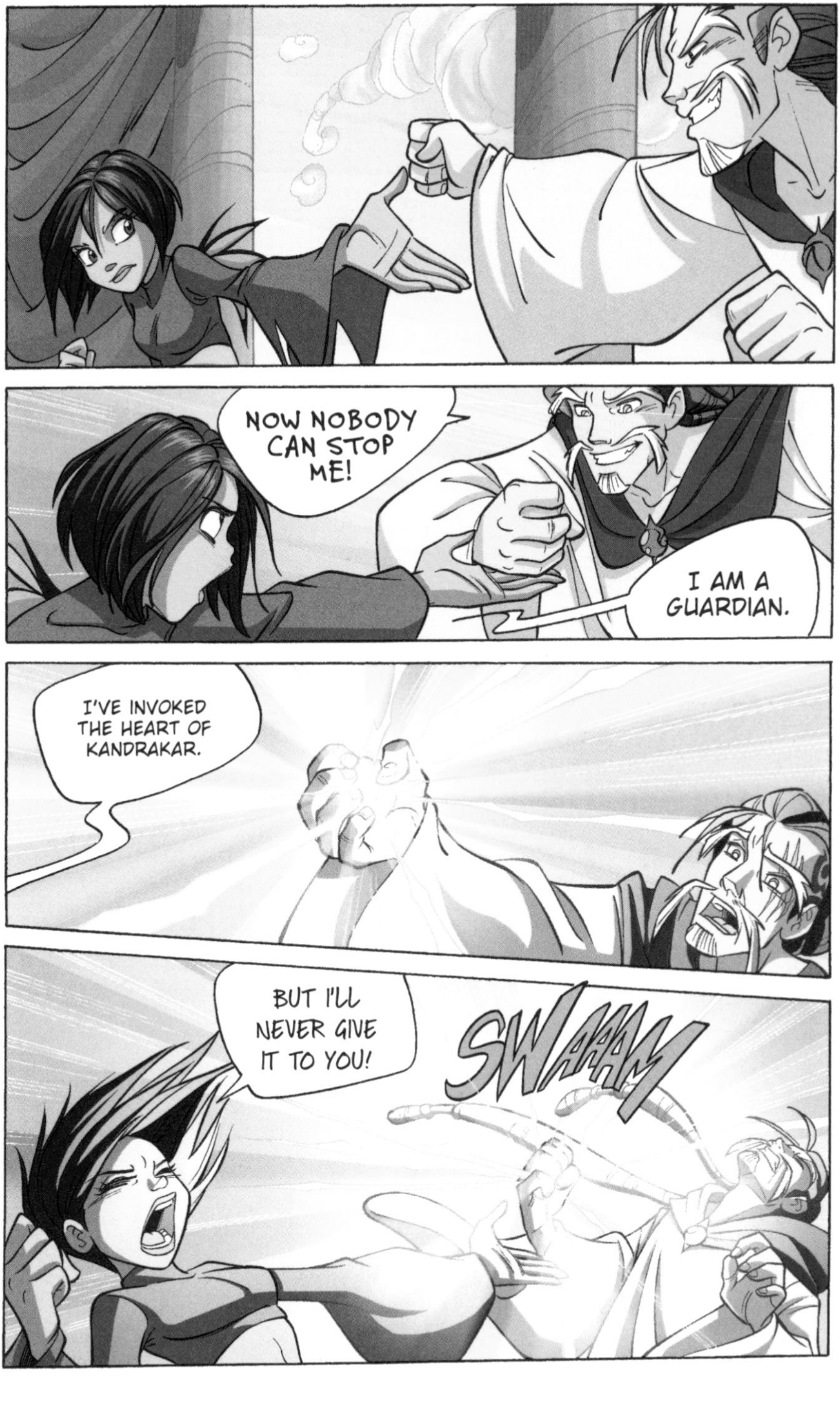
NOW NOBODY CAN STOP ME!
I AM A GUARDIAN.
I'VE INVOKED THE HEART OF KANDRAKAR.
BUT I'LL NEVER GIVE IT TO YOU!
SWAAAM

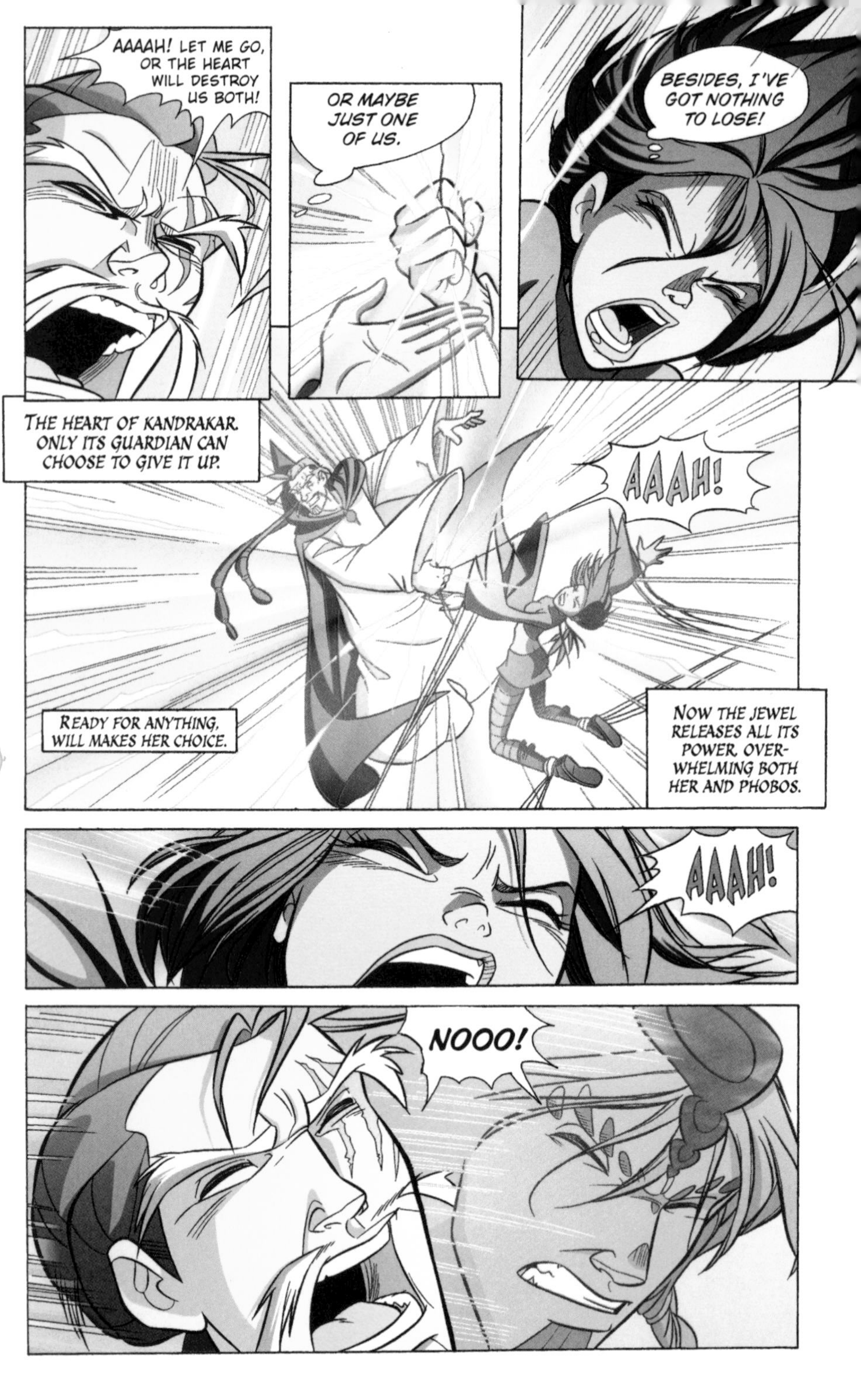
AAAAH! LET ME GO, OR THE HEART WILL DESTROY US BOTH!
OR MAYBE JUST ONE OF US.
BESIDES, I'VE GOT NOTHING TO LOSE!
THE HEART OF KANDRAKAR. ONLY ITS GUARDIAN CAN CHOOSE TO GIVE IT UP.
AAAH!
READY FOR ANYTHING, WILL MAKES HER CHOICE.
NOW THE JEWEL RELEASES ALL ITS POWER, OVER-WHELMING BOTH HER AND PHOBOS.
AAAH!
NOOO!

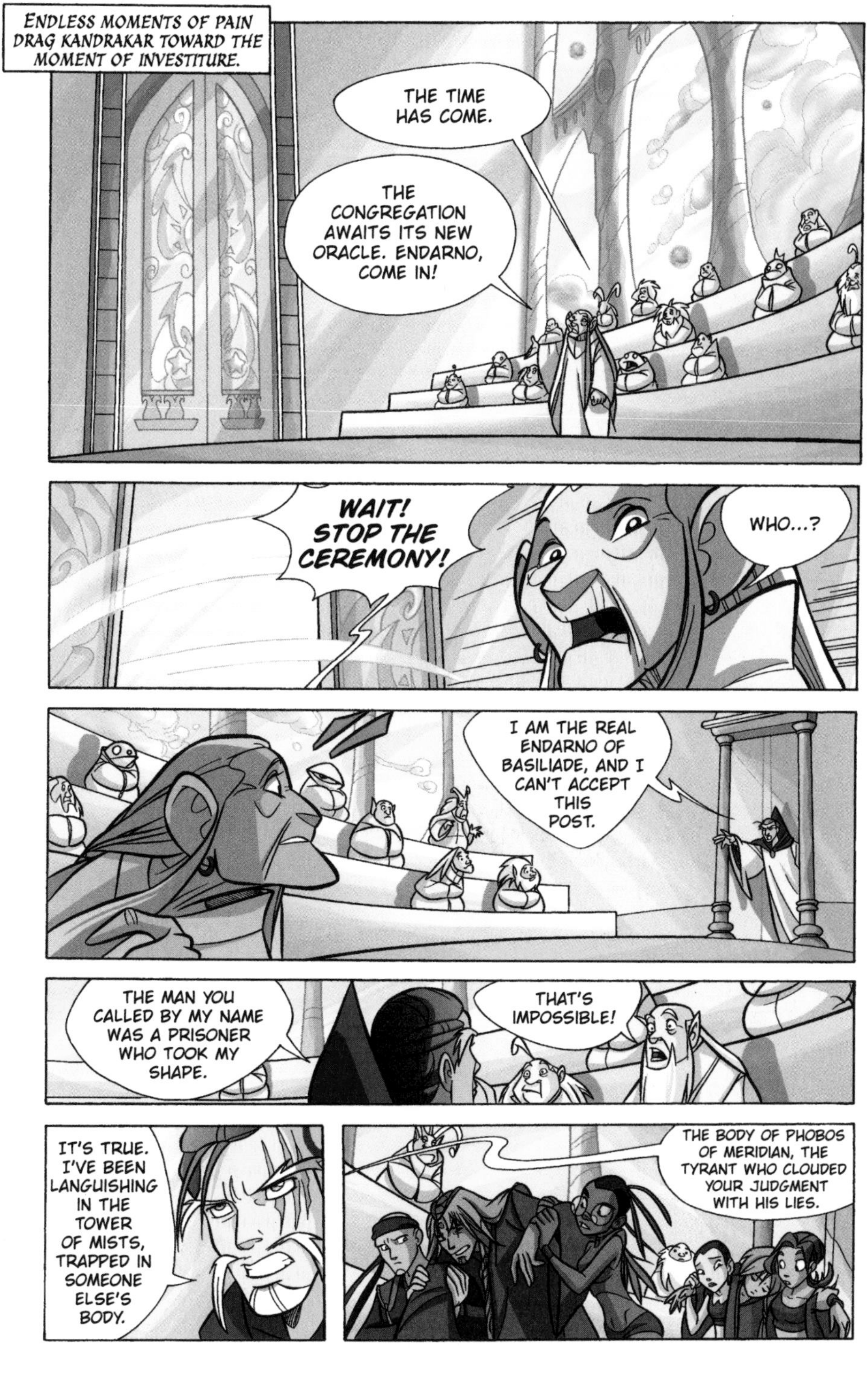
ENDLESS MOMENTS OF PAIN DRAG KANDRAKAR TOWARD THE MOMENT OF INVESTITURE.
THE TIME HAS COME.
THE CONGREGATION AWAITS ITS NEW ORACLE. ENDARNO, COME IN!
WAIT! STOP THE CEREMONY!
WHO...?
I AM THE REAL ENDARNO OF BASILIADE, AND I CAN'T ACCEPT THIS POST.
THE MAN YOU CALLED BY MY NAME WAS A PRISONER WHO TOOK MY SHAPE.
THAT'S IMPOSSIBLE!
IT'S TRUE. I'VE BEEN LANGUISHING IN THE TOWER OF MISTS, TRAPPED IN SOMEONE ELSE'S BODY.
THE BODY OF PHOBOS OF MERIDIAN, THE TYRANT WHO CLOUDED YOUR JUDGMENT WITH HIS LIES.

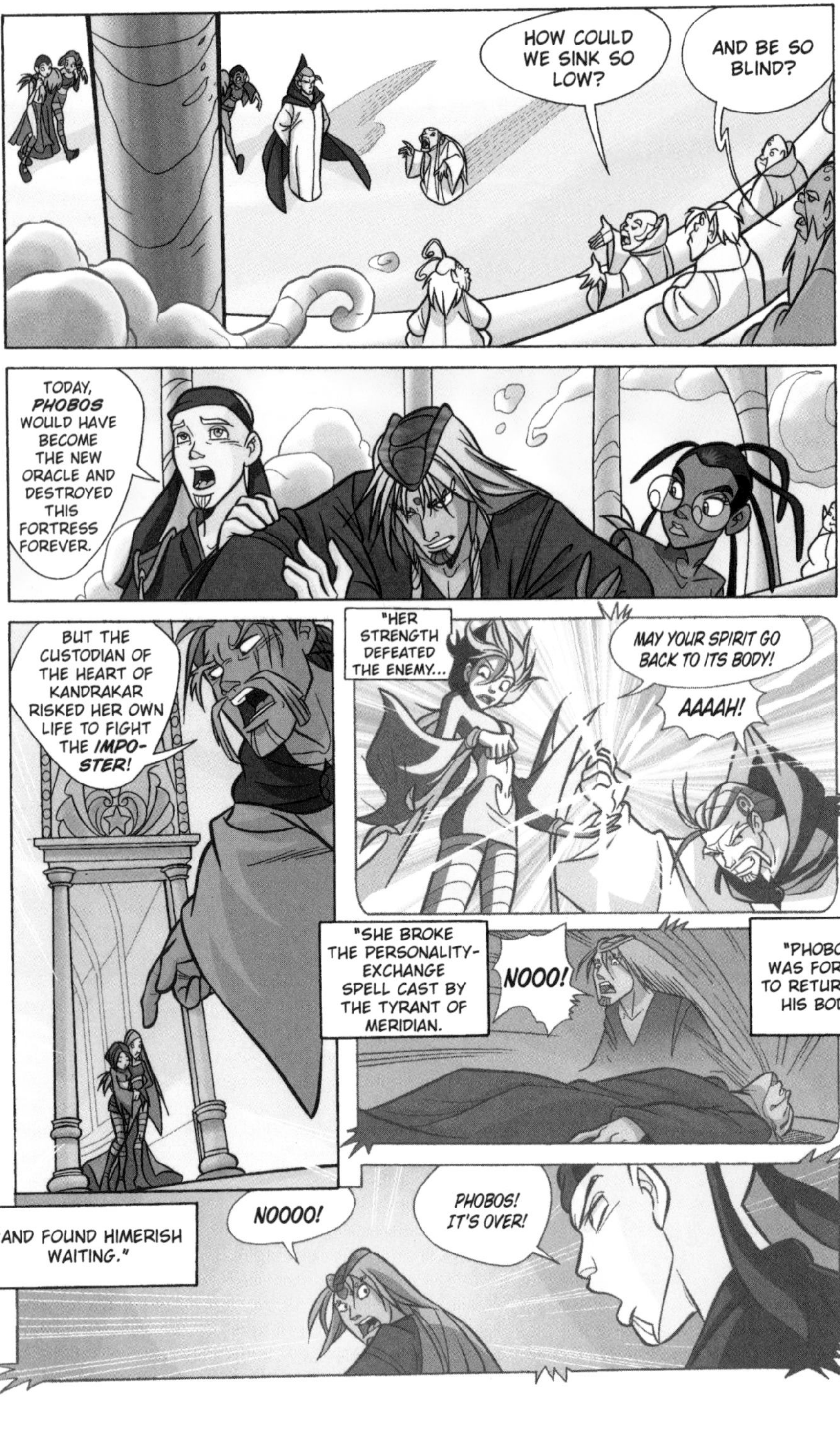
HOW COULD WE SINK SO LOW?
AND BE SO BLIND?
TODAY, **PHOBOS** WOULD HAVE BECOME THE NEW ORACLE AND DESTROYED THIS FORTRESS FOREVER.
BUT THE CUSTODIAN OF THE HEART OF KANDRAKAR RISKED HER OWN LIFE TO FIGHT THE **IMPOSTER**!
"HER STRENGTH DEFEATED THE ENEMY...
MAY YOUR SPIRIT GO BACK TO ITS BODY!
AAAAH!
"SHE BROKE THE PERSONALITY-EXCHANGE SPELL CAST BY THE TYRANT OF MERIDIAN.
NOOO!
"PHOBOS WAS FORCED TO RETURN TO HIS BODY.
"AND FOUND HIMERISH WAITING."
NOOOO!
PHOBOS! IT'S OVER!

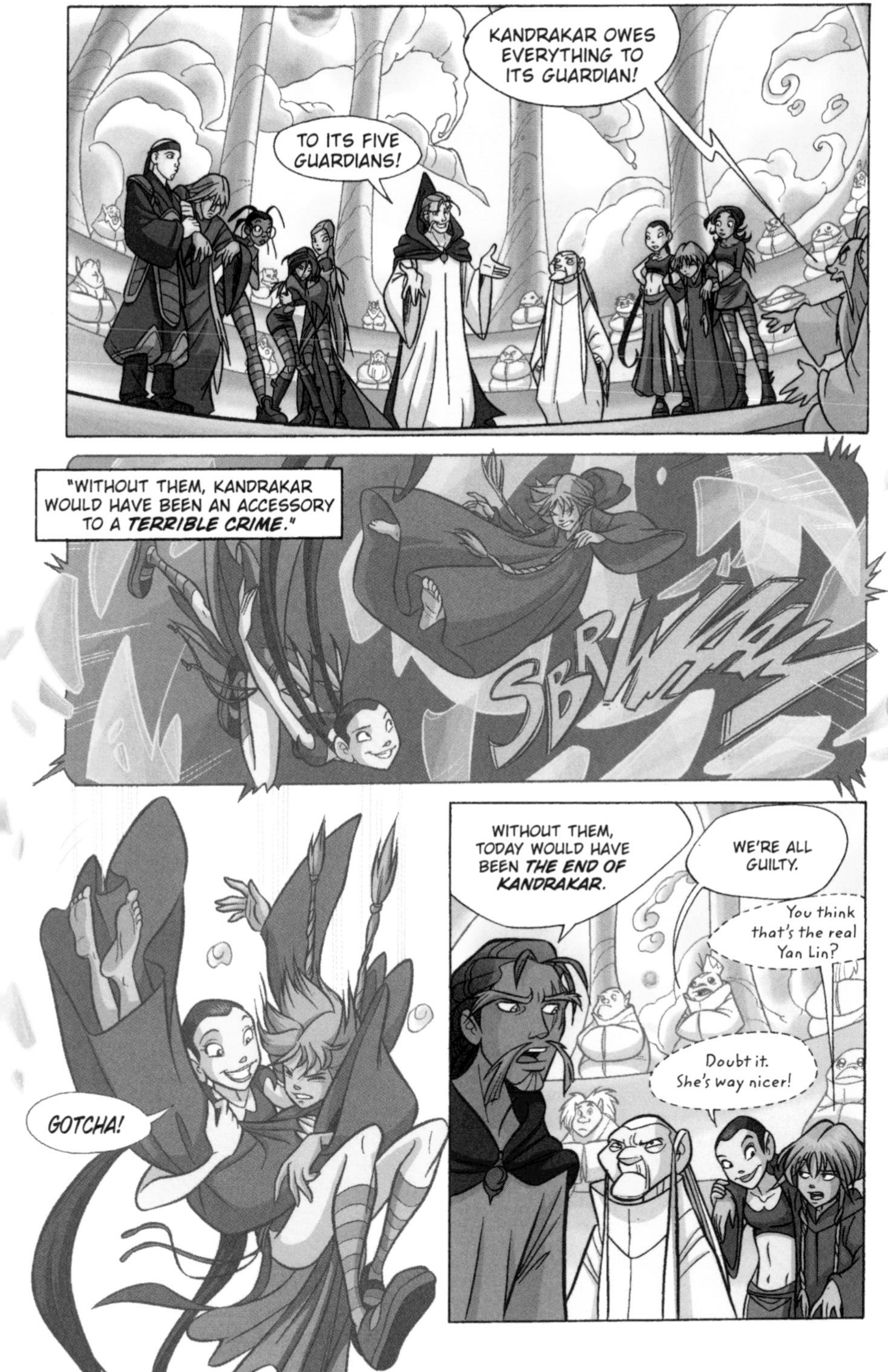
KANDRAKAR OWES EVERYTHING TO ITS GUARDIAN!
TO ITS FIVE GUARDIANS!
"WITHOUT THEM, KANDRAKAR WOULD HAVE BEEN AN ACCESSORY TO A **TERRIBLE CRIME**."
SBRWAAA
GOTCHA!
WITHOUT THEM, TODAY WOULD HAVE BEEN **THE END OF KANDRAKAR**.
WE'RE ALL GUILTY.
You think that's the real Yan Lin?
Doubt it. She's way nicer!

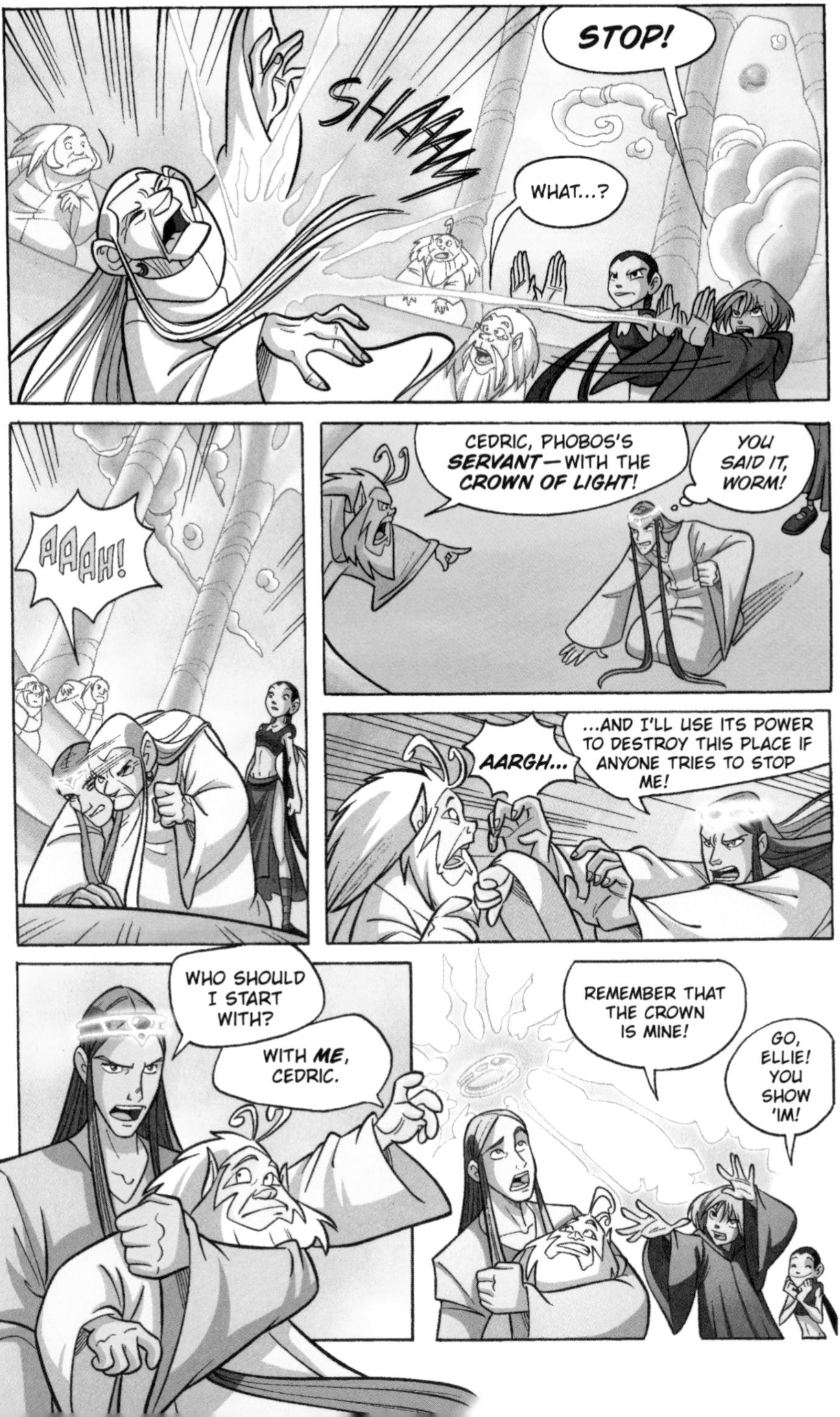

STOP!
SHAAAM
WHAT...?
AAAH!
CEDRIC, PHOBOS'S **SERVANT**—WITH THE **CROWN OF LIGHT**!
YOU SAID IT, WORM!
AARGH...
...AND I'LL USE ITS POWER TO DESTROY THIS PLACE IF ANYONE TRIES TO STOP ME!
WHO SHOULD I START WITH?
WITH **ME**, CEDRIC.
REMEMBER THAT THE CROWN IS MINE!
GO, ELLIE! YOU SHOW 'IM!

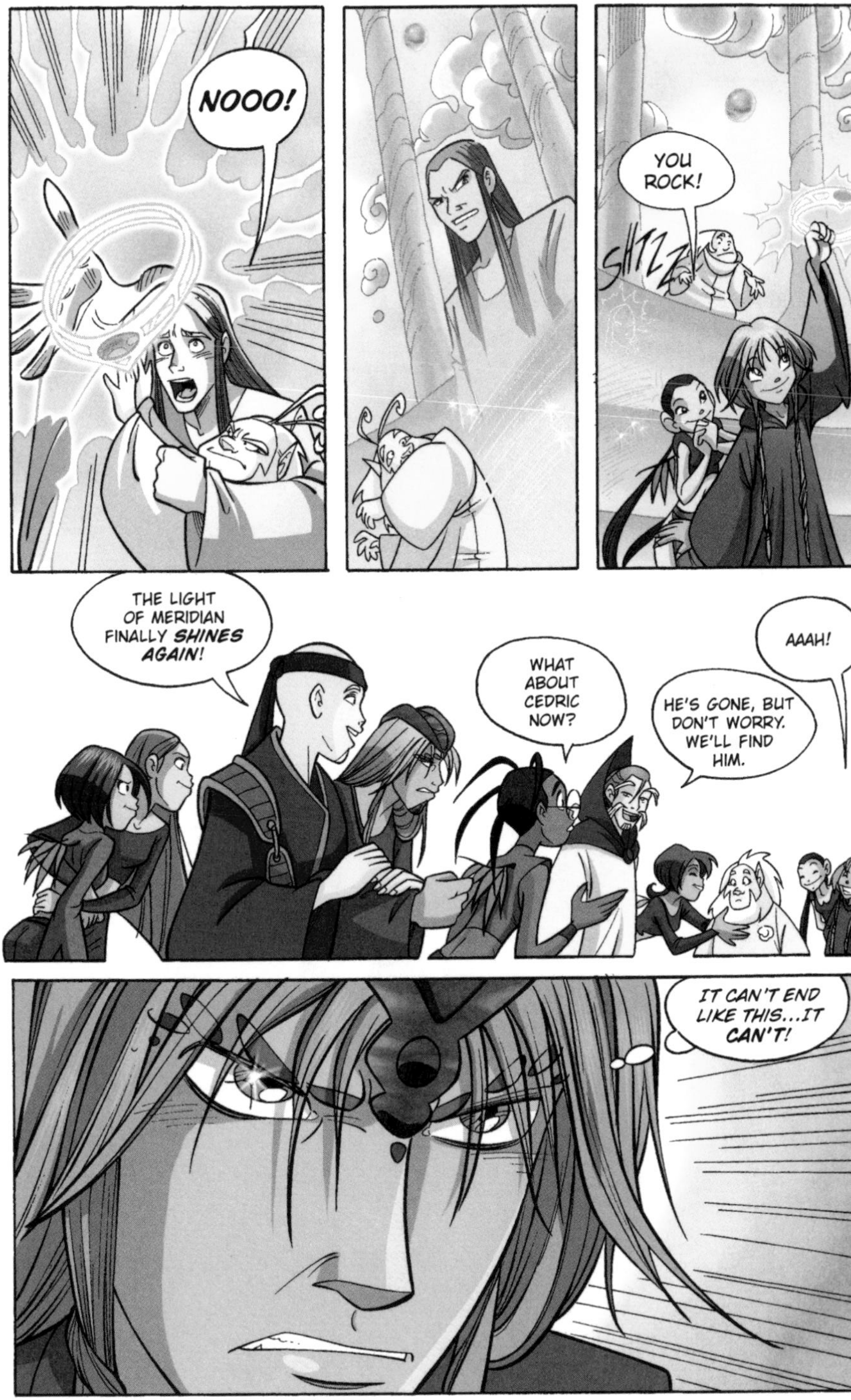
NOOO!
YOU ROCK!
SHIZZ
THE LIGHT OF MERIDIAN FINALLY SHINES AGAIN!
WHAT ABOUT CEDRIC NOW?
HE'S GONE, BUT DON'T WORRY. WE'LL FIND HIM.
AAAH!
IT CAN'T END LIKE THIS...IT CAN'T!

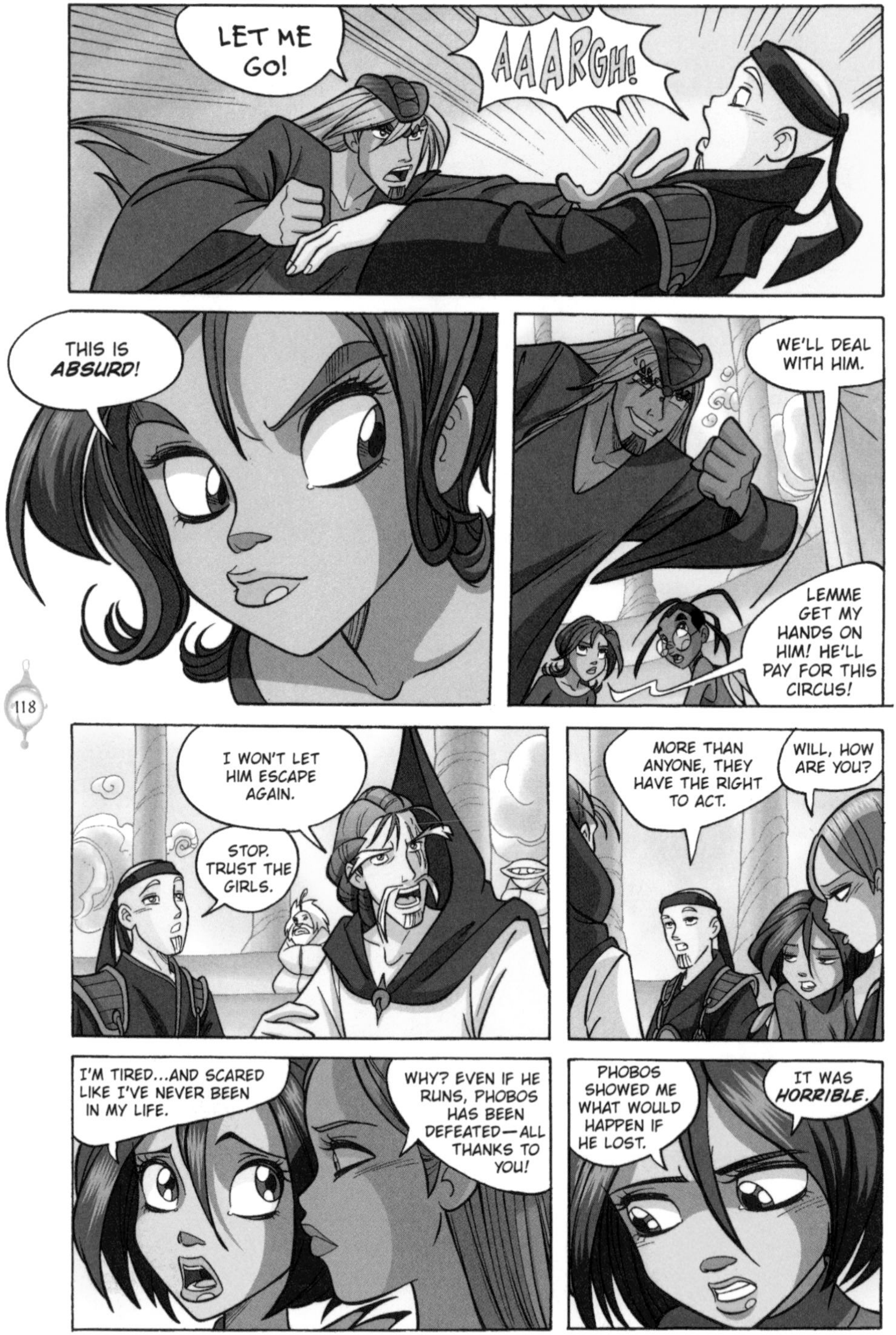
LET ME GO!
AAARGH!
THIS IS **ABSURD!**
WE'LL DEAL WITH HIM.
LEMME GET MY HANDS ON HIM! HE'LL PAY FOR THIS CIRCUS!
I WON'T LET HIM ESCAPE AGAIN.
STOP. TRUST THE GIRLS.
MORE THAN ANYONE, THEY HAVE THE RIGHT TO ACT.
WILL, HOW ARE YOU?
I'M TIRED...AND SCARED LIKE I'VE NEVER BEEN IN MY LIFE.
WHY? EVEN IF HE RUNS, PHOBOS HAS BEEN DEFEATED—ALL THANKS TO YOU!
PHOBOS SHOWED ME WHAT WOULD HAPPEN IF HE LOST.
IT WAS **HORRIBLE.**

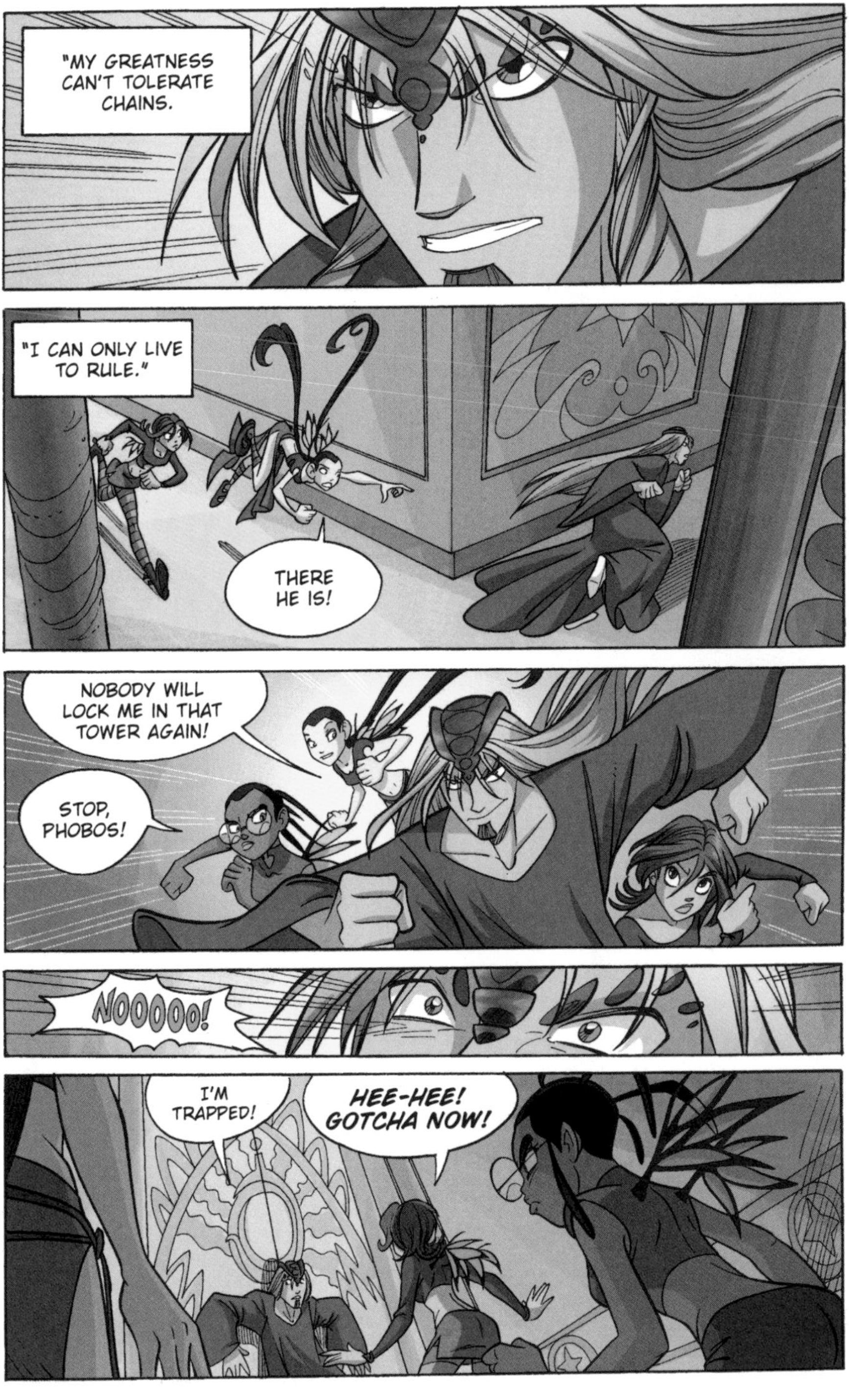
"MY GREATNESS CAN'T TOLERATE CHAINS.
"I CAN ONLY LIVE TO RULE."
THERE HE IS!
NOBODY WILL LOCK ME IN THAT TOWER AGAIN!
STOP, PHOBOS!
NOOOOO!
I'M TRAPPED!
HEE-HEE! GOTCHA NOW!

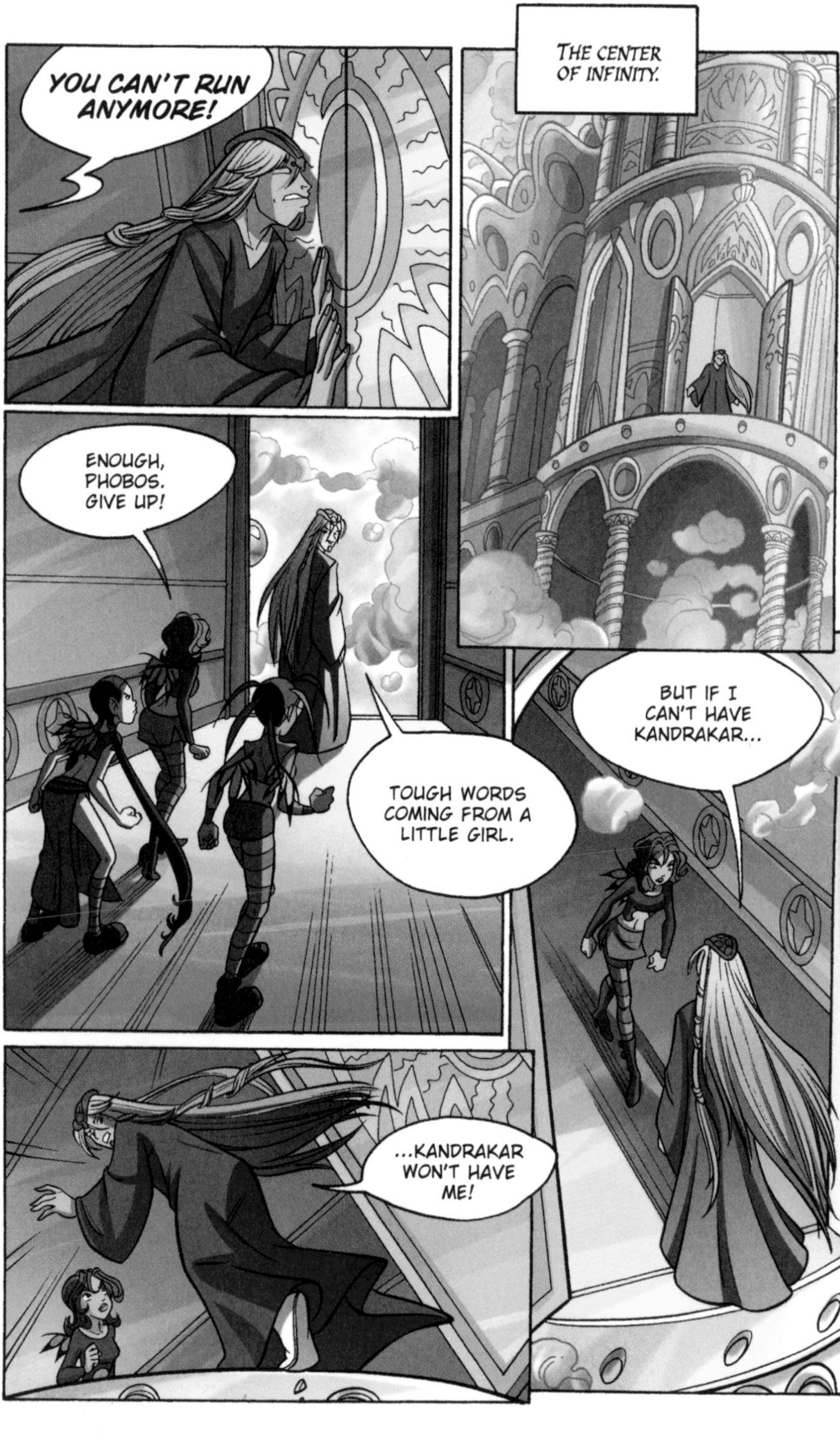
YOU CAN'T RUN ANYMORE!
THE CENTER OF INFINITY.
ENOUGH, PHOBOS. GIVE UP!
TOUGH WORDS COMING FROM A LITTLE GIRL.
BUT IF I CAN'T HAVE KANDRAKAR...
...KANDRAKAR WON'T HAVE ME!

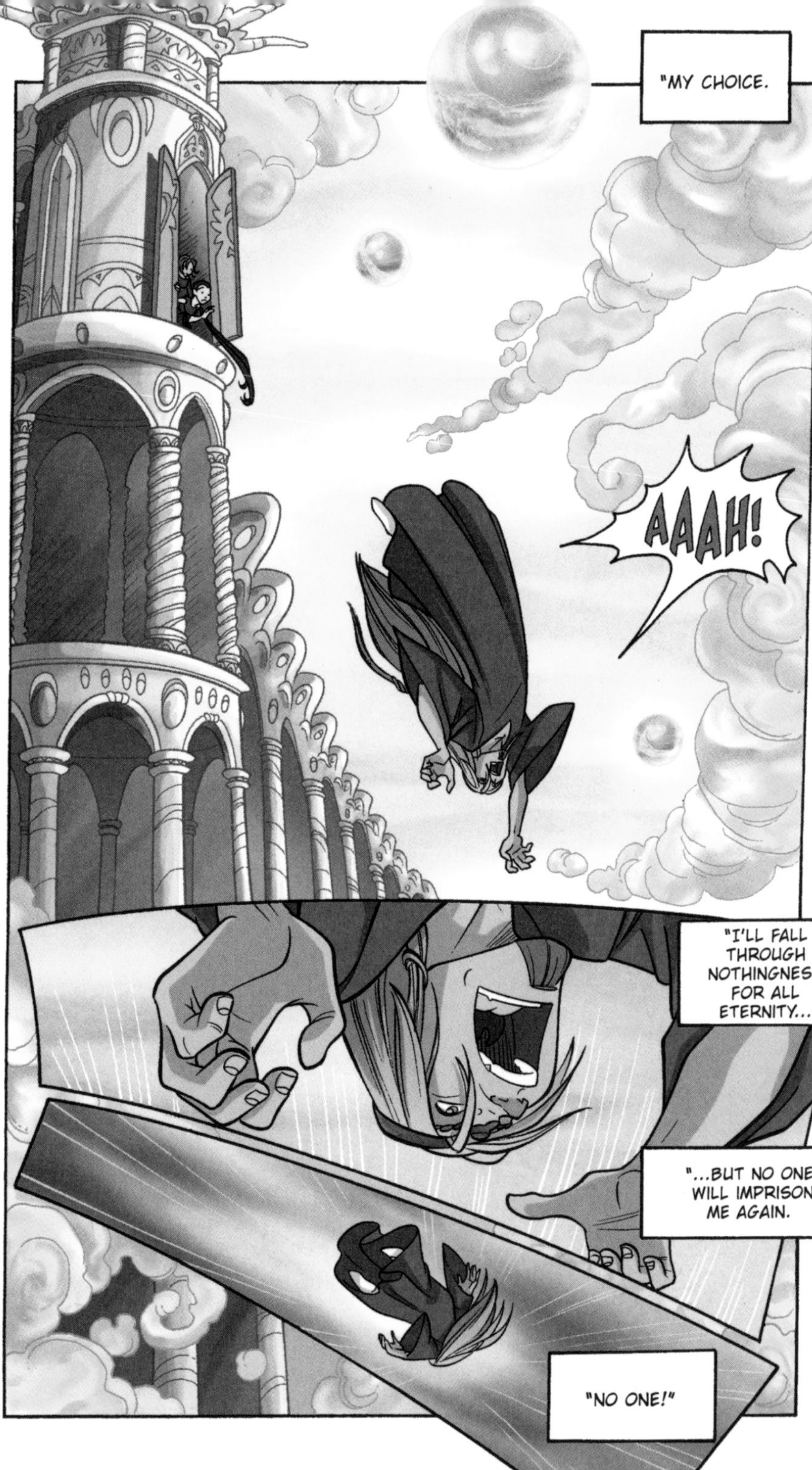
"MY CHOICE.
AAAH!
"I'LL FALL THROUGH NOTHINGNESS FOR ALL ETERNITY...
"...BUT NO ONE WILL IMPRISON ME AGAIN.
"NO ONE!"

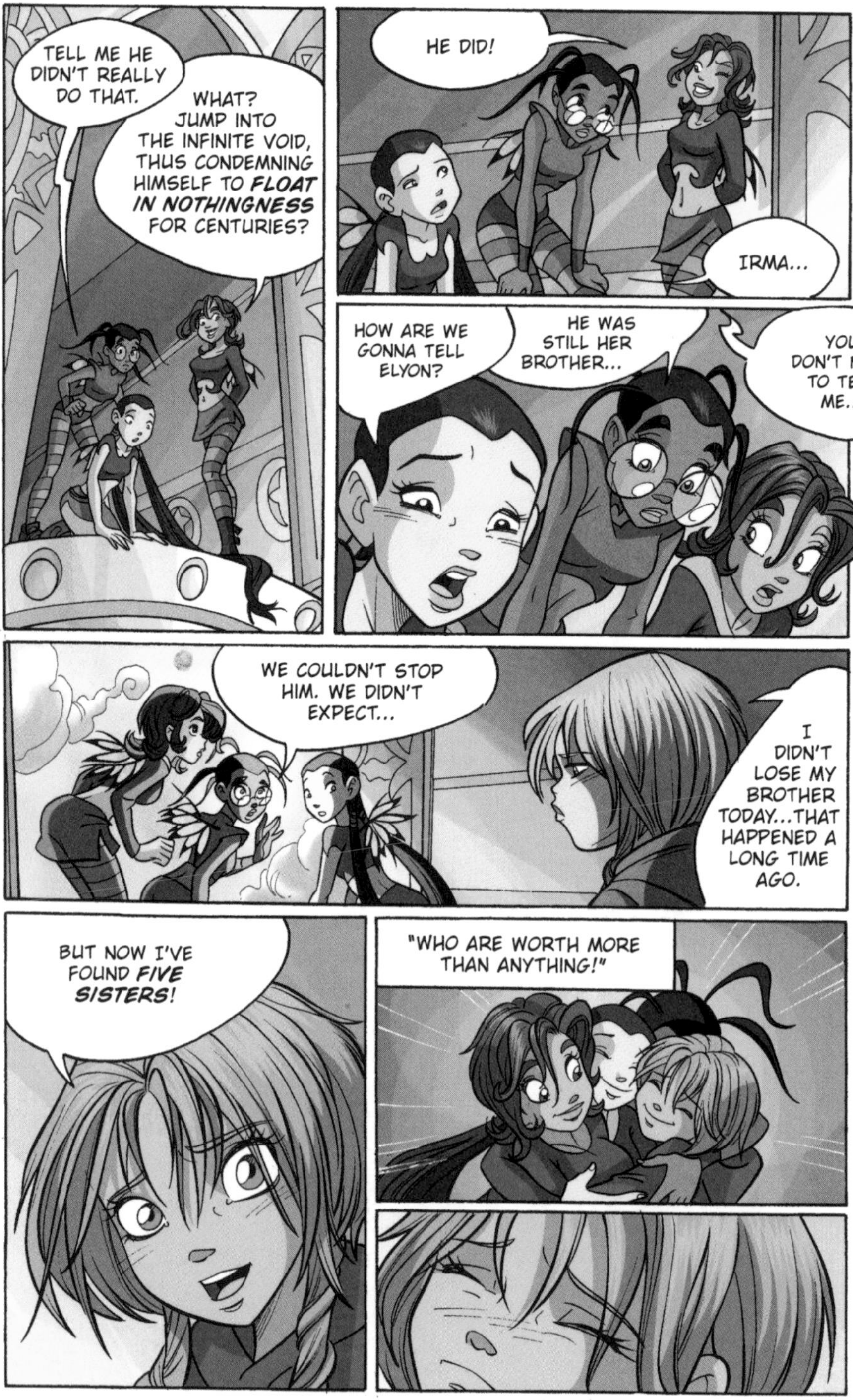

TELL ME HE DIDN'T REALLY DO THAT.
WHAT? JUMP INTO THE INFINITE VOID, THUS CONDEMNING HIMSELF TO **FLOAT IN NOTHINGNESS** FOR CENTURIES?
HE DID!
IRMA...
HOW ARE WE GONNA TELL ELYON?
HE WAS STILL HER BROTHER...
YOU DON'T NEED TO TELL ME...
WE COULDN'T STOP HIM. WE DIDN'T EXPECT...
I DIDN'T LOSE MY BROTHER TODAY...THAT HAPPENED A LONG TIME AGO.
BUT NOW I'VE FOUND **FIVE SISTERS**!
"WHO ARE WORTH MORE THAN ANYTHING!"

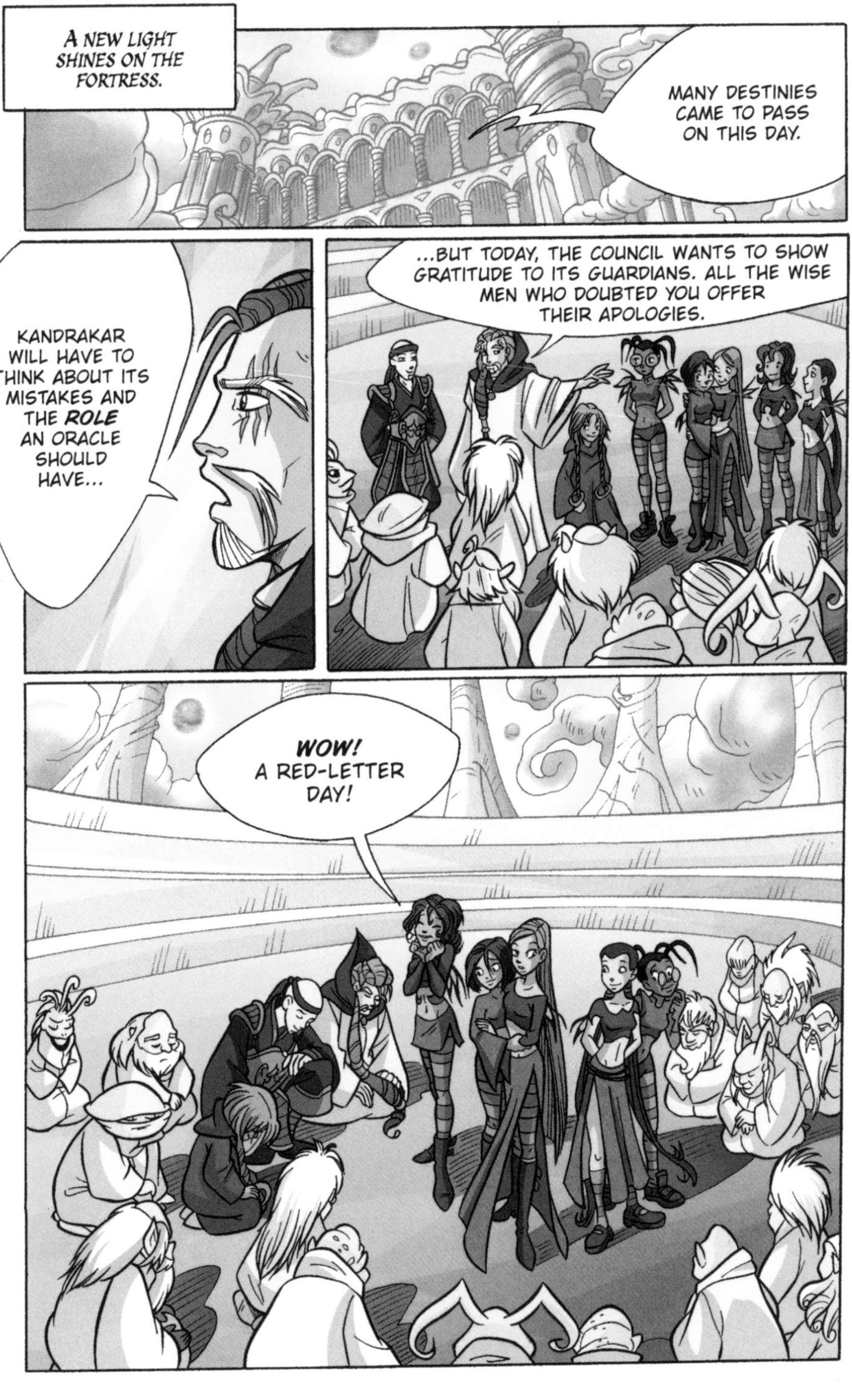
A NEW LIGHT SHINES ON THE FORTRESS.
MANY DESTINIES CAME TO PASS ON THIS DAY.
KANDRAKAR WILL HAVE TO THINK ABOUT ITS MISTAKES AND THE ROLE AN ORACLE SHOULD HAVE...
...BUT TODAY, THE COUNCIL WANTS TO SHOW GRATITUDE TO ITS GUARDIANS. ALL THE WISE MEN WHO DOUBTED YOU OFFER THEIR APOLOGIES.
WOW! A RED-LETTER DAY!

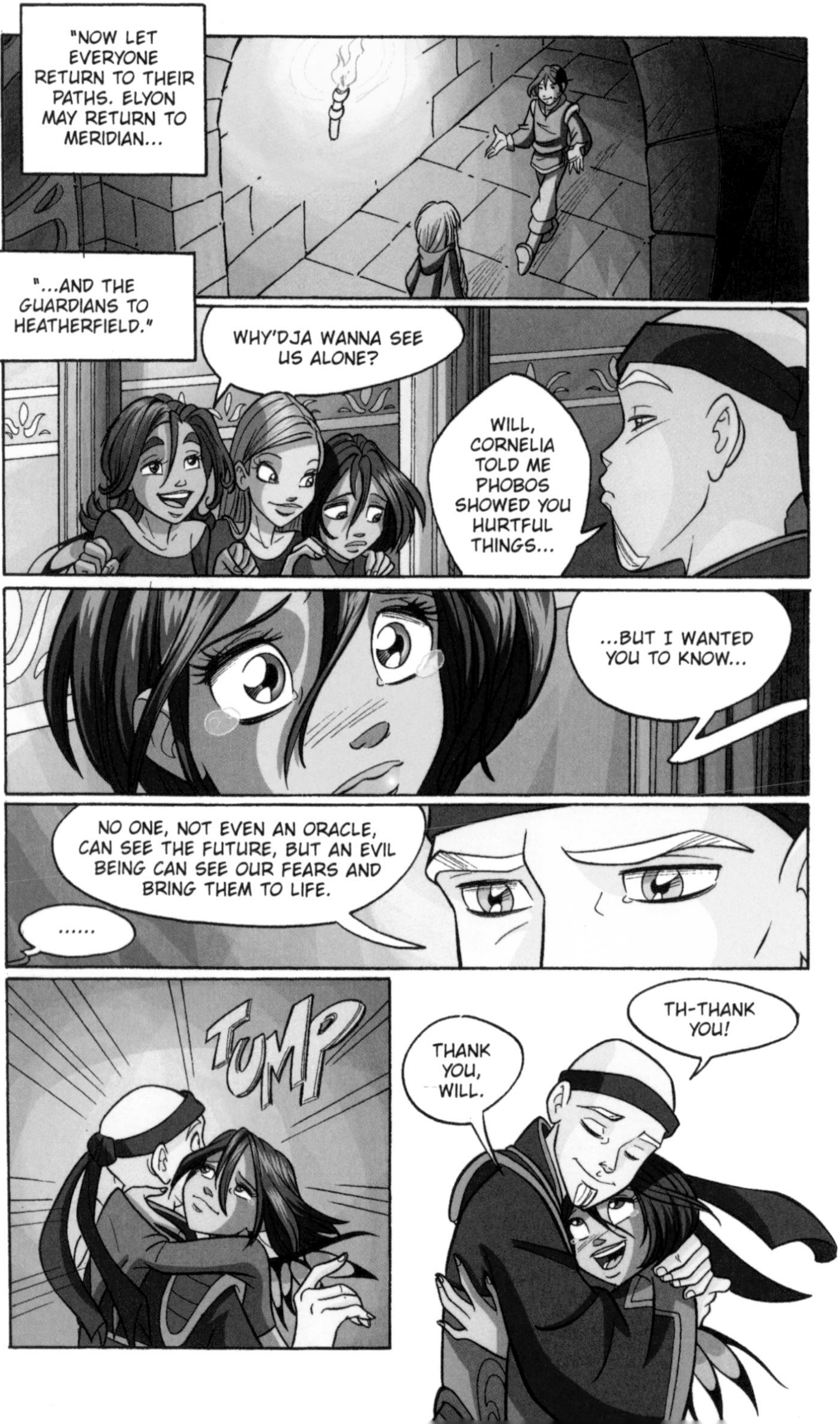
"NOW LET EVERYONE RETURN TO THEIR PATHS. ELYON MAY RETURN TO MERIDIAN...
"...AND THE GUARDIANS TO HEATHERFIELD."
WHY'DJA WANNA SEE US ALONE?
WILL, CORNELIA TOLD ME PHOBOS SHOWED YOU HURTFUL THINGS...
...BUT I WANTED YOU TO KNOW...
NO ONE, NOT EVEN AN ORACLE, CAN SEE THE FUTURE, BUT AN EVIL BEING CAN SEE OUR FEARS AND BRING THEM TO LIFE.
......
TUMP
THANK YOU, WILL.
TH-THANK YOU!

124

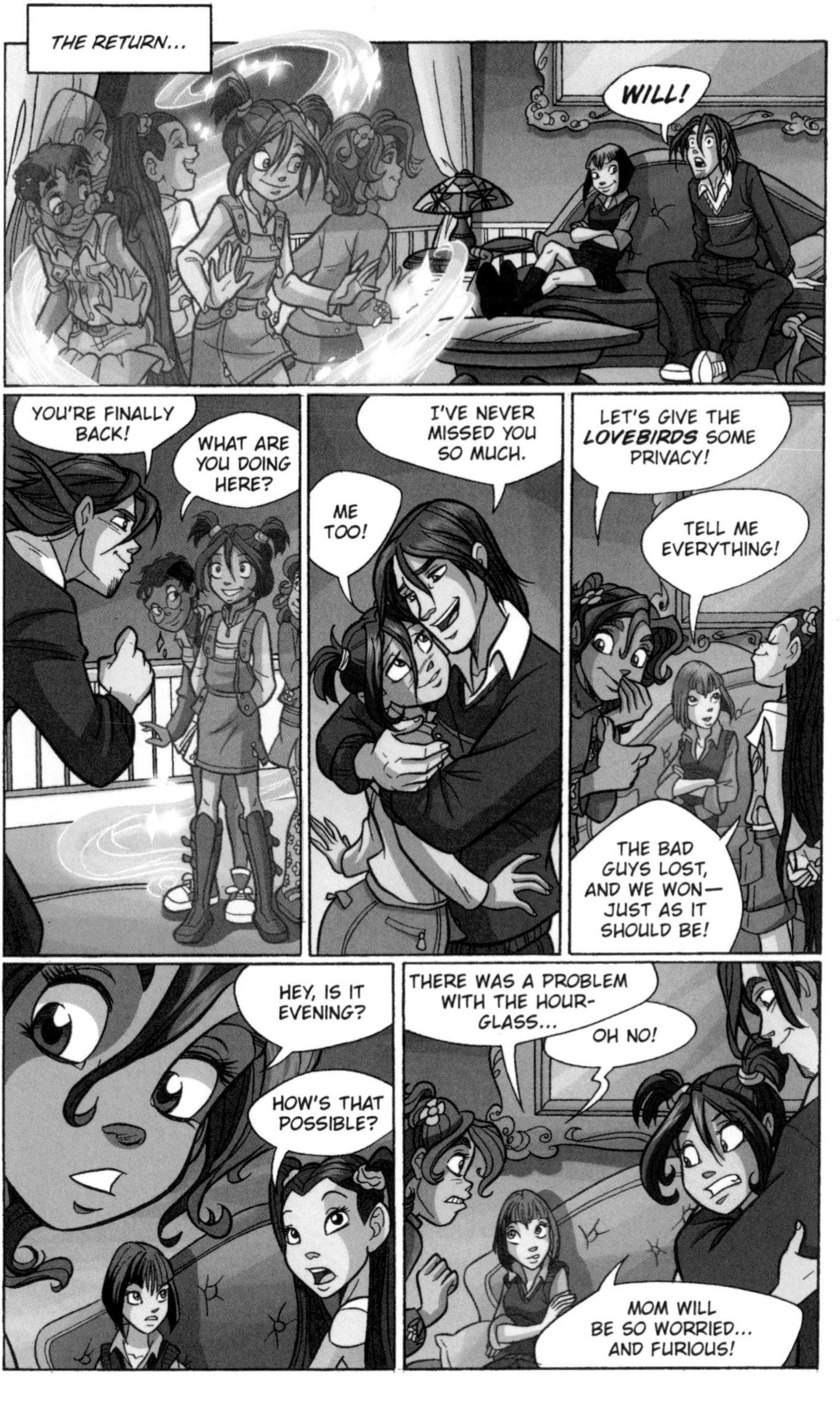
THE RETURN...
WILL!
YOU'RE FINALLY BACK!
WHAT ARE YOU DOING HERE?
I'VE NEVER MISSED YOU SO MUCH.
ME TOO!
LET'S GIVE THE ***LOVEBIRDS*** SOME PRIVACY!
TELL ME EVERYTHING!
THE BAD GUYS LOST, AND WE WON— JUST AS IT SHOULD BE!
HEY, IS IT EVENING?
HOW'S THAT POSSIBLE?
THERE WAS A PROBLEM WITH THE HOUR-GLASS...
OH NO!
MOM WILL BE SO WORRIED... AND FURIOUS!

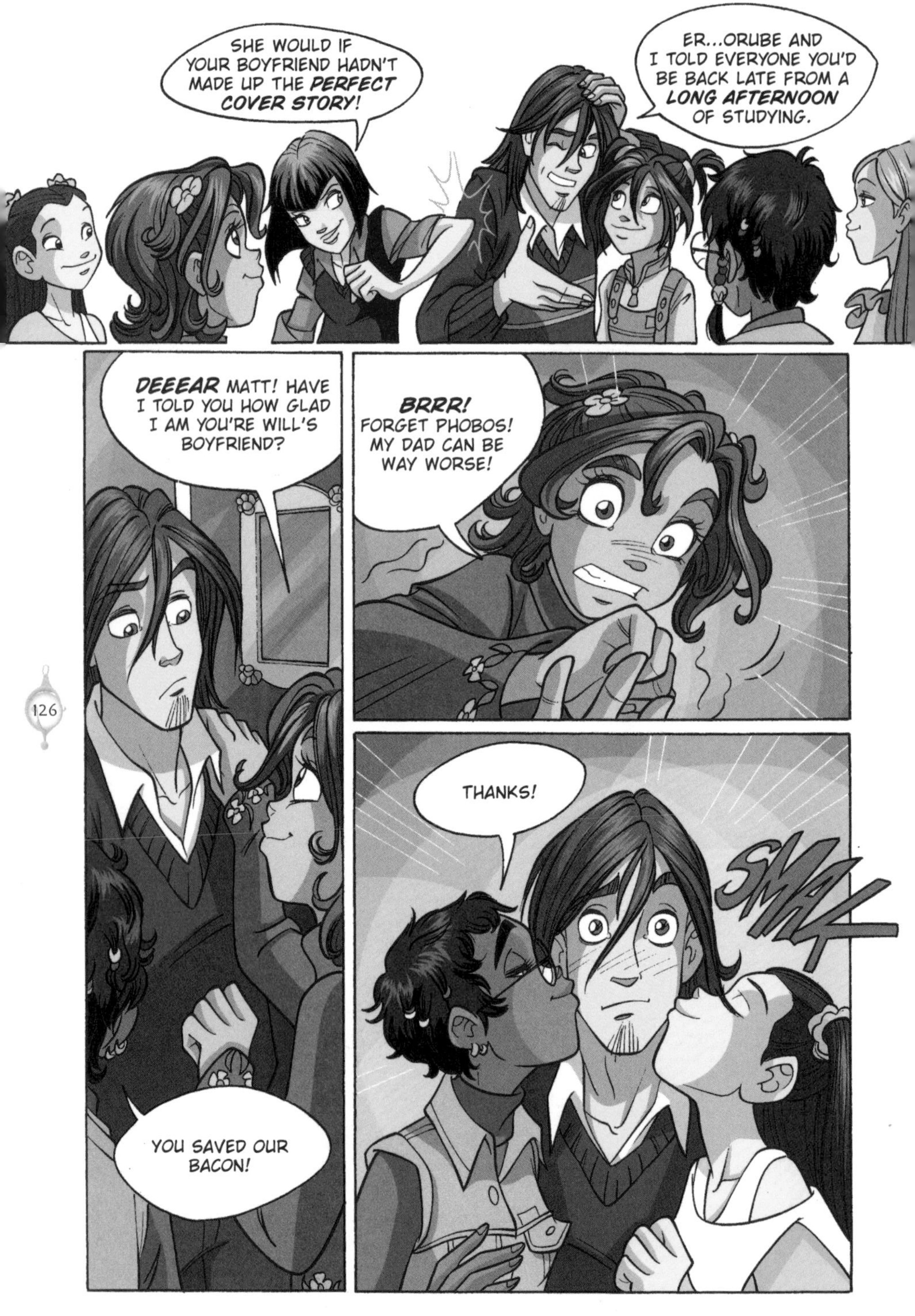
SHE WOULD IF YOUR BOYFRIEND HADN'T MADE UP THE **PERFECT COVER STORY**!
ER...ORUBE AND I TOLD EVERYONE YOU'D BE BACK LATE FROM A **LONG AFTERNOON** OF STUDYING.
DEEEAR MATT! HAVE I TOLD YOU HOW GLAD I AM YOU'RE WILL'S BOYFRIEND?
YOU SAVED OUR BACON!
BRRR! FORGET PHOBOS! MY DAD CAN BE WAY WORSE!
THANKS!
SMAK

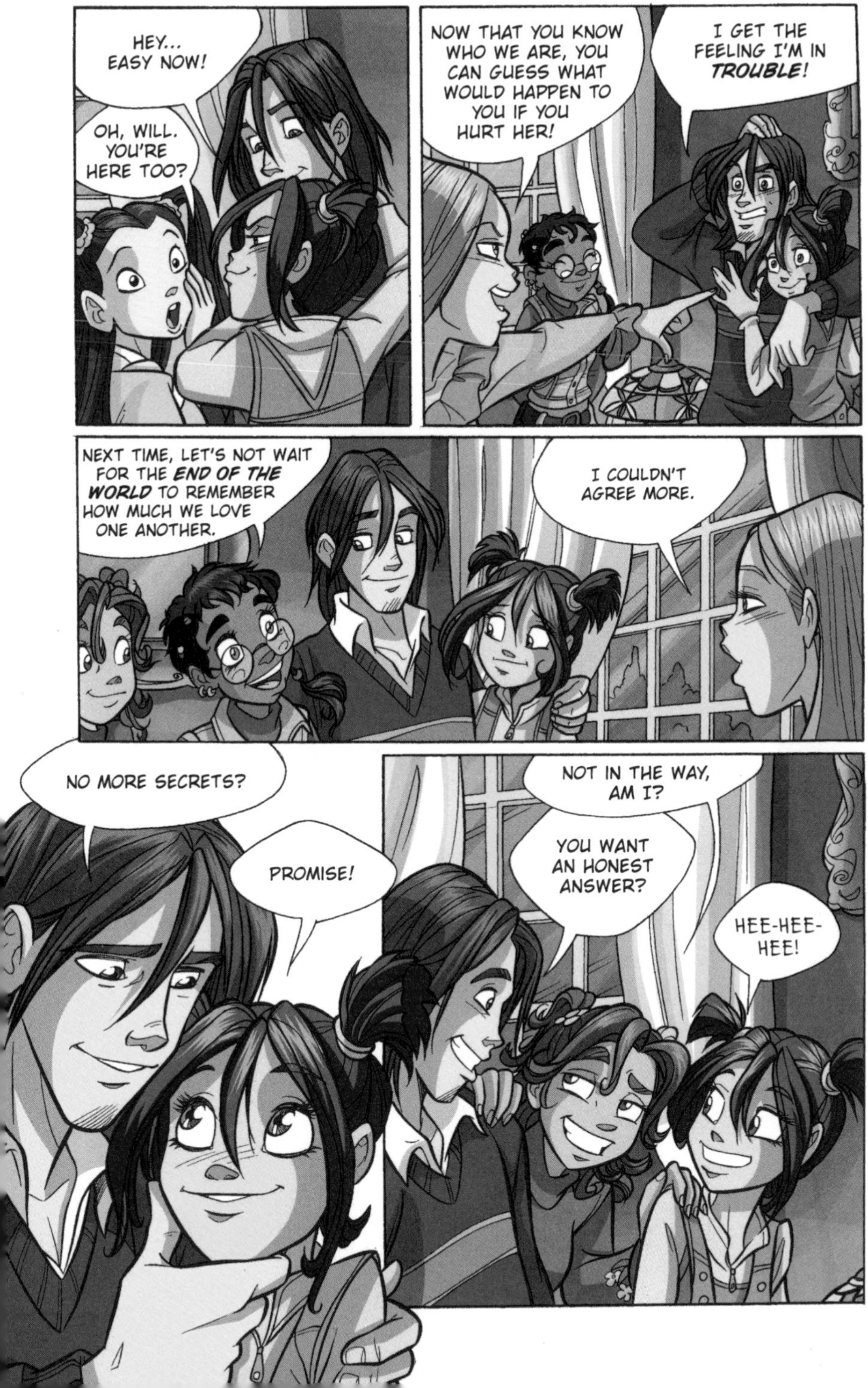
HEY... EASY NOW!
OH, WILL. YOU'RE HERE TOO?
NOW THAT YOU KNOW WHO WE ARE, YOU CAN GUESS WHAT WOULD HAPPEN TO YOU IF YOU HURT HER!
I GET THE FEELING I'M IN ***TROUBLE***!
NEXT TIME, LET'S NOT WAIT FOR THE ***END OF THE WORLD*** TO REMEMBER HOW MUCH WE LOVE ONE ANOTHER.
I COULDN'T AGREE MORE.
NO MORE SECRETS?
PROMISE!
NOT IN THE WAY, AM I?
YOU WANT AN HONEST ANSWER?
HEE-HEE-HEE!

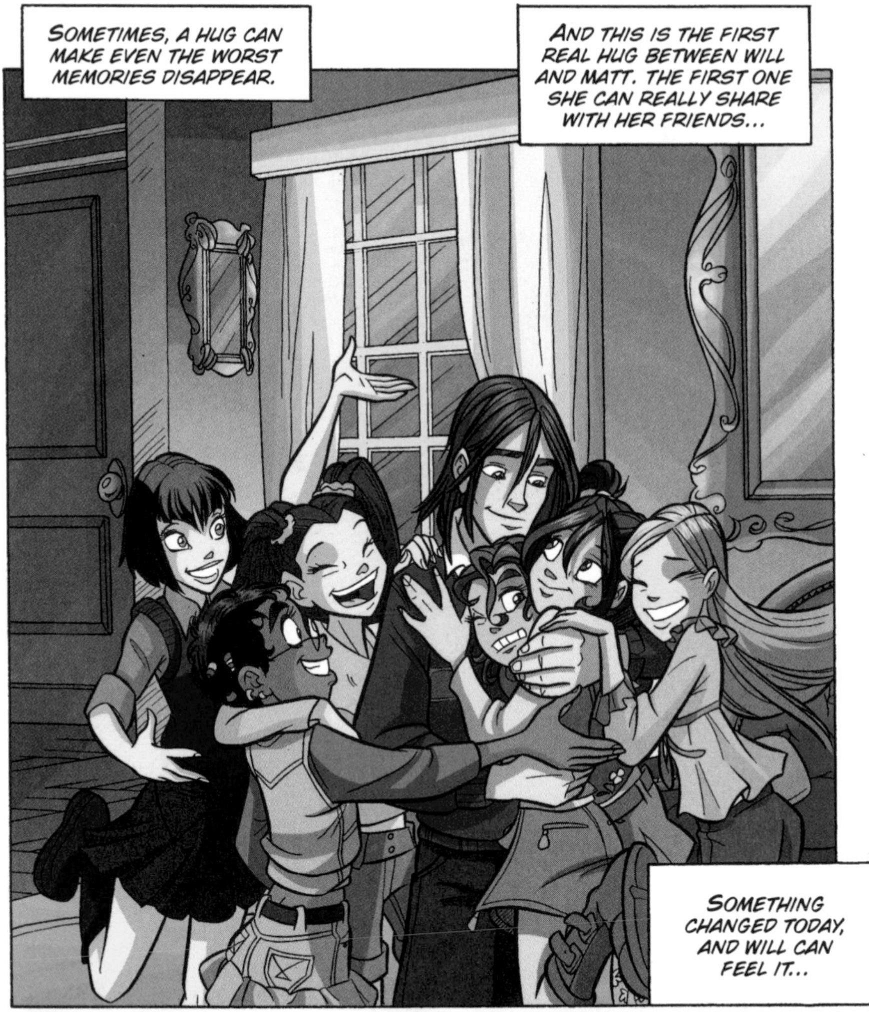
SOMETIMES, A HUG CAN MAKE EVEN THE WORST MEMORIES DISAPPEAR.
AND THIS IS THE FIRST REAL HUG BETWEEN WILL AND MATT. THE FIRST ONE SHE CAN REALLY SHARE WITH HER FRIENDS...
SOMETHING CHANGED TODAY, AND WILL CAN FEEL IT...

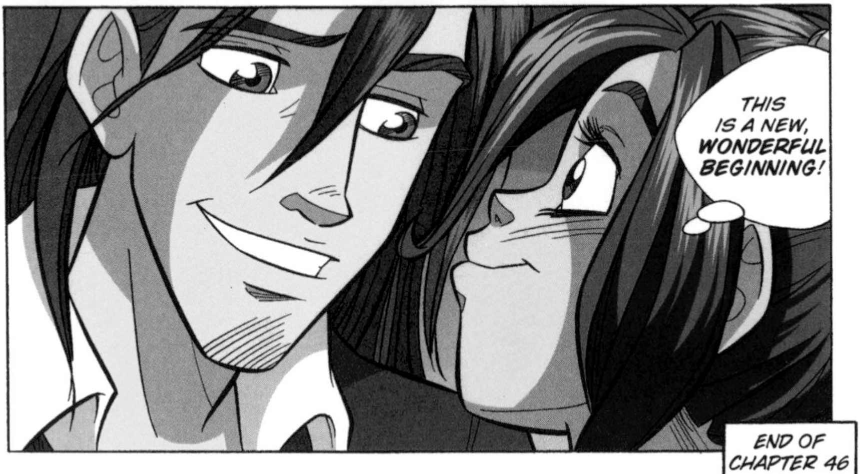
THIS IS A NEW, WONDERFUL BEGINNING!
END OF CHAPTER 46

47

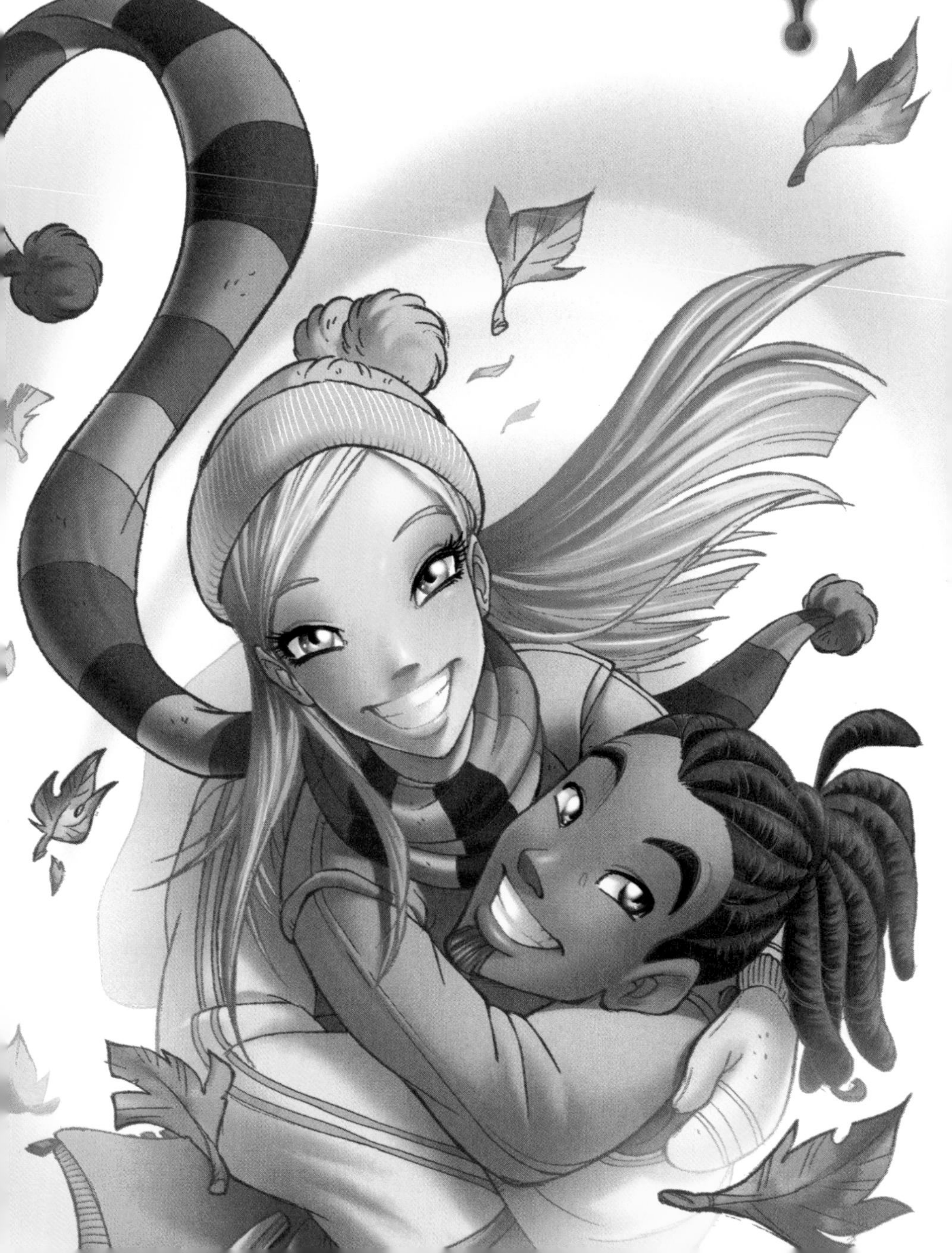

The Sands of Time

"Be it a smile or an invitation, I'll know how to answer."

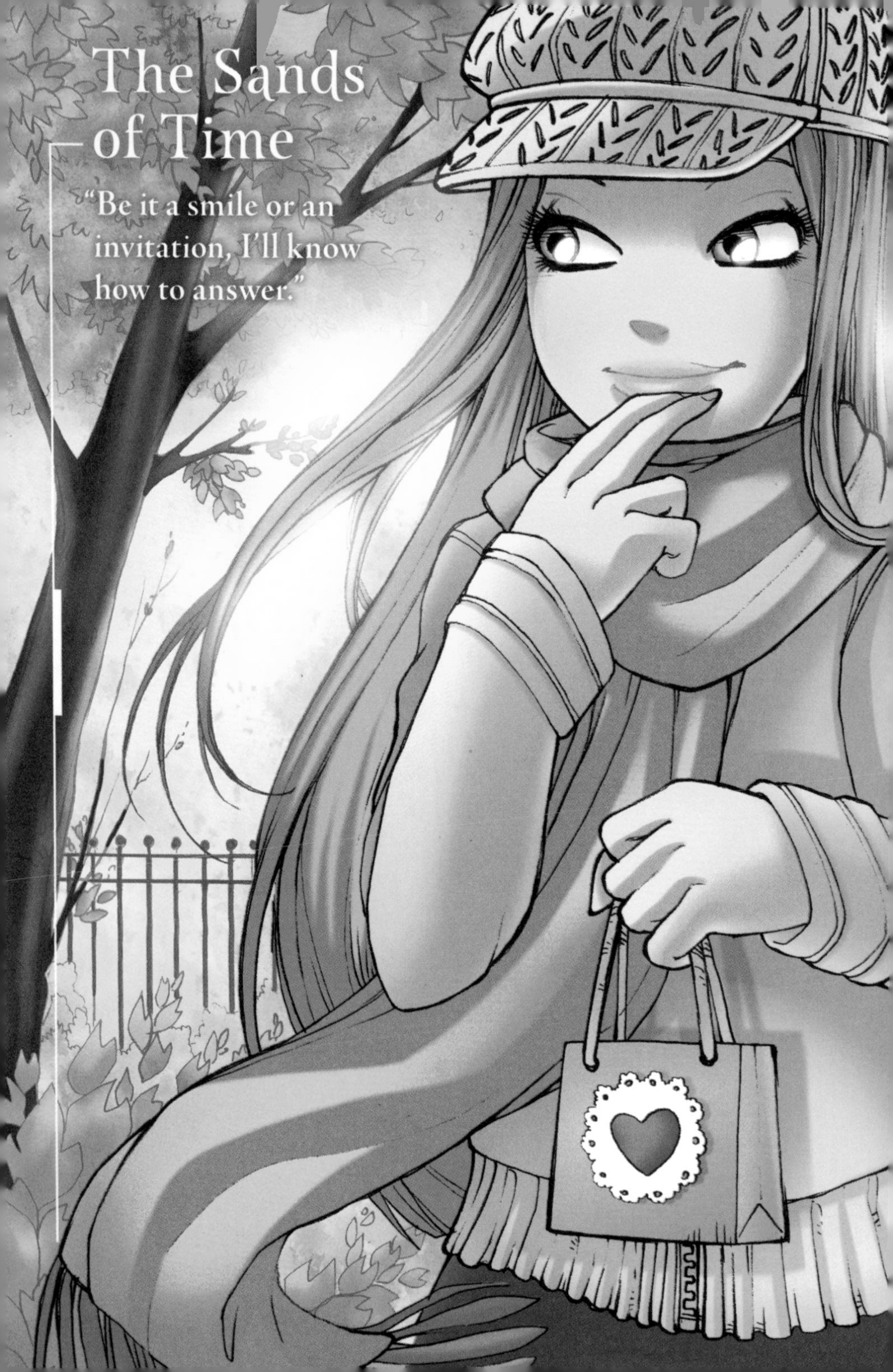

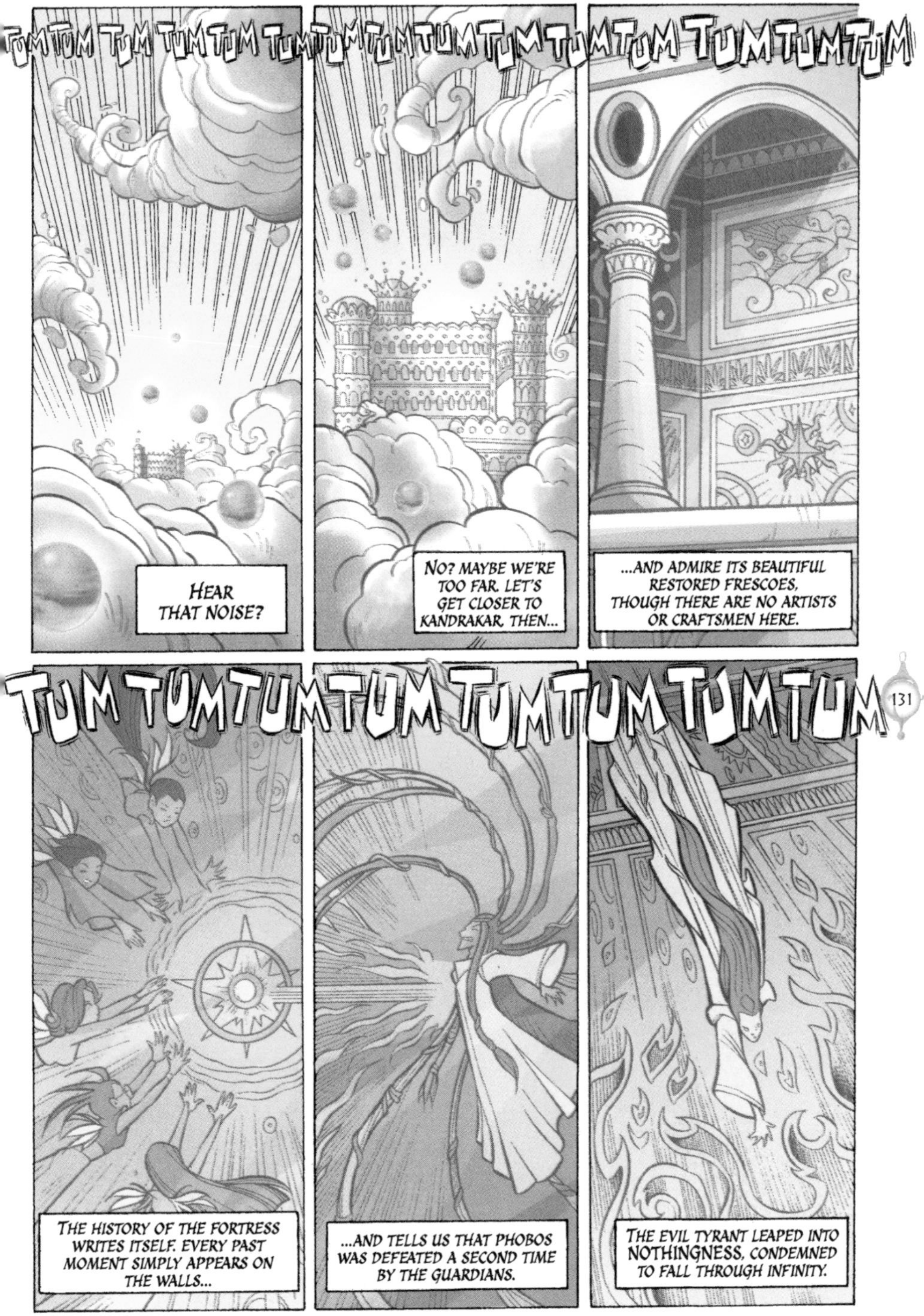
TUM TUM TUM TUM TUM TUM TUM TUM TUM TUM TUM TUM TUM TUM TUM
HEAR THAT NOISE?
NO? MAYBE WE'RE TOO FAR. LET'S GET CLOSER TO KANDRAKAR, THEN...
...AND ADMIRE ITS BEAUTIFUL RESTORED FRESCOES, THOUGH THERE ARE NO ARTISTS OR CRAFTSMEN HERE.
TUM TUM TUM TUM TUM TUM TUM TUM TUM TUM
THE HISTORY OF THE FORTRESS WRITES ITSELF. EVERY PAST MOMENT SIMPLY APPEARS ON THE WALLS...
...AND TELLS US THAT PHOBOS WAS DEFEATED A SECOND TIME BY THE GUARDIANS.
THE EVIL TYRANT LEAPED INTO NOTHINGNESS, CONDEMNED TO FALL THROUGH INFINITY.

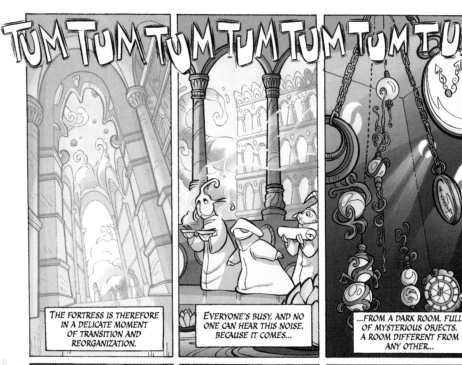

TUM TUM TUM TUM TUM TUM TUM

THE FORTRESS IS THEREFORE IN A DELICATE MOMENT OF TRANSITION AND REORGANIZATION.

EVERYONE'S BUSY, AND NO ONE CAN HEAR THIS NOISE, BECAUSE IT COMES...

...FROM A DARK ROOM, FULL OF MYSTERIOUS OBJECTS. A ROOM DIFFERENT FROM ANY OTHER...

TUM TUM TUM TUM TUM TUM

...REMINDING US THAT, WHILE KANDRAKAR MAY BE AT THE CENTER OF INFINITY, IT CAN'T ESCAPE TIME.

SO WHAT IS THAT SOUND? THE REPETITIVE FALL OF HUGE GRAINS OF SAND...

...OR THE QUICK BEATING...

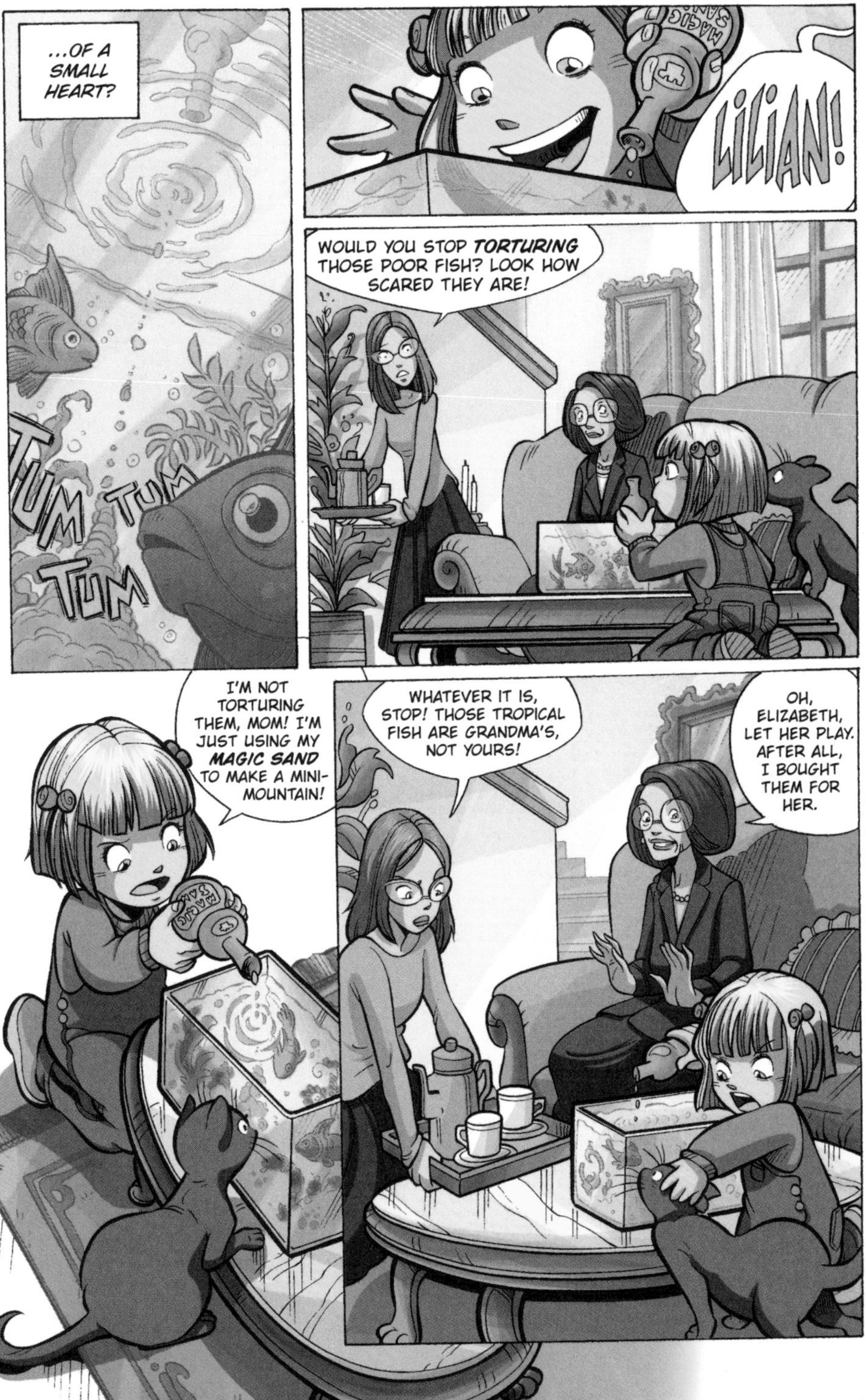
...OF A SMALL HEART?
TUM TUM
TUM
MAGIC SAND
LILIAN!
WOULD YOU STOP *TORTURING* THOSE POOR FISH? LOOK HOW SCARED THEY ARE!
I'M NOT TORTURING THEM, MOM! I'M JUST USING MY ***MAGIC SAND*** TO MAKE A MINI-MOUNTAIN!
WHATEVER IT IS, STOP! THOSE TROPICAL FISH ARE GRANDMA'S, NOT YOURS!
OH, ELIZABETH, LET HER PLAY. AFTER ALL, I BOUGHT THEM FOR HER.

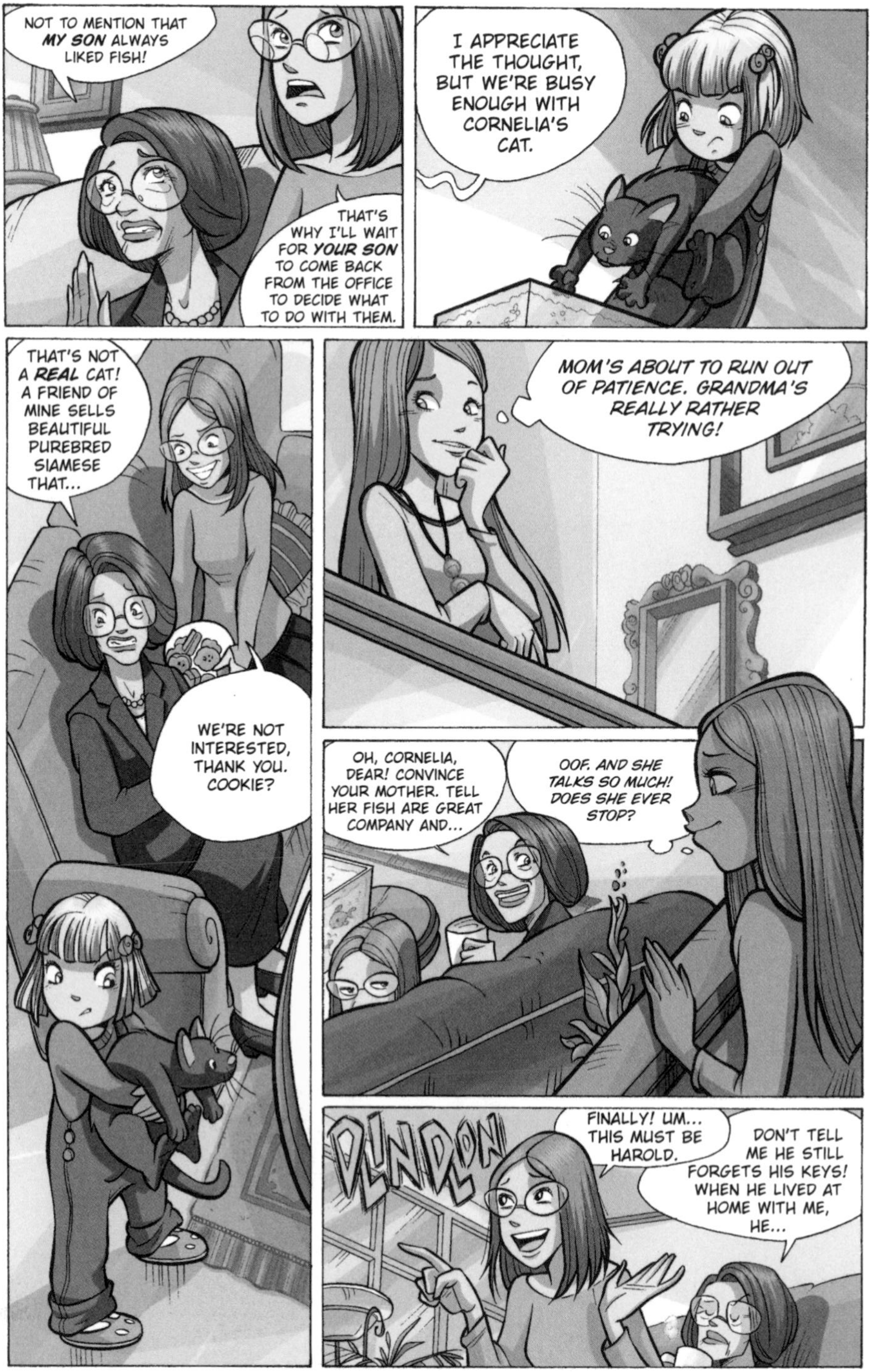
NOT TO MENTION THAT ***MY SON*** ALWAYS LIKED FISH!
THAT'S WHY I'LL WAIT FOR ***YOUR SON*** TO COME BACK FROM THE OFFICE TO DECIDE WHAT TO DO WITH THEM.
I APPRECIATE THE THOUGHT, BUT WE'RE BUSY ENOUGH WITH CORNELIA'S CAT.
THAT'S NOT A ***REAL*** CAT! A FRIEND OF MINE SELLS BEAUTIFUL PUREBRED SIAMESE THAT...
WE'RE NOT INTERESTED, THANK YOU. COOKIE?
MOM'S ABOUT TO RUN OUT OF PATIENCE. GRANDMA'S REALLY RATHER TRYING!
OH, CORNELIA, DEAR! CONVINCE YOUR MOTHER. TELL HER FISH ARE GREAT COMPANY AND...
OOF. AND SHE TALKS SO MUCH! DOES SHE EVER STOP?
DLIN DLON
FINALLY! UM... THIS MUST BE HAROLD.
DON'T TELL ME HE STILL FORGETS HIS KEYS! WHEN HE LIVED AT HOME WITH ME, HE...

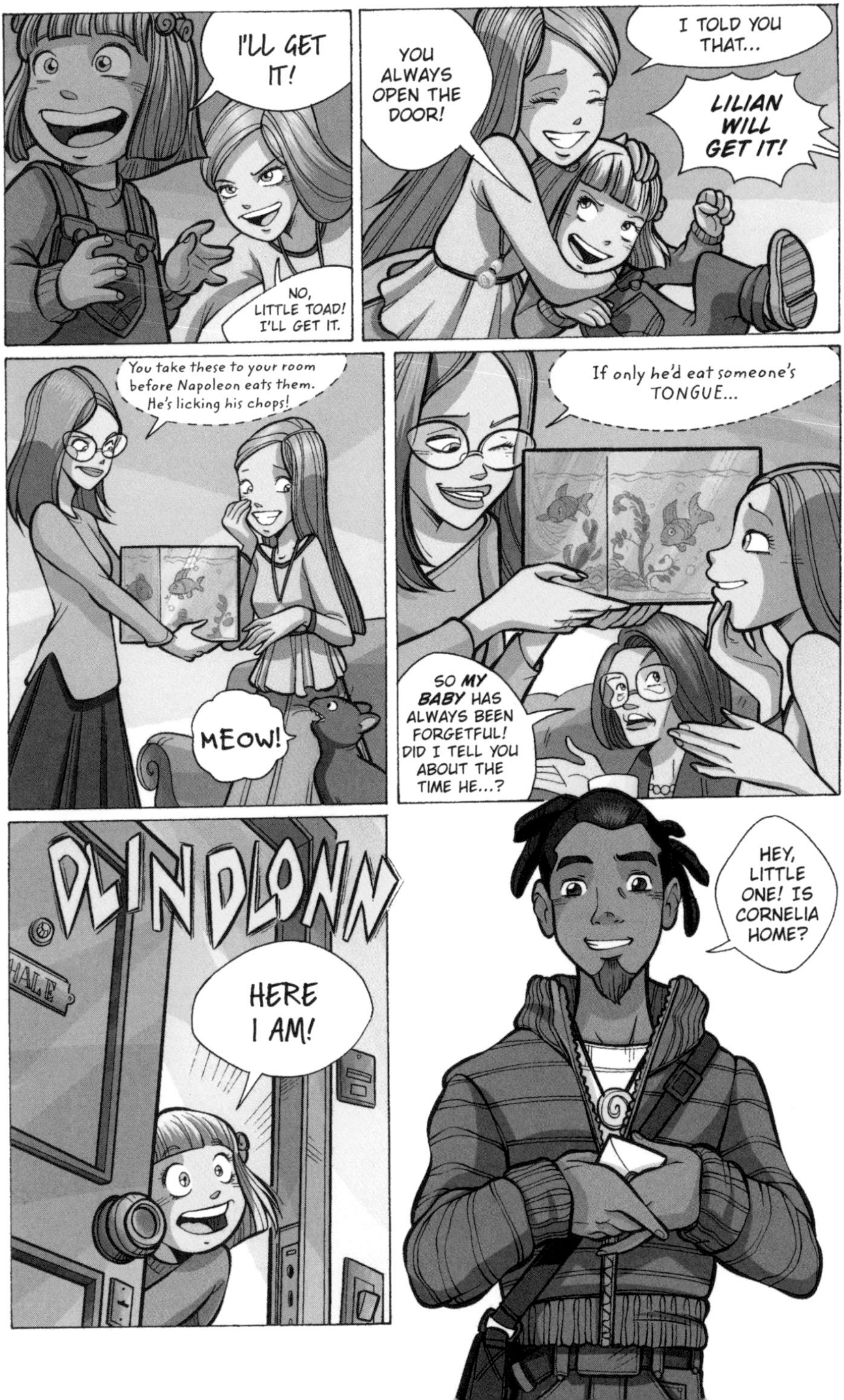
I'LL GET IT!
NO, LITTLE TOAD! I'LL GET IT.
YOU ALWAYS OPEN THE DOOR!
I TOLD YOU THAT...
LILIAN WILL GET IT!
You take these to your room before Napoleon eats them. He's licking his chops!
MEOW!
If only he'd eat someone's TONGUE...
SO MY BABY HAS ALWAYS BEEN FORGETFUL! DID I TELL YOU ABOUT THE TIME HE...?
DLIN DLONN
HALE
HERE I AM!
HEY, LITTLE ONE! IS CORNELIA HOME?

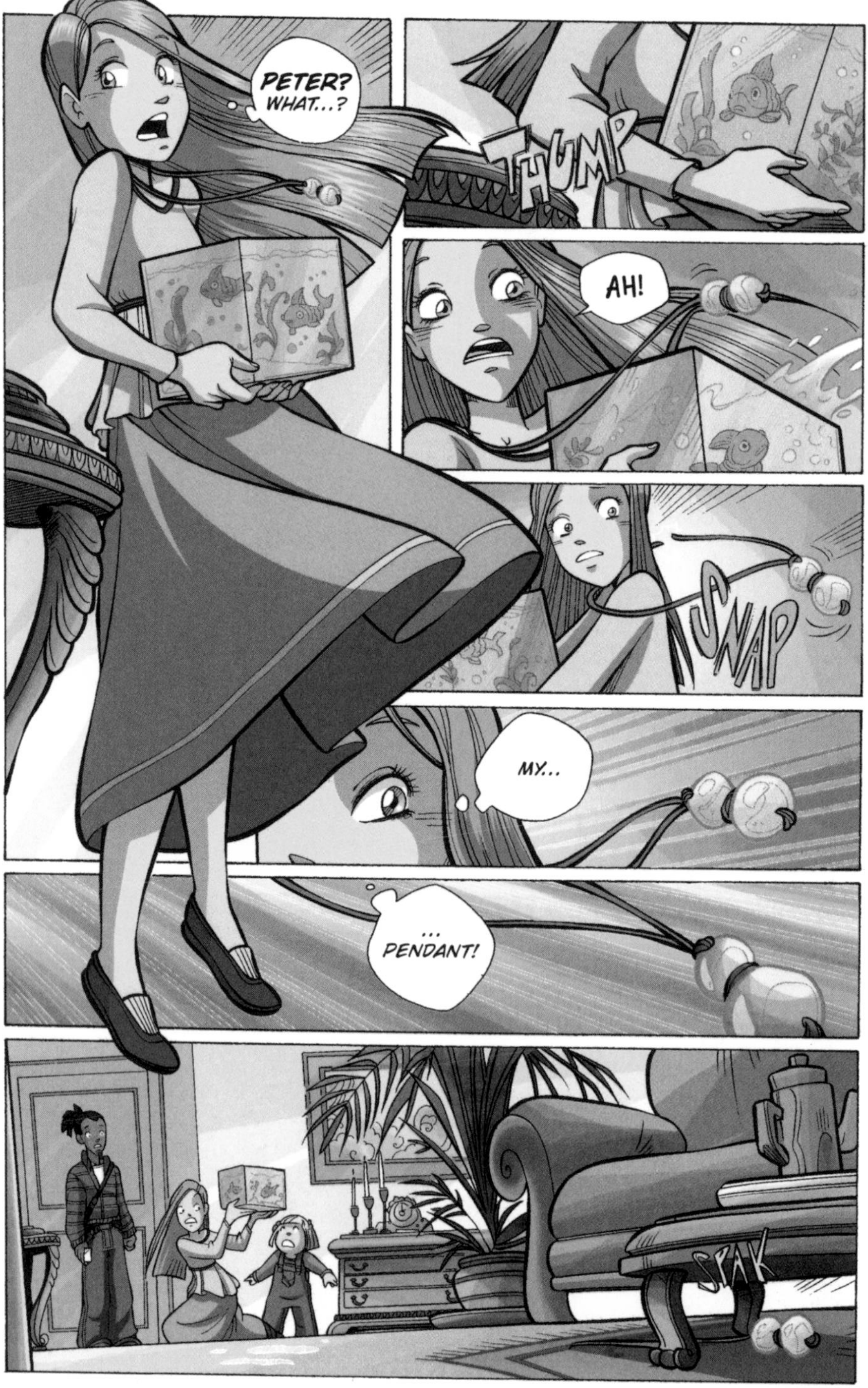
PETER? WHAT...?
THUMP
AH!
SNAP
MY...
... PENDANT!
SPAK

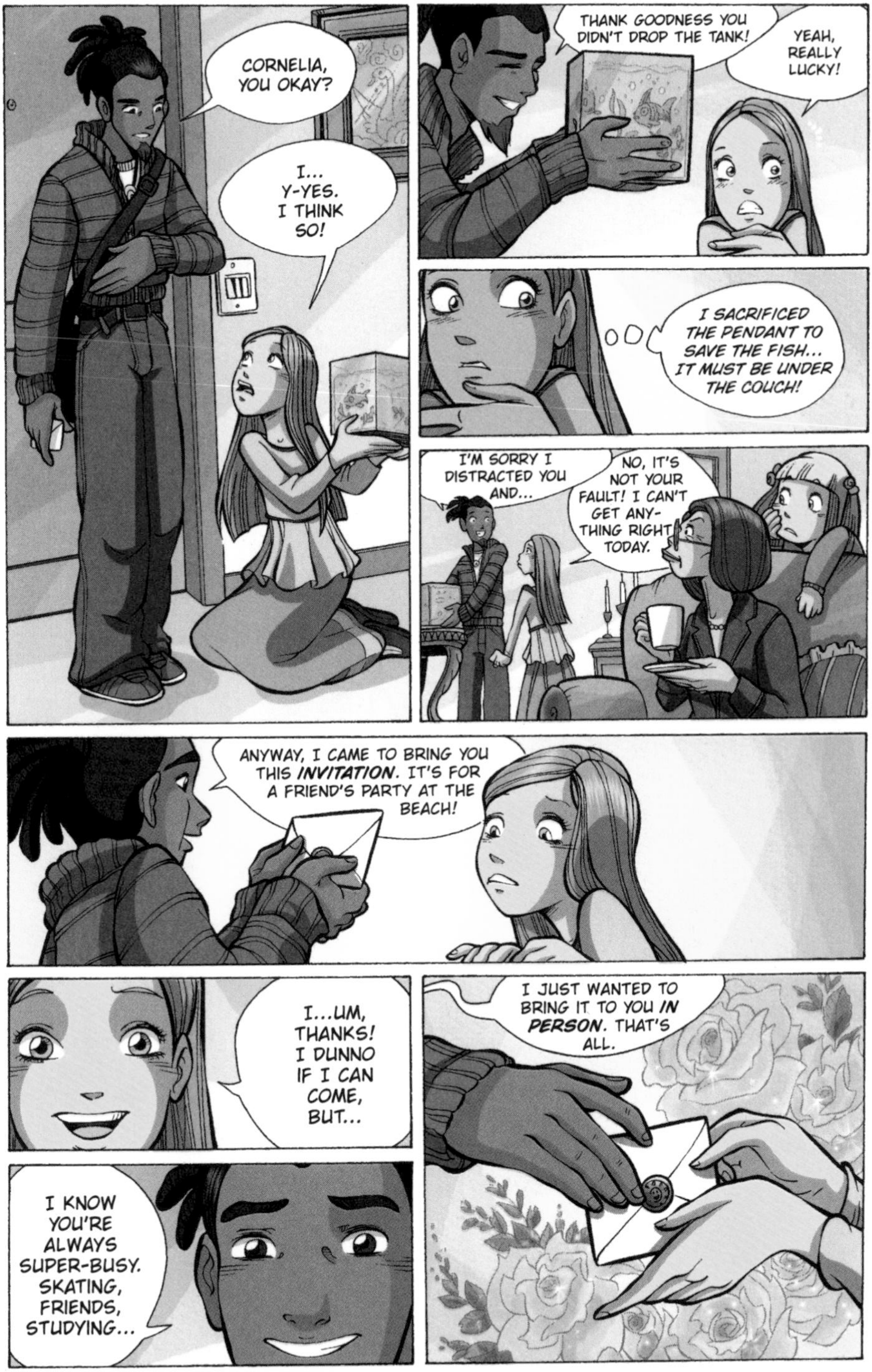
CORNELIA, YOU OKAY?
I... Y-YES. I THINK SO!
THANK GOODNESS YOU DIDN'T DROP THE TANK!
YEAH, REALLY LUCKY!
I SACRIFICED THE PENDANT TO SAVE THE FISH... IT MUST BE UNDER THE COUCH!
I'M SORRY I DISTRACTED YOU AND...
NO, IT'S NOT YOUR FAULT! I CAN'T GET ANYTHING RIGHT TODAY.
ANYWAY, I CAME TO BRING YOU THIS *INVITATION*. IT'S FOR A FRIEND'S PARTY AT THE BEACH!
I...UM, THANKS! I DUNNO IF I CAN COME, BUT...
I KNOW YOU'RE ALWAYS SUPER-BUSY. SKATING, FRIENDS, STUDYING...
I JUST WANTED TO BRING IT TO YOU *IN PERSON*. THAT'S ALL.

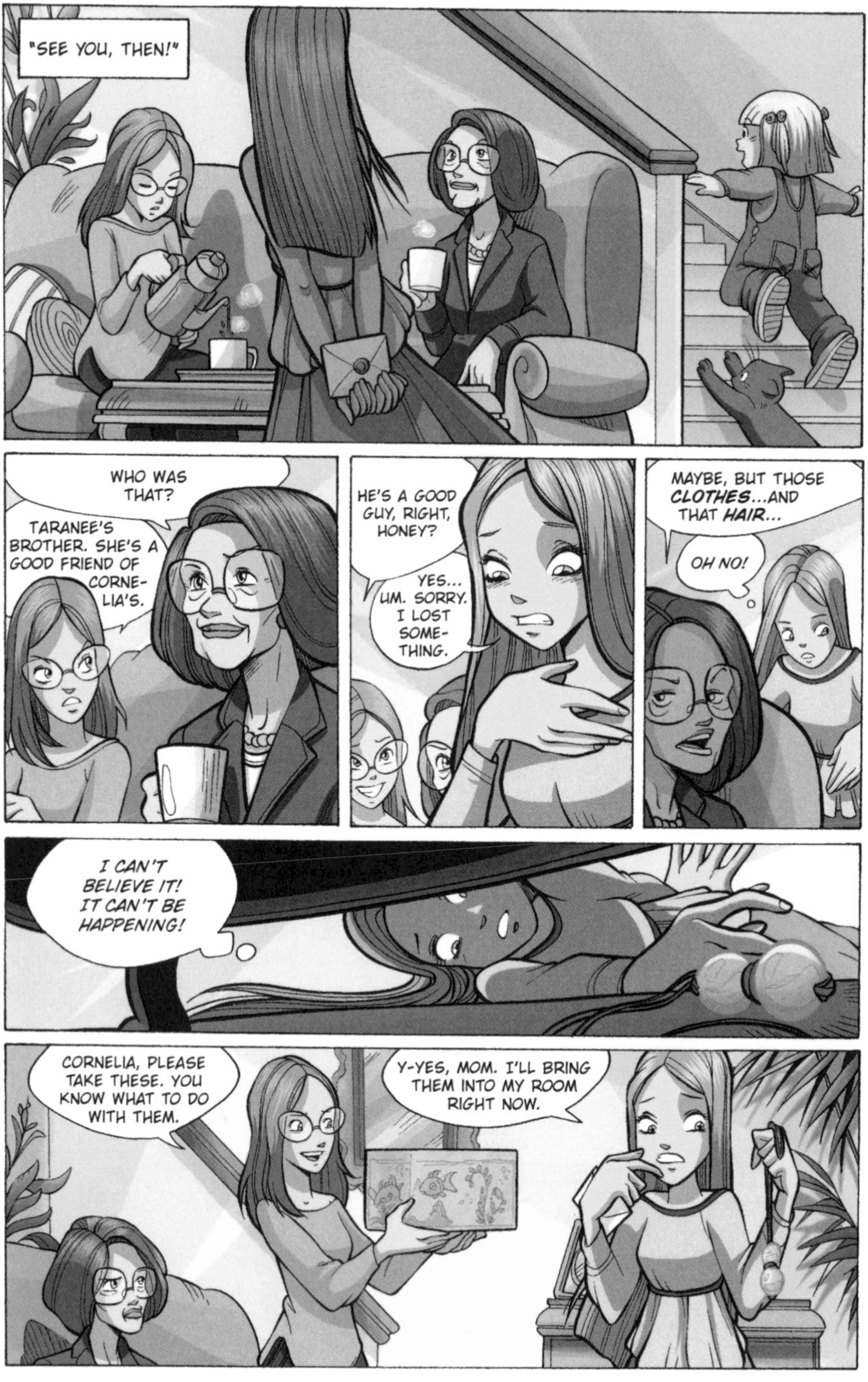
"SEE YOU, THEN!"
WHO WAS THAT?
TARANEE'S BROTHER. SHE'S A GOOD FRIEND OF CORNELIA'S.
HE'S A GOOD GUY, RIGHT, HONEY?
YES... UM. SORRY. I LOST SOMETHING.
MAYBE, BUT THOSE *CLOTHES*...AND THAT *HAIR*...
OH NO!
I CAN'T BELIEVE IT! IT CAN'T BE HAPPENING!
CORNELIA, PLEASE TAKE THESE. YOU KNOW WHAT TO DO WITH THEM.
Y-YES, MOM. I'LL BRING THEM INTO MY ROOM RIGHT NOW.

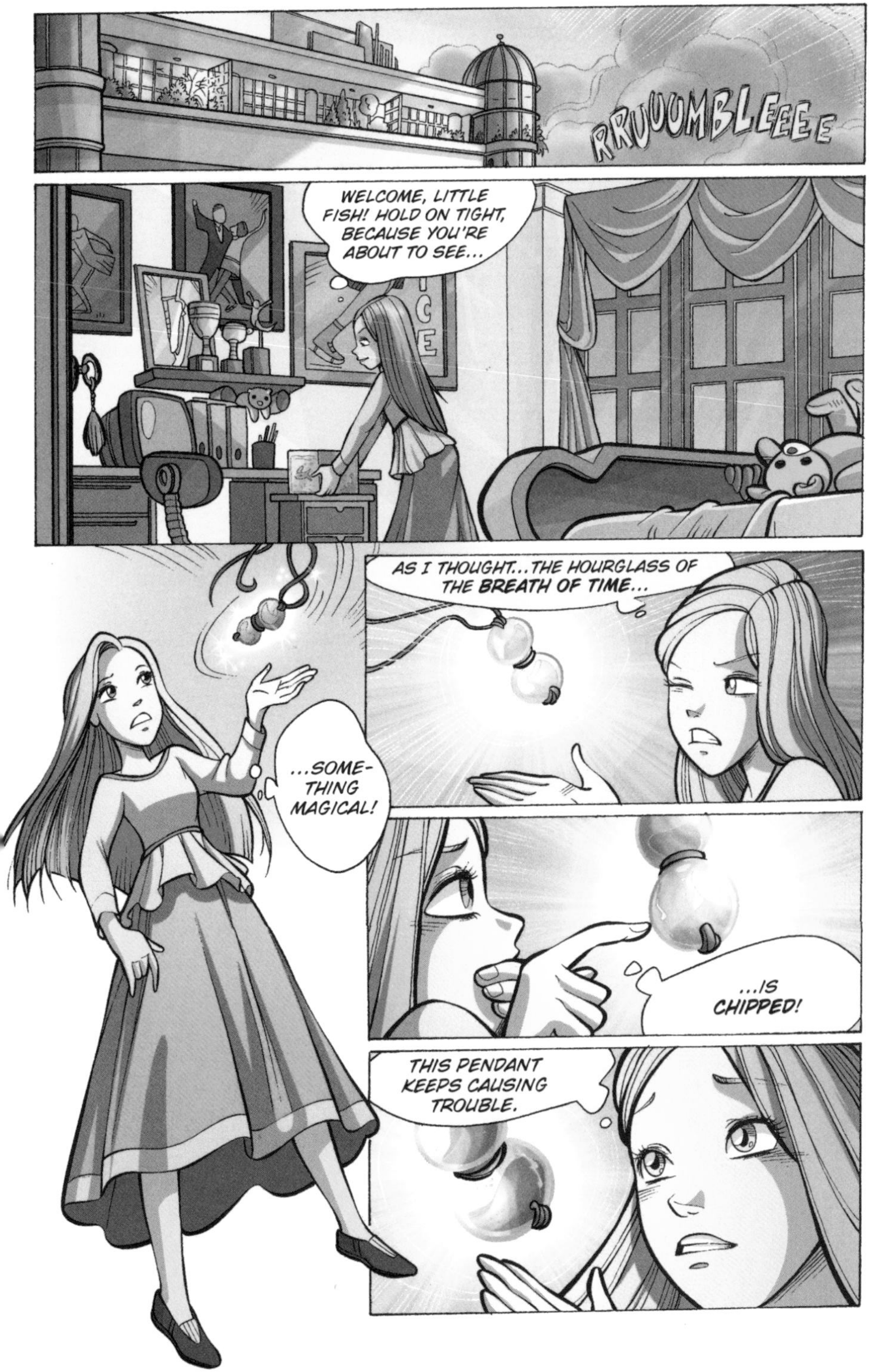
RRUUUMBLEEEE
WELCOME, LITTLE FISH! HOLD ON TIGHT, BECAUSE YOU'RE ABOUT TO SEE...
...SOME-THING MAGICAL!
AS I THOUGHT...THE HOURGLASS OF THE **BREATH OF TIME**...
...IS **CHIPPED!**
THIS PENDANT KEEPS CAUSING TROUBLE.

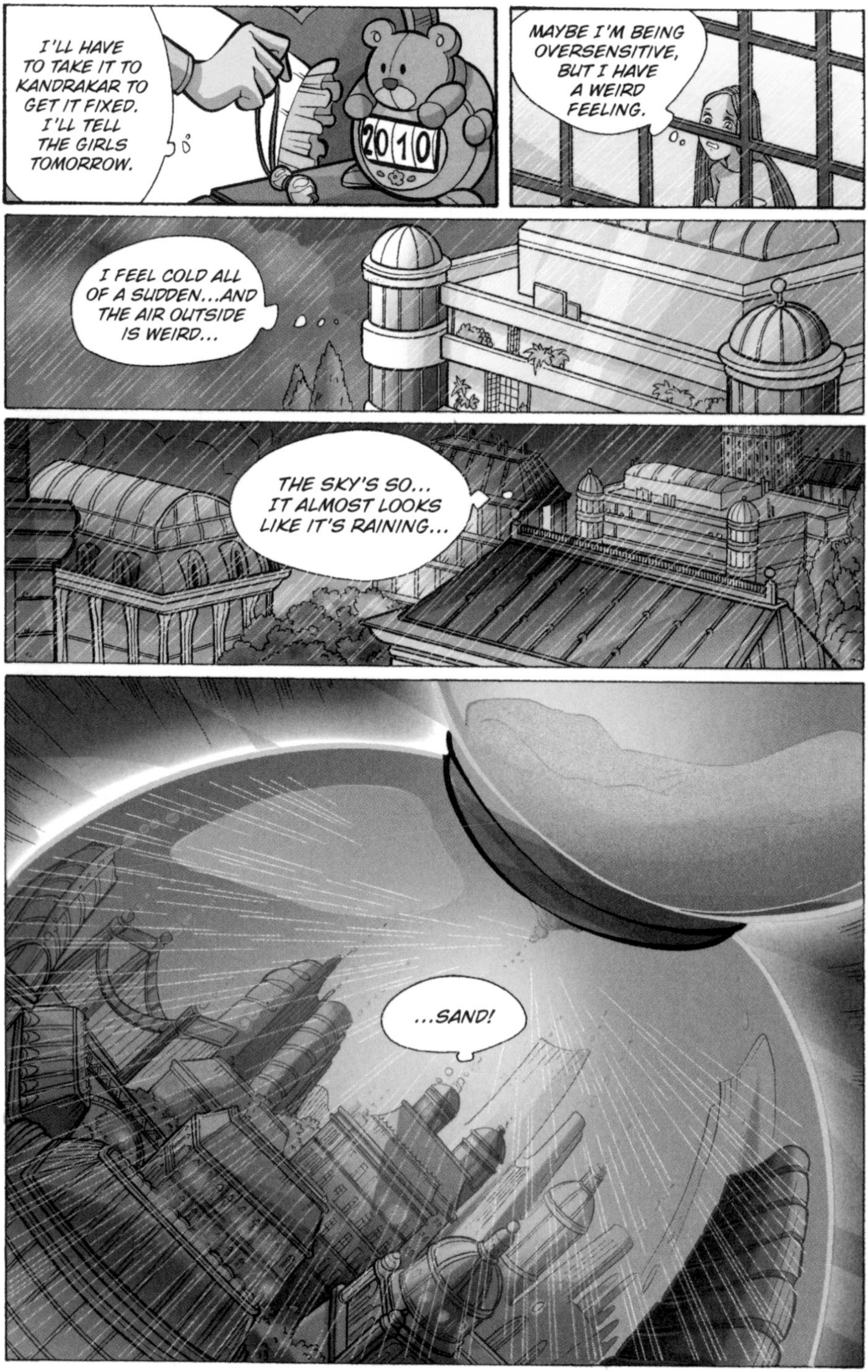
I'LL HAVE TO TAKE IT TO KANDRAKAR TO GET IT FIXED. I'LL TELL THE GIRLS TOMORROW.
2010
MAYBE I'M BEING OVERSENSITIVE, BUT I HAVE A WEIRD FEELING.
I FEEL COLD ALL OF A SUDDEN...AND THE AIR OUTSIDE IS WEIRD...
THE SKY'S SO... IT ALMOST LOOKS LIKE IT'S RAINING...
...SAND!

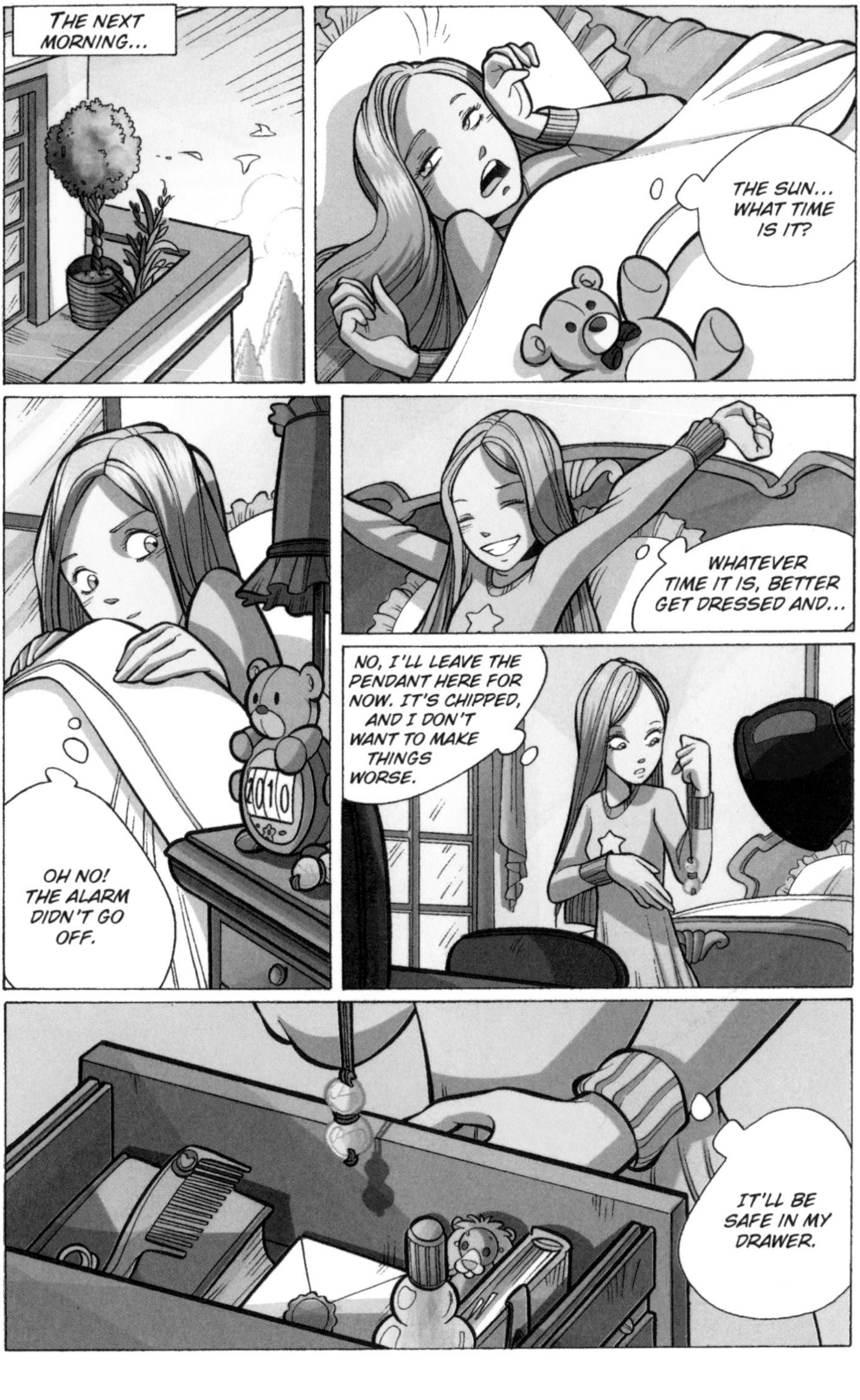
THE NEXT MORNING...
THE SUN... WHAT TIME IS IT?
OH NO! THE ALARM DIDN'T GO OFF.
WHATEVER TIME IT IS, BETTER GET DRESSED AND...
NO, I'LL LEAVE THE PENDANT HERE FOR NOW. IT'S CHIPPED, AND I DON'T WANT TO MAKE THINGS WORSE.
IT'LL BE SAFE IN MY DRAWER.

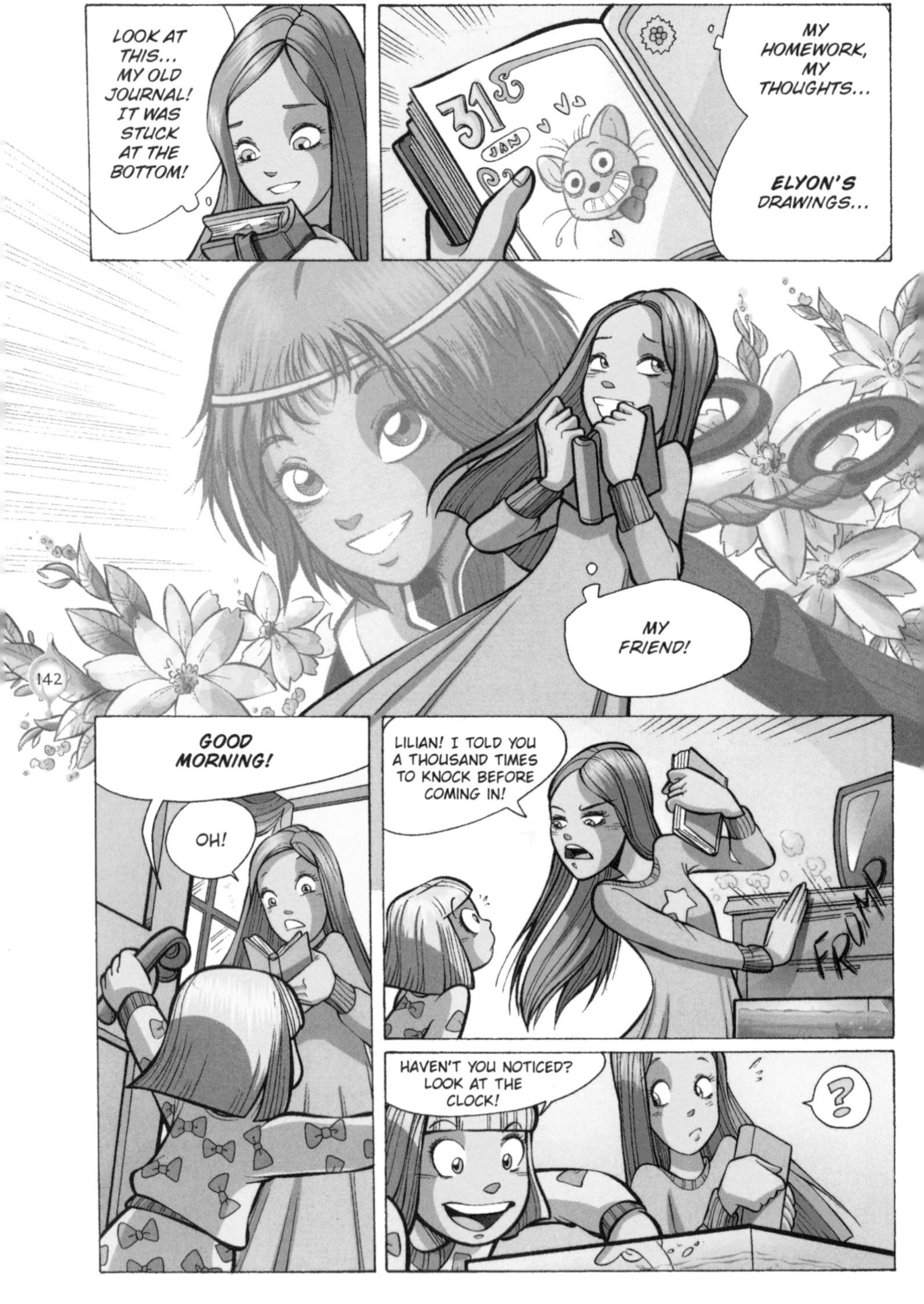

LOOK AT THIS... MY OLD JOURNAL! IT WAS STUCK AT THE BOTTOM!
MY HOMEWORK, MY THOUGHTS...
ELYON'S DRAWINGS...
31 JAN
MY FRIEND!
GOOD MORNING!
OH!
LILIAN! I TOLD YOU A THOUSAND TIMES TO KNOCK BEFORE COMING IN!
FRUMP
HAVEN'T YOU NOTICED? LOOK AT THE CLOCK!
?

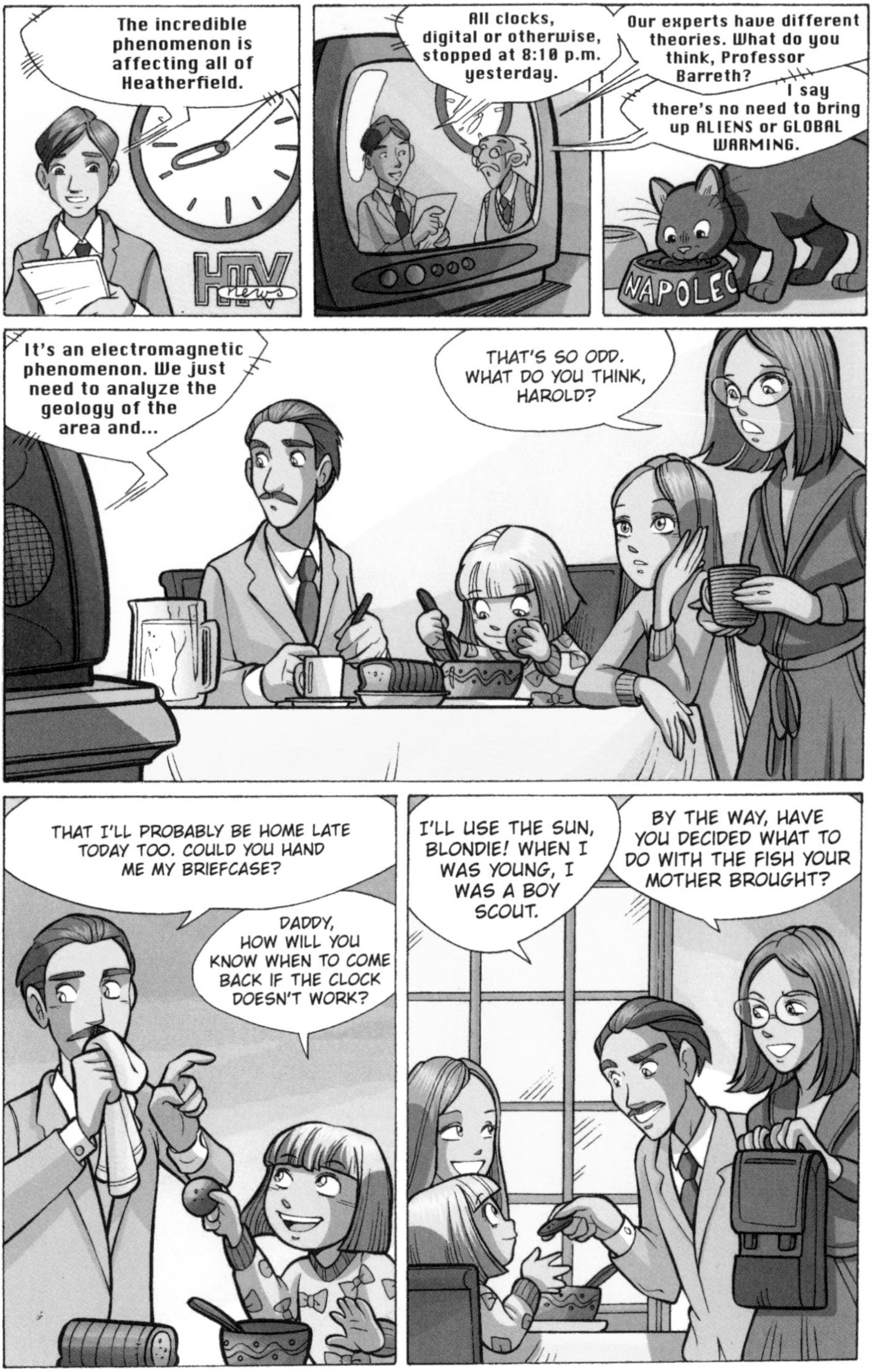
The incredible phenomenon is affecting all of Heatherfield.
HTV news
All clocks, digital or otherwise, stopped at 8:10 p.m. yesterday.
Our experts have different theories. What do you think, Professor Barreth?
I say there's no need to bring up ALIENS or GLOBAL WARMING.
NAPOLEO
It's an electromagnetic phenomenon. We just need to analyze the geology of the area and...
THAT'S SO ODD. WHAT DO YOU THINK, HAROLD?
THAT I'LL PROBABLY BE HOME LATE TODAY TOO. COULD YOU HAND ME MY BRIEFCASE?
DADDY, HOW WILL YOU KNOW WHEN TO COME BACK IF THE CLOCK DOESN'T WORK?
I'LL USE THE SUN, BLONDIE! WHEN I WAS YOUNG, I WAS A BOY SCOUT.
BY THE WAY, HAVE YOU DECIDED WHAT TO DO WITH THE FISH YOUR MOTHER BROUGHT?

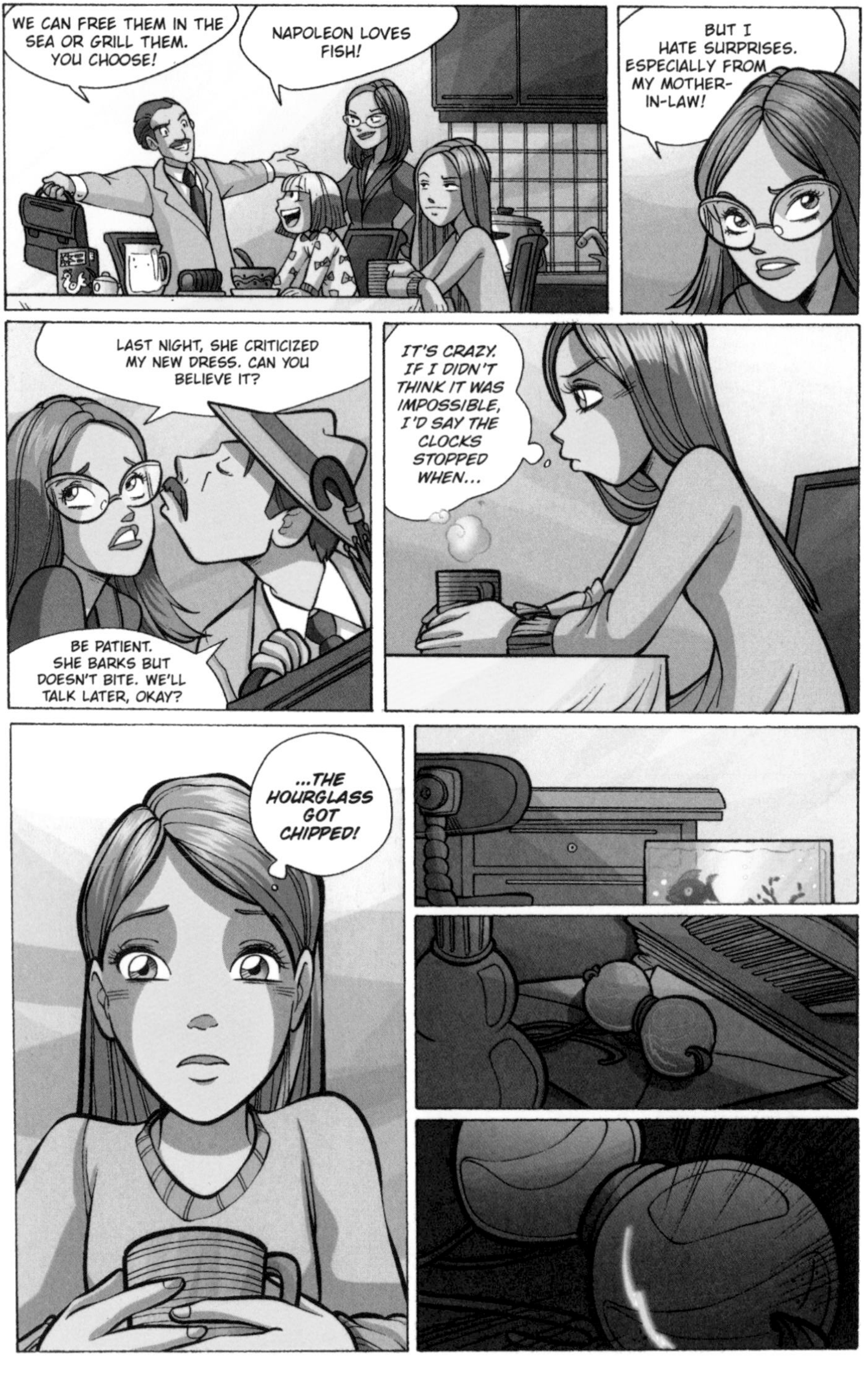
WE CAN FREE THEM IN THE SEA OR GRILL THEM. YOU CHOOSE!
NAPOLEON LOVES FISH!
BUT I HATE SURPRISES. ESPECIALLY FROM MY MOTHER-IN-LAW!
LAST NIGHT, SHE CRITICIZED MY NEW DRESS. CAN YOU BELIEVE IT?
BE PATIENT. SHE BARKS BUT DOESN'T BITE. WE'LL TALK LATER, OKAY?
IT'S CRAZY. IF I DIDN'T THINK IT WAS IMPOSSIBLE, I'D SAY THE CLOCKS STOPPED WHEN...
...THE HOURGLASS GOT CHIPPED!

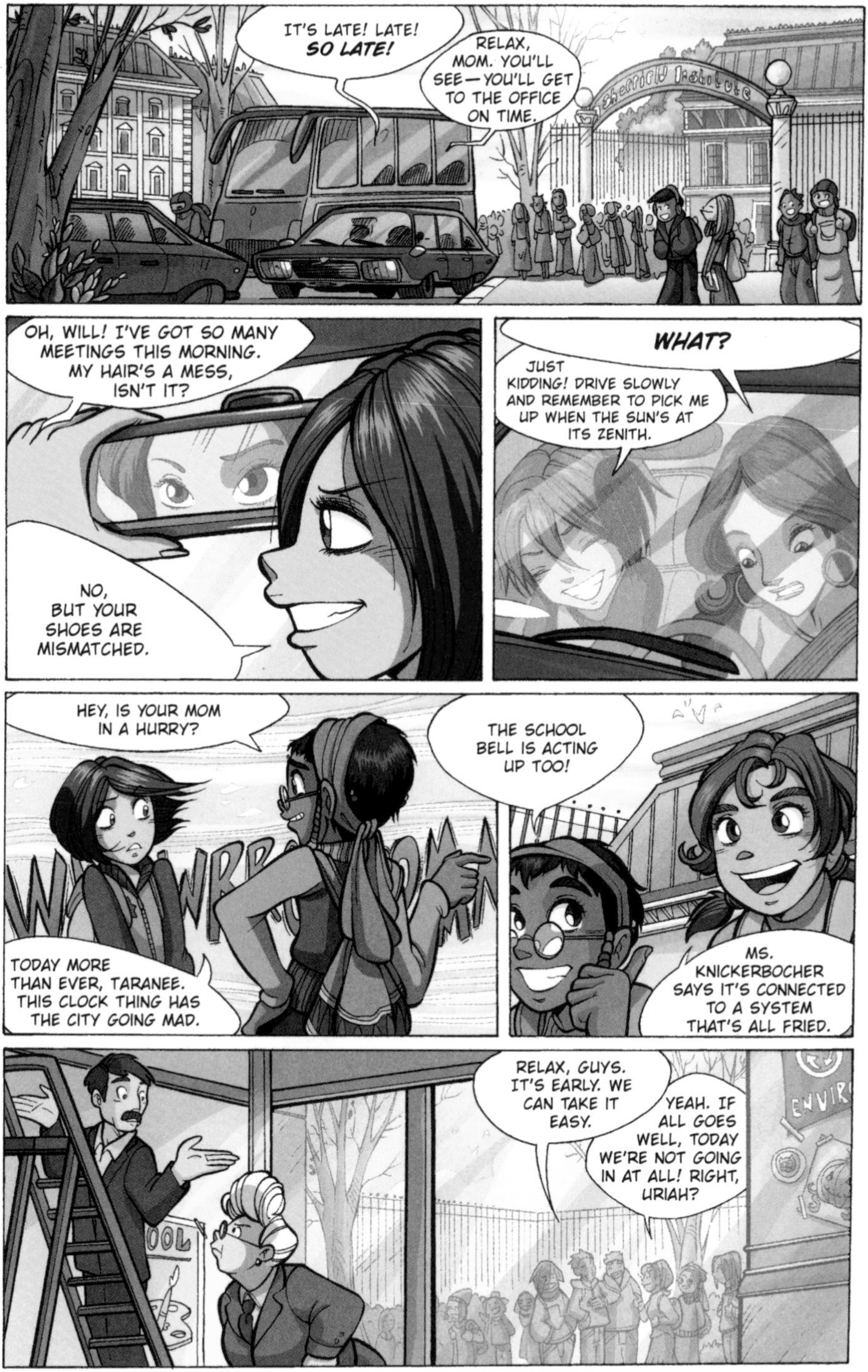
IT'S LATE! LATE! **SO LATE!**
RELAX, MOM. YOU'LL SEE—YOU'LL GET TO THE OFFICE ON TIME.
OH, WILL! I'VE GOT SO MANY MEETINGS THIS MORNING. MY HAIR'S A MESS, ISN'T IT?
NO, BUT YOUR SHOES ARE MISMATCHED.
WHAT?
JUST KIDDING! DRIVE SLOWLY AND REMEMBER TO PICK ME UP WHEN THE SUN'S AT ITS ZENITH.
HEY, IS YOUR MOM IN A HURRY?
TODAY MORE THAN EVER, TARANEE. THIS CLOCK THING HAS THE CITY GOING MAD.
THE SCHOOL BELL IS ACTING UP TOO!
MS. KNICKERBOCHER SAYS IT'S CONNECTED TO A SYSTEM THAT'S ALL FRIED.
RELAX, GUYS. IT'S EARLY. WE CAN TAKE IT EASY.
YEAH. IF ALL GOES WELL, TODAY WE'RE NOT GOING IN AT ALL! RIGHT, URIAH?

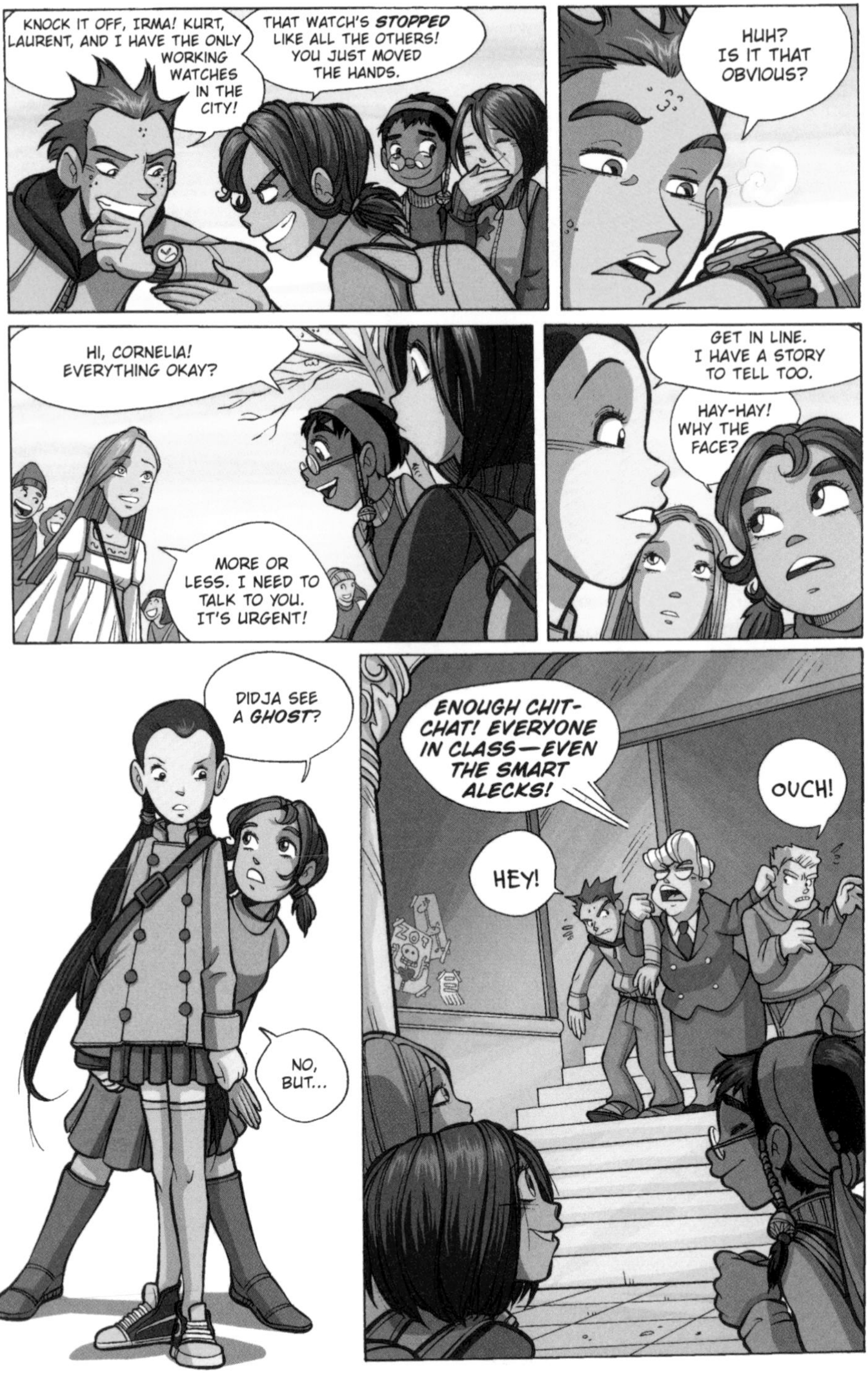
KNOCK IT OFF, IRMA! KURT, LAURENT, AND I HAVE THE ONLY WORKING WATCHES IN THE CITY!
THAT WATCH'S *STOPPED* LIKE ALL THE OTHERS! YOU JUST MOVED THE HANDS.
HUH? IS IT THAT OBVIOUS?
HI, CORNELIA! EVERYTHING OKAY?
MORE OR LESS. I NEED TO TALK TO YOU. IT'S URGENT!
GET IN LINE. I HAVE A STORY TO TELL TOO.
HAY-HAY! WHY THE FACE?
DIDJA SEE A *GHOST*?
NO, BUT...
ENOUGH CHIT-CHAT! EVERYONE IN CLASS—EVEN THE SMART ALECKS!
HEY!
OUCH!

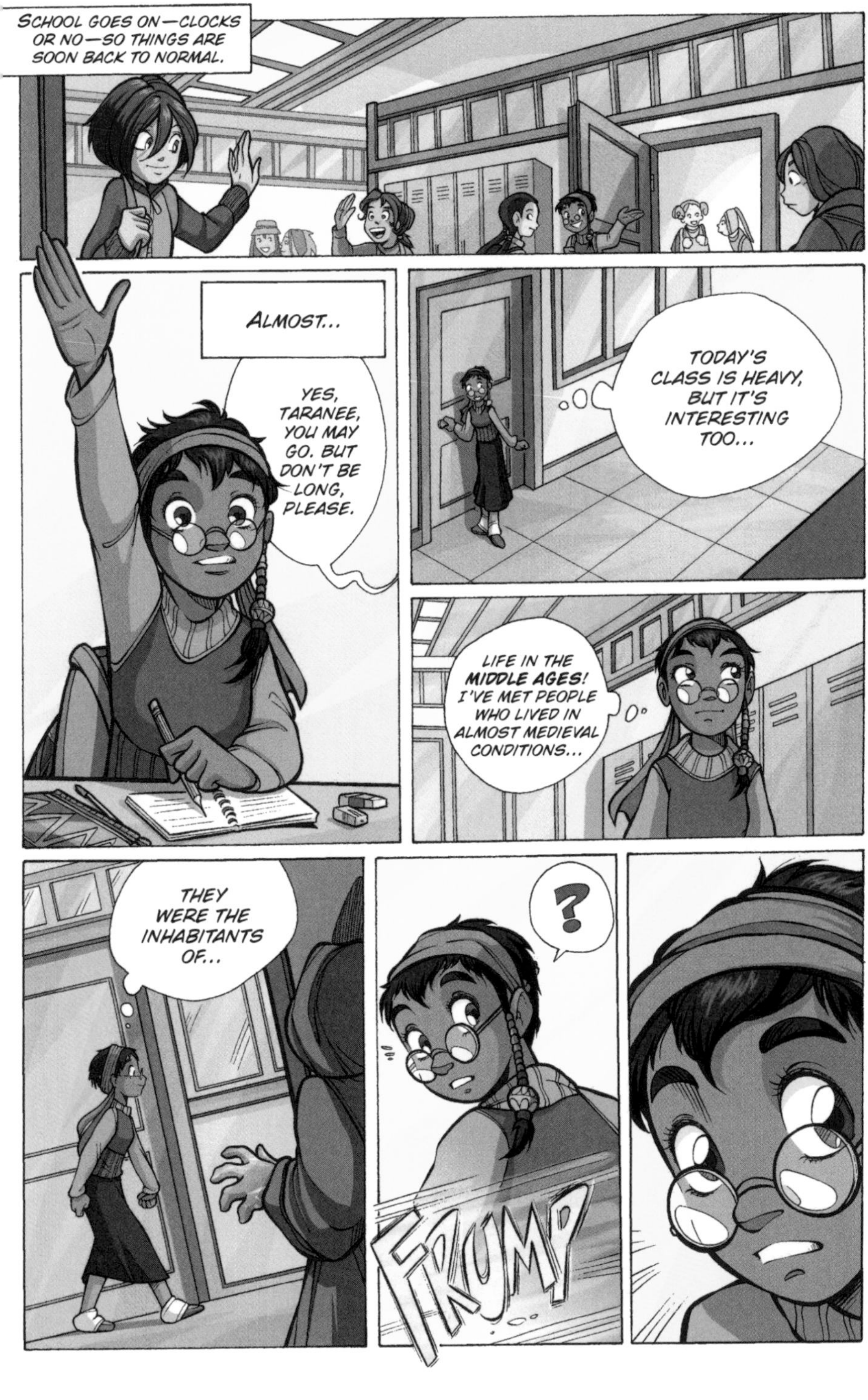
SCHOOL GOES ON—CLOCKS OR NO—SO THINGS ARE SOON BACK TO NORMAL.
ALMOST...
YES, TARANEE, YOU MAY GO. BUT DON'T BE LONG, PLEASE.
TODAY'S CLASS IS HEAVY, BUT IT'S INTERESTING TOO...
LIFE IN THE MIDDLE AGES! I'VE MET PEOPLE WHO LIVED IN ALMOST MEDIEVAL CONDITIONS...
THEY WERE THE INHABITANTS OF...
?
FRUMP

HEY, YOU! WAIT!

THAT SHADOW! AM I HALLUCINATING? I WAS JUST THINKING ABOUT MERIDIAN, AND NOW...

I'M NOT GONNA HURT YOU! I...

D-DON'T...

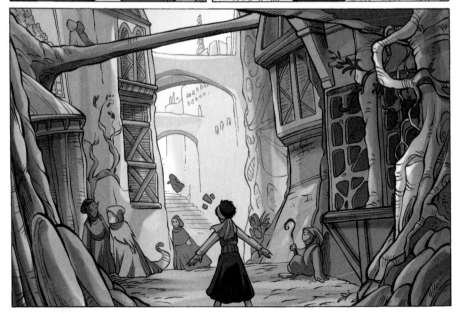

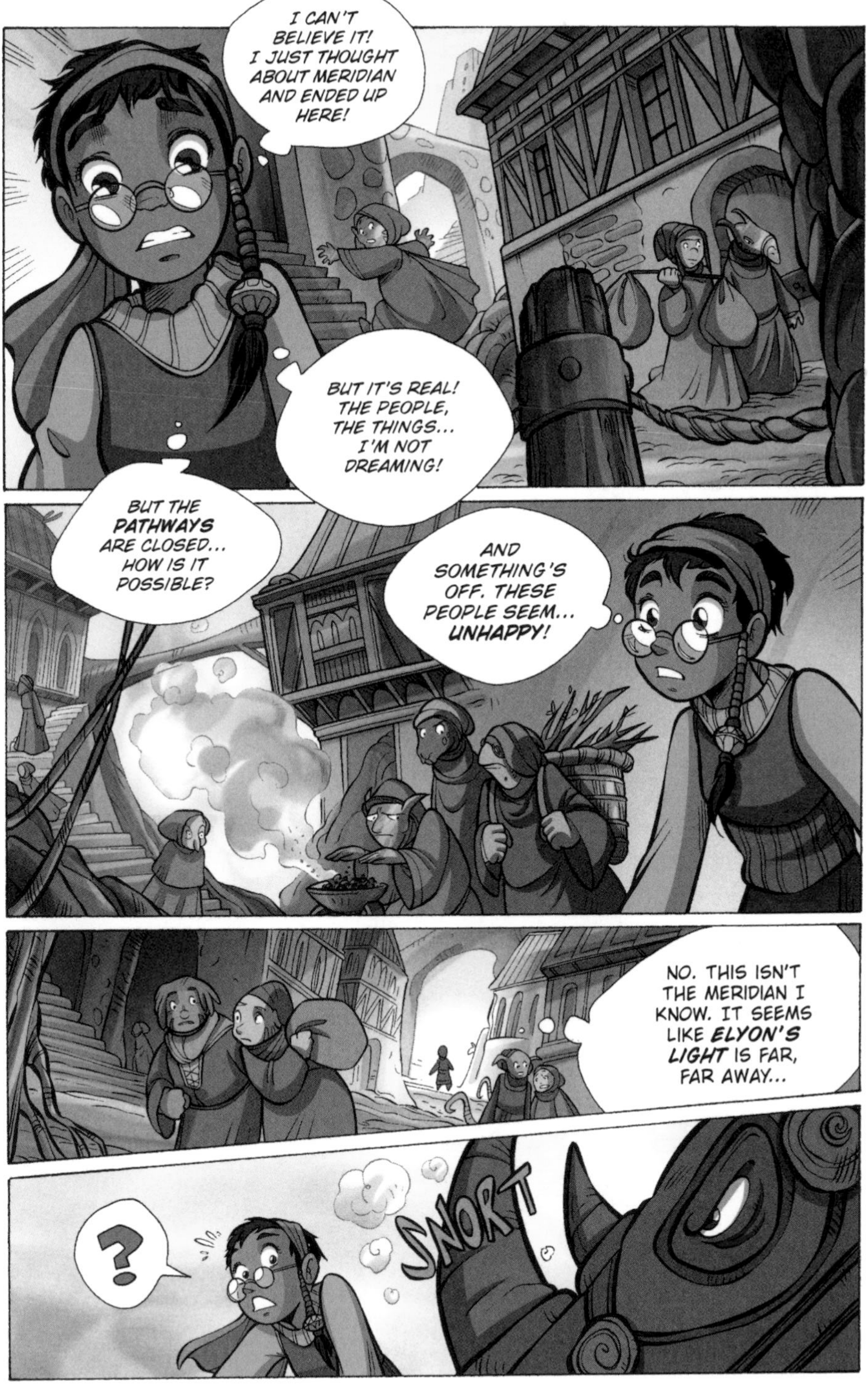
I CAN'T BELIEVE IT! I JUST THOUGHT ABOUT MERIDIAN AND ENDED UP HERE!
BUT IT'S REAL! THE PEOPLE, THE THINGS... I'M NOT DREAMING!
BUT THE **PATHWAYS** ARE CLOSED... HOW IS IT POSSIBLE?
AND SOMETHING'S OFF. THESE PEOPLE SEEM... **UNHAPPY**!
NO. THIS ISN'T THE MERIDIAN I KNOW. IT SEEMS LIKE **ELYON'S LIGHT** IS FAR, FAR AWAY...
?
SNORT

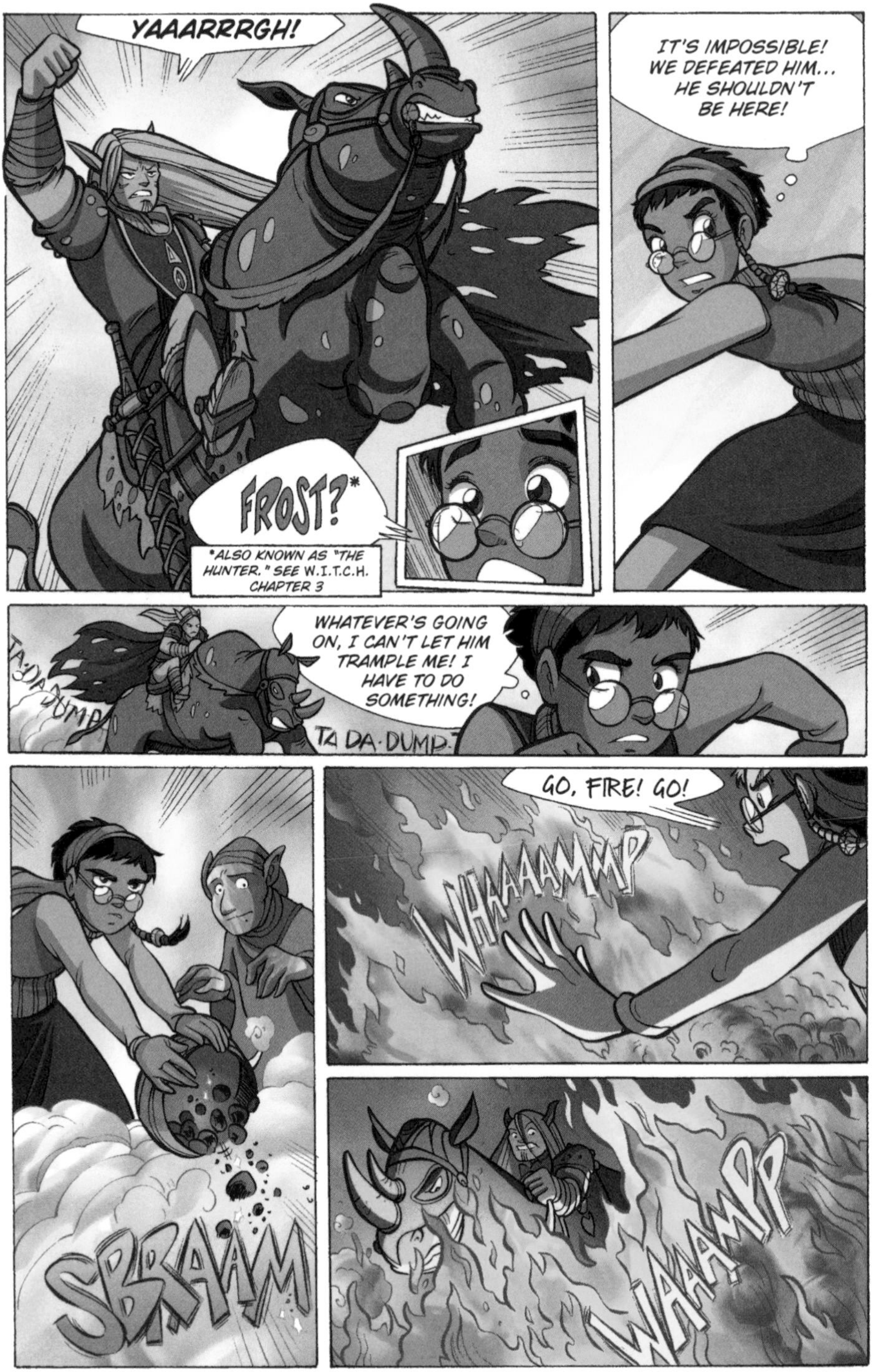
YAAARRRGH!
FROST?*
*ALSO KNOWN AS "THE HUNTER." SEE W.I.T.C.H. CHAPTER 3
IT'S IMPOSSIBLE! WE DEFEATED HIM... HE SHOULDN'T BE HERE!
TA-DA-DUMP
WHATEVER'S GOING ON, I CAN'T LET HIM TRAMPLE ME! I HAVE TO DO SOMETHING!
TA DA-DUMP
SBRAAM
GO, FIRE! GO!
WHAAAAMMP
WAAMPP

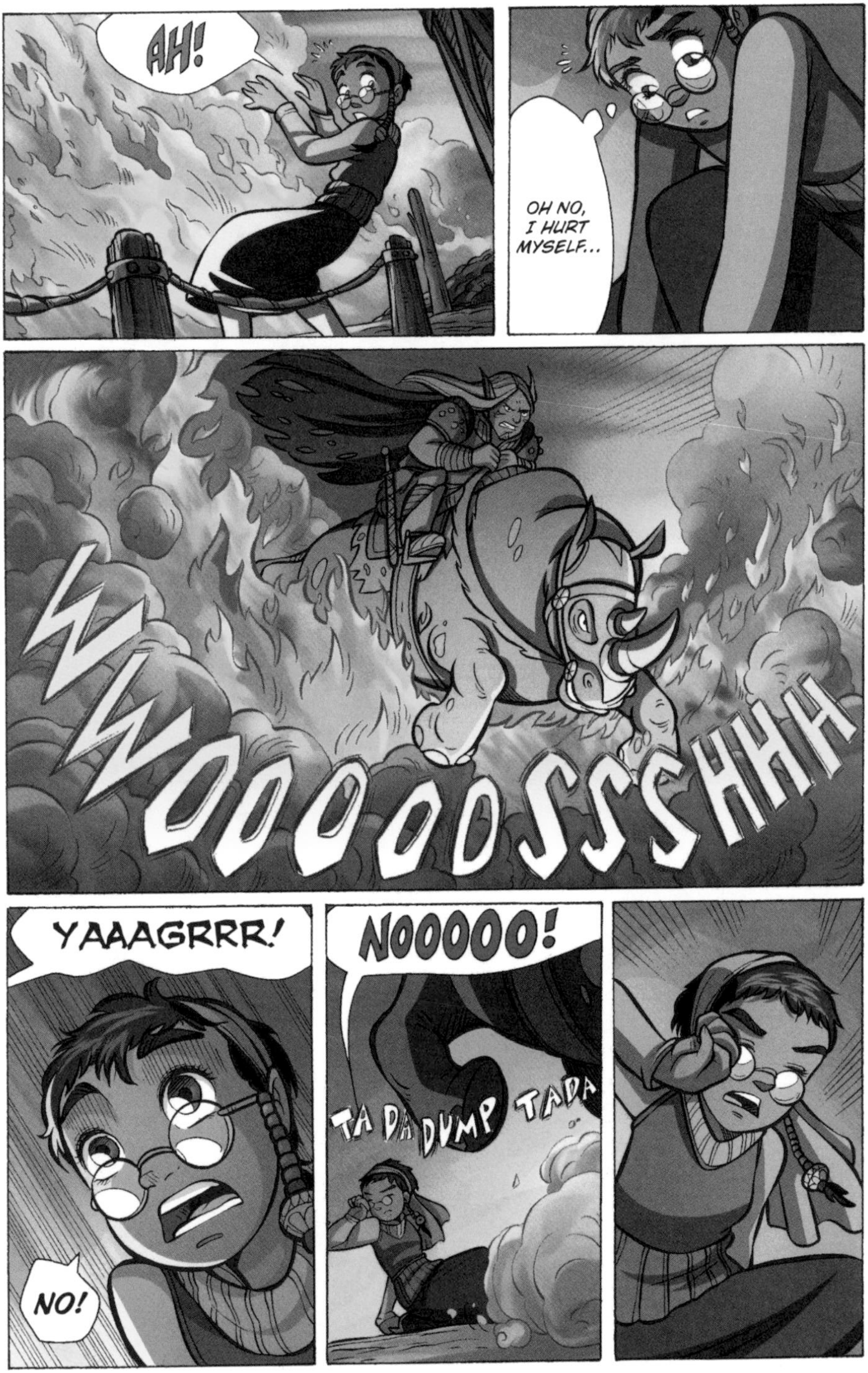

AH!
OH NO, I HURT MYSELF...
WWOOOOOSSSHHH
YAAAGRRR!
NO!
NOOOOO!
TA DA DUMP TADA

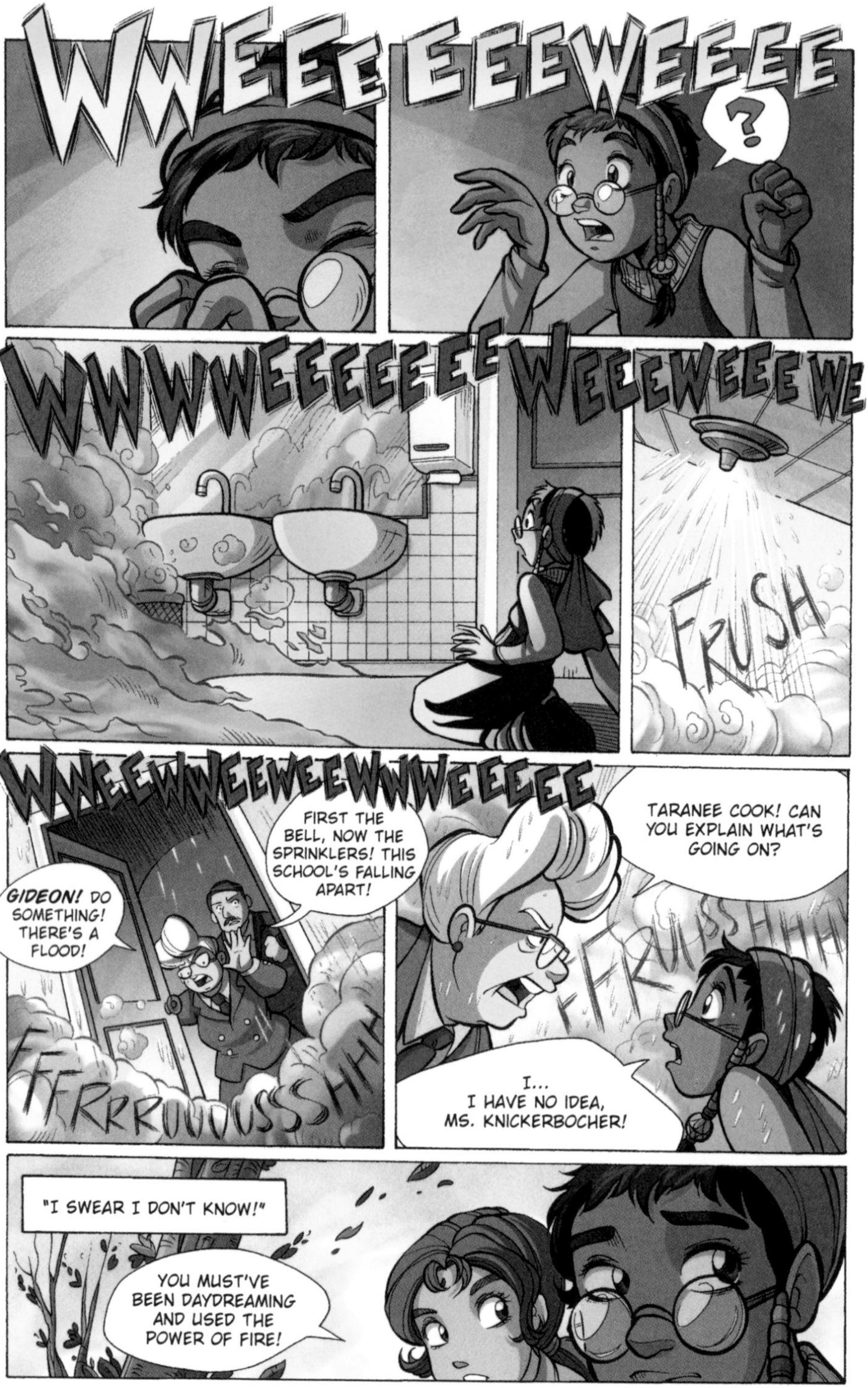
WWEEEEEEEWEEEE
?
WWWWEEEEEEEWEEEWEEEWE
FRUSH
WWEEWWEEWEEWWWEEEEE
GIDEON! DO SOMETHING! THERE'S A FLOOD!
FIRST THE BELL, NOW THE SPRINKLERS! THIS SCHOOL'S FALLING APART!
FFRRRUUUUSSSHH
TARANEE COOK! CAN YOU EXPLAIN WHAT'S GOING ON?
FFRRUUSSHHH
I... I HAVE NO IDEA, MS. KNICKERBOCHER!
"I SWEAR I DON'T KNOW!"
YOU MUST'VE BEEN DAYDREAMING AND USED THE POWER OF FIRE!

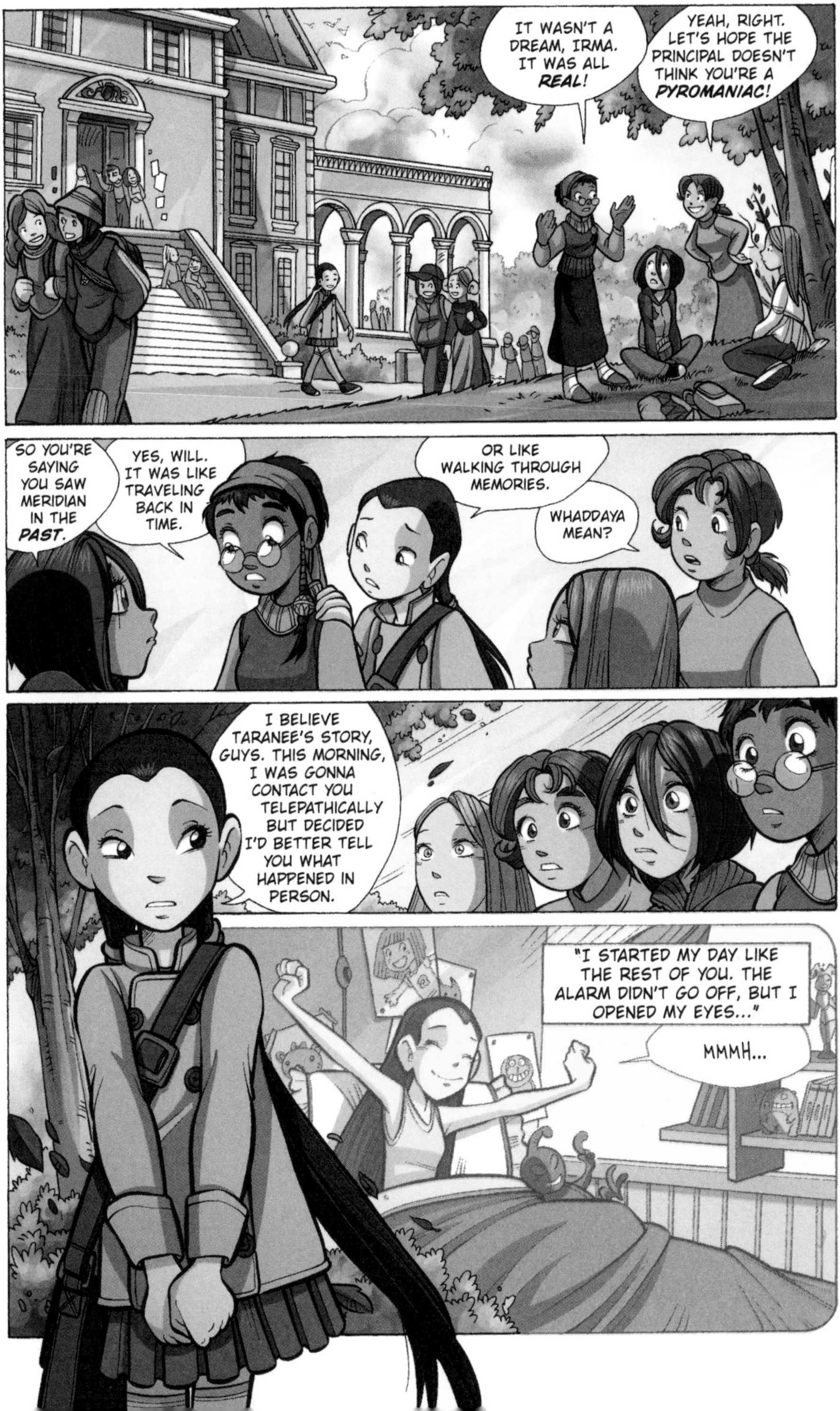
IT WASN'T A DREAM, IRMA. IT WAS ALL REAL!
YEAH, RIGHT. LET'S HOPE THE PRINCIPAL DOESN'T THINK YOU'RE A PYROMANIAC!
SO YOU'RE SAYING YOU SAW MERIDIAN IN THE PAST.
YES, WILL. IT WAS LIKE TRAVELING BACK IN TIME.
OR LIKE WALKING THROUGH MEMORIES.
WHADDAYA MEAN?
I BELIEVE TARANEE'S STORY, GUYS. THIS MORNING, I WAS GONNA CONTACT YOU TELEPATHICALLY BUT DECIDED I'D BETTER TELL YOU WHAT HAPPENED IN PERSON.
"I STARTED MY DAY LIKE THE REST OF YOU. THE ALARM DIDN'T GO OFF, BUT I OPENED MY EYES..."
MMMH...

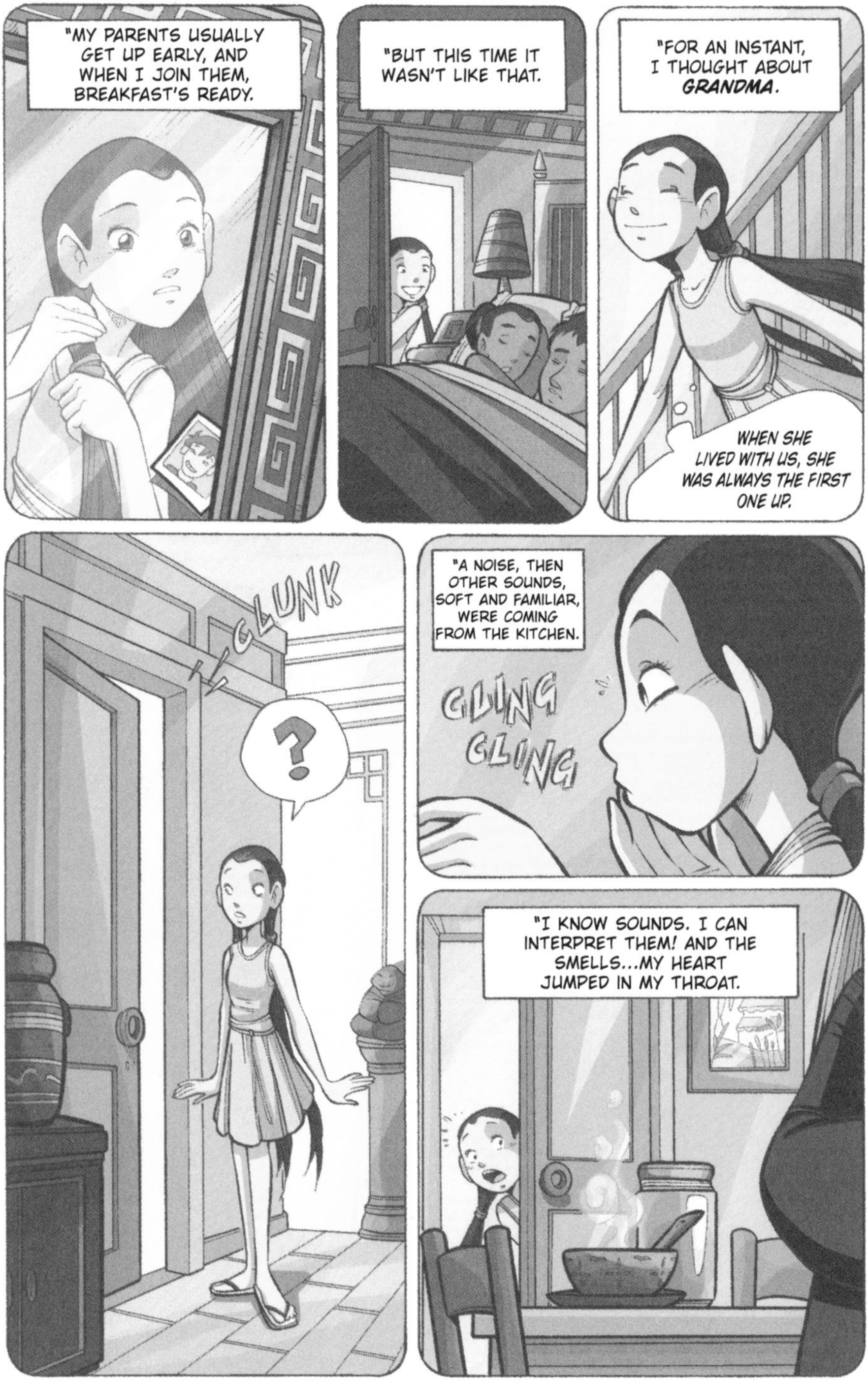
"MY PARENTS USUALLY GET UP EARLY, AND WHEN I JOIN THEM, BREAKFAST'S READY.
"BUT THIS TIME IT WASN'T LIKE THAT.
"FOR AN INSTANT, I THOUGHT ABOUT GRANDMA.
WHEN SHE LIVED WITH US, SHE WAS ALWAYS THE FIRST ONE UP.
CLUNK
?
"A NOISE, THEN OTHER SOUNDS, SOFT AND FAMILIAR, WERE COMING FROM THE KITCHEN.
CLING
CLING
"I KNOW SOUNDS. I CAN INTERPRET THEM! AND THE SMELLS...MY HEART JUMPED IN MY THROAT.

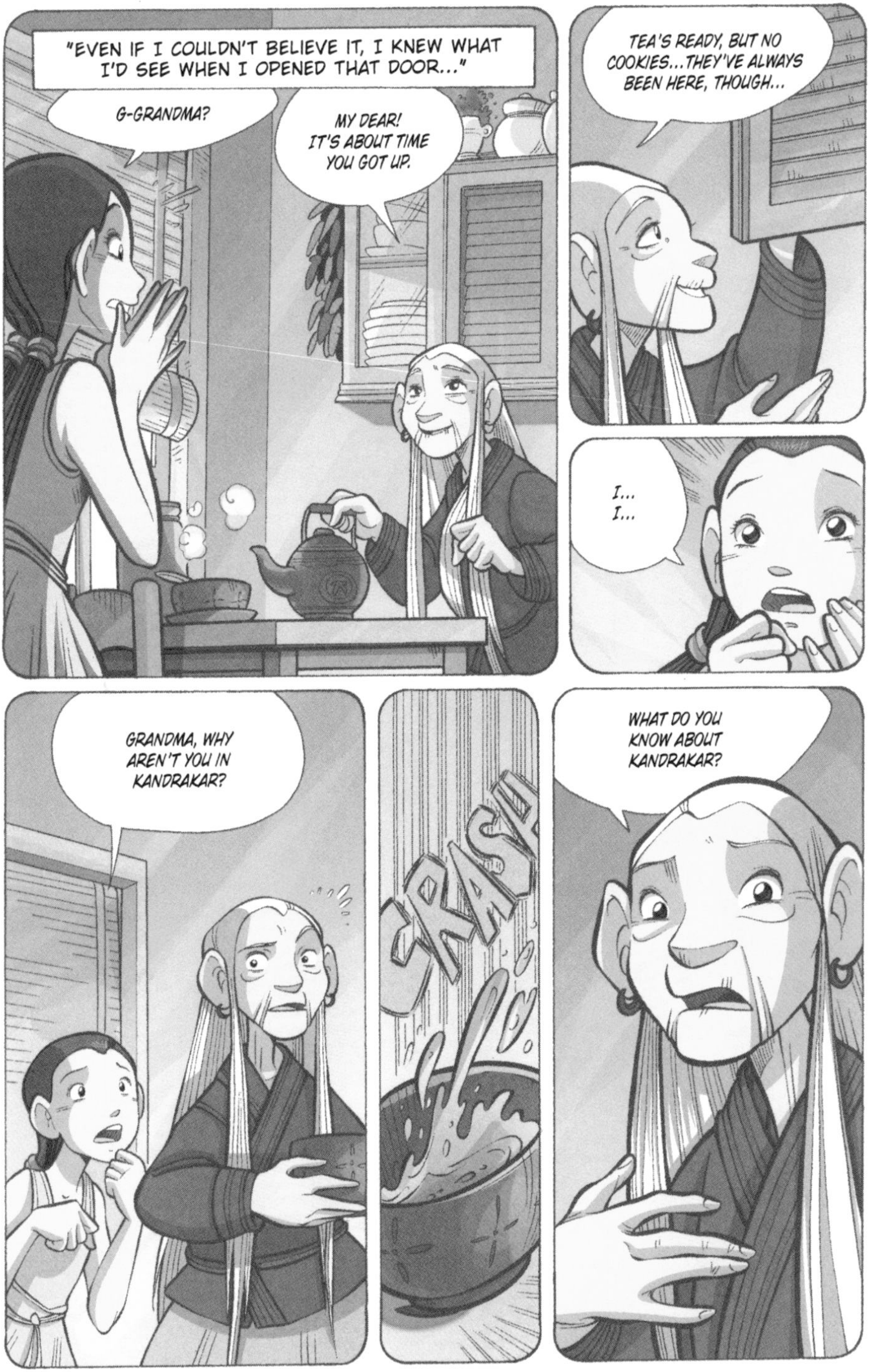
"EVEN IF I COULDN'T BELIEVE IT, I KNEW WHAT I'D SEE WHEN I OPENED THAT DOOR..."
G-GRANDMA?
MY DEAR! IT'S ABOUT TIME YOU GOT UP.
TEA'S READY, BUT NO COOKIES...THEY'VE ALWAYS BEEN HERE, THOUGH...
I... I...
GRANDMA, WHY AREN'T YOU IN KANDRAKAR?
CRASH
WHAT DO YOU KNOW ABOUT KANDRAKAR?

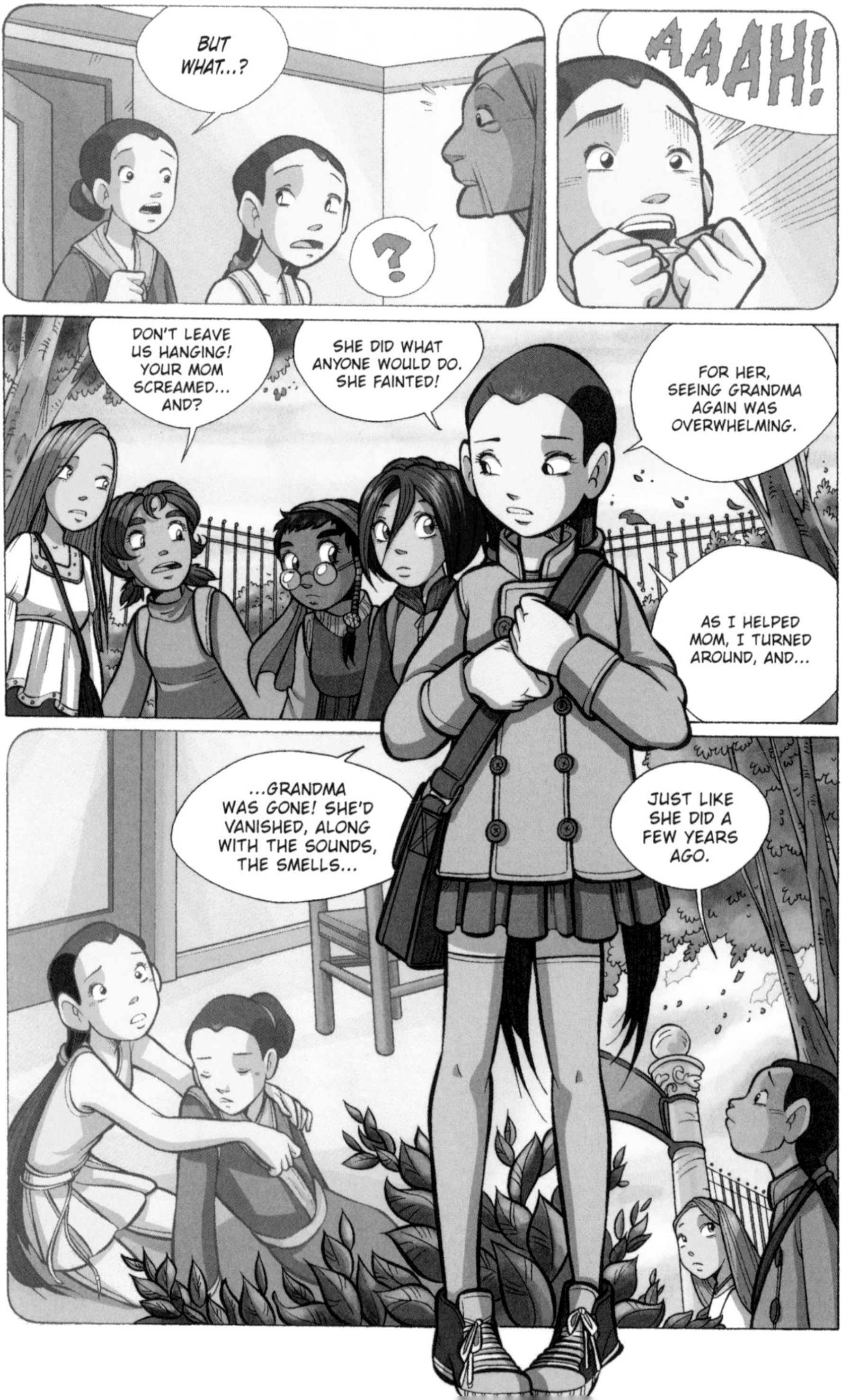
BUT WHAT...?
?
AAAH!
DON'T LEAVE US HANGING! YOUR MOM SCREAMED... AND?
SHE DID WHAT ANYONE WOULD DO. SHE FAINTED!
FOR HER, SEEING GRANDMA AGAIN WAS OVERWHELMING.
AS I HELPED MOM, I TURNED AROUND, AND...
...GRANDMA WAS GONE! SHE'D VANISHED, ALONG WITH THE SOUNDS, THE SMELLS...
JUST LIKE SHE DID A FEW YEARS AGO.

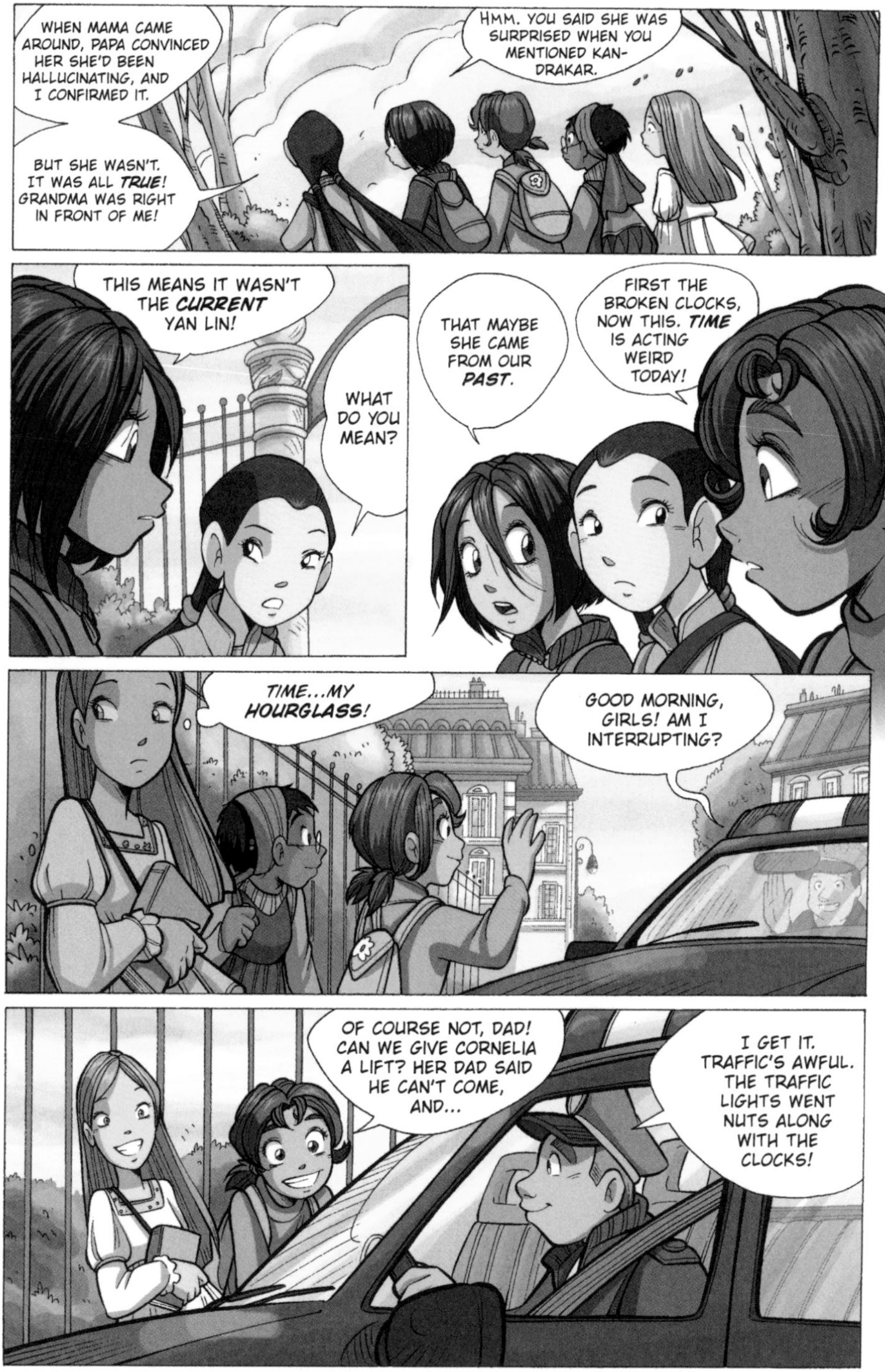
WHEN MAMA CAME AROUND, PAPA CONVINCED HER SHE'D BEEN HALLUCINATING, AND I CONFIRMED IT.
BUT SHE WASN'T. IT WAS ALL TRUE! GRANDMA WAS RIGHT IN FRONT OF ME!
HMM. YOU SAID SHE WAS SURPRISED WHEN YOU MENTIONED KAN-DRAKAR.
THIS MEANS IT WASN'T THE CURRENT YAN LIN!
WHAT DO YOU MEAN?
THAT MAYBE SHE CAME FROM OUR PAST.
FIRST THE BROKEN CLOCKS, NOW THIS. TIME IS ACTING WEIRD TODAY!
TIME...MY HOURGLASS!
GOOD MORNING, GIRLS! AM I INTERRUPTING?
OF COURSE NOT, DAD! CAN WE GIVE CORNELIA A LIFT? HER DAD SAID HE CAN'T COME, AND...
I GET IT. TRAFFIC'S AWFUL. THE TRAFFIC LIGHTS WENT NUTS ALONG WITH THE CLOCKS!

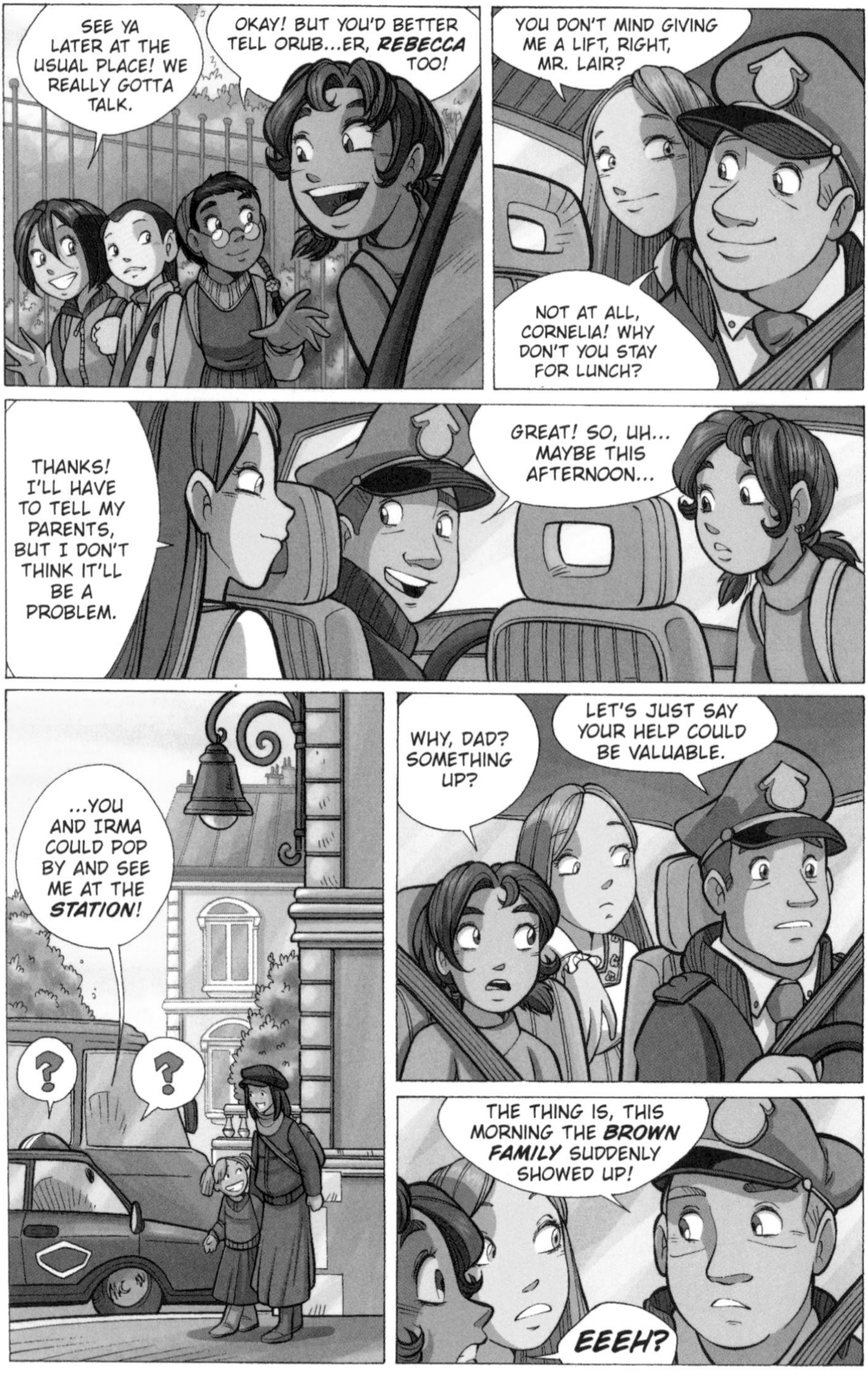
SEE YA LATER AT THE USUAL PLACE! WE REALLY GOTTA TALK.
OKAY! BUT YOU'D BETTER TELL ORUB...ER, REBECCA TOO!
YOU DON'T MIND GIVING ME A LIFT, RIGHT, MR. LAIR?
NOT AT ALL, CORNELIA! WHY DON'T YOU STAY FOR LUNCH?
THANKS! I'LL HAVE TO TELL MY PARENTS, BUT I DON'T THINK IT'LL BE A PROBLEM.
GREAT! SO, UH... MAYBE THIS AFTERNOON...
...YOU AND IRMA COULD POP BY AND SEE ME AT THE STATION!
?
?
WHY, DAD? SOMETHING UP?
LET'S JUST SAY YOUR HELP COULD BE VALUABLE.
THE THING IS, THIS MORNING THE BROWN FAMILY SUDDENLY SHOWED UP!
EEEH?

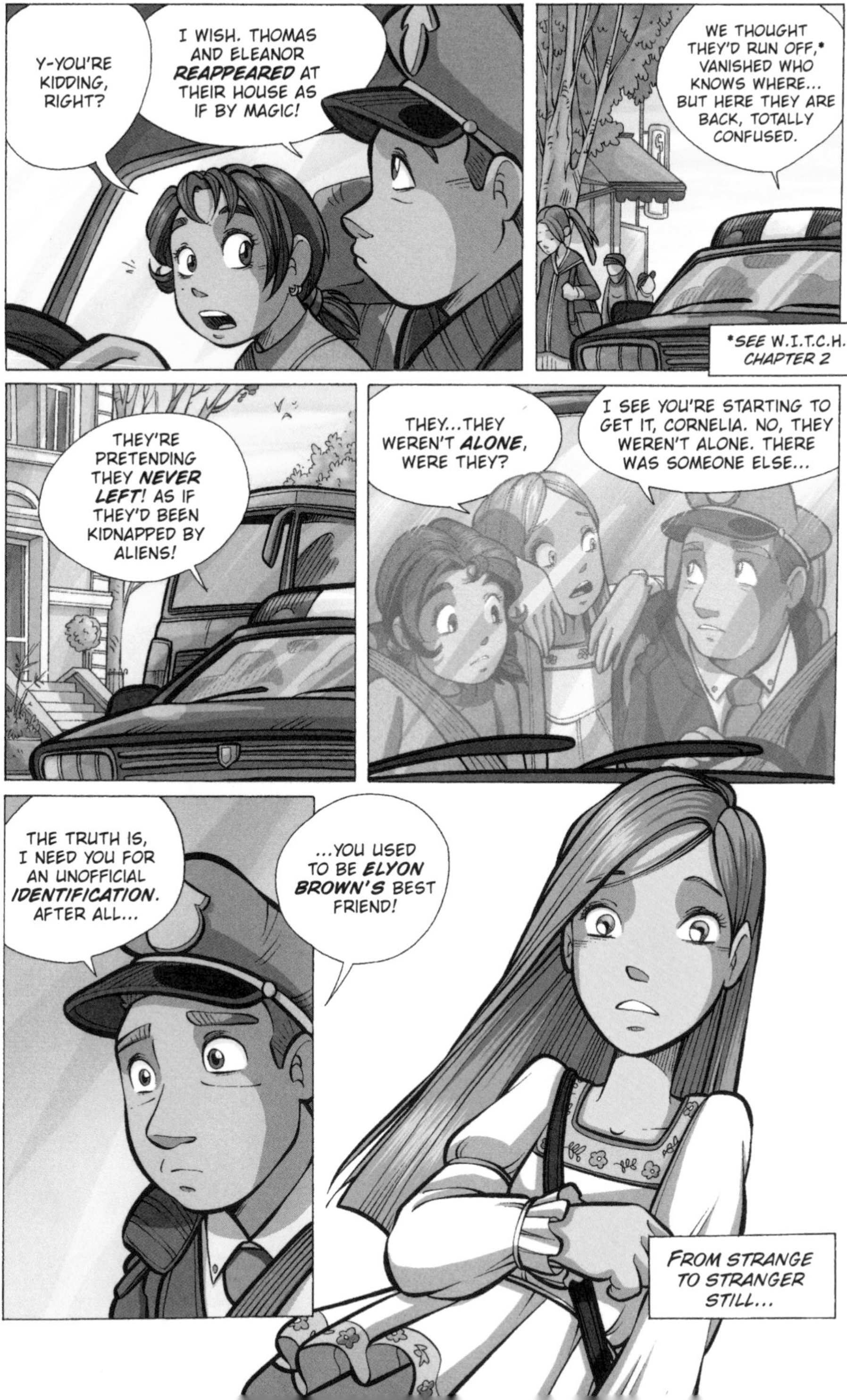
Y-YOU'RE KIDDING, RIGHT?
I WISH. THOMAS AND ELEANOR **REAPPEARED** AT THEIR HOUSE AS IF BY MAGIC!
WE THOUGHT THEY'D RUN OFF,* VANISHED WHO KNOWS WHERE... BUT HERE THEY ARE BACK, TOTALLY CONFUSED.
*SEE W.I.T.C.H. CHAPTER 2
THEY'RE PRETENDING THEY **NEVER LEFT**! AS IF THEY'D BEEN KIDNAPPED BY ALIENS!
THEY...THEY WEREN'T **ALONE**, WERE THEY?
I SEE YOU'RE STARTING TO GET IT, CORNELIA. NO, THEY WEREN'T ALONE. THERE WAS SOMEONE ELSE...
THE TRUTH IS, I NEED YOU FOR AN UNOFFICIAL **IDENTIFICATION**. AFTER ALL...
...YOU USED TO BE **ELYON BROWN'S** BEST FRIEND!
FROM STRANGE TO STRANGER STILL...

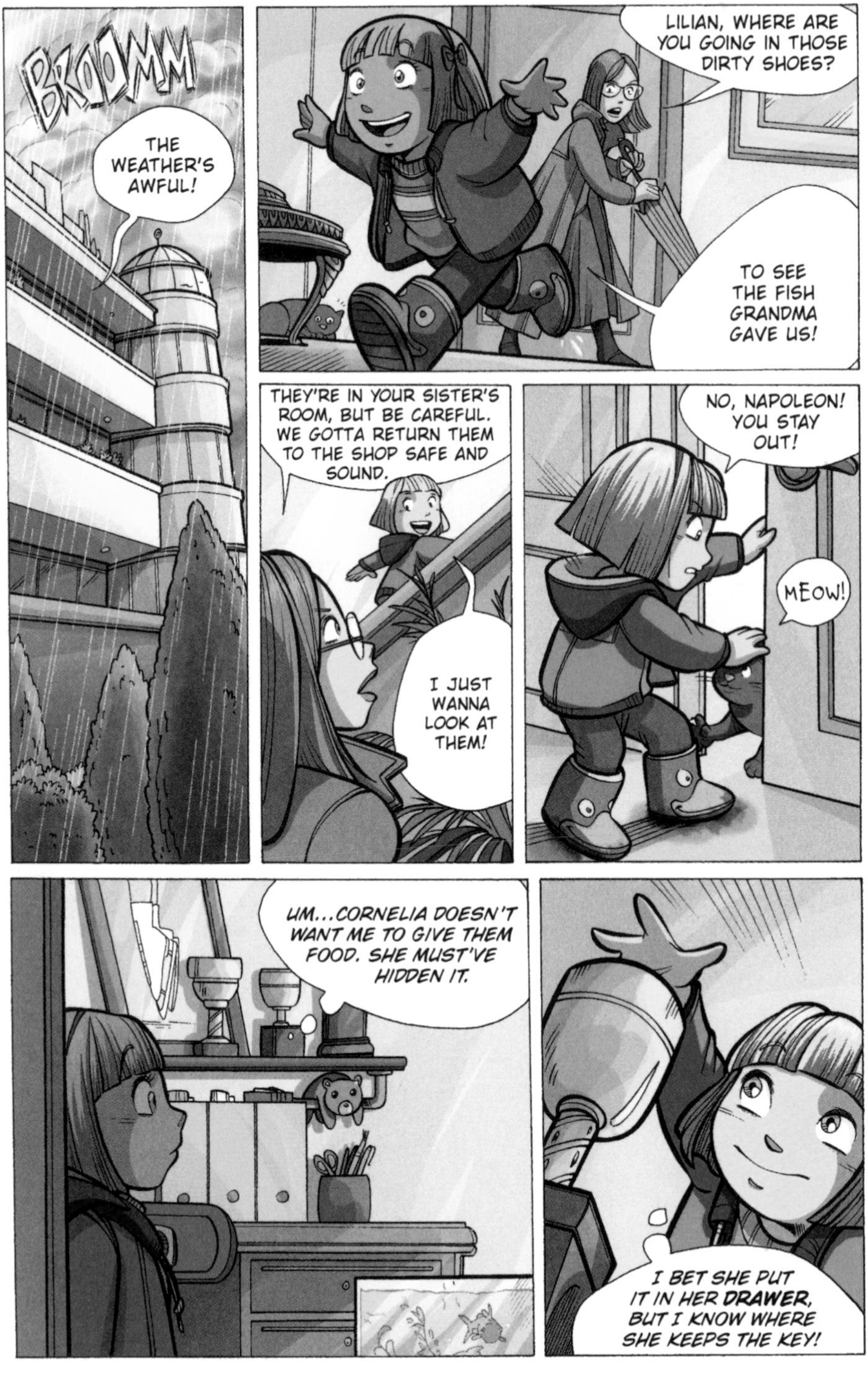
BROOMM
THE WEATHER'S AWFUL!
LILIAN, WHERE ARE YOU GOING IN THOSE DIRTY SHOES?
TO SEE THE FISH GRANDMA GAVE US!
THEY'RE IN YOUR SISTER'S ROOM, BUT BE CAREFUL. WE GOTTA RETURN THEM TO THE SHOP SAFE AND SOUND.
I JUST WANNA LOOK AT THEM!
NO, NAPOLEON! YOU STAY OUT!
MEOW!
UM...CORNELIA DOESN'T WANT ME TO GIVE THEM FOOD. SHE MUST'VE HIDDEN IT.
I BET SHE PUT IT IN HER **DRAWER**, BUT I KNOW WHERE SHE KEEPS THE KEY!

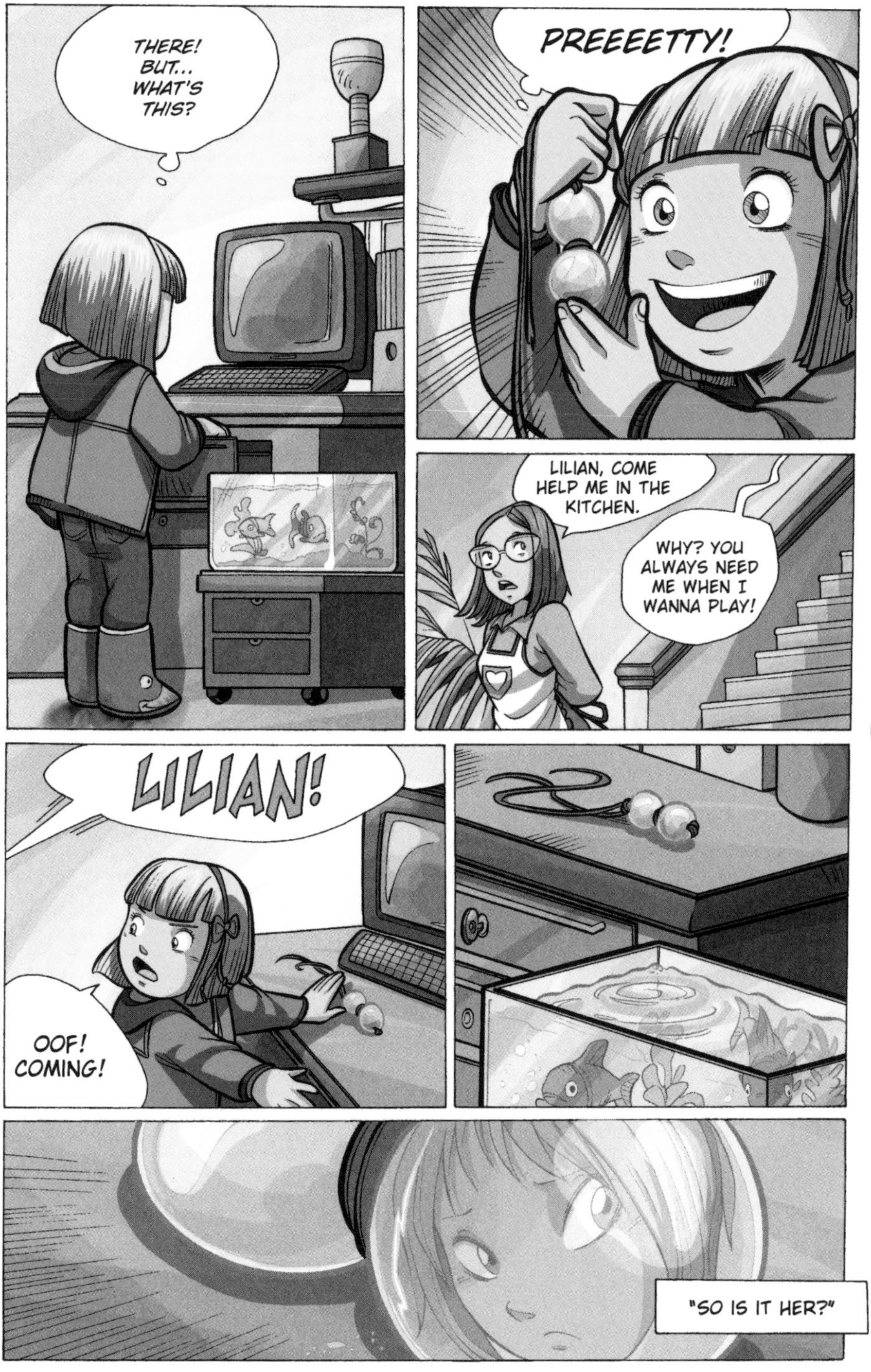
THERE! BUT... WHAT'S THIS?
PREEEETTY!
LILIAN, COME HELP ME IN THE KITCHEN.
WHY? YOU ALWAYS NEED ME WHEN I WANNA PLAY!
LILIAN!
OOF! COMING!
"SO IS IT HER?"

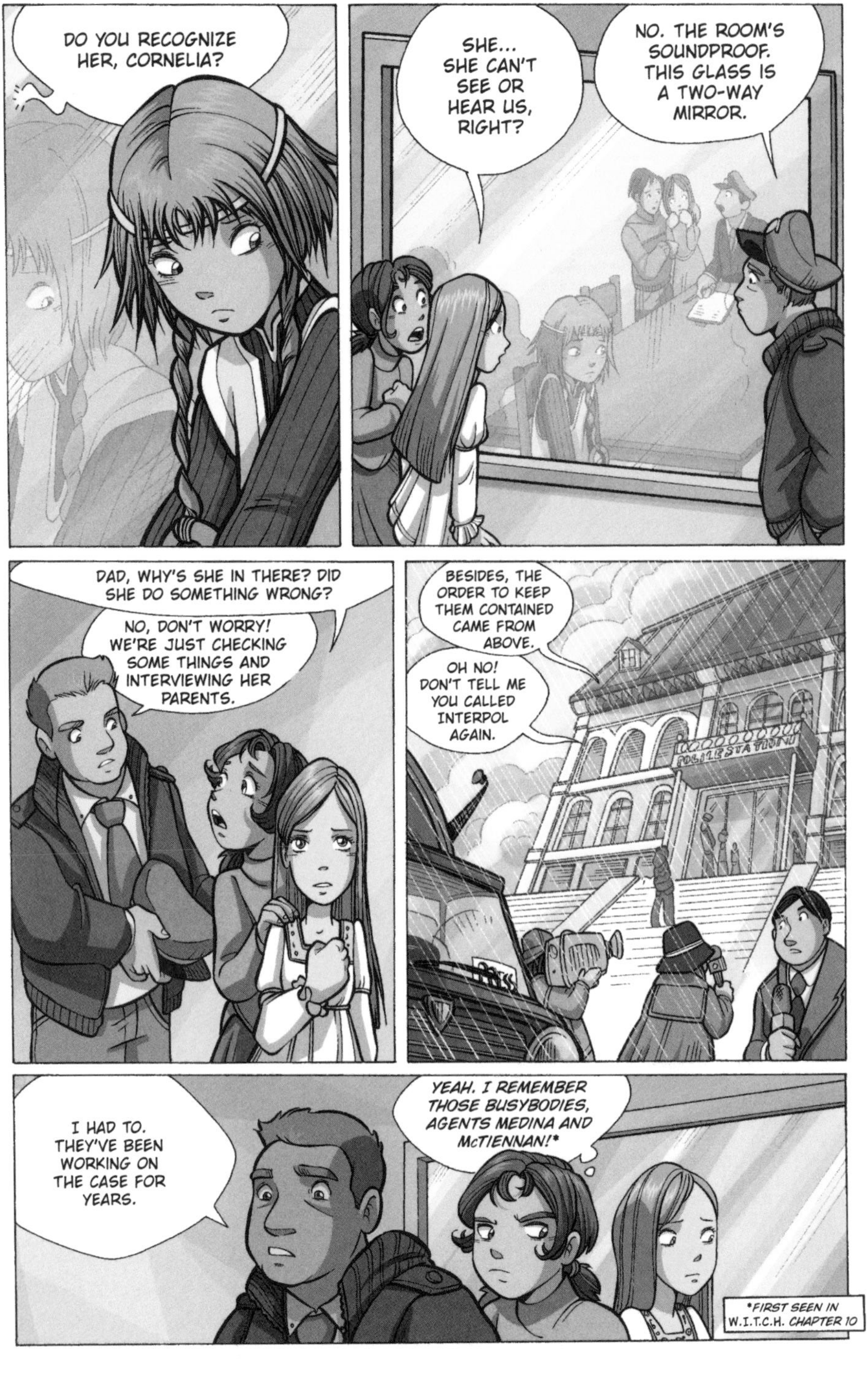
DO YOU RECOGNIZE HER, CORNELIA?
SHE... SHE CAN'T SEE OR HEAR US, RIGHT?
NO. THE ROOM'S SOUNDPROOF. THIS GLASS IS A TWO-WAY MIRROR.
DAD, WHY'S SHE IN THERE? DID SHE DO SOMETHING WRONG?
NO, DON'T WORRY! WE'RE JUST CHECKING SOME THINGS AND INTERVIEWING HER PARENTS.
BESIDES, THE ORDER TO KEEP THEM CONTAINED CAME FROM ABOVE.
OH NO! DON'T TELL ME YOU CALLED INTERPOL AGAIN.
PRESS
I HAD TO. THEY'VE BEEN WORKING ON THE CASE FOR YEARS.
YEAH. I REMEMBER THOSE BUSYBODIES, AGENTS MEDINA AND McTIENNAN!*
*FIRST SEEN IN W.I.T.C.H. CHAPTER 10

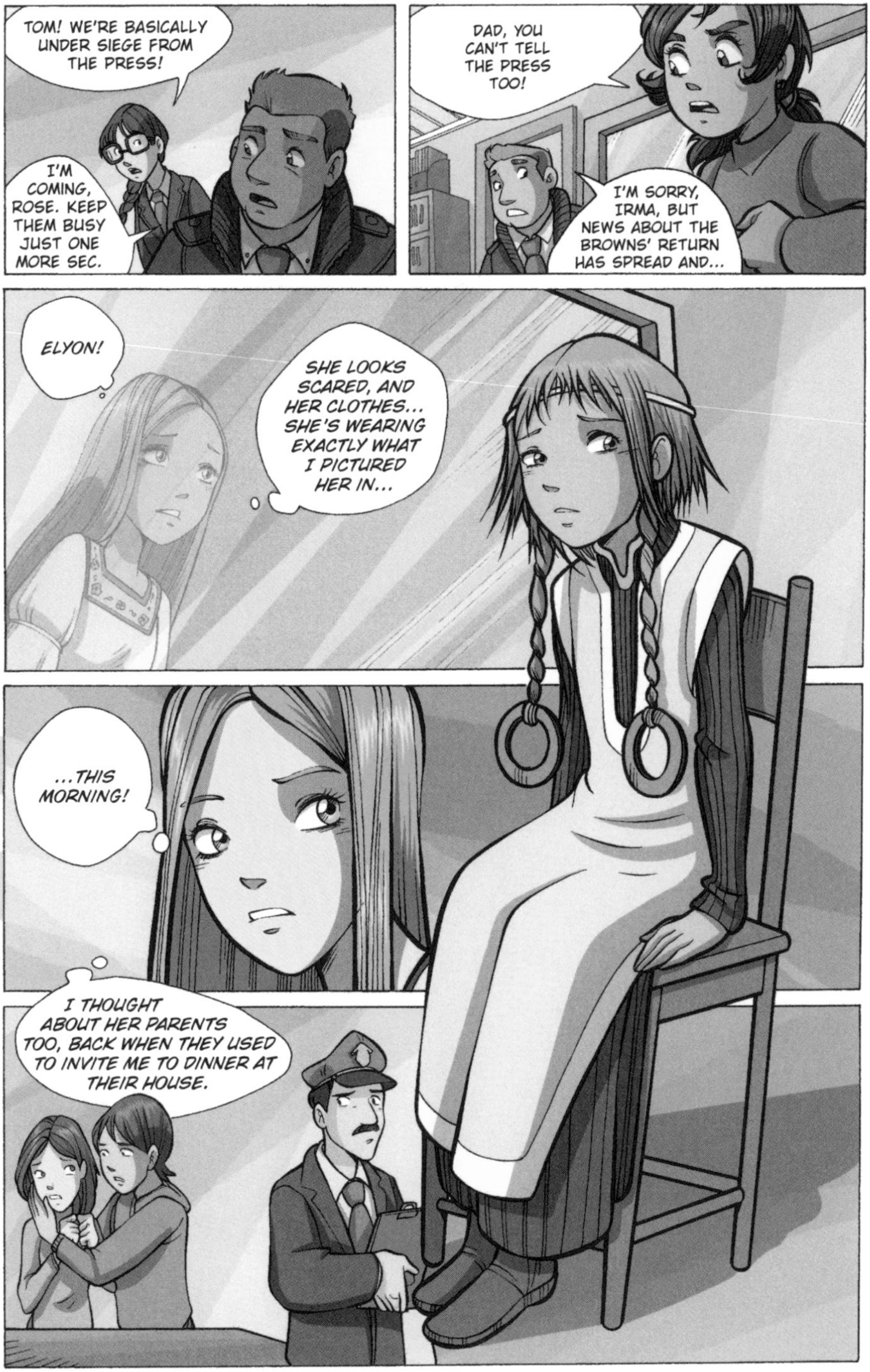
TOM! WE'RE BASICALLY UNDER SIEGE FROM THE PRESS!
I'M COMING, ROSE. KEEP THEM BUSY JUST ONE MORE SEC.
DAD, YOU CAN'T TELL THE PRESS TOO!
I'M SORRY, IRMA, BUT NEWS ABOUT THE BROWNS' RETURN HAS SPREAD AND...
ELYON!
SHE LOOKS SCARED, AND HER CLOTHES... SHE'S WEARING EXACTLY WHAT I PICTURED HER IN...
...THIS MORNING!
I THOUGHT ABOUT HER PARENTS TOO, BACK WHEN THEY USED TO INVITE ME TO DINNER AT THEIR HOUSE.

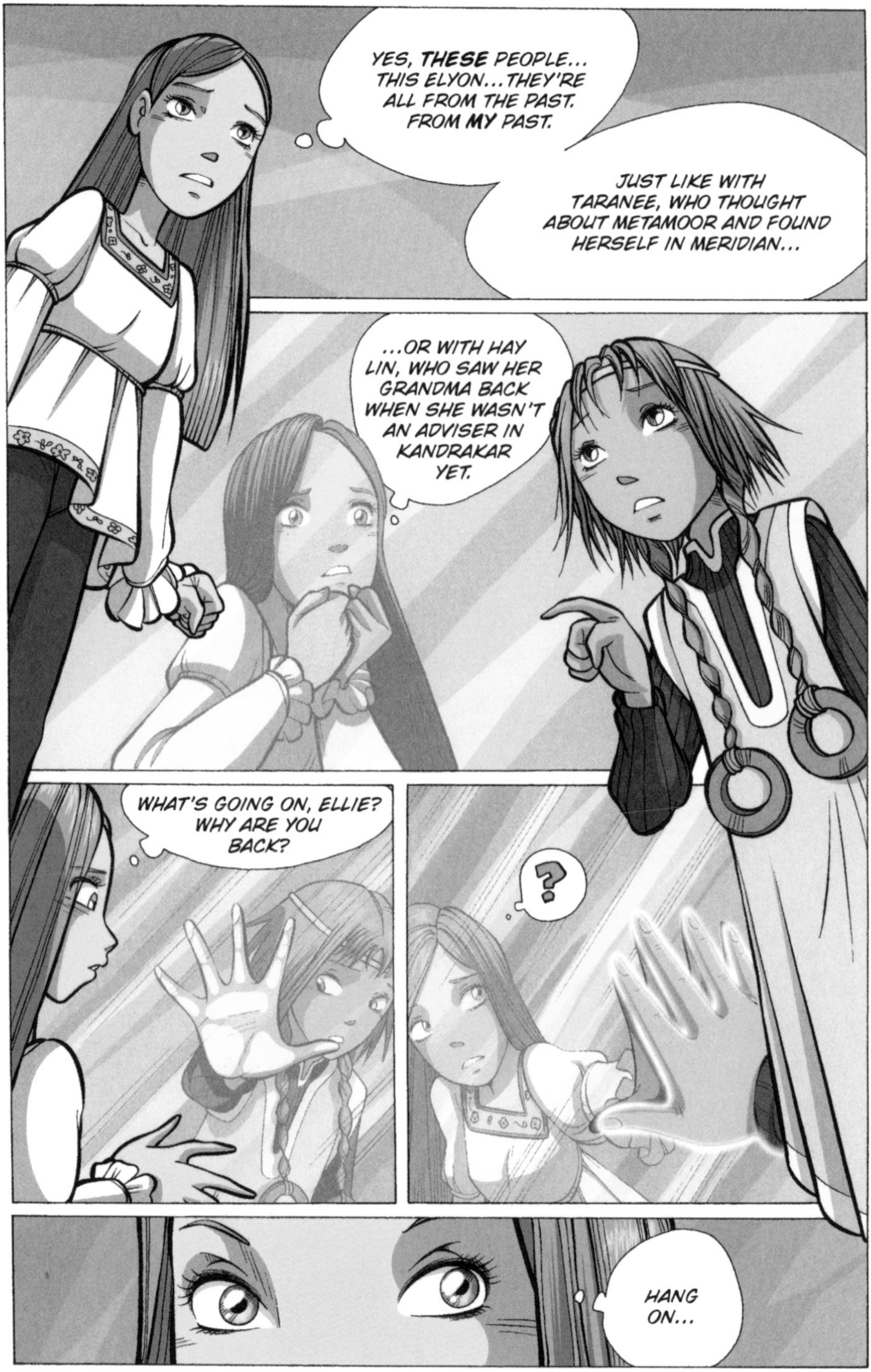
YES, THESE PEOPLE... THIS ELYON...THEY'RE ALL FROM THE PAST. FROM MY PAST.
JUST LIKE WITH TARANEE, WHO THOUGHT ABOUT METAMOOR AND FOUND HERSELF IN MERIDIAN...
...OR WITH HAY LIN, WHO SAW HER GRANDMA BACK WHEN SHE WASN'T AN ADVISER IN KANDRAKAR YET.
WHAT'S GOING ON, ELLIE? WHY ARE YOU BACK?
?
HANG ON...

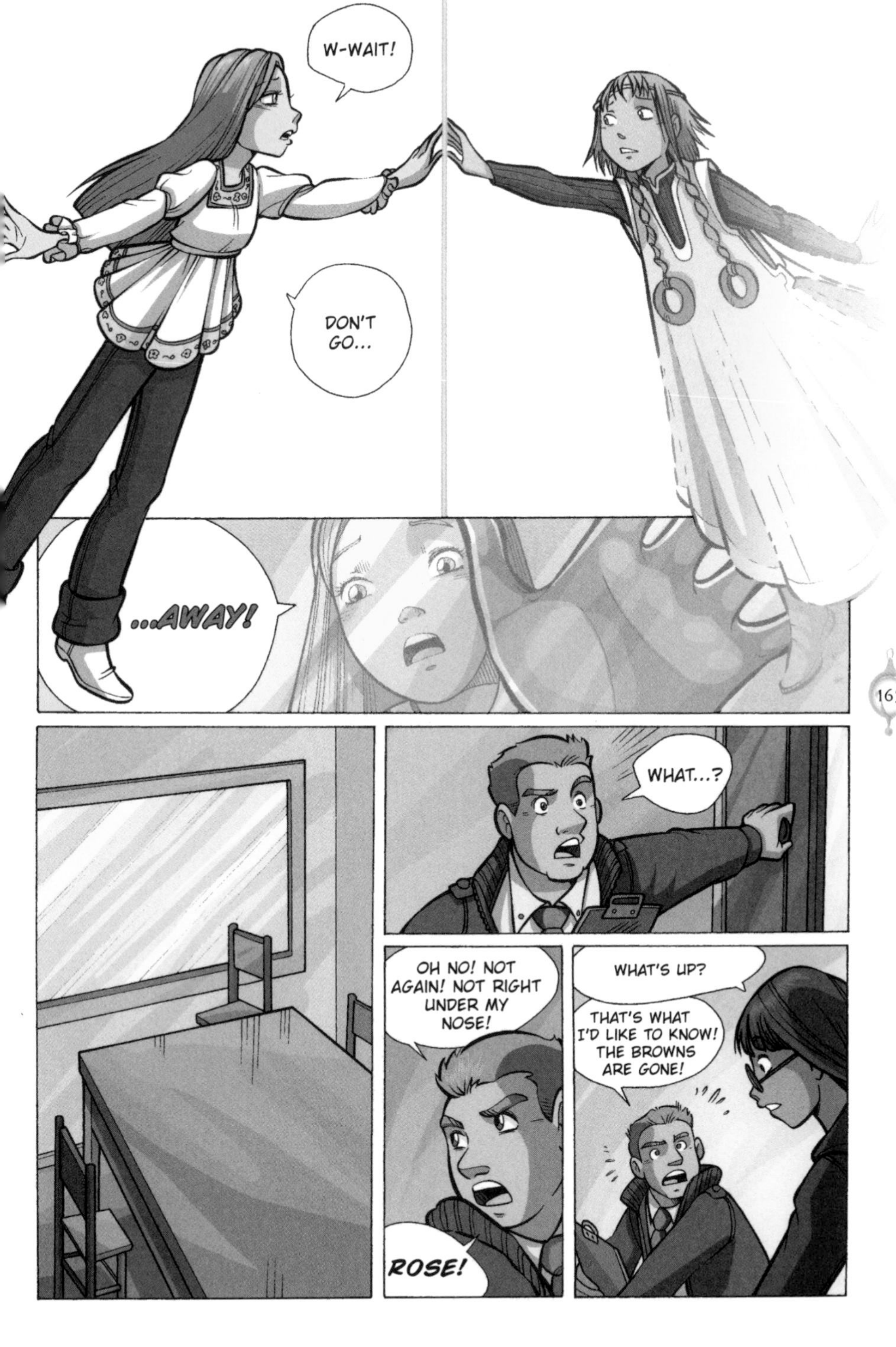
W-WAIT!
DON'T GO...
...AWAY!
WHAT...?
OH NO! NOT AGAIN! NOT RIGHT UNDER MY NOSE!
ROSE!
WHAT'S UP?
THAT'S WHAT I'D LIKE TO KNOW! THE BROWNS ARE GONE!

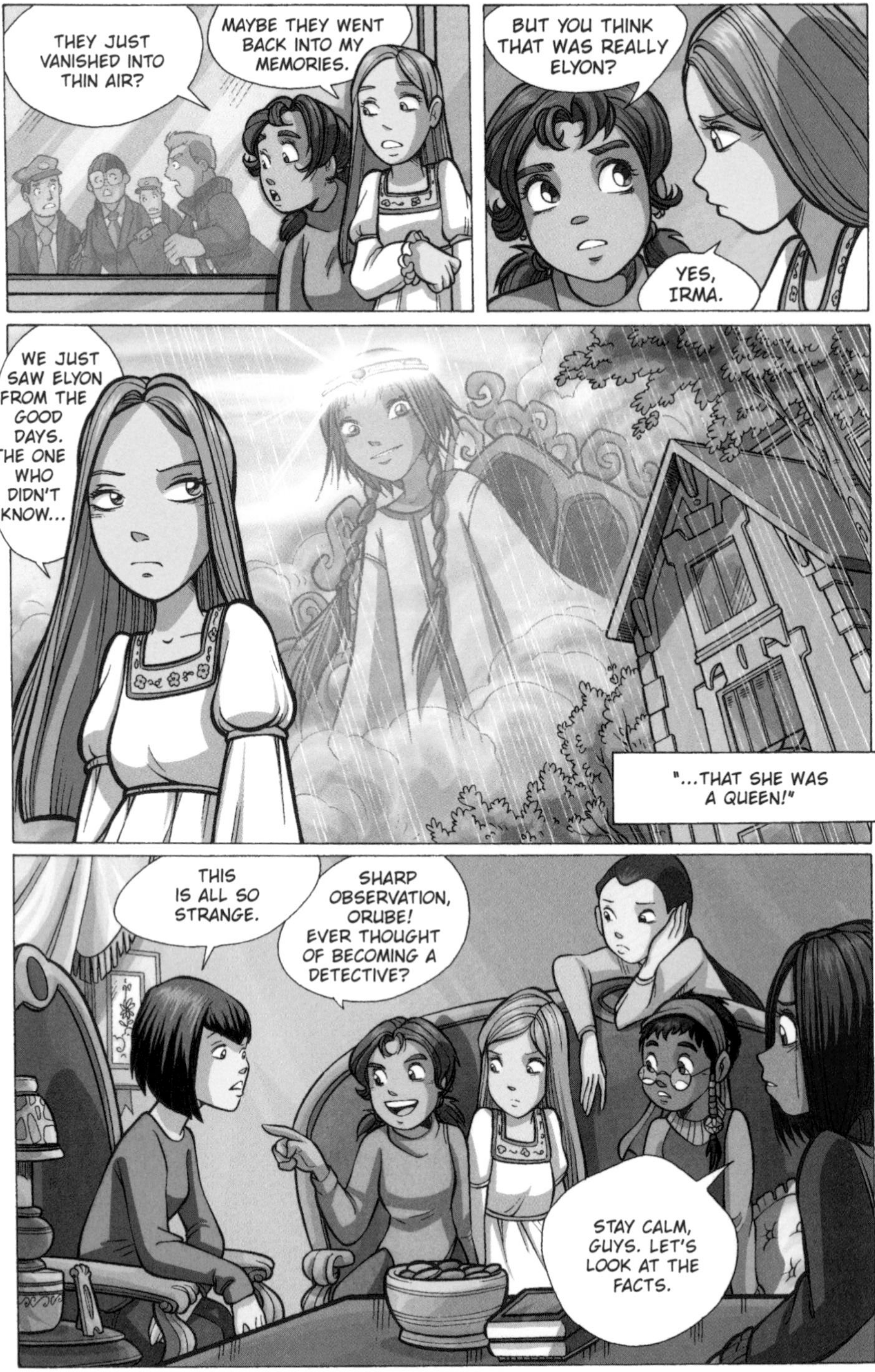
THEY JUST VANISHED INTO THIN AIR?
MAYBE THEY WENT BACK INTO MY MEMORIES.
BUT YOU THINK THAT WAS REALLY ELYON?
YES, IRMA.
WE JUST SAW ELYON FROM THE GOOD DAYS. THE ONE WHO DIDN'T KNOW...
"...THAT SHE WAS A QUEEN!"
THIS IS ALL SO STRANGE.
SHARP OBSERVATION, ORUBE! EVER THOUGHT OF BECOMING A DETECTIVE?
STAY CALM, GUYS. LET'S LOOK AT THE FACTS.

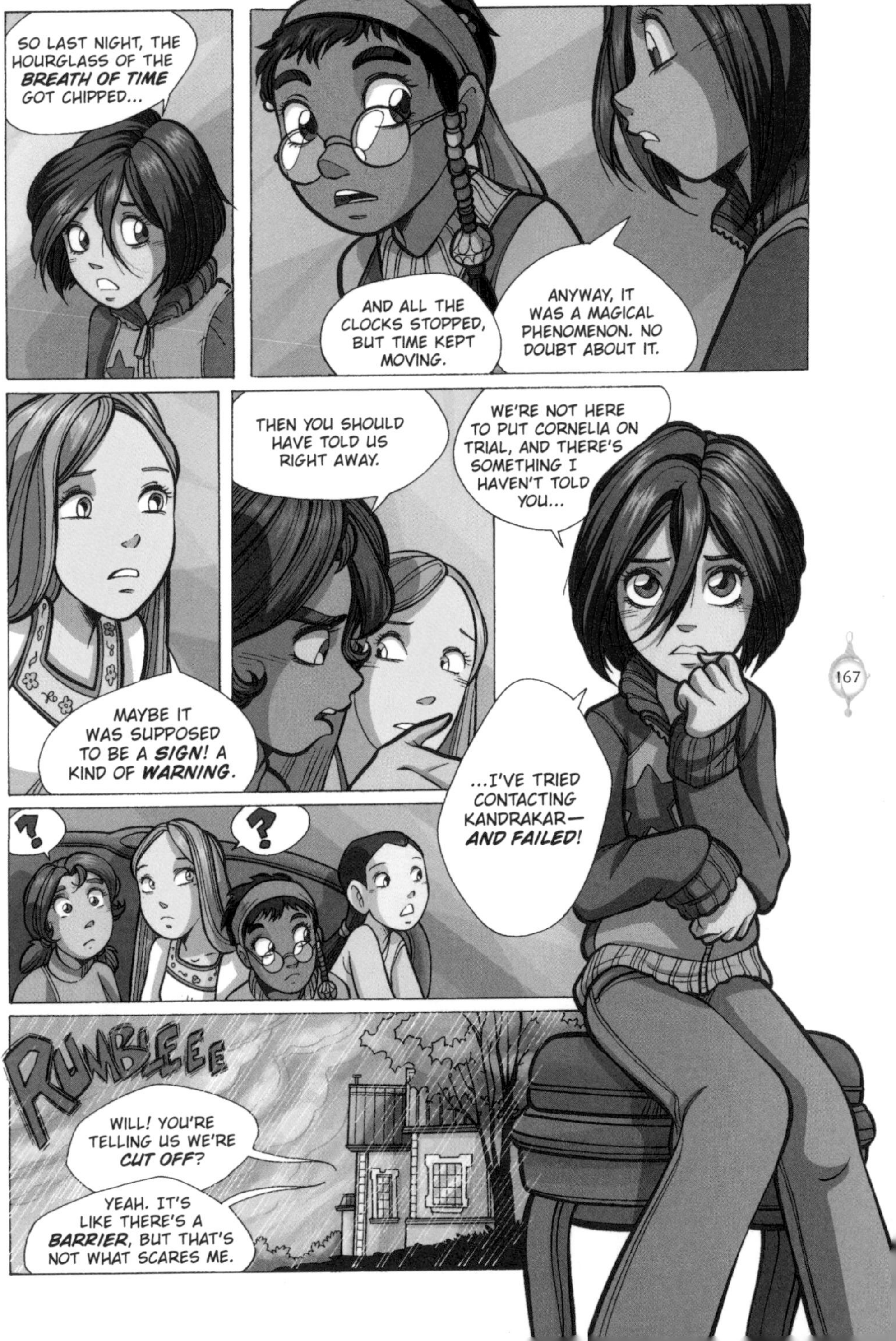
SO LAST NIGHT, THE HOURGLASS OF THE BREATH OF TIME GOT CHIPPED...
AND ALL THE CLOCKS STOPPED, BUT TIME KEPT MOVING.
ANYWAY, IT WAS A MAGICAL PHENOMENON. NO DOUBT ABOUT IT.
MAYBE IT WAS SUPPOSED TO BE A SIGN! A KIND OF WARNING.
THEN YOU SHOULD HAVE TOLD US RIGHT AWAY.
WE'RE NOT HERE TO PUT CORNELIA ON TRIAL, AND THERE'S SOMETHING I HAVEN'T TOLD YOU...
...I'VE TRIED CONTACTING KANDRAKAR—AND FAILED!
?
?
RUMBLEEE
WILL! YOU'RE TELLING US WE'RE CUT OFF?
YEAH. IT'S LIKE THERE'S A BARRIER, BUT THAT'S NOT WHAT SCARES ME.

SOMEHOW OUR MEMORIES ARE *MATERIALIZING*, THAT'S CLEAR...

...BUT THEY'RE NOT *RANDOM*. THEY'RE ALL FROM A SPECIFIC TIME OF OUR LIVES.

FIRST, METAMOOR WHEN IT WAS POOR AND WRETCHED...

THEN, GRANDMA WHEN SHE HADN'T TOLD US ABOUT OUR MISSION YET...

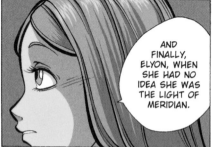

AND FINALLY, ELYON, WHEN SHE HAD NO IDEA SHE WAS THE LIGHT OF MERIDIAN.

THERE. YOU'RE STARTING TO GET IT TOO.

ALL THESE MEMORIES ARE CONNECTED BY JUST ONE THOUGHT...

...JUST ONE *NAME*!

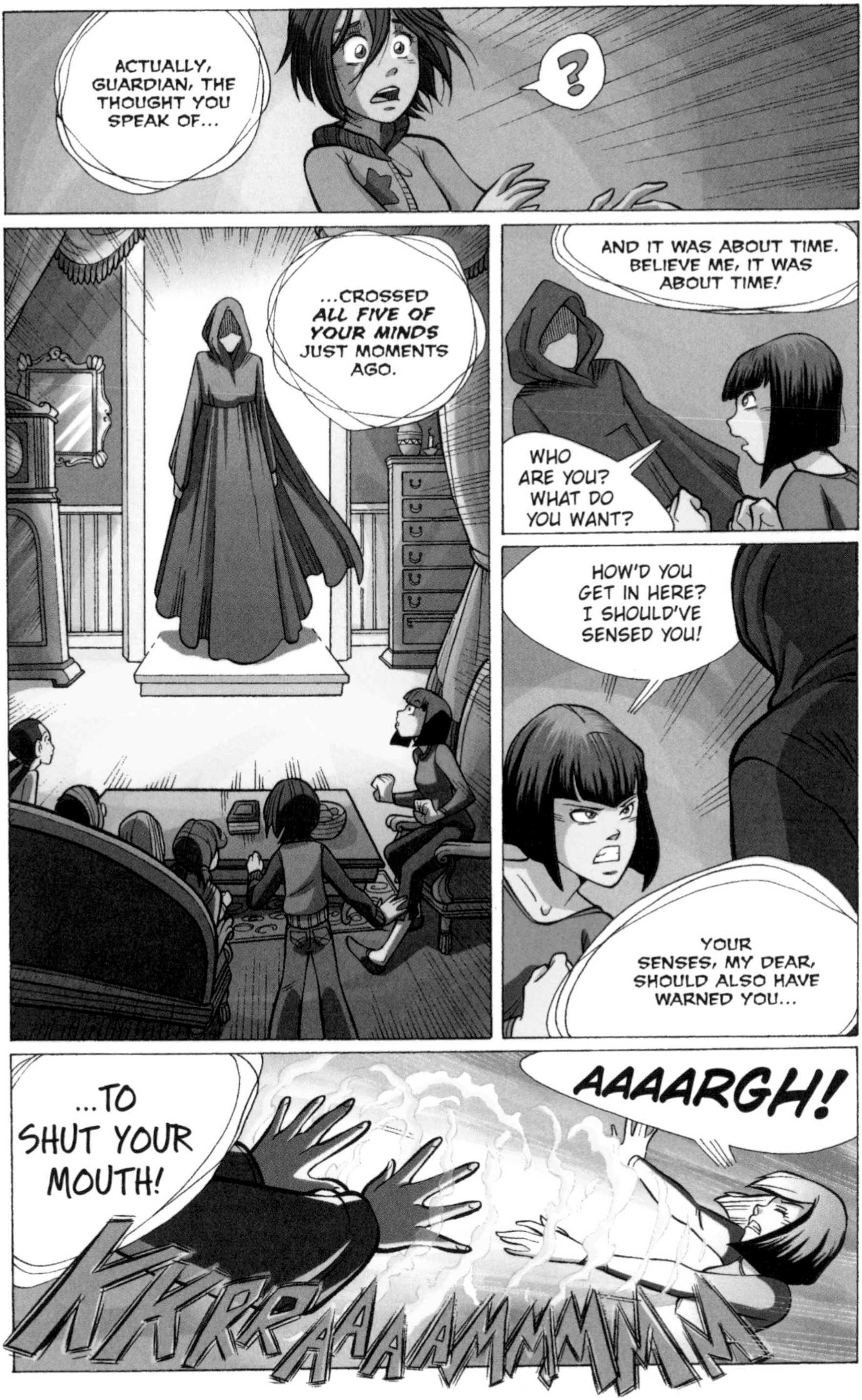
ACTUALLY, GUARDIAN, THE THOUGHT YOU SPEAK OF...
?
...CROSSED ALL FIVE OF YOUR MINDS JUST MOMENTS AGO.
AND IT WAS ABOUT TIME. BELIEVE ME, IT WAS ABOUT TIME!
WHO ARE YOU? WHAT DO YOU WANT?
HOW'D YOU GET IN HERE? I SHOULD'VE SENSED YOU!
YOUR SENSES, MY DEAR, SHOULD ALSO HAVE WARNED YOU...
...TO SHUT YOUR MOUTH!
AAAARGH!
KRRRAAAAMMMMM

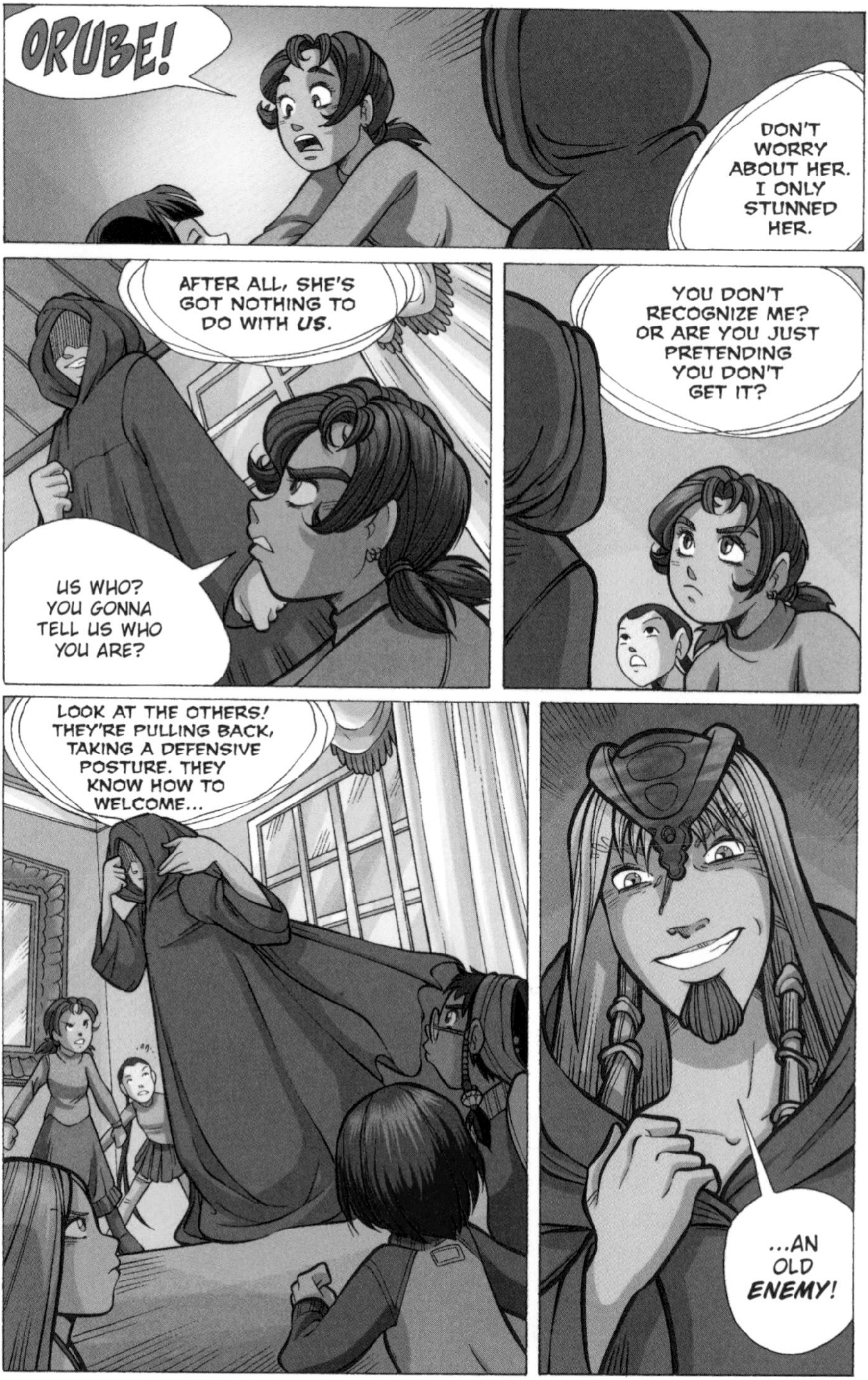
ORUBE!
DON'T WORRY ABOUT HER. I ONLY STUNNED HER.
AFTER ALL, SHE'S GOT NOTHING TO DO WITH US.
US WHO? YOU GONNA TELL US WHO YOU ARE?
YOU DON'T RECOGNIZE ME? OR ARE YOU JUST PRETENDING YOU DON'T GET IT?
LOOK AT THE OTHERS! THEY'RE PULLING BACK, TAKING A DEFENSIVE POSTURE. THEY KNOW HOW TO WELCOME...
...AN OLD ENEMY!

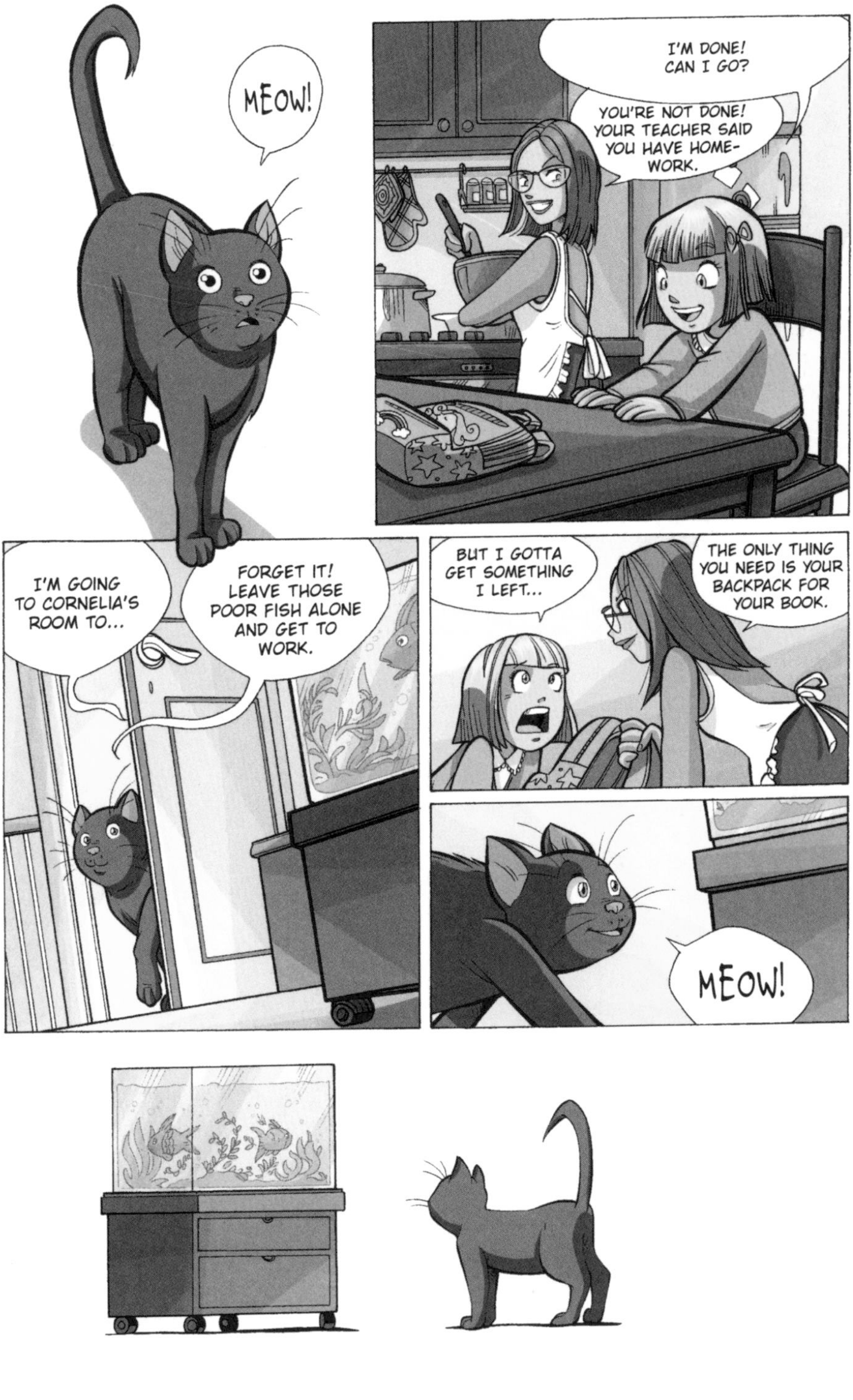
MEOW!
I'M DONE! CAN I GO?
YOU'RE NOT DONE! YOUR TEACHER SAID YOU HAVE HOME-WORK.
I'M GOING TO CORNELIA'S ROOM TO...
FORGET IT! LEAVE THOSE POOR FISH ALONE AND GET TO WORK.
BUT I GOTTA GET SOMETHING I LEFT...
THE ONLY THING YOU NEED IS YOUR BACKPACK FOR YOUR BOOK.
MEOW!

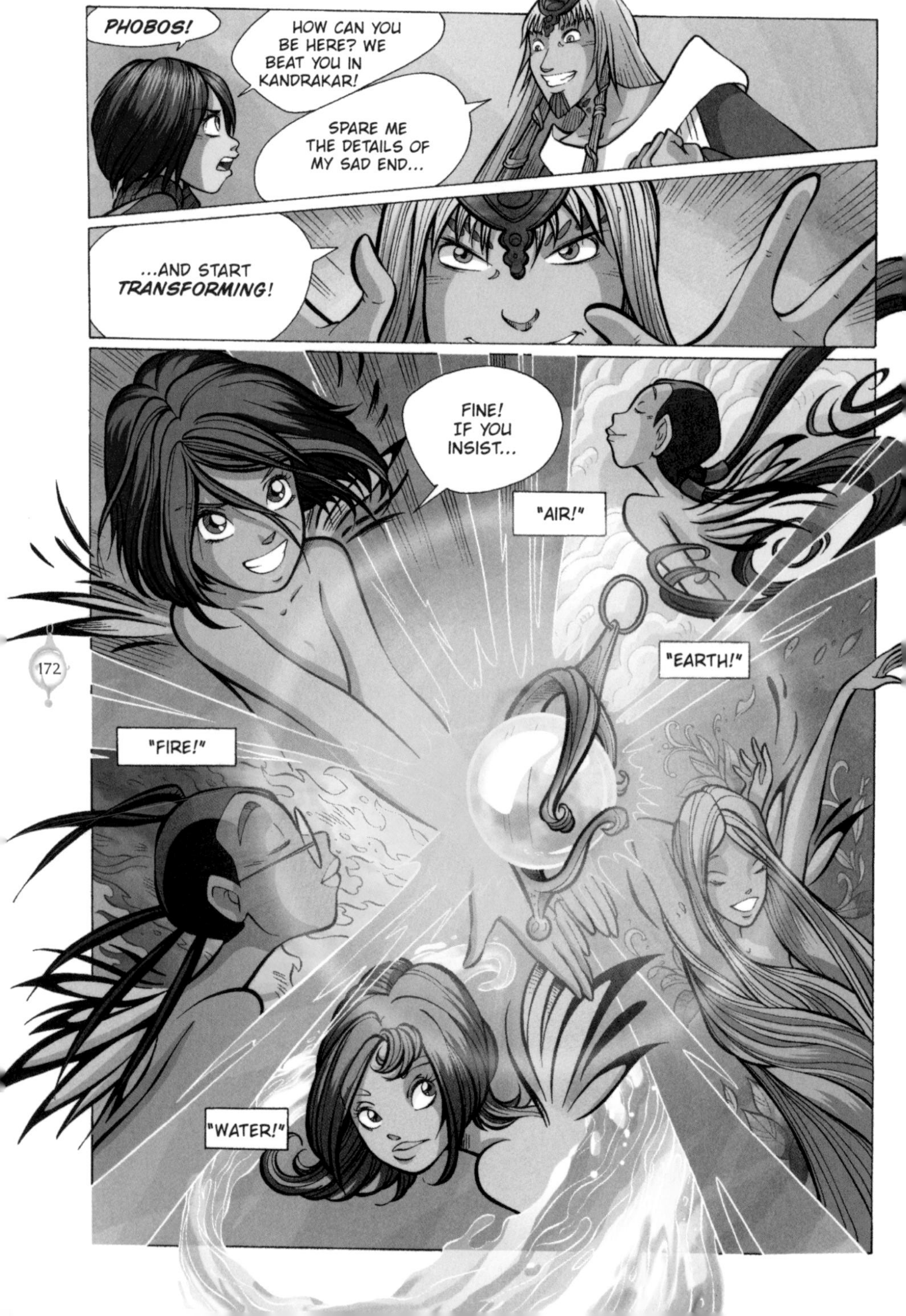
PHOBOS!
HOW CAN YOU BE HERE? WE BEAT YOU IN KANDRAKAR!
SPARE ME THE DETAILS OF MY SAD END...
...AND START TRANSFORMING!
FINE! IF YOU INSIST...
"AIR!"
"EARTH!"
"FIRE!"
"WATER!"

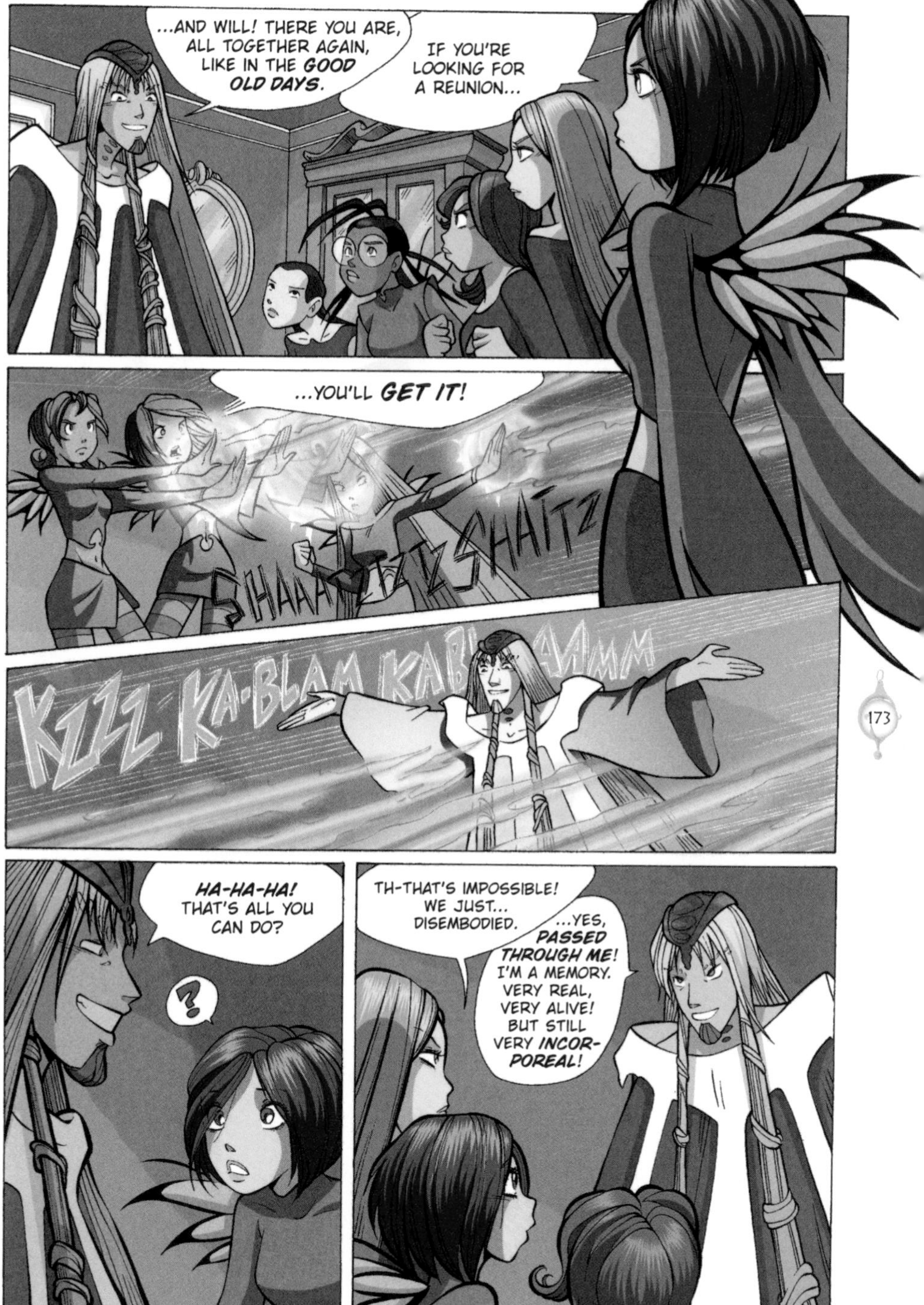
...AND WILL! THERE YOU ARE, ALL TOGETHER AGAIN, LIKE IN THE **GOOD OLD DAYS**.
IF YOU'RE LOOKING FOR A REUNION...
...YOU'LL **GET IT**!
SHAAAZTZZSHAITZ
KZZZ KA-BLAM KABLAAMM
HA-HA-HA! THAT'S ALL YOU CAN DO?
?
TH-THAT'S IMPOSSIBLE! WE JUST... DISEMBODIED.
...YES, **PASSED THROUGH ME!** I'M A MEMORY. VERY REAL, VERY ALIVE! BUT STILL VERY **INCORPOREAL!**

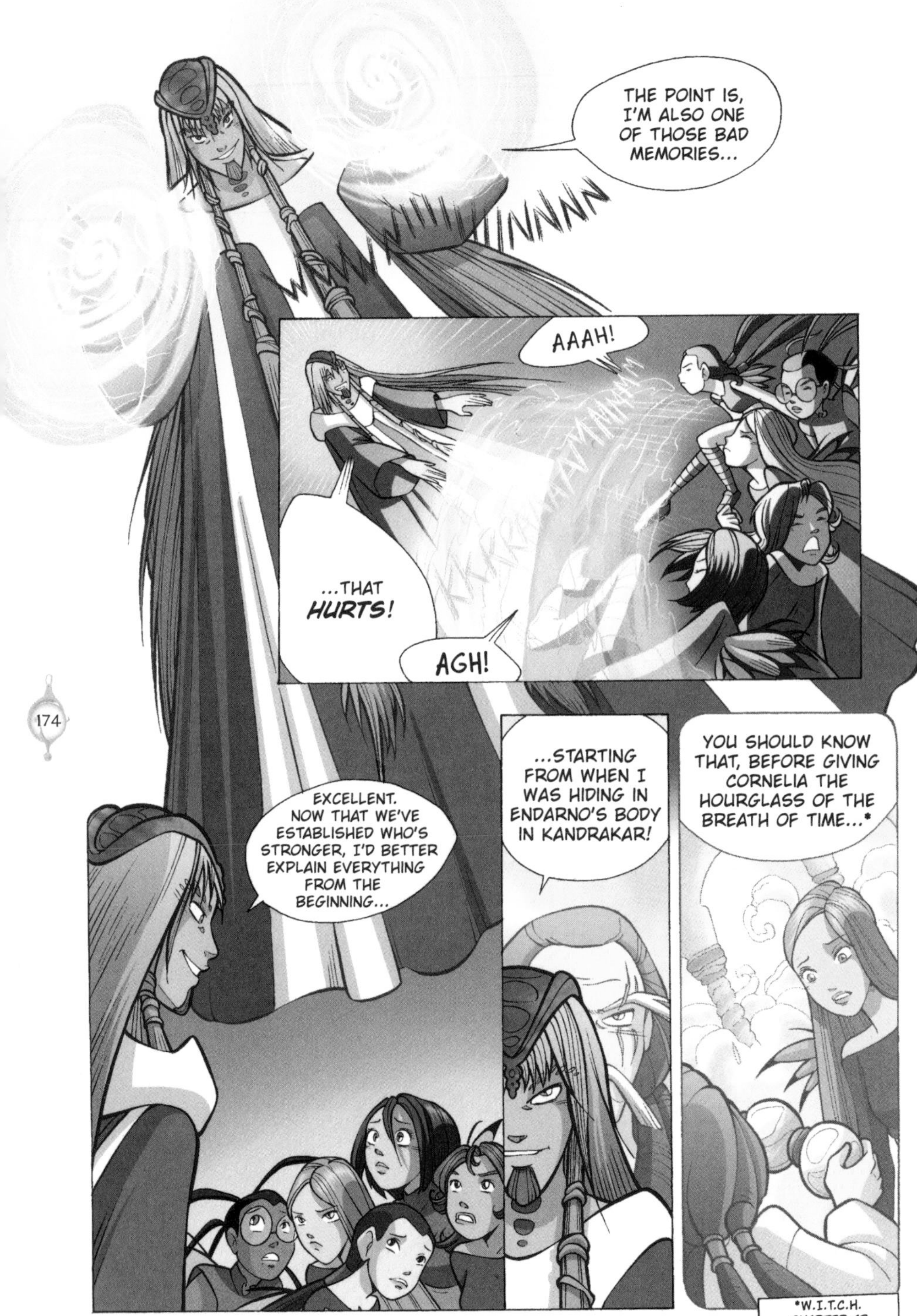
THE POINT IS, I'M ALSO ONE OF THOSE BAD MEMORIES...
AAAH!
...THAT HURTS!
AGH!
EXCELLENT. NOW THAT WE'VE ESTABLISHED WHO'S STRONGER, I'D BETTER EXPLAIN EVERYTHING FROM THE BEGINNING...
...STARTING FROM WHEN I WAS HIDING IN ENDARNO'S BODY IN KANDRAKAR!
YOU SHOULD KNOW THAT, BEFORE GIVING CORNELIA THE HOURGLASS OF THE BREATH OF TIME...*
*W.I.T.C.H. CHAPTER 42

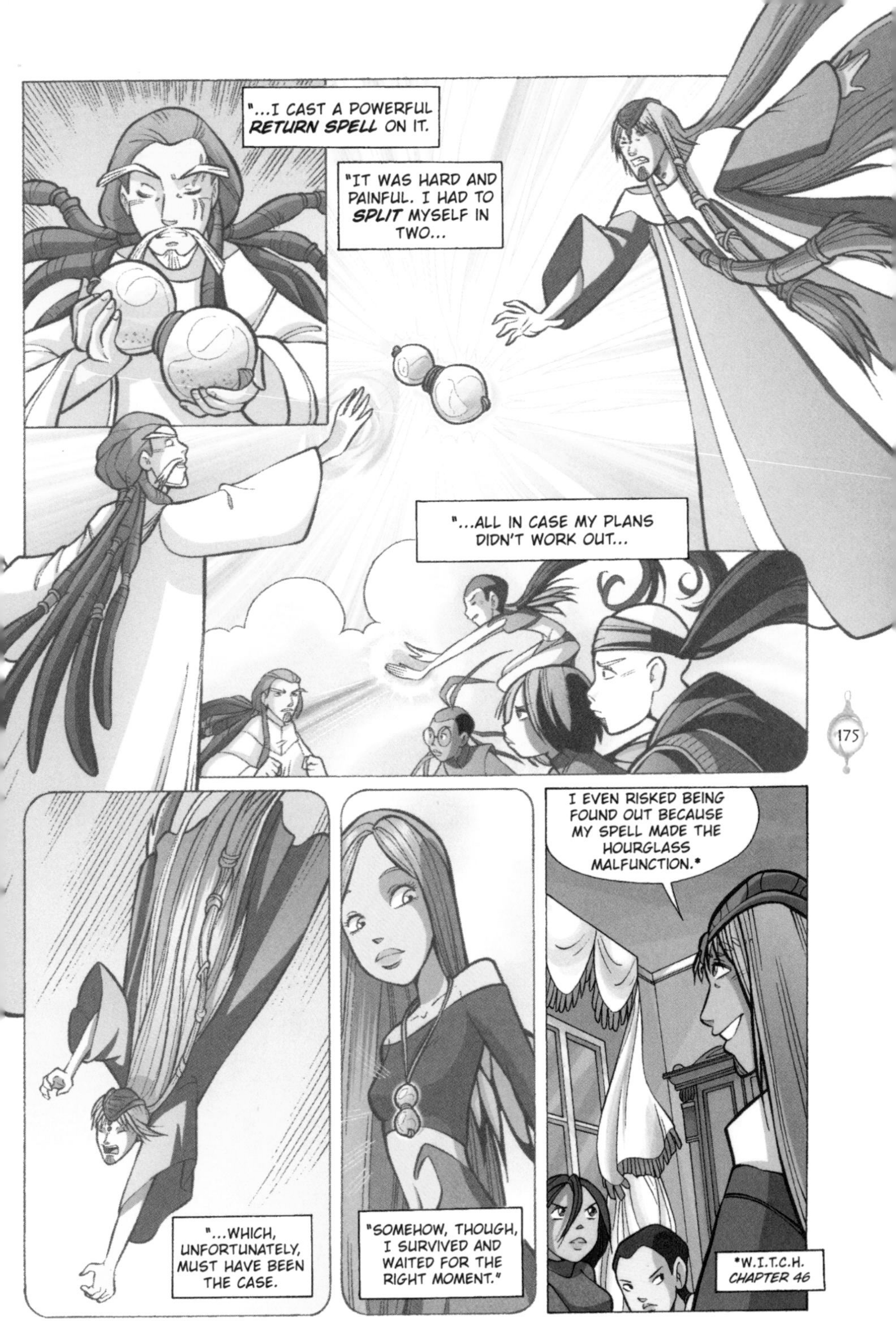
"...I CAST A POWERFUL RETURN SPELL ON IT.
"IT WAS HARD AND PAINFUL. I HAD TO SPLIT MYSELF IN TWO...
"...ALL IN CASE MY PLANS DIDN'T WORK OUT...
"...WHICH, UNFORTUNATELY, MUST HAVE BEEN THE CASE.
"SOMEHOW, THOUGH, I SURVIVED AND WAITED FOR THE RIGHT MOMENT."
I EVEN RISKED BEING FOUND OUT BECAUSE MY SPELL MADE THE HOURGLASS MALFUNCTION.*
*W.I.T.C.H. CHAPTER 46

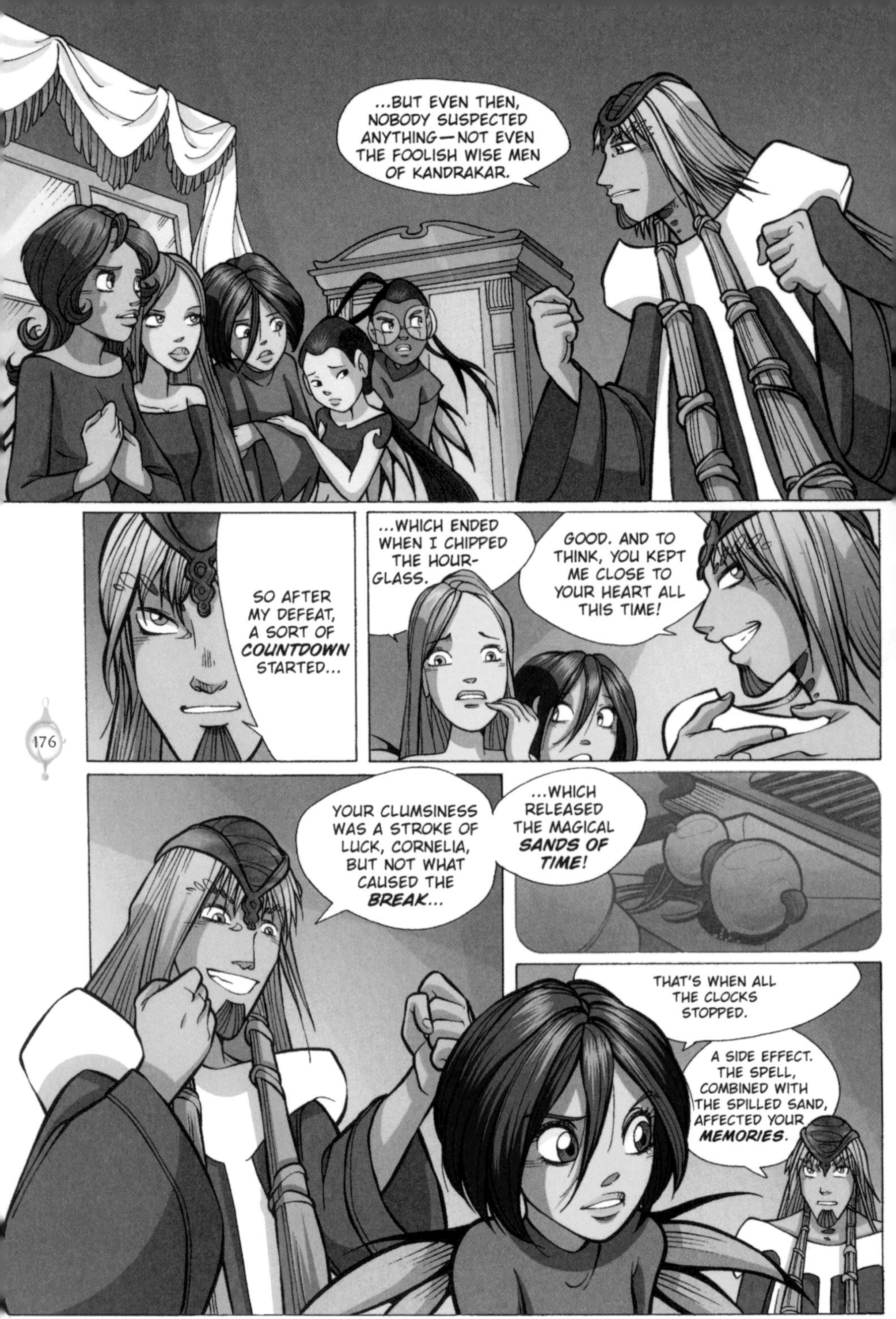
...BUT EVEN THEN, NOBODY SUSPECTED ANYTHING—NOT EVEN THE FOOLISH WISE MEN OF KANDRAKAR.
SO AFTER MY DEFEAT, A SORT OF COUNTDOWN STARTED...
...WHICH ENDED WHEN I CHIPPED THE HOUR-GLASS.
GOOD. AND TO THINK, YOU KEPT ME CLOSE TO YOUR HEART ALL THIS TIME!
YOUR CLUMSINESS WAS A STROKE OF LUCK, CORNELIA, BUT NOT WHAT CAUSED THE BREAK...
...WHICH RELEASED THE MAGICAL SANDS OF TIME!
THAT'S WHEN ALL THE CLOCKS STOPPED.
A SIDE EFFECT. THE SPELL, COMBINED WITH THE SPILLED SAND, AFFECTED YOUR MEMORIES.

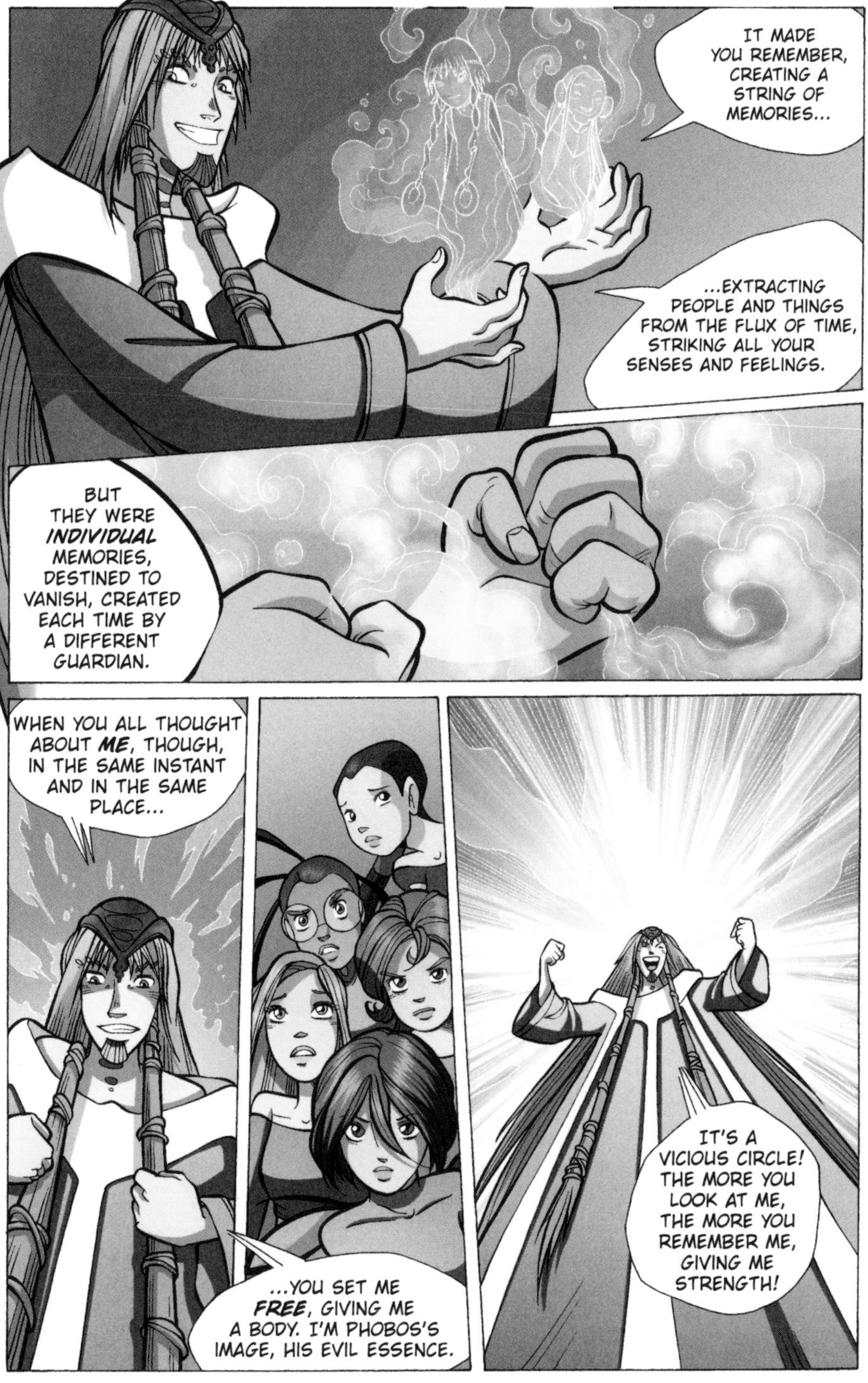

IT MADE YOU REMEMBER, CREATING A STRING OF MEMORIES...
...EXTRACTING PEOPLE AND THINGS FROM THE FLUX OF TIME, STRIKING ALL YOUR SENSES AND FEELINGS.
BUT THEY WERE *INDIVIDUAL* MEMORIES, DESTINED TO VANISH, CREATED EACH TIME BY A DIFFERENT GUARDIAN.
WHEN YOU ALL THOUGHT ABOUT *ME*, THOUGH, IN THE SAME INSTANT AND IN THE SAME PLACE...
...YOU SET ME *FREE*, GIVING ME A BODY. I'M PHOBOS'S IMAGE, HIS EVIL ESSENCE.
IT'S A VICIOUS CIRCLE! THE MORE YOU LOOK AT ME, THE MORE YOU REMEMBER ME, GIVING ME STRENGTH!

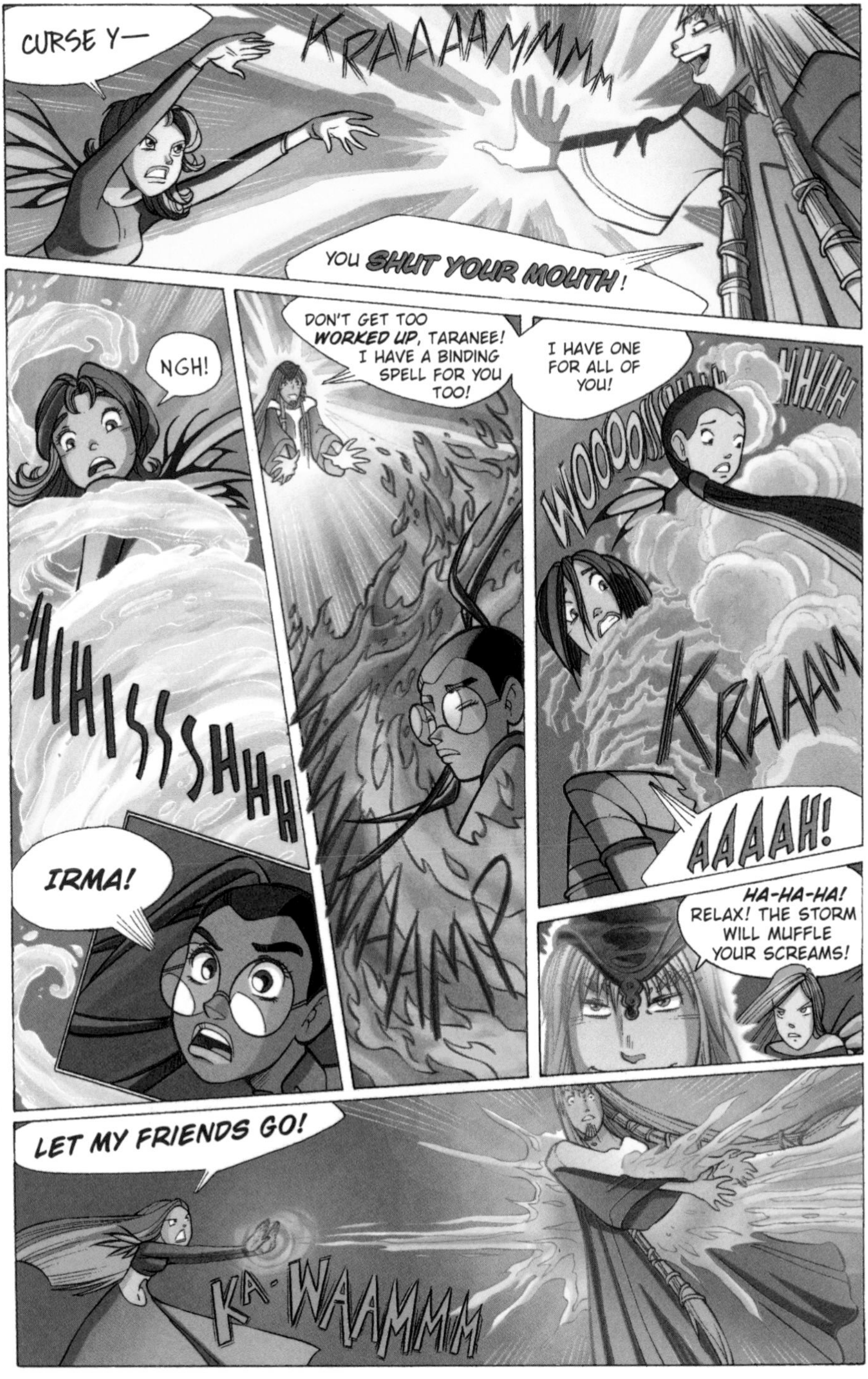

CURSE Y—
KRAAAAMMM
YOU SHUT YOUR MOUTH!
NGH!
HHISSSHHH
IRMA!
DON'T GET TOO WORKED UP, TARANEE! I HAVE A BINDING SPELL FOR YOU TOO!
I HAVE ONE FOR ALL OF YOU!
WOOOOSHHHH
KRAAAM
AAAAH!
HA-HA-HA! RELAX! THE STORM WILL MUFFLE YOUR SCREAMS!
LET MY FRIENDS GO!
KA-WAAMMM

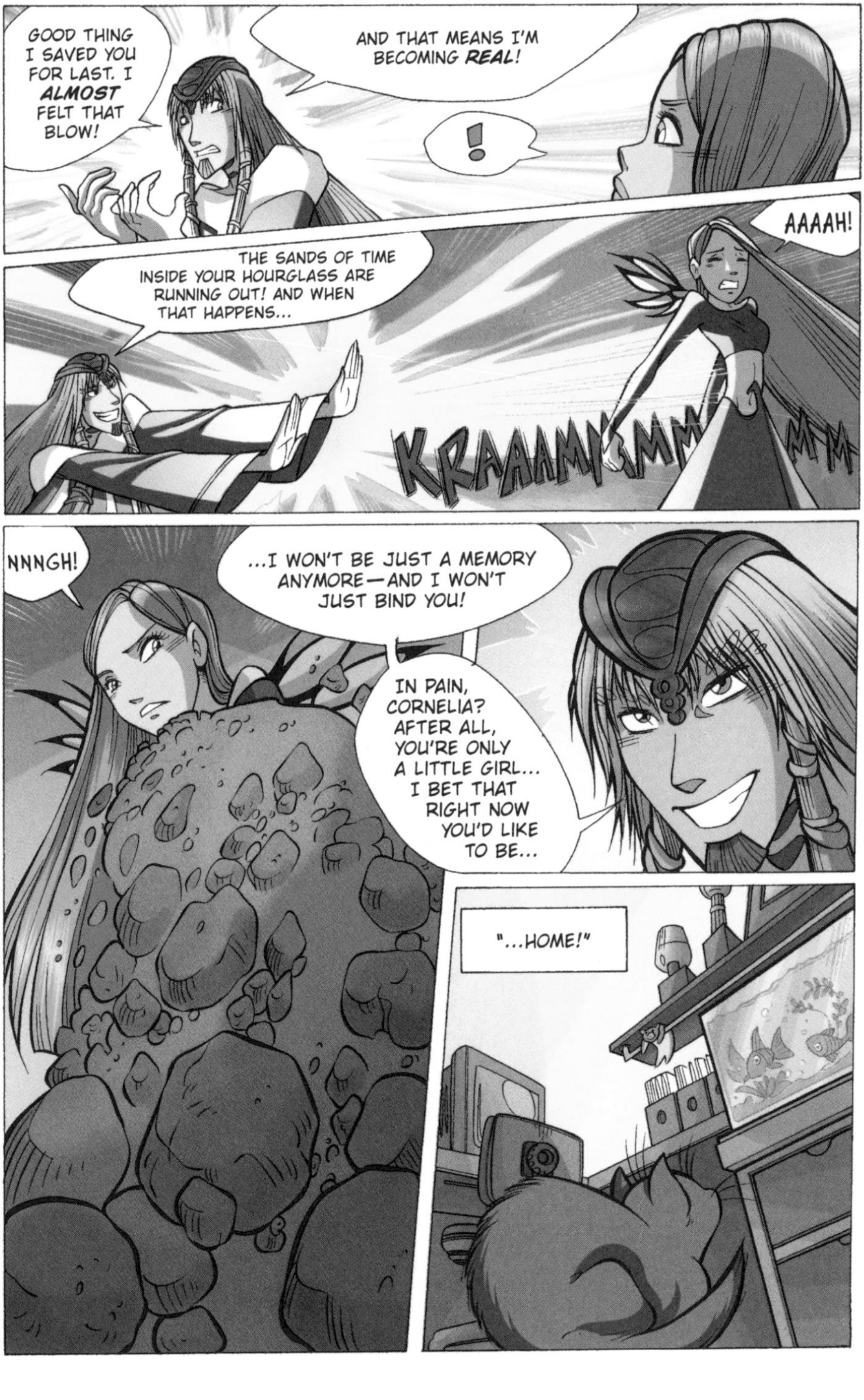
GOOD THING I SAVED YOU FOR LAST. I **ALMOST** FELT THAT BLOW!
AND THAT MEANS I'M BECOMING **REAL**!
!
THE SANDS OF TIME INSIDE YOUR HOURGLASS ARE RUNNING OUT! AND WHEN THAT HAPPENS...
AAAAH!
KRAAAMMMMMMMM
NNNGH!
...I WON'T BE JUST A MEMORY ANYMORE—AND I WON'T JUST BIND YOU!
IN PAIN, CORNELIA? AFTER ALL, YOU'RE ONLY A LITTLE GIRL... I BET THAT RIGHT NOW YOU'D LIKE TO BE...
"...HOME!"

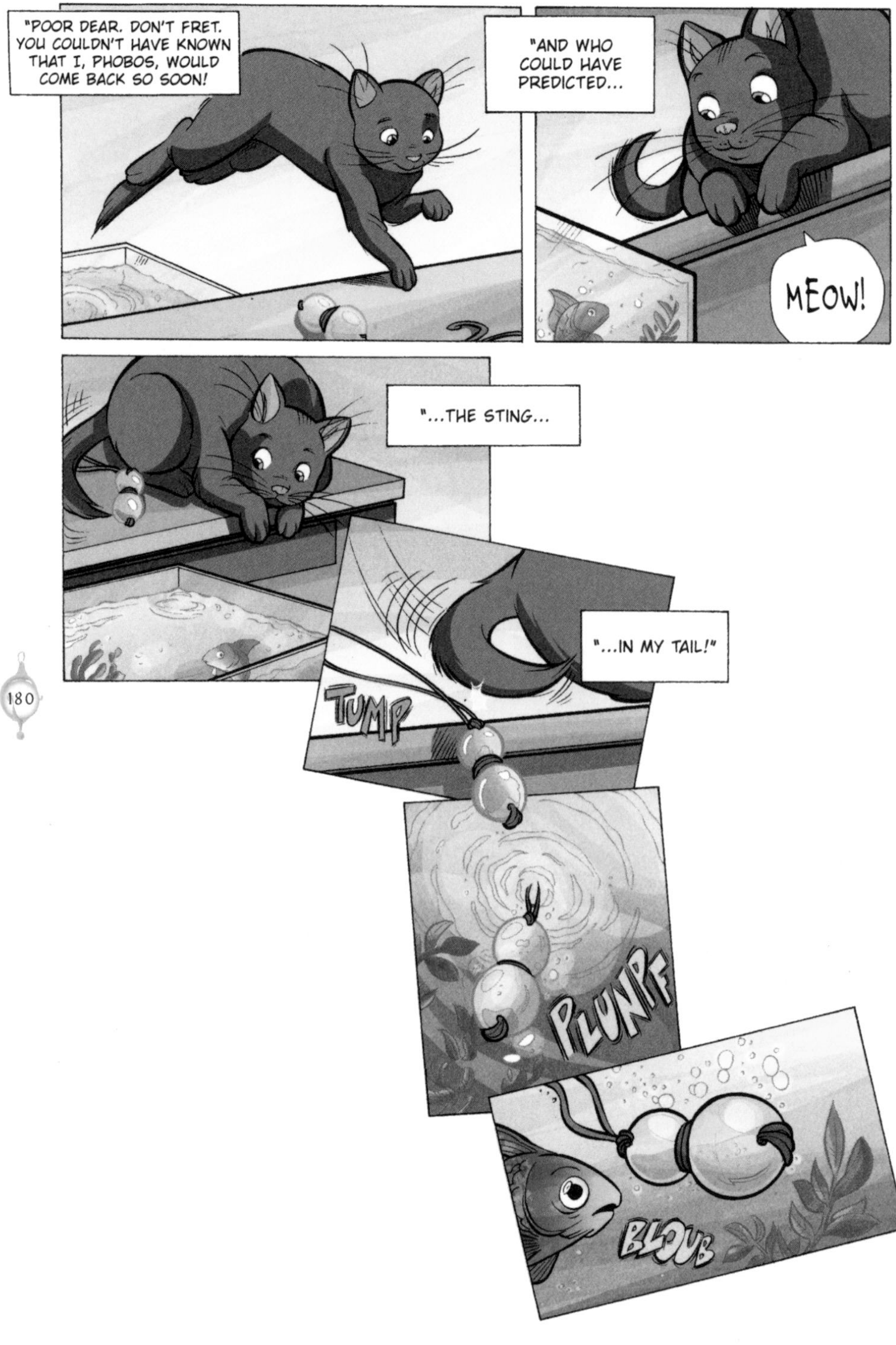
"POOR DEAR. DON'T FRET. YOU COULDN'T HAVE KNOWN THAT I, PHOBOS, WOULD COME BACK SO SOON!
"AND WHO COULD HAVE PREDICTED...
MEOW!
"...THE STING...
"...IN MY TAIL!"
TUMP
PLUNPF
BLOUB

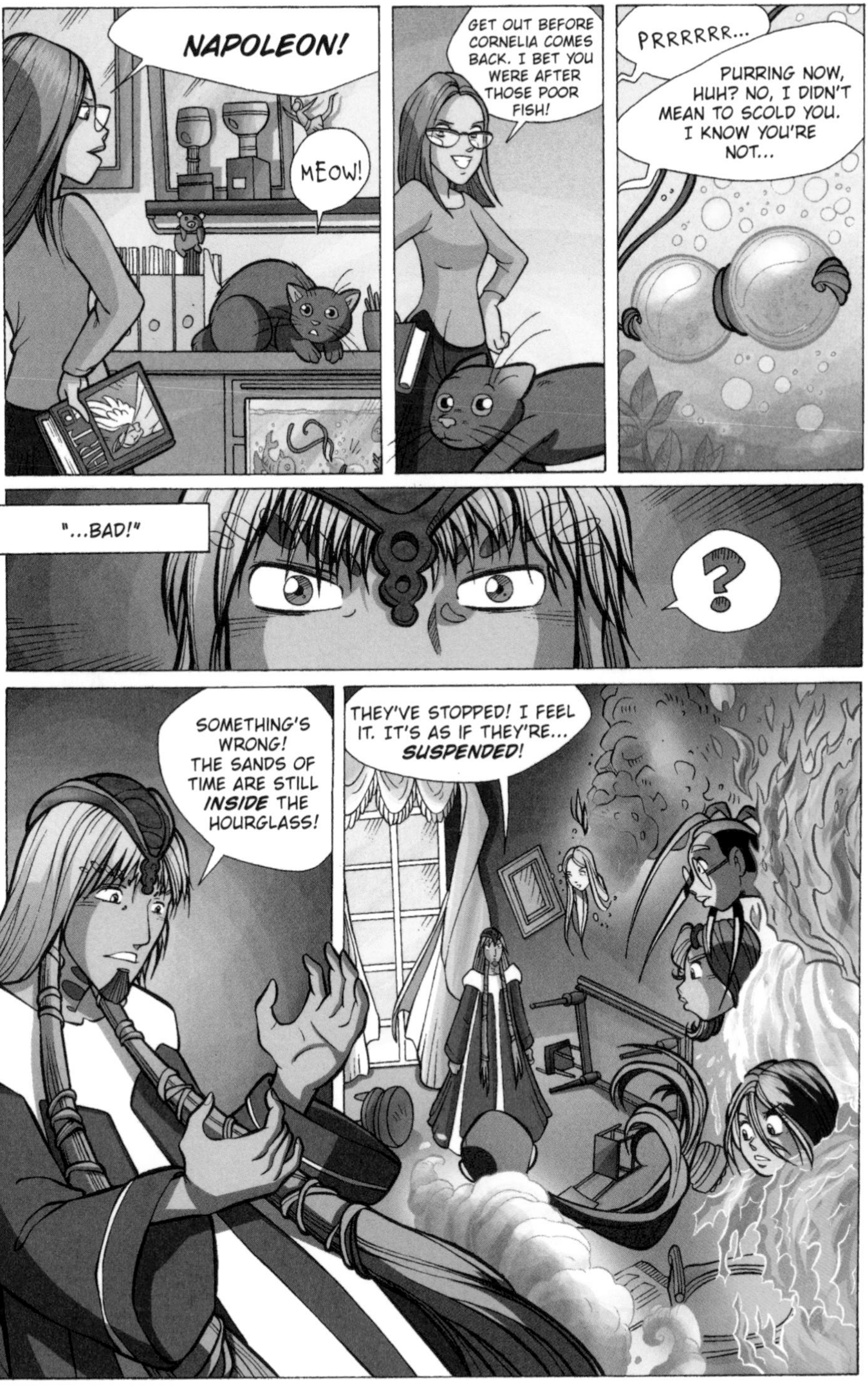
NAPOLEON!
MEOW!
GET OUT BEFORE CORNELIA COMES BACK. I BET YOU WERE AFTER THOSE POOR FISH!
PRRRRRR...
PURRING NOW, HUH? NO, I DIDN'T MEAN TO SCOLD YOU. I KNOW YOU'RE NOT...
"...BAD!"
?
SOMETHING'S WRONG! THE SANDS OF TIME ARE STILL INSIDE THE HOURGLASS!
THEY'VE STOPPED! I FEEL IT. IT'S AS IF THEY'RE... SUSPENDED!

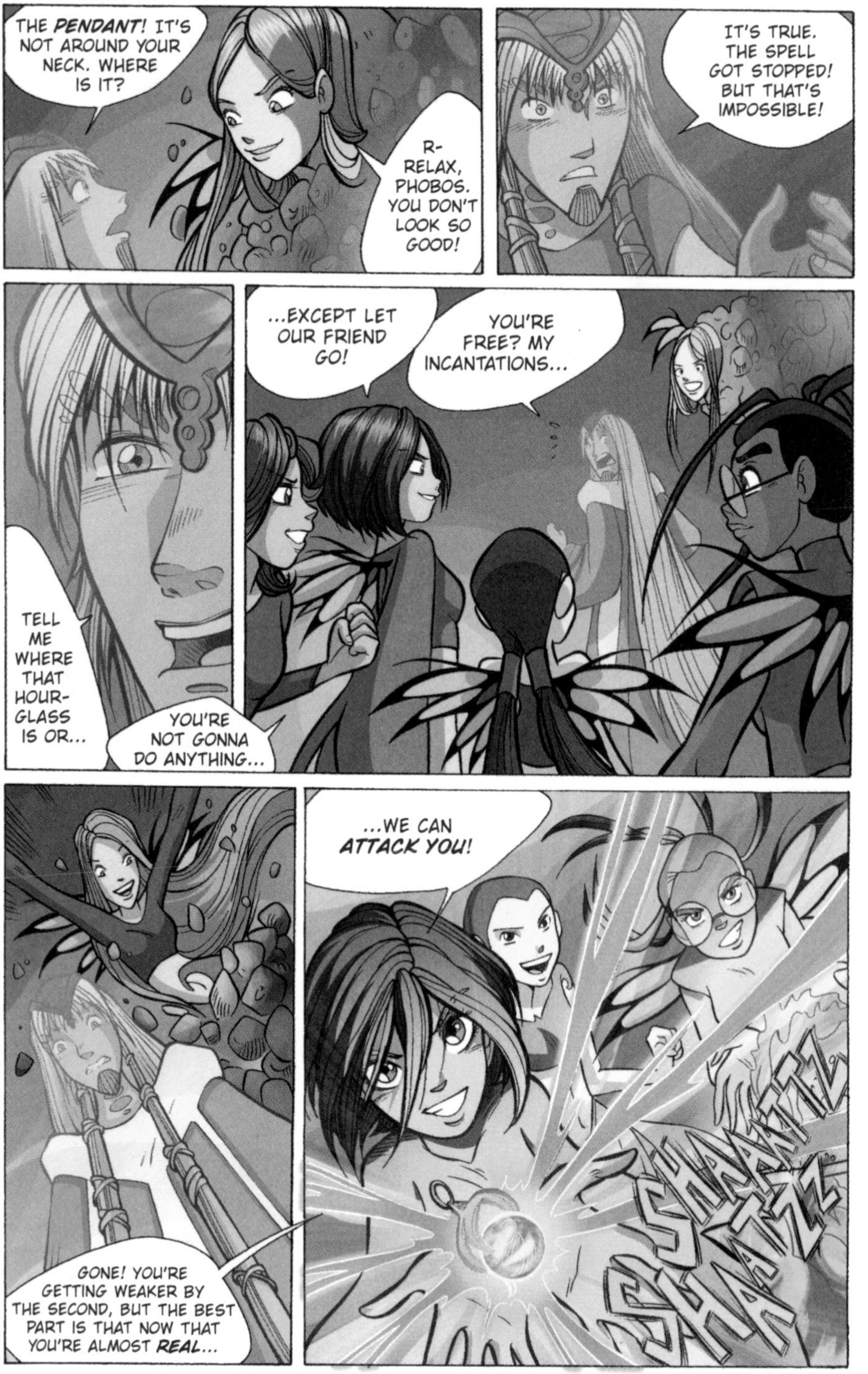
THE PENDANT! IT'S NOT AROUND YOUR NECK. WHERE IS IT?
R-RELAX, PHOBOS. YOU DON'T LOOK SO GOOD!
IT'S TRUE. THE SPELL GOT STOPPED! BUT THAT'S IMPOSSIBLE!
TELL ME WHERE THAT HOURGLASS IS OR...
YOU'RE NOT GONNA DO ANYTHING...
...EXCEPT LET OUR FRIEND GO!
YOU'RE FREE? MY INCANTATIONS...
GONE! YOU'RE GETTING WEAKER BY THE SECOND, BUT THE BEST PART IS THAT NOW THAT YOU'RE ALMOST REAL...
...WE CAN ATTACK YOU!
SHAAAZZZ
SHAZZ
SHA

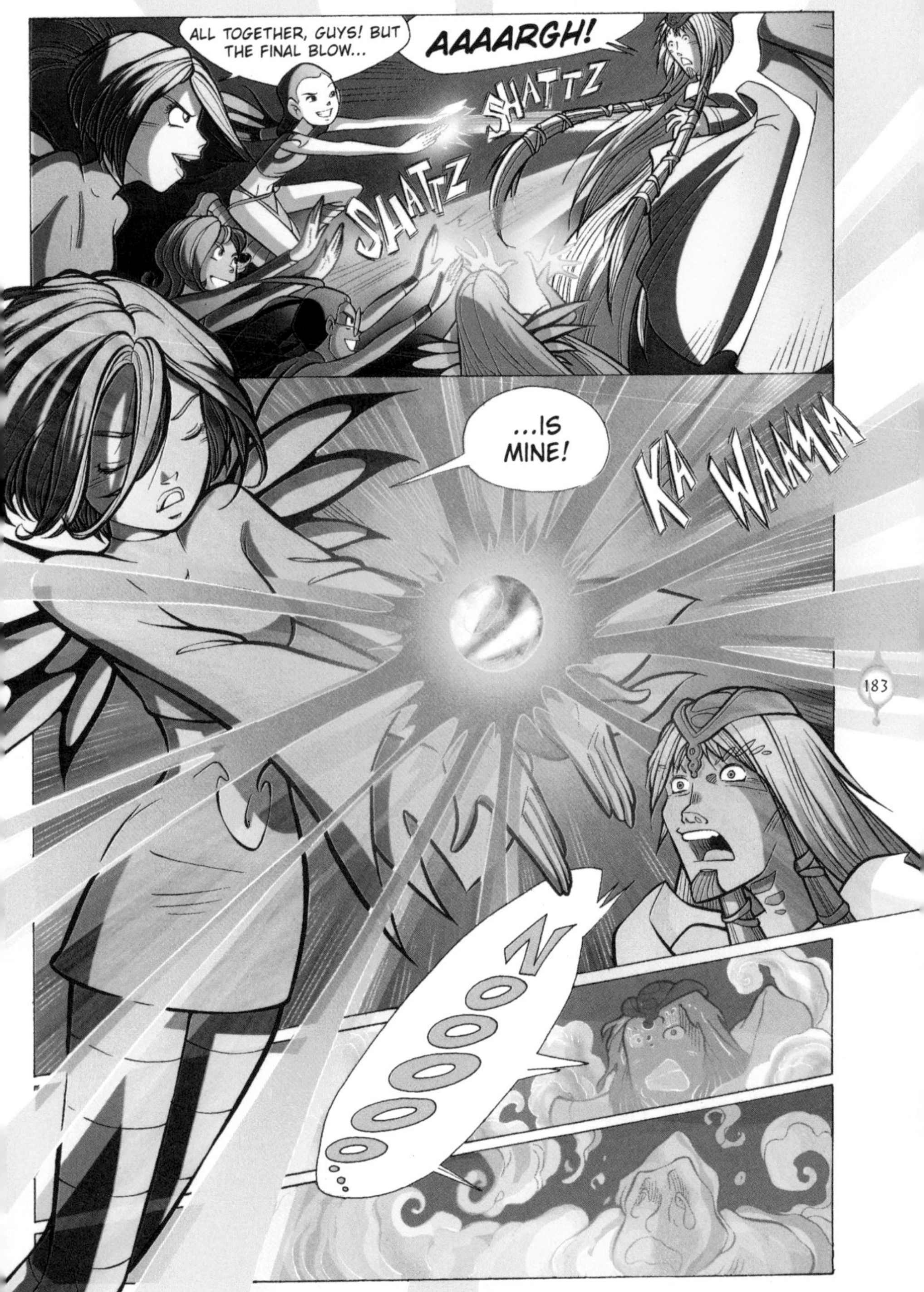
ALL TOGETHER, GUYS! BUT THE FINAL BLOW...
AAAARGH!
SHATTZ
SHATTZ
SHATTZ
...IS MINE!
KA WAAMM
NOOOOOOOO

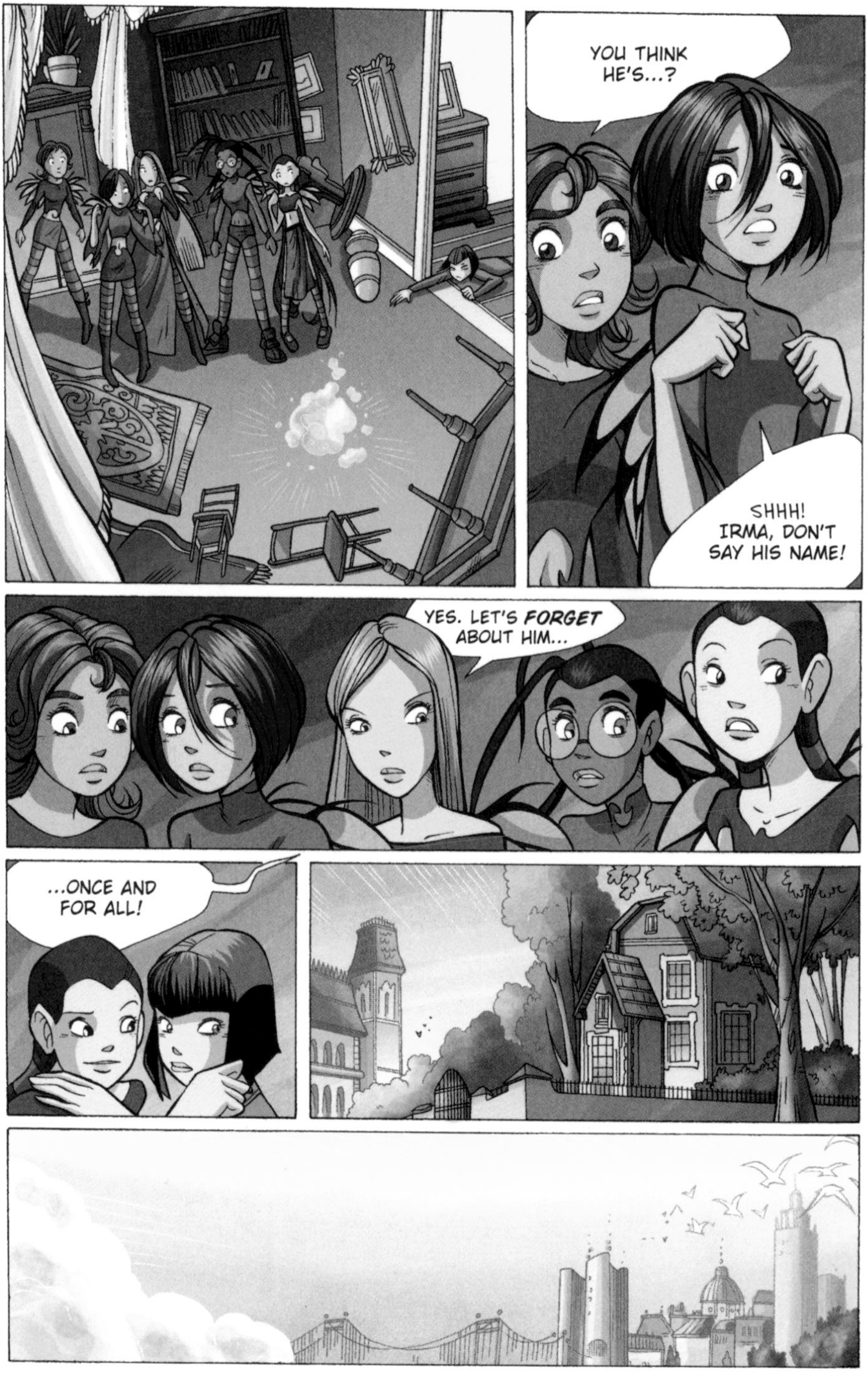
YOU THINK HE'S...?
SHHH! IRMA, DON'T SAY HIS NAME!
YES. LET'S **FORGET** ABOUT HIM...
...ONCE AND FOR ALL!

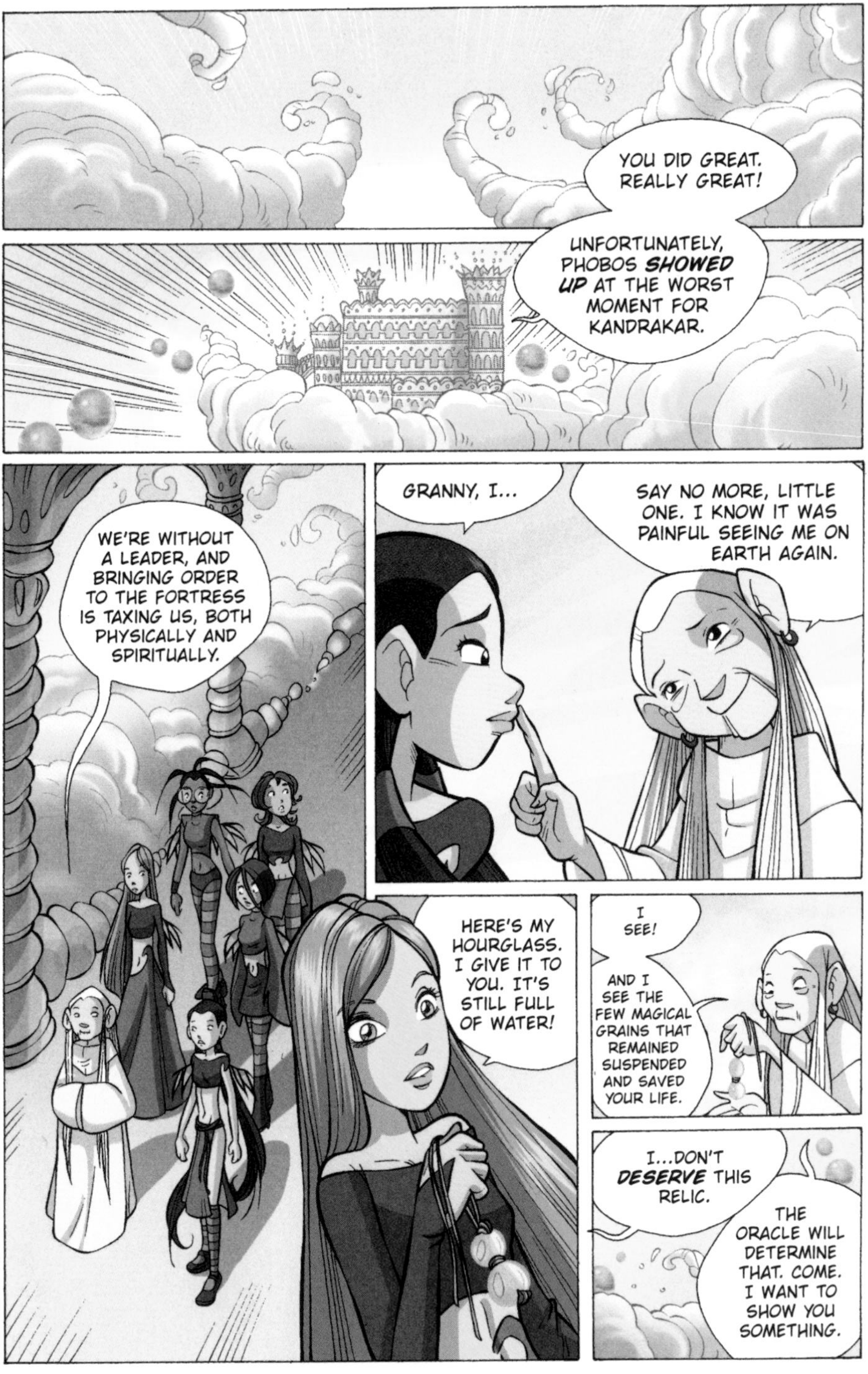

YOU DID GREAT. REALLY GREAT!
UNFORTUNATELY, PHOBOS **SHOWED UP** AT THE WORST MOMENT FOR KANDRAKAR.
WE'RE WITHOUT A LEADER, AND BRINGING ORDER TO THE FORTRESS IS TAXING US, BOTH PHYSICALLY AND SPIRITUALLY.
GRANNY, I...
SAY NO MORE, LITTLE ONE. I KNOW IT WAS PAINFUL SEEING ME ON EARTH AGAIN.
HERE'S MY HOURGLASS. I GIVE IT TO YOU. IT'S STILL FULL OF WATER!
I SEE!
AND I SEE THE FEW MAGICAL GRAINS THAT REMAINED SUSPENDED AND SAVED YOUR LIFE.
I...DON'T **DESERVE** THIS RELIC.
THE ORACLE WILL DETERMINE THAT. COME. I WANT TO SHOW YOU SOMETHING.

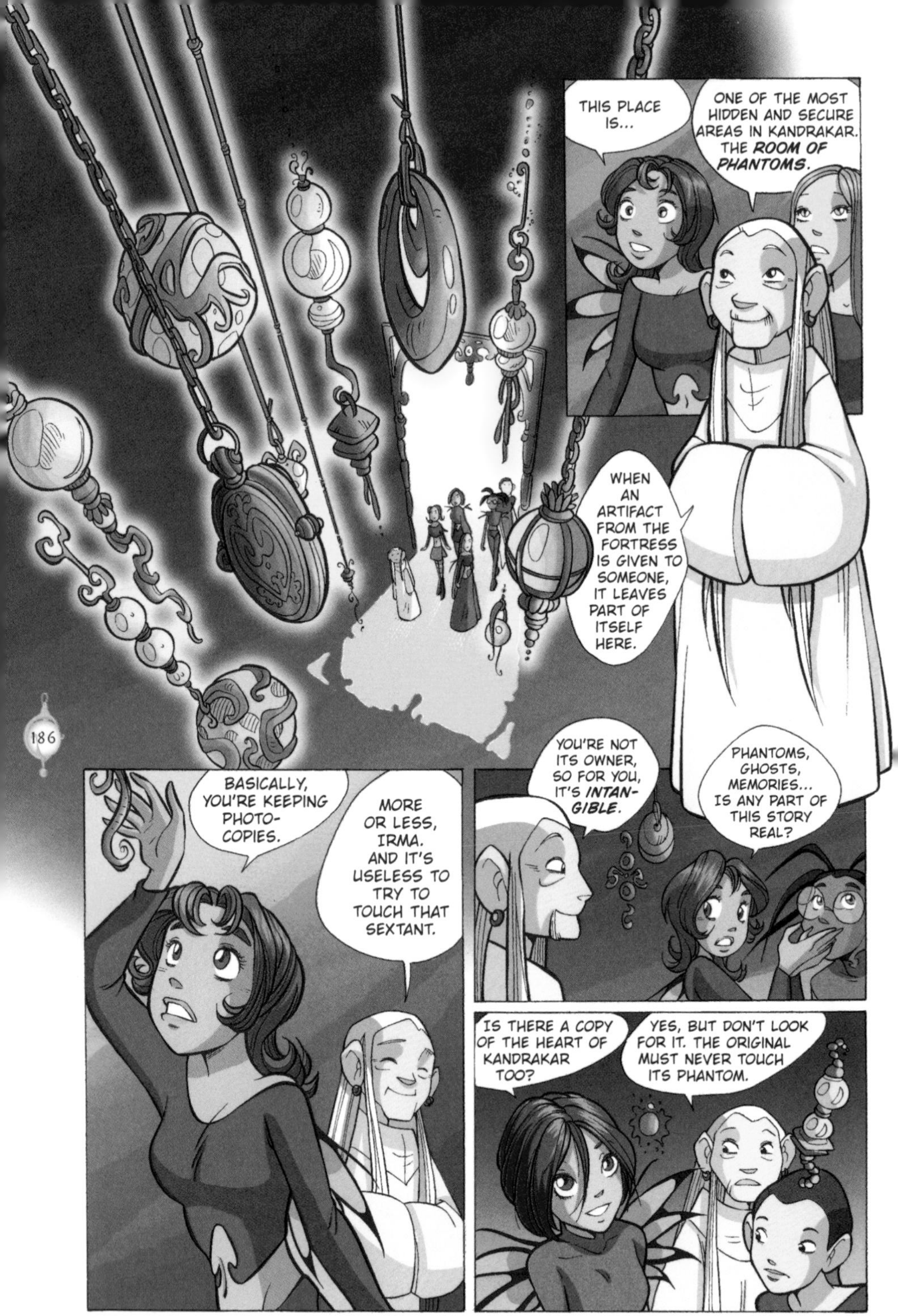
THIS PLACE IS...
ONE OF THE MOST HIDDEN AND SECURE AREAS IN KANDRAKAR. THE ***ROOM OF PHANTOMS***.
WHEN AN ARTIFACT FROM THE FORTRESS IS GIVEN TO SOMEONE, IT LEAVES PART OF ITSELF HERE.
BASICALLY, YOU'RE KEEPING PHOTO-COPIES.
MORE OR LESS, IRMA. AND IT'S USELESS TO TRY TO TOUCH THAT SEXTANT.
PHANTOMS, GHOSTS, MEMORIES... IS ANY PART OF THIS STORY REAL?
YOU'RE NOT ITS OWNER, SO FOR YOU, IT'S ***INTAN-GIBLE***.
IS THERE A COPY OF THE HEART OF KANDRAKAR TOO?
YES, BUT DON'T LOOK FOR IT. THE ORIGINAL MUST NEVER TOUCH ITS PHANTOM.

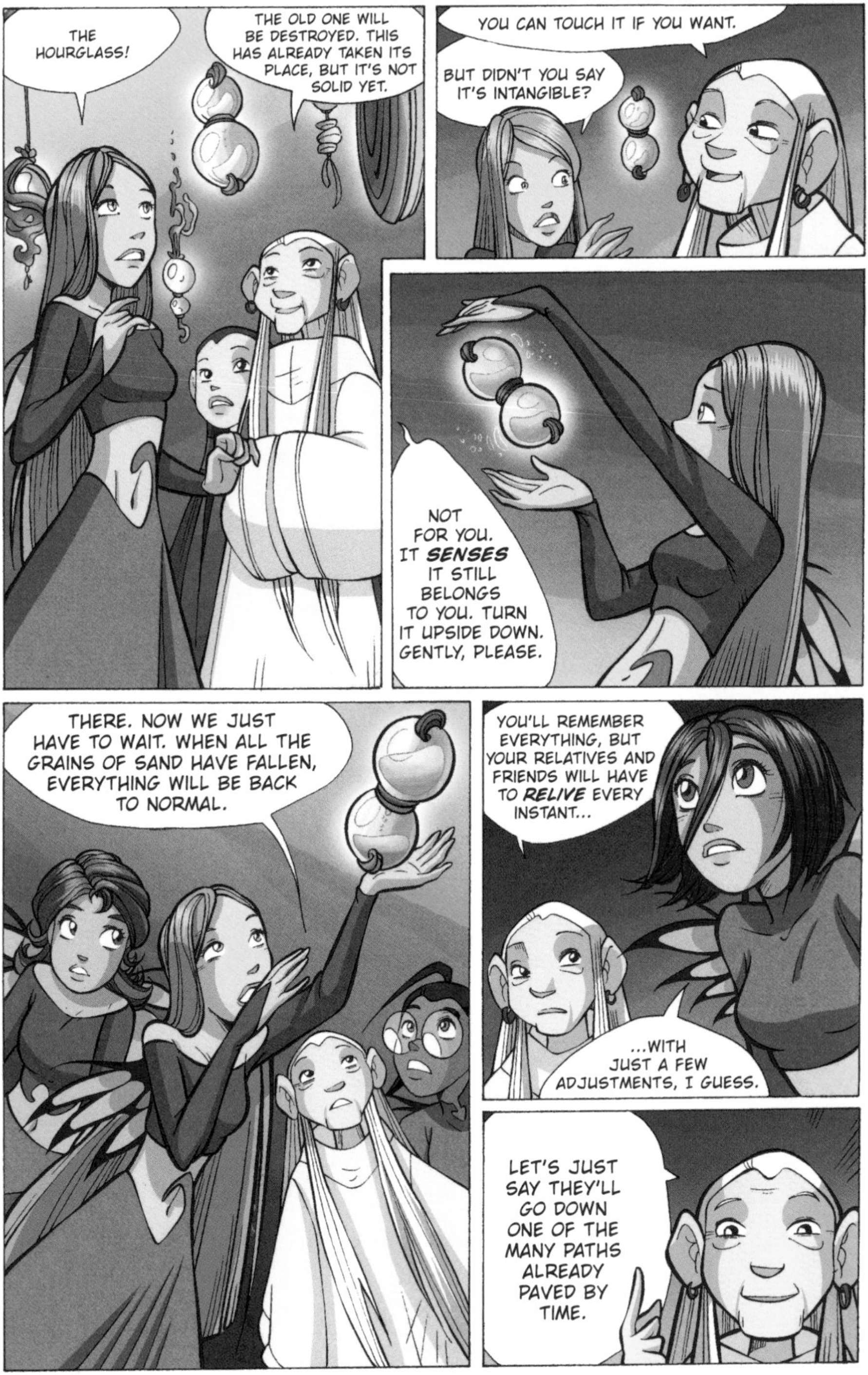
THE HOURGLASS!
THE OLD ONE WILL BE DESTROYED. THIS HAS ALREADY TAKEN ITS PLACE, BUT IT'S NOT SOLID YET.
YOU CAN TOUCH IT IF YOU WANT.
BUT DIDN'T YOU SAY IT'S INTANGIBLE?
NOT FOR YOU. IT **SENSES** IT STILL BELONGS TO YOU. TURN IT UPSIDE DOWN. GENTLY, PLEASE.
THERE. NOW WE JUST HAVE TO WAIT. WHEN ALL THE GRAINS OF SAND HAVE FALLEN, EVERYTHING WILL BE BACK TO NORMAL.
YOU'LL REMEMBER EVERYTHING, BUT YOUR RELATIVES AND FRIENDS WILL HAVE TO **RELIVE** EVERY INSTANT...
...WITH JUST A FEW ADJUSTMENTS, I GUESS.
LET'S JUST SAY THEY'LL GO DOWN ONE OF THE MANY PATHS ALREADY PAVED BY TIME.

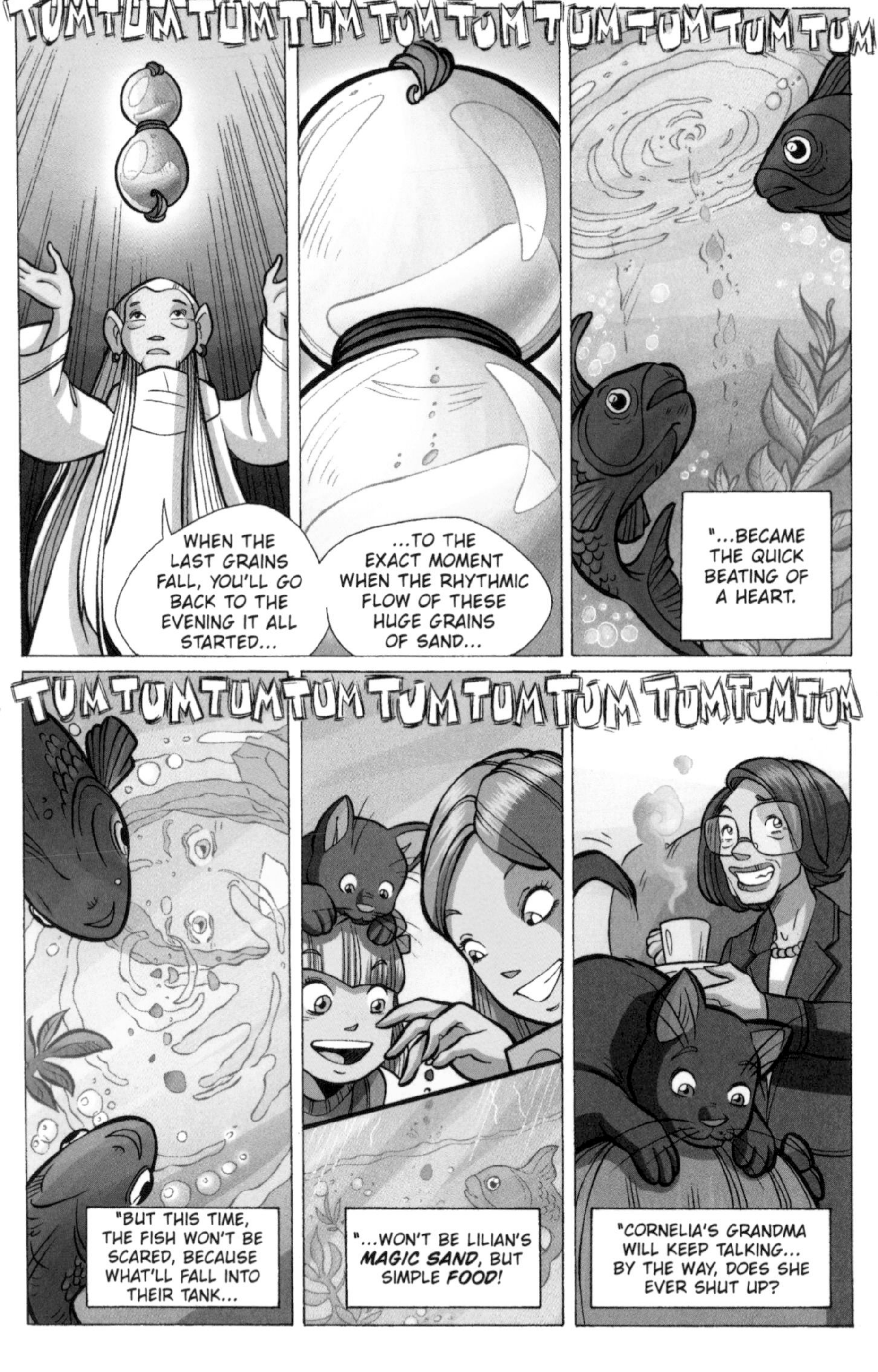
TUM TUM TUM TUM TUM TUM TUM TUM TUM TUM TUM
WHEN THE LAST GRAINS FALL, YOU'LL GO BACK TO THE EVENING IT ALL STARTED...
...TO THE EXACT MOMENT WHEN THE RHYTHMIC FLOW OF THESE HUGE GRAINS OF SAND...
"...BECAME THE QUICK BEATING OF A HEART.
TUM TUM TUM TUM TUM TUM TUM TUM TUM TUM
"BUT THIS TIME, THE FISH WON'T BE SCARED, BECAUSE WHAT'LL FALL INTO THEIR TANK...
"...WON'T BE LILIAN'S ***MAGIC SAND***, BUT SIMPLE ***FOOD***!
"CORNELIA'S GRANDMA WILL KEEP TALKING... BY THE WAY, DOES SHE EVER SHUT UP?

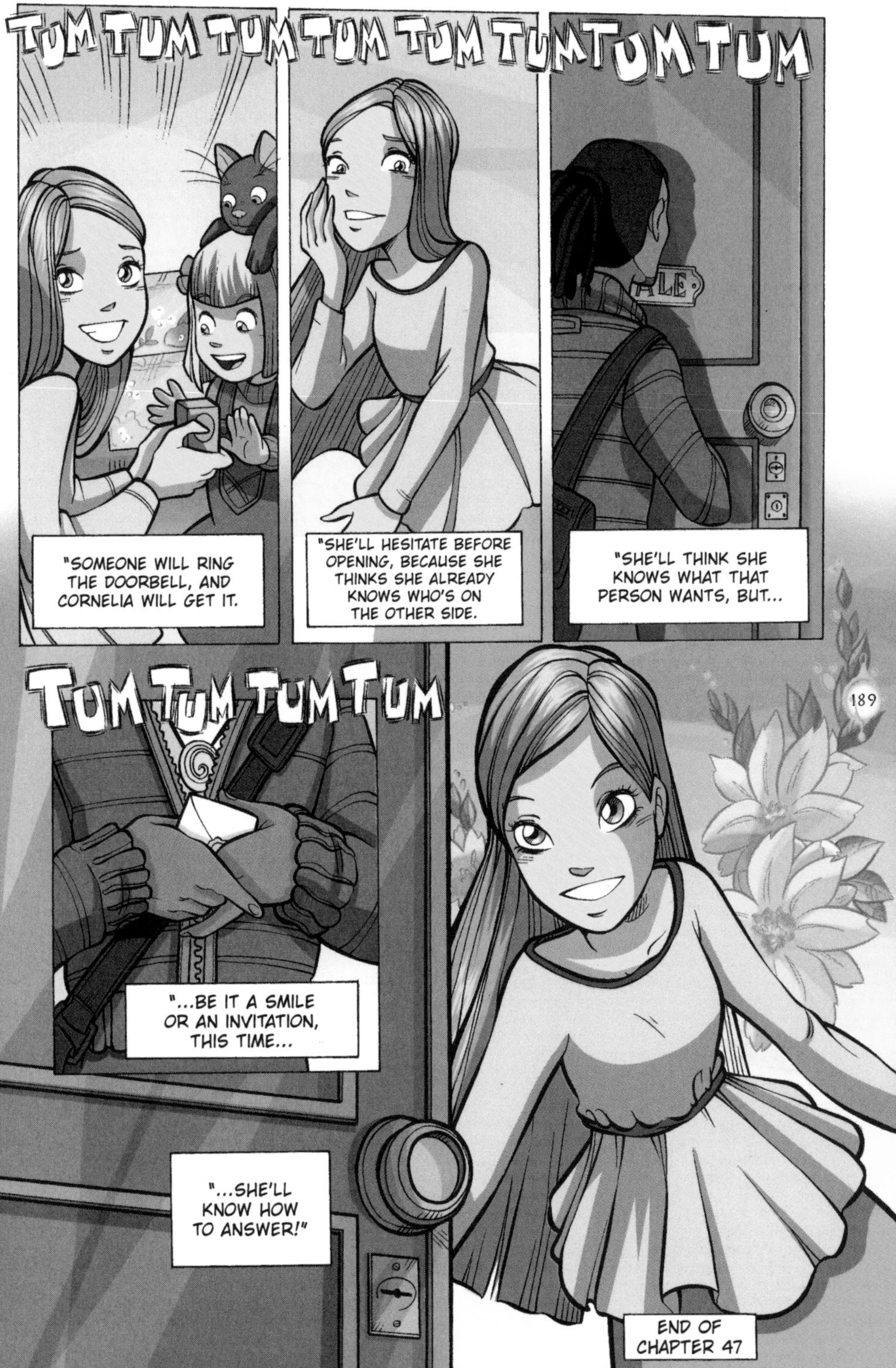
TUM TUM TUM TUM TUM TUM TUM TUM
"SOMEONE WILL RING THE DOORBELL, AND CORNELIA WILL GET IT.
"SHE'LL HESITATE BEFORE OPENING, BECAUSE SHE THINKS SHE ALREADY KNOWS WHO'S ON THE OTHER SIDE.
"SHE'LL THINK SHE KNOWS WHAT THAT PERSON WANTS, BUT...
TUM TUM TUM TUM
"...BE IT A SMILE OR AN INVITATION, THIS TIME...
"...SHE'LL KNOW HOW TO ANSWER!"
END OF CHAPTER 47

W.i.t.c.h.

Will Irma Taranee Cornelia Hay Lin

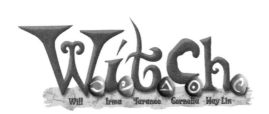

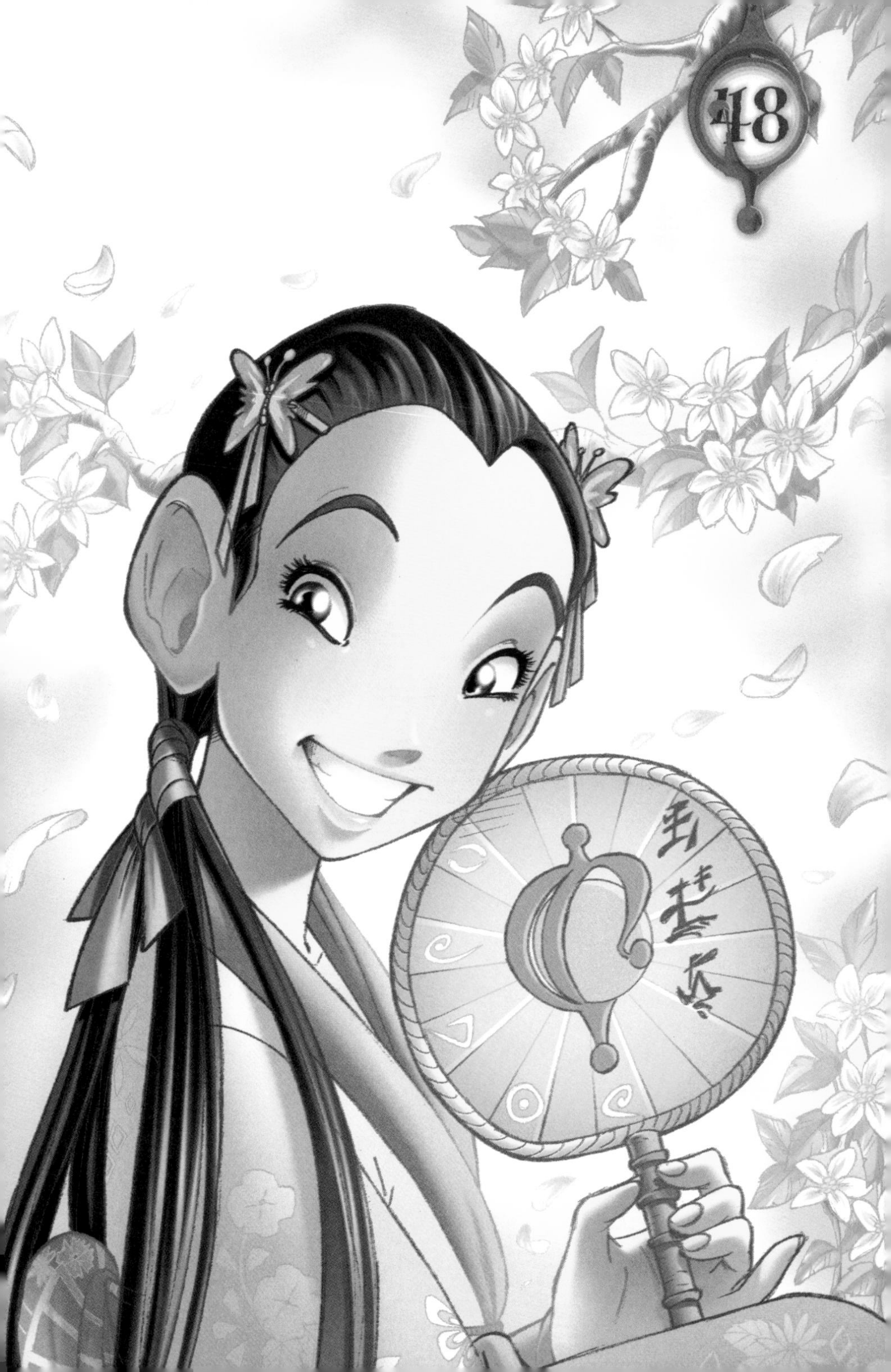
48

New Horizons

"Don't allow the flames of passion to be extinguished..."

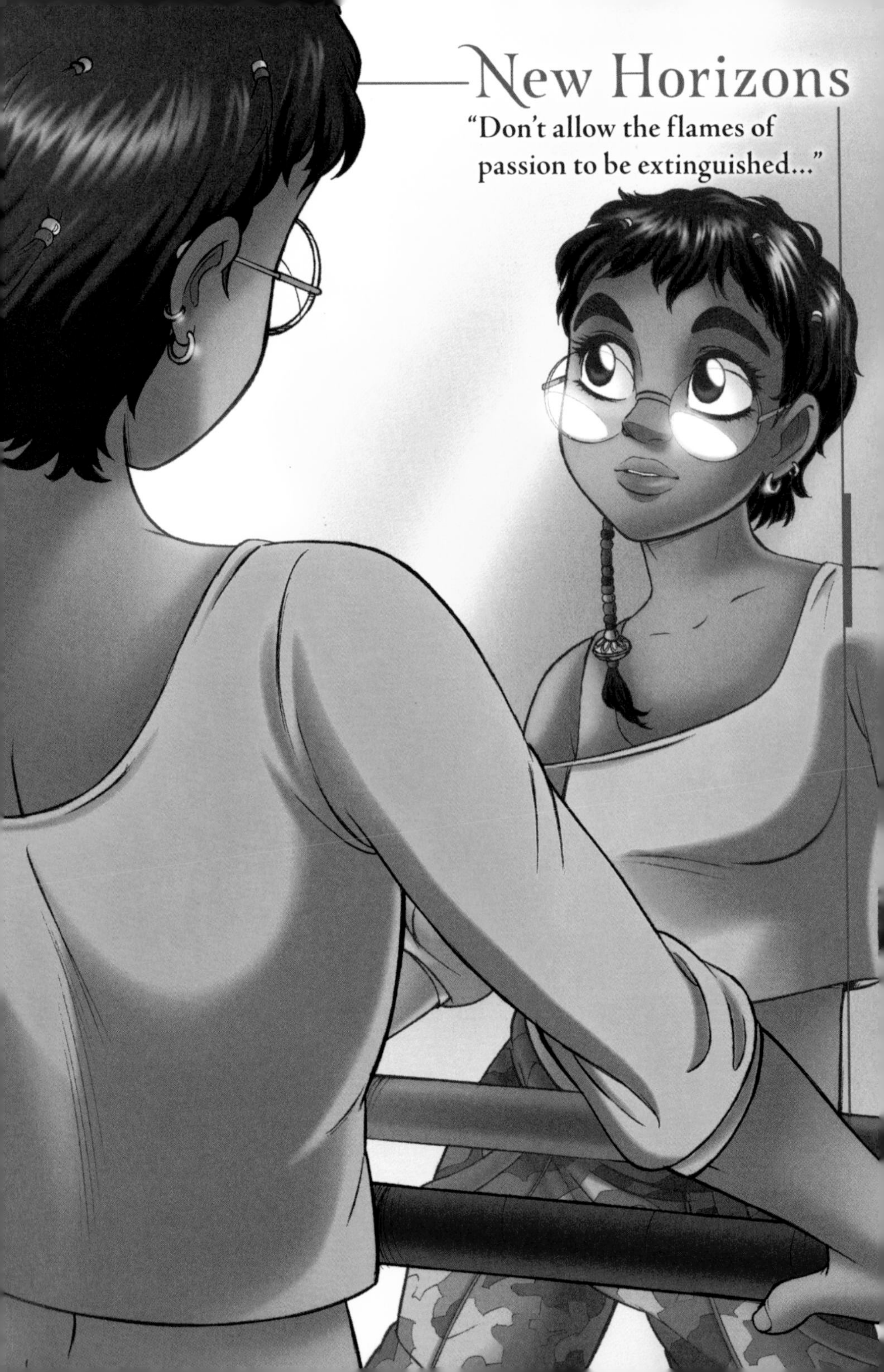

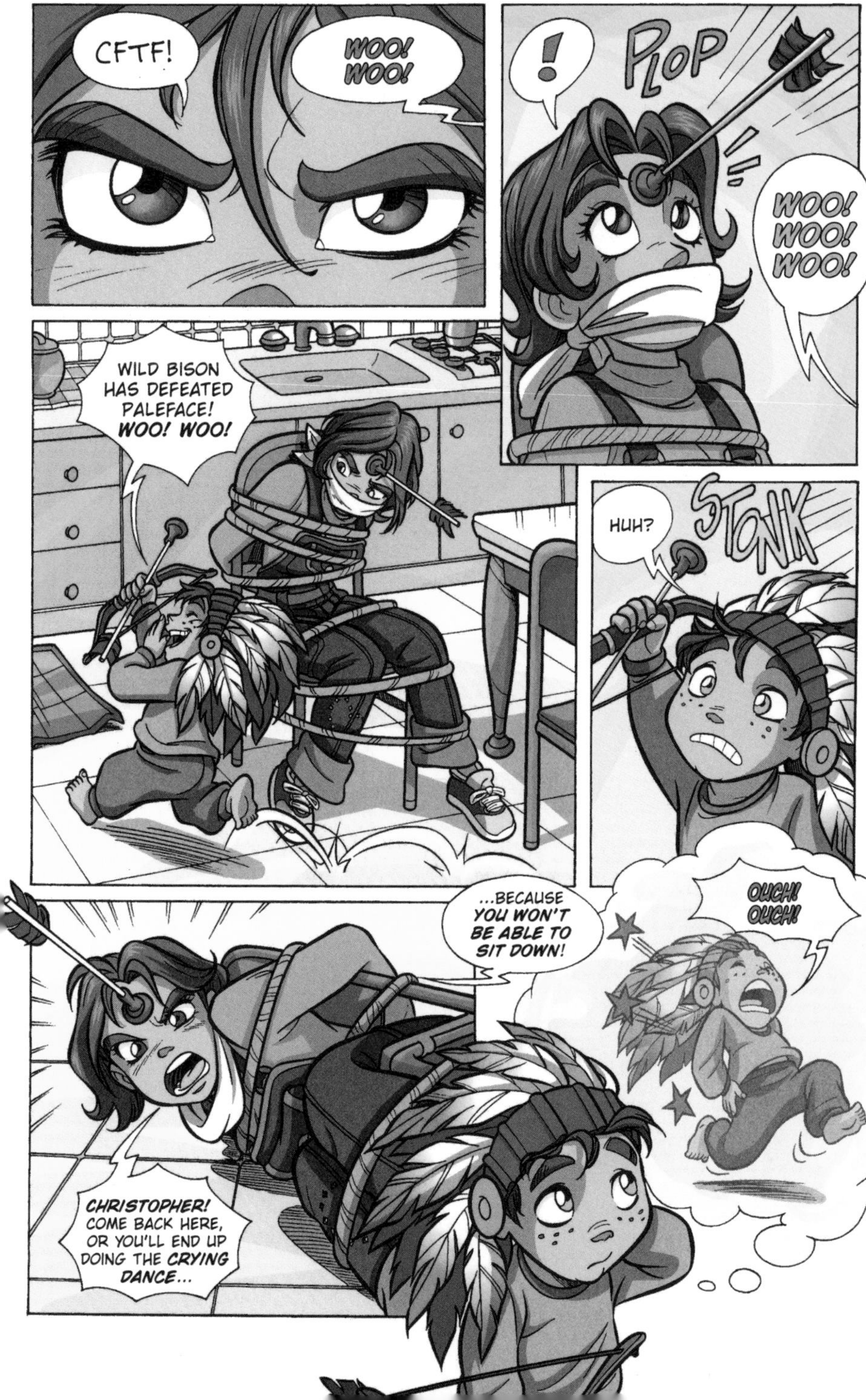
CFTF!
WOO! WOO!
!
PLOP
WOO! WOO! WOO!
WILD BISON HAS DEFEATED PALEFACE! WOO! WOO!
HUH?
STONK
...BECAUSE YOU WON'T BE ABLE TO SIT DOWN!
OUCH! OUCH!
CHRISTOPHER! COME BACK HERE, OR YOU'LL END UP DOING THE CRYING DANCE...

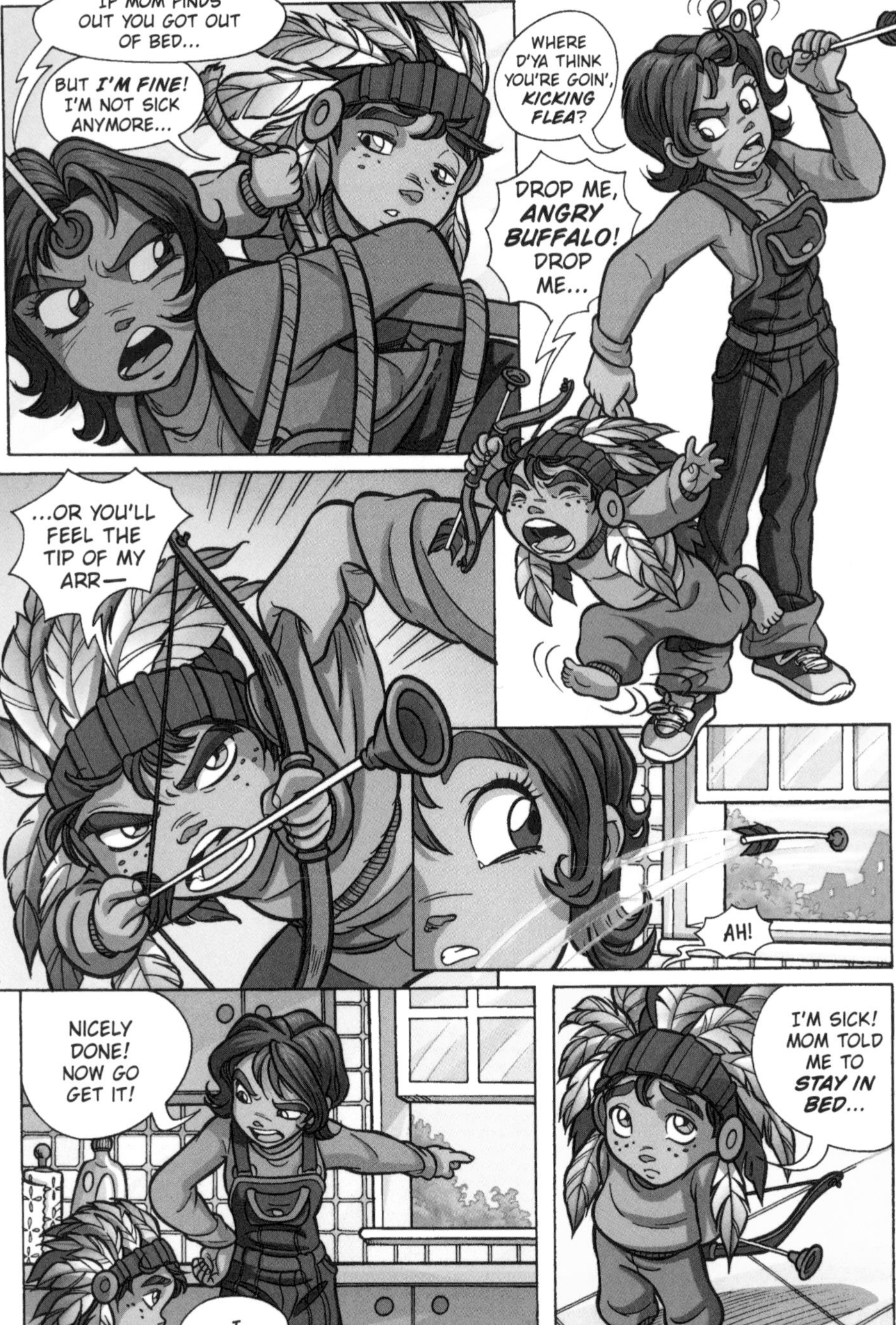
IF MOM FINDS OUT YOU GOT OUT OF BED...
BUT I'M FINE! I'M NOT SICK ANYMORE...
WHERE D'YA THINK YOU'RE GOIN', KICKING FLEA?
POP
DROP ME, ANGRY BUFFALO! DROP ME...
...OR YOU'LL FEEL THE TIP OF MY ARR—
AH!
NICELY DONE! NOW GO GET IT!
I CAN'T...
I'M SICK! MOM TOLD ME TO STAY IN BED...

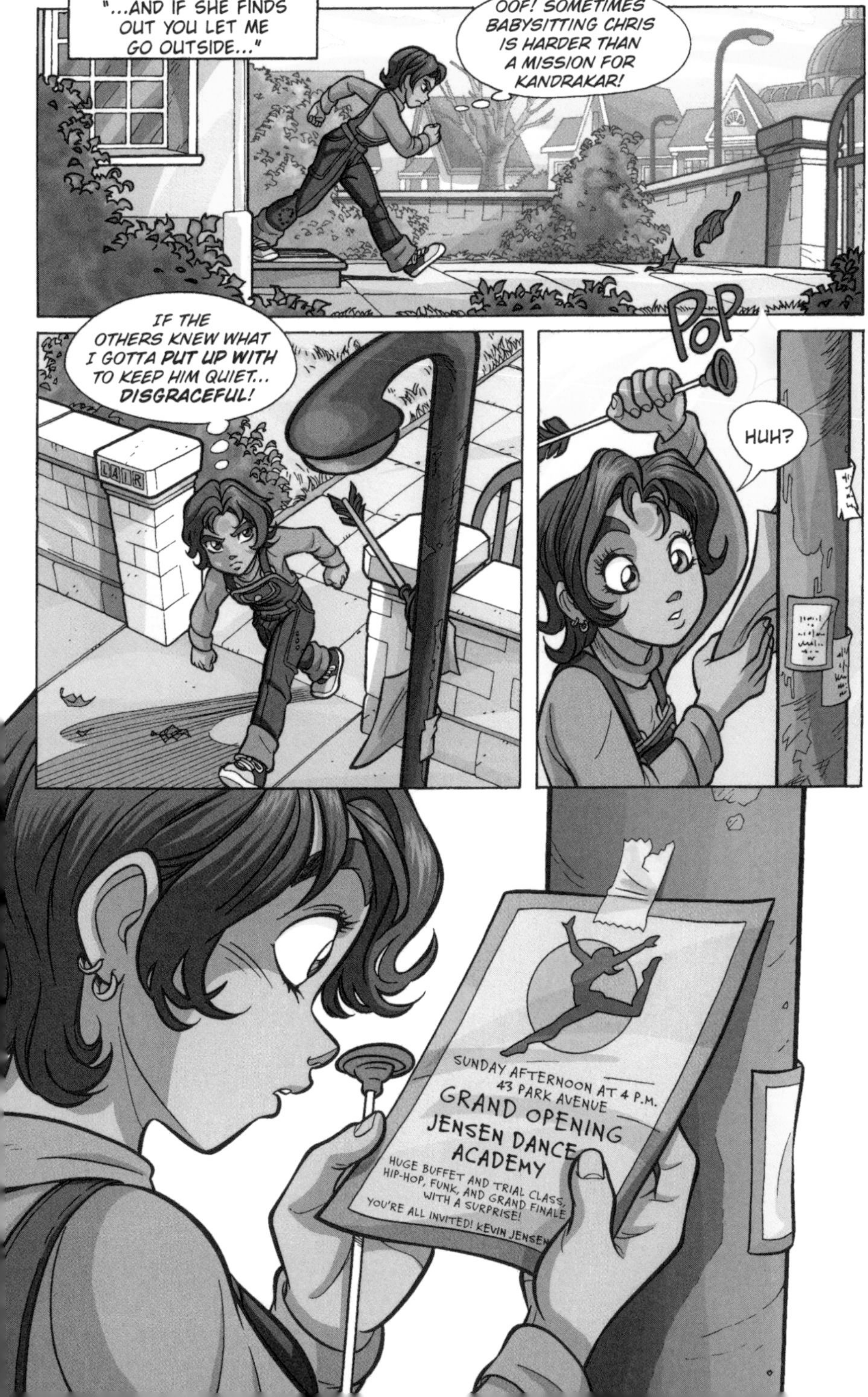
"...AND IF SHE FINDS OUT YOU LET ME GO OUTSIDE..."
OOF! SOMETIMES BABYSITTING CHRIS IS HARDER THAN A MISSION FOR KANDRAKAR!
IF THE OTHERS KNEW WHAT I GOTTA **PUT UP WITH** TO KEEP HIM QUIET... **DISGRACEFUL!**
POP
HUH?
SUNDAY AFTERNOON AT 4 P.M.
43 PARK AVENUE
GRAND OPENING
JENSEN DANCE ACADEMY
HUGE BUFFET AND TRIAL CLASS, HIP-HOP, FUNK, AND GRAND FINALE WITH A SURPRISE!
YOU'RE ALL INVITED! KEVIN JENSEN

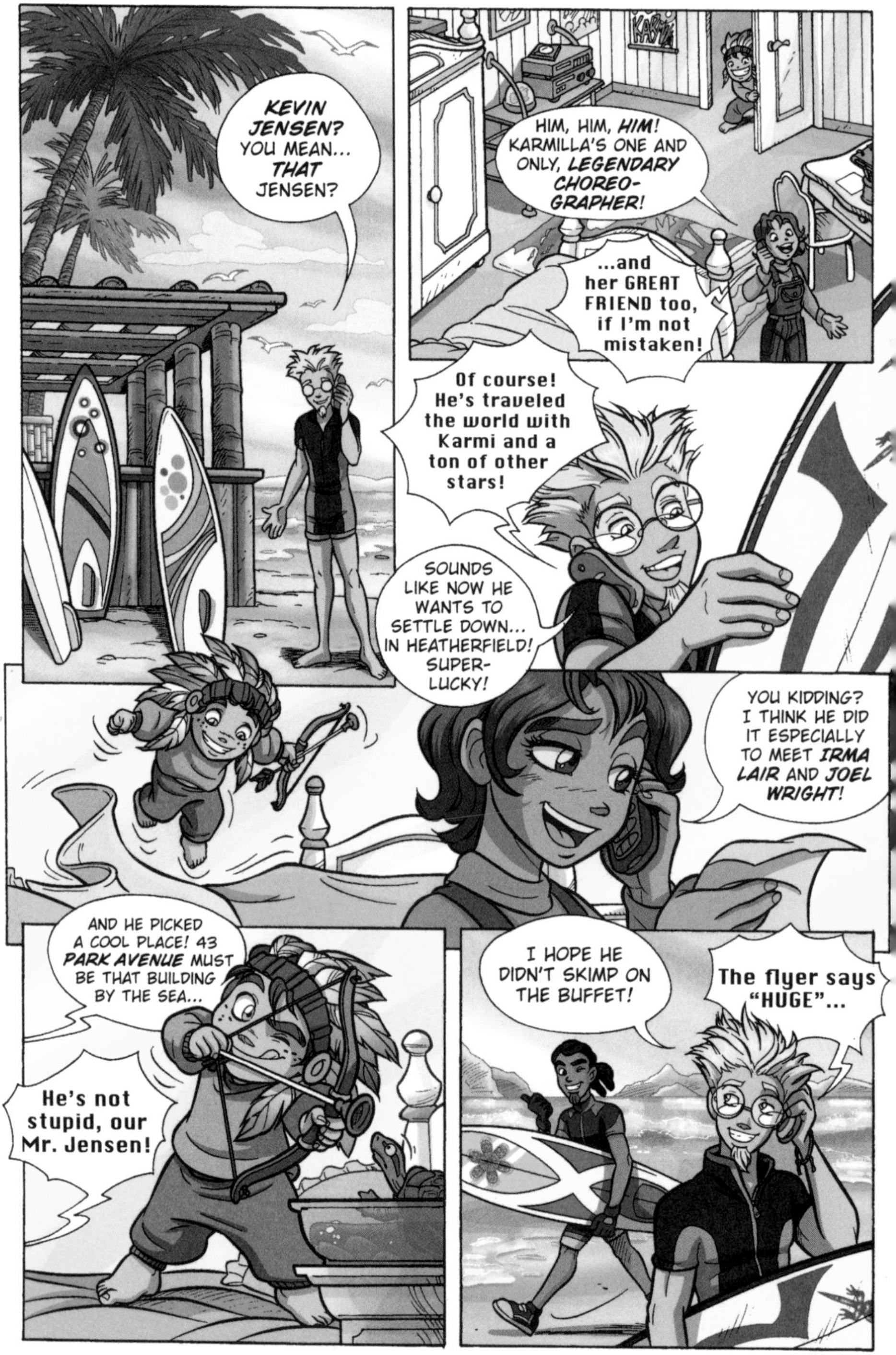

KEVIN JENSEN? YOU MEAN... THAT JENSEN?
HIM, HIM, HIM! KARMILLA'S ONE AND ONLY, LEGENDARY CHOREO-GRAPHER!
...and her GREAT FRIEND too, if I'm not mistaken!
Of course! He's traveled the world with Karmi and a ton of other stars!
SOUNDS LIKE NOW HE WANTS TO SETTLE DOWN... IN HEATHERFIELD! SUPER-LUCKY!
YOU KIDDING? I THINK HE DID IT ESPECIALLY TO MEET IRMA LAIR AND JOEL WRIGHT!
AND HE PICKED A COOL PLACE! 43 PARK AVENUE MUST BE THAT BUILDING BY THE SEA...
He's not stupid, our Mr. Jensen!
I HOPE HE DIDN'T SKIMP ON THE BUFFET!
The flyer says "HUGE"...

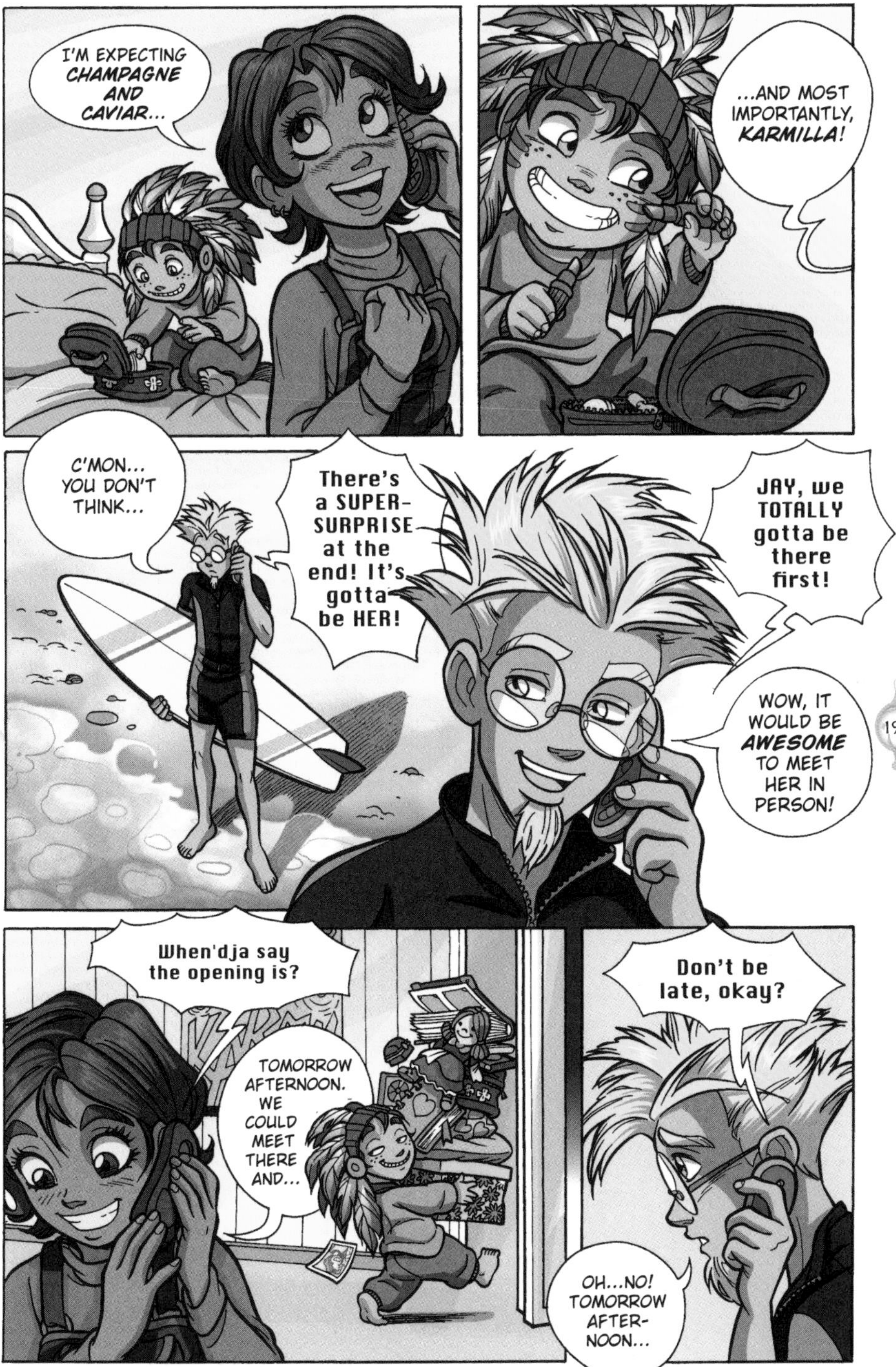
I'M EXPECTING CHAMPAGNE AND CAVIAR...
...AND MOST IMPORTANTLY, KARMILLA!
C'MON... YOU DON'T THINK...
There's a SUPER-SURPRISE at the end! It's gotta be HER!
JAY, we TOTALLY gotta be there first!
WOW, IT WOULD BE AWESOME TO MEET HER IN PERSON!
When'dja say the opening is?
TOMORROW AFTERNOON. WE COULD MEET THERE AND...
Don't be late, okay?
OH...NO! TOMORROW AFTER-NOON...

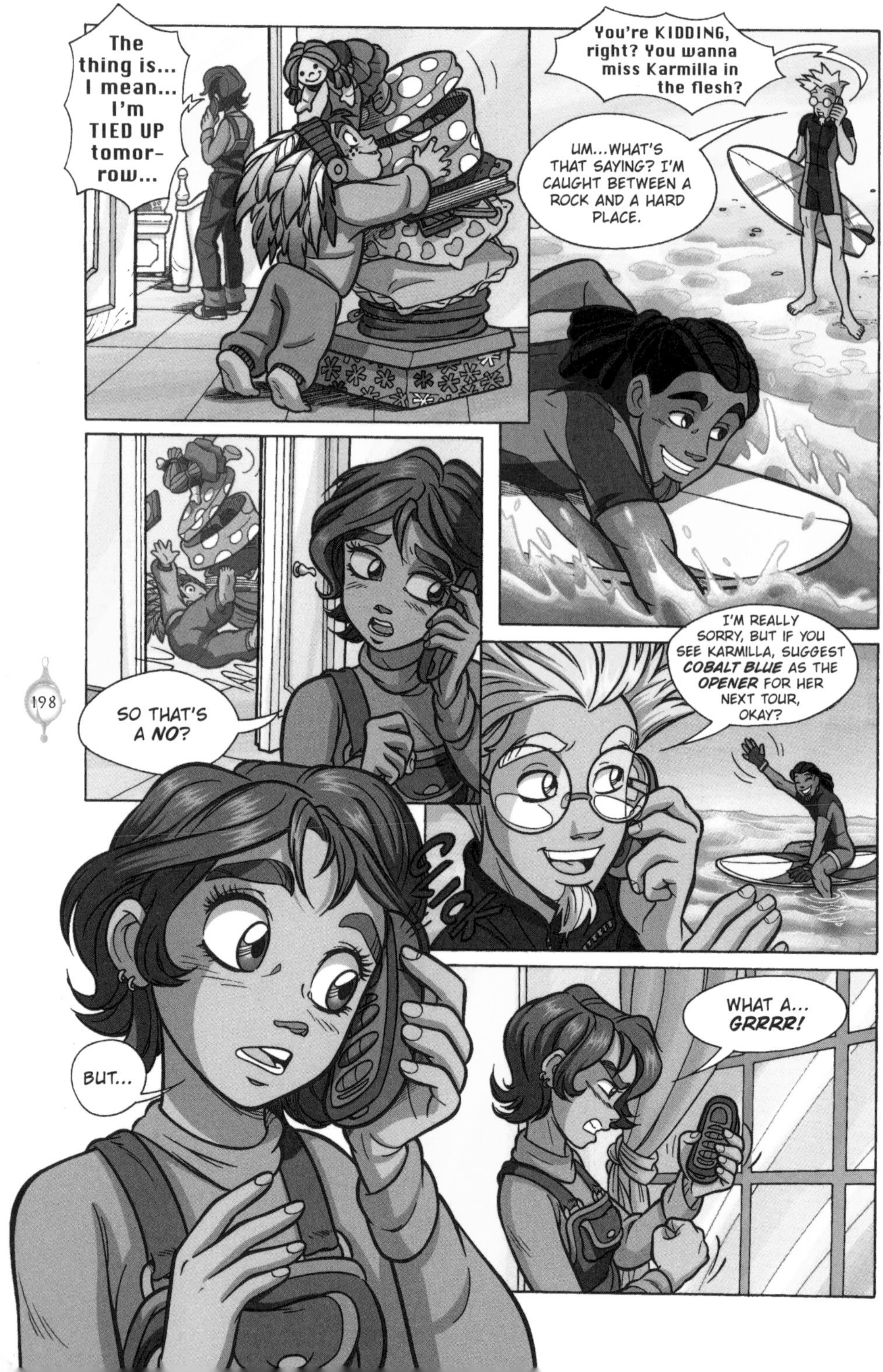
The thing is... I mean... I'm TIED UP tomorrow...
You're KIDDING, right? You wanna miss Karmilla in the flesh?
UM...WHAT'S THAT SAYING? I'M CAUGHT BETWEEN A ROCK AND A HARD PLACE.
SO THAT'S A ***NO***?
I'M REALLY SORRY, BUT IF YOU SEE KARMILLA, SUGGEST ***COBALT BLUE*** AS THE ***OPENER*** FOR HER NEXT TOUR, OKAY?
CLICK
BUT...
WHAT A... ***GRRRR!***

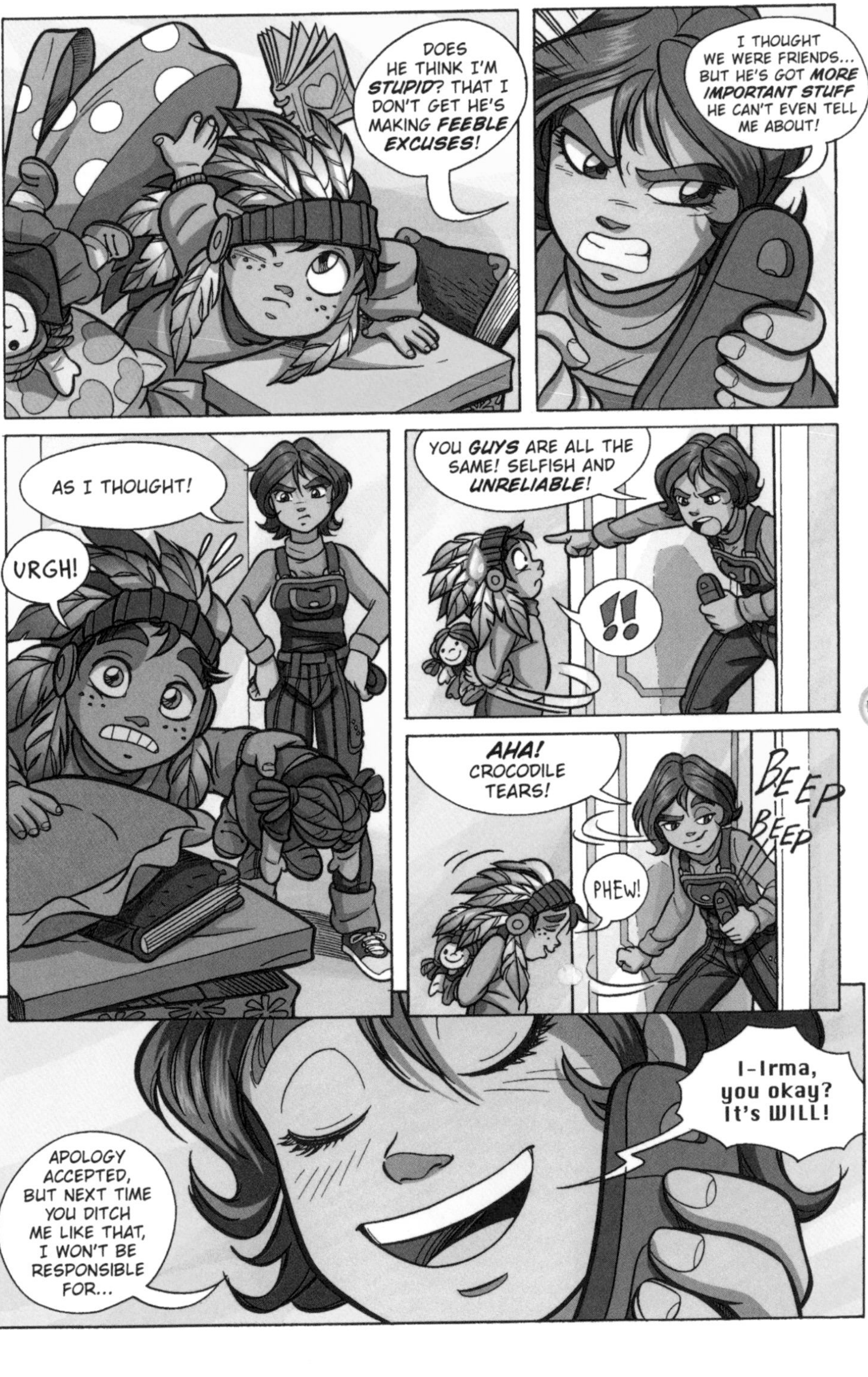
DOES HE THINK I'M STUPID? THAT I DON'T GET HE'S MAKING FEEBLE EXCUSES!
I THOUGHT WE WERE FRIENDS... BUT HE'S GOT MORE IMPORTANT STUFF HE CAN'T EVEN TELL ME ABOUT!
AS I THOUGHT!
URGH!
YOU GUYS ARE ALL THE SAME! SELFISH AND UNRELIABLE!
!!
AHA! CROCODILE TEARS!
PHEW!
BEEP
BEEP
I-Irma, you okay? It's WILL!
APOLOGY ACCEPTED, BUT NEXT TIME YOU DITCH ME LIKE THAT, I WON'T BE RESPONSIBLE FOR...

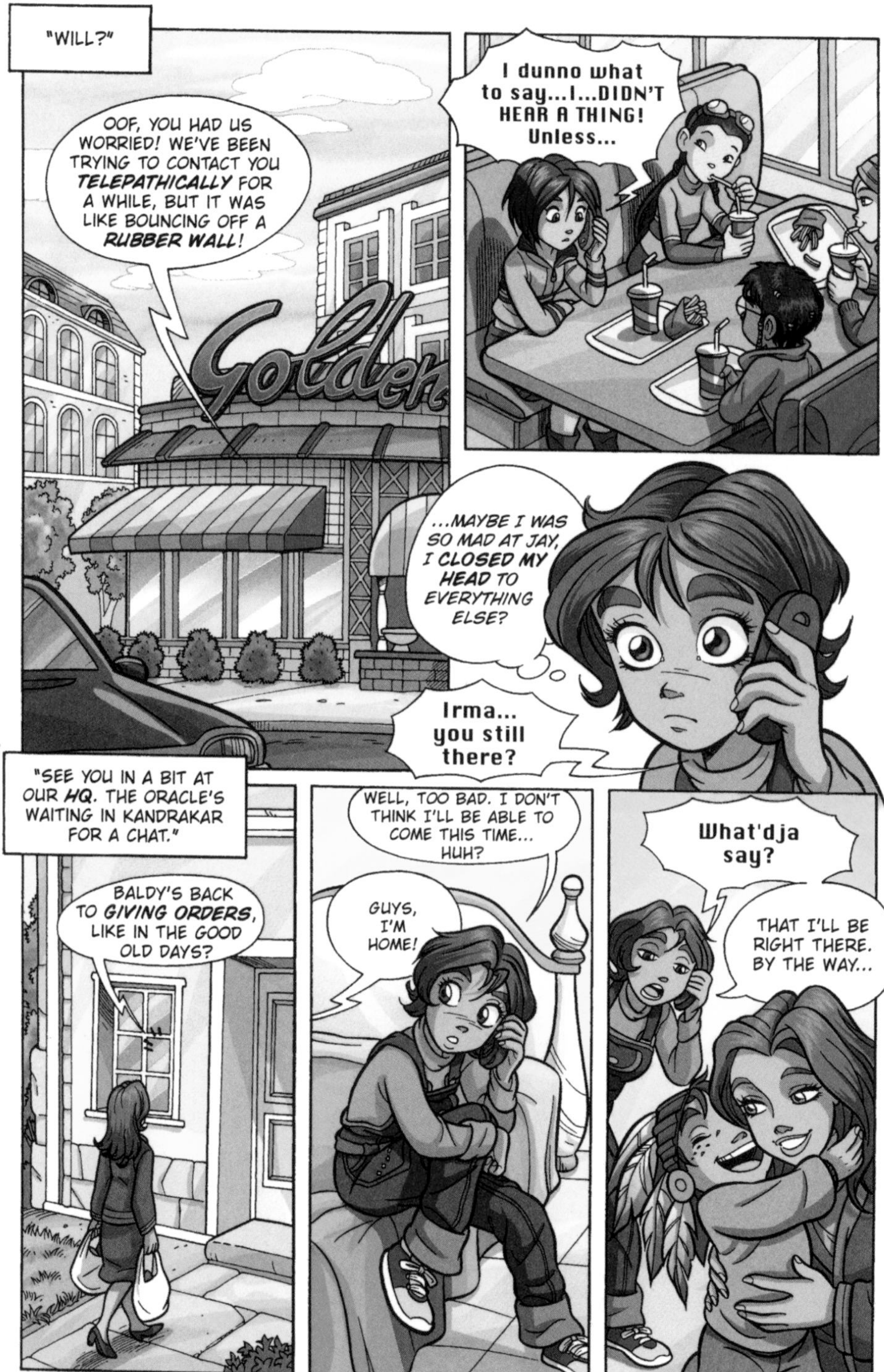
"WILL?"
OOF, YOU HAD US WORRIED! WE'VE BEEN TRYING TO CONTACT YOU TELEPATHICALLY FOR A WHILE, BUT IT WAS LIKE BOUNCING OFF A RUBBER WALL!
Golden
I dunno what to say...I...DIDN'T HEAR A THING! Unless...
...MAYBE I WAS SO MAD AT JAY, I CLOSED MY HEAD TO EVERYTHING ELSE?
Irma... you still there?
"SEE YOU IN A BIT AT OUR HQ. THE ORACLE'S WAITING IN KANDRAKAR FOR A CHAT."
BALDY'S BACK TO GIVING ORDERS, LIKE IN THE GOOD OLD DAYS?
WELL, TOO BAD. I DON'T THINK I'LL BE ABLE TO COME THIS TIME... HUH?
GUYS, I'M HOME!
What'dja say?
THAT I'LL BE RIGHT THERE. BY THE WAY...

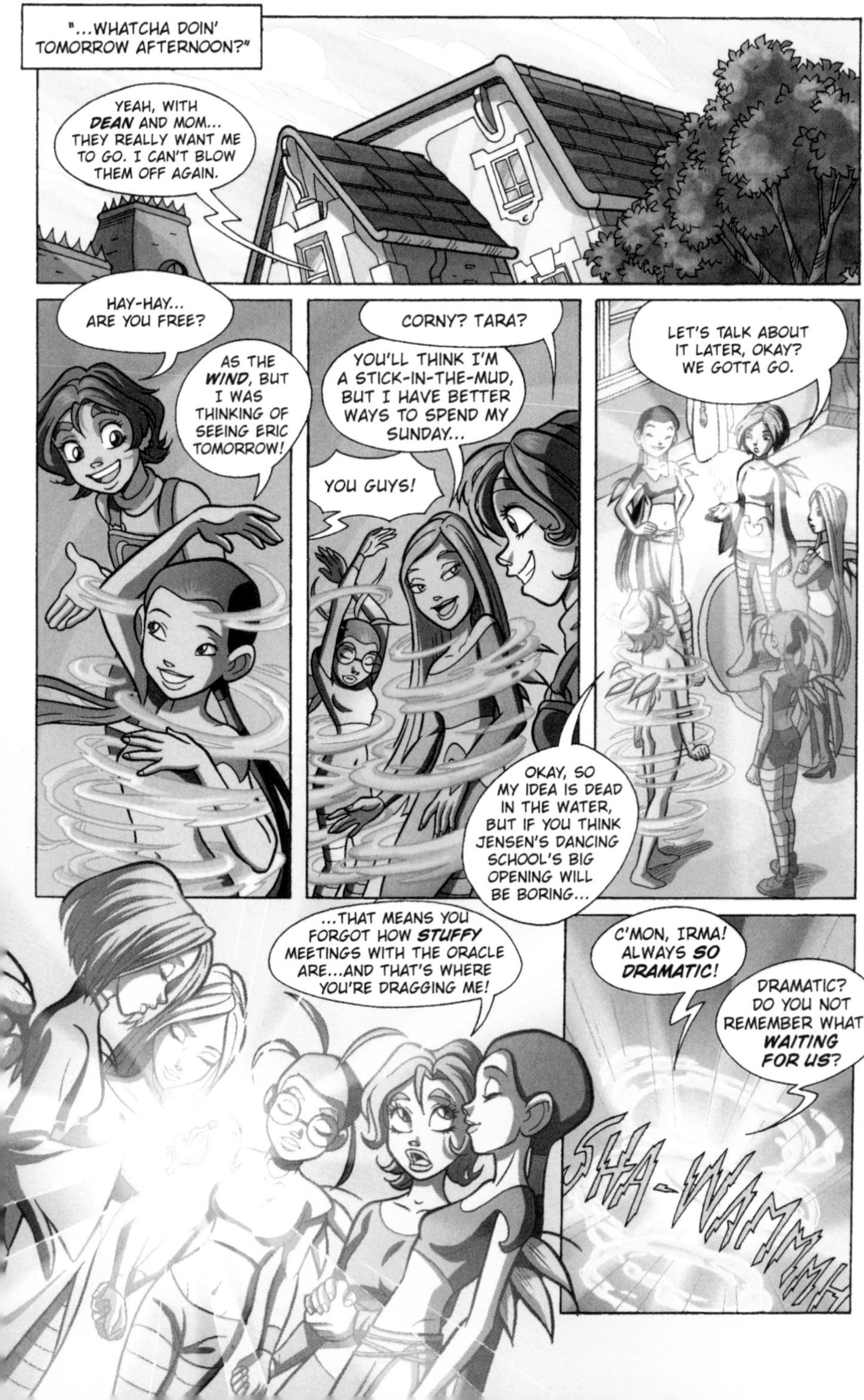
"...WHATCHA DOIN' TOMORROW AFTERNOON?"
YEAH, WITH DEAN AND MOM... THEY REALLY WANT ME TO GO. I CAN'T BLOW THEM OFF AGAIN.
HAY-HAY... ARE YOU FREE?
AS THE WIND, BUT I WAS THINKING OF SEEING ERIC TOMORROW!
CORNY? TARA?
YOU'LL THINK I'M A STICK-IN-THE-MUD, BUT I HAVE BETTER WAYS TO SPEND MY SUNDAY...
YOU GUYS!
LET'S TALK ABOUT IT LATER, OKAY? WE GOTTA GO.
OKAY, SO MY IDEA IS DEAD IN THE WATER, BUT IF YOU THINK JENSEN'S DANCING SCHOOL'S BIG OPENING WILL BE BORING...
...THAT MEANS YOU FORGOT HOW STUFFY MEETINGS WITH THE ORACLE ARE...AND THAT'S WHERE YOU'RE DRAGGING ME!
C'MON, IRMA! ALWAYS SO DRAMATIC!
DRAMATIC? DO YOU NOT REMEMBER WHAT'S WAITING FOR US?
SHA-WAMMM

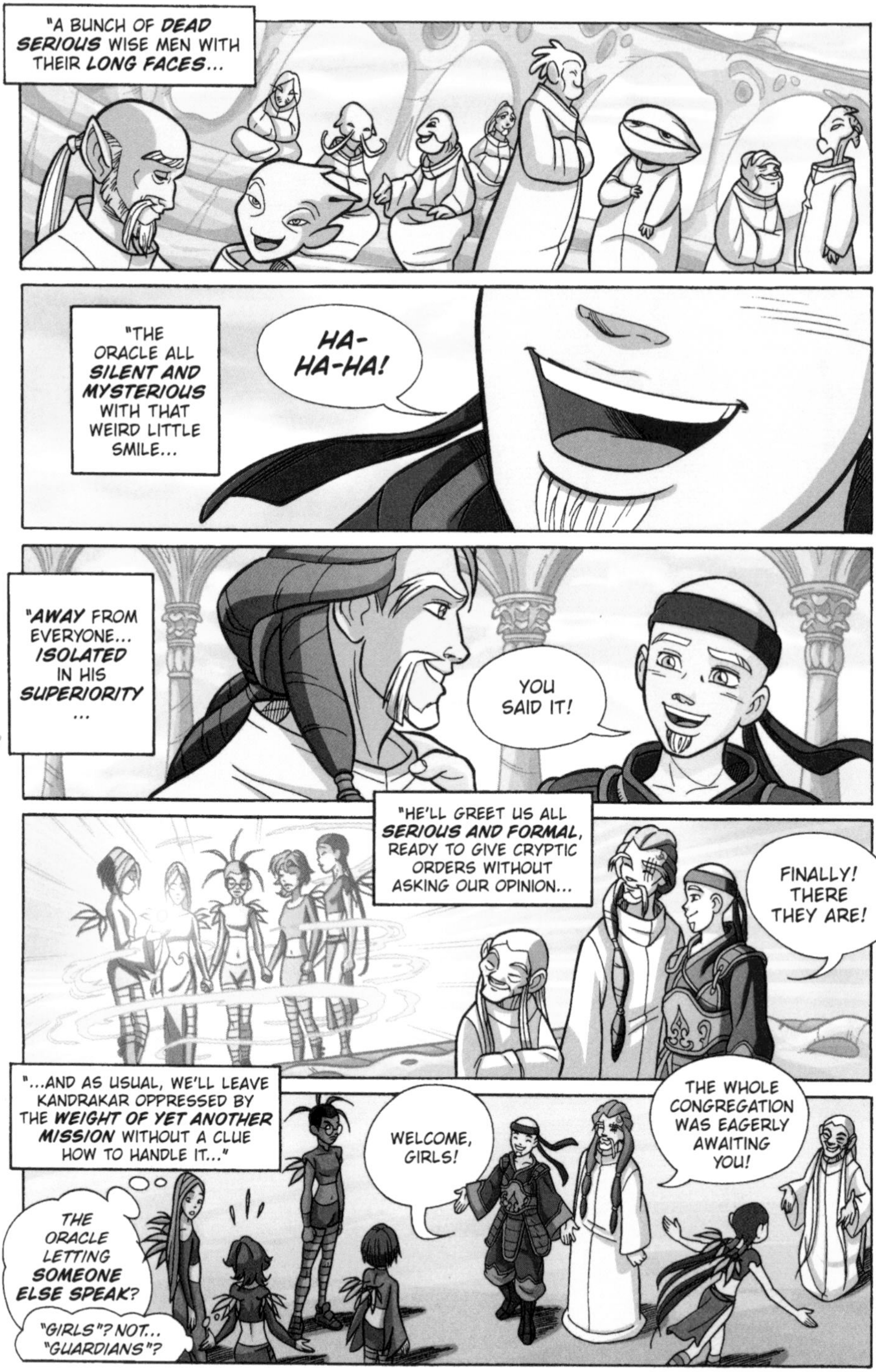
"A BUNCH OF DEAD SERIOUS WISE MEN WITH THEIR LONG FACES...
"THE ORACLE ALL SILENT AND MYSTERIOUS WITH THAT WEIRD LITTLE SMILE...
HA-HA-HA!
"AWAY FROM EVERYONE... ISOLATED IN HIS SUPERIORITY ...
YOU SAID IT!
"HE'LL GREET US ALL SERIOUS AND FORMAL, READY TO GIVE CRYPTIC ORDERS WITHOUT ASKING OUR OPINION...
FINALLY! THERE THEY ARE!
"...AND AS USUAL, WE'LL LEAVE KANDRAKAR OPPRESSED BY THE WEIGHT OF YET ANOTHER MISSION WITHOUT A CLUE HOW TO HANDLE IT..."
THE ORACLE LETTING SOMEONE ELSE SPEAK?
"GIRLS"? NOT... "GUARDIANS"?
WELCOME, GIRLS!
THE WHOLE CONGREGATION WAS EAGERLY AWAITING YOU!

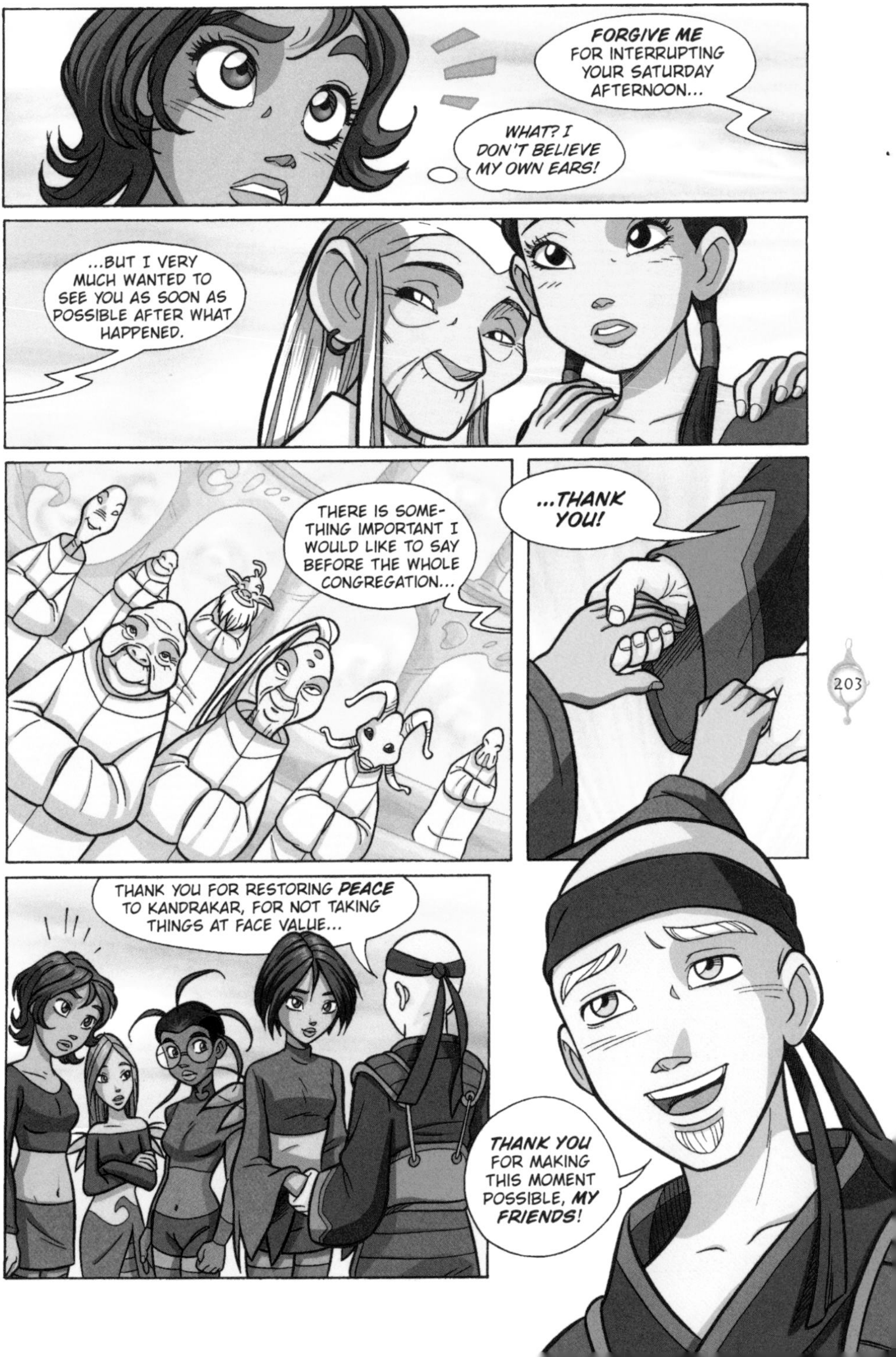
FORGIVE ME FOR INTERRUPTING YOUR SATURDAY AFTERNOON...
WHAT? I DON'T BELIEVE MY OWN EARS!
...BUT I VERY MUCH WANTED TO SEE YOU AS SOON AS POSSIBLE AFTER WHAT HAPPENED.
THERE IS SOME-THING IMPORTANT I WOULD LIKE TO SAY BEFORE THE WHOLE CONGREGATION...
...THANK YOU!
THANK YOU FOR RESTORING PEACE TO KANDRAKAR, FOR NOT TAKING THINGS AT FACE VALUE...
THANK YOU FOR MAKING THIS MOMENT POSSIBLE, MY FRIENDS!

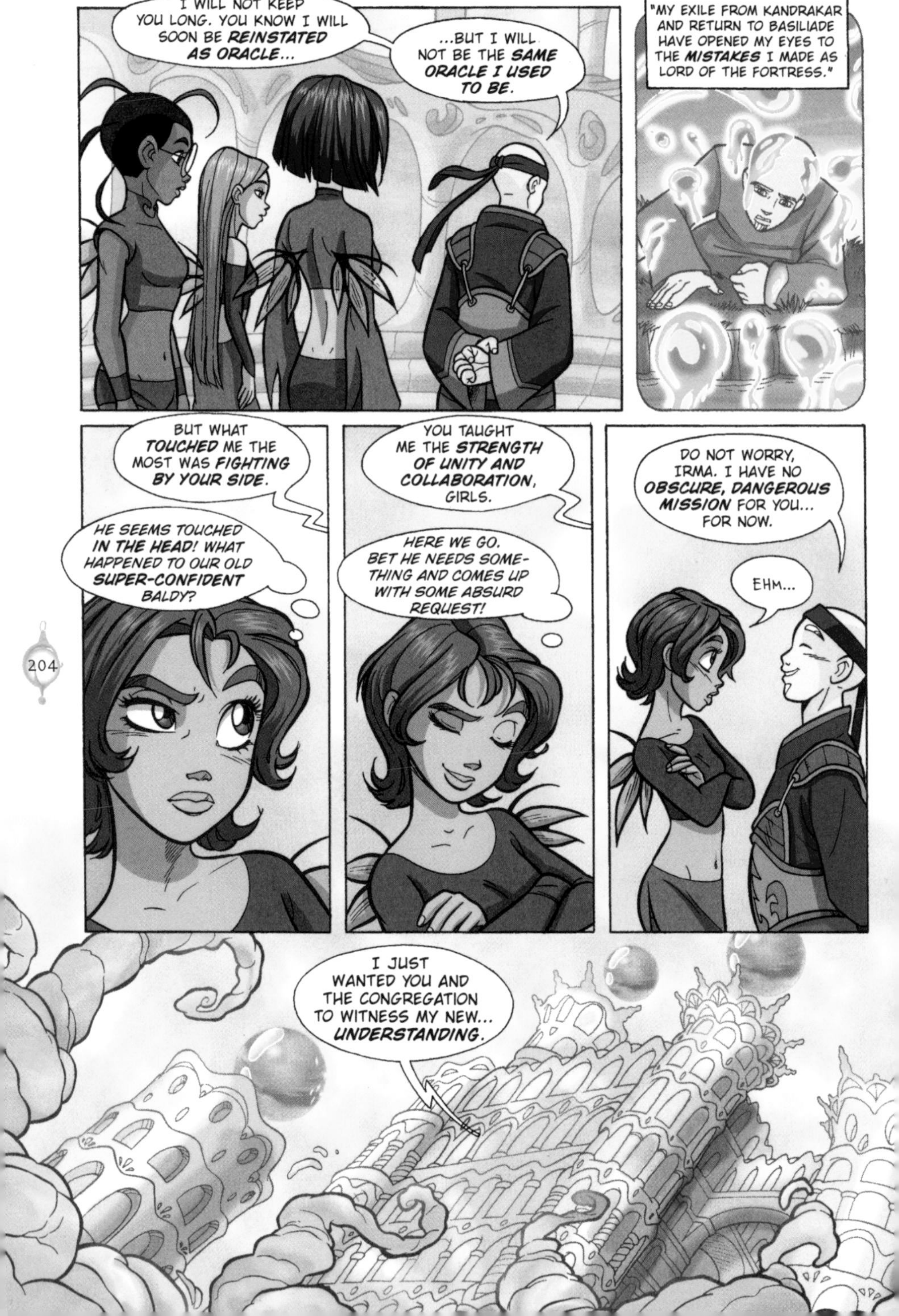
I WILL NOT KEEP YOU LONG. YOU KNOW I WILL SOON BE REINSTATED AS ORACLE...
...BUT I WILL NOT BE THE SAME ORACLE I USED TO BE.
"MY EXILE FROM KANDRAKAR AND RETURN TO BASILIADE HAVE OPENED MY EYES TO THE MISTAKES I MADE AS LORD OF THE FORTRESS."
BUT WHAT TOUCHED ME THE MOST WAS FIGHTING BY YOUR SIDE.
HE SEEMS TOUCHED IN THE HEAD! WHAT HAPPENED TO OUR OLD SUPER-CONFIDENT BALDY?
YOU TAUGHT ME THE STRENGTH OF UNITY AND COLLABORATION, GIRLS.
HERE WE GO. BET HE NEEDS SOMETHING AND COMES UP WITH SOME ABSURD REQUEST!
DO NOT WORRY, IRMA. I HAVE NO OBSCURE, DANGEROUS MISSION FOR YOU... FOR NOW.
EHM...
I JUST WANTED YOU AND THE CONGREGATION TO WITNESS MY NEW... UNDERSTANDING.

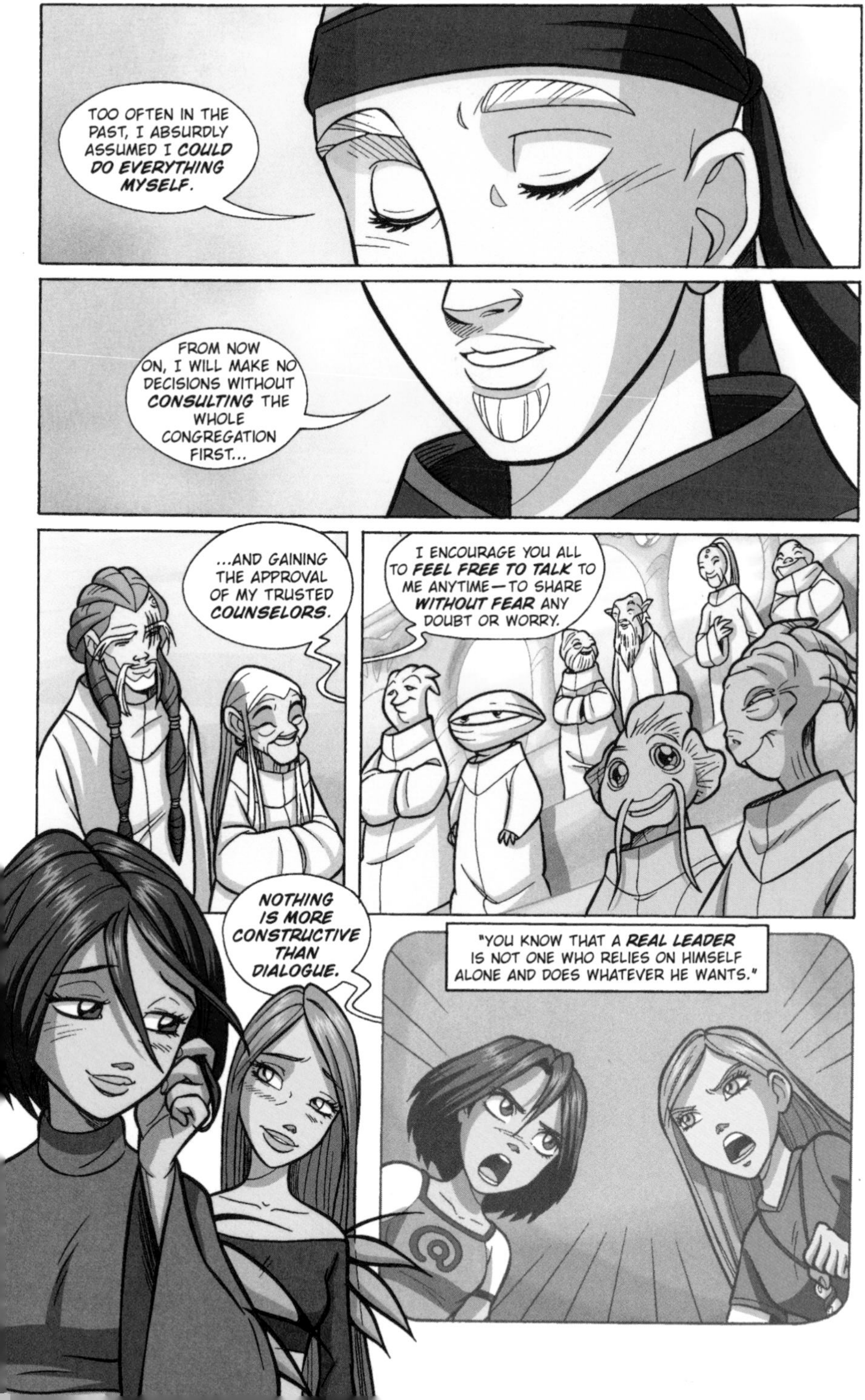
TOO OFTEN IN THE PAST, I ABSURDLY ASSUMED I COULD DO EVERYTHING MYSELF.
FROM NOW ON, I WILL MAKE NO DECISIONS WITHOUT CONSULTING THE WHOLE CONGREGATION FIRST...
...AND GAINING THE APPROVAL OF MY TRUSTED COUNSELORS.
I ENCOURAGE YOU ALL TO FEEL FREE TO TALK TO ME ANYTIME—TO SHARE WITHOUT FEAR ANY DOUBT OR WORRY.
NOTHING IS MORE CONSTRUCTIVE THAN DIALOGUE.
"YOU KNOW THAT A REAL LEADER IS NOT ONE WHO RELIES ON HIMSELF ALONE AND DOES WHATEVER HE WANTS."

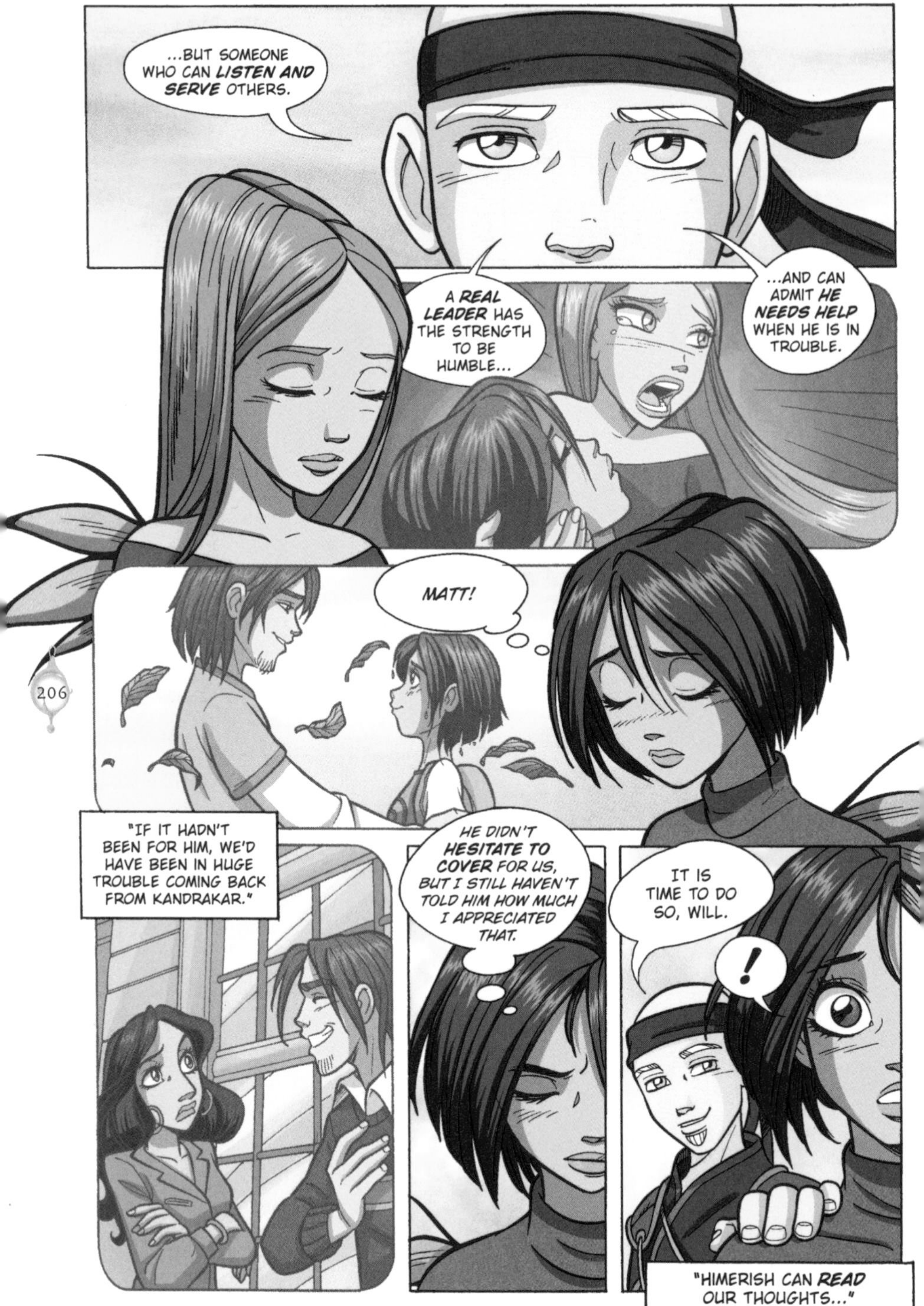
...BUT SOMEONE WHO CAN LISTEN AND SERVE OTHERS.
A REAL LEADER HAS THE STRENGTH TO BE HUMBLE...
...AND CAN ADMIT HE NEEDS HELP WHEN HE IS IN TROUBLE.
MATT!
"IF IT HADN'T BEEN FOR HIM, WE'D HAVE BEEN IN HUGE TROUBLE COMING BACK FROM KANDRAKAR."
HE DIDN'T HESITATE TO COVER FOR US, BUT I STILL HAVEN'T TOLD HIM HOW MUCH I APPRECIATED THAT.
IT IS TIME TO DO SO, WILL.
!
"HIMERISH CAN READ OUR THOUGHTS..."

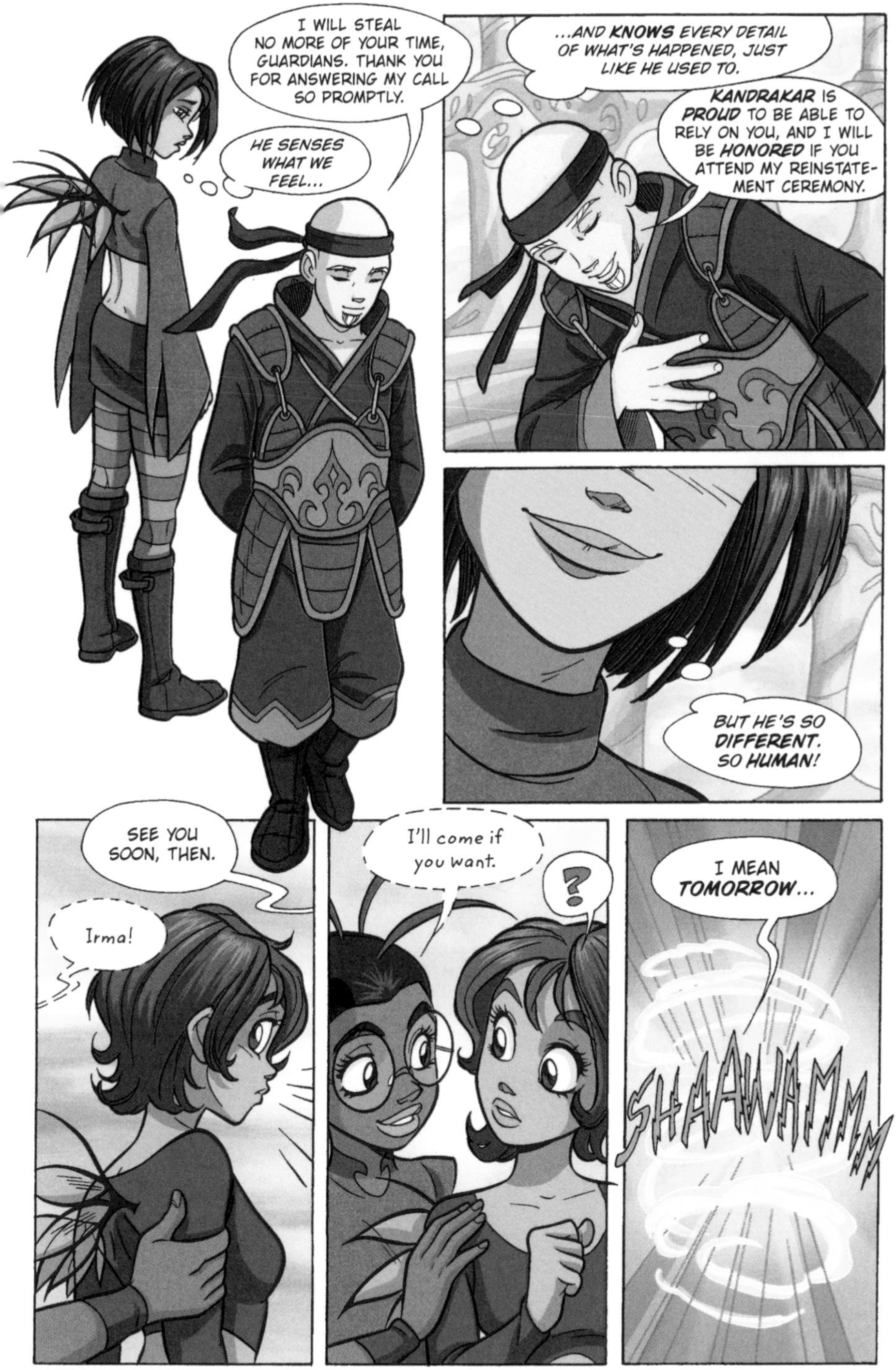

I WILL STEAL NO MORE OF YOUR TIME, GUARDIANS. THANK YOU FOR ANSWERING MY CALL SO PROMPTLY.
HE SENSES WHAT WE FEEL...
...AND KNOWS EVERY DETAIL OF WHAT'S HAPPENED, JUST LIKE HE USED TO.
KANDRAKAR IS PROUD TO BE ABLE TO RELY ON YOU, AND I WILL BE HONORED IF YOU ATTEND MY REINSTATEMENT CEREMONY.
BUT HE'S SO DIFFERENT. SO HUMAN!
SEE YOU SOON, THEN.
Irma!
I'll come if you want.
?
I MEAN TOMORROW...
SHAAWAMMM

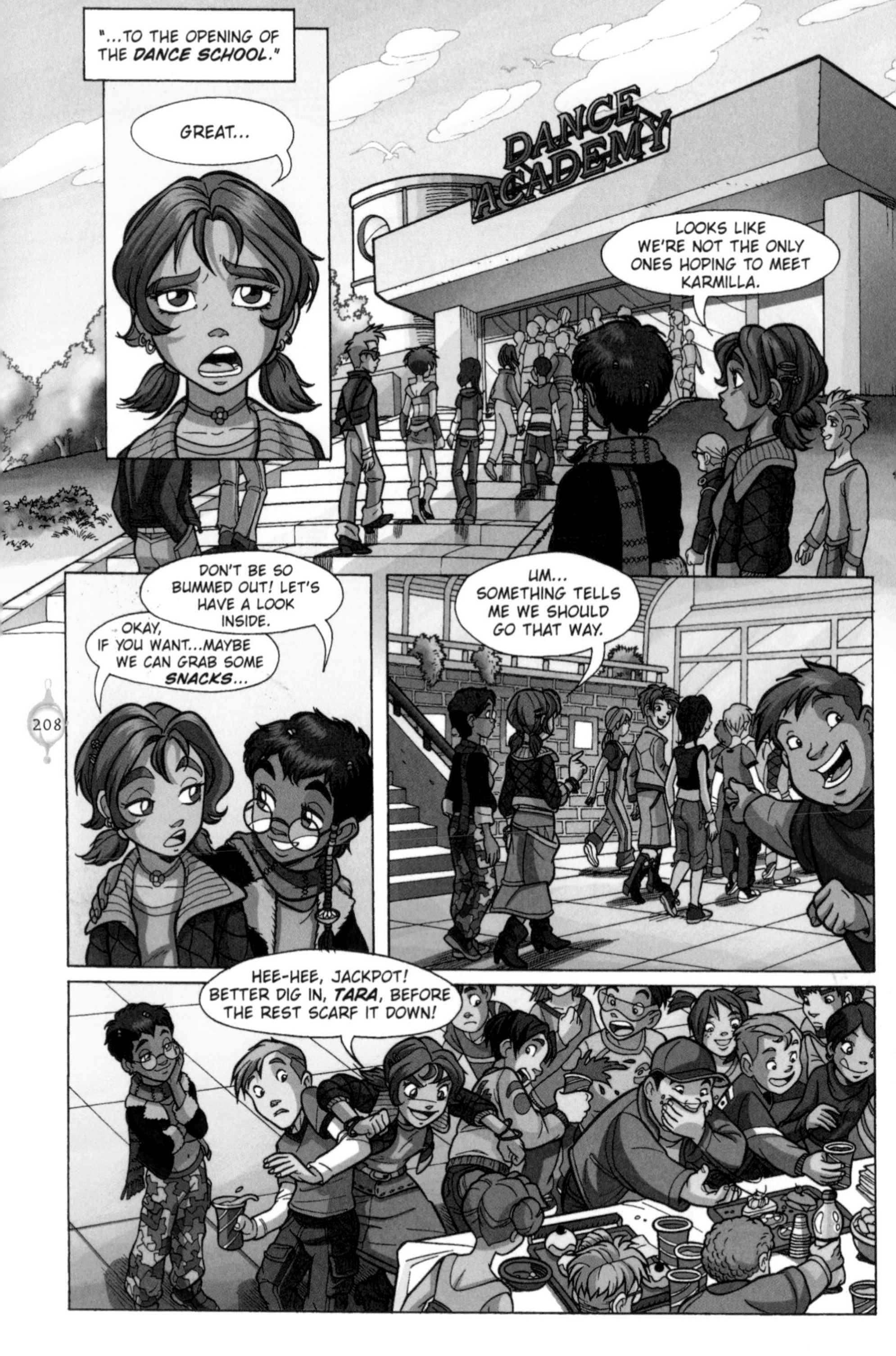
"...TO THE OPENING OF THE DANCE SCHOOL."
GREAT...
DANCE ACADEMY
LOOKS LIKE WE'RE NOT THE ONLY ONES HOPING TO MEET KARMILLA.
DON'T BE SO BUMMED OUT! LET'S HAVE A LOOK INSIDE.
OKAY, IF YOU WANT...MAYBE WE CAN GRAB SOME SNACKS...
UM... SOMETHING TELLS ME WE SHOULD GO THAT WAY.
HEE-HEE, JACKPOT! BETTER DIG IN, TARA, BEFORE THE REST SCARF IT DOWN!

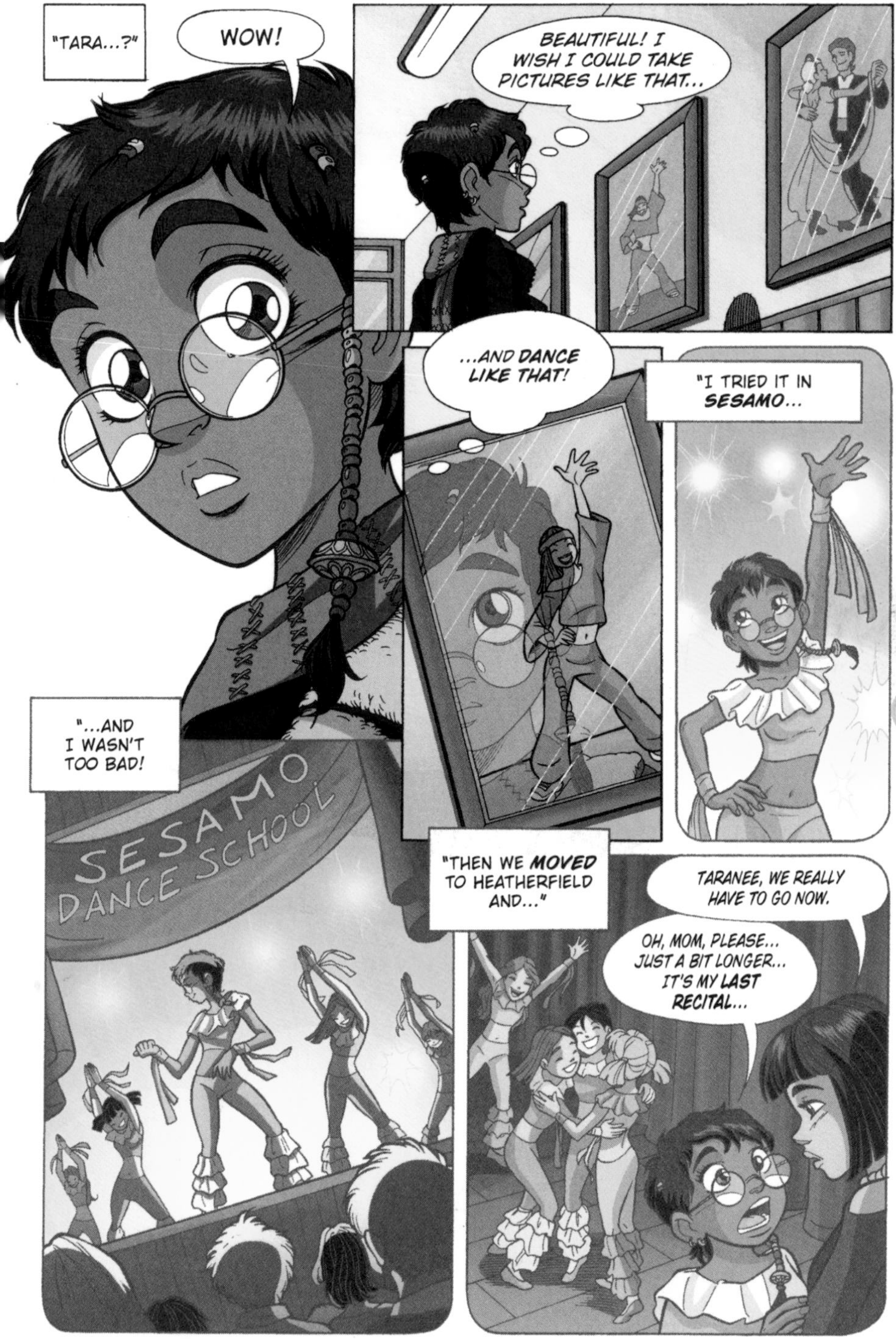
"TARA...?"
WOW!
BEAUTIFUL! I WISH I COULD TAKE PICTURES LIKE THAT...
...AND DANCE LIKE THAT!
"I TRIED IT IN SESAMO...
"...AND I WASN'T TOO BAD!
SESAMO DANCE SCHOOL
"THEN WE MOVED TO HEATHERFIELD AND..."
TARANEE, WE REALLY HAVE TO GO NOW.
OH, MOM, PLEASE... JUST A BIT LONGER... IT'S MY LAST RECITAL...

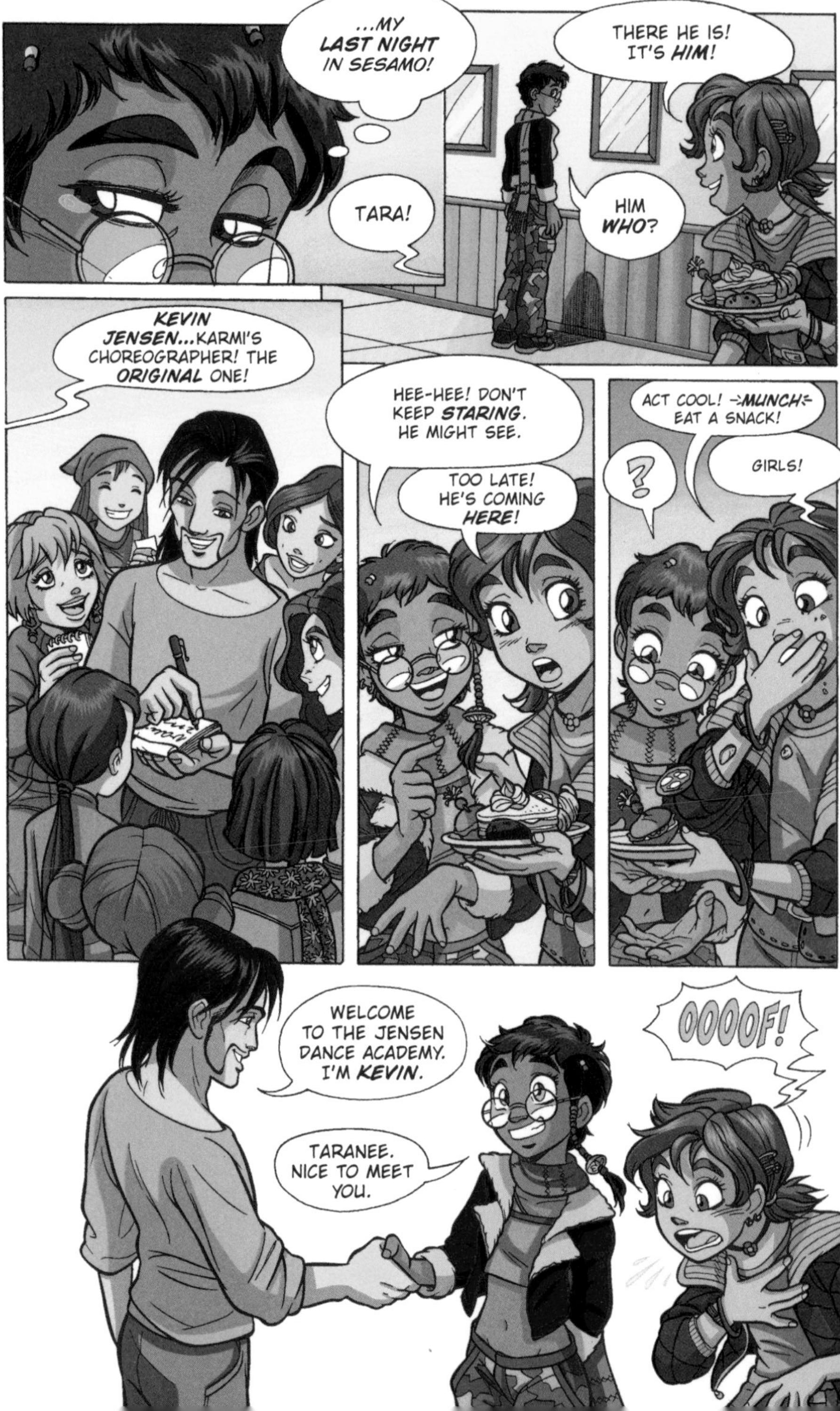
...MY LAST NIGHT IN SESAMO!
TARA!
THERE HE IS! IT'S HIM!
HIM WHO?
KEVIN JENSEN...KARMI'S CHOREOGRAPHER! THE ORIGINAL ONE!
HEE-HEE! DON'T KEEP STARING. HE MIGHT SEE.
TOO LATE! HE'S COMING HERE!
ACT COOL! -MUNCH- EAT A SNACK!
?
GIRLS!
WELCOME TO THE JENSEN DANCE ACADEMY. I'M KEVIN.
TARANEE. NICE TO MEET YOU.
OOOOF!

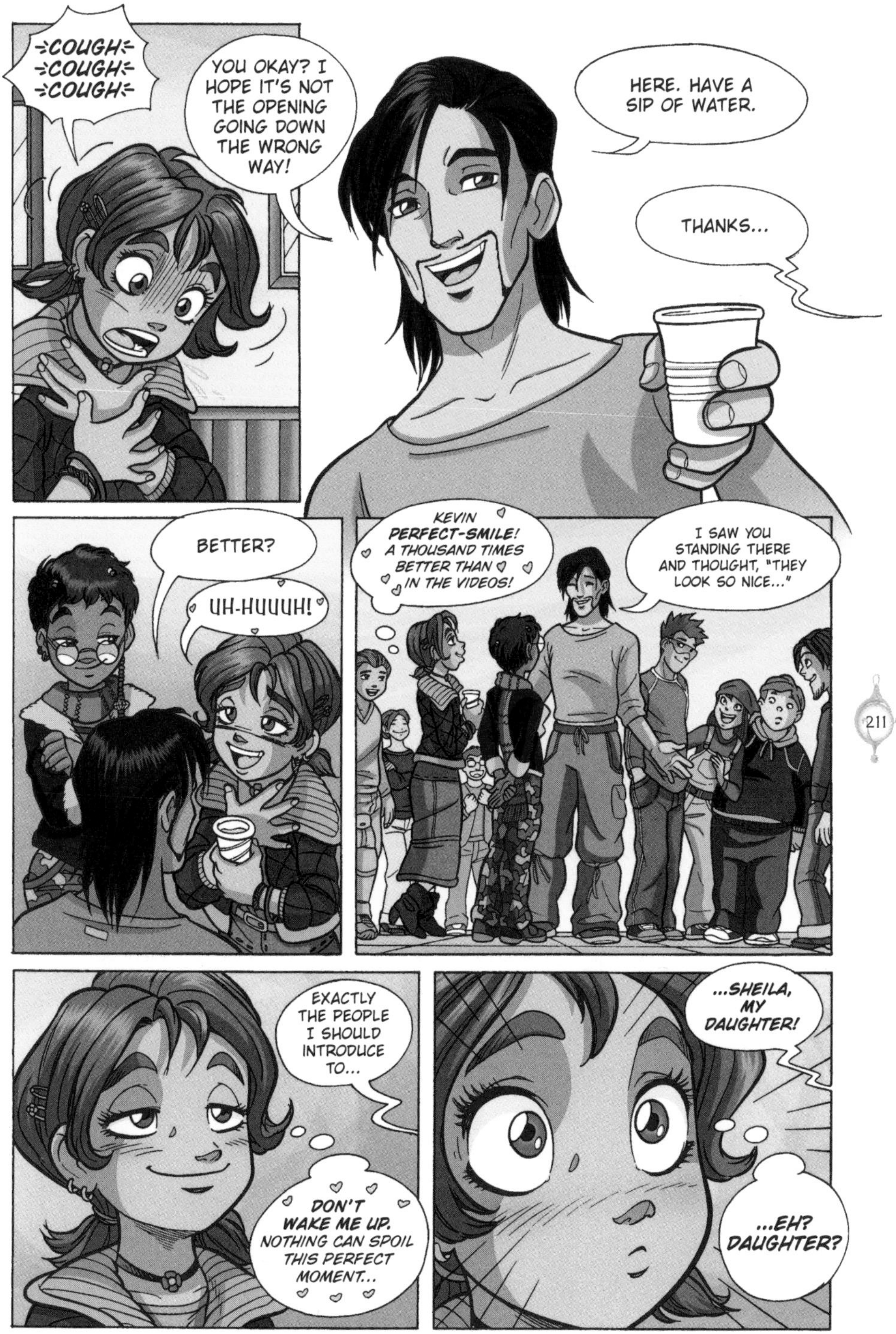

=COUGH= =COUGH= =COUGH=
YOU OKAY? I HOPE IT'S NOT THE OPENING GOING DOWN THE WRONG WAY!
HERE. HAVE A SIP OF WATER.
THANKS...
BETTER?
UH-HUUUH!
KEVIN PERFECT-SMILE! A THOUSAND TIMES BETTER THAN IN THE VIDEOS!
I SAW YOU STANDING THERE AND THOUGHT, "THEY LOOK SO NICE..."
EXACTLY THE PEOPLE I SHOULD INTRODUCE TO...
DON'T WAKE ME UP. NOTHING CAN SPOIL THIS PERFECT MOMENT...
...SHEILA, MY DAUGHTER!
...EH? DAUGHTER?

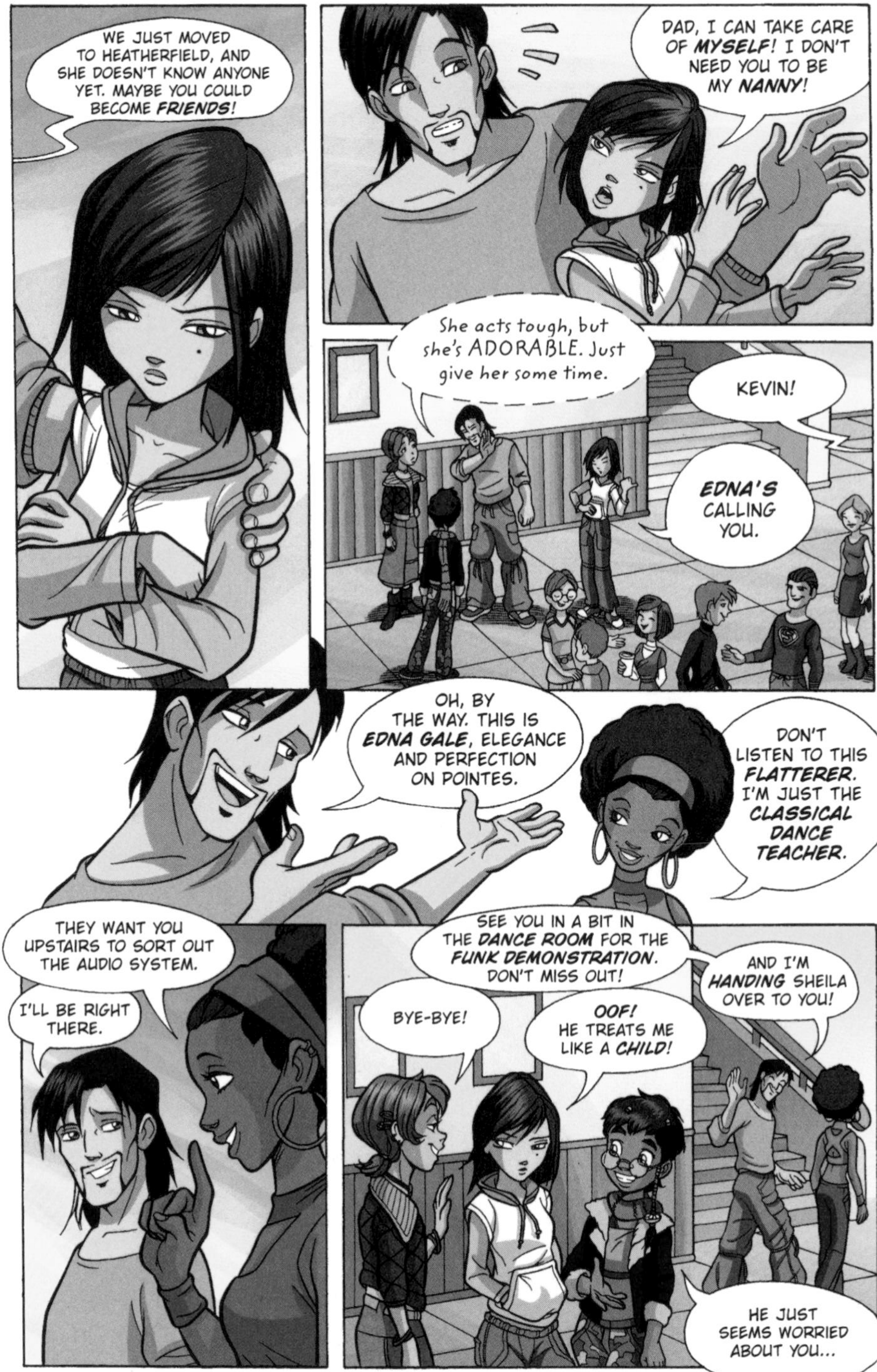
WE JUST MOVED TO HEATHERFIELD, AND SHE DOESN'T KNOW ANYONE YET. MAYBE YOU COULD BECOME FRIENDS!
DAD, I CAN TAKE CARE OF MYSELF! I DON'T NEED YOU TO BE MY NANNY!
She acts tough, but she's ADORABLE. Just give her some time.
KEVIN!
EDNA'S CALLING YOU.
OH, BY THE WAY. THIS IS EDNA GALE, ELEGANCE AND PERFECTION ON POINTES.
DON'T LISTEN TO THIS FLATTERER. I'M JUST THE CLASSICAL DANCE TEACHER.
THEY WANT YOU UPSTAIRS TO SORT OUT THE AUDIO SYSTEM.
I'LL BE RIGHT THERE.
SEE YOU IN A BIT IN THE DANCE ROOM FOR THE FUNK DEMONSTRATION. DON'T MISS OUT!
AND I'M HANDING SHEILA OVER TO YOU!
BYE-BYE!
OOF! HE TREATS ME LIKE A CHILD!
HE JUST SEEMS WORRIED ABOUT YOU...

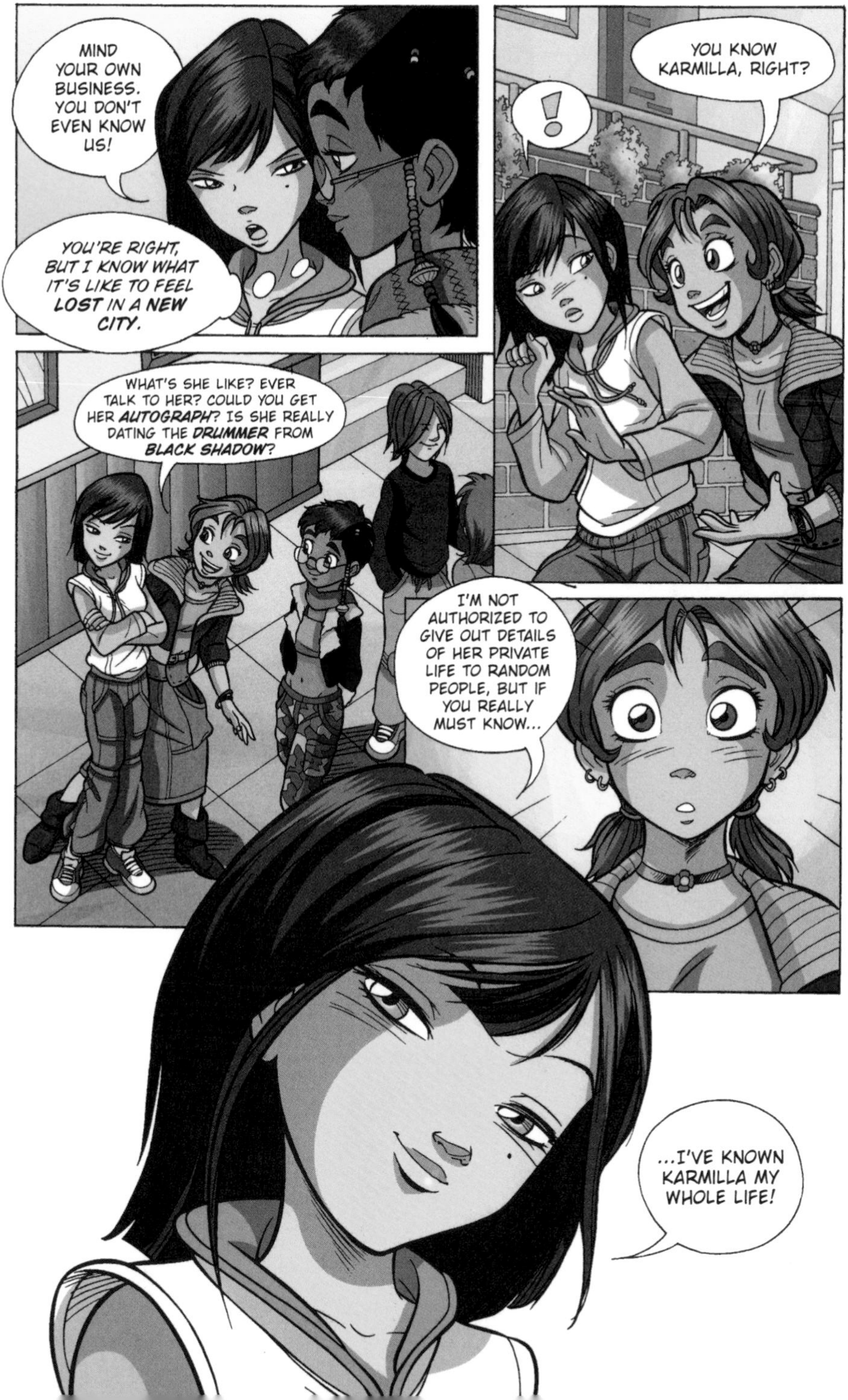
MIND YOUR OWN BUSINESS. YOU DON'T EVEN KNOW US!
YOU'RE RIGHT, BUT I KNOW WHAT IT'S LIKE TO FEEL ***LOST*** *IN A* ***NEW CITY.***
!
YOU KNOW KARMILLA, RIGHT?
WHAT'S SHE LIKE? EVER TALK TO HER? COULD YOU GET HER ***AUTOGRAPH***? IS SHE REALLY DATING THE ***DRUMMER*** FROM ***BLACK SHADOW***?
I'M NOT AUTHORIZED TO GIVE OUT DETAILS OF HER PRIVATE LIFE TO RANDOM PEOPLE, BUT IF YOU REALLY MUST KNOW...
...I'VE KNOWN KARMILLA MY WHOLE LIFE!

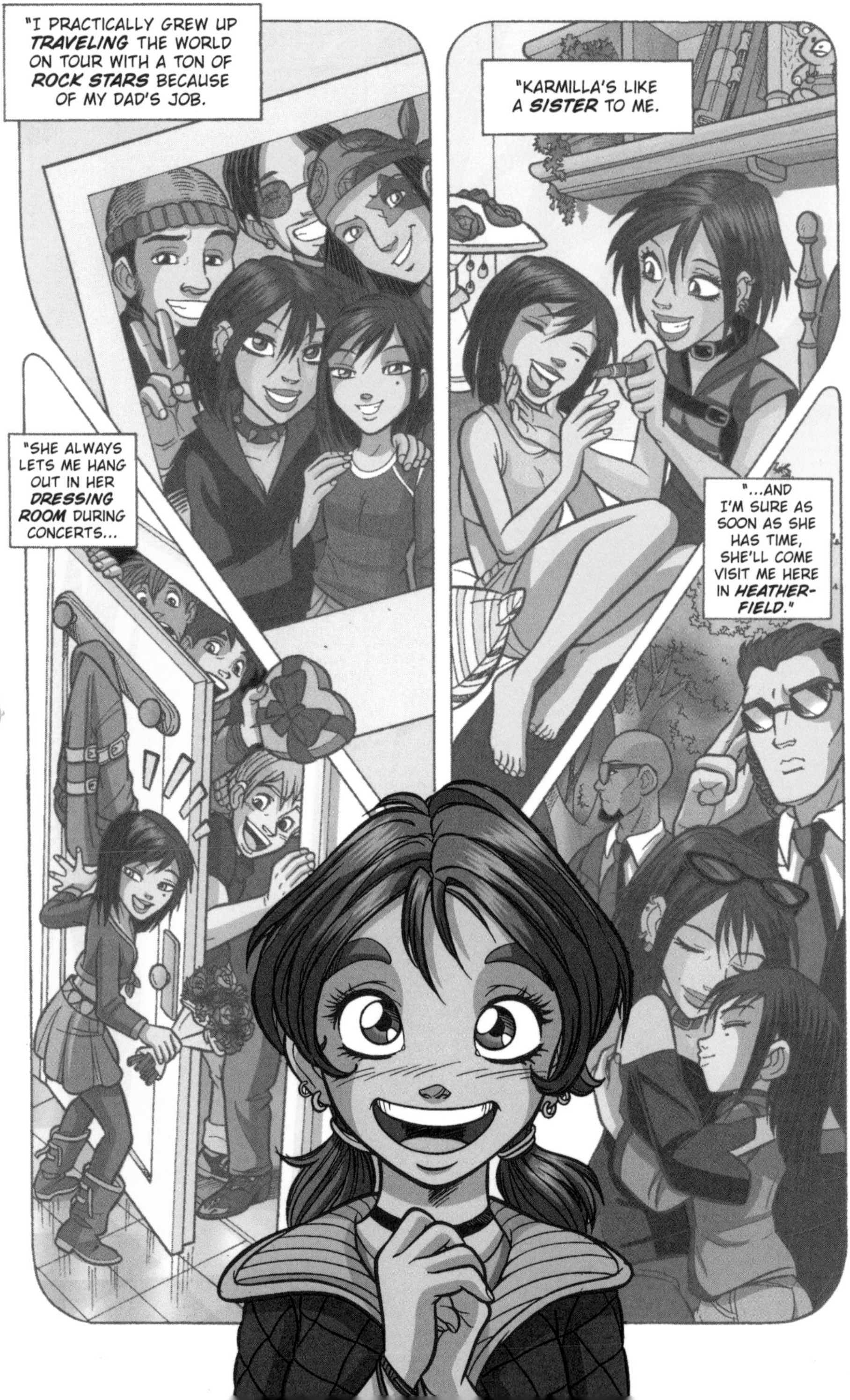
"I PRACTICALLY GREW UP TRAVELING THE WORLD ON TOUR WITH A TON OF ROCK STARS BECAUSE OF MY DAD'S JOB.
"KARMILLA'S LIKE A SISTER TO ME.
"SHE ALWAYS LETS ME HANG OUT IN HER DRESSING ROOM DURING CONCERTS...
"...AND I'M SURE AS SOON AS SHE HAS TIME, SHE'LL COME VISIT ME HERE IN HEATHER-FIELD."

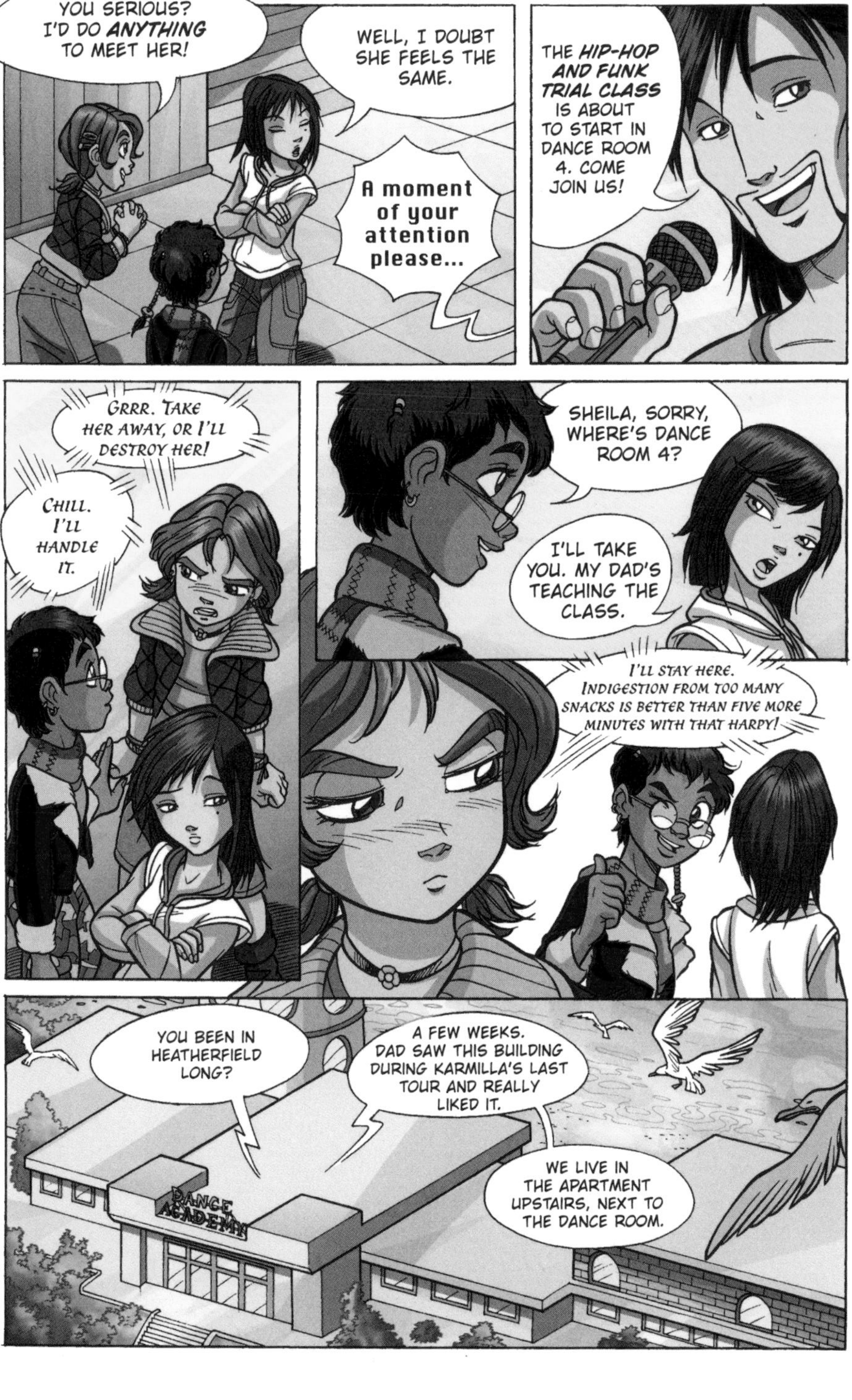
YOU SERIOUS? I'D DO ***ANYTHING*** TO MEET HER!
WELL, I DOUBT SHE FEELS THE SAME.
A moment of your attention please...
THE ***HIP-HOP AND FUNK TRIAL CLASS*** IS ABOUT TO START IN DANCE ROOM 4. COME JOIN US!
GRRR. TAKE HER AWAY, OR I'LL DESTROY HER!
CHILL. I'LL HANDLE IT.
SHEILA, SORRY, WHERE'S DANCE ROOM 4?
I'LL TAKE YOU. MY DAD'S TEACHING THE CLASS.
I'LL STAY HERE. INDIGESTION FROM TOO MANY SNACKS IS BETTER THAN FIVE MORE MINUTES WITH THAT HARPY!
YOU BEEN IN HEATHERFIELD LONG?
A FEW WEEKS. DAD SAW THIS BUILDING DURING KARMILLA'S LAST TOUR AND REALLY LIKED IT.
WE LIVE IN THE APARTMENT UPSTAIRS, NEXT TO THE DANCE ROOM.
DANCE ACADEMY

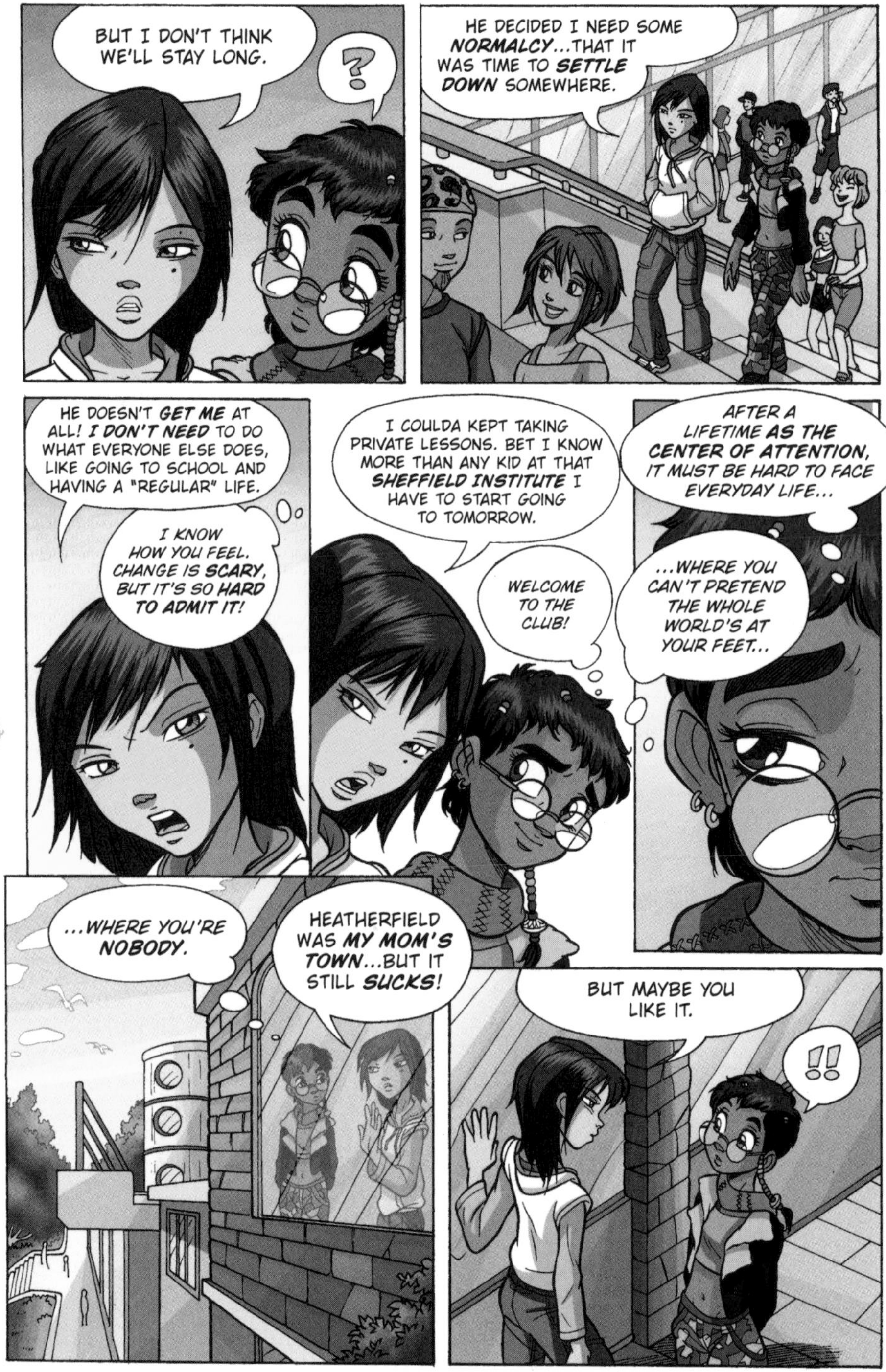
BUT I DON'T THINK WE'LL STAY LONG.
?
HE DECIDED I NEED SOME NORMALCY...THAT IT WAS TIME TO SETTLE DOWN SOMEWHERE.
HE DOESN'T GET ME AT ALL! I DON'T NEED TO DO WHAT EVERYONE ELSE DOES, LIKE GOING TO SCHOOL AND HAVING A "REGULAR" LIFE.
I KNOW HOW YOU FEEL. CHANGE IS SCARY, BUT IT'S SO HARD TO ADMIT IT!
I COULDA KEPT TAKING PRIVATE LESSONS. BET I KNOW MORE THAN ANY KID AT THAT SHEFFIELD INSTITUTE I HAVE TO START GOING TO TOMORROW.
WELCOME TO THE CLUB!
AFTER A LIFETIME AS THE CENTER OF ATTENTION, IT MUST BE HARD TO FACE EVERYDAY LIFE...
...WHERE YOU CAN'T PRETEND THE WHOLE WORLD'S AT YOUR FEET...
...WHERE YOU'RE NOBODY.
HEATHERFIELD WAS MY MOM'S TOWN...BUT IT STILL SUCKS!
BUT MAYBE YOU LIKE IT.
!!

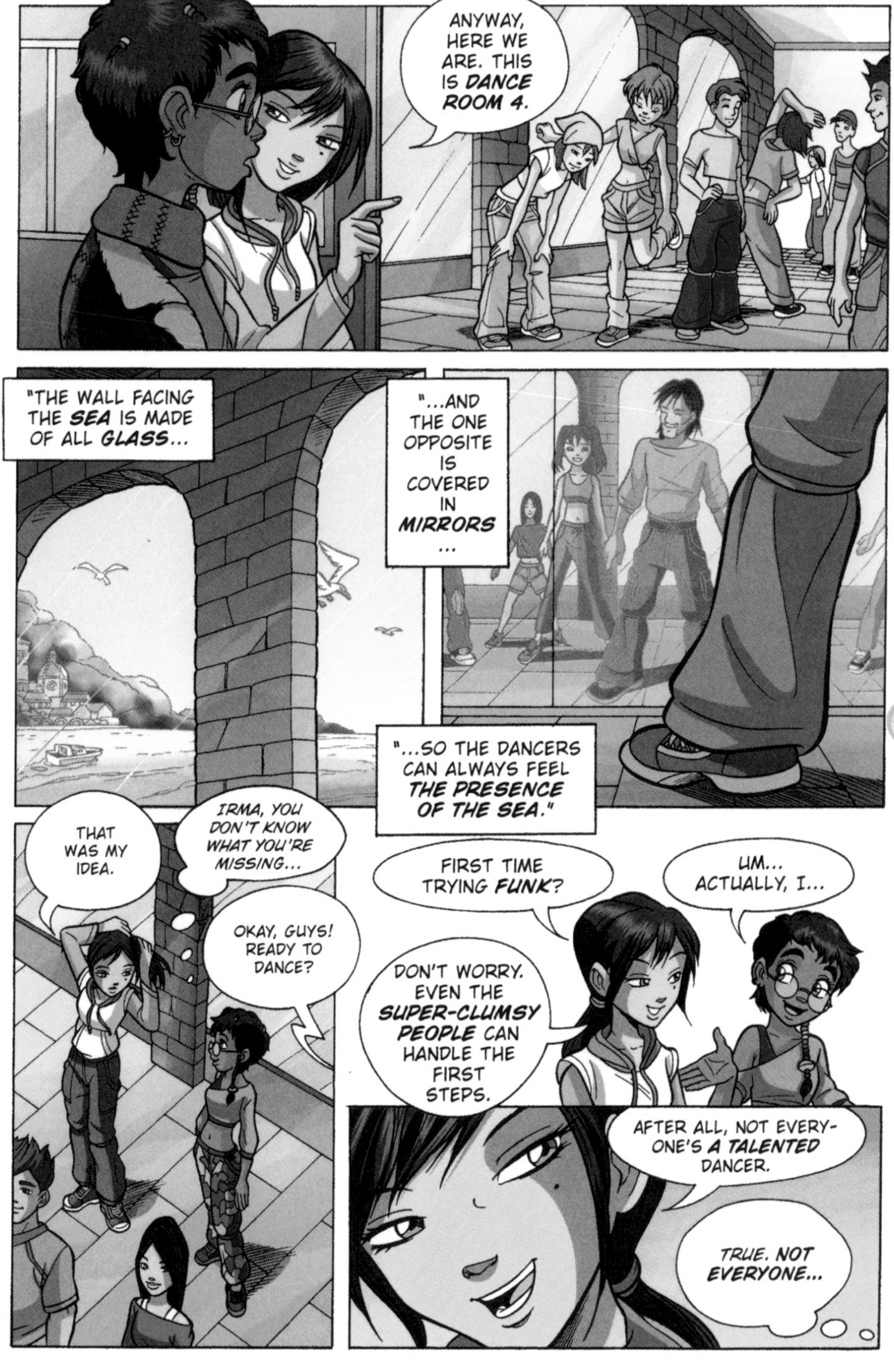
ANYWAY, HERE WE ARE. THIS IS DANCE ROOM 4.
"THE WALL FACING THE SEA IS MADE OF ALL GLASS...
"...AND THE ONE OPPOSITE IS COVERED IN MIRRORS...
"...SO THE DANCERS CAN ALWAYS FEEL THE PRESENCE OF THE SEA."
THAT WAS MY IDEA.
IRMA, YOU DON'T KNOW WHAT YOU'RE MISSING...
OKAY, GUYS! READY TO DANCE?
FIRST TIME TRYING FUNK?
UM... ACTUALLY, I...
DON'T WORRY. EVEN THE SUPER-CLUMSY PEOPLE CAN HANDLE THE FIRST STEPS.
AFTER ALL, NOT EVERY-ONE'S A TALENTED DANCER.
TRUE. NOT EVERYONE...

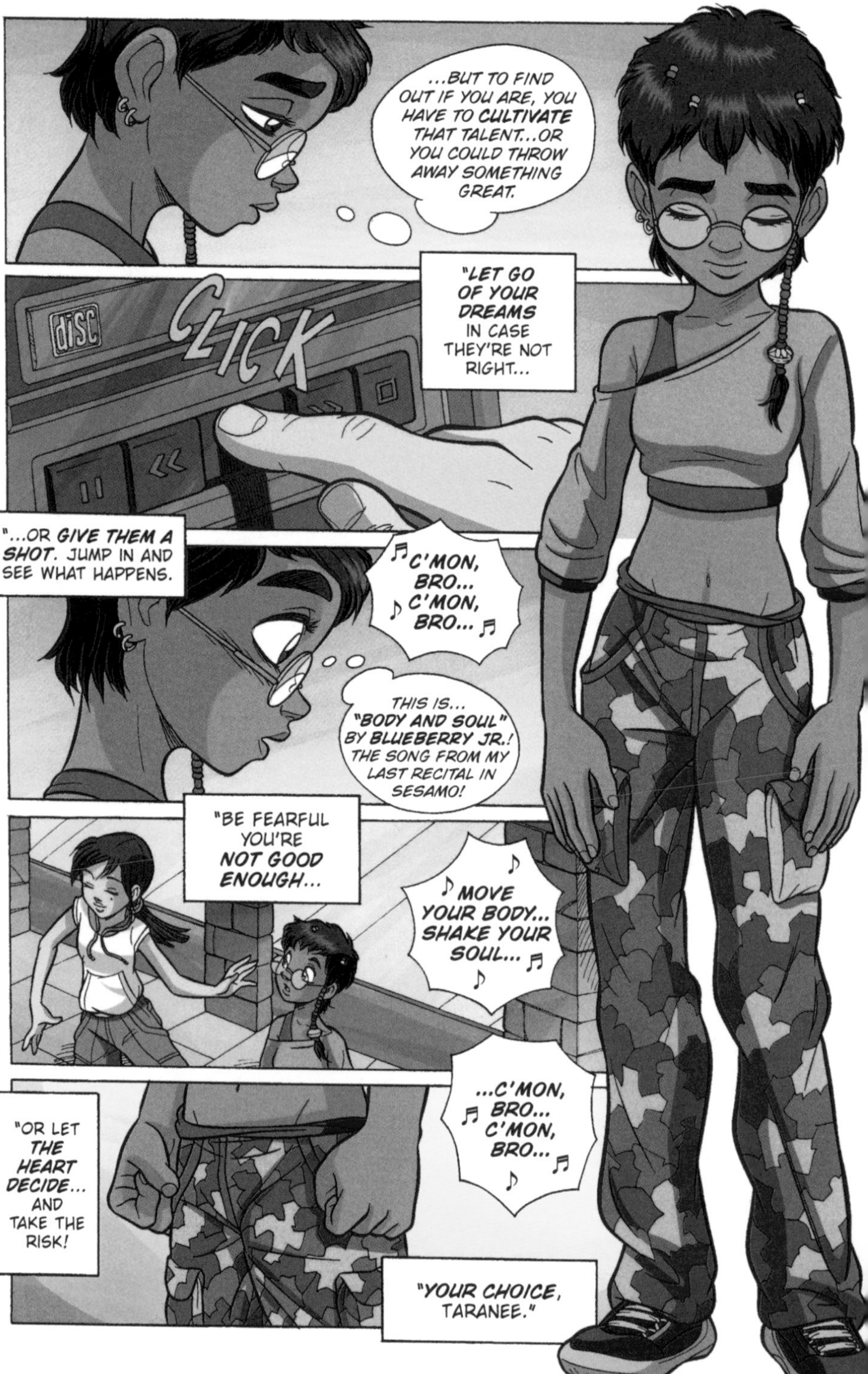
...BUT TO FIND OUT IF YOU ARE, YOU HAVE TO CULTIVATE THAT TALENT...OR YOU COULD THROW AWAY SOMETHING GREAT.
"LET GO OF YOUR DREAMS IN CASE THEY'RE NOT RIGHT...
CLICK
disc
"...OR GIVE THEM A SHOT. JUMP IN AND SEE WHAT HAPPENS.
C'MON, BRO... C'MON, BRO...
THIS IS... "BODY AND SOUL" BY BLUEBERRY JR.! THE SONG FROM MY LAST RECITAL IN SESAMO!
"BE FEARFUL YOU'RE NOT GOOD ENOUGH...
MOVE YOUR BODY... SHAKE YOUR SOUL...
"OR LET THE HEART DECIDE... AND TAKE THE RISK!
...C'MON, BRO... C'MON, BRO...
"YOUR CHOICE, TARANEE."

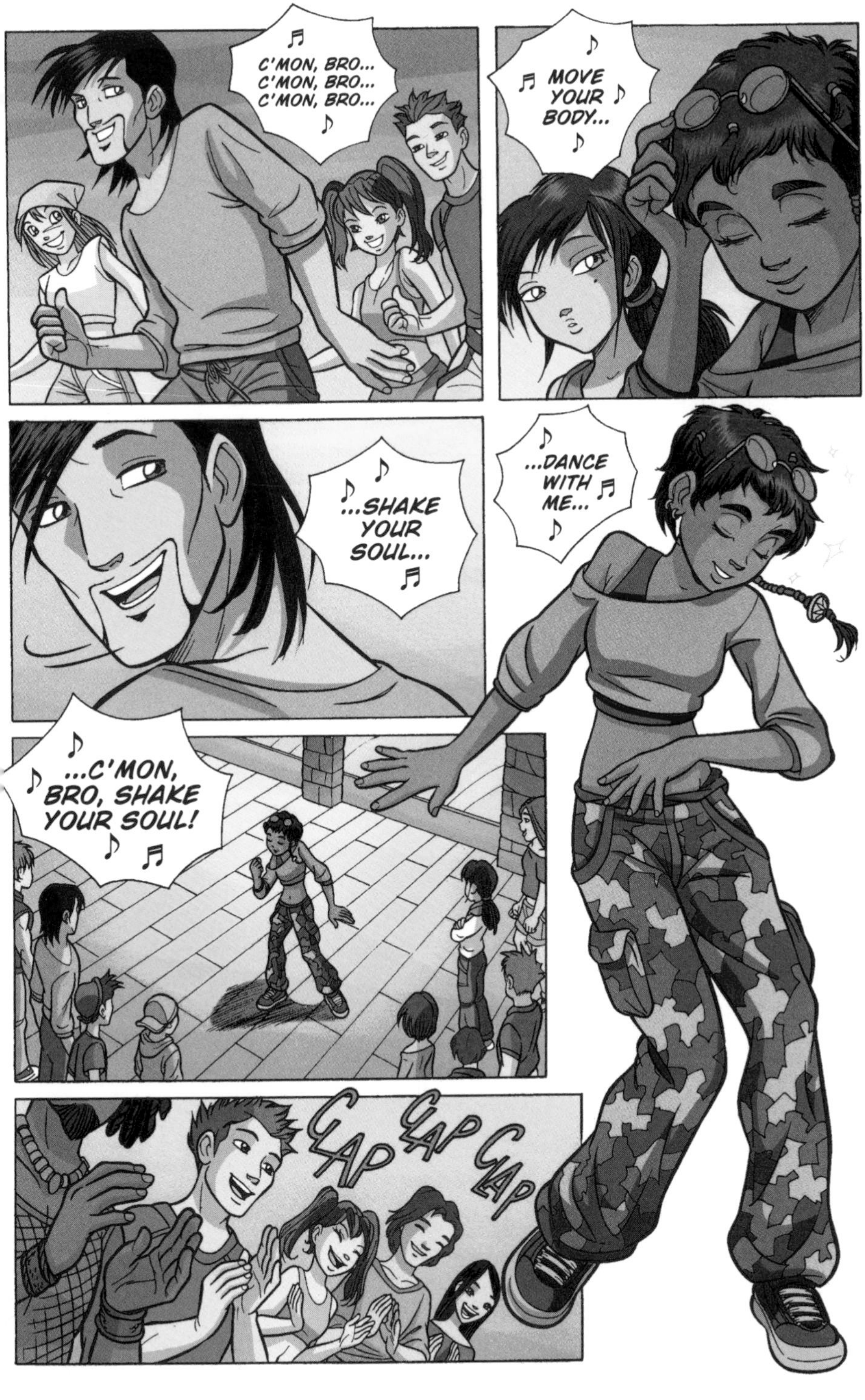

C'MON, BRO... C'MON, BRO... C'MON, BRO...
MOVE YOUR BODY...
...SHAKE YOUR SOUL...
...DANCE WITH ME...
...C'MON, BRO, SHAKE YOUR SOUL!
CLAP CLAP CLAP

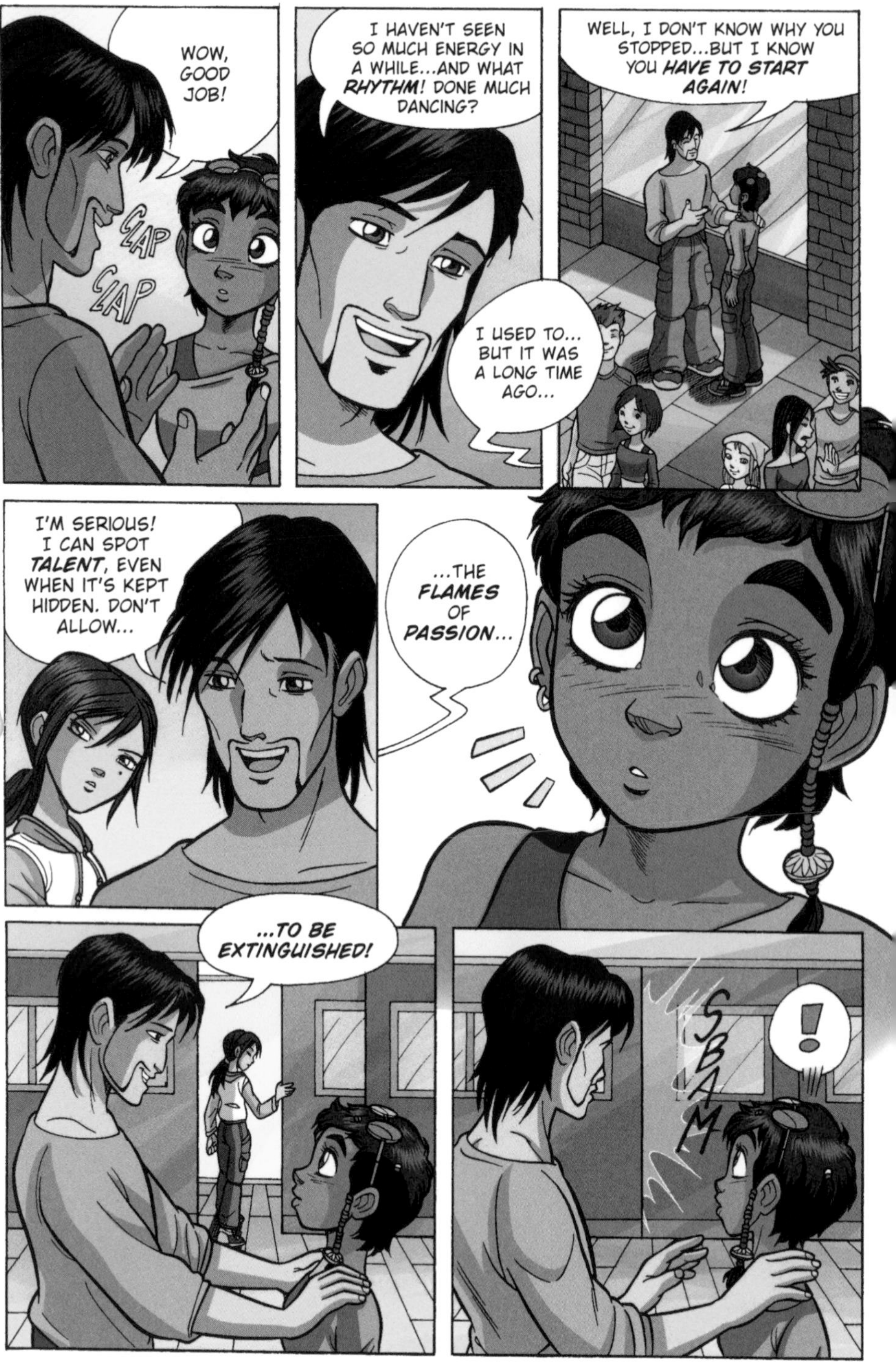
WOW, GOOD JOB!
CLAP
CLAP
I HAVEN'T SEEN SO MUCH ENERGY IN A WHILE...AND WHAT RHYTHM! DONE MUCH DANCING?
I USED TO... BUT IT WAS A LONG TIME AGO...
WELL, I DON'T KNOW WHY YOU STOPPED...BUT I KNOW YOU HAVE TO START AGAIN!
I'M SERIOUS! I CAN SPOT TALENT, EVEN WHEN IT'S KEPT HIDDEN. DON'T ALLOW...
...THE FLAMES OF PASSION...
...TO BE EXTINGUISHED!
SBAM
!

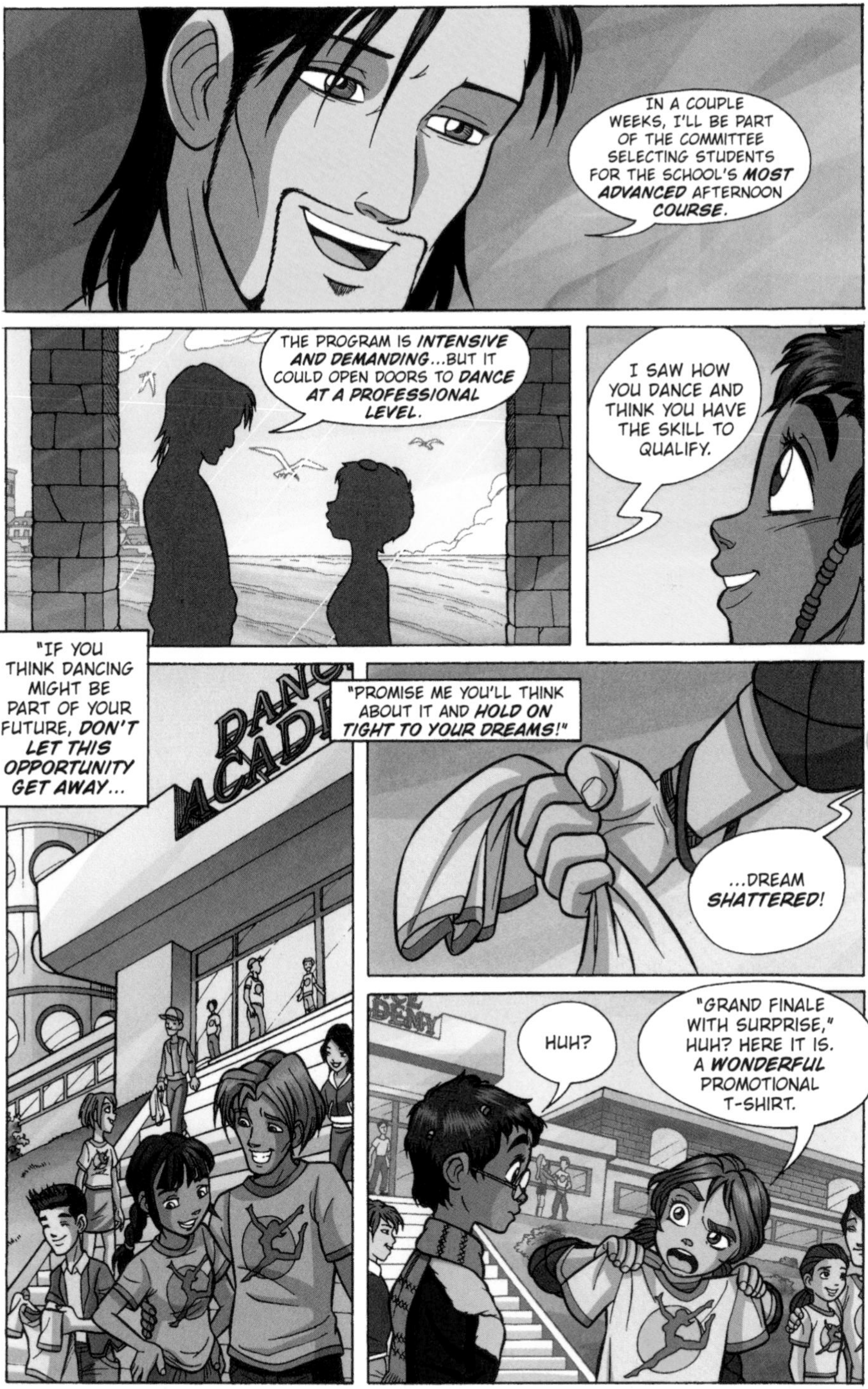
IN A COUPLE WEEKS, I'LL BE PART OF THE COMMITTEE SELECTING STUDENTS FOR THE SCHOOL'S **MOST ADVANCED** AFTERNOON **COURSE.**
THE PROGRAM IS ***INTENSIVE AND DEMANDING***...BUT IT COULD OPEN DOORS TO ***DANCE AT A PROFESSIONAL LEVEL.***
I SAW HOW YOU DANCE AND THINK YOU HAVE THE SKILL TO QUALIFY.
"IF YOU THINK DANCING MIGHT BE PART OF YOUR FUTURE, ***DON'T LET THIS OPPORTUNITY GET AWAY***...
"PROMISE ME YOU'LL THINK ABOUT IT AND ***HOLD ON TIGHT TO YOUR DREAMS!***"
...DREAM ***SHATTERED!***
HUH?
"GRAND FINALE WITH SURPRISE," HUH? HERE IT IS. A ***WONDERFUL*** PROMOTIONAL T-SHIRT.

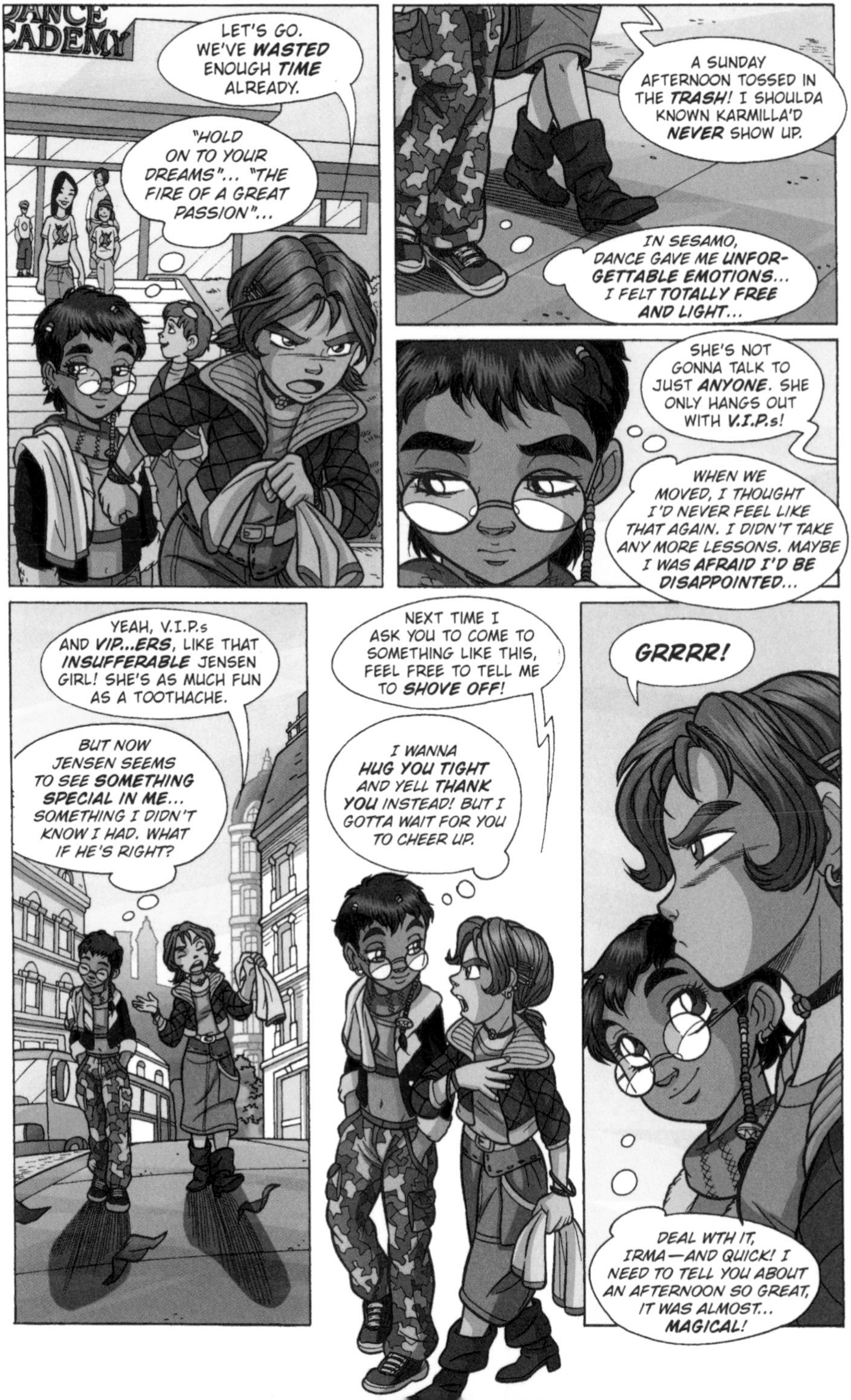
DANCE ACADEMY
LET'S GO. WE'VE WASTED ENOUGH TIME ALREADY.
"HOLD ON TO YOUR DREAMS"... "THE FIRE OF A GREAT PASSION"...
A SUNDAY AFTERNOON TOSSED IN THE TRASH! I SHOULDA KNOWN KARMILLA'D NEVER SHOW UP.
IN SESAMO, DANCE GAVE ME UNFORGETTABLE EMOTIONS... I FELT TOTALLY FREE AND LIGHT...
SHE'S NOT GONNA TALK TO JUST ANYONE. SHE ONLY HANGS OUT WITH V.I.P.s!
WHEN WE MOVED, I THOUGHT I'D NEVER FEEL LIKE THAT AGAIN. I DIDN'T TAKE ANY MORE LESSONS. MAYBE I WAS AFRAID I'D BE DISAPPOINTED...
YEAH, V.I.P.s AND VIP...ERS, LIKE THAT INSUFFERABLE JENSEN GIRL! SHE'S AS MUCH FUN AS A TOOTHACHE.
BUT NOW JENSEN SEEMS TO SEE SOMETHING SPECIAL IN ME... SOMETHING I DIDN'T KNOW I HAD. WHAT IF HE'S RIGHT?
NEXT TIME I ASK YOU TO COME TO SOMETHING LIKE THIS, FEEL FREE TO TELL ME TO SHOVE OFF!
I WANNA HUG YOU TIGHT AND YELL THANK YOU INSTEAD! BUT I GOTTA WAIT FOR YOU TO CHEER UP.
GRRRR!
DEAL WTH IT, IRMA—AND QUICK! I NEED TO TELL YOU ABOUT AN AFTERNOON SO GREAT, IT WAS ALMOST... MAGICAL!

W.i.t.c.h.

Will Irma Taranee Cornelia Hay Lin

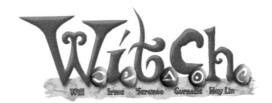

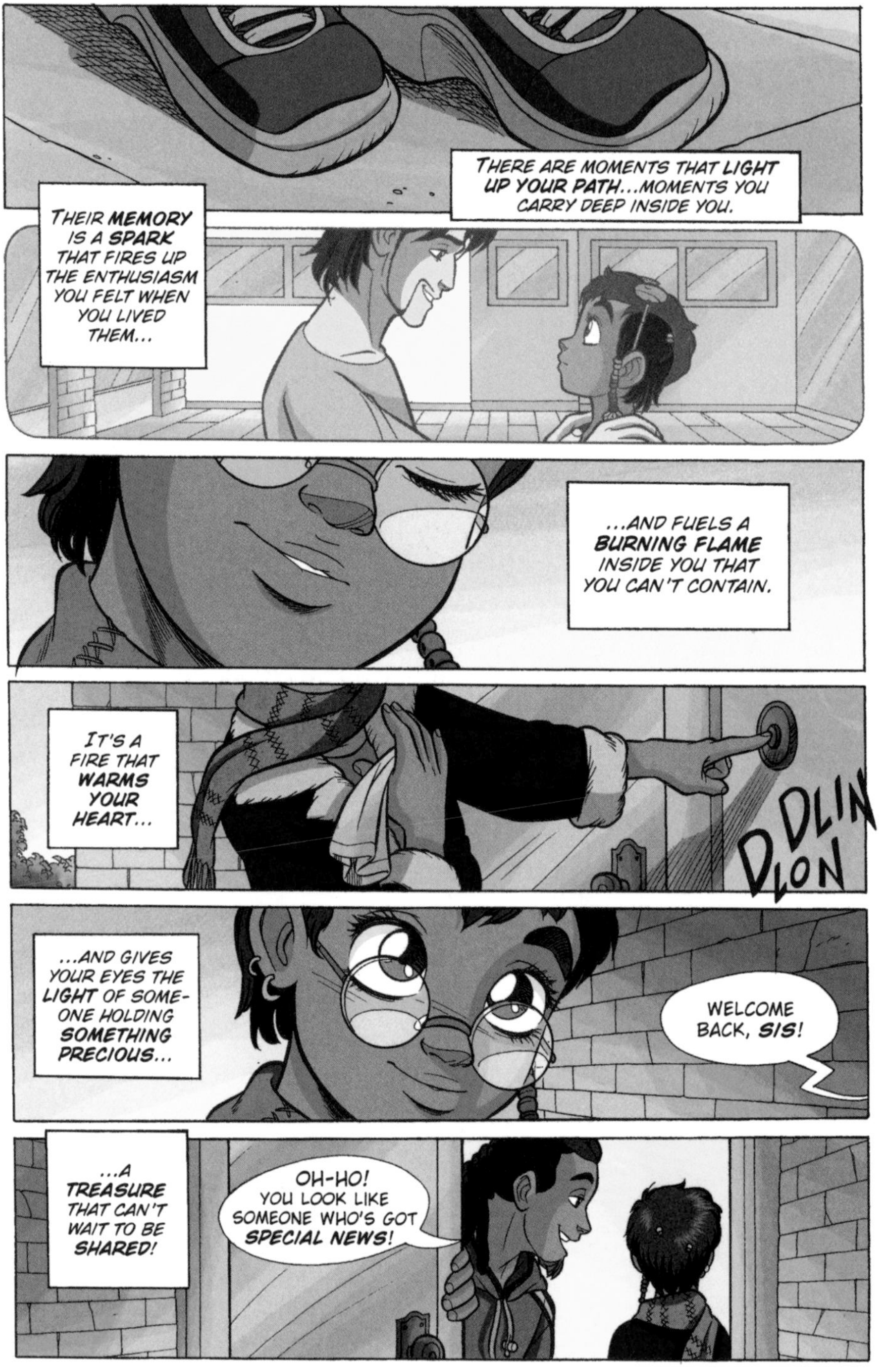
THERE ARE MOMENTS THAT LIGHT UP YOUR PATH...MOMENTS YOU CARRY DEEP INSIDE YOU.
THEIR MEMORY IS A SPARK THAT FIRES UP THE ENTHUSIASM YOU FELT WHEN YOU LIVED THEM...
...AND FUELS A BURNING FLAME INSIDE YOU THAT YOU CAN'T CONTAIN.
IT'S A FIRE THAT WARMS YOUR HEART...
DLIN
DLON
...AND GIVES YOUR EYES THE LIGHT OF SOME-ONE HOLDING SOMETHING PRECIOUS...
WELCOME BACK, SIS!
...A TREASURE THAT CAN'T WAIT TO BE SHARED!
OH-HO! YOU LOOK LIKE SOMEONE WHO'S GOT SPECIAL NEWS!

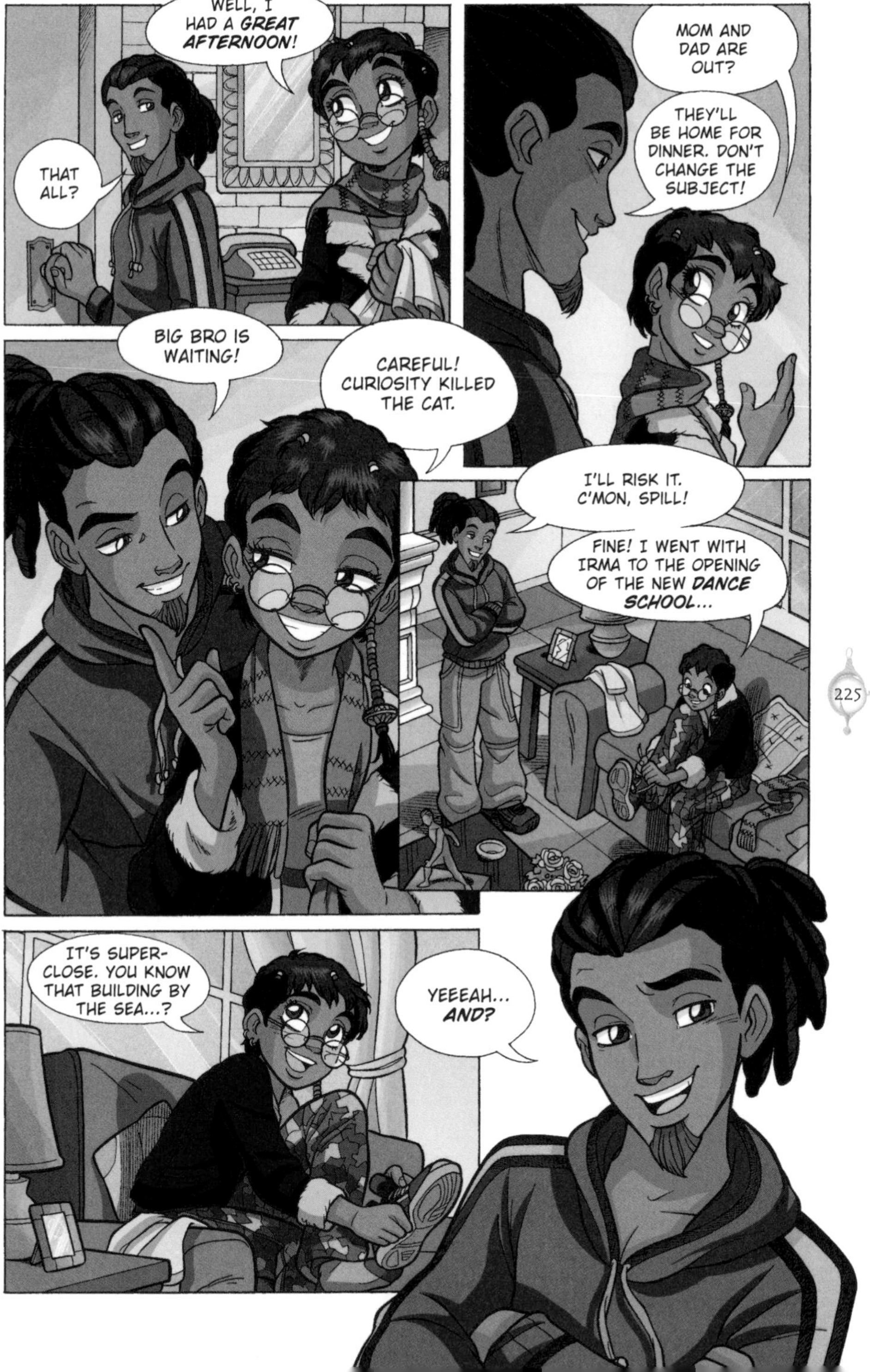

WELL, I HAD A **GREAT AFTERNOON**!
THAT ALL?
MOM AND DAD ARE OUT?
THEY'LL BE HOME FOR DINNER. DON'T CHANGE THE SUBJECT!
BIG BRO IS WAITING!
CAREFUL! CURIOSITY KILLED THE CAT.
I'LL RISK IT. C'MON, SPILL!
FINE! I WENT WITH IRMA TO THE OPENING OF THE NEW **DANCE SCHOOL**...
IT'S SUPER-CLOSE. YOU KNOW THAT BUILDING BY THE SEA...?
YEEEAH... **AND?**

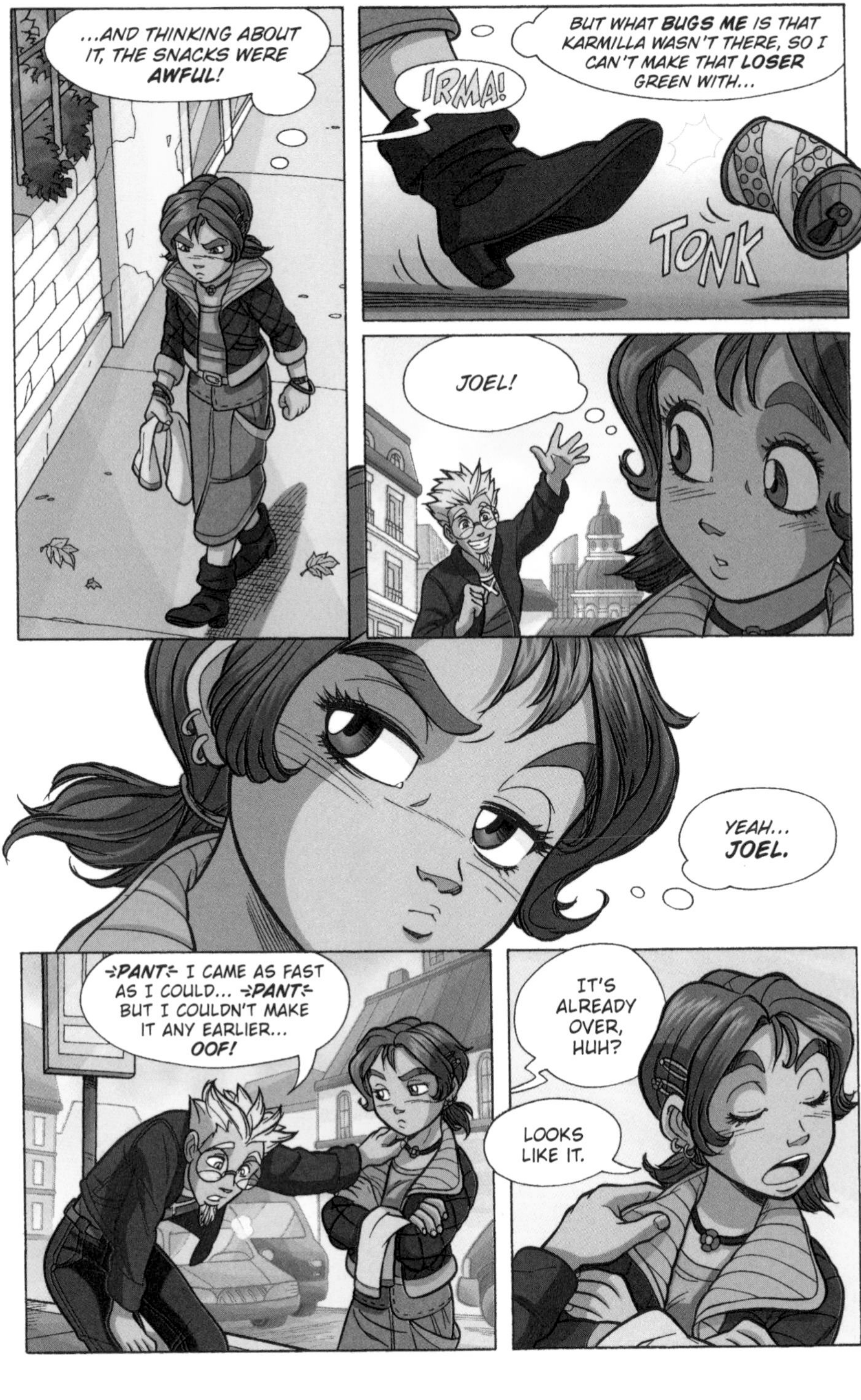
...AND THINKING ABOUT IT, THE SNACKS WERE AWFUL!
BUT WHAT BUGS ME IS THAT KARMILLA WASN'T THERE, SO I CAN'T MAKE THAT LOSER GREEN WITH...
IRMA!
TONK
JOEL!
YEAH... JOEL.
≈PANT≈ I CAME AS FAST AS I COULD... ≈PANT≈ BUT I COULDN'T MAKE IT ANY EARLIER... OOF!
IT'S ALREADY OVER, HUH?
LOOKS LIKE IT.

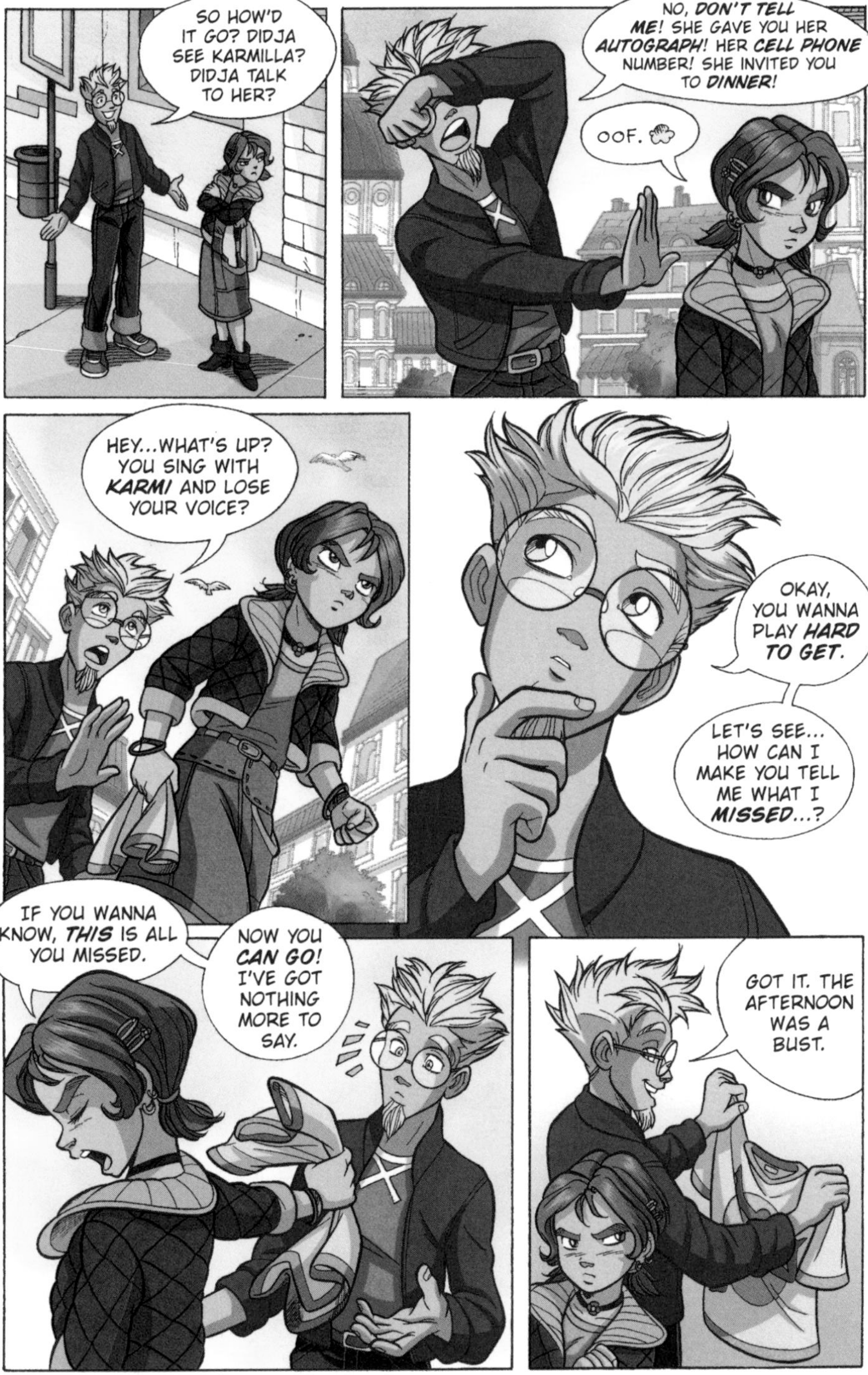
SO HOW'D IT GO? DIDJA SEE KARMILLA? DIDJA TALK TO HER?
NO, DON'T TELL ME! SHE GAVE YOU HER AUTOGRAPH! HER CELL PHONE NUMBER! SHE INVITED YOU TO DINNER!
OOF.
HEY...WHAT'S UP? YOU SING WITH KARMI AND LOSE YOUR VOICE?
OKAY, YOU WANNA PLAY HARD TO GET.
LET'S SEE... HOW CAN I MAKE YOU TELL ME WHAT I MISSED...?
IF YOU WANNA KNOW, THIS IS ALL YOU MISSED.
NOW YOU CAN GO! I'VE GOT NOTHING MORE TO SAY.
GOT IT. THE AFTERNOON WAS A BUST.

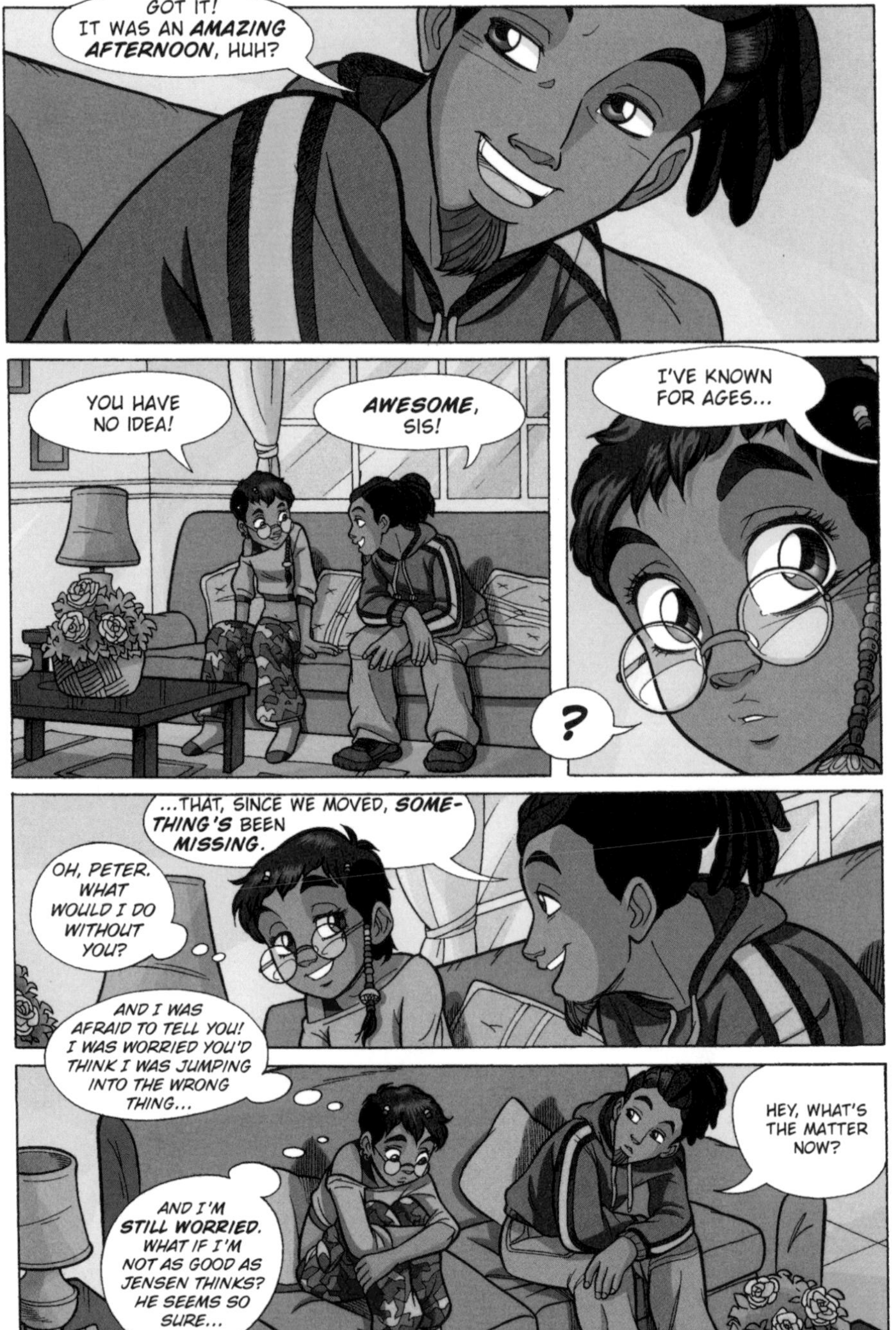
GOT IT! IT WAS AN AMAZING AFTERNOON, HUH?
YOU HAVE NO IDEA!
AWESOME, SIS!
I'VE KNOWN FOR AGES...
?
...THAT, SINCE WE MOVED, SOME-THING'S BEEN MISSING.
OH, PETER. WHAT WOULD I DO WITHOUT YOU?
AND I WAS AFRAID TO TELL YOU! I WAS WORRIED YOU'D THINK I WAS JUMPING INTO THE WRONG THING...
AND I'M STILL WORRIED. WHAT IF I'M NOT AS GOOD AS JENSEN THINKS? HE SEEMS SO SURE...
HEY, WHAT'S THE MATTER NOW?

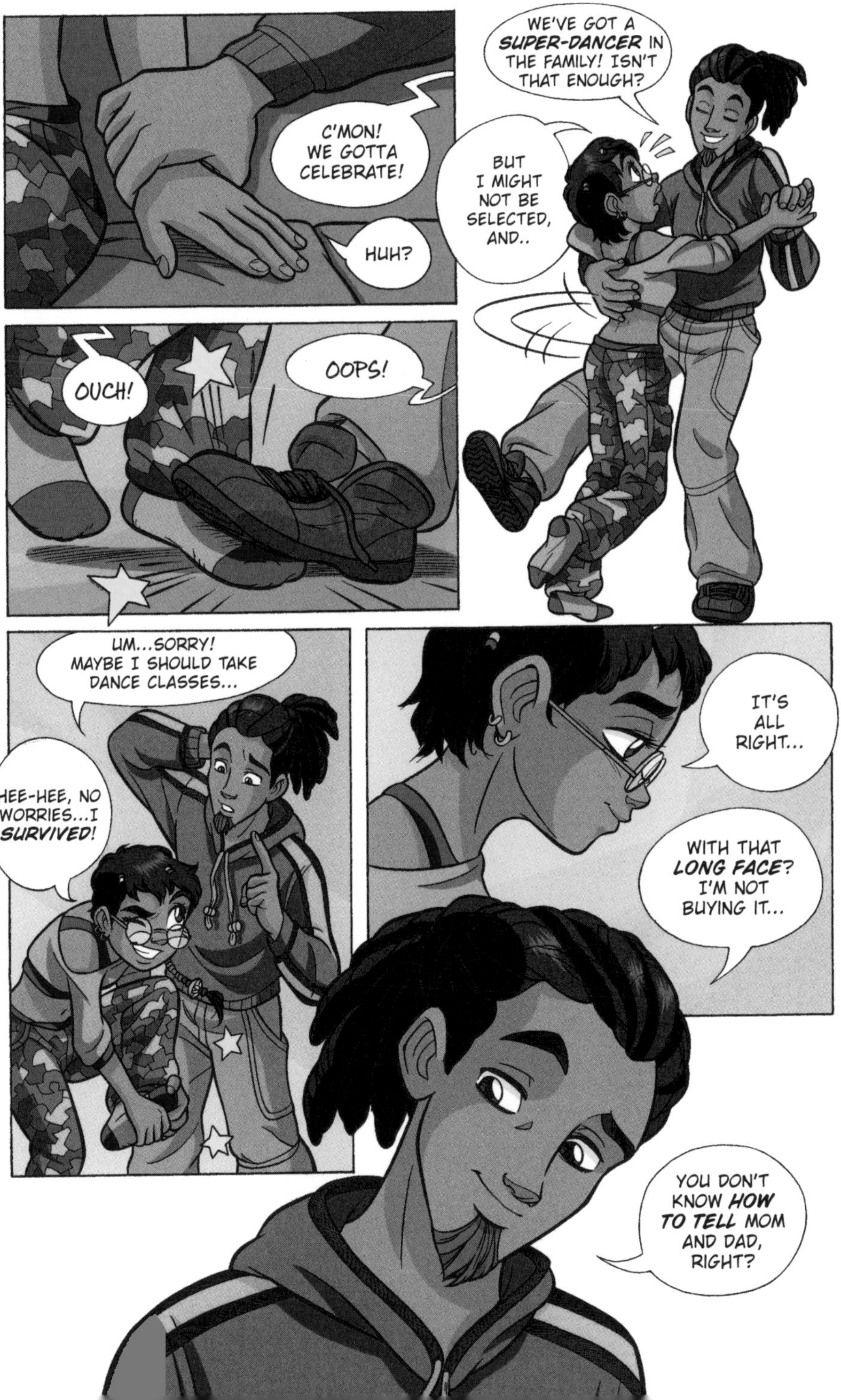
C'MON! WE GOTTA CELEBRATE!
HUH?
OUCH!
OOPS!
WE'VE GOT A SUPER-DANCER IN THE FAMILY! ISN'T THAT ENOUGH?
BUT I MIGHT NOT BE SELECTED, AND..
UM...SORRY! MAYBE I SHOULD TAKE DANCE CLASSES...
HEE-HEE, NO WORRIES...I SURVIVED!
IT'S ALL RIGHT...
WITH THAT LONG FACE? I'M NOT BUYING IT...
YOU DON'T KNOW HOW TO TELL MOM AND DAD, RIGHT?

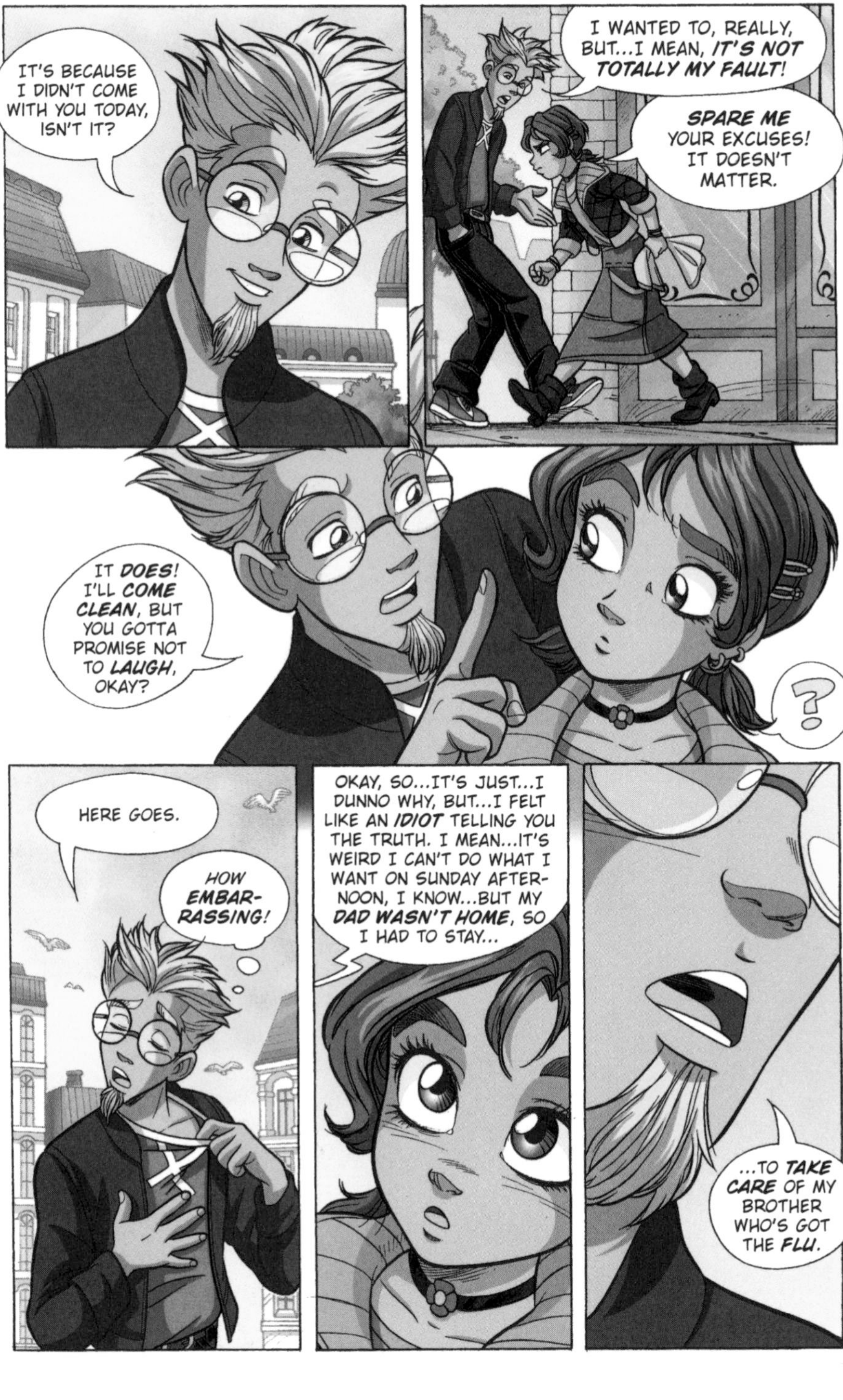

IT'S BECAUSE I DIDN'T COME WITH YOU TODAY, ISN'T IT?
I WANTED TO, REALLY, BUT...I MEAN, IT'S NOT TOTALLY MY FAULT!
SPARE ME YOUR EXCUSES! IT DOESN'T MATTER.
IT DOES! I'LL COME CLEAN, BUT YOU GOTTA PROMISE NOT TO LAUGH, OKAY?
?
HERE GOES.
HOW EMBARRASSING!
OKAY, SO...IT'S JUST...I DUNNO WHY, BUT...I FELT LIKE AN IDIOT TELLING YOU THE TRUTH. I MEAN...IT'S WEIRD I CAN'T DO WHAT I WANT ON SUNDAY AFTERNOON, I KNOW...BUT MY DAD WASN'T HOME, SO I HAD TO STAY...
...TO TAKE CARE OF MY BROTHER WHO'S GOT THE FLU.

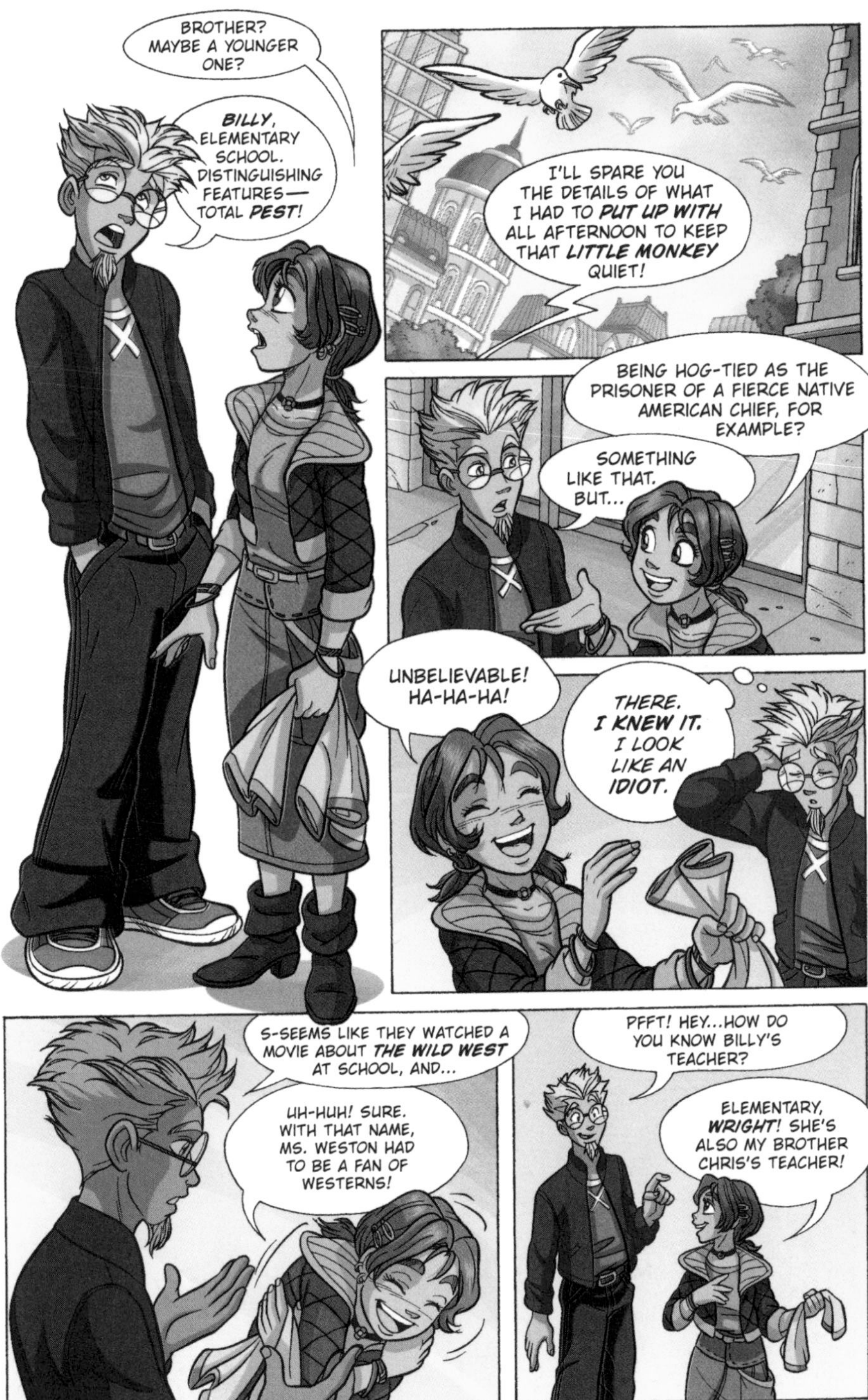
BROTHER? MAYBE A YOUNGER ONE?
BILLY, ELEMENTARY SCHOOL. DISTINGUISHING FEATURES— TOTAL *PEST*!
I'LL SPARE YOU THE DETAILS OF WHAT I HAD TO *PUT UP WITH* ALL AFTERNOON TO KEEP THAT *LITTLE MONKEY* QUIET!
BEING HOG-TIED AS THE PRISONER OF A FIERCE NATIVE AMERICAN CHIEF, FOR EXAMPLE?
SOMETHING LIKE THAT. BUT...
UNBELIEVABLE! HA-HA-HA!
THERE. *I KNEW IT.* I LOOK LIKE AN *IDIOT*.
S-SEEMS LIKE THEY WATCHED A MOVIE ABOUT *THE WILD WEST* AT SCHOOL, AND...
UH-HUH! SURE. WITH THAT NAME, MS. WESTON HAD TO BE A FAN OF WESTERNS!
PFFT! HEY...HOW DO YOU KNOW BILLY'S TEACHER?
ELEMENTARY, *WRIGHT*! SHE'S ALSO MY BROTHER CHRIS'S TEACHER!

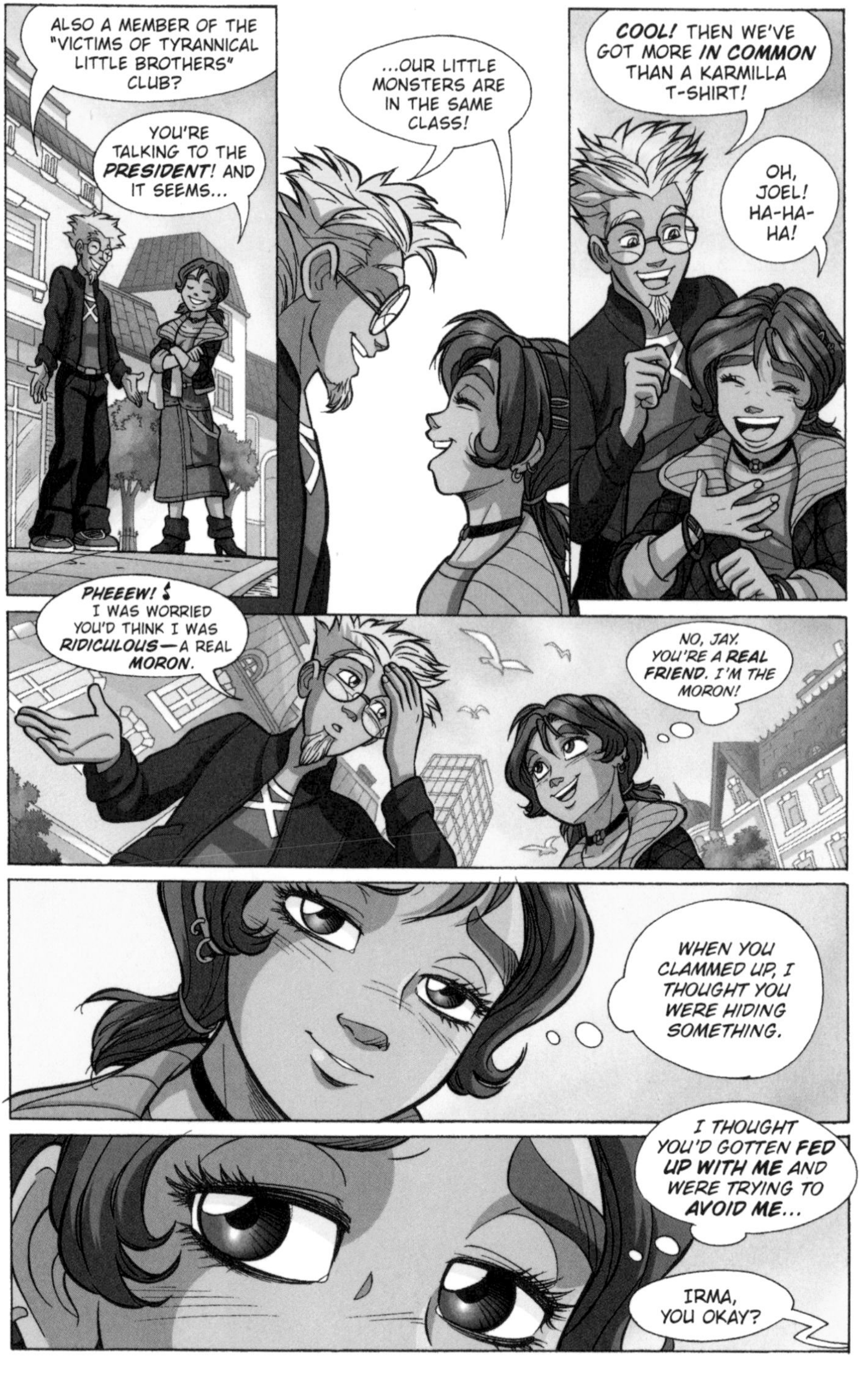
ALSO A MEMBER OF THE "VICTIMS OF TYRANNICAL LITTLE BROTHERS" CLUB?
YOU'RE TALKING TO THE PRESIDENT! AND IT SEEMS...
...OUR LITTLE MONSTERS ARE IN THE SAME CLASS!
COOL! THEN WE'VE GOT MORE IN COMMON THAN A KARMILLA T-SHIRT!
OH, JOEL! HA-HA-HA!
PHEEEW! I WAS WORRIED YOU'D THINK I WAS RIDICULOUS—A REAL MORON.
NO, JAY. YOU'RE A REAL FRIEND. I'M THE MORON!
WHEN YOU CLAMMED UP, I THOUGHT YOU WERE HIDING SOMETHING.
I THOUGHT YOU'D GOTTEN FED UP WITH ME AND WERE TRYING TO AVOID ME...
IRMA, YOU OKAY?

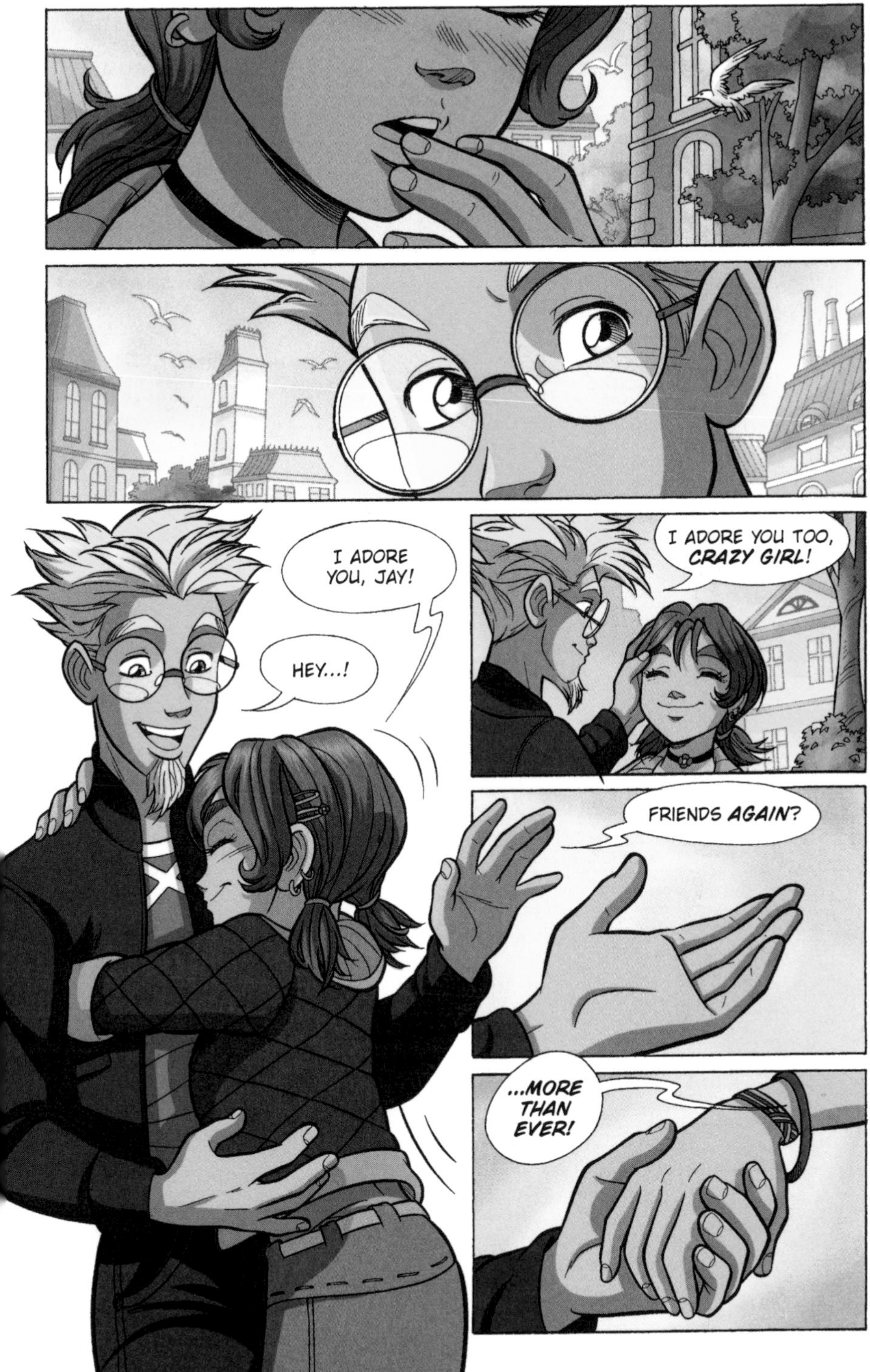
I ADORE YOU, JAY!
HEY...!
I ADORE YOU TOO, **CRAZY GIRL!**
FRIENDS **AGAIN**?
...MORE THAN EVER!

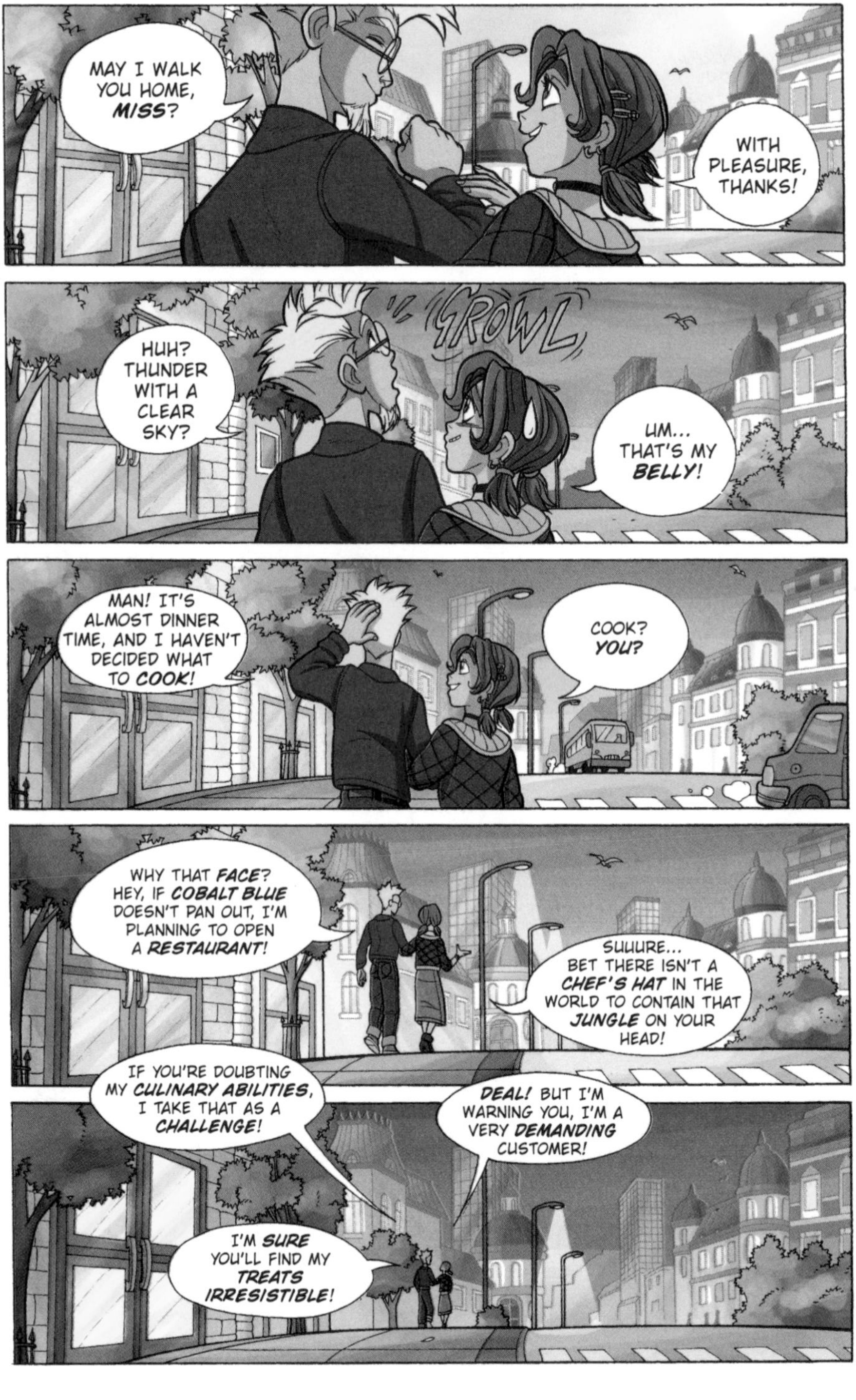
MAY I WALK YOU HOME, **MISS**?
WITH PLEASURE, THANKS!
GROWL
HUH? THUNDER WITH A CLEAR SKY?
UM... THAT'S MY **BELLY**!
MAN! IT'S ALMOST DINNER TIME, AND I HAVEN'T DECIDED WHAT TO **COOK**!
COOK? **YOU?**
WHY THAT **FACE**? HEY, IF **COBALT BLUE** DOESN'T PAN OUT, I'M PLANNING TO OPEN A **RESTAURANT**!
SUUURE... BET THERE ISN'T A **CHEF'S HAT** IN THE WORLD TO CONTAIN THAT **JUNGLE** ON YOUR HEAD!
IF YOU'RE DOUBTING MY **CULINARY ABILITIES**, I TAKE THAT AS A **CHALLENGE**!
DEAL! BUT I'M WARNING YOU, I'M A VERY **DEMANDING** CUSTOMER!
I'M **SURE** YOU'LL FIND MY **TREATS IRRESISTIBLE**!

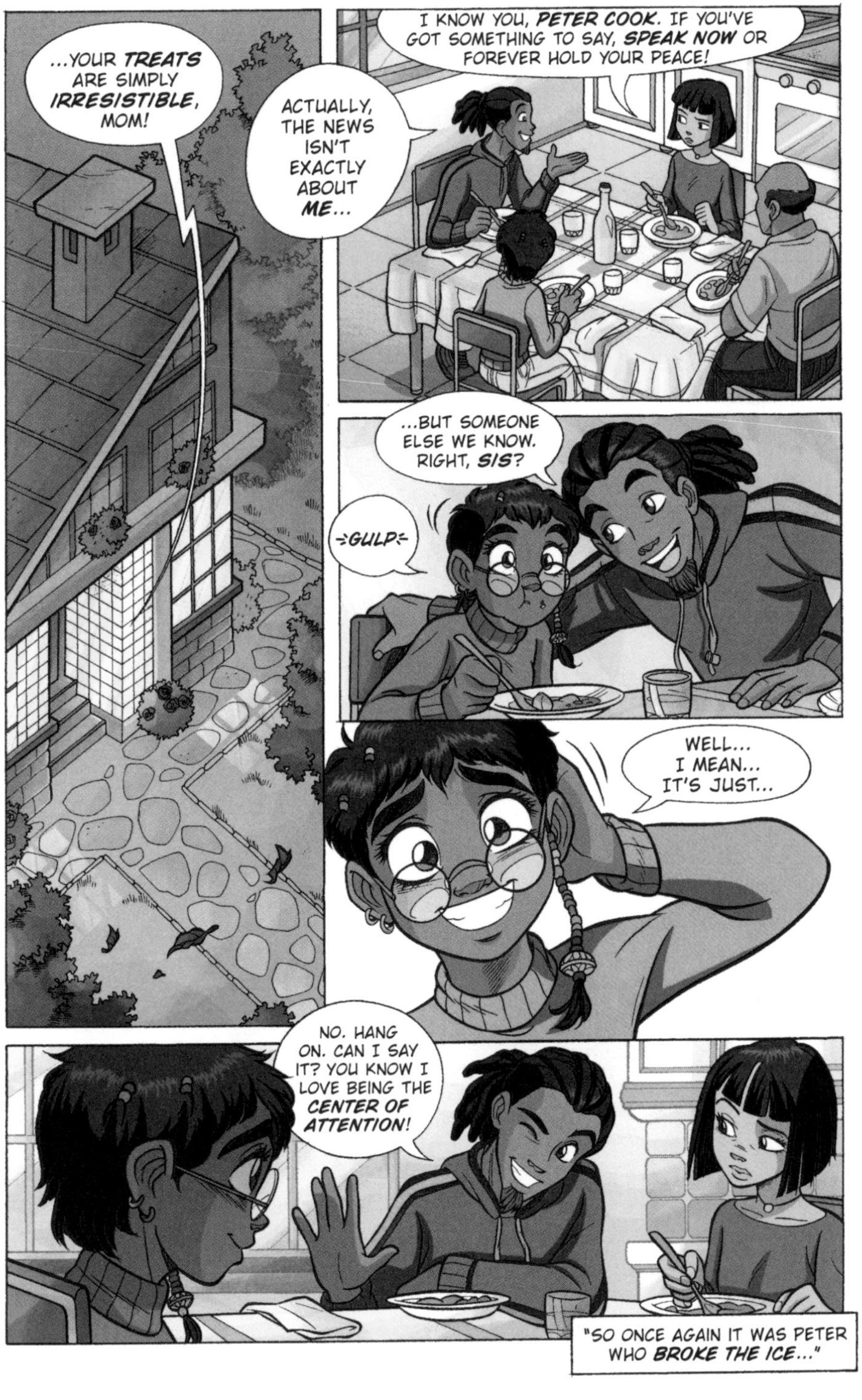

...YOUR **TREATS** ARE SIMPLY **IRRESISTIBLE**, MOM!
ACTUALLY, THE NEWS ISN'T EXACTLY ABOUT **ME**...
I KNOW YOU, **PETER COOK**. IF YOU'VE GOT SOMETHING TO SAY, **SPEAK NOW** OR FOREVER HOLD YOUR PEACE!
...BUT SOMEONE ELSE WE KNOW. RIGHT, **SIS**?
GULP
WELL... I MEAN... IT'S JUST...
NO. HANG ON. CAN I SAY IT? YOU KNOW I LOVE BEING THE **CENTER OF ATTENTION**!
"SO ONCE AGAIN IT WAS PETER WHO **BROKE THE ICE**..."

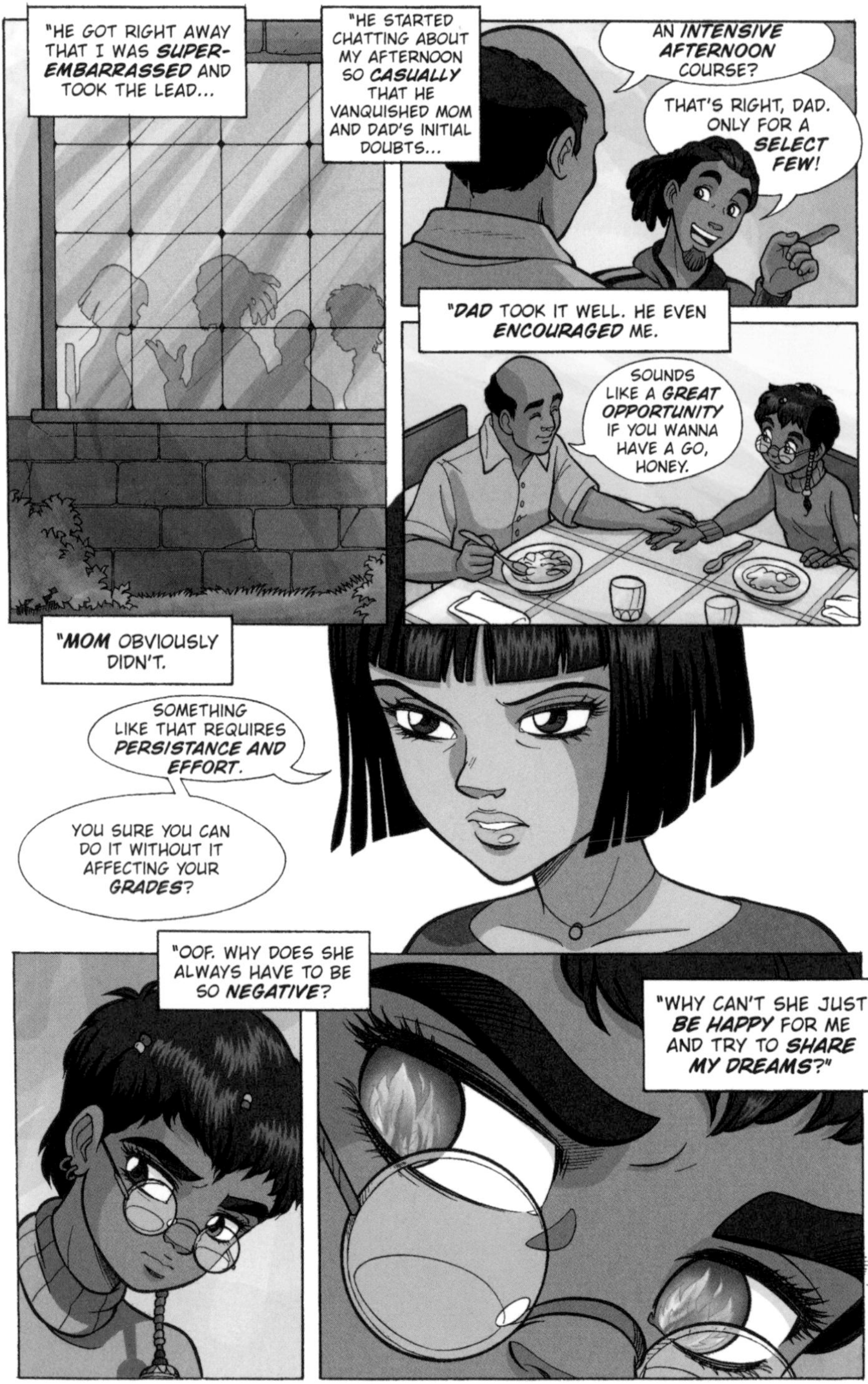
"HE GOT RIGHT AWAY THAT I WAS SUPER-EMBARRASSED AND TOOK THE LEAD...
"HE STARTED CHATTING ABOUT MY AFTERNOON SO CASUALLY THAT HE VANQUISHED MOM AND DAD'S INITIAL DOUBTS...
AN INTENSIVE AFTERNOON COURSE?
THAT'S RIGHT, DAD. ONLY FOR A SELECT FEW!
"DAD TOOK IT WELL. HE EVEN ENCOURAGED ME.
SOUNDS LIKE A GREAT OPPORTUNITY IF YOU WANNA HAVE A GO, HONEY.
"MOM OBVIOUSLY DIDN'T.
SOMETHING LIKE THAT REQUIRES PERSISTANCE AND EFFORT.
YOU SURE YOU CAN DO IT WITHOUT IT AFFECTING YOUR GRADES?
"OOF. WHY DOES SHE ALWAYS HAVE TO BE SO NEGATIVE?
"WHY CAN'T SHE JUST BE HAPPY FOR ME AND TRY TO SHARE MY DREAMS?"

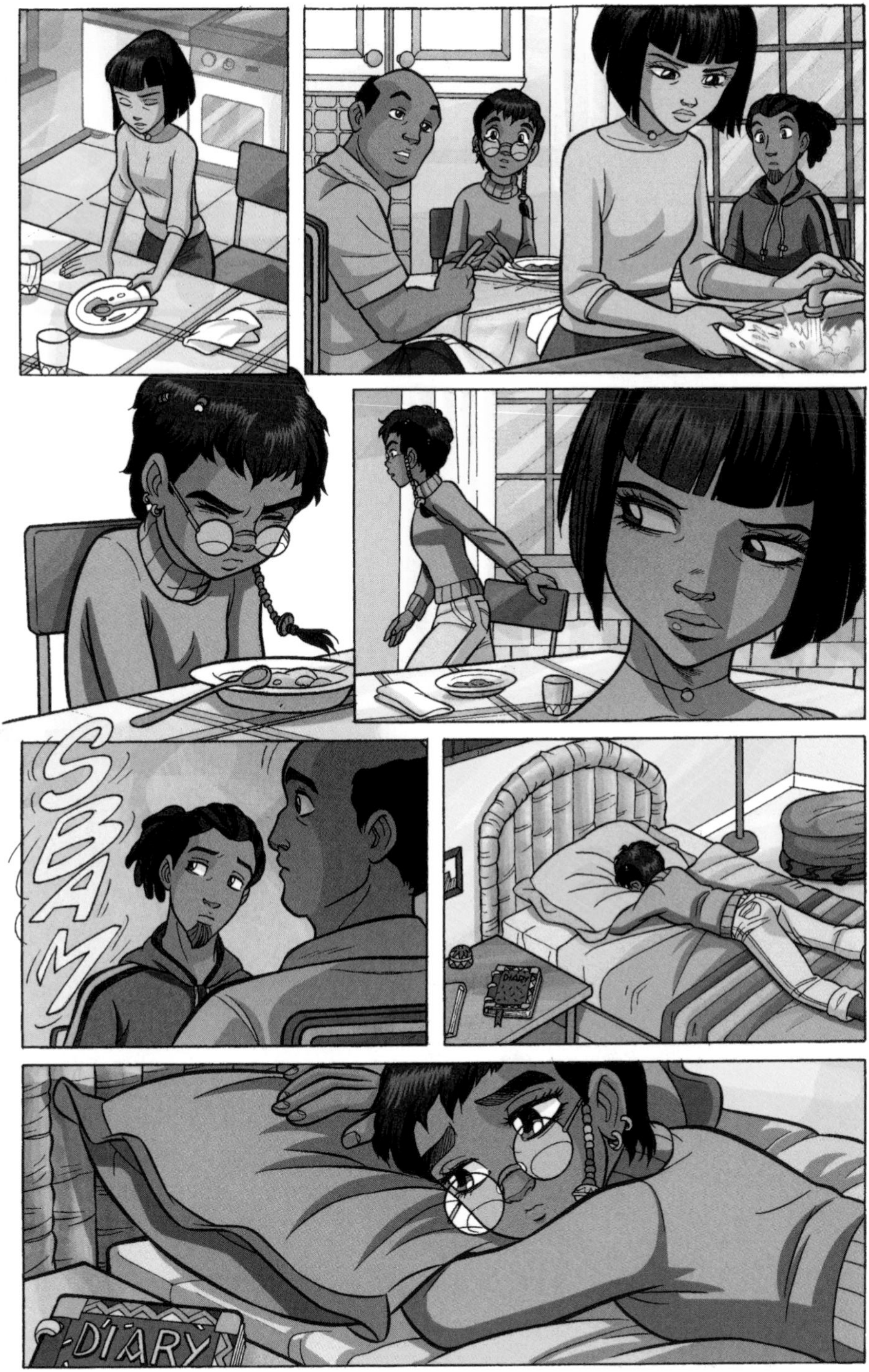
SBAM
DIARY
DIARY

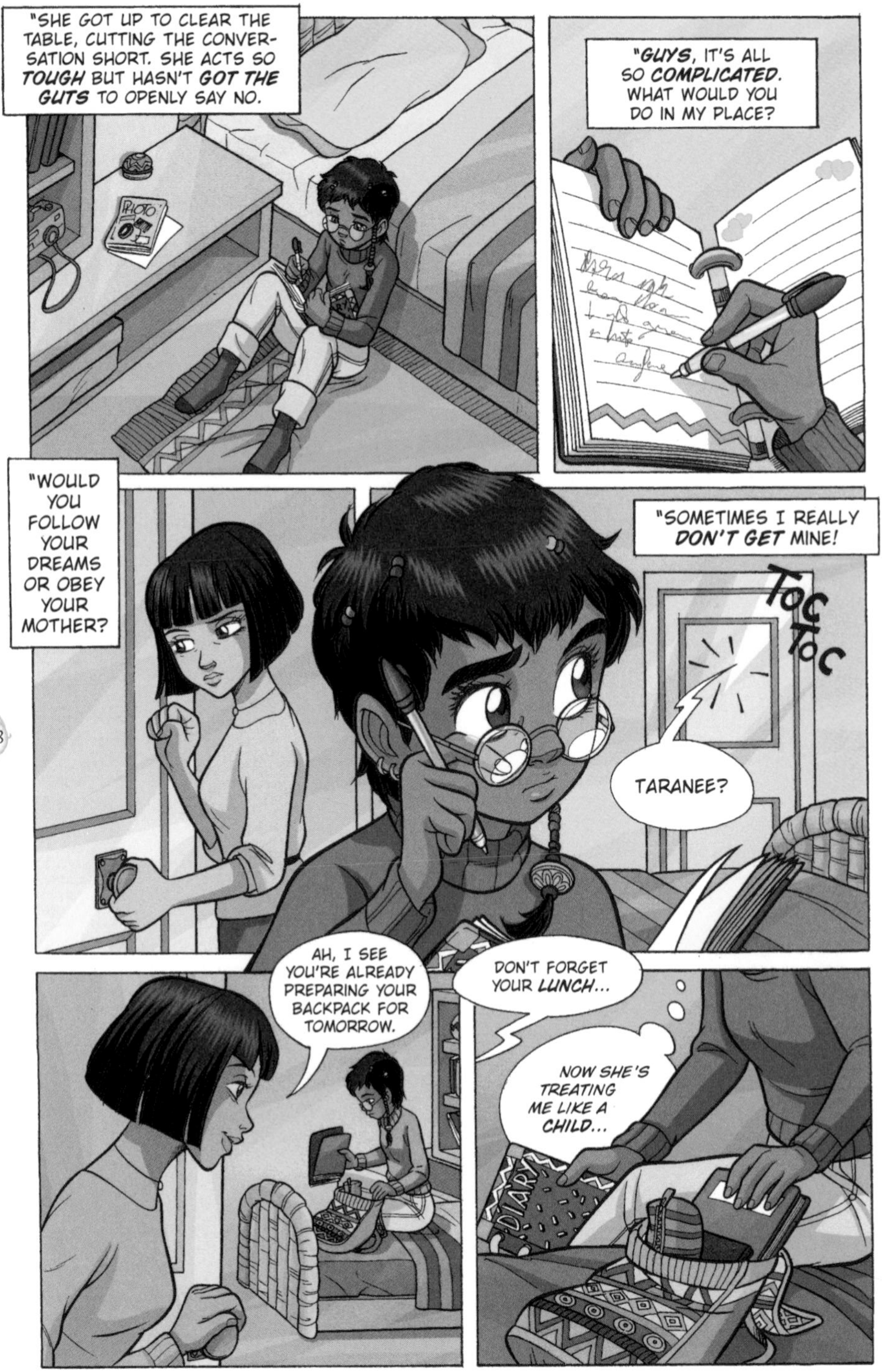
"SHE GOT UP TO CLEAR THE TABLE, CUTTING THE CONVERSATION SHORT. SHE ACTS SO **TOUGH** BUT HASN'T **GOT THE GUTS** TO OPENLY SAY NO.
PHOTO
"**GUYS**, IT'S ALL SO **COMPLICATED**. WHAT WOULD YOU DO IN MY PLACE?
"WOULD YOU FOLLOW YOUR DREAMS OR OBEY YOUR MOTHER?
"SOMETIMES I REALLY **DON'T GET** MINE!
TOC TOC
TARANEE?
AH, I SEE YOU'RE ALREADY PREPARING YOUR BACKPACK FOR TOMORROW.
DON'T FORGET YOUR **LUNCH**...
*NOW SHE'S TREATING ME LIKE A **CHILD**...*
DIARY

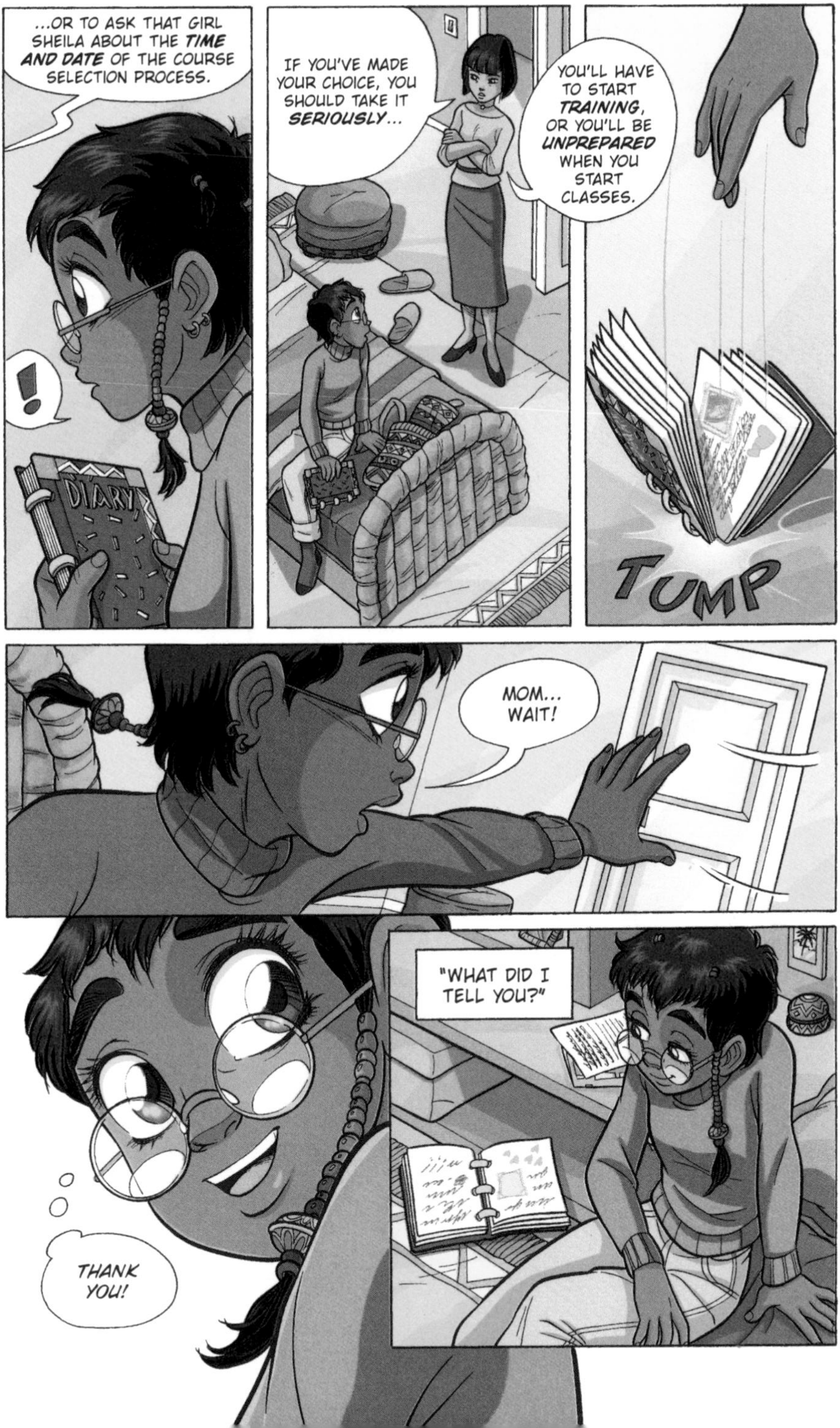
...OR TO ASK THAT GIRL SHEILA ABOUT THE **TIME AND DATE** OF THE COURSE SELECTION PROCESS.
!
DIARY
IF YOU'VE MADE YOUR CHOICE, YOU SHOULD TAKE IT **SERIOUSLY**...
YOU'LL HAVE TO START **TRAINING**, OR YOU'LL BE **UNPREPARED** WHEN YOU START CLASSES.
TUMP
MOM... WAIT!
THANK YOU!
"WHAT DID I TELL YOU?"

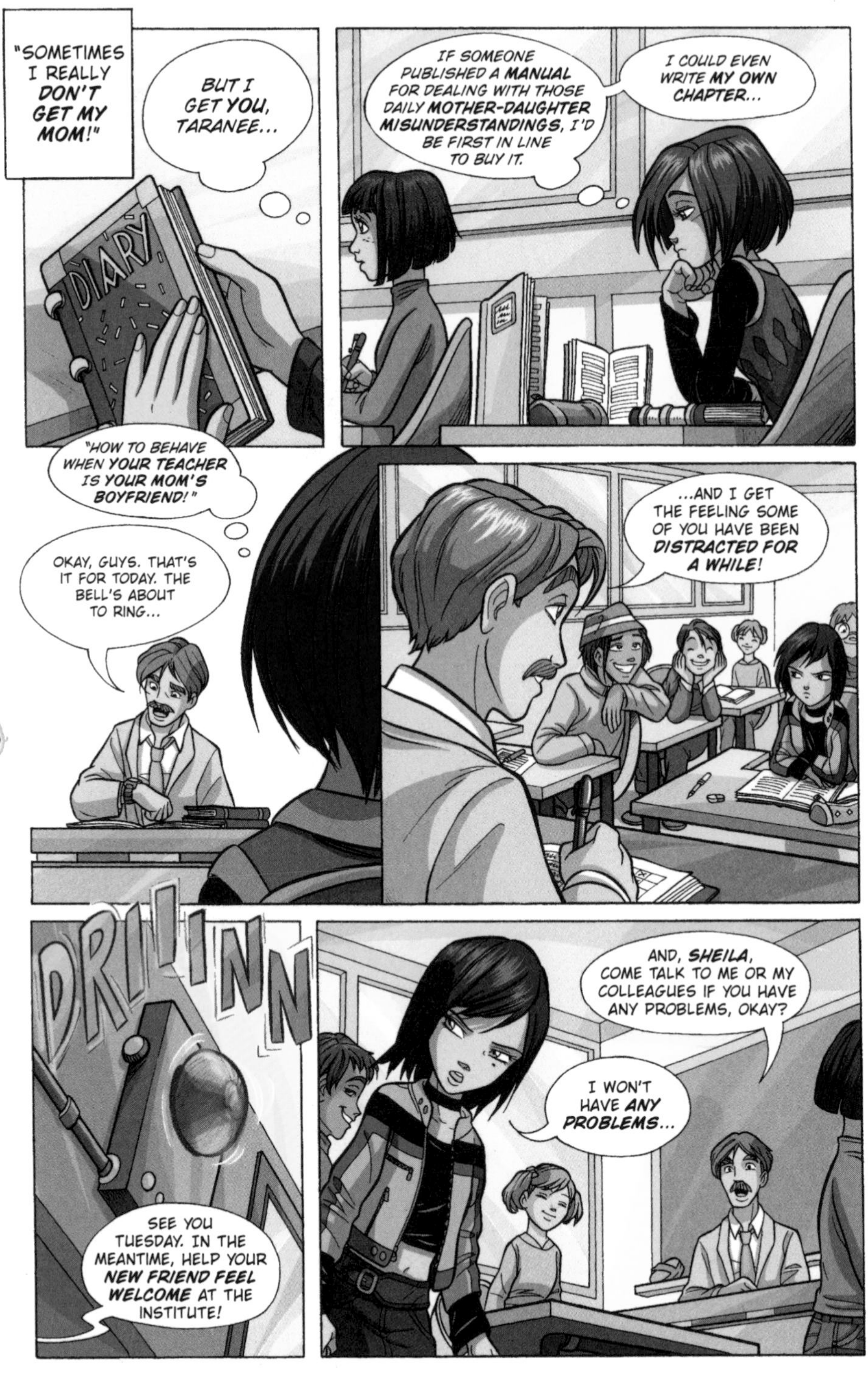
"SOMETIMES I REALLY DON'T GET MY MOM!"
BUT I GET YOU, TARANEE...
DIARY
IF SOMEONE PUBLISHED A MANUAL FOR DEALING WITH THOSE DAILY MOTHER-DAUGHTER MISUNDERSTANDINGS, I'D BE FIRST IN LINE TO BUY IT.
I COULD EVEN WRITE MY OWN CHAPTER...
"HOW TO BEHAVE WHEN YOUR TEACHER IS YOUR MOM'S BOYFRIEND!"
OKAY, GUYS. THAT'S IT FOR TODAY. THE BELL'S ABOUT TO RING...
...AND I GET THE FEELING SOME OF YOU HAVE BEEN DISTRACTED FOR A WHILE!
DRIIINN
SEE YOU TUESDAY. IN THE MEANTIME, HELP YOUR NEW FRIEND FEEL WELCOME AT THE INSTITUTE!
AND, SHEILA, COME TALK TO ME OR MY COLLEAGUES IF YOU HAVE ANY PROBLEMS, OKAY?
I WON'T HAVE ANY PROBLEMS...

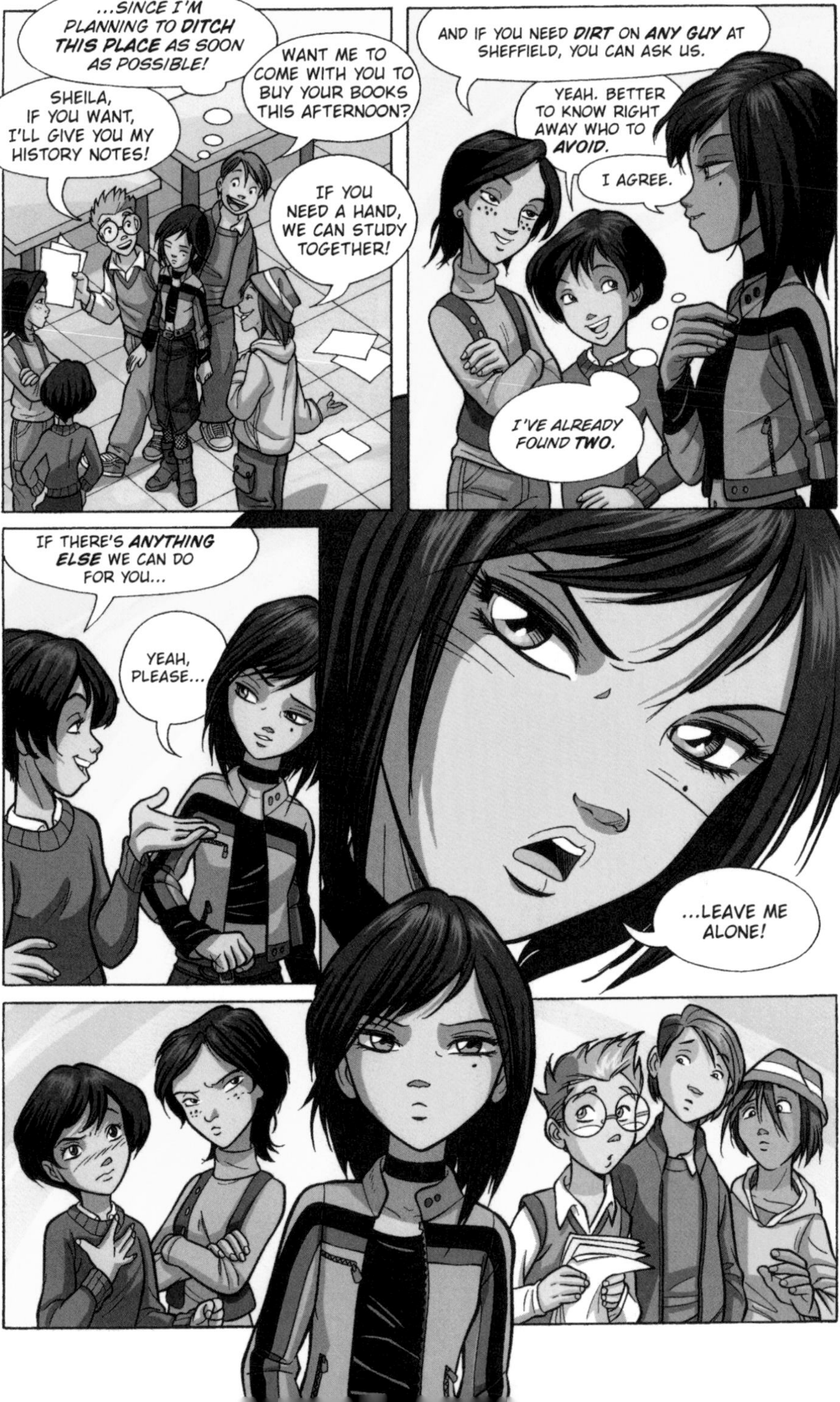
...SINCE I'M PLANNING TO DITCH THIS PLACE AS SOON AS POSSIBLE!
SHEILA, IF YOU WANT, I'LL GIVE YOU MY HISTORY NOTES!
WANT ME TO COME WITH YOU TO BUY YOUR BOOKS THIS AFTERNOON?
IF YOU NEED A HAND, WE CAN STUDY TOGETHER!
AND IF YOU NEED DIRT ON ANY GUY AT SHEFFIELD, YOU CAN ASK US.
YEAH. BETTER TO KNOW RIGHT AWAY WHO TO AVOID.
I AGREE.
I'VE ALREADY FOUND TWO.
IF THERE'S ANYTHING ELSE WE CAN DO FOR YOU...
YEAH, PLEASE...
...LEAVE ME ALONE!

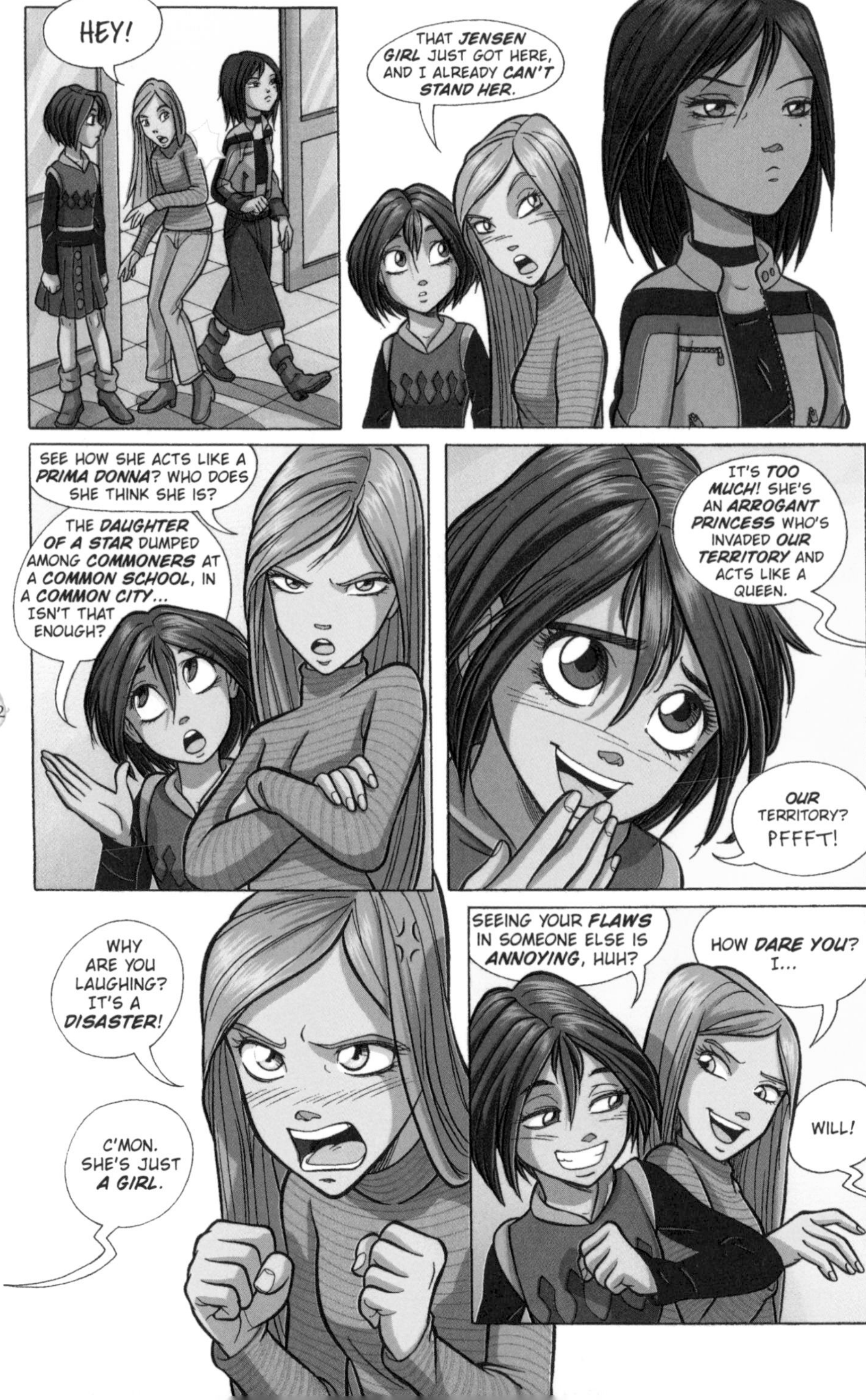
HEY!
THAT JENSEN GIRL JUST GOT HERE, AND I ALREADY CAN'T STAND HER.
SEE HOW SHE ACTS LIKE A PRIMA DONNA? WHO DOES SHE THINK SHE IS?
THE DAUGHTER OF A STAR DUMPED AMONG COMMONERS AT A COMMON SCHOOL, IN A COMMON CITY... ISN'T THAT ENOUGH?
IT'S TOO MUCH! SHE'S AN ARROGANT PRINCESS WHO'S INVADED OUR TERRITORY AND ACTS LIKE A QUEEN.
OUR TERRITORY? PFFFT!
WHY ARE YOU LAUGHING? IT'S A DISASTER!
C'MON. SHE'S JUST A GIRL.
SEEING YOUR FLAWS IN SOMEONE ELSE IS ANNOYING, HUH?
HOW DARE YOU? I...
WILL!

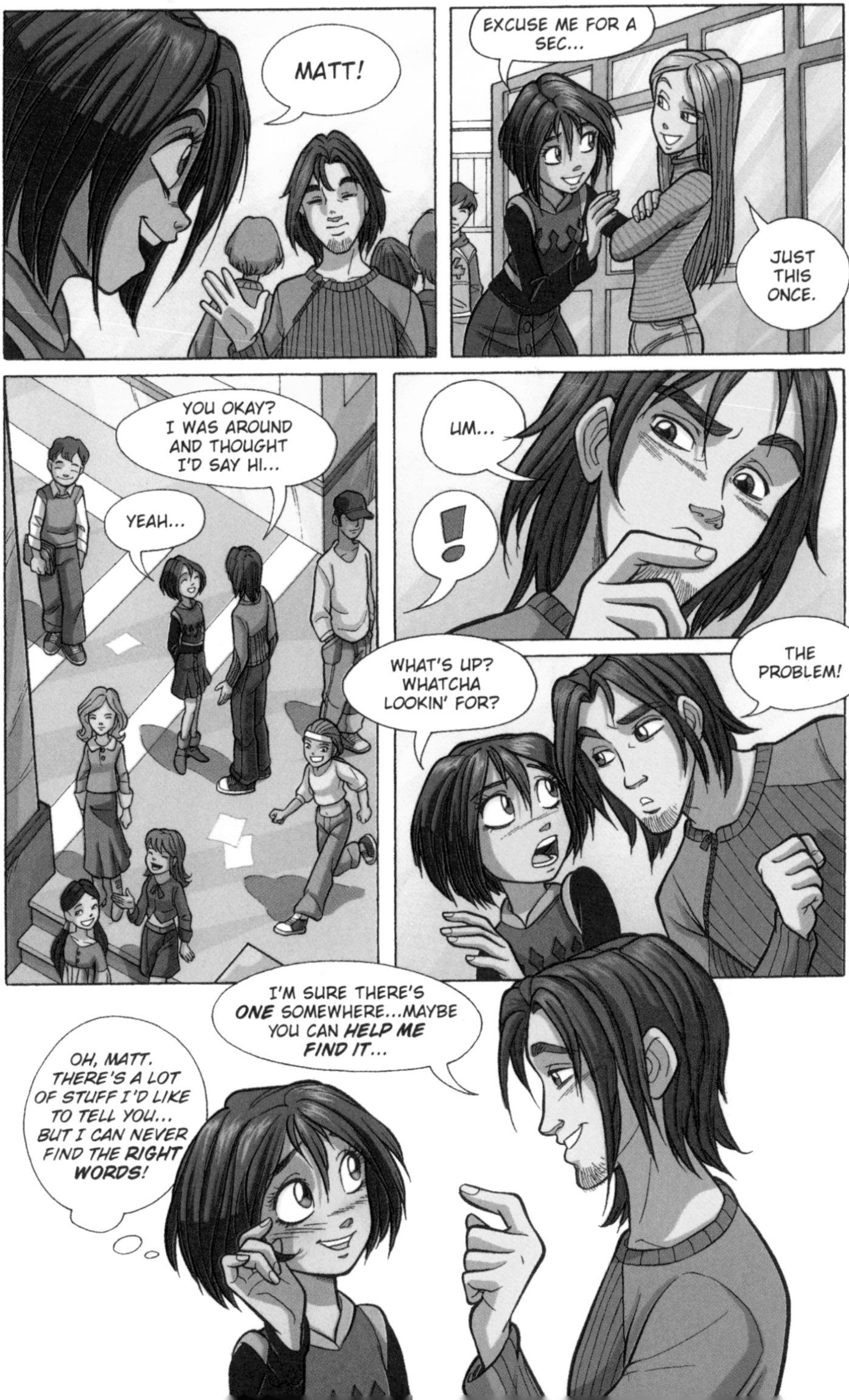
MATT!
EXCUSE ME FOR A SEC...
JUST THIS ONCE.
YOU OKAY? I WAS AROUND AND THOUGHT I'D SAY HI...
YEAH...
UM...
!
WHAT'S UP? WHATCHA LOOKIN' FOR?
THE PROBLEM!
OH, MATT. THERE'S A LOT OF STUFF I'D LIKE TO TELL YOU... BUT I CAN NEVER FIND THE RIGHT WORDS!
I'M SURE THERE'S ONE SOMEWHERE...MAYBE YOU CAN HELP ME FIND IT...

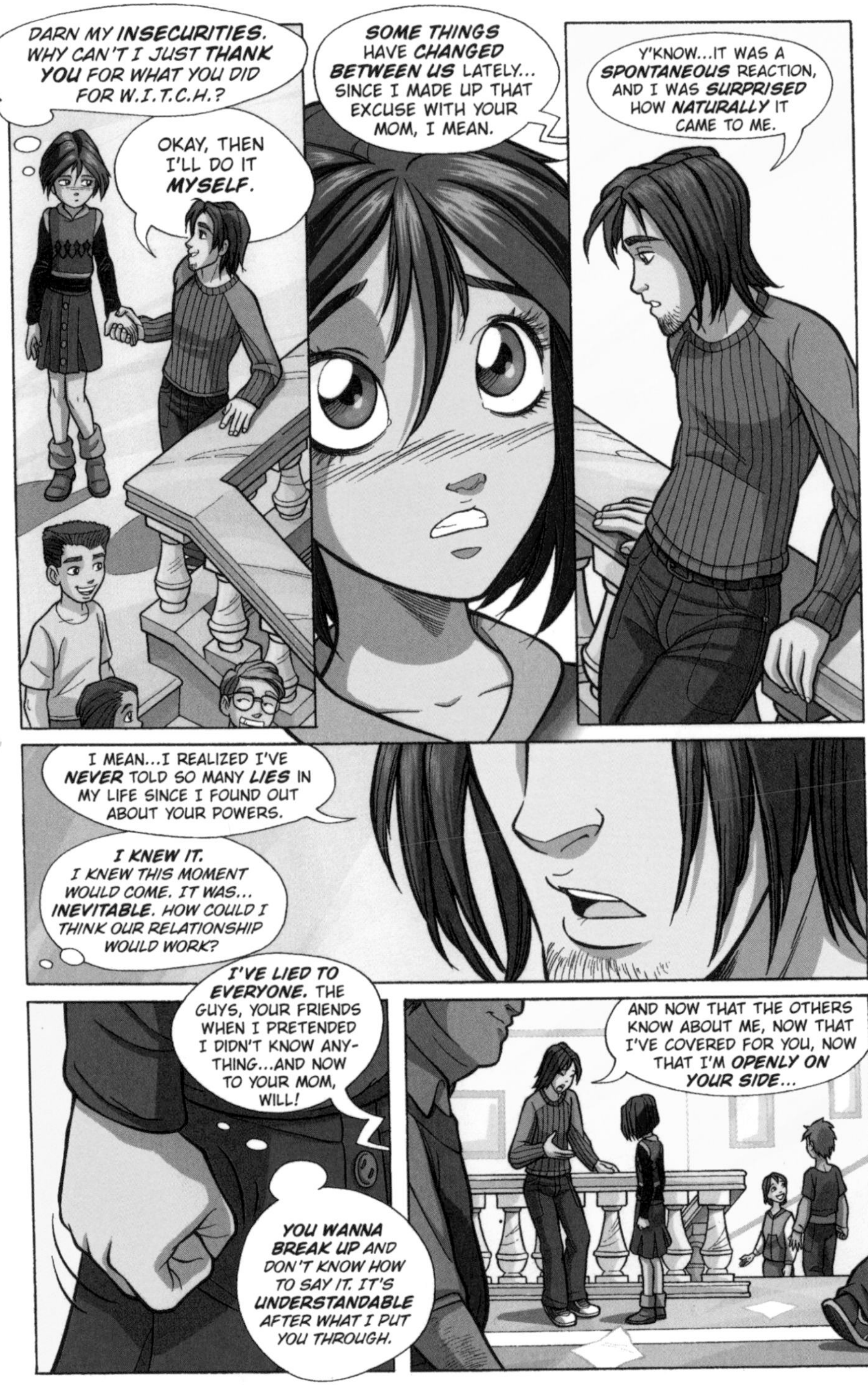
DARN MY INSECURITIES. WHY CAN'T I JUST THANK YOU FOR WHAT YOU DID FOR W.I.T.C.H.?
OKAY, THEN I'LL DO IT MYSELF.
SOME THINGS HAVE CHANGED BETWEEN US LATELY... SINCE I MADE UP THAT EXCUSE WITH YOUR MOM, I MEAN.
Y'KNOW...IT WAS A SPONTANEOUS REACTION, AND I WAS SURPRISED HOW NATURALLY IT CAME TO ME.
I MEAN...I REALIZED I'VE NEVER TOLD SO MANY LIES IN MY LIFE SINCE I FOUND OUT ABOUT YOUR POWERS.
I KNEW IT. I KNEW THIS MOMENT WOULD COME. IT WAS... INEVITABLE. HOW COULD I THINK OUR RELATIONSHIP WOULD WORK?
I'VE LIED TO EVERYONE. THE GUYS, YOUR FRIENDS WHEN I PRETENDED I DIDN'T KNOW ANY-THING...AND NOW TO YOUR MOM, WILL!
YOU WANNA BREAK UP AND DON'T KNOW HOW TO SAY IT. IT'S UNDERSTANDABLE AFTER WHAT I PUT YOU THROUGH.
AND NOW THAT THE OTHERS KNOW ABOUT ME, NOW THAT I'VE COVERED FOR YOU, NOW THAT I'M OPENLY ON YOUR SIDE...

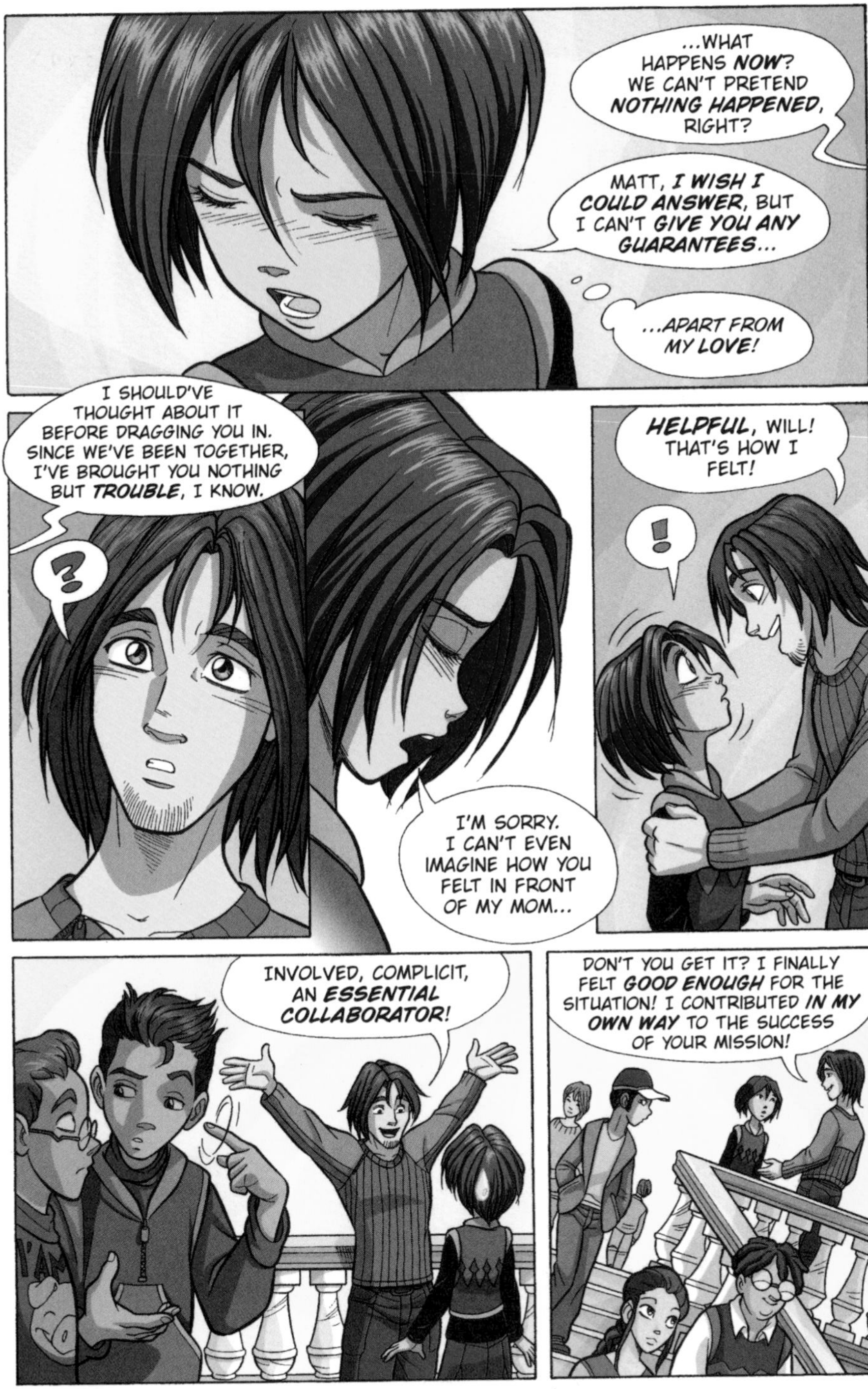
...WHAT HAPPENS NOW? WE CAN'T PRETEND NOTHING HAPPENED, RIGHT?
MATT, I WISH I COULD ANSWER, BUT I CAN'T GIVE YOU ANY GUARANTEES...
...APART FROM MY LOVE!
I SHOULD'VE THOUGHT ABOUT IT BEFORE DRAGGING YOU IN. SINCE WE'VE BEEN TOGETHER, I'VE BROUGHT YOU NOTHING BUT TROUBLE, I KNOW.
?
I'M SORRY. I CAN'T EVEN IMAGINE HOW YOU FELT IN FRONT OF MY MOM...
HELPFUL, WILL! THAT'S HOW I FELT!
!
INVOLVED, COMPLICIT, AN ESSENTIAL COLLABORATOR!
DON'T YOU GET IT? I FINALLY FELT GOOD ENOUGH FOR THE SITUATION! I CONTRIBUTED IN MY OWN WAY TO THE SUCCESS OF YOUR MISSION!

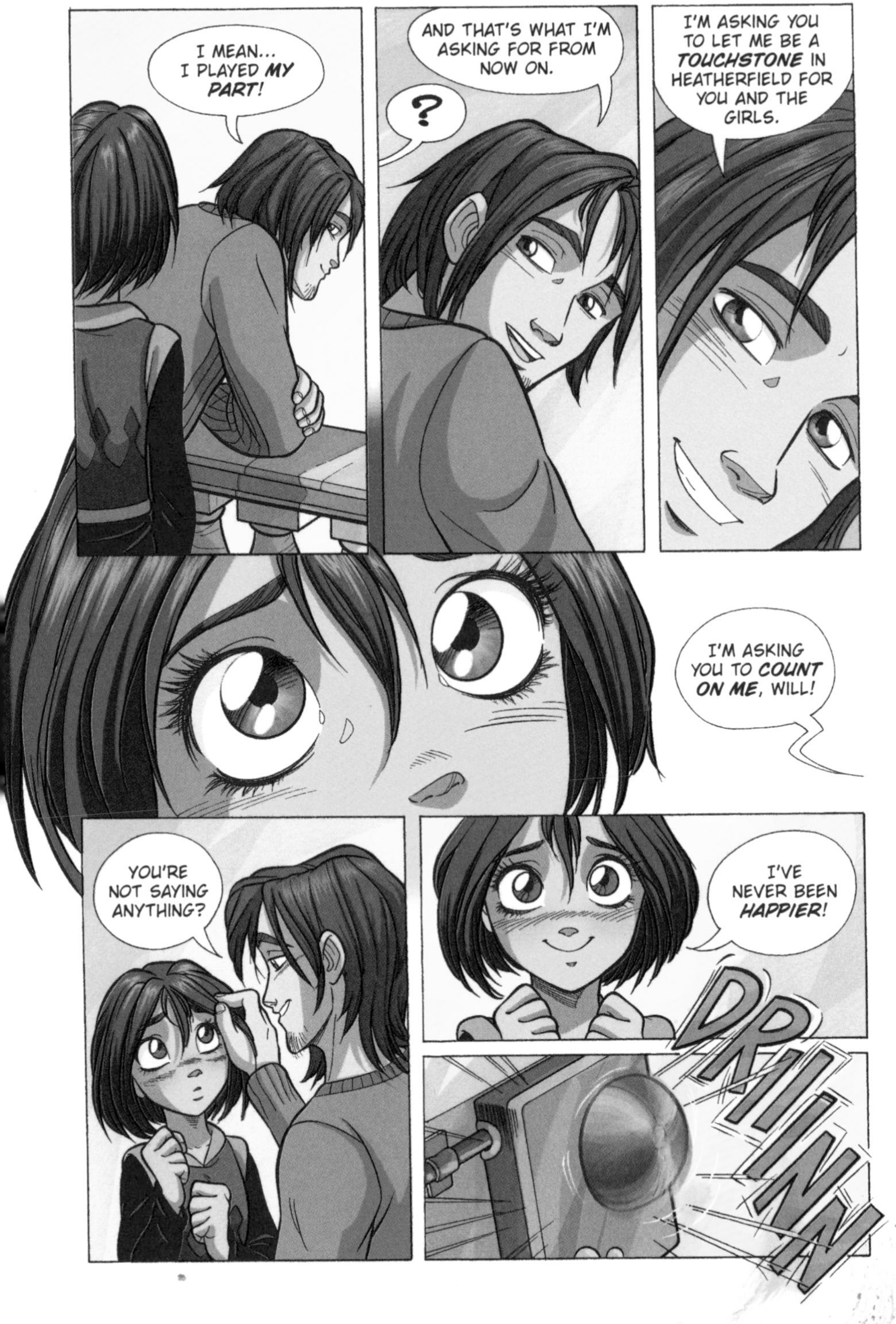
I MEAN... I PLAYED **MY PART**!
AND THAT'S WHAT I'M ASKING FOR FROM NOW ON.
?
I'M ASKING YOU TO LET ME BE A **TOUCHSTONE** IN HEATHERFIELD FOR YOU AND THE GIRLS.
I'M ASKING YOU TO **COUNT ON ME**, WILL!
YOU'RE NOT SAYING ANYTHING?
I'VE NEVER BEEN **HAPPIER**!
DRIIINN

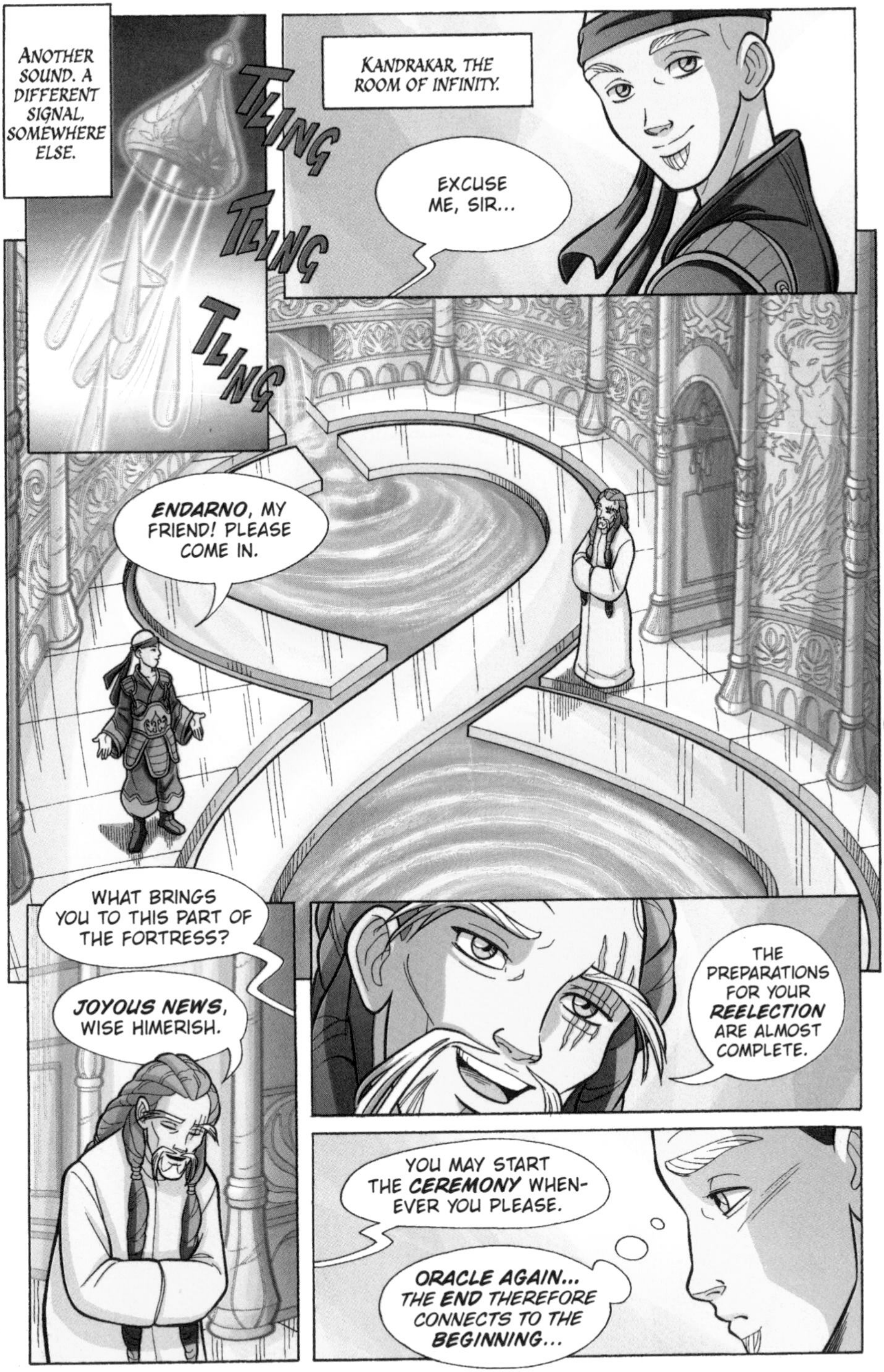

ANOTHER SOUND. A DIFFERENT SIGNAL, SOMEWHERE ELSE.
TLING TLING TLING
KANDRAKAR, THE ROOM OF INFINITY.
EXCUSE ME, SIR...
ENDARNO, MY FRIEND! PLEASE COME IN.
WHAT BRINGS YOU TO THIS PART OF THE FORTRESS?
JOYOUS NEWS, WISE HIMERISH.
THE PREPARATIONS FOR YOUR REELECTION ARE ALMOST COMPLETE.
YOU MAY START THE CEREMONY WHEN-EVER YOU PLEASE.
ORACLE AGAIN... THE END THEREFORE CONNECTS TO THE BEGINNING...

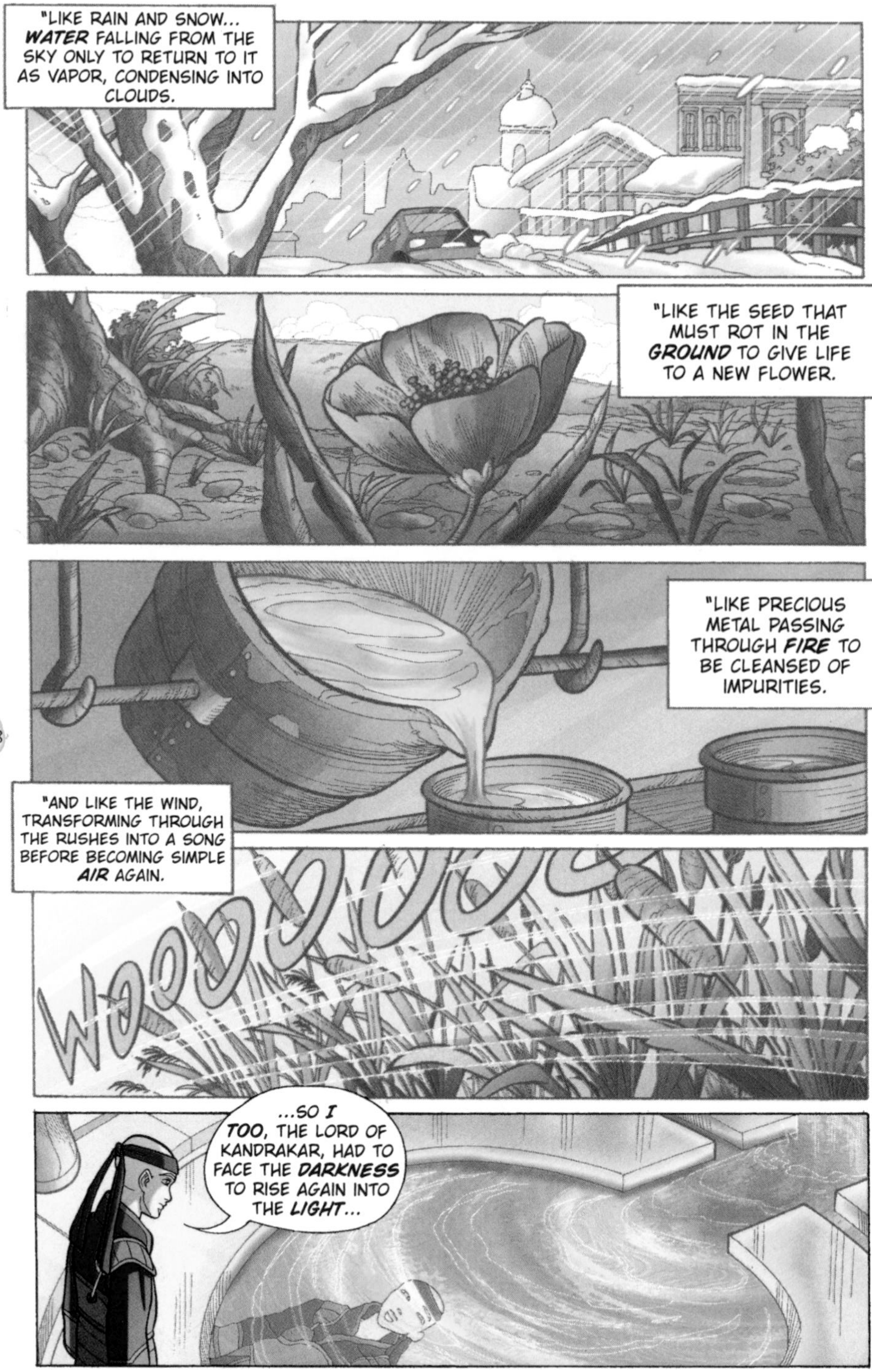
"LIKE RAIN AND SNOW... WATER FALLING FROM THE SKY ONLY TO RETURN TO IT AS VAPOR, CONDENSING INTO CLOUDS.
"LIKE THE SEED THAT MUST ROT IN THE GROUND TO GIVE LIFE TO A NEW FLOWER.
"LIKE PRECIOUS METAL PASSING THROUGH FIRE TO BE CLEANSED OF IMPURITIES.
"AND LIKE THE WIND, TRANSFORMING THROUGH THE RUSHES INTO A SONG BEFORE BECOMING SIMPLE AIR AGAIN.
WOOOOOOO
...SO I TOO, THE LORD OF KANDRAKAR, HAD TO FACE THE DARKNESS TO RISE AGAIN INTO THE LIGHT...

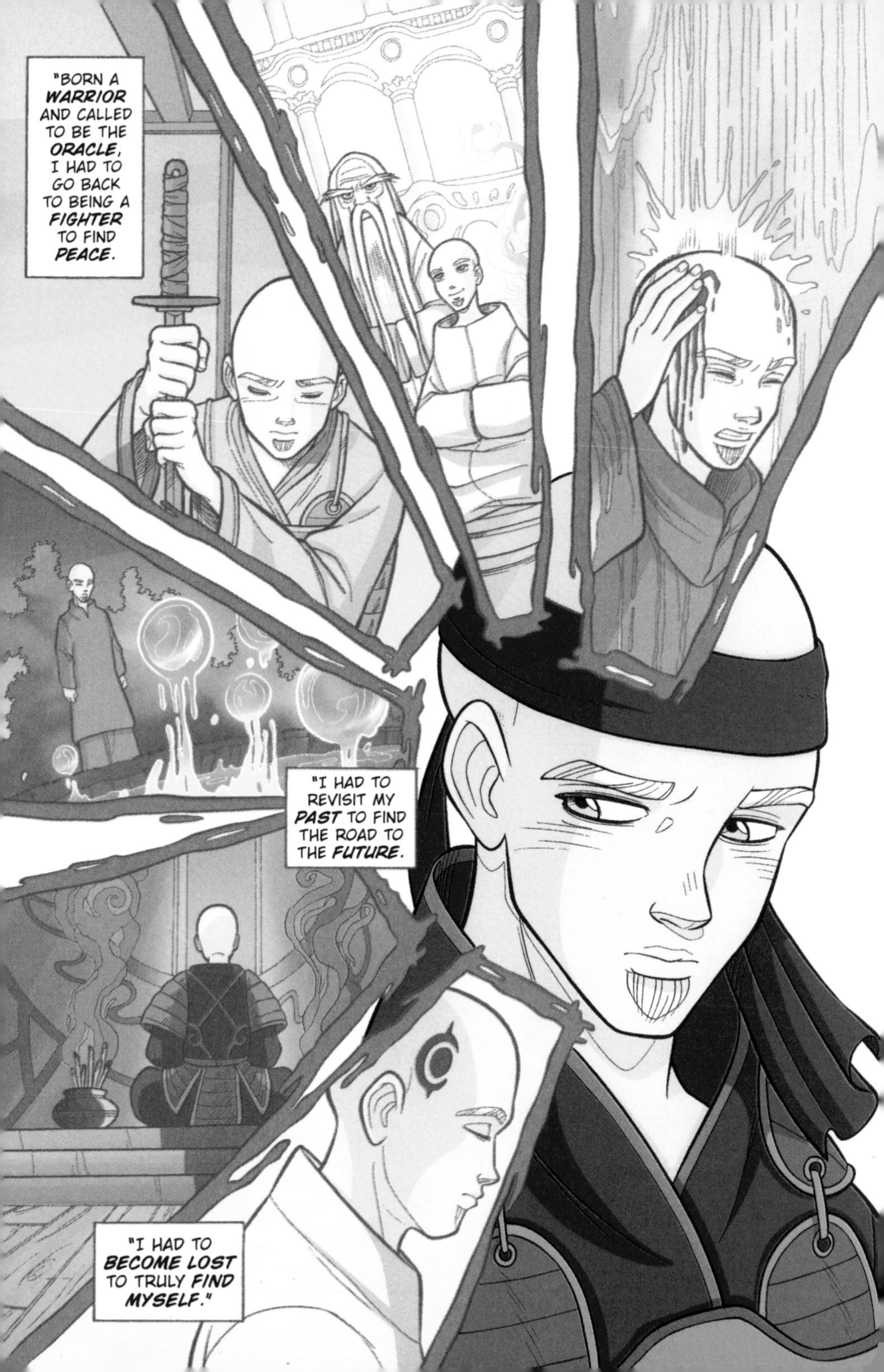
"BORN A **WARRIOR** AND CALLED TO BE THE **ORACLE**, I HAD TO GO BACK TO BEING A **FIGHTER** TO FIND **PEACE**.
"I HAD TO REVISIT MY **PAST** TO FIND THE ROAD TO THE **FUTURE**.
"I HAD TO **BECOME LOST** TO TRULY **FIND MYSELF**."

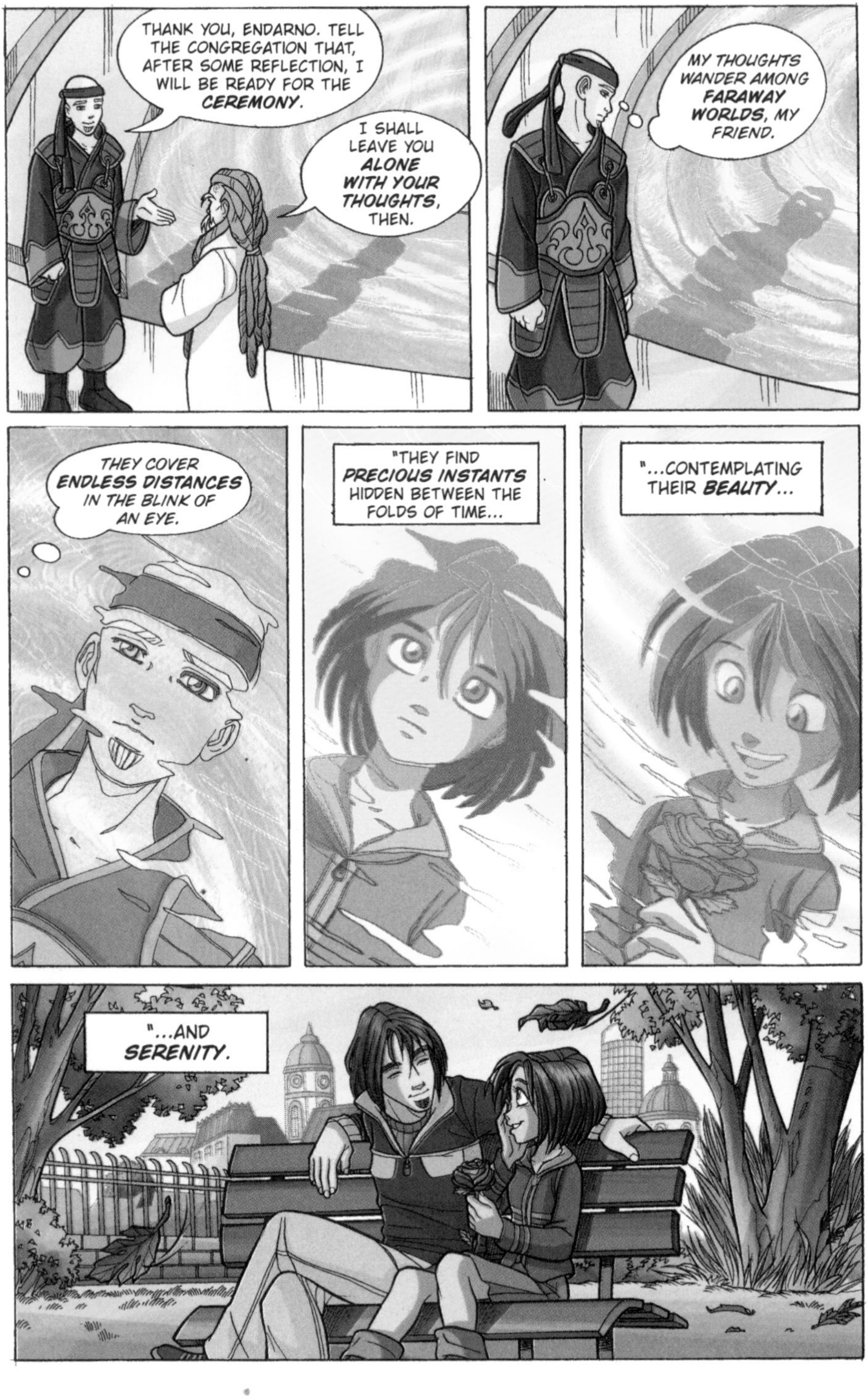
THANK YOU, ENDARNO. TELL THE CONGREGATION THAT, AFTER SOME REFLECTION, I WILL BE READY FOR THE CEREMONY.
I SHALL LEAVE YOU ALONE WITH YOUR THOUGHTS, THEN.
MY THOUGHTS WANDER AMONG FARAWAY WORLDS, MY FRIEND.
THEY COVER ENDLESS DISTANCES IN THE BLINK OF AN EYE.
"THEY FIND PRECIOUS INSTANTS HIDDEN BETWEEN THE FOLDS OF TIME...
"...CONTEMPLATING THEIR BEAUTY...
"...AND SERENITY.

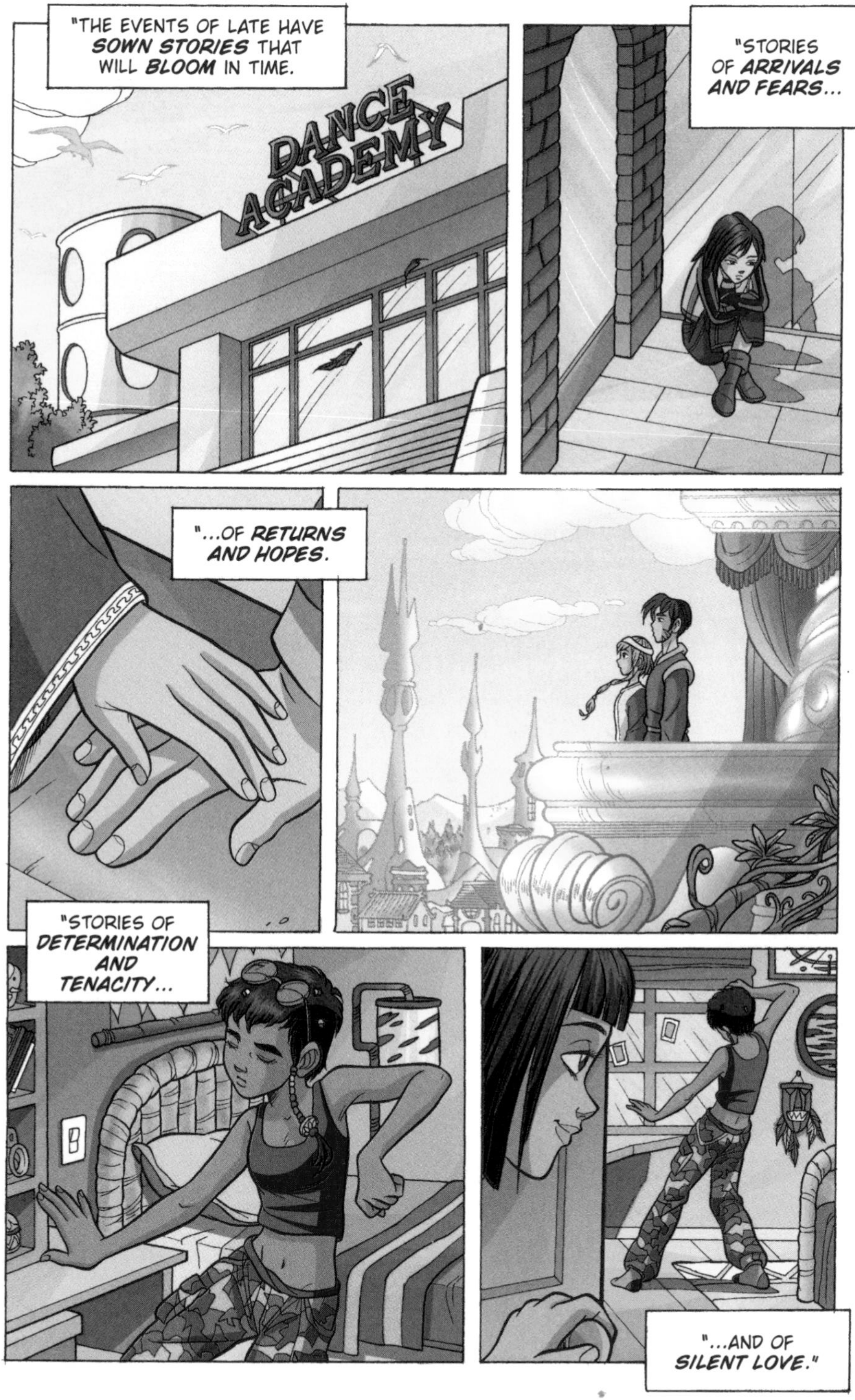
"THE EVENTS OF LATE HAVE SOWN STORIES THAT WILL BLOOM IN TIME.
DANCE ACADEMY
"STORIES OF ARRIVALS AND FEARS...
"...OF RETURNS AND HOPES.
"STORIES OF DETERMINATION AND TENACITY...
"...AND OF SILENT LOVE."

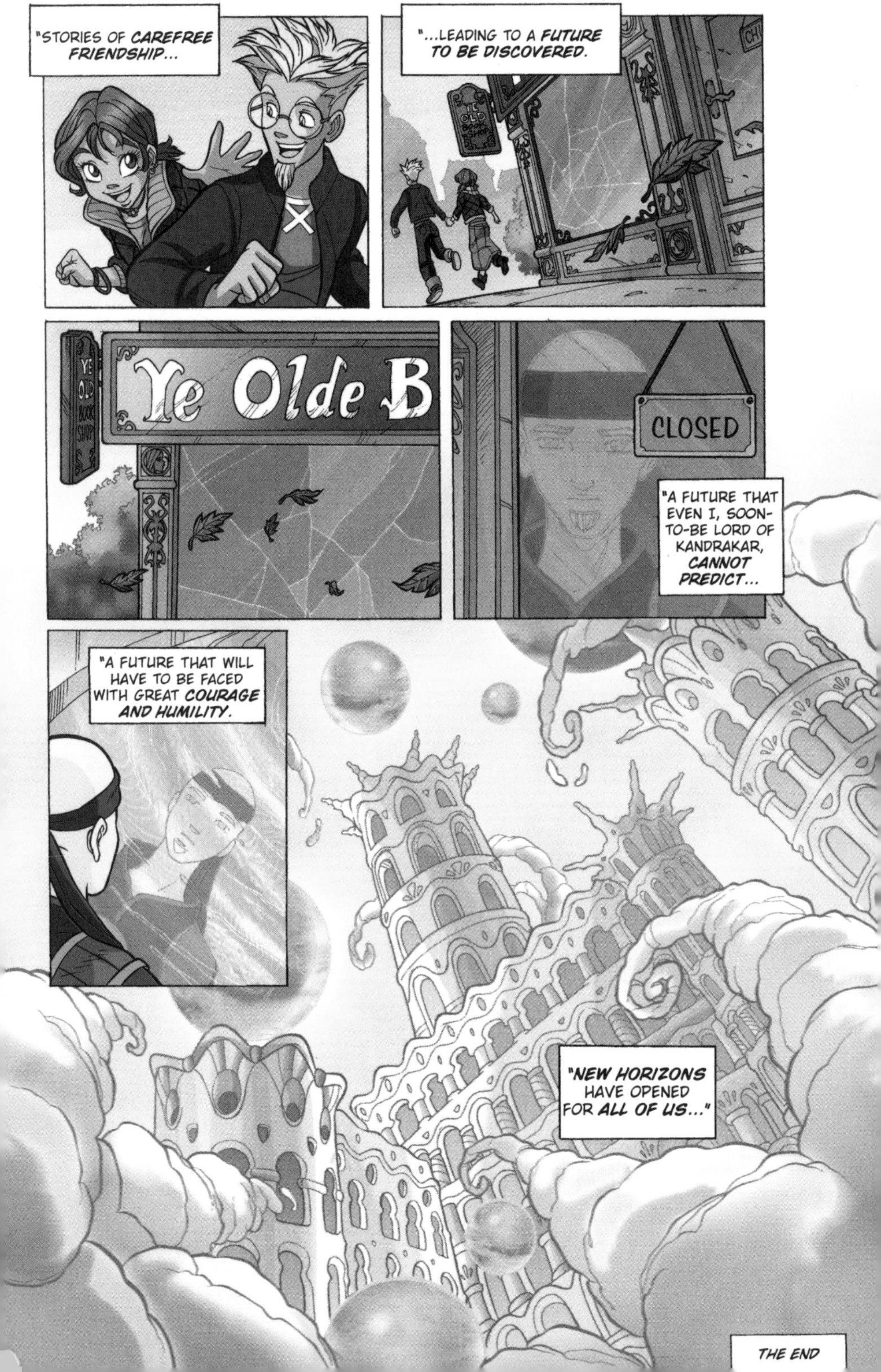
"STORIES OF CAREFREE FRIENDSHIP...
"...LEADING TO A FUTURE TO BE DISCOVERED.
YE OLD BOOK SHOP
Ye Olde B
YE OLD BOOK SHOP
CLOSED
"A FUTURE THAT EVEN I, SOON-TO-BE LORD OF KANDRAKAR, CANNOT PREDICT...
"A FUTURE THAT WILL HAVE TO BE FACED WITH GREAT COURAGE AND HUMILITY.
"NEW HORIZONS HAVE OPENED FOR ALL OF US..."
THE END

Read on in Volume 13!

W.i.t.c.h.

Will Irma Taranee Cornelia Hay Lin

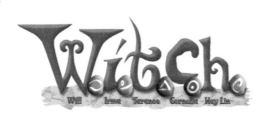

Endarno

Origins

Endarno comes from Basiliade, where he was a brave and noble warrior from the Shanta tribe back when Basiliade was in the throes of a war between tribes. Endarno showed great courage rebelling against Sharr, the leader of his tribe, to bring peace back to Basiliade. At the time, he saved the life of the man who would go on to become the Oracle.

Against the Oracle

For a long time, Endarno was the Custodian of the Tower of Mists, Kandrakar's prison, where he became a victim of Phobos's cruel plans. In his quest for revenge, Meridian's tyrant managed to possess Endarno's body, taking over his mind and imprisoning the Custodian in his place.

Endarno-Phobos leads the "rebellion" against the Oracle, putting him on trial and bringing his actions into question, and finally managing to have him kicked out. He eventually succeeds in being elected as the new Oracle. Can W.I.T.C.H. thwart Phobos's cruel plan?

W.i.t.c.h.

Will Irma Taranee Cornelia Hay Lin

Part IV. Trial of the Oracle • Volume 3

12

Series Created by Elisabetta Gnone
Comic Art Direction: Alessandro Barbucci, Barbara Canepa

W.I.T.C.H.: The Graphic Novel, Part IV: Trial of the Oracle © Disney Enterprises, Inc.

English translation © 2018 by Disney Enterprises, Inc.

JY
1290 Avenue of the Americas
New York, NY 10104

Visit us at yenpress.com
facebook.com/yenpress
twitter.com/yenpress
yenpress.tumblr.com
instagram.com/yenpress

First JY Edition: September 2018

JY is an imprint of Yen Press, LLC.
The JY name and logo are trademarks of Yen Press, LLC.

The publisher is not responsible for websites (or their content) that are not owned by the publisher.

Library of Congress Control Number: 2017950917

ISBNs:
978-0-316-47713-0 (paperback)
978-1-9753-0187-3 (ebook)

10 9 8 7 6 5 4 3 2

LSC-C

Printed in the United States of America

Cover Art by Giada Perissinotto
Colors by Andrea Cagol

Translation by Linda Ghio and Stephanie Dagg at Editing Zone
Lettering by Katie Blakeslee

DOUBLE DECEPTION

Concept and Script by Giulia Conti
Layout by Giada Perissinotto
Pencils by Monica Catalano
Inks by Marina Baggio and Roberta Zanotta
Color and Light Direction by Francesco Legramandi
Title Page Art by Giada Perissinotto
with Colors by Andrea Cagol

THE STRENGTH OF COURAGE

Concept by Paola Mulazzi
Script by Silvia Gianatti and Paola Mulazzi
Layout by Manuela Razzi
Pencils by Flavia Scuderi
Inks by Marina Baggio and Roberta Zanotta
Color and Light Direction by Francesco Legramandi
Title Page Art by Manuela Razzi
with Colors by Andrea Cagol

THE SANDS OF TIME

Concept and Script by Bruno Enna
Layout and Pencils by Paolo Campinoti
Inks by Santa Zangari
Color and Light Direction by Francesco Legramandi
Title Page Art by Giada Perissinotto
with Colors by Andrea Cagol

NEW HORIZONS

Concept and Script by Teresa Radice
Layout by Gianluca Panniello
Pencils by Davide Baldoni
Inks by Marina Baggio
Color and Light Direction by Francesco Legramandi
Title Page Art by Davide Baldoni
with Colors by Francesco Legramandi